EAST AND WEST

BY GERALD GREEN

FICTION

Not in Vain
Karpov's Brain
Murfy's Men
The Chains
Cactus Pie: Ten Stories
The Healers
Holocaust
Girl
An American Prophet
The Hostage Heart
Blockbuster
Faking It
Tourist
To Brooklyn With Love
The Legion of Noble Christians
The Heartless Light
The Lotus Eaters
The Last Angry Man
The Sword and the Sun

NONFICTION

My Son the Jock
The Stones of Zion
The Artists of Terezin
The Portofino PTA
His Majesty O'Keefe
   (with Lawrence Klingman)

TELEVISION DRAMA

Wallenberg: A Hero's Story
Holocaust
The Last Angry Man
Kent State
   (with Richard Kramer)

EAST
AND
WEST

GERALD
GREEN

DONALD I. FINE, INC., New York

Library of Congress Catalogue Card Number: 85-81167
ISBN: 0-917657-56-X

Manufactured in the United States of America
10 9 8 7 6 5 4 3 2 1

This book is printed on acid free paper. The paper in this book meets the guidelines
for permanence and durability of the Committee on Production Guidelines for Book
Longevity of the Council on Library Resources.

CHARACTERS

The Tamba Family

Goro Tamba, a servant at the Imperial Palace

Hisako, his wife

Masao Tamba, eldest son, an army officer and war hero, "The Dragon of Shansi"

Kenji Tamba, second son, "Master Cold Rice"

Saburo Tamba, youngest son, a student

Yuriko Tamba, only daughter

The Varnum Family

Dr. Adam Varnum, a medical missionary in Japan

Dr. Cora Varnum, his wife, a Swiss national, also a physician at the Shibuya Ward Clinic

Julie Varnum, their niece

Christopher Varnum, her brother, a war correspondent

The Sato Family

Colonel Hiroshi Sato, a military "outlaw"

Michiko, his daughter, wife of Masao Tamba

Others

Lt. Ed Hodges, United States Marine Corps

Hans Baumann, German journalist in Tokyo

Hideo Kitano, husband of Yuriko Tamba, a naval officer

Kingoro Hata, a politician, the "man of broad face"

Professor Adachi, Kenji Tamba's teacher, or *sensei*

Satomi, owner of the Plum Blossom geisha house

For Jack Arbolino
United States Marine Corps Reserve, Major
Tarawa and Saipan

and

To the memory of Philip Bayer
United States Marine Corps Reserve, First Lieutenant
Tarawa and Peleliu

Honeymoon of a newly wedded couple is interrupted by the Japanese attack on Pearl Harbor catching them up in the passion of two nations at war.

KENJI TAMBA · MAY, 1941

North of Tokyo in Toshima Ward the bus halted to allow a troop of schoolboys to cross the street.

I could not help smiling at them—shave-headed, shiny-faced kids in dark blue brass-buttoned uniforms and dark blue caps. They of course brought back memories of my own childhood, and I sensed a sorrow and elation all at the same time. Elusive and saddening, the lost years of youth. And yet if we've learned wisely from them, if we can contemplate good memories, the past can be gratifying.

The boys entered a shabby elementary school, with a parched lawn, cracked windows, a drab and plain building.

On a gravel square outside the entrance door stood a stone statue. I bowed my head to the monument.

"Thank you, Kinjiro," I said.

An old woman sitting next to me laughed. "Ah, Kinjiro Ninomiya. Do you like him?"

"He was my hero."

Let me explain. One finds this statue outside many Japanese schools. Kinjiro is a legendary youth, always depicted carrying a load of firewood on his back and a book in his hand. He was poor and had to work hard, but his desire to learn was unquenchable and he achieved a good deal in life. The statue is a reminder—as it always was to me—that education and hard work go together.

I was now in my twenty-third year, and felt a heavy load had been lifted from my back, and that the long hours of study, of reading, arduous days in classrooms and laboratories had brought their own reward.

9

Only a few hours ago, in the office of my sponsor at Tokyo Imperial University I had learned that my scholarship for graduate study in America had come through. Trying to suppress my elation, I had deflected Professor Adachi's praise.

"You deserve it, Kenji," Professor Adachi had said. "Your career is moving forward. Are you pleased that you will be returning to America?"

I told him I was. I had spent my last two undergraduate years at the University of Oregon (also via a government scholarship) and now thanks to the generosity and kindness of His Imperial Majesty, our emperor, I was to pursue my doctoral studies at the University of California in Los Angeles.

Professor Adachi was affectionately referred to by his students as the Last Confucian, and in fact was one of Japan's leading sociologists. The teachings of Confucius, stressing education, ethical behavior, right thinking and right living, were at the heart of Professor Adachi's philosophy. He was an inspiration to me throughout my years at Tokyo Imperial University, and (as I believe this narrative will reveal) at a later and dangerous time in my life.

"Well, good-bye, Kenji," he said, "you will like Los Angeles. It gives off a magical odor of orange blossoms and gasoline. There is nothing like it anywhere in the world. Dissimilar yet strangely harmonious . . ."

We laughed and I bowed deeply to show my respect for a great *sensei.* He was, indeed, a teacher in the noblest sense of the word.

Now, on the noisy clattering suburban bus I thought of how I had tried to please my parents, my teachers, the emperor and my nation by being a scholar who hoped some day to serve his government.

The bus moved on and I smiled at the statue of poor Kinjiro laboring under his load of firewood. The bus dropped me at the main gate of the Musashi Training Barracks, an army camp fifteen miles north of Tokyo.

It was a flat dusty area, bordered with those incredibly productive patches of farmland from which our people manage to raise so much rice, vegetables and fruit. We seem to have a genius for taking barren earth, what appear to be useless scraps of land, and nurturing them into fertility. I saw two old women, bent forever at the waist from years of cultivating the hard soil, and realized how lucky I was to be a member of a middle-class family, the recipient of the finest education my country could offer, and now honored with the gift of three more years of study in America, a country I had come to admire almost as much as my own.

I crossed the macadam road to the sentry box. On either side ran an endless chain-link fence crowned with barbed wire. Above the main gate was a gaudy sign reading MUSASHI BARRACKS and beneath it a depiction of the man the training post was named for—Miyamoto Musashi, the greatest sword fighter in our nation's history, a sixteenth-century warrior, philosopher, artist and poet.

Musashi was represented rather crudely, standing at ease (beware, opponent) long sword in his right hand, short sword in his left, in the *Happo Biraki* attitude, which meant that in spite of his relaxed, almost somnolent appearance there was no possible opening for an attack on him. (I have tried to explain Musashi's hold on the imagination of the Japanese, especially on our youth, to my American friends, and the closest I can come is that he was a sort of combination of Jesse James, Henry James and William James. A remarkable mixture, I grant you. Or perhaps a cross between Wyatt Earp and Ralph Waldo Emerson . . . I confess this sounds like nonsense but there is much truth to it. We expect our great soldiers and *samurai* fighters to be poetic, artistic, aware of higher goals, having lofty visions and philosophical concepts. I also confess that our expectations are often betrayed. And sometimes, when it involves family, it can be very painful. But more of that later.)

The sentry on duty checked his ledger, found my name, bowed deeply to me (in spite of my civilian clothes) and let me pass. Obviously he was impressed to learn that I was the younger brother of Captain Masao Tamba, the "Dragon of Shansi."

Masao was three years older than me. He was a career officer and had been in combat since the start of the war with China in 1937. Although only a junior officer, his reputation for leadership, for raw courage and strategic genius had already marked him for greatness. His patron and future father-in-law, Colonel Hiroshi Sato, had told me that there were limitless heights Masao could rise to.

I wondered some about this as I crossed the dusty hard-packed parade grounds, past a sea of flapping tents and peeling buildings. Shave-headed recruits, stocky boys having the look of peasants, ran at double-time around the perimeter of the field. Others were put through a tough obstacle course—rope climbing, crawling under spiked wires, vaulting fences, straddling beams. Noncommissioned officers barked out orders, abused them with curses and insults, whacked at their naked backs with canes. It was no easy life being a Japanese soldier, and I was guiltily aware that my position as a scholar had so far exempted me from it.

Beyond the barracks was a vast open field, misted over with dust and baking under an unusually hot May sun. The air was charged with yellow particles that made me sneeze. I saw the running, climbing, panting young men as if hazed, almost underwater.

Some days earlier my brother Masao, much against his will, had been recalled from active duty in China to supervise the training of recruits. The truth was that the war against the Chinese had not been going too well in spite of newspaper and radio claims of endless victories. There was grumbling at home about the "Chinese quagmire," the continuing drafting of young men, the rising casualty tolls.

At this time—late May of 1941—it was known among the military that the battle for southern Shansi Province had actually been a failure if not a defeat. Our best troops, led by courageous officers like my brother, had managed to cross the Yellow River, but most of the Chinese had slipped away into the Jiewing Mountains. (Later, during my years in America, I would learn that the Chinese, poorly educated and badly equipped, had fought bravely for their ancestral lands. Our own press had always characterized them as stupid and cowardly.)

A new commanding general, Neiji Okamura, had been sent to Shansi, a man who devised the "three-all" policy to deal with the Chinese—burn all, loot all, kill all. These rules of his applied equally to civilians and soldiers. The command change included a rotation of officers who had served for over two years in China, and my brother Masao was among those sent home to oversee training, boost morale and help staff officers plan for the future.

On a parched soccer field a battalion of skin-headed bare-chested youths in tan gym shorts and sneakers now stood waiting their turn in combat exercises. Inside a large hollow square of men six pairs of contestants battled one another with eight-foot bamboo poles. Wearing reed helmets and padded vests, they lunged, parried, used the poles as swords or bludgeons. I'd played at this form of *kendo* as a high school boy and I can tell you it is no pleasure to get thwacked—even wearing a padded vest—with a flexible whistling length of hard bamboo.

Standing in a grandstand was my brother, Captain Masao Tamba, and his future father-in-law, Colonel Hiroshi Sato. Several steps below them four noncommissioned officers were shouting at the contestants to be more aggressive, to fight like Musashi—no mercy, no quarter, no retreat.

Masao and Colonel Sato wore tunics spangled with campaign medals and ribbons, and each carried long curved officers' sword. As I walked toward the grandstand feeling out of place in my white cotton shirt and gray trousers, a pallid civilian amid *samurai,* I couldn't help but notice the contrast between Masao and Colonel Sato.

My brother was a tall man, beautifully muscled, graceful and elegant in his movements. He was also very handsome—long-headed, with a square jaw, features that seemed almost carved from yellow ivory. He moved like an athlete, gestured little and exuded what the Americans call "command presence."

Colonel Sato was rotund and pot-bellied. It had been years since he had had a field command. He had grown soft on too much sake and rich food and too many evenings with whores. He was attached to the Imperial General Staff, but I was never quite certain what his job was, who he reported to, or why he had so much influence. Never mind, at the time it was enough for me to know that he admired my older brother, had helped along his career and was eager to see Masao married to his only child, a beautiful talented young woman named Michiko.

Thwack.

Crack.

Bamboo smashing against chests, limbs, reed helmets. One of the half-naked combatants fell, tried to roll away, absorbed a blow to the head, struggled to his feet. A sergeant blew his whistle. Six more teams took over, flailing at one another with the poles, shouting, grunting. As I watched I had a mental vision of another painting of Musashi I'd seen— the *kendo* fighter wielding two long poles in combat, his narrow face angry and intense, his tunic flowing, his agile legs clothed in billowing scarlet pants. Should you ever see this painting (it's a nineteenth-century work by Kuniyoshi) note the lean intense face and you'll have an idea of how my brother Masao appeared to me.

An emaciated-looking young man—we must have been scraping the barrel for China recruits—wilted under the first blow given him by a bruiser, dropped to his knees and actually started to cry.

I watched, holding my breath, as Masao, in his dress uniform and sword, came down from the grandstand, stopped the fighting pairs and walked to the fallen young man.

"You are not hurt."

"I am, sir. I am ill—"

I could believe him. He looked consumptive.

"You were barely struck."

"My stomach is in pain, sir, I cannot hold food—"

Masao responded with two swift kicks, driving his leather boot into the boy's ribs. The youth scuttled away, tried to get up and collapsed.

"Get to your feet," Masao said. "Hold your pole above your head. *Both* hands. Now run around this field twenty times."

The boy bowed deeply to Masao, who did not acknowledge the gesture but turned to the other men, who were standing at rigid attention with their bamboo poles at their sides.

"War," Masao told them, "is not for weaklings. Strength is survival. When you get to China you will learn. Sergeant, resume the exercises."

Masao then walked among the combatants, and his expression became abruptly gentle, warm. Theirs—and his—was a holy dedication.

I approached the grandstand, stood to one side, and tried to catch Colonel Sato's eye. He had met me several times, including at the *miai*, the formal "get-acquainted" session when Masao and his future bride Michiko and their respective families gathered around a restaurant table to exchange pleasantries and make judgments about the compatibility of the couple. In my brother's and Michiko's case it was a foregone conclusion that they would marry. Colonel Sato was a force, a man with dark and important secrets. He had known Masao since February 1936, during the tragic events in Tokyo that brought them together, and which I'll talk about later. My family was socially several cuts below the Satos. Michiko was beautiful and, if not rich, the daughter of an influential military officer who was personally shepherding Masao's career.

I caught the colonel's eye and bowed.

"Ah, Kenji. A surprise seeing you here. Thinking of enlisting?" He barely smiled. Behind his dark glasses I saw no eyes.

"No, sir, but I have good news I wanted to tell Masao."

"Good, good."

The shrug of indifference was in his voice. My standing as a scholar meant nothing to Colonel Sato. He knew little about me—and cared less, I suspect—including my ability in languages, my years in America. He was purely a soldier, and nothing more. My exposure to American ways and my association with so-called liberals or intellectuals like Professor Adachi would have brought down only his contempt. Colonel Sato was a follower of *Kodo-Ha*—the Imperial Way—which was pretty much what the military extremists said it was. Conquest, the domination of Asia (and why not the world?) all done in the name of the emperor, who, if Adachi was right, was never in agreement with this attitude. No wonder Colonel Sato had little use for me.

Masao was addressing the men now, speaking in a soft yet resonant voice. Somehow when my brother spoke people became silent. The air itself, traffic sounds, the whistle of the wind seemed stilled.

"Your life has meaning only if you are willing to give it to His Majesty. We are the children of the sun. We fight for the living god who rules us with kindness and generosity. Some of you will soon be in China. You will be asked to give your lives, to fight bravely, never to retreat, *never* to surrender."

Colonel Sato was nodding his bald head in punctuation of Masao's speech. Suddenly my brother took off his tunic and sword and picked up a bamboo stave, then approached a big man who had earlier proven himself the best *kendo* fighter.

"You," Masao said, "you will fight me."

I swallowed, found my voice, spoke to Sato. "Masao isn't wearing armor. No helmet. How can he—?"

"Don't be concerned."

The sergeant ordered the recruits to move back and Masao and the big man squared off, legs apart, arms extended. It seemed unequal—one good blow could smash my brother's ribs, crack his skull. I looked at his handsome face with that odd mixture of sensitivity and fierceness in the eyes—*Musashi's eyes*—and wondered (as I did so often) how we could be so different.

"Captain Tamba is the best hand-to-hand fighter in the Fifth Division," Sato said.

I wanted to say: Yes, he practiced on me when we were kids. But I held my tongue. As Masao and the recruit circled one another I tried to remember if I had ever won a fight from Masao. Only three years separated us in age. I was just as tall, a bit thinner but a decent athlete. Still, he always got the best of me and I wondered if I lacked something. At least *once,* I thought, I ought to have beaten him . . .

It was astonishing the way Masao—without helmet, unarmored—handled the bigger man, a powerful fellow, muscles bulging from his limbs, a chest like an oaken cask. Masao was not only parrying blows with the expertise of a fencing master but was delivering a lecture on Musashi's technique and philosophy to the troops as he fought.

"Brilliant," Sato said. "The only officer I know who could do this."

"I maneuver my opponent so that the sun is behind me," Masao was saying. And, indeed, he had done just that. The big man looked hesitant.

"There is free space on my left. Rear unobstructed. My right side is occupied with my weapon. I move my enemy to the left . . ."

Which he did with short thrusts and feints, parried by the recruit who was brave and skilled as well.

"The first method. *Ken No Sen.* The attack. Be calm, move in quickly." And with blinding speed Masao swung the pole into the man's middle, making him gasp and double over. But he caught his breath and gave Masao a savage smack to the thigh. Masao didn't flinch. He advanced again, saying, *"Tai No Sen.* The enemy attacks but he is in disorder. I can see his spirit is in collapse, I am the hawk, he is the pheasant—"

With lightning moves Masao then crashed his stave against the man's knees, watched him bend, then drove the pole against the base of the soldier's spine. The man fell face forward in the dust. The whole contest couldn't have lasted more than a minute, and most of the time my brother was delivering a *lecture.*

Only the padding had saved the man's life. The sergeant and two other noncoms got him to his feet. Stunned, the recruit took off his helmet and bowed to Masao, *thanking* him for the honor of having the daylights beaten out of him.

Masao returned the bow and told the man he had fought well, that he was the kind of soldier the emperor was depending on to bring Japan victory in China. And then he ordered the battalion dismissed.

Masao saw me then and smiled as we bowed to each other. I'd gotten into the habit of shaking hands, even embracing my friends in America. Now at home in Tokyo I often had to catch myself since public touching of skin was regarded as disgusting.

"I have good news, brother."

Sato smiled. "I thought perhaps Kenji was joining us."

Masao didn't join in the teasing. I have to say that he always treated me with respect even though as the oldest son he was a king, a god in our house. Even my father, a gentle, somewhat confused person, often deferred to his oldest son.

"Your scholarship?" Masao said.

"It's been approved by the council on Education. Everything paid for, transportation, tuition, lodging. I'm to leave in two weeks so I can start the summer session."

"At the school you wanted?"

I walked with him and Sato—who seemed bored if not annoyed— toward the officers' quarters.

"UCLA. In Los Angeles. A great university."

"That's good," Masao said. "We serve the emperor in many ways."

Sato put in, "What are you studying?"

"Political science. Especially the American political system."

The colonel said nothing to this as we walked along the gravel path. And once again I felt somehow inferior, a lesser man in my civilian clothing, not worthy of the two soldiers with me, my brother and his future father-in-law resplendent in their medals, boots, spurs and long swords. Yes, I *knew* better, but I was also Japanese—born and bred. One didn't shake off one's heritage so easily . . .

"I can see where such knowledge might be of value to us," Sato said.

"Yes, Kenji is practically an American," Masao said. "He was two years in the state of Oregon. He speaks English like an American. He likes their food. He passes for a Nisei. Isn't that right, Kenji?"

If there was any mockery or displeasure in my brother's voice I didn't hear it. I think he was genuinely praising me for an accomplishment, and I felt embarrassed. We don't like to be praised.

"Tell me," Sato said. "Do Americans demean us? How do they treat the Japanese who have settled there?"

"Well, there is some prejudice. It isn't entirely good for many Japanese-Americans. But these matters aren't easy—"

"They humiliate us," Sato said. "I know. I have met American officers. They call us yellow monkeys. And this from a mongrel people . . ."

I knew enough about Colonel Sato's background, about the dark and bloody events in his past, not to make an enemy of him by arguing, especially now that he was to be my brother's father-in-law . . . We were entering the officers' quarters now, a lavish, far cry from the flimsy dust-covered tents the recruits lived in.

"Master Cold Rice," Masao said to me affectionately, "come on to the baths with us."

Flattered, I confess, to be included, I agreed. We crossed the lobby and Masao went to a bulletin board to study some war dispatches that had been posted. There was good news from China. General Okamura had announced that an entire Chinese army had been massacred in Shansi and that attacks were being launched against Chinese communist armies in the north.

"What did your brother call you?" Sato asked me.

"Master Cold Rice."

"Ah, the younger son, the one who gets fed last when the rice is cold."

I smiled. "That's right, sir. As you know, there are two children younger than me—my sister Yuriko and little brother Saburo. But somehow they always got to eat before I did."

All of which amused Sato. "That's good, that's very good. Master Cold Rice."

Masao had rejoined us and suggested we bathe, enjoy a massage and have dinner. As I said, I was honored to be accepted into this military world . . . a world I could never be part of.

We soaped and shaved on wooden stools, then soaked in the steaming hot tub along with female bath attendants, all of us nude but with no suggestion of sex, fondling, flirting or embracing. It was restorative, a welcome relief from the dusty training field.

Although I'd been included in the officers' bath—we were lying now on massage tables where cunning female hands kneaded and slapped our bodies—my brother and the colonel still tended to ignore me. I was, after all, an outsider.

"It will go the way we wish," Colonel Sato was saying.

"How soon?" Masao asked.

"Oh, months. Perhaps by the end of the year."

"Faster than we thought."

I listened, puzzled.

"Yamamoto has drawn up his plan already," Sato said. "Sometime in January he presented it to the chiefs of staff. It is bold, ingenious."

Masao grunted as the masseuse bent his long legs, cracked the joints. "What was their reaction?"

"The usual. It's strange. Yamamoto himself needs a bit of stiffening. He's a genius but he's also fainthearted. He has a brilliant strategy but he's afraid it may be a long war . . ."

At that moment I had no real idea what they were talking about. Apparently some grand plan was in the making, perhaps a naval assault against the Soviet Union north of the Japan Sea. In any case I held my tongue, enjoying the tingle of the girl's clever feet as she walked on my spine, massaging each vertebra with enlightened toes.

What especially puzzled me still was that both my brother as a cadet and Sato as a captain had taken part in the army mutiny of February 26, 1936, a mere five years earlier. One would have thought that this would have shamed them forever, that they would have been cashiered, court-martialled, maybe even jailed. But no. In the curious way these matters work in Japan, both had retained their commissions, remained on active service and were still important parts of the war machine that so dominated our national life.

I will be talking more about this 1936 mutiny later, but now I'll only say that certain young officers of the First Division, permeated with the extremist notions of *Kodo-Ha*—the Imperial Way—and angered by what they perceived to be corruption, cowardice and inaction on the part of the government, rebelled against their commanders, who, they argued, were insufficiently aware of the dangers of "liberalism and communism" in Japan. These junior officers issued a manifesto calling for the murder of "villains who surround the throne." They would save the emperor from his own evil advisers. Fourteen hundred officers and men were involved, and they assassinated cabinet ministers, high-ranking officers, even wives. Among those murdered by the 1936 mutineers was Viscount Saito, Lord Keeper of the Privy Seal, a gentle old man who was close to the emperor. At one point they even talked about doing away with Hirohito himself. *Yes.* This is a fact. Professor Adachi has shown me secret papers about the 1936 mutiny. In the end the mutiny was suppressed and fifteen officers were executed, eighty were jailed. But most went free, were hidden for a while, then allowed to rejoin the army. Sato, who always had a knack for working behind the scenes, was never indicted or even mentioned. My brother, then only a cadet, was pardoned along with many others. What these junior officers wanted was a confrontation and war with Russia, the United States, Britain, the Netherlands, and anyone else who blocked the way of Japan's destined . . . as they saw it . . . rule of Asia. These aren't fuzzy speculations invented by Adachi and other democrats. It was a case of what we Japanese call *gekokujo*—rule by men of lower rank who enforce their will on superiors. Yes, my brother Masao had been a part of it, and I could say I wish he had not been, but even now I could not condemn him. Easy to criticize a group, a movement. Not so easy your own brother, the eldest in the family, the one you had looked up to all your young years. And to whom, in a way, you still did . . .

Colonel Sato excused himself and got up from the massage table, his belly resembling a pumpkin as he waddled out to get dressed. He always seemed to be off to meetings and dinners, usually in brothels and geisha houses, where he conducted his business. It was years since he had commanded troops. Now he lived the combat life vicariously through my brother, who would soon marry into the Sato family.

Masao was stroking the naked thigh of the masseuse, a plain woman, flat-faced and bowlegged. My masseuse was prettier, shy with pale skin and bobbed hair.

"Kenji," my brother said, "are you looking forward to going back to America?"

"Oh . . . yes."

"You must know a great deal about them."

"I suppose so. They're an easy people to know, they don't hide things, even from strangers."

"But they hate strangers, don't they? They hate us, isn't that right? They look down on us."

In this Masao was like so many of our military, who couldn't seem to overcome a sense of inferiority. It was always assumed that the *gaijin*—the foreigner—looked down on them. I tried to tell Masao that this wasn't the case, at least not the way he saw it.

"Have you slept with their women?"

The masseuses giggled.

"No."

"Never?"

"Never."

"Were you tempted?"

"Many times. But I was an outsider. I took an American girl to a movie a few times but I never danced with one. Remember, Masao, I had to work hard. The first year I spent as much time on my English as I did on my courses."

He smiled across the massage tables as the girls smoothed our backs with rose-scented oil, stroked and kneaded muscles, making our nerves vibrate with pleasure.

"I would like to make love to an American or an Englishwoman," he said solemnly. "One with long pale legs, long thighs and high round buttocks. Of course no *gaijin* woman can equal the beauty of our women. Especially in the nape of the neck. No women in the world have such necks as ours. But just once . . ."

"Maybe you'll get your chance," I said, not knowing what else to say.

"Maybe you could do it first and let me know how it is. For one thing, they do smell different, correct? They smell from too much meat-eating. They smell like cheese or boiled milk. Isn't it odd? You'd think that the *gaijin*, who are supposed to be so intelligent, would at least invent a perfume to disguise that odor."

Masao's masseuse laughed happily and turned him over. We were the only clients in the massage room now. "Oh, you are a funny man, Captain Tamba . . ."

I wanted to ask Masao a lot of things . . . about Colonel Sato, and how it was that the colonel and Masao could stay in service after they had been part of a mutiny. And why Sato's star was rising even though he had been an accomplice in the assassination of a Lord Keeper of the Privy Seal. But I said nothing. It was not the time. Would it ever be, I wondered . . .

Masao's masseuse now drew a curtain between the two tables and soon I heard a rhythmic hard breathing, laughter. The girl was gently, artfully stroking Masao's member with her silken fingertips, the finishing touch, the ultimate relaxation. I could see shadows behind the flimsy cotton drape, and in a minute or so I heard three loud explosions of breath and saw my brother's body jackknifing forward.

"Would you like the same?" my masseuse asked.

I am not a prude. I have at times gone to whores. As a boy I masturbated as much as any youth. (We attach no shame to the act, none whatsoever). But I wasn't at ease. My body had been soothed by the girl's hands, but somehow I didn't want to let loose an inner part of me, not here in this officers' gymnasium, to smear the girl's hands and trickle onto my stomach.

I was too much with my thoughts about Masao and his sponsor. I kept wondering what their secret power was . . . why they had been able to do what they had done and still go untouched?

* * *

Later I said good-bye to Masao at the barracks gate. "What wedding present would you like from me?" I asked him.

"Master Cold Rice," he said warmly. "Always looking to please someone. Our parents, me, Yuriko and Saburo. You have a generous nature."

"You are my older brother, Masao. My respect is due you."

"Any gift will be fine, Kenji. But the best gift? To serve the emperor. Your knowledge of the enemy will be—"

"The enemy? Who? We are fighting in China."

"Oh, Kenji, there are many enemies. Our people are not aware of them yet . . . but they will be."

"But I must give you a gift."

"Then pray for me, that I will soon be back with my troops in China, that our armies will be victorious. And then to fight again."

"Where?"

"Wherever His Majesty asks us to go."

I hesitated a moment. "I'm told he's a man of peace, that he opposed the wars in Manchuria and China—"

"The lies of traitors, Kenji. That is why we must protect him, and know his mind, obey his divine will."

There was little more I could say without an argument. But was it the emperor's divine will that an army division should mutiny, kill officials, threaten others, even talk about killing the Son of Heaven himself? There are times, I knew, when logic doesn't apply, when lies become truth . . .

Masao and I bowed to each other. I would next see him at his wedding. I wished him a thousand good wishes and the blessings of all the gods, all eight million of them.

MASAO TAMBA · JUNE, 1941

That evening I dined with Colonel Sato, soon to be my father-in-law, at the senior officers' club in Tokyo.

The dinner was not exactly memorable—roasted eel in a hot vinegar sauce and pickled *daikon*—but some of the colonel's comments were.

He was upset by a new report to the League of Nations concerning alleged atrocities committed by our army (indeed, our very own division) during the occupation of Nanking in 1937. He had a copy of it and he read from it as we sipped green tea and ate honey-sweetened *tofu*.

"Why now?" I asked. "Nanking is an old story."

Sato shook his head. "All part of the Western conspiracy to blackguard us. It proves they are looking for excuses to make war and fight on China's side."

"Why have they waited four years?"

"Why? They keep yammering about this Nanking affair, these so-called atrocity stories. China is ready to collapse, the whole rotten structure crashing around Chiang's head. So the United States and Britain feel they have to distract the world from the truth of it."

I nodded. In 1937 I had been a second lieutenant in the Shanghai Expeditionary Army. Colonel Sato, then a captain, was my company commander in a special assault unit. Only a year earlier Sato and I had been involved as so-called mutineers in the February 26 incident. Some of our comrades in that patriotic attempt to purify Japan in the emperor's name had been executed, others jailed. Sato and I were among the fortunate ones. After a reprimand—his family was connected with one of the old *samurai* clans from Kyushu—we were restored to active duty. Indeed it was felt by the Imperial General Staff that men of such courage and daring, who would try to seize the government—for the most noble of reasons—were worthy of the most vital and dangerous assignments.

Once called assassins and blackmailers, we now were the cutting edge of the China war. In four days our division routed a Chinese army of 100,000. Nanking was ours.

I recalled these events of four years ago—the massed bayonet charges, the enfilading fire by our machine guns and rifles, the way the barefoot Chinese fell in windrows or took to their heels—as I scanned the League of Nations document that Sato had brought.

"It is garbage," he said. "Lies and propaganda. We will ignore it."

I read on, knowing that these statements were not all lies, were at least partly the truth. But why should we have been ashamed of it? I challenged myself. War is about death. Death to the enemy. The quicker one gets it over with, the faster the enemy succumbs, the better it is for all concerned.

> . . . Japanese officers engaged in *samurai* fights with unarmed
> Chinese soldiers. Each officer killed more than one hundred
> Chinese before tiring of the sport . . .

. . . Young women, mature women, aged women were raped
over and over by Japanese soldiers, beheaded if they were
considered ugly. Eyewitness testimony . . .

. . . Several instances of huge numbers of Chinese men, bound in
large groups, doused with gasoline and set on fire . . .

Testimony from surviving members of Nanking's foreign colony,
British, Germans, French and Americans state that these were not
random acts by enlisted men running amok but a calculated plan
by Japanese officers to use execution, rape and torture as a means
of subduing the Chinese people . . .

Chinese men were used as targets for bayonet practice . . . others
were roasted, buried alive, burned to death with industrial acid . . .

Accurate statistics are hard to come by, but it is estimated that
200,000 civilians were slaughtered . . .

I put down the report. "We did no more than fulfill General Okamura's
policies," I murmured. "Kill all, loot all, burn all."

Sato ran his pudgy hand over his shaved crown. "We had no choice,
Masao. The Chinese, even though they are our cousins, are barbarians.
Their insistence on fighting us proves it. Perhaps there were some excesses,
but war is not a tea ceremony."

"And we *did* try to control our men later," I said. "The world just
won't understand that most of our army consists of ignorant peasant boys
not much above farm animals. We train them harshly because that is the
way of *bushido*. We beat them, we teach them to obey, to fight, to die. It's
not unnatural for them to let loose their anger on the enemy."

Sato raised his hand. "Never mind, that is of less account, Masao, than
the fact that once one suffers defeat one is shamed forever. Defeat is death.
One has no rights. The Chinese, damn them, can't seem to understand
this. As for savages like the Americans and the British, it is not worth
explaining to them."

We smoked American cigarettes, sipped rice brandy. I reflected on the
Chinese captives I had bayonetted. They had died stoically, and I silently
saluted them.

"My brother Kenji thinks differently," I said.

"Kenji? That firefly? What can he have to say about a soldier's code?
About the rules for a *samurai?*"

"He says that Japan also has a tradition of kindness. Of honor, of
obligations and duties—"

"Who would contest that? But what your brother fails to comprehend
is that these rules apply to Japanese, and to friendly guests. To our family,

our friends, our neighbors, and yes, to visitors. But once we depart from
our own soil and go to battle on foreign soil, all such rules are invalid.
They do not apply."

"Yes, well, I suppose Kenji has spent too much time with Americans.
At the university he came under the influence of liberals and socialists, like
that fellow Adachi I once met."

"I don't know him. Probably some greasy-palmed doddering old
scholar. Some say we'll dig them out of the universities, root and branch.
Doesn't your brother understand that it was a prince of the Imperial
blood, General Asaka, who ordered us to kill civilians in Nanking?"

"It's not common knowledge, sir. Some wonder if His Majesty was
informed—"

"Who remembers? Who cares? Suppose His Majesty was not informed." He belched. "The emperor had his sources, peace-faction cowards. They poisoned his mind. He asked for lenient and generous treatment of the people of Nanking. By that time we'd already killed all we
had to. Split them like chickens. The emperor is a kind man. He did not
understand that killing a Chinese is like stepping on an ant."

We finished the bottle of brandy, and Sato soon fell off his cushion,
drunk. I had the orderlies help me carry him to a taxi. I imagine we made
quite a sight, each of us bedecked with medals and ribbons, each bearing
our long swords. But no shame attached to the colonel's drunkenness. I
was honored to bear my future father-in-law to his home. He was a
widower and had a maid and a cook and an unmarried daughter—my
future wife Michiko—to look after him, not to mention several mistresses.

In the taxi he stirred, yawned, and kept repeating, "Kill all, burn all,
loot all."

YURIKO TAMBA · JUNE, 1941

My brother Masao and his bride, my friend Michiko Sato, were married
on a hot windy day at a Shinto temple in Ueno Park, north of the
city.

Uneo Park was always one of my favorite places—soft green lawns,
gardens, forests, stone lanterns, *torii* gates, museums. It is so lovely that
on the most crowded weekend or holiday you have a sense of peace and

quiet. Not that I mind crowds, we Japanese are never happier than when we're getting lost in hordes of our beloved countrymen.

Anyway, Ueno Park is also a center for our religious life. It's located in the northeast corner of Tokyo, a direction on the compass that is most likely to bring bad luck. Here, Kenji would say, we embark on one of those delicious Japanese paradoxes so dear to our philosophers. Because of this unlucky location, the ancient rulers of Edo—the old name for Tokyo—erected many temples and shrines here to ward off evil forces. In 1626, for example, the shogun built the Kan-ei Buddhist temple to protect against malevolent demons. And so instead of being unlucky Ueno became very safe and secure.

Well, the ceremony for the marriage of Michiko and Masao was brief and rather somber, I thought. The Shinto priest in his orange robe and black hat spoke the sacred words in the old court language. The bridal couple solemnized the ceremony by signing the civil register, then drank the traditional nine sips of sake and the guests all joined them.

I was twenty years old, younger than Masao and Kenji, and six years older than my brother Saburo. Everyone said I looked like a perfect young Japanese lady in my maroon-and-yellow kimono and a dark gold *obi*. My hair was done in the old-fashioned style, jet black, and decorated with a strand of pearls. I know it sounds immodest, but I don't think I ever looked prettier, not even at my own wedding that would come a year later. Maybe it was because I was so happy on the day Masao got married, and so sad at my own wedding . . .

"June isn't a lucky month for weddings," my brother Kenji said, "but I wish them well."

"They had no choice," I told Kenji. "Masao is going back to China . . ."

"Why are October and November the best months for a wedding?" he asked me. He was always testing me, quizzing me.

"The harvest is in and the heat of the summer is over. Am I right?"

"You are right, little Yuriko."

I remember how dazzling the bridal couple looked. I had to catch my breath when I looked at them. Masao wore a blue dress uniform and all his campaign ribbons and medals . . . His long sword rested lightly on his leg. His boots gleamed. And he was so handsome. Like Kenji, he had a long strong face, although Masao did not smile as easily as Kenji.

Michiko Sato wore an antique white brocade kimono made of the finest heavy silk that had belonged to her grandmother, a lady-in-waiting to the Meiji emperor. It was as elaborate as any in the Tokyo museum of costume, and must have been very heavy. On her head Michiko wore the broad, stiff white-silk hat, the *tsuno-kakushi*, "horn hider," to hide the horns of jealousy. What this really means is that the wife will never become angry or jealous if the husband goes to another woman for . . . well, you understand.

People were passing by the newly married couple now, bowing and paying compliments. No one shook hands or kissed the bride. We consider such touchings of flesh unsanitary.

I stood there with Kenji and my younger brother Saburo, all of us happy for Masao and Michiko. A long table was piled high with wedding presents, all magnificently wrapped . . . no one in the world can wrap packages the way we do. They teach us young girls how to do it when we're in high school, and some say we create works of art with paper and ribbon. Colonel Sato, father of the bride, had arranged for every guest to receive a small gift, beautifully wrapped in small red *furoshiki*s, the scarves we use for decorative packaging.

I noticed that Colonel Sato stood a little apart with some high ranking officers who were friends of his. One was a sickish looking man, Commander Endo from the Imperial Navy. The men in uniform talked in loud voices and turned their backs on the other people.

"Quite a collection," Kenji said to me.

"Collection?"

"The bride's father's friends. Every one of them a member of the Cherry Blossom Association."

"Oh? They like flowers?"

"Other things. Like war and mutiny."

"How do you know so much?"

"Never mind . . . but I think the colonel also belongs to the Blood Pledge Association and the Golden Pheasant Academy."

I was such an innocent. "It's nice he is so important and that Masao has married into the family. We're humble people alongside Colonel Sato."

Kenji smiled that warm, tolerant smile of his.

But it was true that our own parents, Mr. and Mrs. Goro Tamba of Shibuya Ward, did indeed seem ordinary in comparison to the starched medal-covered officers who had come to honor the bridal couple.

My father was standing with some of his people from the Imperial Palace, where he was a subvalet working for the chamberlain. His were housekeeping duties—looking after linens, cutlery, furniture, serving refreshments to guests. I suppose it was humble work, but the fact that it was associated with the palace and that he often got to see His Majesty made his job more than an ordinary steward's.

My father was also a gentle man. Most Japanese husbands . . . I don't like to admit it but it's true . . . are tyrants in their homes, but I can't remember my father ever losing his temper or even raising his voice. Yes, he did expect to be waited on and served in his own house, but he was never mean or thoughtless.

I heard him say to a colleague, "My son Masao gives us all great joy and honor," and the man said, "Yes, there is no greater honor than to fight for the emperor." Another added, "Let us pray the Chinese are beaten soon, so that Masao may enjoy his home and produce many male children and continue the Tamba name."

They all drank to this, laughed, talked about the weather, the good auspices that that meant, the good news about the imminent victory in China.

My mother Hisako was rather tall for a Japanese woman, slender and graceful. She was fair-skinned and long-headed like my three brothers. (I'd inherited the round rosy face of my father). There are supposed to be two main physical strains among us Japanese—the long-heads and the round-heads. Well, the longs dominated in our family.

Ordinarily my mother wore a plain gray house kimono and little makeup. Today, though, she was resplendent in an heirloom—a blue-green and lavender kimono over a hundred years old and worn only on the most important occasions. I knew she would wear it again at my wedding—although at the time there was no one in sight as a possible husband for me.

Saburo was fourteen and a tease and was yanking now at my *obi* to get my attention. When I turned to see what he wanted he made a funny face and ran off. As the baby of the family he got away with all sorts of mischief. He wasn't a bad kid, but with Kenji about to leave and Masao moving out, well, I didn't relish the idea of being tormented by him. He wore his dark blue schoolboy's uniform with brass buttons, and the peaked cap of the student. He was, I might add, as skinny as a bamboo shoot, but not nearly as tough. Dr. Adam Varnum said that Saburo had weak lungs and that the Tokyo air was bad for him.

It's funny about my three brothers . . . Masao was, naturally, the king of the house. An eldest son always is. He would carry on my father's name and inherit all his wealth. Masao had been raised to believe he could do no wrong and get anything he wanted. A bright student, he was awarded a scholarship to the military academy, just as Kenji became a government scholar at Tokyo Imperial University a few years later. The difference was that Masao was constantly praised, spoiled and given his way. Poor Kenji, actually much brighter than Masao, was always "Master Cold Rice"—the

younger son who gets fed last. I was, they said, a cute baby girl and then
an "adorable little lady," and I guess in a way I was kind of spoiled too.
Saburo, youngest and sickly, was also allowed to have his way. But "Number Two" Kenji, as nice as he was, as smart as he was, was somehow
overlooked by my parents. He didn't complain. He studied, won prizes,
had friends, learned to speak English and French and happily accepted
his scholarly life. He'd already spent two years in the United States at the
University of Oregon and would be returning in a week or so for graduate
studies in California. How I envied him his travels . . .

Saburo was tugging at Kenji's tan suit jacket and hooting at him—
"Firefly!"

Kenji laughed and shook a finger at Saburo. Of course it was Saburo's
way of teasing, of making a comparison between Masao—all boots and
medals and sword—and Kenji the student. There is a legend that poor
country boys who want to do well in their studies will catch fireflies, put
them in a glass jar and study far into the night by the light of the little
bugs. Hardworking students are often given firefly lapel pins to reward
their good work. Not surprising that Kenji, who could stay up half the
night reading, was nicknamed "Firefly" by his school chums.

Sometimes I thought Kenji was too nice for his own good. I wish, for
example, that he would have yanked Saburo's ear or been able to join in
the conversation my father was having with his palace friends, or at least
have a few words with Colonel Sato's Black Dragons or whatever they
were. But he was too polite to intrude. He was also kind enough to stay
with me and my friends. That wasn't very Japanese for a male, but then,
Kenji was unusual in his way. I loved him very much.

KENJI TAMBA · JUNE, 1941

Random memories of Masao's wedding . . .

How beautiful Yuriko was, a jewel. She put all the women there to
shame, including her friend Michiko Sato, who was also a beauty but had
a certain resigned look about her. In Yuriko's eyes I saw something else.
I hoped life would treat her well.

My dad got drunk early but he held his sake well, and his buddies from
the palace—an assortment of stewards, cooks, bakers—helped prop him up.

Colonel Sato came in force, a military man down to his high heels. That fellow Endo, the naval officer, was said to have Admiral Yamamoto's ear, or so Professor Adachi told me. A loud bunch of junior officers, full of opinions, loud voices, much slapping of thighs and fondling of sword hilts.

There was one political person there, a man named Kingoro Hata, a distant cousin of my mother's. He was a deputy in Parliament elected from western Tokyo. He had a big belly and a shaved head and he affected a monocle. He would have been a pompous ass if it weren't for the fact that he represented the National Founding Association. They were a right-wing group, at one time given to violence, murder, torture and blackmail. Lately, according to Adachi, they had scrubbed up their image and were receiving considerable financial support from respectable big business interests. Hata himself was in some kind, or kinds, of business, making commissions, investing, putting people in touch with one another. He was what we Japanese call "a man of broad face"—influential, ambitious, and not too savory. He was the only civilian who was allowed to mingle with Colonel Sato and his military guests.

The Shinto priest got up on the dais and offered a prayer and toast to the emperor: "To the glory of Tenno Heika, our divine majesty, the Son of Heaven, our living god. We give him our lives and souls forever and we pray that this young couple, Masao Tamba and Michiko Sato, will live long and happy lives and fulfill all their duties to His Majesty and always gladden his heart."

We raised our cups of sake, Masao and Michiko bowed, then everyone else did. I smiled at Yuriko and Saburo. All three of us felt a rush of pride at being kin to Captain Tamba. Thoughts of Nanking and what might have happened there had for the moment left my mind.

Then Colonal Sato stepped to the dais. He was not a man to let a Shinto priest take the spotlight on his daughter's wedding day. Looking as if his chest would burst and splatter the crowd with his ribbons and medals, he proclaimed:

"In this marriage are united two families, Tamba and Sato, servants of the Son of Heaven. Michiko, my daughter, serve this great soldier Captain Tamba well. Do his bidding, give him sons. For in soldiers like Captain Tamba lies the future of Japan." Sato raised his glass. "To Japan and our divine ruler—Japan, first in the world!"

At the edge of the pavilion on the lawn stood the only Caucasians at the wedding. They'll figure prominently in my story so I will talk a little about them now. They were a married couple, both physicians and in their late forties. Dr. Adam Varnum was a Californian. His wife, Dr. Cora Varnum, was Swiss. They were Quakers and had come to Shibuya Ward over twenty years earlier to open a clinic. Although technically they were medical missionaries they did nothing to try to convert us but instead devoted their lives to serving the people of the district. They had delivered both my sister Yuriko and my brother Saburo, and had seen Masao and me through measles, scarlet fever, and any number of bruises, sprained ankles, bee stings and the other usual ailments of two active boys. The Varnums were fine people. My family felt close to them and were grateful to them, but they could never be close friends the way our Japanese neighbors were. It didn't seem to bother the Varnums. They were the kind of people who lived to serve others, never bragged about it or made a fuss over it, and found their satisfaction in their work. They had no children, which was too bad, since they loved kids. One could always find youngsters playing outside the Shibuya Ward clinic.

Although both Adam Varnum and his wife were fluent in Japanese (they even spoke with a Tokyo accent) they seemed left out of the ceremonies now, the toasting and drinking and congratulating. I walked toward them, bowing to Colonel Sato and his clique and not missing a certain coolness from them.

As I walked the length of the pavilion I could see across the greensward of Ueno Park that a typical Japanese celebration, a *matsuri,* was approaching us. A crowd of half-naked young men, dressed only in breechclouts and headbands, powerful bodies gleaming with sweat, were chanting and bearing a shrine, a *mikoshi.* Bystanders refreshed them with cups of sake as the *matsuri* made its way around the pavilion and the guests stopped to admire the young men. The ceremony was in honor of a local god. The priest came out of the cover of the pavilion to bestow a blessing on the runners. Other young men waited to relieve those who tired. It was considered a great honor to bear the *mikoshi.* I can remember Masao staying forever under the back-breaking wooden poles that supported the ornate eagle-crowned little house where the god dwelled, determined not to let anyone take his place.

"See those guys?" Saburo said to Yuriko. "They're dancing just for Masao."

"They are not. It's for the god."

He tugged at her *obi,* stuck his tongue out and ran off to follow the shrine-bearers.

"A beautiful day," Cora Varnum said to me. "Masao is so handsome. And I had no idea Michiko was so lovely. She's like a painting, or a figure on a silk screen."

"The *samurai* deserve the best," I said.

Dr. Varnum nudged me. "Scholars should do just as well . . . Excited about your return to America?"

I told him I was. They already knew my plan to spend two or three years at UCLA in American studies, trying to learn about the United States political system. Upon getting my Ph.D I would return to the Ministry of Education, where I had held a temporary job as Professor Adachi's assistant.

"You must write to us," Cora said.

"Of course I will."

Dr. Adam Varnum—he was a burly rumpled man, a one-time football player—fumbled in his vest pocket and brought out a prescription blank that he'd written a name and address on.

"Our niece. She's at UCLA. A senior or junior, I'm not sure. You must look her up, Kenji."

I looked at the scratchy scrawl. Like all doctors he prided himself on unintelligible penmanship. Dr. Adam Varnum surely would never become a calligrapher.

Julie Mary Varnum. It was followed by an address in a town called Glendale and a telephone number. In my mind was a vision of some unattainable American girl. What in the world could she want with a strange fish like Kenji Tamba? But I thanked the Varnums and said I would send her their regards.

"She's very pretty," Cora Varnum said. "And smart. Her father is Adam's older brother."

"It will be an honor to meet them," I said.

My father, stiff and a bit flustered, was approaching now with Colonel Sato a step behind him. My father may have been an employee of the Imperial Palace but he was clearly the social inferior of Colonel Sato. Sato did not let people forget his rank and power, and wasn't above hinting at those mysterious associations in his past. My father wore his frock coat, stiff collar, ascot and striped trousers with a certain touching aplomb. He wore this same getup on many palace occasions and I was glad to see he carried it off as well as Sato in his display of medals and long sword.

It was obvious that my father wanted Sato to meet our American friends, probably to show that we weren't just another ordinary family in Shibuya Ward.

My father bowed to the Varnums, and they, longtime residents of Japan, returned the bow.

"A fine day, a lovely wedding, and a handsome couple," Adam Varnum said. "Goro, my wife and I wish you and your family great happiness."

My father bowed again. "You are most kind." He turned to Sato. "Allow me the honor of presenting the father of the bride, Colonel Hiroshi Sato of the Imperial General Staff. He asked to meet you."

Sato did not bow but the Varnums did.

"Dr. Adam Varnum, Dr. Cora Varnum, Colonel Sato," my father went on. "Colonel, these two American friends are our neighbors and have looked after our health for many years."

"Two doctors?" Sato asked. "Man and wife?"

"It gets confusing, colonel," Cora said.

I thought I detected a film of hostility on the colonel's face. Rigid, bound to old ways and codes, he had trouble imagining a married couple (even though, of course, they were *gaijin*) both practicing medicine. Moreover it was evident that their splendid command of the Japanese language irked him. Why, I'm not certain. Sato was one of those turned-in supernationalists who considered all that was Japanese as sacred, inviolate and inherently incomprehensible to outsiders.

"Ah, two physicians . . ."

A small attractive woman with a round rosy face and light brown hair worn short with coquettish bangs, Cora Varnum smiled, then said as if to reassure him, "I'm in charge of women and children, colonel. My husband is a general practitioner and does our administrative work."

"And I have the privilege of fixing the hot-water boiler when it breaks down," Adam Varnum said.

Colonel Sato only looked offended. "Can't you find a decent plumber?"

"Oh, yes," Adam said, "but I enjoy working with my hands."

Masao, leaving Michiko to her admiring bridesmaids, approached us. "Strong hands, colonel," Masao said. "Dr. Varnum can throw a baseball better than I can."

Adam Varnum wagged a finger at my brother. "You weren't bad yourself, Masao. Only you insisted on throwing that cheap ball I gave you against my garage door. How many times did I have to chase you and Kenji?"

"We only wanted you to come out and play with us," Masao said.

How different Masao could be at times . . . With Dr. Varnum and his wife he seemed the least hostile of men.

"Masao's right," I added. "You never got around to teaching us to hit a curve ball."

"To be honest," Dr. Varnum said, "I was no good at it myself. There's a trick to it." He assumed a batting stance, held an imaginary bat in his huge corded hands. "Fellow at USC tried to teach me once. Turn your left shoulder slightly into the pitch, wait for the ball to start to drop . . . I forget the rest."

We all laughed. The sight of this husky gray-haired man, his powerful fingers stained with nicotine (or was it iodine?), reliving his youth was funny and endearing.

"I am told you have been in Tokyo for more than twenty years," Sato said. "What brought you here?"

"Our faith," Cora said.

"Oh?"

I said quietly, "The Varnums are Quakers, colonel."

"Ah, a sect? Like our Zen Buddhists?"

"Similar . . . but not quite," Dr. Adam Varnum said. "We're a rather odd lot. We go on believing in peace and brotherhood and trying to be of some help to the less fortunate."

"Very noble," the colonel said. "Too bad the realities of the world do not permit many of us to live by such ideals. The Buddha also taught such concepts, but they are as elusive as a white fox in a field of snow." He studied their faces. "So . . . you like Japan?"

Adam Varnum could be tough and direct in spite of his Quaker forbearance. For a moment he seemed to be studying the blaze of ribbons on Sato's tunic, ignoring the colonel's military cronies, including Commander Endo, who had gathered to stare at the *gaijin* guests. Then, with an edge to his voice, Adam said, "We like the people here. We hope we've been good guests in your country."

"I am sure you have been," Sato said. "But as perhaps Masao has explained to you, it is difficult for us to accept the generosity of foreigners. An obligation is a sacred duty. If someone does us a favor or assists us or gives us a gift we are obliged to repay him. We are honor-bound to outdo the giver. So you see, doctor, acts of kindness that are put upon us can become a burden . . ."

Adam, who had heard all this before and who knew our customs well, turned now to his wife and smiled. "Well, my dear, it seems we'll have to be less attentive to our patients. Maybe cut down on medication, set only half a broken bone or remove part of an appendix. That way they won't have to suffer the sorrows of heavy obligations."

Blank looks adorned the faces of my father, Sato, and the military people. But Masao and I, who knew the Varnums well, tried to break the tension. Masao said, "Dr. Varnum, you could never act that way. And I must say I never felt sorry about the way you taped my ankle or put a splint on my wrist."

It occurred to me that just about everyone had delivered a toast except my father, his mind cluttered as it was with tableware inventories and laundry lists. I urged my father to give his own toast now.

"A speech?"

"Yes, I spoke to the priest."

"You had no right to do so."

My mother edged up. "Kenji, respect your father."

"I am showing respect by asking him to speak, mother."

My father shrugged and walked to the center of the pavilion, and as we left I overheard Colonel Sato asking his new son-in-law, "These Quaker people . . . they don't believe in war?"

"No violence of any kind," Masao said.

"Interesting . . . I wonder how many Americans are Quakers . . . ?"

Ignorance, I thought . . . dangerous ignorance. Sato in his plot-thickened brain might be thinking of a war against a nation of unarmed peace-loving cheek-turning Quakers. Dangerous . . .

My father was raising a cup of sake, and nervously fussed with his steamed spectacles and starched collar.

"Tears of joy fill my eyes today. I have more pleasure than my heart can bear. Today the Tamba family of Shibuya Ward incurs heavy obligations, burdens we shall bear all our lives . . ."

Adam and Cora Varnum were standing behind me and I heard her say, "Obligations again."

My father went on: "To be joined to the great family of Colonel Sato, a *samurai*, a hero, is so beautiful that I cannot contemplate it. Now we offer to Colonel Sato another *samurai*, my son Masao Tamba."

The military applauded. But everyone knew that Sato was an armchair soldier. My brother had earned his reputation in battle. (I confess that in the light moments of this occasion thoughts of the men and women in Nanking were shut out of my mind).

"But all of this, this wedding, this happy day, this marriage of a soldier and a soldier's daughter serves one purpose—to fulfill the desires of our majesty, the Son of Heaven, our divine ruler."

Shouts of *"Kampai"* and more toasts to the emperor. Then an open carriage drawn by a pair of matched coal-black horses drew up to the edge of the pavilion, and Michiko, in white robe and broad white hat, was helped into it by her bridesmaids (who included my sister Yuriko), Masao following her.

Little brother Saburo ran to the side of the carriage and shouted at Masao, "The sword, the sword . . ."

Laughing, Masao drew his curved sword and held it over his head. Everyone laughed and clapped. A wedding party, a honeymoon, a first night of love, did not seem the occasion to be brandishing a weapon but nobody objected as the carriage horses trotted away and they were off to Lake Hakone and a country inn.

My mother Hisako wept, but was stoical. She refused any comfort from Yuriko or from me. Masao, of course, was her favorite. He always had been. And as is our tradition, she seemed to enjoy her sorrow.

Sometimes it was like a three-ring circus, that summer of 1941. The kids were getting nervous. All the war talk. But no one believed it. Not really.

All over the UCLA campus you'd see signs that said OHIO. Or boys wearing buttons that said OHIO, meaning Over the Hill in October, and "over the hill" meant to go AWOL or to desert. October was when a lot of draftees' time was up. Not many guys wanted to stay in the army. There was a lot of "America First" talk on campus from conservative students, and a lot of "Stay out of Imperialist War" talk from the left-wingers, although some changed their tune after Germany invaded Russia.

My boyfriend Ed Hodges, who'd just graduated, had decided to take a commission in the Marine Corps. There was a Corps training program right on campus, and I'd see Ed in his cadet suntans and overseas cap doing close-order drill on the practice football field with young men from UCLA and other California schools. Ed had this notion that if he was going into service—the draft was going to be extended—he might as well go "first class" as an officer and as a Marine. What he really wanted was to go to law school (he'd been accepted at Stanford) but he knew he'd have to do his service first.

You read a lot about how footloose and crazy we were back in 1941 before the war began . . . goldfish-swallowing, consuming musical records, stuffing ourselves into phonebooths, jitterbugging. Gals in pleated skirts, Peter Pan collar blouses, bobbysox and saddle shoes. Guys in zoot-suits, pointy shoes, crewcut hair . . . Sure, a lot of that went on, but the smarter ones like Ed and my friend Carol Andrus and my brother Chris—they saw something coming and started to get serious and make plans early.

I can remember sitting in the shade of some pin oaks at the edge of the field watching Ed and his buddies do the fancy steps of close-order drill while their D.I., Sergeant Ralph Guzzo, a dark stocky man in a campaign hat, bellowed orders. With me were my brother Chris, a year and a half older than I am (I was twenty-one with a year of college remaining) and Carol Andrus, who was Chris's age.

> *Count cadence, count!*
> *Count cadence, count!*
> *One, two, three, four,*
> *One, two—three, four!*

The sounds of the massed voices echoed across the campus. In counterpoint a group of "America First" students, some I knew, were parading

around the perimeter of the field, carrying signs that demanded an end to
the draft and that America stay out of Europe's wars.

> *Roosevelt, Willkie,*
> *Wallace, Taft,*
> *End the draft, end the draft!*

One guy—Van Dyke Ord, a Phi Gam—toted a sign that read VETER-
ANS OF FUTURE WARS. Another guy held up one that read WHY
DIE FOR ROOSEVELT? They tried but couldn't outshout the Marine
company. I still get a chill when I think of the marching chant:

> *You had a good home when you left,*
> *You right!*
> *You had a good home when you left,*
> *You right!*
> *Sound off, one, two . . .*

There were other verses that Ed and his buddies marched to, including
one about a character named Jody—the one who dodged the draft, stayed
home and got all the girls. (I think this started with black soldiers—in
those days we called them Negroes.)
   I said to my brother Chris, "What if they're right and we're all wrong?"
   "About what?"
   "Oh, staying out of the army. No more wars. America First."
   "Maybe they are."
   Chris, chewing on a blade of grass, took hold of Carol's hand. My
brother, to tell the truth, didn't seem much committed to anything except
his career and himself. He'd been an editor of the campus newspaper, the
Daily Bruin. Summers, he'd worked as a news assistant at a Los Angeles
radio station, and he'd tried his hand (with no great success) at freelance
magazine writing. I'm not sure he was a very good writer, but he was
ambitious, energetic and determined to be a journalist. Carol meanwhile
was frowning and shouting something at the antiwar, antidraft marchers.
I don't think they heard her, or if they did, I doubt they cared a damn.
   "They should be told off," Carol said. "There are lot worse things than
wearing a uniform or serving your country."
   "Everybody stand up and salute," Chris said. "Listen to the army brat."
   "That's a *compliment* as far as I'm concerned," Carol said.
   Not surprising . . . Carol's dad was a retired master sergeant, regular
army, who'd fought in the World War and had done his years of service
in the Philippines, the Canal Zone, the Hawaiian Islands. He was widowed
and ran an automotive spare parts business. He didn't have much money

but he'd still managed to send Carol and her older sister through college and was very proud of them. Carol was a whiz at science, she was going to enlist in the Army Medical Corps and train for a commission as an army nurse.

"They'll never lay a glove on me," Chris said.

"Maybe they should," Carol told him. "teach you to obey orders."

"War correspondents get deferred. I'll tell the world about our brave guys getting blown apart. Give the public what it wants—"

"Oh, you really can be horrid," she said, and yanked her hand away.

"Hey, if I get drafted I'll never make officer and then *I'll* have to salute *you*. I can't do that."

"Your brother's nuts, Julie," Carol said.

"And selfish." I smiled when I said it, but I also half meant it. Which made me nervous.

The ROTC company had finished its drill, ending with a dramatic flourish, split-second routine done with rifles called a Queen Anne salute, then were ordered to stack arms and given a break.

Ed broke from his ranks—he was a platoon leader and carried the guidon—and trotted over to us.

"Man," Chris said, "you guys march like you're serious. Tell the truth, Hodges, didn't you enlist so Uncle Sam could pay your law-school tuition?"

My brother could be a real pill. "He did not. And you're *not* funny," I said.

The protesters had set up a ladder that a young man mounted and was now shouting that America had better stay out of Europe's wars. The draft, lend-lease, FDR, anything that smacked of intervention was evil and stupid.

"Tell 'em, Trotsky," Chris yelled at them, apparently unaware of the irony that his own position wasn't exactly gung-ho for the war.

The four of us started to walk away, me walking ahead with Ed—God, I'd known him since I was four years old and he was six—Carol and Chris trailing us, Chris putting his arm around her shoulders and Carol taking it off. Carol was a dark girl with long dark brown hair and intense brown eyes. She had a kind of solemn manner . . . I think it came from all that moving around when she was little . . . and had a million stories about being an army sergeant's kid in "the Zone" or "the Islands." Her mother had died when Carol was ten.

Chris was fair, like me, thin, loose-limbed with a certain arrogance in his walk and manner. Right now he was teasing Carol.

"Hey, can't we play Judy Garland and Mickey Rooney? That's what college people do in the summer, hold hands, smooch—"

"Hands *off,* Chris. We're *supposed* to act like adults."

"Which calls for adultery."

"Not funny."

"My folks went to La Jolla for the weekend. My sweet sister's going out with Ed . . . How about you and me and Glenn Miller and Artie Shaw having a private party—"

"No."

"Why?"

"Because I have to get ready for my trip to San Francisco, I'm going to take the exam to be an army nurse. All clear, smart guy?"

"I'll be damned, you're serious."

"Just as serious as you are about your career, Chris. So let's ease off, see where we're going, not complicate it. Okay?"

"It ain't so complicated, lady," Chris said. "It's easy."

"Not for some of us."

"You'll be sorry when I win the Pulitzer Prize."

"I hope you do. I mean that, Chris."

"He never quits, does he?" Ed said. We had stopped in front of Royce Hall. I was taking two summer courses—Social Psychology and Latin American Civilization. Actually I had no career in mind. In those days young women got their degree, got married, had kids and took care of the house.

"It's fairly harmless," I said, "although sort of boring. He really likes Carol, I think."

"Well, meet another guy who won't quit."

"You? Edward Hodges, Jr.? Whoever said you did?"

We stood in the warm June sunlight. Ed was tall and strong in his uniform, the sun lighting his beach-tanned face. Now he was offering me a Marine pin—globe, anchor and eagle.

"Take it."

"I can't, it's not fair—"

"I won't hold you to anything. No promises, no deals. *Nada.* "

"Don't, please, Ed. I'd hate to hurt you."

"You? Julie Mary Varnum? How could you ever hurt me or anybody else, for that matter? Remember, I've known you since you were five years old."

"Four. God, what a bully you were. The terror of Glendale."

"I'm trying to make up for it. Come on, Julie. Wear the pin for old Ed."

"But . . . everything's so unsettled . . ."

"Look, I may not get to law school for a long time. I may like being a jarhead, I may stay in forever. We can't count on anything. There are all kinds of latrine rumors. Fast commissions, shipping us out . . . that's why I want us to be engaged. Now."

"Ed, you know how much I like you. The only boy on the block who let me play on the softball team . . ." I smiled when I said it.

"Purely selfish, kid. You were a great outfielder. Not to mention catch. You still are."

There was always something winning, something innocent about Ed. What today they call "up front." "Okay," I said. "I'll wear the pin, but—"

"That's my center fielder," and he kissed my forehead before I could develop the "but."

I decided to try to make light of it. "Can I pull rank on people now? Including my insolent brother?"

"Absolutely. You are now a gyrene, junior grade."

"I'm not sure I'll be too good at it. I always hated to take orders—or give them."

"It's going to work out just fine . . . just so long as there's a fighting chance for Edward Hodges, nonfighting Marine."

I brushed his lips with mine. "We'll leave it at that, old buddy," and went to class feeling not a little guilty and mixed up. Which, of course, was the way most everything seemed back then in 1941.

MASAO TAMBA · JULY, 1941

My wife and I enjoyed a brief honeymoon at a rustic old-fashioned inn on Lake Hakone. It was especially good to spend time in a quaint old gabled building that once served the *daimyo*, the feudal lord, as a stopping place on his marches to Tokyo.

It was a curious old place, with an overhanging second story with elaborately carved and wide-projecting eaves. The kitchen was huge, and a fragrant wood fire burned in the huge fireplace. (In Tokyo we used charcoal).

The rooms were also large—eight- or ten-*tatami* mat size, without furnishings or ornamentation but with pillars made from the finest darkened cypress wood and walls and doors of translucent rice paper. There was also a stone garden to rival the Ryoanji of Kyoto.

Waited on by a dozen well-trained servants, we took our simple meals in the room.

Michiko proved to be a companionable woman. She took off my clothing, helped me dress, saw to it that I had the best *futon* and pillow, chastised the servants when they were laggard and did not complain when I engaged her in sexual intercourse more than she expected. Unfortunately, she reacted very little and seemed a bit ashamed of offering me her body. But a fine body it was—fair and unmarked and bud-breasted, with legs properly chunky, thick-ankled and slightly bowed, the way we Japanese men like them.

We walked on woodland paths, admired the waterfall, collected botanical specimens for pressing but did not talk much. Which pleased me. I cannot abide talkative women.

Once back in Tokyo we moved into a four-room house much like my parents', with a main room of ten-*tatami* size. It was a gift from the colonel as part of Michiko's dowry, and Kingoro Hata was also involved in it . . . I believe that to curry favor with my father-in-law he had arranged for him to buy the house at a low price by threatening the owner with a tax increase. Hata had a way of getting things done. As for myself, I detest business dealings—money, stocks, bonds, all that boring and tainted business that takes one's mind off important things such as war and national destiny.

Colonel Sato had postponed my return to China so that I might sit in on meetings of the Imperial General Staff as his aide. In that tense summer of 1941 these meetings became more frequent, longer and with angry arguments breaking out, followed by visits to the Imperial Palace to brief the emperor, the Prime Minister Prince Konoye, the Lord Privy Seal Kido and other important government officials. All day long the black limousines came and went across the Ishi-Bashi stone bridge and through the Niju-Bashi Gate, driving about the greening flowering grounds of the royal enclosure, circling carp ponds, wooden bridges, rose gardens. Ladies-in-waiting would bow to the generals and admirals as they rode by, flags waving in the breeze. Gardeners and maintenance workers tipped their hats and lowered their heads. Riding with Colonel Sato, I thought of the irony of my father working inside the palace as a dispenser of dishes and linen while his son was privy to command decisions and these displays of respect.

As a young boy, along with my brother Kenji, three years younger than me, I occasionally was taken into the palace grounds for a special treat. My father would be as proud as a peacock as he showed us the flocks of semitame birds, the sloping Cyclopean walls, the massive fortifications, the peaked roofs of the emperor's dwelling and offices, as well as the willows and cherry trees. It was a fairyland to me, a domain built for a god on earth, the Son of Heaven, the direct descendant of the sun goddess Amaterasu, founder of our race . . .

"Here lives our god," said Colonel Sato solemnly as we rode in an official staff car with Commander Endo, chain-smoking nervously. Endo was a secret official of the Anti-Red Corps, an anti-communist, anti-Soviet spokesman who favored an immediate declaration of war against Russia. He branded as lies the report that in 1939 a Soviet division had mauled our best troops in a Manchurian border incident. He also seemed unaware that his "strike north" faction, advocating war with Russia, was losing ground to those in the military who wanted to "strike south" and attack Malaya, the Dutch Indies, Hong Kong, the Philippines and all those nations of Asia ruled by the tyrants of the West, *including* the United States.

"A God, yes," said Endo, and chuckled.

"Commander Endo finds that funny?" I asked. I may have been a mere captain but I knew I had the power and the right to ask such a question . . . my combat record, my days in the field were much greater than Endo's and my father-in-law's combined. It occurred to me that they seemed to spend more time plotting and scheming than fighting . . .

"Commander Endo means to say," Colonel Sato answered me, "that the notion of godhead is a recent one. We of the Imperial Way, who know His Majesty's heart, decided that he is a god. Such belief helps inspire the people. Anyone who opposes us can be accused of heresy, blasphemy and atheism. The emperor, I might add, does not seem to mind the arrangement."

"I see . . ." In fact I was bothered but put it out of my mind and was grateful that I was a fighting man, a field soldier, not a desk man who spent his life at meetings.

We assembled on the lawn outside the Imperial offices, where we were served soft drinks and tea, and I caught sight of my father passing among us with a tray. A few of those present knew he was my dad, but they made no point of it. Our family may have been low in rank, but I had vowed that I would elevate us. I am proud that the Japanese are less class-bound than, let us say, the British. The sons of courtesans and geishas and peasants, even illegitimate children, can rise on the basis of sheer merit.

"Manchuria, Manchuria," Sato was saying.

I was at the rear with some junior officers, and waited to hear more.

"A bloody good time that was," Commander Endo said.

"Yes," Sato went on, "the old Kwangtung army . . . there was a gang of *samurai* for you. Took matters into our own hands. When Tokyo dragged its feet, dilly-dallied, cleared its throat but couldn't talk we took the war to the Chinks. And the emperor approved."

That was not what my brother Kenji had said. Kenji's version—he could have been jailed for saying it publicly—was that the Kwangtung army was a collection of rebellious hotheads who defied Tokyo, the emperor, Parliament, the General Staff and waged an illegal war against Manchuria. I wondered . . .

"The *fait accompli,* as the French say," Sato went on, "that's what does it. How could anyone object after we'd cleaned up Manchuria and driven the Chinese out?"

"We should have kept moving north," Commander Endo said. "Right into Russia. To Moscow."

Others agreed, some apparently did not. I was glad to see that the meeting was about to begin, but there was a last-minute change. Junior officers like myself were to wait outside, so I took the opportunity to chat with my father, who was bursting with pride to see me at the palace, even if, as I told him, my role there was to carry Colonel Sato's notebook.

"Oh, it is more than that, my dear Masao. *You* do *him* honor. You were the hero of Nanking. You fought at Shansi and Shanghai. Yes, my eldest, you do us *all* honor."

I smiled and bowed, then introduced some of my fellow officers to him. I was not ashamed of his being a servant. Not in the least. And I believed my record in the field made me a better man than most of them—paper-pushers . . .

In an hour or so the conference ended, and I got into the staff car, sitting in front with the driver. Sato and Endo sat in the back. They appeared flushed with excitement as we drove through the palace grounds again, wound our way to the Ishi-Bashi Gate and then into the heart of the teeming, heat-hazed city.

"It went well," my father-in-law said. "His Majesty understood our wishes. I think we may expect an outcome that will suit us."

Endo coughed. "Russia, Russia, *that* is the way to move—"

"I am afraid not, old comrade. This will not be like the Kwangtung army in Manchuria. This must be a concerted effort from Tenno Heika down to the lowest private. We must have the entire nation with us."

"To strike south?" I asked.

Sato nodded. "There is no longer any dispute."

"The prime minister was his usual dithering ineffectual self," Endo said irritably. "Damned fool acts like an Englishman."

"Never mind, Prince Konoye will side with us," Colonel Sato said. "As you say, he is a weakling. He will faint at the sight of a bared sword."

"I thought Yamamoto was at his best," Endo said.

He was talking about our one true naval genius, Admiral Isoroku Yamamoto.

"What did he say, if I may ask?"

"He was persuasive and precise with His Majesty," Colonel Sato said. "He agreed with Tenno Heika's desire for peace with the United States and the other Western powers, but also said that the best way to ensure peace was to prepare for war."

Endo added, "That spineless Konoye kept mumbling about His Majesty being a man of peace and that every diplomatic road must be explored and so on. Of course everyone—Yamamoto, Sugiyama, Nagano, all of them, bobbed their heads. Men of peace, each and every one, the hypocrites."

Colonel Sato made a clucking sound that reminded me of a contented hen. "I thought it was wise of them not to inform His Majesty that since January Yamamoto has had ready a plan to attack Pearl Harbor without warning."

"Yes, why trouble His Majesty?"

I was silent. I had much to reflect about. This was startling news.

JULIE VARNUM · JULY, 1941

Good lord, what *airheads* a lot of us were, we didn't have a *clue* about what was happening. Even with my friend Ed Hodges and so many others in uniform we refused to believe that anything threatening was around the corner. Our newspapers and radio weren't much help either. Oh, there were reports about the war in China, about the Japanese occupying French Indo-China (without a protest from defeated France), stuff about an oil embargo against Japan, diplomatic meetings and so on . . . but hardly anyone really thought about war . . .

I can remember a time jitterbugging in a campus hangout with Ed, Chris and Carol. Chris had landed a job as a radio reporter for an outfit called California Broadcasting and was having a big time covering sewage commission hearings and stories about cats stuck in trees. As he swirled and bounced on the dance floor to Benny Goodman's "String of Pearls"

I could hear him bragging to Carol, "You're having the privilege, lady, of lindying with the new third-string reporter for California Broadcasting. Impressed?"

Carol was leaving the next day for San Francisco. "It sounds absolutely marvelous."

"Never mind, my day's a-comin'. So far I've gotten six minutes' air time . . . a fire on Oliveras Street, a story on the next orange crop and a piece on a new traffic light in Pasadena. It's a start . . ." And so saying, my brother the comedian cupped a hand to his ear like a radio announcer and in deep, honeyed tones said, "This is Chris Varnum, reporting to you live from the new dog pound on Laguna Beach . . ."

As Ed and I danced by—Ed seemed a little downcast that night—I heard Chris trying to make out with Carol, asking her to go to the Phi Gam house for a little sack time.

She refused him, as she always did.

"Not even for a short happy course in radio reporting?"

"Not ever. Give it up, lover."

Ed and I switched hands. My plaid skirt flared. I kicked out my saddle shoes and he did some neat steps in his Marine cordovans. We were both trying to hide a sense of unease . . . there were rumors Ed's unit would be shipped to a Marine base any day . . . "My dear brother," I said, "is still after Carol to . . . you know. He just won't quit."

Ed twirled me around, came back to me. "Neither will I."

Benny Goodman. Glenn Miller. Tommy Dorsey. Artie Shaw. The songs are still in my head. "String of Pearls." "Moonlight Serenade." "The Angels Sing." "Moonlight on the Ganges" . . . they don't make them like that any more . . .

YURIKO TAMBA · JULY, 1941

Miai is a getting-acquainted session for the families of a possible wedding couple to meet, look each other over, see if the man and woman get along. Just before my brother Kenji left for the United States a *miai* had been arranged at the Bamboo Forest restaurant on the Ginza for me and my family to meet the young man they had selected for me along with his parents.

I hope I'm not being conceited when I say I was pretty, dressed well and had a good high school education. Our family might not have been socially important but my father did work at the palace and my brother Masao was an army captain and a hero. The young man's family, the Kitanos, were a rank lower. Mr. Kitano was a post-office employee. His son Hideo, my intended husband, was a twenty-two-year-old ensign in the Imperial Navy.

Hideo had been "discovered" by Mr. Kingoro Hata, a member of Parliament, and a friend of my family's. He seemed to have a finger in everything. I knew he was a friend of Colonel Sato, Masao's father-in-law, and that he had a lot of influence. He told my father he expected no fee for serving as our *nakoodo.*

We rode in Mr. Hata's black Chevrolet to the Bamboo Forest, Mr. Hata driving and my father and Kenji sitting up front with him. My mother, my little brother Saburo and I sat in the back. Masao had gone back to China a few days earlier, and my mother was still sniffling over it. She was especially worried about him . . . newly married as he was and always risking his life . . .

"Our detectives ran the usual check on the Kitanos," Hata said. "No insanity, no criminals. Mr. Kitano had an uncle who was once jailed for bankruptcy. His wife had an aunt who died of tuberculosis in 1933. Other than that they are honest healthy people and as you will see, young Hideo Kitano is handsome, healthy, intelligent and has a fine career in the navy ahead of him."

It was and still is customary for both families in a *miai* to make these investigations of one another. No one is offended by them. Mr. Hata had been his usual efficient self, but of course he wasn't quite telling the truth. I had seen a photograph of Hideo Kitano and even in his white uniform he looked like a monkey.

We passed the Meiji shrine, the Akasaka detached palace, the National Diet building and then we all bowed our heads as Mr. Hata drove by the Imperial Palace. I felt sweaty and hot in my new heavy silk kimono that my mother had scrimped and saved for. It was lovely, though, and had a design of pink chrysanthemums on a gray background.

Young Hideo, Kingoro Hata told us, was serving aboard the aircraft carrier *Akagi,* and that his assignment to such a warship proved he was an exceptional young man. I said nothing, but thought privately that it proved nothing about him as a person. "And they had us investigated?" my father asked.

"And came up with nothing of consequence. The matter of Mrs. Tamba's cousin, the one who drowned on the ferryboat, was discovered but they didn't seem concerned that it may have been suicide. Let me tell you, the fact that Yuriko here is the sister of Captain Tamba means a great deal to them."

"As it should," said my father.

"The lad's navy career *is* important," Hata said. "I predict that you'll be hearing important news about our navy very soon. It will honor your family to have a member associated with the fleet. Believe me."

I don't know what imp got my tongue, but I did a very un-Japanese thing . . . I said what was really on my mind. "He looks funny in the photograph . . ."

"*Yuriko,*" my mother said. "Be quiet."

Saburo giggled. "Like a baboon." Even Kenji smiled but said nothing.

"That's enough," my father said quietly. "We want no foolish jokes from any of you." He looked at Kenji. "I will depend on you, in the absence of your older brother, to bring good manners and pleasant conversation to this *miai.*"

Kenji nodded gravely, but seemed to be holding back his amusement.

We sat stiffly in Western-style chairs, four-legged contraptions with hard backs, around an oval table with a gleaming white silk cloth on it.

Kingoro Hata and Kenji were the only members of the *miai* who seemed at ease in the hard chairs . . . most Japanese really hate them and find them painful. How can *anyone* prefer sitting for hours with legs dangling below and feet planted on the floor to a soft cushion close to the *tatami,* back free, legs crossed, buttocks in happy contact with the ground? My spine started to ache and the circulation in my left foot stopped. I was sweating. My parents controlled the twinges I knew they must be feeling, but Saburo squirmed like a hooked trout, kept going to the bathroom and making faces.

Mr. Hata, at the head of the table, did most of the talking. Oh, he loved to talk, and kept boasting about his friendship with cabinet officers and how he had helped Masao's career and how Japan's navy was the best in the world. I sat between my parents, Kenji was next to my father and Saburo next to my mother. Hideo Kitano, my intended monkey, sat directly opposite me between his parents. They were plain people . . . Mrs. Kitano's father, an aged, wrinkled, retired grocer from Osaka who spoke with a typical Osaka drawl which sounded funny to the rest of us, sat next to her and kept dozing off. He couldn't really be blamed. It was a boring luncheon. Now I knew why *miai*s are so often failures, and why potential married couples never get together or find anything worthwhile in their intendeds at these meetings.

"The old ways are certainly the best," Hata boomed out, then clapped his hands and ordered the waitress to pass the sake bottle again. He seemed to be able to drink huge amounts of rice wine and not get drunk, while my father and Mr. Kitano after two cups were a bit tipsy.

Another waitress brought a large platter of dried cuttlefish and smoked eel on a bed of seaweed and we all helped ourselves.

"It is hard to eat sitting up so high," Saburo said. "I wish I could sit on the floor."

"Rest your back against the chair," Kenji said. "Relax your legs."

"It's easy for you," Saburo said. "You spent so much time in America you can sit up like a *he na gaijin* (a funny foreigner)."

Everyone laughed, and Kenji took it in good humor.

Hata went on, "Yes, the old ways are the best. I don't mind sitting in a chair or even sleeping in a bed on four legs when I travel abroad but these romantic ideas of love, of marrying for love, are dangerous."

My father agreed quickly—too quickly, I thought—and Mr. Kitano said that love was nonsense. Considering his son, I thought guiltily, he had a good point.

The old man, Hideo's grandfather, shut his eyes and snored ever so softly, which I thought was the best comment of all.

"There are actually young people today," Hata said loudly, "young fools I should say, who are infected by Western films and magazines and believe they must be in love to marry. What stupidity. As if *they* know what love is."

"Some do," Kenji said quietly. "In America—"

"But *not* in Japan," Hata cut him off. "It's a mockery of tradition, of the way of the gods. The only good marriage is an arranged marriage. Parents know better than children." To which the two sets of parents smiled, sucked in their breath and nodded energetically, quick to agree with the *nakoodo*.

A vast platter of steamed sea bream was now served, cooked in ginger root and scallions, and was delicious. My future husband (assuming all went well with the *miai*) was shoveling fish into his mouth as if waiting for his ship's siren to call him to a battle station.

Yes, he was quite ugly. It's wrong, I know, and even sinful to attach importance to a person's physical appearance . . . Kenji taught me that we should never mock or criticize or shun people who are not favored with an attractive appearance, and Baron Hideyoshi, after all, our great ruler, was also a strange-looking man. When people said the baron looked like a monkey he replied with a grin, "No, all the monkeys in the world look like *me.*"

Actually Hideo seemed to be slow-witted but hiding some kind of hurt

or anger. He talked slowly, softly. His smile looked false to me, although
I think he was pleasantly surprised to see how I looked.

"Wait till you meet Captain Tamba," Hata was saying to him.

"My oldest son," my father added proudly. "You and he will have
much in common."

"I read about him in the newspaper last week," Hideo said.

"Ah, yes, in *Asahi Shimbun,*" my father said.

Now what was odd about this last bit of conversation was that both
were, well, *lying.* There had been no newspaper article about Masao. He
had been mentioned in a magazine article on the China war a year ago.
That was all. But Hideo had invented the article and my father built on
it by even naming the newspaper. Each knew the other was lying but it
was considered good manners that advanced good relations between the
families.

"Tell us about your other sons," Mr. Kitano said. He was a hunched
man with the pasty look of a clerk who stamps papers all day.

My father looked at Kenji and Saburo and shrugged.

No one was shocked. Second and third sons don't amount to much in
Japan.

"But I understood that the second son is studying in America," Mrs.
Kitano said nervously. "He must be intelligent—"

Hata broke in. "A scholar, my dear Mrs. Kitano. The bride's family
produces not only a great soldier, but scholars too."

Hideo leaned across the table, grinned at me and said, "Do you like the
movies?"

I said I did.

"Gary Cooper?"

"Yes, he's nice."

"Clark Gable?"

"He's also nice."

"I like American cowboy pictures and *samurai* movies."

Silence for a moment, then Hideo switched the fascinating conversation. "The food in the navy is terrible, they don't wash the rice correctly
and it comes out in wet lumps. I'm always constipated."

"Yes, a frequent problem in the services," said Mr. Kitano sagely.

"But a small sacrifice to make in the defense of our nation," put in Hata.

Kenji had on his shy smile throughout the uncomfortable *miai.* As
always he understood me and I could sense his feelings for me . . . He saw
that I didn't care for Ensign Kitano and wanted to help me out of this
arranged marriage, but he was only a second son and he was leaving the
country. And if Masao had been there and had known my true feelings

he would never have stood in the way of my parents' plans for my marriage. It was the way of our world and I was obliged to obey it whether I liked it or not.

Hideo was still talking, this time about how much he liked home-cooked meals—a huge plate of rice with a heavy helping of grilled bluefin tuna and a side dish of salty radishes. He seemed to be ordering his marriage menu before the ceremony.

"Yuriko is a very good cook," my mother said, reading the message.

One look at my soft pale hands was enough to tell anyone that I wasn't much around a kitchen, but it was wrong to hurt anyone's feelings, let alone those of a prospective groom, so everyone pretended to believe the obvious lie, including me. Kenji, though, caught my eye with a wink. He knew exactly what I was thinking.

Over the tea-flavored ice cream—by this time our backs and legs were screaming for release from the dreadful Western chairs and we longed for the security of a wood floor, a *tatami* mat and a cushion—my father, Mr. Hata and Mr. Kitano exchanged toasts, the meal ending with a final, inevitable toast to the emperor.

Three days later, through Mr. Hata, both families gave their assent to the wedding of Miss Yuriko Tamba and Ensign Hideo Kitano. I was never consulted. When I dared to tell my mother I thought Hideo homely, dull and frankly beneath me, I was quickly silenced.

KENJI TAMBA · JULY, 1941

The day before I sailed for San Francisco I visited the Doctors Varnum to say good-bye. Their whitewashed stucco clinic, different in appearance from the surrounding gray wooden buildings, was only a few blocks from our house in Shibuya Ward.

The neighborhood, once middle class, was now congested, homes needing repair. Small shops and ateliers—comb-makers, dyers, potters—had displaced families. The street was covered with gravel and pocked with rain holes.

On the cracked side wall of the clinic someone had pasted a colored poster exhorting people to work harder and support our soldiers in China. Japanese troops were shown bayoneting a fire-spouting Chinese dragon. It was odd in those days how little of the war seemed to touch our people. No one talked much about it. Some kids were tossing an old taped baseball in front of the Shibuya Ward clinic . . . to them a future in the army was the last thing on their minds . . . A grounder skittered past my feet, I fielded it and tossed it back to a small boy who grinned at me, then bowed. A bow is not only a thank you, it's respect too.

Dr. Adam Varnum was a curious man. Although I had been told that Quakers are peaceable people he had a hot temper, and although he was fond of the Japanese he could also be impatient and even brusque with us. (His wife Cora, on the other hand, was even-tempered and easygoing. They joked about it . . . her reasonableness, she said, came from being Swiss, a small nation that had somehow survived the violence around it.)

As I entered the clinic, a plain white building badly needing paint, I realized that a minor crisis was erupting in the waiting room. Two local women were shouting at a third woman who cradled a sickly infant in a cloth sling.

"She's a dirty *Eta*," one of the women said. "Look at her—filthy, her hands are stained."

"Dung carrier," said the second woman. "Filthy one, *out.*"

The *Eta* people, perhaps two million of them, live in isolation from the rest of us. They are like the untouchables of India, a people of obscure origin, whose very name when written in ideograms means "much dirt." They are perhaps descendants of aboriginal people, or Koreans, or a lower feudal class dating back to antiquity. In any event they are universally despised and are assigned degrading jobs such as carrying buckets of human excrement or cleaning animal hides. Laws had been passed to abolish discrimination against these unfortunates but prejudice lingers and this miserable *Eta* woman in Dr. Varnum's waiting room was causing huge upset in the other women.

Dr. Varnum came bursting now through the door, his white coat flying, a cigar clenched between his teeth.

"Mrs. Kida, Mrs. Kuroda, *stop,*" he said. "This woman is entitled to medical care—"

"She's an *Eta.*"

"She's dirty."

"She also has a sick child. Now be still. I run this clinic. If you want medical care you'll do as I say. She stays. Is that clear?"

The women moved as far away from the *Eta* as they could, but they did not leave . . . Japanese women appreciate a strong male presence, even in a *gaijin.*

Dr. Varnum noticed me then and invited me into his office. As we walked through the examining room toward his study he asked me, "Weren't those idiotic customs prohibited by law years ago?"

"In 1871, as a matter of fact," I said, "but bad habits are hard to get rid of."

He studied his malodorous cigar. "Need I be reminded. Cora says it's a wonder anyone comes here anymore, the way I foul the air with smoke."

Cora Varnum was examining a teenage girl who looked tubercular while her mother looked on somberly. As I watched I wondered what had brought the Varnums here, to a strange country, to devote their lives to helping foreigners.

In Dr. Varnum's office, a dark musty room looking out on a neglected garden, I looked once again at the photographs on the wall—physicians he admired such as Maimonides, Sir William Harvey, Jenner, Ehrlich. Dr. Varnum's heroes were men of peace who tried to heal people instead of conquering them . . .

He offered me one of his cigars as he said, "So, the Imperial Scholar is about to return to the scene of his early triumphs. What do your sponsors expect of you, Kenji?"

"To become an expert on the American political system, I think."

He nodded. "May I be my usual subtle self?" He dragged on the cigar, lost himself in a blue haze. "Your leaders could use a stiff dose of medicine called democracy. I hope some day you can inject them with a vaccine against military conspiracies."

Much as I liked him *and* what I had seen of America, I was still a Japanese . . . and felt obliged to defend my country, though it wasn't always easy. "We have a constitution and a Parliament—"

"Both ignored every day by your military. Kenji, you know damn well who runs Japan. And it isn't the emperor."

"Well . . . that may be partly true, but—"

Dr. Varnum got up then and paced the small room. "I'm worried, Kenji."

"China?"

"Something much worse. It's in the air. You can smell it."

"My brother says the war in China is almost over, we'll win, we'll make peace—"

"And?"

"We'll be strong enough to make some arrangement with the Americans and the British and the Dutch. We'll get our rightful place in Asia . . ." I instantly regretted those last words that seemed to tumble automatically out of my mouth.

Dr. Varnum smiled at me as if I were a student doing lessons by rote,

which was close to the truth. I was still conditioned by my early upbringing and education. The Imperial Scholar had a good deal to learn. "The
old jingoistic stuff I read in the newspapers every day. Japan will unite the
Eight Corners of the World Under One Roof. Nice and neat."

"Well, we *are* an Asian power. Why should we be denied our rights?"

"What rights?" He tossed his cigar out the window. "Nanking? Killing
and raping thousands of Chinese? What can Asia expect from an army like
that? Come on, Kenji. You were in America. You *saw* the evidence—
newsreels and photographs, the newspapers . . ."

"Masao insists those stories are lies, publicized by the Americans to
embarrass us—"

"You agree with him?"

"I'm not sure . . . but I just can't believe that our soldiers killed all those
civilians—"

He faced me. "I'd swear you Japanese are two people. I've lived here
more than twenty years. I've found you gentle, tolerant and grateful. The
people of the ward have accepted Cora and me and become our friends.
And yet I'll be damned if I really understand the Japanese."

"I hope you understand *me.*"

"I mentioned friends, Kenji. You are our best friend."

Cora appeared in the doorway then. "I need you, Adam. Cut out the
jawing and help me set a splint."

"I was telling Kenji how much we'll miss him."

"Yes," she said quickly. "We talked about it last night."

Adam put his arm on my shoulder. "We have no children, Kenji. We
wanted them but . . . you, your brothers, your sister, but especially you,
Kenji, we like to think of you as our son. Okay?"

"Better than a son," Cora said, laughing. "I never had to diaper you
or spank you. We just shared a lot of good times."

"Yes," I said, "I remember when we saw the American baseball team
that came here. Lefty O'Doul. And Babe Ruth. It was a good time." I
bowed. "I am very fond of both of you. My American family." And
because two years in America had made me less resistant to touching and
kissing people I loved, I was able to hug Adam and let Cora kiss me on
the cheek.

Cora left then, and Adam gave me an envelope. "Here's a picture of my
niece Julie. And her address and telephone number. Look her up when
you get to Los Angeles."

"Do you have any message?"

"Just greetings from her aunt and uncle."

And then we said our final good-byes. In the street I opened the envelope and my heart sank. Dr. Varnum's niece was truly beautiful, much too much for me. She had an oval-shaped face, long blond hair, a warm smile. I wondered if I would find the courage ever to speak to her.

JULIE VARNUM · JULY, 1941

Looking back, it seems damned eerie the way life went on—summer session, dating, softball games. It was still fun being young, and in California, and full of hope and plans and no fear of the future, even if it was only dimly perceived.

The first time I saw Kenji was at a pickup softball game on campus. It was a hot, dusty day but no one seemed to mind. It must have been a Sunday because Ed was free of his Marine ROTC training. Chris, intrepid reporter, covering PTA meetings and fires, had shown up and the two of them had organized a game.

I was sitting with Carol Andrus and some others under the shade of cottonwood trees and watching the game. Carol had just passed her entrance examinations for the medical corps. Ed Hodges had asked again that we be engaged and, feeling like a rat, I'd said no.

The sounds of that hot summer day linger in my mind . . . so clear, so real, so incredible . . .

No hitter, no hitter!

Double-play ball!

Throw it past him, Chris baby!

Chris was pitching. Ed was playing first base. There was this new student, a young Japanese, playing second base. He wore a baseball cap, and a T-shirt that said YOMIURI GIANTS, whoever they were. He was also devastatingly handsome.

At first I didn't take much notice of him. There were always a lot of Oriental students at UCLA, most of them Nisei born in the United States. As a matter of fact, the runner taking a lead off first base, Frank Yasuda, was a Nisei who'd been in one of my classes the previous semester. He talked slangy Californian and ran the 440. So a new Japanese face—or Korean, or Chinese, or Filipino—didn't make any special impression on anyone. What I remember is that the young man playing second base seemed very solemn through all the jabber of the players talking it up, yelling encouragement to Chris. Chatter was definitely not his game.

I remember the batter hit a hard ground ball to Ed, who was playing wide of first base, Ed scooped the ball up, turned and was going to try for a first-second-first double play (my dad has always been a great fan and I played a lot of softball when I was growing up). Yasuda, charging toward second, ran into the new Japanese student and knocked him on his rear so hard he dropped the ball Ed had thrown and both runners were safe. Yasuda helped him to his feet, dusted him off and asked him if he was all right. Everyone laughed when the new guy bowed. We thought he had to be kidding.

Carol said to me, "They're really funny."

"Who?"

"The Japs. That guy at second—he got knocked down, had his teeth rattled and he *bows,* for God's sake."

Chris had come off the pitcher's mound and was shouting at the second baseman. "You okay?"

"Oh, yes. Fine. Thank you."

"You ever play this game before?"

"Oh, yes."

"Well, don't get beaned by a pop fly. Protect yourself at all times."

Everybody laughed, including me, and the second baseman bowed again, this time to Chris.

When the teams changed over, Yasuda was talking to him. Nisei? Sansei? No, the real thing. From Tokyo. And where'd he learn such perfect English? Oregon, he said. Oregon?

I got a good look at him as he came to bat in the next inning. He was tall and thin with a long beautiful face and gentle eyes. His skin was a sort of pale gold. If I sound like I was impressed, I was. Just looking at him did something to me.

It became a close game. Ed's team was trailing by a run when the new student came to bat with a man on second base. My brother Chris said to Ed, "Why don't we pinch hit for him? He hasn't got the ball out of the infield yet."

The Japanese turned and said, "That's all right. I am a little out of practice."

Ed. For all his big talk he could not hurt anyone's feelings (which, by the way, made it even harder for me when I turned him down). "Go on," he said. "Just try and make contact."

He stepped into the batter's box, took some practice swings, dug in as if he knew what he was doing, and this time he did . . . slamming the first pitch deep and on a line between the center and the left fielders. We all cheered and the runner scored easily from second. Tie score. The YOMI-URI GIANTS shirt flew around the base path and charged for homeplate with the winning run. The left fielder made a good throw, the shortstop relayed it to the catcher, but the Japanese refused to slide into him. He just bumped into the catcher, real gentle—and was tagged out. Our side lost by a run in extra innings.

Chris and Ed and a few others were, understandably, I guess, annoyed. The new man came over quickly and apologized. He looked so pathetic standing there, wondering what he'd done wrong, that I invited him to join us for Cokes. . .

"You should have slammed into the guy," Chris said later when we were in a booth in a luncheonette in Westwood. "Knocked him down. Good God, man, you were the winning run."

"I didn't want to hurt him—"

"You're the one ended up with the strawberries. Look at your right arm."

I was sitting with Ed across from Chris and Carol. Kenji—his name was Kenji Tamba—sat on a bentwood chair facing us. It was almost as if we were a jury or something. As Chris had said, his right arm was red and raw and bleeding a little, but he didn't seem to mind. In fact he acted as if his injury were somehow an affront to us. (It would take a very long time for Kenji to lose this sort of hat-in-hand attitude toward Americans. It bothered me then, and sometimes when he still behaves that way it still bothers me.)

"I'm a guest in your country. And it was only a game."

The others looked sort of blank, so I spoke up. "He's right. So we lost, so what?"

"You play to win in Japan, don't you?" Ed asked him.

"Yes."

Chris arched his eyebrows. "Ask the Chinese."

An embarrassed silence followed, broken by Carol asking how come Kenji's English was so good, since he was a *real* Japanese from Tokyo, not a Nisei. He told us then about his two years in America, and years of study at the Tokyo Imperial University. But mostly he was reluctant to talk about himself. When we all introduced ourselves we did it with first names only (very California)—Julie, Chris, Carol, Ed. I mention this because Kenji was looking at me curiously, trying not to be rude but somehow unable to take his eyes off of me, and for a moment, being the modest creature I am, I wondered if he thought he'd seen me before, which of course was hardly likely.

"Excuse me," he said. "Is it possible your second name is Varnum?"

"Yes . . ."

"I know your aunt and uncle in Tokyo. I know them quite well."

"You know Uncle Adam and Aunt Cora?"

"They are my dear friends." And suddenly he relaxed, became expansive. It was a pleasure to see him drop his self-effacing manner, and I thought how much nicer he looked when he smiled and laughed. He truly was delicious-looking.

Kenji filled us in on my Uncle Adam and Aunt Cora, how they ran the local clinic for more than twenty years, how Aunt Cora had delivered his younger sister and brother and how the Varnums had taken care of the Tamba family for twenty years. The doctors, he said, were considered true friends of the local people, spoke Japanese fluently and were part of the community. They had been the only Westerners to attend the wedding of Kenji's brother . . .

"I . . . I thought it was you," Kenji said nervously, "your uncle showed me a photograph . . ."

Chris, who seemed annoyed by this familiarity, asked, "They show you my photograph? They're my aunt and uncle too."

Kenji either missed Chris's annoyance or chose to ignore it. "I'm afraid not. But they send you both their greetings."

"I'm *stunned.* Chris, can you imagine? Kenji, tell me all about Uncle Adam! Does he still smoke those awful cigars and lose his temper?"

"I have orders to bring him two boxes of White Owls."

Chris seemed to warm up some at that. "How are they doing?" he asked Kenji.

"They're fine—"

"What about anti-American feelings?"

Kenji seemed uneasy. "It . . . it really doesn't show up among ordinary people. Besides, everyone in Shibuya considers your uncle one of us."

"I'd love to see them again, it's been nine years since they were back here."

"Dr. Varnum said he taught you some Japanese," Kenji said. "Both of you."

"Sorry," Chris said. "Forgot mine long ago."

"Well I remember some. *Ohayo*—good morning. *Konnichiwa*—hello. *Konnbanwa*—good evening. *Arigato*—thank you."

"That's terrific," Kenji said. He was sounding very all-American.

Carol smiled at him. He *was* hard to resist. But was he playing a role, I wondered, or was he really the friendly young man, trying hard to be at home in a strange environment?

Chris said rather rudely, "How about the one word I know? *Sayonara?*"

"Take it easy," Ed said.

But the dig wasn't lost on Kenji. He seemed to duck his head slightly, then got up. "I must study. You're all very kind to include me." He bowed to Ed. "Thank you for letting me play on your team. Next time I'll slide into the catcher." Again a tiny bow. "Thank you for the pleasure of your company, I hope to see you again."

"Hey, man, you don't have to bow to us," Ed said.

"It's a sign of respect. Friendship is an obligation we don't take lightly. Good-bye."

"Very cute," Chris said after he left. "A real Nip. Even Yasuda was fooled by him. The guy's probably got the plans to the San Diego Naval Base tattooed under his left arm."

"Oh, come on," Carol said, "he's okay. They all do a lot of bowing."

Ed and I both said we liked him, that he seemed to be a nice guy.

Chris shrugged. "It was the *way* he bowed that got me. Heels together, back straight. Imperial Scholar, my eye. That was all military."

I hoped Chris was kidding, because all I knew was that I wanted to see Kenji Tamba again, to talk to him, to know more about him. I've always been drawn to men who act gentle, who are polite. Ed was like that. So was Kenji Tamba.

MASAO TAMBA · AUGUST, 1941

I was glad my tour of duty in China was cut short. The war had become a series of bloody skirmishes. Worst of all, the Chinese had developed a cowardly technique of so-called warfare that was new to us. They operated behind our lines. I had no real fear of them but it was not my concept of warfare. When I was wounded by shrapnel from an artillery shell—a laceration of my left calf—I was pleased when Colonel Sato arranged for me to return to Tokyo and join in planning new campaigns, battles that would far exceed in global importance the war with the cowardly Chinese.

But those damned guerrillas . . . who could imagine that an opium-smoking, lazy, filthy nation of idlers could have given us so much trouble? The Chinese should have welcomed us. After all, we were their cousins. We came to help them, but they never seemed to learn.

Instead they wrecked our trains. They would pull out rail spikes at places where the track curved or on railway bridges, the trains would fall, our men would be killed or ambushed by hiding partisans . . . I managed to devise a way of combatting this by sending light trains ahead with special scouts on them to look for missing spikes. Now listen to what the Chinese bandits did next . . . they replaced the iron spikes with wooden ones painted to look like steel and were able to support the weight of the light trains. But when our heavy troop trains passed over them the pegs broke and the trains were derailed. In one month alone we lost over two hundred men this way. Again, not *my* idea of proper warfare, these hit-and-run tactics. I call it the way of cowards. My men were *soldiers,* trained to fight in the field, to face the enemy head-on. Craven sneaks hiding in peasant clothing, poisoning wells and dynamiting rails, were not soldiers. They were criminals, to be treated as such. On one occasion we caught four of these so-called partisans after they had blown up an ammunition dump. I ordered them set afire. I did not enjoy it . . . it was a necessary example.

The truth was that the war with China was dragging on. We were caught in a vast sea of mud, winning battles, but our goal of conquest was farther from us every day. Someone said we were like men trying to plow the ocean. He was right.

The high command was planning an autumn offensive against Changsha, and my division would be one of the spearhead units. I was now attached to the Eleventh Army and we were determined to destroy the Chinese will to fight. Optimism was high. The Germans had invaded the Soviet Union and it was felt that Russia's hands were tied and Stalin was in no position to help out Chiang Kai-shek or intervene. We could strike China full force without looking over our shoulder at the Reds. On the other hand the Americans and British were pouring economic aid into China, the Burma Road had been reopened and when we occupied southern Indo-China the Americans and the British froze our assets, hurting our foreign trade. There was even talk of an oil embargo against us. In spite of all this the Changsha offensive was launched. I couldn't wait to smash into the enemy lines and be done with these damn guerrillas. Waiting for us was the army of the Chinese Ninth War Zone, one of Chiang's best, and as I've said, in one of the first probing artillery barrages I was wounded and Colonel Sato ordered me back to Tokyo, for as he put it, "more vital duties for His Majesty."

My new home in Tokyo was a gift from the colonel, a pleasant house on a shaded sidestreet about a mile north of my parents' home. Simple and graceful, with unpainted wood walls, a thatched roof, a veranda facing the street and a rear porch looking out on a garden, its main room was a ten-*tatami* chamber with *shoji* screens and sliding doors. Wall closets stored *futons* and cushions and pillows. In the center of the room was the usual *kotatsu,* a well with a hibachi placed in it for warmth. The kitchen was at the rear, as was a splendid new wooden bathtub with an exterior metal heater for the charcoal. There were two extra rooms, one for storage, the other for guests. I liked the simplicity and barrenness . . . I am, after all, a soldier, I can live anywhere and I need very little. I could live out of a rucksack and a blanket roll very easily.

The one adornment was a beautiful *tokonama,* the alcove that displays a scroll with a poem on it, usually hailing a new season or holiday. Our honored guests were always seated with their backs to the *tokonama.* There was also a sacred *stele* and a floral arrangement reflecting the time of year. Next to the *tokonama* was a polished *tokobashira,* a column of dark mahogany that was also sacred.

My kid brother Saburo spent a lot of time hanging around our house even when I was away and I suspect he had a crush on Michiko . . . partly because she was my wife—Saburo worshipped me—and a colonel's daughter. Saburo badly wanted to be in uniform but he was sickly and too young for the military academies. Actually, he was never the student that Kenji and I had been. He daydreamed and once told me (no shame attached to it) that he masturbated three and four times a day.

I had been home now for about four days. My leg wound was only flesh-deep and had been cauterized, stitched and bandaged. In a day or two I would start attending conferences (I hated them) at the War Ministry. Sato told me that the older men wanted more views on strategy and weaponry from young officers who had been in the field.

I was dressing for a dinner with Colonel Sato and Kingoro Hata when Saburo came slouching into the house. (My wife, naturally, was not invited to the dinner. We do not take our wives out at night. It is simply not done. Michiko did not expect to be wined and dined around town. Her place was in our home and the shops.) Michiko was buttoning my tunic when Saburo, in stocking feet, grabbed my sword, yanked it from the scabbard and started lunging at the paper wall. "Dead Chinese! Dead Russians!"

"The sword, radish-nose."

"Watch me, Masao. I see the enemy. I hold down his shadow."

"Give your brother his sword," Michiko said.

"Yah, yah, I don't take orders from women."

It took me three seconds to disarm him, flip him over and prod him with my foot. "Weak," I said. "No muscles."

I jammed the sword into the scabbard and turned sideways to look at myself in the mirror. Normally I don't give a damn about a starched tunic, shiny boots, and rows of medals. I like it best when I'm in combat garb, dusty and sweaty.

"Where are you going next, Masao?" Saburo asked. "Indo-China? Russia?"

"I go where I'm sent, lizard."

"I want to go with you. I hate school. I hate the kids. They're shit-heads."

"Saburo," Michiko warned.

"I'll say anything I want. This is Masao's house now, not yours."

"Please, Masao, tell him not to insult me."

"He means no harm."

Saburo grabbed my sleeve. "Please, Masao. Take me. Enlist me in your company."

"You'd wet your pants."

"I want to kill Chinks." He picked up a broom and leveled it at me in *kendo* fashion. "Fight," he said. "I dare you."

I grabbed a feather duster and squared off with him. "All right. Show me how Musashi would fight a bigger man," I said.

He circled me. "Head erect. Forehead and the space between the eyes unwrinkled. Instill vigor from the shoulders down."

"Very good, runt. Brace your abdomen so you don't bend at the hips."

We swung at each other. I parried his blows lightly as if brushing away a fly. We came perilously close to the room divider made only of rice paper.

"Please, no," wailed Michiko. "Every time he comes here—"

We paid no attention to her. "Learn to look at both sides without moving your eyeballs," I told him. "Musashi says, a gaze that is wide and broad but does not stray."

Saburo tried to put on the fearsome gaze of the *samurai* but he went cockeyed, and as he did so I knocked him head over heels with one thrust of the duster handle. As he fell his broomstick went ripping through the new *shoji,* leaving a rent a foot long.

Michiko looked on miserably. Like all Japanese wives she was in charge of the household and its expenses, my government check was sent directly to her, she held the purse strings. It was a perfect arrangement and it left me free for my evening pleasures.

"So what?" Saburo crowed. "Your father has plenty of money. He's an armchair officer anyway. Not like Masao."

"I don't like his tongue," Michiko said. "Tell him."

"He means no harm." I lifted Saburo off the ground and shook him a little, then sent him home with a friendly swat on the rear end and told him he had to run more, exercise with weights, eat more red meat, that in a few years he might qualify for cadet training if he worked hard at developing himself.

To my surprise, Michiko asked me where I was going. That is really not the business of a wife.

"I told you. To see your father and Kingoro Hata."

"I mean . . . where?"

"At the Plum Blossom."

"The woman Satomi's place?"

"Yes, yes. The food is excellent and they have the best *koto* player in Tokyo."

She had shown rare daring in asking me where I was going. It could have been to a brothel and it would not have been her business, nor would she have had the right to nag.

"I worry about you," Michiko said. "Your wound. The bad food you ate in China. Maybe you have beri-beri."

"I am *fine*. Goodnight."

Michiko slid across the floor on her knees and opened the door for me, her head touching the floor. She stayed in that position until I left.

Michiko accepted. Her concern was to keep me happy and give me male children. My sister Yuriko, on the other hand, was showing a disturbing tendency to think too much about herself. I suspected Kenji, with his American ideas, had infected her mind. She even told people she didn't like her future husband Hideo and that she would run away if she had to marry him. I dismissed such talk as the maunderings of an immature woman but I did not like to hear it. I told her she should take Michiko as her example. Actually Michiko was talented at depicting flowers and worked mostly in *sumi*—Chinese black ink that can portray tones from light gray to black. She would mix it with rice paste to give her paintings a special luster. Someone once said that if she had spent more time at it she could have become a *sumi* master. I don't know. It was not the most pressing consideration on my mind.

The Plum Blossom House was located in an alley in Akasaka so narrow the taxi could not get through to the entrance and I had to get out at the corner, where I ignored two harlots in gaudy kimonos who motioned to me, and walked the short block to Satomi's establishment. There was no sign outside, just a yellow lantern with a painting of a blossom on it.

Geisha houses, contrary to ill-informed Western thought, are not broth-els. One goes there to dine, drink, meet friends, hear music, see traditional dancing and be served by graceful, witty, elegant women in traditional dress. It is a place for men of means and influence and character. Of course, special favors may be granted to special clients. A wealthy man "sponsor" may have a particular geisha he has a fondness for. A room may be reserved for his pleasures, but such arrangements require a great deal of influence, and money, and the acquiescence of the geisha mistress.

Satomi was Kingoro Hata's mistress and business partner—a tall and angular woman with a long hard face, handsome in a mannish sort of way. Kenji used to say that she had a jaw like a gunnery sergeant. But she was attractive as a finely cut stone is, and was clearly a woman of intelligence and business acumen.

Waiting for me in Satomi's house were Hata and my father-in-law. Hata was a part owner, and Colonel Sato was a frequent client for whom favors —a toothsome girl and a darkened room—were always available. Many of the colonel's military friends like Commander Endo and certain politi-cians of the right as well as sympathetic journalists and businessmen often joined him at the Plum Blossom. At the moment, the Plum Blossom was less a geisha house than a house of assignation for patriots meeting in these *machiai* to plot strategy. Our political enemies (like Kenji's senile teacher Adachi) say it implies shady and corrupt dealings and that geisha and sometimes whores who host these meetings influence their clients. One's enemies say a great many vicious things. One can live with it. While they talk we act.

Hata and the colonel, dressed in silk kimonos, were lying back on purple *futons.* I was helped out of my uniform by a *maiko,* an apprentice geisha, helped into a similar coat and then joined the older men in one of the private rooms. There was a rather noisy party going on in the main room, so Satomi closed the doors and proceeded to supervise the geishas attend-ing us.

For the evening's entertainment Satomi had imported three Kyoto-trained geishas from the Gion district who performed a delicate *sambaso* for us as we sipped sake and nibbled at delicious broiled shrimp marinated in ginger sauce.

It was restful to the soul and the senses in this dimly lit room. The *shoji* screens were pale and shimmering. On one wall was a fine depiction of Fujiyama. Three seated geisha musicians, the *jikata,* accompanied the dancers with classical *samisen* music. The dancers wore lavish *desho,* formal kimonos, and skillfully manipulated their ivory fans.

"Ah, the *sambaso*," Hata said. "Lovely. Has its origins in Shinto rites. Correct, Satomi?"

"Yes, sir."

Colonel Sato asked the geisha mistress, "What are they dancing now?"

The three young women—hard black wigs, jeweled combs, purple-and-scarlet kimonos—had changed to a different series of dainty steps, a slower rhythm. "The *gaku*, colonel."

Sato drained his cup. Satomi refilled it. He and Hata got drunk quickly, began to snicker, laugh, undo their coats. I do not know why, but we Japanese seem to have little tolerance for alcohol. Sake is, after all, only rice wine, yet two or three cups can turn strong men into blubbering children.

Hata smiled at me. "You're quiet tonight, captain. Are you enjoying the entertainment?"

"Very much."

Hata nodded. "Satomi knows about your exploits. The dance is for you."

I thanked him. To tell the truth, I was not sure I much liked Kingoro Hata. He was, after all, no soldier. But he did support us, and when the colonel and I were in danger after the February 26 incident in 1936 he came to our defense along with other patriots who saw Japan's future as clearly as we did. He had had dealings with Colonel Sato dating back to the time of the Kwangtung Army in 1932. Sato told me that Hata had invested in jute mills in Manchuria after the conquest and had cut in various officers who had aided him. Kenji said that in America they would call Hata an operator. I thought I understood why.

The conversation now got around to the honored practice of the deflowering of virgins. Satomi, pressed to discuss it by Hata, said that in the good old days all geisha apprentices were required to lose their virginity at the hands of a wealthy patron, that it was an honor much sought after by the young women. The patron, the *danna*, would pay the house generously for the right to deflower some tender young woman. As for the girl, she would be lovingly initiated into womanhood, and if she were lucky she might even acquire a lasting and profitable relationship with her *danna*.

"The whole ceremony is called the *mizu-age*," Hata said, taking up Satomi's account. "When I was young I participated in several such experiences. The girl would be kept in isolation in a darkened room for a week. Every night one of the older geishas placed three eggs on top of the *futon* near the apprentice's head. I would follow, entering the room and breaking the eggs. I would eat the yolks and then rub the whites between the young beauty's thighs. I would start mid-thigh and each night work my fingers and the egg whites closer to the heavenly crevice, then into it, rubbing the whites gently into her lower lips. By the end of the week the child would be well-oiled, relaxed and ready for my noble entry."

Satomi laughed, a sound like the clinking of coins. "And of course Mr. Hata would be well prepared, having eaten twenty-one raw egg yolks."

"Quite well prepared. One night I came to orgasm four times in an hour. Unfortunately such days are gone forever."

"But not for our young heroes," Sato said. "Is it true, Satomi, that the ceremony of the *mizu-age* is dying out?" *Koto* music drifted about me, made by an older woman squatting in the corner and plucking at the lyrelike instrument.

"Sadly the girls come to us with more knowledge now," Satomi said. "Some have been deflowered. Others don't like the idea. In the old days a man was not required just to be wealthy but to be skilled with hand and member. Today all the girls want is money, to be set up in teashops. Very sad."

We must have been getting drunker and drunker . . . Mount Fuji seemed to be rising and falling, the sounds of the *koto* came to me only faintly, Hata was rambling on about the joys of being kissed below and above by two women at the same time, about the use of dildos, about how to masturbate with a feather and so on . . .

Suddenly he and Colonel Sato began to argue. I think it started when Hata said to me, "Don't fall in love with your wife, captain. You'll only ruin a good servant." My father-in-law promptly said that his daughter was no servant. Hata backed down and tried to apologize, but the colonel was not accepting. "Why the hell aren't you in uniform if you're such a big patriot?"

Hata was not a man easily embarrassed. In his line of work, a thin skin was an unaffordable luxury. "I have many important duties, as you know. We both serve His Majesty in different ways. You and your son-in-law as soldiers, I as someone who knows the emperor's mind. I can tell you, it is a full-time job keeping peace-faction traitors away from him. And then there are my business interests, all of which serve the war effort . . ."

Colonel Sato belched loud enough to be heard in Shibuya Ward. "You lie. The last batch of uniforms you sold the army—millions and millions of yens' worth—were no good. The seats wore out. The seams came apart."

I looked surprised, which I was.

"A cheating contractor," Hata said. "He will be dealt with, I assure you."

"You're a profiteer," Sato said. "If men like Captain Tamba didn't offer their lives to the emperor you'd be a dried dog turd."

Hata still could not be insulted. He winked at Satomi, who refilled the glasses and ordered the musicians to keep playing. "Forgive me, colonel," Hata said smoothly, "but the military isn't the only string to Japan's bow."

"It's the only one that matters," I put in. Colonel Sato smiled his approval of me. I knew that men like Hata—profiteers connected to business and industry—worked hand-in-glove with the military, but I also realized they were motivated by greed as much as by patriotism and love for the emperor.

During all this political jabber, Satomi had retired to an inner room. Now she returned, went to the floor, bowed, and addressed me.

"Captain Tamba, we have prepared a *mizu-age* for you."

I hesitated. After all, the father of my wife was reclining three feet away.

"Go to it, my boy," Sato said. "Michiko will understand." And as I got to my feet, Hata called out, "My pleasure will be as great as yours, captain." A damn peculiar thing to say, I thought.

Another geisha came forward to help Satomi convey me to a rendezvous with the virgin.

"Sure she's still got her maidenhead?" asked Sato.

"I guarantee it," Hata told him. "I have paid for everything. Your son-in-law will be satisfied."

"It's true what they say. You are a man of broad face."

They laughed as they watched me approach the rear room. Satomi and her geisha kneeled and opened the doors. Inside in faint blue light, in a room containing only a *tatami* mat and *futons,* a washstand, and a vase of roses, reclined a girl of fifteen. She had a hard porcelain face, emotionless eyes, and wore the costume of the apprentice geisha.

I knelt beside her and she promptly began to undo my coat. Three eggs rested on the pillow.

"Yolk for you, white for me," the girl said.

"I'm not a damned cook," I said. "I'm a soldier." And drunk at that. I smashed the eggs on the floor and fell on top of her.

Later the colonel and Hata told me that while I was with the *maiko,* they had gotten into a drunken argument. (I obviously was too far gone in alcohol and sex to have overheard it.) It seems that as the colonel went on accusing Hata of being a bloodsucker and war profiteer Hata struck back by naming all of the militaristic secret societies that my father-in-law patronized, and in the process checked off alleged assassinations and blackmailings he had been involved in.

Sato said such acts, though exaggerated, were committed only to help create a new Japan, to bring the Eight Corners of the World Under One Roof, to grant His Majesty the divine rule of the earth to which he was entitled.

Hata had snapped back that such talk was mystical bullshit by a bunch of dwarfs. Pure *gekokujo,* the slime at the bottom ruling the top. Colonel Sato proceeded to call Hata a swindler who would screw a locust, that he and his men put their lives on the line for His Majesty. Hata reminded him about the killing of Finance Minister Takahashi, accused him of being involved. Apparently Sato admitted it but said no court had ever found him guilty.

While all this was going on—they were too drunk to come to blows—I was making love once more to the *maiko.* In retrospect, I decided she either was an accomplished actress or truly enjoyed her work. At one point she stuffed a silken cloth in her mouth. To keep from shrieking with joy?

When I was exhausted and satisfied, she thanked me. She had bled very little and assured me I had given her no pain, only deep pleasure. She then bathed me from the basin with perfumed water and patted me dry.

I allowed myself to be dressed by the women and taken home in a taxi. Michiko met me at the door and she and the driver helped me inside. I vaguely remember Michiko undressing me and washing off my body. She was, indeed, a good wife in every way, lavishing *amae* on me.

Do not tell me we Japanese men are not fortunate in our women. But of course *we* have a culture.

JULIE VARNUM · AUGUST, 1941

Ed, just a week away from getting his commission, had said his good-byes to his mother—she was widowed and worked in the Glendale post office—and I was the only one at the downtown Los Angeles bus station to see him off.

"No big deal," Ed said. "Pendleton's just down the highway. I'll get my bars, do my time and be back in a jiffy. And maybe you'll change your mind then."

"We'll see . . ." You didn't give a flat no to a man going off to the service.

"They say a married Marine is a better Marine. Gives a guy something to fight for. Wife, apple pie, the picket fence."

I felt real bad. "Ed, you know how much I like you—"

"Maybe you'll like me better with gold bars?"

"Don't be dumb. I like you, period."

We chatted sort of casually about impersonal stuff, to keep from getting too mushy. I had summer session to finish, then another semester, so I'd have my degree in January of '42. I had no plans beyond that. Teaching, maybe. I'd always liked working with children . . . "I'm sorry you won't get to law school," I said, and meant it.

"Yeah . . . no law school, no wife, no happy college days. UCLA is the kind of place that spoils you. They shot too many movies there. Sun, lawns, trees, those red brick buildings. And who could believe Westwood Village? Strictly Mickey Rooney territory." He took hold of my arms. "Julie . . . it's been the best four years of my life. And you made it for me."

"I'm glad." God, that sounded awful.

"Know what I think our problem was?"

I waited.

"We knew each other too well. Neighbors, highschool, college. Oh, I dated other girls the first two years and you saw other guys, until I tried to preempt the field. But, you know, it was like we were kidding around. Lots of memories, though, good things we did . . . maybe we can pick up. I mean, they say there may not even be any war. Maybe it's all propaganda. Kenji thinks so too . . ."

"I hope he's right." The bus driver was honking. "You'll miss your bus." I was crying then.

"Maybe I missed one already."

I tried to ignore that.

"They give us a few days leave after we're commissioned. I'll be back."

"We'll look forward to it, shavetail." I wondered if he heard the "we."

"There are worse things than being an officer's wife, Julie. And if there's no war I do my service, go to law school, and we're right on schedule again. Okay?"

I smiled and kissed him. He hugged me and then hopped aboard the bus. We waved to each other as it pulled away. Walking back, I realized how much Ed had always meant to me, a big brother and a friend. The sad thing was he wanted it to be something more. Deep down I think I knew this just wasn't in the cards . . .

Carol Andrus once told me about the time my brother visited her in San Francisco, and I've embroidered some of it with my imagination . . .

Chris was a persuasive, energetic fellow. He was reed-thin, hyper. His minor job with California Broadcasting, he was convinced, would lead to bigger things. He was cocky, bright, handsome and very aggressive. Career and sex were what mattered to him. Even as a teenager he had the nerve to whistle at women, anyone from age fourteen to forty-five.

How *exactly* he broke Carol down I don't know. She'd gotten her commission in the Army Medical Corps. Chris had gone to San Francisco to celebrate with her—her father, the old master sergeant, and her mother had come and gone—and managed to get her into a hotel room. And to make love to her.

The way I got it from Carol it was sort of low comedy. After they'd done it Chris leaped from the bed and got on the phone to call his office in L.A., phoning in a story about new security measures at the Embarcadero in San Francisco. Having just professed his love for Carol, he now just as quickly forgot all about her. Sex was over, back to career.

Carol, of course, was furious. She was sorry she'd given in to him. Oh, she liked him, but she never felt they were in love . . . actually, she confessed later, they'd had too many drinks at the top of the Mark Hopkins Hotel, and the drinks plus the excitement of her new career and his comical bragging about his life as a radio newsman—*Wow! Maybe a war correspondent!*—well, she let herself be led to a hotel room . . . "I guess I liked the idea at first, the adventure, the secrecy, the intimacy. But listening to him reading his story to an editor in L.A., well, that was too much." My big-deal brother even hauled out the old Hemingway thing . . . "If it feels good, it's moral," he told her. And then got out his typewriter, set it on a table and started to peck away at another story he'd dug up—the reactions of the Japanese community to the threats of war. Carol said she felt naked even once she'd gotten dressed. When she closed the room door behind her, all she heard was the clicking of his typewriter. Some farewell to arms, I thought, and could have murdered my brother when I heard this.

Until, that is, I remembered how young, and innocent, we all were back then in that summer of '41.

MASAO TAMBA · SEPTEMBER, 1941

Colonel Sato took me for dinner to a private room in a seafood restaurant off the Ginza after I had finished a long boring session with some junior officers. The subject had been amphibious landings, something about which I knew little or nothing.

The colonel had been at the palace with the General Staff and was telling me about the meeting that morning with Tenno Heika.

"Konoye was his usual belly-talking self," my father-in-law said irritably, then ordered an assortment of *sashimi* for us, making sure that the bluefin tuna and the yellowtail were market-fresh and that his favorite chef was on duty.

"Weak in the knees?" I asked.

"He's scared shitless of Sugiyama and Nagano. Not to mention the lower ranks like Endo and myself. I really think that ass-kisser Konoye is pro-American. He's got some notion that if he made a visit to Roosevelt he could avoid a war. We had to remind him that we had the goods on him. He's been in bed with the right-wingers for years. He even formed the Imperial Rule Assistance Association to exalt the Divine Way. Now he's getting the runs."

"A man of no spine," I said.

The colonel agreed, then told how the emperor entered and sat on his thronelike chair in front of the gold screen. All rose and bowed. General Sugiyama minced no words. Diplomacy was failing. Roosevelt, misled by people like Secretary of State Hull, was pushing Japan to the brink. Impossible demands regarding China were being made. The freezing of Japanese assets. Restrictions on Japan's navy. And worst of all, the oil embargo. Without oil our warships were paralyzed. It was necessary to strike quickly, seize the oil-rich Dutch East Indies, take over Malaya for its rubber, control the perimeter islands. And if necessary . . , this was kept from Tenno Heika . . . a lethal strike at the heart of the prime enemy, the United States. Sugiyama said that the purposes of war with the United States, Great Britain and the Netherlands were to expel the influence of the three countries from East Asia, to establish a sphere for the self-defense and the self-preservation of our empire and to build a new order in Greater East Asia. He was very impressive.

A day earlier the emperor had queried the military about the dangers of a protracted war with the United States, a country he seemed to admire, although he liked the British and their system even more, probably because he'd visited there as a young man . . . he still favored, my father told me, a British breakfast of bacon and eggs and at one time affected *plus-fours* and *golf.* The China incident, the emperor had pointed out, was supposed to last only a month and had now dragged on for four years, with no end in sight. When reminded that "China is vast," the colonel said he responded, and quite acidly for him, being a mild-mannered man, that the Pacific was even vaster.

General Sugiyama and others had argued politely that lightning strikes could immobilize and terrify the enemy. The securing of island bases for a defense line together with the seizing of oil and other natural resources would guarantee Japan's ability to fight on. Once the United States realized this, he told His Majesty, the enemy's diplomats would realize that the wind was in Japan's favor and would influence Roosevelt to seek terms. But His Majesty kept asking, usually through a surrogate like Konoye, what steps were being taken to pursue a diplomatic solution. The generals and admirals had to avoid a direct answer. In the nation's interest, they had long ago decided on war and nothing would be allowed to stop them.

Then, of all things, he went on, Hirohito read a *haiku* that had been composed many years ago by his grandfather, Emperor Meiji, who is credited with bringing us into the modern age.

> *All the seas everywhere are brothers to one another,*
> *Why then do the winds and waves of strife rage*
> *Violently over the world?*

Once they had regained their composure, the admirals and generals agreed that diplomatic means should be exhausted, though fortunately they knew we were poised for attack.

"Doesn't His Majesty realize that war must come?" I asked.

"Who knows? Who can know the mind of a god? Anyway, Sugiyama and the others said they would give Konoye six weeks to negotiate an acceptable agreement with the United States. If by October 15 Roosevelt still does not abandon his demands on Japan, then war will have to come."

"What do you think, sir?"

"Masao, my dear son, there will be a war. There is no stopping us. We have planned and prepared and waited for this, and we are going to fight, and we are going to win."

"May the gods be on our side."

"Where else can they be? Only Japan is a god-descended nation. No other people are so blessed."

Sato then went off to make a phone call and returned with news that one of his spies had learned that that evening Prince Konoye, our tremulous prime minister, was meeting with the American ambassador, Mr. Grew, to request a meeting with Roosevelt.

"Yes," Sato chuckled, "they are meeting at the home of Konoye's mistress. There will be no secrets kept from us. Let Konoye confer with Americans, let him get on his knees to Washington. Things will go our way."

KENJI TAMBA · SEPTEMBER, 1941

I was excited to discover that Miss Julie Varnum, the doctor's niece, was in my class in American Constitutional History. It was a graduate course but undergraduates were allowed to sit in. It was taught by Professor Aaron Shapiro, a stout bald man who scribbled energetically on the blackboard and as a result was usually covered with chalk dust.

I don't remember how it came up, but in a discussion of democracies someone had made the point that even democratic governments can rule colonial systems, which seemed to be a paradox. I was asked by Shapiro to give some examples.

"The British in India," I said. "The Dutch East Indies."

A student named Pat—he was a friend of Ed Hodges—said that maybe some of those people, the Indians, the East Indians, were better off under European rule.

I said nothing.

Julie raised her hand. "Isn't it a question of *how* they're ruled?"

I could not help staring at her. She was so beautiful. Not in a cosmeticized way but naturally beautiful—clear tanned skin with highlights of red, long blond hair, eyes a remarkable blue.

Professor Shapiro said, "Yes, Miss Varnum. One could argue that there are good colonial governments and bad ones." Then he asked *me* to comment. I said that whether the governments were good or bad, the subject peoples usually didn't appreciate them. There was, I felt, a growing movement all over the world to replace foreign powers with governments representative of the people.

Pat called out, "They why doesn't Japan get out of China?"

I said nothing.

"Mr. Tamba?" said the professor.

"My country—Japan—is a Pacific power. Just as much as the United States or Britain or the Netherlands. We are only asking for a sphere of influence like yours and theirs."

"Then Japan wants to colonize these countries—the Philippines, Malaya, China, anything she regards as within her sphere?" Professor Shapiro was friendly but challenging.

"I'm not certain colonizing is exactly correct," I replied. "As Asians the Japanese seek a co-prosperity area. Cooperation, the liberation of native populations—"

Pat hooted at that. "Like your guys liberated China? Come on, Tamba, you've seen the photographs. How many Chinese civilians did you knock off? That's *liberation?* And bombing civilians, starving out villages?"

There was a hush, only the sound of Professor Shapiro pacing behind his desk.

"Mr. Tamba?" he asked. "Do you want to respond?"

"All armies, all governments, make mistakes," I tried. "One of the problems is that the Western powers will not give Japan a hearing—"

"Japan had a chance at the League of Nations," Julie said, "and you walked out." I was startled and upset to hear her join in this.

Shapiro smiled. "Not Mr. Tamba personally, Miss Varnum. But you do raise a good point."

Pat took it up. "And what did your government do? You made a deal with Hitler and Mussolini. The Axis. *Buddies.* And a nonaggression pact with the Russians. I can see what's coming—"

"What?" the professor asked.

"I don't know, but it sure won't be a tea party." Pat looked at me as if I were the enemy.

I continued to be upset that Julie Varnum seemed to be one of my adversaries too. "China was invaded in 1937," she said.

"And Manchuria in 1931," Professor Shapiro added.

"Right," she said. "Japan's had enough time to explain why it did these things."

I was blushing deeply—yes, we yellow-skinned people can blush—and I was tongue-tied. All eyes in the class seemed to be fixed on me.

"Many . . . many of our leaders feel that we have been denied a proper role in Asia," I said, now almost by rote. "It is not appropriate for Westerners to dominate trade. We are brothers to all Asian peoples—Chinese, Koreans, Malayans. We ask only an opportunity to develop our relationships with them. The United States has responded by freezing our assets, denying us oil and asking us to humiliate ourselves in China by giving up what we gained in a terrible costly war—"

"Hey, *buddy*," Pat called out, "the Chinese didn't invade *you*. You invaded *them*. Get it right."

The class laughed.

To save me further embarrassment Professor Shapiro tried to divert the argument. "What do you think, Mr. Tamba? Is a diplomatic settlement possible?"

I hesitated. "One must always hope that is the case. I must tell you that the Japanese people have no stomach for a war. Many of them are sick of the fighting in China. They have good feelings about the United States and they admire Americans. We look on America as a friend—"

"With a friend like that who needs enemies?" Pat again. And more laughter.

I felt ashamed. A Japanese would normally have nursed the hurt, sought revenge, submerged himself in humiliation. But this was America. And as much as I liked to think I had come to know America and Americans, it was obvious that we were still centuries and cultures apart. My final answer was silence.

Outside the classroom Julie Varnum walked up to me. We had always exchanged good mornings, news about Ed, news of her aunt and uncle.

"Hey, Kenji," she said, "I'm sorry. I wish I could have sided with you but I can't agree on some things. We Americans, as you may have noticed, have big mouths."

"Thank you."

"I thought, though, and don't get mad, that you sounded sort of defensive."

"I suppose I was. I can appreciate that there's antagonism toward me, especially when people learn that I am—what did your brother Chris call me?—the real McCoy."

"Yes, but like the professor said, *you* didn't invade China. Other guys did."

We started walking toward the library. It was hot, breezy, dusty. California has desert, people seem to forget. But I liked the summers—the haze, the smell of blossoms and cut grass, the nearby beaches. Our conversation got around to my brother Masao. Julie seemed interested in him, in fact, in all of my family. Maybe she felt sorry for me, I thought.

"He's a war hero," I said. "One magazine article called him the Dragon of Nanking."

"Why?"

"His company helped capture the city. A hundred men routed five thousand Chinese. Masao led the attack. He has no fear."

"Do you?"

"I've never been tested as a soldier. The truth is, I feel a little inferior to him. My studies and my job with the Ministry of Education exempt me from service. I realize the emperor and the government need scholars, men for our civil service, but while I enjoy a stroll in Los Angeles with a pretty girl my brother risks his life. It isn't so easy to retain my self-respect."

"Well, for heaven's sake, you shouldn't feel *that* way. People do what they're best at . . . Do you like your older brother?"

"Oh, yes. I respect him."

She cocked her head and sort of winked one eye. "I detect a note of hesitancy, Kenji."

"He is an oldest son. That means that next to my father he is the most important person in the house. He gets his way. He gets the best food, the best place to sleep. When I was little I was called 'Master Cold Rice'—always fed last. Now you must understand that all Japanese children are terribly spoiled, especially boys. But an oldest son—he is a god."

"But that's unfair. A scholar is every bit as good as an infantry captain."

"It's kind of you to say that. The military tradition is not so strong in your country, but among us there is no nobler profession than that of the warrior, the *samurai.*"

"All that swordplay and people looking angry and bodies churning? The stuff I saw in the prints in the oriental art collection?"

"It is part of our heritage."

We stopped under a grove of linden trees and sat on a stone bench. I had trouble not staring at her tanned throat, her broad high forehead, the gentle blue eyes. Once she turned to wave to a friend and I gasped at the sight of the nape of her smooth neck. As you may have heard, the back of a woman's neck is her most sensual and erotic part to a Japanese man. This sudden rush of feeling for her seemed to communicate itself, and she turned to look at me. "Why are you so quiet?"

"Forgive me. It is just that . . . you are so lovely . . ."

"Thank you. But tell me about your *samurai.* And why a soldier like your brother is so all-fired important."

"He's . . . he's like Musashi."

"Musashi?"

"The most famous of our sword fighters. He was a legend. A poet, an artist and a warrior. He was the greatest expert with long sword, short sword, ball and chain, bamboo pole, any variety of armed combat. Something like your Jesse James or Buffalo Bill. Every schoolboy worships Musashi and reads his book."

"Did you?"

"When I was ten years old. But . . ." I must have looked a bit dubious.

"Uh-oh. An anti-Musashiist?"

"Not quite, but I admit I could never revere him the way Masao did, or model my life after his."

"Why?"

White and yellow butterflies skipped among the trees and hedges. I recalled as a boy how I had made a collection of moths and butterflies . . . and how Masao had smashed it, calling it "girl's work." I put the unwelcome thought out of my mind . . . "I learned that one of Musashi's victories, one that he bragged about, was over a thirteen-year-old boy. He cut his head in half."

"Good lord, what a creep."

I smiled at her. "I guess I was not intended to be a warrior. It was lucky for me that I was a good student."

To my astonishment—I think I must have shivered—she rested her hand on the back of mine. "Kenji . . . do you miss your family?"

"Very much. Especially my sister Yuriko. She's a wonderful girl. Full of life, fun. But it's good being on one's own, learning, making new friends . . . I hope I've made a friend in you."

"I think you just might have . . . friend."

What could I possibly say that was up to that? We got up and walked. Peaceful, green all around us, and I had a twinge of guilt. After all, Masao might be dying on some muddy field in China . . .

"May I . . ."

"Yes?"

"Would . . . would you honor me by going to the movies with me tonight?"

Julie laughed. It was like soft music. "Only if you rephrase the question. You're not a diplomat *yet.* Try a simple 'would you like to go to the movies?' "

"Yes, that's what I meant to say," and I actually started to bow. Then caught myself. "Please notice, Julie. I'm at least learning not to bow so much."

"Duly noted . . . now just name the time and place."

"Ten minutes to eight o'clock? At the Westwood Cinema?"

With a glint in her eye, a look that poked fun at me yet was altogether warm and friendly, Julie bowed and said, "I'd be honored, Master Cold Rice."

I left her in a daze. I knew I would not be able to concentrate on my studies. The truth was, I had been rehearsing this daring deed for a week. How else would I know what theater I wanted to go to, and what time to be there?

At first I did not tell my family that I was "dating" an American girl. When I had been at the University of Oregon I had been reclusive, almost a hermit, associating with Nisei students and a handful of Japanese. I saw a Japanese girl from time to time, but she was a zoology student and seemed more interested in reptiles than me. As for American girls, I was afraid to speak to one. They seemed like goddesses—so tall and fair and free. So now I did not write to my family for a while that I had dated Julie, or was beginning to see her regularly—in class, at brown-bag lunches on campus, on weekends. That hot, hazy summer of 1941 I knew I was falling in love with her, a knowledge that often depressed me because I was certain that she could never be mine.

I did write to her uncle, Dr. Adam Varnum.

I could envision him sitting in his dim study, the eyes of his medical heroes staring down at him from the wall, the smoke from his awful cigars filling the room with a bluish fog as he read my letter . . .

> My dear Dr. Varnum,
>   This has been a busy and exciting time for me. I am taking seventeen credits toward my doctorate in political science. It is hard work, but my labors are made easier by the friendliness of teachers and fellow students, notably your charming niece, Miss Julie Varnum. She is a kind person and shows a real interest in Japan, our customs, my family. We met a month ago. Her boyfriend is named Edward Hodges and he is about to receive his commission as an officer in the Marine Corps. He has been friendly also, as was your nephew Chris. (He now has a job as a radio reporter).
>   I trust all is well in Shibuya Ward, that the patients are not overwhelming you, and that the Tokyo summer is not too humid. Please send my sincerest good wishes to Cora. I have not forgotten the two boxes of White Owls.

Years later, Dr. Varnum told me that as he read the letter he sensed that there was more between his niece and myself than I was saying. He felt good about it but hesitated to hint at his suspicions when he wrote to me.

Saburo, the imp, was reading from his history book:

> We are an island nation. We have never been defeated in battle
> and we never will be. Japan is the only nation in the world to be
> descended from a god, the sun goddess Amaterasu, and to be ruled
> by a living god. We are a nation that is victorious, invincible and
> destined to rule Asia. That is why we are superior to any other
> nation and should protect this godlike quality . . .

We were enjoying dinner. My mother had cooked an enormous bowl
of exceptional rice—white, moist, each grain gleaming—and had served
it with small fried crabs and slices of roasted mackerel. There were side
dishes of pickled turnips and spicy eggplant.

Our family was much smaller now. Although Masao was in Tokyo
he lived in his own house with Michiko and worked long hours with
Colonel Sato. Kenji had left and we would not see him for perhaps two
long years.

"The mackerel is very sweet," my father was saying.

My mother bowed and served him a second portion. "It was caught this
morning."

Miso, the clear soup with tiny clams, was served last. For dessert we
ate more rice drenched in sweetened green tea.

"I hope Kenji gets enough rice to eat in California," I said idly.

"Oh, he told me they grow a lot of rice there," my mother said.

"It can't be as good as ours," said my father.

"Kenji says we import American rice," I said, defending America,
Kenji and California.

"Yeah," Saburo put in, " we feed American rice to pigs and chickens."

My mother, bustling from kitchen to the main room, shuffling on her
scuffs, hair messy—it was a dreadfully hot autumn and the house was
airless and humid—remembered that a letter had just arrived from Kenji.
She never liked to upset my father or distract him from the joys of his
evening meal, but now with the low table cleared and all of us properly
squatting on cushions, she handed him the letter.

He smiled at the strange stamp—a portrait of the American President
George Washington—and carefully opened the envelope. "The second
son," my father said. "He is good to write to me."

"That is his duty," my mother said.

"It's because Kenji loves us," I said. "I miss him."

My father read:

> Honored father and mother:
> I am quite well and hope that this letter finds all of you in good
> health. The teachers work us hard here. I took two summer
> courses to get ahead of my schedule and did well in both of them,
> being awarded an *A* and an *A*-minus, *A* being the highest grade
> one can receive. I live in a small but comfortable room and it is
> odd to be sitting in chairs with legs again and sleeping on beds so
> far off the floor. Now, in September, I am carrying a full schedule
> of courses—eighteen credits, which is a great deal—and I spend
> many hours reading, studying and talking to my teachers, who are
> very kind.
> UCLA is a beautiful school, with many fine buildings, green
> lawns and trees. It is very hot and dry here, but I have been
> swimming in the Pacific Ocean, which is nearby, several times. I
> have a few Japanese friends. They are all Nisei, born here and very
> American, although they like to hear me talk about the old ways
> and how Japan is today.

At this point my father's brow turned into a row of furrows. He adjusted his eyeglasses, squinted, pursed his mouth. Clearly something was upsetting him.

"Is anything wrong?" my mother asked.

"He is seeing a *gaijin* woman," my father said icily. He gave me the letter, apparently unable to confront what to him was tragic news. "Yuriko, you read it."

I took the letter from him and went on:

> I have met a fine young American woman. She is the niece of Dr.
> Varnum and her name is Julie Varnum. She is a senior in the
> undergraduate program. I have taken her to the movies and to the
> beach. She is very kind but I cannot see her too often because of
> my work. Also, she has a boyfriend, another student, who is going
> to be a Marine officer—

Saburo howled. "Yow! He's got an *American* girlfriend! Wait till Masao finds out!"

My father's lip trembled. "Hisako! When Kenji was in Oregon did he spend time with American women?"

"I don't recall," she said.

"This is very bad."

"They only went to the movies and the beach—"

"Yuriko, do not offer your opinions."

"Yeah, stay out of it," Saburo, my little brother, put in.

My mother, seeing my father's upset, filled his sake cup.

My father could not be derailed. "In Oregon? Did he . . . ?"

"Yes," I said. "He went out with a Nisei girl named Sally. Her real name was Sachiko. I believe she was studying to be a doctor."

"But she was Japanese. It is wrong of him to have anything to do with American women." My father got up, straightened his robe and shuffled off to the garden. At times like this I was sorry he was a servant, even a servant of the emperor. He always seemed bowed, defeated. No wonder Masao, who was all courage and command, meant so much to him.

"Wrong, wrong," my father said as he sat on the stone bench and lit a cigarette. "I must write to Kenji not to get involved with the woman."

Saburo jumped up, began bouncing a rubber ball against the side of the house, and as he did said, "Masao says the worst thing a Japanese can do is marry a black person. After that, Asians. Chinks and Koreans and Indo-Chinese are almost as bad. White people are the least bad but they're bad enough."

A fast learner, my brother. When the dishes were done—it takes a Japanese housewife about three minutes to clean up, just a bit longer than it takes her to transform a living room into a bedroom—my mother and I sat in the garden with my dad. Neighbors, who had heard some of the commotion through the paper walls and the open veranda, peered over the wooden fence, dying to find out what the fuss was about.

My father spoke in a low voice. "I will write to Kenji tomorrow. I will ask Masao to write to him. Second son is a government scholar. He owes the emperor everything. If he carries on with this woman, even if she is related to Dr. Varnum, he may end up disgracing us."

My mother nodded vigorously, knelt at my father's feet, took off his slippers and began to massage his feet.

I felt I had to speak up. "I think Kenji has the right to pick his friends. He is allowed to see Americans, and that includes American girls."

"You will speak when spoken to," my mother said. "Don't upset your father."

Saburo hooted at me. "Yeah, nobody cares what you think."

But I would not be quiet. "If Kenji says she's a good woman, I believe him."

"Be *still*, Yuriko." My mother was on her knees, bent double, still stroking my father's feet.

With a twinge of disgust I saw myself in that position, doing the same for Hideo Kitano's feet. My fiancé, a man I did not love or even respect, was on sea duty. I had not seen him for almost a month, and wondered how I would feel married to him. The very idea depressed me, until I thought of Kenji and felt some hope for him. I decided to write to him without telling my family.

"At least that woman in Oregon," my father muttered, "at least she was a daughter of Nippon."

"Kenji will understand," my mother said. "He will not marry a *gaijin*. He is too intelligent to do that. He is an Imperial Scholar."

MASAO TAMBA · SEPTEMBER, 1941

I was sick of staff meetings, planning sessions during which I smoked too many cigarettes and developed a harsh cough. The war in China was not going the way we had anticipated. The damned Chinks, barefoot, badly armed, poorly led by corrupt generals, were actually fighting back.

Chiang Kai-shek had ordered three of his best divisions to protect the city of Zhengzhou, the target of our autumn offensive, and we wiped out one division, more than ten thousand men, but we paid such a heavy price that even after taking the city we were too wounded to advance and so the offensive failed. One of our politicians said publicly—and was reprimanded for it—"We see no end in sight."

Still, these matters did not overly concern my superiors on the General Staff and at the War Ministry. They were moving on to a new theater, greater battles, a destiny they declared the gods had ordained.

We now had a new prime minister, Hideki Tojo. I confess that I never fully trusted him . . . he was a slippery, cunning man, at one time chief of staff of the Kwangtung army and Prince Konoye's war minister. Now he succeeded Konoye as prime minister and we all knew and were pleased with what that meant—we, the military, were in charge, no longer would timid civilians stand in our way. We may not have approved of the man, but what his coming to power signified was very much to our liking.

Curiously Tojo was not all that enthusiastic about the prospect of war with the United States. He was more in love with money, and for years had been subsidized and promoted by the industrial and business interests. In fact, he was the kind of corrupt person that we young officers had tried to oust in February of 1936, but he at least seemed pliable and sympathetic. "He's a whore," was Colonel Sato's evaluation, "and he will open his legs when we pay him to."

As for the emperor, he attended some staff conferences, seated in front of his gold screen, nodded and accepted our analyses of the world situation. Tenno Heika, though, never failed to ask that diplomatic channels be kept open and let it be known through aides like Lord Privy Seal Kido that he did not want war. But our god now seemed to be like the olden emperors, subject to the iron desires of a new shogunate—the generals. And I was part of it.

One very hot night at the ministry, as we labored late into the evening, poring over maps of the Pacific and discussing our options, Admiral Yamamoto appeared. We all immediately rose and bowed to our great strategist—a modest, plain-looking roundish man with calm intelligent eyes. What a life his had been . . . he had fought in the Russo-Japanese war, at the historic victory of the Straits of Tsushima, had attended the London Naval Conference, had a wide range of experiences, civilian and naval. He had even spent a year at Harvard University, and been posted to Washington.

Yamamoto studied our contour maps, our order of battle, and smiled. "Do any of you feel that the United States will collapse without a fight?"

The highest ranking general in our group said, "She will not collapse, but after the early defeat and the loss of her navy, she will sue for peace."

Yamamoto shook his head. "You do not know Americans. May I inform you that I am supporting every effort by Prince Konoye to contact the Americans, to explore a peaceful settlement of our differences."

"We are in accord," said the general, whose special talent was saying the right thing at the right time.

Yamamoto looked us over, then said bluntly, "We will give them hell for a year or a year and a half, gentlemen. But after that, I guarantee nothing." . . . Some of us were shocked. Colonel Sato was frozen at his desk. Others looked at the ceiling, doodled with their pens. To hear the genius of our navy speak this way was very disturbing, especially since he was known as a most honest and forthcoming man . . . "A final word, gentlemen," the admiral said. "Read the life of Abraham Lincoln. The finest of all American presidents. A rare man, a great man of purpose. He committed errors but that never detracted from his humanity. It inspired feelings of warmth toward him. He was capable of forgiving the mistakes of others, and so his subordinates and the American people forgave him his mistakes. I have read six biographies of Lincoln and have come away with greater admiration for him each time."

He looked at us with a compassionate, almost wistful smile. This was a man who had seen a great deal of war, of destruction, of death, and yet he admired an American president for his warmth and forgiveness. It was strange . . .

"Carry on," he said, and left us quickly. With more to think about than we had bargained for.

JULIE VARNUM · SEPTEMBER, 1941

I had been dating Kenji for several weeks since we'd gone to the movies. It would be a lie if I said I wasn't taken with him from the start. And I'd obviously had my effect on him . . . I'd even gotten him to stop bowing and apologizing so much. Maybe Kenji's only fault was that he was *too* good . . . he was considerate, helpful, and very intelligent, and his stories about Japan, his family, his upbringing constantly intrigued me. Oh well, why not stop beating around the bush . . . I was falling in love with him. And the *real* reasons, the basic ones, were probably as elusive as they always are in these things. Once one of my art history teachers at UCLA told me that most art criticism is too analytical, too intent on interpretation, attempts to explore and reduce art to an essay. Wrong, wrong, Professor McPhail had said. The test of a great work of art was its immediate impact on the viewer. You should see it and react. A *gestalt*, he called it, an overall sense of the work should arouse you, move you, give you an emotional and aesthetic boost.

And that's the way it was for me and Kenji. I couldn't explain how or why it happened. Ed Hodges, after all, was one of the finest men I ever knew . . . handsome, kind, bright, gentle . . . but I never was in love with him. I'm convinced Kenji and I knew we were in love after that first date. It wasn't just that he was so attractive—darn near beautiful, as a matter of fact—and graceful and smart and *different,* and so polite and anxious to please me . . . it was the elusive something else. I know this all sounds a bit soppy, but I've never heard even the hotshot philosophers do much better, just fancier.

There was no problem, though, in identifying what Kenji felt about meeting my parents—sheer terror. I tried to tell him they weren't fancy or rich or snobby, that like the Varnums that he knew so well and felt easy with, they were Quakers. Our house was a low white stucco bungalow in Glendale, my father was an insurance-claims adjuster, a modest job, and he didn't even have a college education. My mother had once taught home economics in a junior high school. Chris and I commuted from home to UCLA—no ritzy out-of-town colleges, no elegant wardrobes and neither of us had joined a sorority or a fraternity. There was no money for that kind of stuff in Walter Varnum's family. All of this reassurance did little good . . . right up to the last minute, as we walked down the street to my home, Kenji was nervous, convinced my parents wouldn't like him.

"And you're still wearing Ed's Marine pin," he said. "They will think I am an intruder. They'll want you to marry Ed—"

I quickly told him I had no such intentions, and that as much as I loved my parents they would *not* pick out my husband.

He smiled, seemed to relax a bit at that. "It's so different from what happens in Japan. Americans are lucky. You have so much freedom. Our lives are defined before we're born."

"I couldn't live that way, and I bet you won't be able to either . . ."

We had turned onto the flagstone path between two low rows of privet that led to our home. I suppose it wasn't exactly a thing of beauty . . . squat heavy gables, stumpy wooden pillars on the porch . . . but I loved it. Kenji stopped now. His Adam's apple was dancing. He was sweating.

"Maybe your parents won't like the presents I brought them."

"Well, we won't know till they open them. Come on, Kenji, a little of that old *samurai* courage, please. Quakers like *everybody*. And forgive everything."

At last I'd made him smile. "You're joking, you always do when I'm upset."

"One of my many talents," I said, and pushed him along to the house.

My parents, of course, were as nervous as Kenji, for all their religious philosophy and good manners. My father was a patient, accepting man but had always been in the shadow of his older brother Adam, who'd attended medical school, married a European and gone off to an adventurous life in the Orient. My mother was more outgoing. For many years she'd worked for Quaker missions, helping raise money for their projects among American Indians, mostly the Navajo.

When I introduced Kenji to mother and dad he of course bowed, then extended his hand.

"Am I supposed to bow back?" my father asked.

"No, no, please. It was wrong of me to use our custom. Julie is trying to cure me, but . . . It was an act of respect, I hope I have not annoyed you—"

"Julie's friends are always welcome here," my mother put in quickly, the diplomat of the affair.

"Of course," my father said, "and I understand you know my brother Adam. That makes you doubly welcome."

I could see Kenji fighting against the impulse to bow again as we went from the tiny foyer into the living room.

"Oh, yes, sir, I've known Dr. Varnum and his wife since I was a small boy," Kenji was saying.

"Good, good, we'll have a drink and talk about him, and about Japan."

I was surprised to see Kenji accept a light scotch and water. On dates with me he drank only what my mother, in her midwestern way (she was from Minnesota) referred to as "temperance." He'd also told me that Japanese men get drunk very fast. Maybe, though, a drink would relax him. Not to mention me.

"Tell me about Adam," my father said.

Kenji became eased up some as we sat in the parlor, and as he sipped scotch he talked about my aunt and my uncle, the clinic, how Cora had delivered his brother Saburo and his sister Yuriko, how Adam had so often taken care of illnesses, bruises, fractures, sprains for the four active Tamba children, especially Masao, the wildest. "Your brother is very much respected in Shibuya Ward," Kenji said. "We are slow to accept foreigners but he and his wife are looked on as almost Japanese."

My father shook his head. "When Adam went to Japan twenty years ago it was supposed to be a three-year hitch."

"Hitch?"

"A tour of duty," my mother said.

"I suspected he'd stay on from the tone of his letters. He likes your country and the people very much. It's sort of like they cast a magic spell over him."

Kenji looked puzzled. "Magic . . . ?"

"Yeah . . . a sort of witchcraft, no disrespect intended, of course. Adam and Cora could have had fine careers here in California. My brother was at the top of his class at Stanford Medical School and Cora had a fine education in Europe. But the Society of Friends asked them to start that hospital, the one near your home, and, well, it's all a bit of a mystery to me . . . or maybe the mystery is Japan."

I could see Kenji didn't quite know how to answer that, but he usually managed to say something diplomatic and he came through again. "I think we are less a mystery when people get to know us," he said. The ambassador couldn't have said it better.

I began helping my mother set up the table with fried chicken, corn on the cob, fresh sliced tomatoes—huge and ruby-red—freshly made cole slaw. We were, I suppose, not only American, but all-American. I could see that Kenji was winning my father over—he had that quality, he was no empty flatterer but just naturally agreeable and very anxious to please —sometimes too much.

My father motioned to Kenji to come to the table, then raised his glass. "I think we should drink to something."

My mother joined them and raised her glass of ginger ale. "To peace. That's what we all wish for."

Kenji said quickly, "Yes, I agree."

"All right, to peace," my father said.

We raised glasses. Kenji said, *"Kampai."* And when we all looked confused he added, "It means a dry cup."

"To the point," my father said, not knowing what else to say.

My father went on to say that Quakers weren't really supposed to drink intoxicating beverages, but he winked at the law now and then. "Besides, both the Old and New Testaments are full of wine tippling."

Kenji smiled. "A most broad-minded attitude. In moderation, liquor can be a comfort."

I half-frowned at him. "Kenji? Can you please do me a favor and *stop* talking like a Berlitz school record. Okay?"

"Have I said something wrong?"

"No, not at all . . . but you don't have to be so formal. You sound as if you were addressing the Japanese Parliament." I realized quickly that I was being a little harsh with him, but it got under my skin a little, seeing *him* so proper. Like I said, if he had a fault it was being too perfect. Maybe my problem was that he sometimes made me feel like a primitive by comparison.

My mother rode to the rescue. "I think Kenji expresses himself beautifully," she said. "It's truly remarkable the way he's mastered English. Don't you agree, Walter?"

"No question . . . in fact, his English is better than mine."

Kenji—he couldn't help it—promptly bowed his head, as always uncomfortable with compliments. "You mustn't praise me. It really is not hard to learn a foreign language. I had two years in Oregon. Americans are so friendly. They like to help. I'm afraid we aren't that helpful, and our language is almost impossible to learn."

With these exchanges of across-the-sea amenities over, the meal proceeded well. Kenji pecked at the corn on the cob . . . I was sure he was wishing for rice while he amused my parents with stories about Japanese eating habits. No people on earth, he said, love their native foods the way the Japanese do. His teacher and sponsor, Professor Adachi, once went to spend a year of study in France and took along with him ninety pounds of Japanese specialties—dried squid, pickled plums, seaweed, cartons of special rice, rice wafers, bean curd . . . enough to keep him happy while he lived in Paris, the world's most renowned culinary center.

After dinner, sitting in the living room over coffee, Kenji gave my parents the presents he'd brought along—small boxes elaborately wrapped in red-and-gold paper.

My father's gift was a handsome lacquered stud box. "Kenji, you won't be offended if I keep paper clips and rubber bands in it, will you? I'm not much for studs."

Kenji laughed. "Not at all, sir. A gift is at the bidding of the one who receives it. I think it would make an excellent receptacle for paper clips."

"There goes that Berlitz record again," I said. "Loosen up, Kenji, you're not in class." This time I smiled when I said it.

My mother, a pretty woman, wore no makeup and styled her hair in naturally curled gray bangs . . . actually, she looked a little like the pictures I'd seen of Mamie Eisenhower. She was knocked out by the tortoise-shell combs Kenji gave her. "Oh, these are so lovely . . . you shouldn't have . . ."

"I chose poorly," Kenji said, "forgive me."

I could have strangled him. Later I would learn about the Japanese obsession with gift-giving, obligations, debts and so on. All terribly complicated, and, frankly, sort of a pain in the neck.

"Where did you find such beautiful things?" my mother asked.

The scotch was doing its work and relaxing him, I thought, as he said, "We Japanese have our own network. One of the gardeners at UCLA told me he had a cousin in Riverside who had a gift shop with excellent Japanese imports."

"You went all the way to Riverside to buy these?" I asked.

"If they please your parents it is worth a journey five times as long."

Ah, Kenji . . .

My father now proceeded, as he did with all visitors, to show his old family album that rested on the oak buffet. Kenji was interested to see that although we were Quakers, many of my dad's ancestors had been soldiers, and my father explained that it was my mother (a Meriwether of Massachusetts) who had brought him into the Society of Friends. He also pointed out an old faded engraving of his most illustrious ancestor, General James Varnum of Rhode Island, standing proud in brass-buttoned coat, three-cornered hat, white weskit, the purple sash of a general officer in the Continental Army. We also got the obligatory recital of battles the general had fought in . . . Red Bank, Monmouth, Rhode Island. "He was also a teacher, a lawyer and a writer," my father was saying, "but his greatest claim to history was that he was the first officer in the Continental Army to urge the freeing of slaves and their enlistment as soldiers. In fact it was my esteemed ancestor James Varnum who influenced Washington to form the famous Black Regiment."

"A black regiment?" Kenji was obviously intrigued by that.

"You bet. It liberated slaves at a time when Rhode Island was a state where slavery was much the fashion. Newport was one of the biggest slave ports in America. James Varnum's idea was to give these men their freedom with their rifles, so he had his officers go around the countryside buying Negroes, then inducting them into his regiment and handing them, along with their new uniforms, certificates of freedom. Now that's a contribution to our history I am really proud of.

I applauded gently. "Hooray! Kenji, you have to forgive my dad. Every new visitor has to get the James Varnum Memorial Lecture."

"It is an inspiring story," Kenji said. "I like your ancestor very much, Mr. Varnum. A soldier but also a scholar and a man of principle. He did not feel that the color of a man's skin was a reflection of his character, or that any man should be penalized for being of a different race. Yes, I like that..."

I thought he said that last with a special depth of feeling. I think my father caught it too as he closed the album, putting to sleep the dusty pictures of Varnums past—soldiers, teachers, businessmen. Sometimes I felt that dad, in his job with the insurance company, felt he had let down his illustrious forebears. Which made me mad and was maybe why I didn't like to see him dredging up the glories of his family's past.

"And what happened to General Varnum and his Negro soldiers?" Kenji was saying.

"Oh, James Varnum died at forty. When the revolution ended Washington rewarded him with a judgeship in Ohio. As for the Black Regiment, it fought gallantly in Rhode Island, then sort of disappeared. Some historians say that if Varnum's plan had been continued slavery might have ended much earlier and spared us the horrors of the Civil War."

"It is a pity," Kenji said.

"What is?" I asked.

"That good and reasonable men are so often ignored. Somehow they have trouble making themselves heard when violent men take over."

Was he thinking of his brother? That holy horror he'd told me about, the Dragon of Nanking? . . .

All in all I must say that the evening was a success. Just the opposite of what Kenji and my parents had worried it might be. I walked Kenji to the street and made a date to meet him for lunch the next day . . . we were both brown-baggers . . . just outside Royce Hall.

Back in the house, my father said, "He acts as if he's stuck on you. What does Ed think of him?"

"What's that got to do with anything?"

"Ed's a good judge of character, and I thought—"

"Ed likes him, they played on the same softball team."

"And Chris?" my mother asked.

"Dear brother Chris tends to like only himself and people that can do something for him. I don't think he feels one way or the other about Kenji."

"Oh, he's very nice, dear," my mother said, "don't misunderstand us."

"Of *course* not," I said, and wondered if the annoyance I felt had gotten across. I worried that the next thing I'd hear was how they were only interested in my welfare . . . Fortunately, dad went right to his old upright Zenith radio for the eleven o'clock news from NBC. George Hicks was reporting that there was a special Japanese envoy in Washington and that all signs pointed toward an agreement between Japan and the United States.

"Are you going to see Ed this weekend?" my mother asked, not much interested in the news.

"I don't think so . . . got tons of studying, summer session is real tough, mom . . ."

"Will you be seeing Kenji again?"

"I may. And then again I may not." I tried to smile brightly.

I didn't fool her for a minute, but thank God she let it go at that.

I listened to a later newscast in my room, read the chapter on the House of Representatives in Bryce's *The American Commonwealth.* The last thing I heard before I switched off the radio knob and got ready for bed were reports of Japanese naval maneuvers in the western Pacific. They were being discounted in Washington.

It barely registered on me. All my thoughts were on the next day, on seeing Kenji again.

YURIKO TAMBA · OCTOBER, 1941

Hideo, my gorgeous fiancé, was still at sea, and for that I was grateful. He was serving on the aircraft carrier *Akagi,* and it seemed to me that he was already married . . . to the ship.

I was told yesterday by my parents that they had been in touch with Hideo's parents, the Kitanos, and that the families had decided that as soon as Hideo got his next shore leave we would be married.

I was not, as you can understand, thrilled. The more I thought of Hideo the more I envied Kenji in America. Maybe some day I could visit him . . .

Later I would learn that Hideo's letters—very few—traveled back to me all the way across the Pacific. He never said he loved me, that would have been unmanly. Still, he was not different from any of our men, so I should not have blamed him.

Most of his letters were about how tough his officers were to him, and how he in turn, had to beat and punish the enlisted men under him. They were stupid peasant boys, he wrote, and responded only to punches and kicks. He and his bunkmate, an ensign named Mori, were the best karate and judo experts in their group and gave exhibitions for the other officers. The seamen learned to obey Hideo and Mori or get their brains beaten out.

Hideo also told me that he kept my photograph on his footlocker and that Mori and the other junior officers mocked him for this sentimental failing. He also boasted to them that I was the daughter of a palace "official" (quite a promotion for my dad) and that he would marry into the family of the famous Captain Tamba.

About what his *Akagi* was doing, or where she was bound, he said little. I assumed his letters were censored. Life on board, he said, was exhausting, long hours, hard work. He also said something peculiar that made me laugh . . . unlike most of what he wrote. He said that they did not dump their garbage overboard but packed it away in big sacks and stowed them on the lower decks. What a smell, I thought. Also, from time to time, he said, they observed radio silence. He and Mori had no idea why.

They would, as it turned out, soon learn.

JULIE VARNUM · OCTOBER, 1941

Kenji and I now began to see each other every day. We seemed to *need* one another. For sure, we were happy when we were together, lonely when we were apart. At night he would call me from his dorm, where he studied for endless hours, and when he did I was always a little breathless, hear-

ing his soft, somehow intimate voice. No doubt, I was falling in love with
him.

My brother Chris, now a full-fledged radio correspondent, came back
one weekend. He didn't see Kenji—he stayed one day and then had to
cover the dedication of an airplane factory in San Diego—but let me know
he disapproved of my dating Kenji . . . "Nice enough guy, Julie, but if
things keep going downhill he'll be in jail or back in Japan. Where does
that leave you?"

Chris told me the navy officers he'd gotten friendly with in San Francisco felt that the Japanese were planning some aggressive action in the
Pacific, that the first strike most likely would be against the Dutch to get
hold of their oil-rich islands. The navy guys also assured Chris that "those
flat-headed yellow-skinned monkeys" wouldn't stand a chance against the
United States Navy. Their ships were made of tin and their airplanes of
balsa wood. "The Nips will have a short but interesting war," was the
byword among our navy brass.

"Kenji says he can't imagine a war," I told him.

"Well, not against us, anyway," Chris said. "But if the Japs land on
Java, or try to grab some other Dutch islands it'll put us on the spot. That
takes the bite out of our oil embargo, and who knows what's next?"

Chris had more uncomplimentary things to say about the Japanese,
calling them midgets, puppets who bowed too much and had been conned
by a lot of junk about a god-king, a divine right to rule the world. Look
at them in America—cooks, gardeners, dirt farmers . . .

I decided to let him talk and not argue. There wasn't much point in it,
and I knew he'd just say my feeling for Kenji had blinded me.

Before Chris left we had lunch in a Mexican restaurant in Westwood
Village, and as we were leaving, Carol Andrus walked in with a man in
an army uniform. He looked like he was in his late thirties, heavy-set, bald
and with a mustache. She was in uniform too—a first lieutenant in the
Army Medical Corps—and I noted that the man she was with also wore
the caduceus lapel insignia of the medical corps.

"Hey, Carol," Chris said, "I thought you were shipping out."

"Hi, Chris. And Julie!"

She introduced the man with her then . . . Herbert Kahn, a major, chief
surgeon at the military hospital near San Francisco. Carol worked for him,
she told us.

Major Kahn had a ruddy, smiling face. "Yes, I've heard a lot about both
of you," he said. "You're the reporter, right?"

"Right." Chris seemed cool, obviously sensing as I did that Carol and
the major had a relationship that went beyond scalpels and sponges.

"Covering the defense build-up?" Kahn asked after an embarrassed moment of silence.

"What there is of it."

Chris had to drive down to San Diego, I had a class, but I wished we could have stayed a while longer. I'd always liked Carol, who was always sort of high-strung and now more so than ever, sensing Chris's hostility to the major.

Major Kahn asked Chris if his network was sending him out to Hawaii or the Philippines, where the action, he said, seemed to be developing.

"No, I'm too valuable covering rabid raccoons and schoolboard meetings. I guess I'll just have to wait until you guys heat it up so I can play war correspondent."

"Sure . . . well, nice to have met both of you," and he forced a smile.

As we left I could see Major Kahn guiding Carol to a booth, one hand touching her back.

"Carol looks great," I said as we walked into the burning daylight of Los Angeles, "and you were rude."

"What am I supposed to do? Congratulate the little lady on getting herself a major? The guy looks as if he could be her uncle. Major Herbert Kahn. Big deal."

I squinted through the yellow light as we walked to Chris's old Ford. "Look here, dear brother, Carol doesn't owe you a thing. Your little interlude in San Francisco was your big deal. And you weren't very interested in her feelings. She's a free agent, just like you."

"Okay, okay, I'm a rat. But I really like her . . . so now she's got herself a major, the guy probably's married with four kids and a practice in Fresno and—"

"You are something, Chris. All you ever did was proposition Carol. She's got feelings. Like most of us she wants to be more than just . . . just a receptacle for some man's convenience."

"Who said no? What am I, a monster?" He started the motor, slammed his hand down against the steering wheel. "The truth is, I realize now I really like her, and seeing her with that pill roller . . . it's as if I was being compared to him, the guy's got to be forty, and I'm not as good, is the message I got from her. You think I'm jealous?"

"I think you have an overactive imagination."

He dropped me at my classroom . . . I knew Kenji was inside . . . kissed me good-bye and said he'd try to drop by again on his way back from San Diego.

Poor Chris, he had had to lose something before he could appreciate it. I had no intention, I told myself, of losing Kenji Tamba . . .

* * *

That night Kenji and I went to see a revival of *Gone With the Wind*. I'd told him about Chris's brief visit and about his feeling that Japan might attack the Dutch islands but wouldn't stand a chance fighting the U.S. Kenji agreed but said he hoped there wouldn't be any fighting, period. He didn't look too happy when he said it, and for a minute I wondered if he knew something our people didn't—I quickly put *that* out of my mind.

Movies are great for losing yourself. And there was none better than the saga of Tara. The problems of our world disappeared so long as we were with Rhett and Scarlett and Ashley . . .

Afterward we ambled down Westwood Boulevard and Kenji bought us ice-cream cones. I knew he had no money for luxuries, but kept my mouth shut. It would have humiliated him to offer to pay. Instead I asked him if he'd liked the movie.

"Yes . . ."

Not exactly a four-star review, I thought, and said how much I loved Clark Gable.

"He . . . confused me a little."

"How?"

"He was courageous, a man of action and intelligence. But he was not a patriot. He refused to fight with the Confederates like Ashley and the other Southern gentlemen."

"He was a realist, he saw that war against the North couldn't be won."

"But if the Southerners felt they were right he shouldn't have mocked them."

"But they *weren't* right. They were protecting slavery. And Rhett knew thay had to lose, that a war would only bring suffering to everyone in the South."

"But if one is fighting for an honorable cause and loses, one still has done the right thing—"

"Do you really believe that?"

"Yes . . . our greatest national legend, the story of the forty-seven *ronin,* teaches us that."

"*Ronin?*"

"It means feudal warriors, *samurai.* These warriors had lost their lord and became impoverished wanderers. Their sovereign was betrayed by an evil lord and condemned to kill himself. So these forty-seven warriors swore they would avenge his death. Their leader was a brave and cunning man named Oishi. He and the others bided their time, and he pretended to be a drunken shiftless vagabond so that no one would be afraid of him. The *ronin* all became beggars, waiting for the moment of revenge."

"I'm sorry, but that doesn't exactly seem heroic to me—"

"*Samurai* are trained not to flinch from their obligations."

I wanted to say that if I heard another word about obligations I would be *obliged* to scream. But I listened and kept such thoughts to myself.

"Confucius, who was a man of peace, taught that a man cannot live under the same sky with the slayer of his father. That is what the *samurai* believe."

"I can guess what's coming," I told him. "Please don't make it too gory. At the moment I'm enjoying my butter pecan."

Kenji didn't react to that feeble humor but went on with his story ... "Oishi and his followers tricked the evil lord. They killed him, chopped off his head and placed it on their dead master's grave. And so the debt of honor was paid."

"Okay, okay, I surrender—"

Now he did smile but persisted to the bloody end of the tale, to how the shogun ordered all forty-seven of the *ronin* to commit ritual suicide by *seppuku,* ripping open their bellies. I added my own flourish by throwing what was left of my cone into a trash bin.

"The lesson," Kenji said, "is not to shock but to show that once a path is decided upon one must dedicate oneself totally to that goal."

"What if halfway down the path you find out it's the wrong one, not the one you thought it was?"

That seemed to stump him, and I realized again that although he had been exposed to a lot of American education and traditions, in many ways he still thought like a Japanese ... and of course why should it have been otherwise?

"That never occurred to me," he said finally.

My less than enthusiastic reaction to the tale of vengeance indicated a change of subject, so we shifted back to the movie. Kenji said he was confused by the love story in *Gone With the Wind* ... "Scarlett didn't love Rhett, did she?"

"No, she was in love with Ashley."

"But she married Rhett because he was rich, correct?"

"Yes, and just maybe she was a little in love with him too. He certainly loved her, which has its effect on any female . . ."

"It was confusing. An arranged marriage would have solved everything."

Again his Japaneseness . . . He spoke almost too proper English, he could hit a baseball, he liked ice cream and steak, but deep down inside was Japan and its ways . . . "Why an arranged marriage, for Scarlett or anyone else?" I countered.

"They could have been man and wife but never have been troubled by love."

"*Troubled?*" I said it so loud that two women studying the sportswear in Bullock's window jumped. "Love is *trouble?*"

"My parents had an arranged marriage. As did Masao. My sister will have one. They work out."

"How can anyone be happy with a wife or husband someone else picks for him?"

"It doesn't exactly work that way. If one truly detests the proposed partner there are ways of saying no."

"What if you only find that out after the marriage? Like maybe the guy doesn't squeeze the toothpaste from the bottom? Or the woman saves old pieces of bread till they grow mold? There's that path of action you can turn away from again? You can't turn back?"

"Marriages in Japan are not a problem. A wife learns quickly that her duty in life is to please her husband. If she doesn't he can divorce her as easy as paying a bill."

"What about *her* rights?"

He said quietly, "She has the right to be a wife and mother. Is that so bad?"

He didn't mean to annoy me, I knew, but all this was curling my teeth. "You mean the husband has no obligation to please?"

"His obligation is to hand over his wages, to keep her in clothing, food and a house, and encourage her to raise good children . . . I know this sounds severe to you, but most Japanese wives are quite content. They know they are the ones who run the house. They always have the love of the children even if the husband is not affectionate. In fact, it is considered unmanly to like one's wife too much. Other men will make fun of a man who is too attentive to his wife."

I halted at the corner of LeComte. "Kenji, are you leveling with me?"

"No, but please, Julie, don't be so upset. No one could ever think of treating someone like you in that manner." He stopped, seemed to grow tentative . . . "Many European women marry our men—diplomats, teachers—and they lead happy lives. I assume they are treated differently."

We were under a streetlight now, and I could see the serious, almost sad look that had come over him. He took my hand, kept looking at me until I began to feel uneasy.

"You are so beautiful, Julie. The most beautiful woman I've ever seen. Not just your face. All of you . . . your spirit, your soul."

I said nothing. I think I was shaking a little. From anyone else these words would have sounded laughable. From this man they sounded like what they were . . . his exact, honest feelings. He took my arm now as we crossed the street, and his hand was firm, warm. We strolled the campus this way, its green lawns and flagstone paths deserted for the weekend.

"You shouldn't pay me so many compliments," I finally was able to get out, and realized the irony . . . after all, only a little while ago I was the one thinking how hard it was for him to accept compliments. Maybe it was turnabout and I was getting Japanese . . .

"I am acting dishonorably," he said. "Ed is my friend. He loves you and wants to marry you. I apologize for my rudeness—"

"You weren't rude, for God's sake."

"Presumptuous, then?"

He almost sounded like a small boy. He did not, however, look at me like one. No question, this was a man.

"When I am too familiar with you I am disobeying the Buddha's truths."

"Oh, Kenji, Confucius and Buddha in one night?"

He laughed then, and so did I. "Buddha teaches that the cause of suffering is craving and that the cure for suffering is the elimination of craving." He held me close as he talked. "I must stop talking about my desires—"

"I'm not complaining. Tell that to Buddha."

We were in a dark corner of the campus in back of the library. He pulled me closer. He kissed me, and I could swear that as he did his eyes were damp.

"I love you," he said.

I answered by kissing him back, and he lost all his Oriental reserve, kissing my face, my neck, my eyes and my forehead. Whoever said that Japanese men don't know how to kiss or find it revolting are crazy. I responded. Oh yes, I admit it. His body was slender, lean, whippy. His skin glowed in the dim light. But when I drew away he reverted to an old habit and bowed.

"That hinge in your back, Kenji . . ."

"Hinge?"

"The one that keeps bending you over. It has got to be put out of commission. I can't stand a man with a hinge."

I kept a straight face when I said it, and it took him a little while to realize I was kidding. When he did he put his arm around my waist and smiled almost shyly. Kenji was never given to outright laughter. He was always reserved.

"Please understand me, Julie. If nothing more ever happens between us, I will always remember this night, your face, that you let me kiss you—"

I put my fingers to his lips, silencing him, and when we walked on it was I who took his hand.

YURIKO TAMBA · OCTOBER, 1941

My brother Masao was suddenly gone to Malaya and Singapore, in civilian clothes and, I was to learn later, with a passport that said he was Ichiro Tsurumi, a salesman for a ball-bearing company. The civilian garb confused me, but in two weeks I was caught up in the excitement of Michiko's discovery that she was pregnant, the news coming, of course, from Dr. Varnum.

"I hope it is a boy," Michiko said. "Masao would want that."

"No guarantees," said Dr. Adam Varnum.

We always giggled at the way he spoke Japanese. It was perhaps rude of us, especially since he was such a kind man. But we can't help laughing at the way *gaijin* speak our language. Masao says it is like seeing a trained monkey. No matter what the monkey does—ride a bicycle, walk on stilts, eat from a plate—it is never quite right and is always funny.

"I'm sure it will be a son," I said as I helped Michiko dress.

Dr. Cora Varnum came in then. "What makes you so sure, Yuriko?"

"A man like Masao must have someone to carry on his name and pray at the altar for the repose of his soul."

She frowned. "My gracious, Masao isn't dead."

"Well, a son must keep the family scrolls and photographs and the house," Michiko said. "If a father cannot pass these things on he feels his life has been empty."

Cora didn't seem very impressed with that, so I added how Masao once told me that he *had* to have a son.

"Michiko, if you have a girl he'll take her and like her," Cora said, and walked out briskly to examine an old woman who had fractured her ankle.

Michiko then turned to me. "I'm so excited . . . the worst thing for a wife is not to have children. And if this baby's a girl we'll keep having them until a boy arrives. I can't wait to have a son, see him marry, and then have a daughter-in-law that I will be able to order her about."

My dear sister-in-law, sometimes she amazed me. To want a son so that she could one day lord it over a daughter-in-law . . . well, I suppose she's not the only married woman who feels that way. But to me it seems too much like getting even. I tried, though, to hold my tongue. Japanese women are not supposed to have unconventional ideas. Besides, Michiko always seemed more put upon than most . . . She'd been Colonel Sato's only surviving child, and a girl at that, which was a double affront to the colonel. His son died in infancy, and his wife committed suicide out of shame. Kenji told me the colonel visited the Floating World and kept a mistress. Sato was very close to Masao, as you might expect, and looked on him as a son.

"It hasn't been easy for her," Kenji once told me, "being the surviving daughter, not to mention what her father is . . ." When I asked what that meant he put me off and said he'd explain it someday.

Before he left Masao had said any child of his would be born in the military infirmary for officers and nowhere else, but I had taken it on myself to bring Michiko to the Varnums' clinic when she started vomiting and missing her period. Masao would just have to live with it.

When their offices finally emptied the Varnums invited Michiko and me into their garden for tea. Michiko was shy, she rarely met foreigners but had heard about the Varnums from me for a long time.

"I will pray to Buddha for a boy," she said softly.

"I hope he comes through for you," Adam Varnum said, and lit up one of his famous smelly cigars that he claimed helped kill the aphids that attacked his rose bushes.

"So we'll save a bed for you here, Michiko," Cora said.

Michiko only bowed her head, too shy to speak up, so I told them that Masao wanted his child born in the army hospital, meaning no offense to either of them.

"Ah," Adam Varnum said, "he's afraid of too much contact with the *gaijin?* I'm surprised. After all, he knows me better than any doctor in Tokyo, including those in the military."

This time we both bowed our heads.

Adam Varnum seemed suddenly dispirited . . . "It's in the air, I can feel it—"

"Adam, *please.* The girls have nothing to do with all that."

And so it seemed as we sat there like two delicate hothouse flowers in our flowered kimonos. "Don't embarrass our visitors, Adam . . . Well, it was a pleasure to examine Michiko and find that she is pregnant and healthy. Masao has the right to take her to any hospital he wants." Dr. Adam got red in the face but took out his anger on his cigar, puffing on it until there was a cloud around him.

As for a fee, we knew in advance that the Varnums would accept none. Besides, they considered the Tamba family close friends, almost relatives. I think Dr. Adam was the only foreign person in the world that my father could be open and frank with—as frank as a Japanese man can be. So there was no fee, but Michiko had brought for the Varnums one of her paintings, a watercolor of a *torii* gate in Ueno Park, a summer scene with trees in full leaf, the sun glowing through the branches.

"For both of you," Michiko said, and bowed again. "For your kindness."

"It's *beautiful*," Cora said. "You have talent, Michiko. I shall hang this in our office to remind us of your generosity."

"Oh, please . . . you must not thank me too much," and Michiko blushed.

Dr. Adam shook his head. "Here it comes, the obligations. See if I have it right, Michiko. I placed a *giri* on you. My wife examined you as a favor and asked for nothing in return. But this burdened you with the obligation to return the favor with precise equivalence. Right?"

Michiko covered her mouth to hide her smile. "You are correct, doctor. Yes, the *giri* from you was the examination. I thought that one of my paintings would be a proper *giri* in return. Now we are even. We have honored one another. I can only hope my humble painting is sufficient." She was perfectly serious when she said it, and Dr. Adam realized it.

Michiko left then to shop and to see if there was a letter from Singapore from Masao. I stayed on with the Varnums and told them about the letter we'd gotten from Kenji and how happy he was to have met their niece.

"Yes, Kenji has written us too. He and our niece Julie have become friends. Did he send you a photograph of her?" Dr. Adam snuffed out his cigar and shredded bits of tobacco into the rose bed . . . made good fertilizer, he once said.

"No, I think that would have upset my parents more than the letter. My father is afraid that Kenji might—"

Dr. Adam waved his hand. "Tell your father not to worry, that Julie's engaged to some fella she's known for years."

Meanwhile Cora had found a black-and-white photograph of their niece, and I could see that she was a pretty woman with a high forehead and long blonde hair. There was a strong line to her mouth, and I thought her eyes spoke of a woman who knew her own mind. I responded to that, and I could also see why Kenji would like her. Maybe more than he was saying in his letters . . .

"Julie says he's one of the brightest students in the department, makes friends easily *and* is a good baseball player. I'll take credit for the last— I coached him."

I reverted to custom, smiled politely, bowed and accepted a small box of hard candies from America to take home. I then promised to bring them a jar of my mother's pickled plums to dissolve this new *giri*. Dr. Adam said that much as he loved us, sometimes he wanted to break our necks out of frustration. "You people just don't know when to quit," he said. History would take care of the irony in that comment.

MASAO TAMBA · OCTOBER, 1941

The news that my wife was carrying a child was welcome indeed as I returned from my swing through Malaya, eager to get to work and convey my knowledge to my superiors.

As Mr. Tsurumi, salesman, I had the run of the cities, walked freely around Singapore, dined at the Raffles Hotel and took hundreds of photographs. The British never ceased to amaze me with their laxness, their smugness, their presumption that their white skin and so-called traditions insured their survival. Well, they were in for some *bloody* surprises.

We gathered in one of the planning rooms at the War Ministry around a huge contour map of the Malayan peninsula. I was feeling very good— anxious to work, determined to be seconded to an infantry division, happy about the impending birth of my first child. I had bought Michiko magazines about romantic love and erotic practices, hoping that such stimulation would render her body more prone to produce a male child. Certain herbs were also recommended to influence the sex of the fetus and I instructed her to drink these with hot water every day.

"Malaya," Colonal Sato was saying. "What a prize. Rubber, tin, all sorts of resources. If we take it we can laugh at the United States' refusal to sell us raw materials."

And so we planned the invasion of Malaya down to the last detail—rafts, barges, tanks, and the cheap handy man-powered bicycle . . . we would pedal our way into Singapore.

After the first briefing session Sato informed me that I was to be promoted to major and would command several of the assault units that would go ashore at Kota Bharu. We would be part of one of General Yamashita's three invasion forces. In my group five thousand of our best-trained men, many of whom had been in China with me, would storm the beaches, wipe out defenders and go on to besiege Singapore.

"The coastline is meagerly defended," I told Sato and his colleagues. "The Indian troops are badly trained, lacking in morale. Under no circumstances can they be depended on to die for British officers and the British flag."

"And Singapore?" a general asked.

I pointed to the contour map. "The guns point south to the sea. They are powerful guns but they cannot be swung around. Fixed positions. For reasons that elude me, the British have never envisioned an attack from the north."

"But the causeway," the general said. "Three hundred feet of causeway . . ."

"If the British have any sense they will blow it up," Colonel Sato said. He looked at me. "Major, what then?"

"If the Japanese army cannot get across three hundred feet of shallow water it does not deserve to cross the Pacific."

They seemed strangely cautious. We had, after all, talked, and talked, and talked about this war and now I saw hesitation and faint hearts. *Why?* I think it was psychological. The British and Americans had looked down their big noses at us for so long, called us yellow apes, so humiliated us, that our leaders found it difficult to believe that we really could rain death and destruction on them and bring them to their knees.

I had no doubts and I so informed all of them. Our time had come. God-ruled, god-descended, we were about to bring the Eight Corners of the World Under One Roof. They sat there like impassive Buddhas. I had no idea whether my message had gotten through.

JULIE VARNUM · NOVEMBER, 1941

We did so many things that hot dry autumn. People tend to forget how windy, dusty and warm a Los Angeles autumn can be. In those days there was little smog and haze, but the heat lingered, reminding us we lived in a transformed desert.

Kenji and I went to movies, studied together, took bike trips, played tennis (Kenji was terrific) and swam at Santa Monica and Malibu.

Kenji kept his blend of Americanization on the outside and Japanese at the core . . . the combination an added fascination for me. He taught me a few more words of Japanese each time we got together. Speaking the language, at least getting to know basic expressions and conversational usages, wasn't too hard, but I never learned to read Japanese or write it. I confess it was beyond me. Kenji assured me I wasn't alone, that the number of Westerners truly fluent in Japanese was probably less than a thousand. Even expert translators had problems, he said. Word order was often reversed; clear statements became obscure; polite phrases became insulting; and a remark, even though translated literally, might take on an entirely different thrust. I began to realize why the Japanese, especially in their contracts with foreigners, used so many smiles, bows and intakes of breath in place of language that could be easily taken the wrong way. Kenji told me their complex language also went with such Japanese attitudes as a suspicion of verbal skills, a belief that people can understand each other without too much talking, the desire for decision by consensus and a deeper desire to avoid confrontations on the personal level. The Japanese, Kenji said, preferred to waltz around a subject, use analogies, poetry, suggestions . . . none of our American cards-on-the-table, let's-be-frank-about-things, let's-lay-it-on-the-line. He said that the emperor's reading of his grandfather's poem about troubled seas in an effort to halt the militarists was a perfect example of this avoidance of direct language.

We continued our cultural exchange during a picnic the next week on a cliff above the beach at Trancas. We'd taken a bus from Westwood Village, hiked across hills covered with dry prairie grass, found a rocky ledge overlooking the brown-gray Pacific Ocean.

Kenji had prepared a Japanese lunch, complete with sake.

"We even have two alphabets," he said, sounding, I thought, rather pleased.

"Congratulations. Most of us have trouble with one." I smiled brightly and sampled some crunchy, salty red stuff on a ball of rice. Kenzo told me it was a pickled plum, and I allowed as to how it was . . . different. To tell the truth, the array of pickled radish, cabbage, turnip, carrot and plum was sort of hard to take for a bred-in-the-bone Californian raised on fresh crisp vegetables from the local market. My mother, health-minded and penny-watching, frowned on any canned or preserved food and it took her years to allow a carton of frozen peas into the house.

"Try the fried eel," Kenji was saying.

I nibbled at a bit of brownish-gray fatty meat, finessed the rubbery dried squid.

Kenji, after a few tries at educating me on the way Japanese could be transcribed into English, went back to food, although it was obviously not what was really on his mind . . . the old Japanese ploy of sneaking up on the subject at hand.

"How is the eel?" he said while looking into my eyes.

"Like an eel." Two could play the game.

"We think it brings good luck to eat an eel."

"For everyone except the eel."

He smiled. "If you don't like the eel or the squid or the pickled plums, just eat the rice. I cooked it myself. Did you know that rice is a gift to the Japanese people from our sun goddess?"

"Only the Japanese? How about for anyone else who eats rice?"

"Oh, they're allowed to have it too. But we honor our rice with seven different names."

"A rose by any other name . . ."

"What?"

"I'm sorry, I was being a wise guy."

"My picnic is a failure."

"No, stop it. I love it here, and I love being here with you. And you can fill my sake cup."

As he did he kissed my arm, then my neck. "I love you, Julie. I am not afraid to say it. It's considered a sign of weakness for a man to say this, especially to a wife, but I am not afraid. I'm no samurai—"

"Kenji, will you please shut up," and before he could apologize I pulled him to me and kissed him full on the mouth . . . sighed at the delicious feathery touch of his lips. It was my last move of the day. I could feel his hands trembling slightly as he stroked my back.

"Your family . . . would they . . . ?"

"Accept you?"

"A yellow man? A foreigner?"

I stroked his face. Skin like cool silk. "It wouldn't be easy, Master Cold Rice."

He nodded. "It will be the same, even harder, for my family. We Japanese are polite to gaijin but in our hearts we dismiss them. We don't dislike them, we just don't think they matter. After all, we are ruled by a living god, the descendant of gods. How can any foreigner be as good as we are?"

"*And* you've got seven different names for rice. *You* don't believe that stuff, Kenji. People are people. And this *gaijin,* descended from nothing more than a couple of very mortal Westerners, happens to be in love with you."

He gasped, kissed my hair, then most of the rest of me . . .

Later we lay in the afternoon sun, holding one another, me kissing his ear. "This is better than rice, isn't it?"

That night I told my parents what I had known for some time, that I was in love with Kenji Tamba and intended to marry him.

We were in our backyard, dad trimming some rambling rose bushes that had run wild and were now withered and brown in the wake of the dry autumn.

"I can't believe you're serious," was his first reaction.

"I am. Very serious. Kenji asked me to marry him."

"Then you will tell him it is *out of the question.*"

"Mother, I—"

"Of course you'll tell him that, dear." She put down the Sunday magazine section of the Los Angeles *Times.* It was five days old. She complained that she never got a chance to read it. Sunday papers lasted a week, sometimes two, in our house.

"I want your blessing," I said. "I love Kenji, believe that."

I was sitting on an old peeling swing that Chris and myself, and Ed and Carol, had played on so many times when we were kids. A shiver passed over me. All the memories of my safe sunny life in California . . .

"What about Ed?" my mother finally said.

"I don't love Ed, mother. I've always admired him and liked him, he's a terrific guy, but I feel very differently about Kenji. We *love* each other. Oh, mother, when you get to know him better . . ."

My mother sat across from me in the glider and reached out for my hands. "Julie . . . you've always had this headstrong streak in you. I think both your father and I are open-minded people, but you know so little about Kenji, about his family, his future . . ."

"I know that I love him. That still counts, doesn't it?"

My father set down his shears, wiped his hands on a rag and walked toward us. His tired freckled face distressed me. I knew he thought of me as his little girl, his princess, and it hurt me to see him hurt.

"You are not in love, Julie. You're fascinated with Kenji's differentness. It's not enough. I don't care about skin color or anything that superficial. I care about you, the kind of life you'd be letting yourself in for. Your Uncle Adam has written us about Kenji's Japanese friends. They're foreign to us, to you, in more ways than their appearance. They look at life differently. You're young and vulnerable, darling. And forgive me for being boring and practical, but how would you two live? What would you live on? Where would you live—?"

"I'll get a job, and we can live anywhere."

My mother was really upset now. "And not get your degree? And what kind of a husband lets a young wife support him?"

"It'll only be until he gets his doctorate."

My father looked grim. "That would, I suppose, be typical. Everything for the man. The woman becomes an appendage, a servant. I know about these Asian marriages. I've had some contact with our own local Japanese. The wives are little better than maids and cooks."

"But Kenji isn't like that."

My father began raking. "So he says, so he may even think . . . Adam says that as much as he likes his Japanese friends they're xenophobic, clannish. They don't take to strange wives and children of mixed races. Julie, can't you see what you're letting yourself in for?"

"I'm not worried. Plenty of people right here in L.A. get divorced and are miserable. We'll manage. After Kenji gets his Ph.D. . . . he's really brilliant, daddy—"

"His brilliance won't help much if there's a war. And there may be one, according to some pretty informed people. Chris says things are heating up. What then? Where do you go? How do you think his family will look on you, if, God forbid, you and he are on opposite sides in a war?"

"I don't care, we love each other—"

"It's not enough."

"What about all those wonderful Quaker ideals about brotherhood that I was raised on? Aren't we supposed to consider all proposals, respect the views of minorities?"

"We are doing that," my father said, "but we are also being practical—"

"Are you telling me not to marry Kenji? That you forbid it?"

". . . I am," my father said.

"Forgive me, I love you both, but this is my decision. Please don't look so *unhappy*. Your daughter has just become a woman."

It was my mother who allowed a smile through her tears, came over and hugged me. And before I could say anything more, my father did the same. How about that for parents?

YURIKO TAMBA · NOVEMBER, 1941

One rainy evening I came back from an interview at a shipping office to find Saburo being bullied by some of his schoolmates.

Saburo was undersized but he always seemed to be in the thick of fights. My mother said he ate nothing and would never be strong and it was no wonder he was picked on. As for Saburo, he seemed to live on air. "Eating is of no importance," he would say. "Quick eating, quick emptying, that's life." Where he learned such a crazy notion, and at his age, I don't know. Maybe from his *samurai* books. He liked to say he was just like a *samurai*, a big man who did not need food or sleep or warmth. "I can put a toothpick between my teeth and feel as if I've had dinner," bragged my kid brother. His schoolmates ragged him mercilessly over his defeats, but he wouldn't be put off.

As I turned into our drizzly, misty street, lights glowing in the row of wooden houses, I saw my tenacious brother wielding two wooden swords *samurai*-fashion, confronting a much taller boy who also was brandishing two wooden swords. They were churning around in the muddy street, circling, lunging, thwacking each other with the wooden weapons.

"Musashi says hit the enemy in one timing," Saburo was calling out.

"I'll Musashi you, mouse turd."

"Musashi says use the Body Strike, hit the enemy through the gap in his guard—"

"You prick, I'll knock your sword through your head."

"Musashi says make your body like a rock and ten thousand things cannot touch it—" Saburo said as he ducked and swung the long sword.

"Rock, huh? You're a pile of crap," and the bigger boy yanked the long sword from Saburo's hand, broke it over his knee and came for Saburo's throat. My brother may have been a first-class pest, but he was a fearless pest. He held out the short sword now, shouting, "Musashi teaches that one can win with the strategy of one cut . . ."

His opponent's answer was to kick Saburo in the crotch, shove him into the mud. Then he flipped him over, sat on him and pushed his face into a puddle. "Eat dirt, Musashi."

"*Stop,*" I screamed. "Leave him alone."

"Let me up, pig."

"Go home and play with dolls."

The others hooted. "Yeah, what would Musashi do?" And one taunted "He thinks he's a bigshot because of his brother. Stick him in the mud for keeps."

"Get your hands off him," I told them. "That's enough . . ."

I should have saved my breath. Instead of thanking me for trying to help him, Saburo kicked me in the shins. "Don't you ever do that again," he screamed. "Don't you *dare* humiliate me in front of my friends!"

"He would have strangled you . . ."

"I don't care, no woman has the right to butt in, I fight my own battles—"

I tried to grab him but he kicked me in the thigh and ran away. I suppose I should have known better . . . what worse disgrace for a *samurai* than hiding behind a lady's kimono?

Our mailman, a sweet old fellow named Ozaki, came limping down the street just then and Saburo saw fit to turn his anger and frustration on him. At least he would never hit an older man, that was forbidden and we all liked old Mr. Ozaki, but Saburo, blinking away tears, danced around the postman shouting unintelligible commands.

"All right, little warrior, do me a favor and take the mail," and Mr. Ozaki proceeded to sort out a packet of letters . . . "A letter from brother Masao. And one all the way from America from brother Kenji. And plenty of bills."

Saburo grabbed the packet and ran past me, no doubt muttering *samurai* oaths as he went.

If Kenji's letter about meeting Julie had upset my parents, this one almost sent them into hysteria, followed by a deep depression.

My father was seated on a floor cushion, eyes glued to the *Asahi Shimbun*'s front-page editorial accusing the United States of trying to strangle Japan and if that didn't work, of getting ready to go to war against us. My mother was flicking dust from one shelf to another and my father kept sneezing.

We all gathered around the floor cushions then to listen to my father read Masao's letter, mailed from any army post office so we had no idea where he was. Security was very tight. We were at war in China, we were occupying French Indo-China, there were constant rumors of invasions to come . . .

Masao's letter, it turned out, was vague, told us little. Mostly he exhorted the family to dedicate itself and work for the emperor. He did say he was "at sea" with his battalion and would soon have good news for us. He paid tribute to our father and ended invoking *Yamato Damashii*— the spirit of Japan, unconquerable, ordained by the gods to rule the earth.

My mother then asked my father to read Kenji's letter also. Father had

tossed it aside and was sipping tea, having no interest in the letter. He told
me to read it.

How well I remember that letter:

> Beloved and honored family, I have come to a great decision in my
> life. I ask your blessing. I have asked Dr. Adam Varnum's niece,
> Miss Julie Mary Varnum, to marry me. She has consented. She is a
> good and kind woman and I am sure you will welcome her to the
> family Tamba—

My father dropped his cup, splashing hot tea on his kimono. My mother
rushed to dry him off but he pushed her away and ordered me to read on.

> . . . We love and respect each other, and I hope, honored father
> and mother, you will be happy with my choice of a wife. This has
> not been an easy decision for me. I have struggled with my
> conscience but I know I am doing the right thing and I—

My father held his hand up. Usually a mild man, he was now altogether
out of character. "The *fool*. Do not read any further, I will get ill. He
wants to dishonor us. I must stop him, I'll call the Minister of Education . . . they can cut off his scholarship, he *cannot* do this stupid
thing . . ."

And then he was out of the house heading toward Adam and Cora
Varnum's, and I went with him, even though he was hardly aware of my
presence.

When Dr. Varnum read the letter he seemed to hesitate before speaking.
Babies were yowling in the office, Cora was talking to a local woman,
giving her a prescription.

"So," Dr. Adam said, "it seems our families will be closer than ever."

My father shook his head. "I cannot regard Kenji's decision as an
occasion for rejoicing."

"Why not? They're splendid young people."

"I appeal to you, doctor. Tell your niece not to do this. It can only cause
harm."

"Goro, I can't do that. I'm an ocean away from Julie. Besides, it's none
of my business."

"Doctor, you have lived in our country long enough to know us. We
are who *we* are, and you are who *you* are. That is the way it is and the
way it should be."

"With all due respect, Goro," Dr. Adam said carefully, "you know that

there are many intermarriages between our people that have been successful. Some of your diplomats have married Western women. Many American men find happiness with Japanese wives."

"Your exceptions prove the rule. Besides, it has happened too soon.
They cannot know each other—"

"Is that your only problem with this?"

"No, I admit it is not. I have a position at the palace. A minor one but
it means a great deal to me and to my family. A *gaijin* in the family might
be the end of my employment. And there is Masao. Colonel Sato has told
me that there is no limit to how high he can rise in the army, even in the
government. Japan's future is with the army, Sato says. Look at our new
prime minister. Mr. Tojo was a general . . . Dr. Varnum, I do not intend
to insult your niece. But Colonel Sato says that it is not impossible that
Masao will be a member of the general staff. Masao will not like it—"

"He isn't Kenji's father. You are."

Dr. Adam was one of the rare *gaijin* who could talk that way to one
of us. "Doctor, do you say you won't write your niece and tell her to give
up my son?"

"No. I will not. If nothing else it would be presumptuous of me."

My father got up and bowed. "You have always been honest with me
and I will be honest with you, doctor. I cannot give this marriage my
blessing. It is against the way things should be."

He said it like a sentence. I felt terrible, seeing these two good men so
miserable. But I could say nothing. I might have had thoughts not common to most Japanese women, but I still could not speak them. That too
was "the way things should be."

JULIE VARNUM · NOVEMBER, 1941

It wasn't easy, but nobody ever said it would be, or should be. I had
to tell Ed about my decision to marry Kenji, and there was no good way
to do it. Everybody agreed it was something I had to do, my family, and
Kenji too. In fact, Kenji insisted on it . . . he said, in his solemn way, that
it would not be fair to write or call Ed in camp. I had to do it in person,
Ed deserved that much.

So I took the bus to Camp Pendleton, and believe, me, it was the hardest thing I'd ever done. Actually, after he got over the shock of it when I first told him, Ed surprised me by the way he took it, asking only that I keep his Marine pin, that is, if Kenji wouldn't mind. That last was about the only bitterness he let out, though I was sure he must have felt plenty more than he was letting on to. He even, just before I left, made a joke, saying that most guys had to go overseas to get Dear John letters. He was getting one in person ahead of time. He forced a smile when he said it, and I had to fight to keep back the tears. I really cared about him, and hated to see him standing there looking too brave, and so miserable.

His last words were, "Hey, congratulate Kenji for me, okay?"

I turned away quickly and got on the bus before I started bawling.

Kenji and I were married on December 2, 1941, in the Friends Meeting House in Glendale.

It was a small wedding. From my family there were my parents and Chris and a few cousins, aunts and uncles. Most of my mother's family were in Minnesota. Daddy's brother Uncle Adam, of course, couldn't come. Kenji had no relatives at all there. Our friend Frank Yasuda came, all spiffy in his ROTC uniform. We also invited Professor Shapiro.

The time and place of the wedding was fixed by three members of the committee on ministry and counsel, and here we were, on this chilly gray day, in the Friends Meeting House, facing one another in front of the meeting.

Frank Yasuda gave Kenji the ring—a plain, narrow gold band. We began with several minutes of silent prayer, seeking to find what the Friends call "a state of religious fellowship." Nervous in my white linen dress and white pumps, I doubted that I'd attained that lofty state. Kenji looked solemn in his tan suit, white shirt and blue-and-buff UCLA tie. His coal-black hair was parted at one side, a few strands falling over his forehead.

I almost dropped my bouquet of purple amaranthus when I got up to face Kenji in front of the meeting. He smiled at me, I nodded. I could see my brother Chris, who looked distinctly unhappy. My parents looked resigned, clearly making great efforts to hide their displeasure.

Kenji and I held each other's right hands. He took a deep breath and began to say our vows:

"In the presence of God and before these our friends, I take thee, Julia Mary, to be my wife, promising with divine assistance to be unto thee a faithful and loving husband so long as we both shall live."

My mother was crying. I squeezed Kenji's hand and repeated his words, substituting "wife" for husband.

We then added some of our own touches, a common practice at Quaker weddings.

Kenji said, "Let us both be guided by the noble eightfold path. Right knowledge . . ."

I replied, "Right intention."

"Right speech."

"Right conduct."

"Right means of livelihood."

"Right effort."

"Right mindfulness."

"Right concentration."

As we kissed I could hear Chris asking the professor, "What was that all about?" and could have killed him.

"Teachings of the Buddha. I've heard worse rules."

Frank Yasuda whispered, "It's worked for twenty-five hundred years."

Transportation for our honeymoon was a rusting Ford that Kenji borrowed from Frank Yasuda's older brother, a Nisei farmer in Arcadia. Farm dust, bits of vegetables and pebbles resisted our efforts to dislodge them before driving south to Coronado Beach and the famous old hotel there. Inside was okay, except for a huge rent in the seat with a spring sticking through.

Actually we'd have been happy on a scooter. For the trip south I was decked out in a lavender suit with matching round hat, and Kenji was very American on the outside—in a checked sports jacket and beige slacks. My parents had scraped up three hundred dollars as a wedding gift, money I knew dad could ill afford. From Kenji's family—nothing. Not a word, a phone call, a telegram. It shamed him, which maybe was the idea . . .

We didn't let any of this affect our high spirits as we drove on Route 101 south to San Diego, listening to a scratchy car radio, turning off newscasts and singing. Well, mostly I sang and Kenji smiled.

I rested my head on his shoulder, let my hand linger on his leg, and gave out with:

> *Jim doesn't ever bring me pretty flowers*
> *Jim doesn't try to cheer my lonely hours*
> *Don't know why I'm so crazy for him . . .*

Some day I know that Jim will up and leave me
Then even if he does you can believe me . . .
I'll go on carrying the torch for Jim . . .

"This Jim will never leave you, beloved wife," Kenji said like a solemn oath.

"Just try it, buster." My fingers played at the back of his neck and right ear. I still marveled at how smooth his skin was and loved to run my hand against the grain of the short stiff hairs at his neck. "See, wiseguy? Yankee woman is allowed to like male back of neck. You Japanese haven't got a patent on necks, right?"

"Right."

"Good. Now we can have our first argument."

We were going through coastal towns, rolling farms, empty wild areas, pine groves, and stony mountains, getting glimpses of the Pacific . . . "You said you wouldn't let me work, that I was supposed to stay in college and get my degree. But that was before Shapiro offered me this neat job of research assistant."

"I cannot let my wife work. I would bring dishonor on you and myself if that became known to my sponsors—"

"Better dishonor then, sweetheart. I know how little you get from your sponsors. We can't live with my family—that's o-u-t, out. I found this studio apartment in West L.A., perfect for us, we can bike to classes. And we do need some things—like furniture, dishes. We didn't do too hot, my love, in the wedding-gift department."

"We'll live Japanese-style. No furniture. Sleep on mats. Eat sitting on floor cushions. One bowl apiece, one set of chopsticks apiece. We simplify, save money, live like kings—"

"On rice three times a day?"

"Maybe four."

"Not for this Mrs. Tamba. Look—I'll work, earn money, in a year you'll have your doctorate and you'll get a terrific job in Washington, London, who knows? We'll be terribly sophisticated and international—"

"We won't be so sophisticated if my wife works. I truly want you to graduate, Julie."

"I truly can do both. I'm a woman of parts. Very versatile." . . . and I proceeded to kiss his ear, stick my tongue in it, nibble its golden edge, at the same time letting my hand stroke his thigh.

"Oh, please. Oh, stop. We'll have an accident."

"Give up? Wife can work?"

"I give up. Surrender . . . just stop, please. Later. Please . . . you can do anything you want . . ."

I purred, we drove on. A clear-cut victory for our side.

KENJI TAMBA · DECEMBER, 1941

Others may have questioned my marriage to Julie, I never did. I admit, though, that part of the attraction was our difference. But who cared why or how much this or that had to do with what we felt for each other?

I craved her—not only as a sexual partner but as someone I could share my life with, someone who knew *other* things. And she found the same in me. By nature a curious person, she was eager to learn, travel, expand her knowledge of the world. We were convinced that our differences would only strengthen the bonds. The truth is, I must add, that Julie was more confident about this than I was. Driving down to Coronado that cool December day I began to worry . . . yes, I am a worrier . . . that maybe she had gone into this to test herself, to rebel. When I said as much she kissed me and said, "No, no, it's called love, Mr. Tamba."

"I hope I am worthy of—"

"Stop. *Stop.* Just stop being the nicest guy on the block. You're allowed to get mad, even to be selfish."

"I will work very hard to be bad if it pleases you," I said, feeling quite proud of myself for this display of humor. Julie promptly rewarded me with a pinch on my thigh that nearly drove us off the road.

I would later learn that at nearly the very moment Julie and I were on our honeymoon drive to Coronado Beach the decision had been made to strike the United States, the date set. The fleet had long been underway, an armada sailing in deadly silence, moving toward Hawaii. Elsewhere in the Pacific other ships of our navy were sailing for the Philippines, Malaya, the Dutch East Indies, Hong Kong . . . The warlords, the outlaws, the modern *samurai* had won out. Resistance to them had collapsed. Behind the warlords the outlaws threatened, bullied, blackmailed, demanded vengeance, an end to humiliation, and the assertion of Japan's divinely ordained right to rule the Pacific.

Only on December 1 was His Majesty informed that the strike against America was set for Sunday, December 7. Colonel Sato and others, including the naval aide Endo, were briefed by General Sugiyama after a meeting with His Majesty.

Sato asked if the emperor had been pleased.

Sugiyama responded evasively, saying only that the emperor again requested that negotiations for peace be continued up to the last minute. If acceptable terms could be reached with the United States, would it be possible to call the fleet back?

And the response? asked Sato.

Sugiyama and Admiral Nagano, the chief of the naval staff, were again evasive. In the roundabout way that the language is used by our officials, some hope was left in the emperor's mind while at the same time not admitting the impossibility of calling back the greatest war armada ever assembled. His Majesty also asked that if war proved unavoidable the Americans be notified in advance of the strike against Hawaii. Sugiyama said that this request of His Majesty would "most regrettably" have to be ignored.

The outlaws were now firmly in charge.

JULIE TAMBA · DECEMBER, 1941

Ed must have gotten my letter just a day or two before the Japanese invaded Wake Island. I would learn later how he was sitting in the shade of a camouflage net with two of his gunnery sergeants, men who became his close friends.

Ralph Guzzo, his old D.I., was now a master sergeant in Ed's platoon. Guzzo was from the Bronx, a former amateur boxer and high school football player who had picked the Marines as a career. His best buddy was a gangly blond boy from Gadsden, Alabama, as fair as Guzzo was dark, named Verne Goodwin. A staff sergeant, Goodwin played the guitar and sang hillbilly songs about longing for his "blue tick hound" and his "red dirt farm."

Ed read my letter to him sitting behind sandbags looking out at the Pacific.

Guzzo and Goodwin could read the hurt in Ed's face, and knew the letter he held in his hand was the source of it. Around them in the sandbagged antiaircraft emplacements other Marines baked in the fierce sun of the atoll, waiting . . .

Ed called my letter a "Dear Jack." A "Dear John," he said, was when your girl told you it was all over. Well, he'd already known that when he shipped out. My letter was the official confirmation—a "Dear Jack."

He couldn't bring himself to tell Guzzo and Goodwin that I had married a Japanese. When they pressed him about who had stolen his girl Ed just said he was an okay guy, much as he hated to admit it.

It was hot, filthy humid, a breeze blowing from the west, a hint of rain. The radio reports were dull, unrevealing. Intelligence didn't seem to know anything . . .

YURIKO TAMBA · DECEMBER, 1941

I was sitting this cold wintry day in the upstairs room by myself reading a romantic novel. We Japanese keep romance out of our lives as if it were a disease. A man never touches his wife's hand in public, or even in their living room. Young couples rarely touch each other, let alone kiss. It's not considered *manly*. No wonder we Japanese women read a lot of romantic novels, mostly sad but so beautiful . . . lords and ladies, warriors and maidens, doomed sweethearts who have to commit suicide together or are banished or die of longing for one another. My book was titled *Fatal Kisses*, about a lord who goes blind and spends his life seeking the love of his youth and so on. Well, at least it helped take my mind off a future lifetime with Hideo . . .

As I read I could hear my parents in the garden, my mother busily raking the gravel around the rocks and shrubs, my father talking . . . of course he did none of the chores . . . as he sat on the veranda steps smoking.

"You will catch cold," my mother was saying. "I will go in the house and get you a coat and a shawl—"

"No, I'm fine." He dragged on his cigarette. I feared he was becoming addicted to tobacco. (I was forbidden to smoke but my brothers and father were allowed to.) I think that Masao's long absences and Kenji's marriage to an American woman upset father more than he would admit.

"You look worried," my mother said. "Have I offended you?"

"No, no."

Hisako said, "It is the times . . . Masao is somewhere, and Yuriko's fiancé is at sea and Kenji is so far from us across the ocean . . ."

"Yes, I wish Kenji had come home. He should not have gone to America."

"But he is a good son. A scholar."

"It is not enough. He has lost respect for us. I could tell it in his last letter. Perhaps he will still come to his senses and divorce the *gaijin.*"

My mother said nothing to that as my father batted his arms against the cold . . . a gentle man, prematurely bald with gray fuzz around his ears and steel-rimmed eyeglasses.

After a long pause my father admitted something else was bothering him, and my mother urged him to tell her what it was, could she help . . . ?

"Well, at the palace . . ."

"Yes?"

"I am laughed at, scorned."

"Why?"

My father cleared his throat and turned his back to my mother. "I . . . I do not have a mistress." Having gotten it out he rushed on. "Of all the valets and even subvalets I'm the only one, they gossip behind my back. They call me Tamba the priest, Tamba the hermit. And these are men of lower rank, some who never get a glimpse of His Majesty. Yet they have mistresses."

"Maybe they are only bragging?"

"No, they tell the truth."

My mother continued raking pebbles, artfully arranging them to simulate waves. She had a fine artistic touch, and a world of patience and tolerance. I felt terribly sorry for her . . . And then angry. Was this to be my life too?

"Dear husband, if it will make you happy," she said, "please arrange as you like. She will be what she will be, I will remain what I am."

"Oh, fine. I am pleased. I'll talk to Kingoro Hata tomorrow. He knows how to handle these matters."

What was odd about this conversation was not that my mother agreed to my father taking on a mistress but that he even bothered to consult her.

Among his peers it was considered unmanly and foolish to involve a wife at all. My mother's reaction, never mind what she may have felt, was *expected.*

I've heard stories, and I am sure they are true, of a mistress bursting into a home when she had a complaint, financial or otherwise, and belly-aching to the husband *and* wife that she was being badly treated. The usual reaction of the man was embarrassment. Not that he was ashamed of the "other woman" but that he was being shown up as a poor provider. The wife shrugged and told the husband to be more generous. We Japanese may imitate but we are *not* the same as you.

Humming now, my father even deigned to help my mother pick up dead leaves. He was delighted, it would be a step up in prestige for him, it would cheer him up. And my mother understood.

Such were the trivial winds before the storm.

JULIE TAMBA · DECEMBER 7, 1941

It was a Sunday, a little chilly but sunny, the last day of our honeymoon at the Coronado Beach Hotel near San Diego.

It had really been a week out of this world. We splurged some, spending a good chunk of our wedding-gift money for the room. We walked the beach, drove into Tijuana and bought presents for our family, played tennis, and made love as if a law were about to be passed against it.

In the secret privacy of our room overlooking the ocean, I'd tease Kenji. "Hurry up, government scholar," I'd giggle. "The state legislature is going to prohibit this. It's too good to be legal."

He'd look confused at first, then laugh and hold me close.

We found out, to our delight, that we were both passionate people. But there was more . . . we were happy just to be with each other. Walking the beach or strolling through Torrey Pines or down the sunny streets of Tijuana looking in shop windows . . . we were just full of joy and pleasure in each other.

We drew stares at the hotel, a marvelous old wooden place with cupolas and turrets. The manager looked suspiciously at us but Kenji's fine manners and perfect English melted him. Once I thought he'd ask to see our I.D.'s but I cut him off at the pass when I indicated our wedding bands and informed him we were indeed Mr. and Mrs. Tamba.

Ah, that last morning. The pain, the terror . . .

We were both awake. It was ten o'clock, maybe later. We were lolling in bed, cuddling, resting in the spoon position, his strong lean figure—my golden man—pressing against mine, his hands on my thighs, my right hand reaching back to touch his.

When he kissed my neck I shivered.

"It's like candy," he said.

"Oh, you oriental sadists. A back-of-the-neck fetish. What if I had an ugly neck?"

"I'd divorce you."

"Oooh, no more." I spun around and attacked him with my hands, my lips. "See how you like it, wiseguy. See how you like being kissed, licked and tickled all at the same time."

"No, no, please . . . *yes* . . ."

Naked now, we held each other, held onto each other . . . I never wanted it to end, at the moment believed it never would. Thoughts race at times like these . . . and I thought briefly of the erotic Japanese prints I'd sneaked looks at in the college art library. Lord knew, Kenji was a lot better-looking than those head-shaved sneaky-eyed cruel-looking types in their flapping kimonos. And I never exactly went for the way the Japanese printmakers rendered what I believe is politely referred to as the male member . . . all wrinkled and oversized and sort of menacing-looking. More like a weapon than a source of love. Maybe it was that *samurai* craziness, the Musashi nonsense. Maybe they really thought that love was just an extension of war. Thank God all Japanese didn't . . . Kenji especially.

After we'd made love and lay close together, me moaning happily . . . is that a contradiction? . . . Kenji breathing deeply, I said, "I always wanted a man with skin like gold . . ."

"You mustn't compliment me too much. I'm still full of disbelief."

"*Why?* About what?"

"That you would have me."

"We're in love, that's a pretty good reason."

"I still get nervous about you, think of losing you."

"No chance, friend. I adore you. I also crave you. Still don't believe it? Are you still going to get all fouled up with obligations and honor and all that stuff? How about some guilt? Might as well go all the way—"

"No, no guilt." He kissed me. "This has been the happiest six days of my life. I wonder if I can ever be so happy again."

"We'll work on it." I got up, put on a robe, fussed with my hair. I wore it long then, ash-blonde, above my ears forming a sort of pile over my forehead. Very 1940s. "I decided last night, Kenji. I want a Japanese house someday. Just the way you described it. *Tatami* mats, *futons,* cushions. Plus a garden with fruit trees and rocks, a foyer where people take off their shoes and put on slippers, a kitchen where I can cook, a *tokonama* for family photographs and a Buddha."

"And rice three times a day?"

"I'll cram rice into you until you turn into a paddy."

He got up, put on his black *happi* coat. We stood on the balcony and looked out at undulant gray waters. Kenji was abruptly quiet, thinking, I suspected, about his family. They had never even acknowledged our marriage, and I knew it hurt him, though he tried to explain it away . . . It had all happened so quickly, he said, they had no time to learn to accept it . . .

We wrapped our arms around each other, not moving. The ocean was hypnotizing, almost. Our idyll somehow held an undercurrent of fear.

I broke the spell with some semiserious chatter . . . "Look, husband, I'll keep a Japanese house, we Quakers like to keep things simple. But Japanese wife, no, sir." That brought him back to my shore. "I won't walk three paces behind you or lug packages or slide across the floor to open doors. And a whole lot less bowing than you're used to. Maybe none at all."

He didn't rise to the bait.

"Julie, you will get no argument from me today. Or tomorrow. We'll keep the good things, like the cherry blossoms in the spring. It's a beautiful custom. We walk among them. We write poems about them. We picnic and drink sake. We don't take the blossoms for granted. We thank nature for them."

"It sounds great . . ." I said, and wondered how long before I would see for myself . . .

"Well, my lover," I said, "until the cherry blossoms, how about we take a ride into the mountains and see what we can see across the ocean . . . might even spot a cherry tree . . ."

We began to dress lazily . . . I was in my bra and panties . . . when we heard shouting from the patio below.

The Japs, the bastards—

They bombed Hawaii—

It's on the radio—sank all our ships—

We're at war, we're at war—

I quickly slipped on a dress and ran to the balcony and shouted to some people below. "What *happened?*"

A fat man in a checked shirt yelled back: "Turn your radio on. The Japs bombed Hawaii!"

People were milling around, disbelieving, shaken—the way I was.

Kenji—he was frozen. At first he couldn't speak, then as if to himself . . . "I was afraid this would happen, I didn't want to believe it but the signs were there . . . my brother . . ."

I came to him. We silently hugged each other, he kissed my hair.

Our idyll was over. Without speaking, we began to pack. Kenji turned on the radio that was on the night table. It was true, all right . . .

". . . Without warning, Japanese ships and planes early this morning launched a massive sea and air bombardment of the United States naval base at Pearl Harbor. The loss of American life is heavy. More than a thousand servicemen are believed dead and many thousands wounded or trapped in sunken warships. At least a dozen ships are reported sunk or severely damaged. A Japanese broadcast monitored in San Francisco quoted Tokyo government sources as saying that a state of war now exists between the United States and the Empire of Japan . . ."

"*Fools,*" Kenji said, and turned it off with an angry twist of the knob.

"What do you think it will mean for us . . . for you . . . ?" Already knowing the answer but not wanting or able to face it.

He shook his head, slumped to the bed, held his head in his hands.

"Maybe it's a mistake? A fake report?" I said inanely, knowing it wasn't, that this was no Orson Welles repeat.

He kept shaking his head. "I couldn't allow myself to believe that it would happen . . . but it has . . . it's true . . ."

"*Why?*" I asked. "I thought they were still talking, negotiating in Washington. What happened?"

He got up then and held me, and for him made the speech of his life. "Whatever happens, Julie, I love you. Know that."

"Well, my friend, my husband, I love you too. And you know that." I even managed to force a smile, which didn't last long as we finished packing.

It was no pleasure checking out. People stared at Kenji. *The enemy?* That well-dressed young man who spoke excellent English, and with the blonde American wife?

On the drive back to L.A. we kept the radio on, and the news got worse and worse. There had been Japanese attacks and invasions all over the Pacific. It was as if they were trying to eat up everything they could reach —Malaya, Hong Kong, Thailand, the Dutch East Indies . . .

"Greater New East Asia Co-Prosperity Sphere," I mumbled, after a newscaster had read the text of a Japanese communiqúe. "What the hell does *that* mean?"

"Conquest. The military has taken over. It's their fancy term."

"But . . . they . . . Japan can't win, they can't beat us—"

"They think otherwise." Kenji paused, frowned. "My brother . . . I wonder where he is—"

"I'm worried about *you. Us.*"

Kenji touched my cheek. "We'll be okay. You must not worry."

For that moment I almost believed him.

Masao Tamba · december 15, 1941

Our assault against the British in Malaya was a model of swift coordinated warfare. We landed almost unopposed at Kota Bharu and started rolling south as most of the Indian troops discarded their weapons and fled. I didn't blame them. Why should they have fought for the British, their arrogant whey-faced mincing masters? I detest them. Say this for them, though, to service their rubber plantations the British had built excellent blacktop roads along which we sent our light tanks, trucks and battalions of bicycles in a tropical downpour. The Indians—Sikhs, Rajputs and Punjabis—tried to make a stand but were massacred or surrendered. After we captured the Alo Star airfield our planes came in low and our pilots strafed them. At times our vehicles could not move, the roads were so clogged with dead Indian soldiers.

It was a lesson for me on how easy it was to send the enemy into retreat with only a sword charge. They had ample firepower, but I organized a striking unit of crack officers and led them into the field of fire yelling and waving swords. Colonal Tsuji, watching the defenders of Malaya scatter, said, "We now understand the fighting capacity of the enemy." He almost spat out the words.

Defeat was like some sort of contagion, a wind-borne disease among the British and their colonial troops. They actually threw away their guns and ran. The native Malayans and Chinese appeared amused by the cowardly retreat of the so-called defenders. They cheered us as our tanks rolled on unchecked toward Singapore. This will be hard to believe, but at one point my advance patrol, moving ahead of the main column, came on a group of Britons *playing cricket,* oblivious to the war.

Our intelligence reports said the British had a *three-to-one* advantage in manpower over us, but we were confident . . . the Indian soldiers hated their commanders, many of our men were battle-hardened veterans of China, we had tanks and artillery. The British had little and had maintained what they had poorly. They thought that heavy ordnance was of little value in jungle warfare, but they had stupidly forgotten their own excellent roads.

I told my battalion officers that night that the day of the white man in Asia was ending. We were sitting in a leaky tent drinking sake and eating mounds of rice. With only a marginal loss of men we were on our way to the conquest of Malaya.

The next morning we left the road for the jungle, silently surrounded an Indian army barracks and forced its surrender after a brief fire-fight. Our enfilading machine-gun attack threw them into panic and they quickly gave up. They were men of a Rajput regiment, fine soldiers. I pitied them, to have let the British use them and rob them of their honor. We cut several dozen to pieces as they came running out of the barracks, used strings of firecrackers at their rear to spread confusion.

Under the dripping trees about a hundred had surrendered, squatted on their haunches in the claylike ooze. They were shamed, silent. Some were wounded. The battle for Malaya and Singapore was all but won. Our planes were within striking distance of the "Lion City."

Three British officers now emerged from the barracks, their hands on their heads. I watched as my men prodded them with their bayonets. We made the English squat on their backsides in the mud and the Indians that had been under their command were told to stand up so they towered over them. (Rajputs, one must admit, are a handsome people, and along with the Sikhs and Gurkhas had been the backbone of the Indian army.)

A dispatch rider on a motorcycle came up, sloshing through the mud, dismounted, bowed to me and reported that resistance was crumbling on the trunk road too. My strategy was clear—hit the main bodies of Indian and British troops with aerial bombing and strafing. If the enemy dug in I would send patrols into the jungle to outflank and surround them as the road to Singapore was being cleared.

I spoke some English, not as good as Kenji's but good enough to tell the British prisoners what I thought of them . . . "You English do not even fight. It has taken us exactly three days to overrun Malaya. Your soldiers run, they refuse to die for you . . ." I felt like spitting on them. They were as we had always known, arrogant and cowardly. Quite a combination.

I went on to tell them about Japanese victories in Hawaii and the Indies, and all through it they just stood there, three white men in filthy tunics and shorts, unarmed, humiliated.

I turned then to the Rajput prisoners. "Why do you fight at all for such rulers? You have no reason to fight for cowards who have betrayed you. Look at us. We are Asians, we are your brothers. You must throw the English out and join us. You will quickly see the wisdom of being friends with Japan."

The Indians studied the wet earth, said nothing. No doubt because they felt humiliated and betrayed.

A British captain—a thin man with yellow hair—finally spoke up. "I must protest this treatment of my officers. It is contrary to the rules of war. We are not to be humiliated in this fashion—"

I nodded at a sergeant, who understood his duty. He and two enlisted men grabbed the captain and dragged him toward the barracks.

"Bloody bastards, sodding yellow apes. You'll pay for this—"

The officer was soon out of sight. When a volley of shots sounded seconds later, the other British officers stood mute, not even able to get themselves together to protest. I asked them if they too would like to say anything. They did not. I then built on their shame with the news that their battleships the *Repulse* and the *Prince of Wales* had been sunk in the Gulf of Siam by Japanese torpedo bombers. The British now had no navy left in the Pacific.

I could, of course, have shot them, but that would have been too easy for them. "Since the worst punishment a soldier can have is the shame of defeat and failure to give his life," I told them, "you will be allowed to survive so you may live forever with your disgrace."

I then ordered the Indians to get up, and the prisoners began a long march through mud and rain to a temporary camp. I watched them for a moment, then raised my sword and called out to my troops, "On to Singapore . . ." It was a great day for me, and for Japan.

JULIE TAMBA · DECEMBER 23, 1941

What could I say to my parents? To anybody? It was a few days before Christmas, when we were supposed to be joyful, celebrating the birth of

Our Lord. Instead we sat in my parents' home in Glendale wondering
what in God's name would happen next.

Kenji—no surprise—had changed. He was solemn, withdrawn. I knew
he felt guilt, as though he had somehow tricked me into the marriage
knowing all the while that a disaster beyond our control would strike us.
Of course that wasn't the case, and I didn't feel that way for a minute.
Which wasn't to say that others felt as sure as I did.

My father lit his pipe, let it go out, put it aside. "I said I wouldn't
indulge in I-told-you-so's, Julie, but I'm sorry, I just can't say nothing,
pretend that the situation isn't . . ."

Kenji and I were sitting alongside but not close to each other on the
sofa. In front of my parents he was reluctant even to hold my hand. He
purposely left a "proper" space between us. We were living in my room
then . . . small and barely accommodating two grown people, including
my single bed. At night he would only hold me, afraid to make love
. . . as though he had no right to . . . my *husband.* I was mad clear through
at prejudice, stupidity . . . above all the damned *unfairness* of it. Kenji and
I were husband and wife—*not* Japanese and American. Why couldn't they
just accept *that* . . . ?

My mother spoke up now. "Julie, you are . . . well, impetuous. You
always were like that, doing things on a dare, taking chances—"

"I didn't take any *chances,* mother. Kenji and I are in love, and we're
married. Please everybody remember that."

Kenji looked at her, at my father. "There is nothing on this earth I
would not do for your daughter . . ."

"Then perhaps you would consider a divorce—"

I caught my breath. "*Daddy.* How dare you say that?"

He got up and walked to the window. What was he looking for? A way
to apologize might be in order, I thought. "Have either of you the *faintest*
idea what kind of life you're heading into?"

"Christopher," my mother put in, "says that it's only a matter of time
before . . . aliens are rounded up and put in prisons. What will you do
then?"

"I'll go wherever Kenji goes, like I promised in my vows."

My father's voice rose now. "No, no, you won't. We won't allow it—"

I was fighting back tears. "Daddy, *don't,* don't make it worse than it
is. Kenji isn't responsible, for God's sake. He thinks what Japan has done
is a terrible thing, a mistake—"

"*Mistake?* It was a damnable sneak attack. You heard what the president said . . . A day that will live in infamy!"

"Don't blame Kenji. He had no more to do with it than you or I."

My father drew in his breath, set his cold pipe down and appeared to be bracing himself. "I am not so sure about that—"

"Daddy, I won't listen—"

"You have to. He's a *government* scholar. A *Japanese* government scholar. His expenses and tuition are paid for by a treacherous government. He has been protected and financed at the highest levels of that government. I am sure that by Japanese standards he's a fine fellow. A father who works at the palace. A brother who is a war hero. But his emperor and his government are responsible for the cold-blooded sneak-murder of thousands of Americans. I don't believe for a moment they'll behave any better as this war goes on. The Quaker missionaries in China have provided us with chapter and verse on atrocities committed against civilians. Not a few hundred killed but tens of thousands. Horror stories I can't even find it in myself to repeat . . ."

Kenji finally said something . . . "Much of what you say is true, sir, but we are not all the same—"

"Dammit, I don't trust you . . . those people," my father said, ignoring Kenji's painful attempt to appease him.

"Kenji isn't any of those things," I said in anger, "and you know it, or ought to."

"Mr. Varnum, I respect you, I won't argue with you. This is your home . . ." He got up and turned to me. "I think it would be better if I went to our room while you talk about this."

"*No.* You stay here—"

"Young man," my father said, "have the decency to give my daughter a divorce. Your lives will be full of nothing but misery if you don't—"

"I won't *hear* of it," I said. "Kenji?"

His face set. "Nor will I, sir. We are man and wife."

We went to our room. Up to now he had still been studying, planning to get his graduate degree. I already had decided to quit UCLA and work for Professor Shapiro. The professor called my job "research." Actually it would be routine secretarial work, but I wanted the money. I wanted us to live alone, *not* with my folks. Kenji and I tried to joke, feebly, that we would need little food to survive—lots of rice, a dab of fish, a slice of vegetable . . .

We heard the doorbell ring, a man speaking to my father. A few seconds later my father called upstairs. "Kenji, someone to see you."

The two of us came downstairs. A slender man in a gray suit was standing in the foyer. He smiled an official smile. "I'm Special Agent Watterson, Federal Bureau of Investigation. Are you Mr. Kenji Tamba?"

Kenji said he was. His face was drained.

"Mr. Tamba, you are required to register with the Bureau as an enemy alien—"

"He's no enemy," I cut in. "He's my *husband* and—"

"I appreciate your feelings, Mrs. Tamba, but those are the regulations. Mr. Tamba, could you give me a few minutes and fill out this questionnaire?"

My parents looked stricken. They hadn't bargained for this, but on the other hand it was the sort of thing they'd been afraid of for me. Kenji answered a series of questions, signed some papers and was given a new I.D. card to go with his green card.

"What happens now?" I asked.

"Procedures are being discussed by the government. For the time beir your husband is not to leave the Los Angeles area."

About the same time the FBI was declaring my husband an enemy alien, my old flame Ed Hodges, I would later learn, was going through his own far worse hell on Wake Island.

On midday, December 7, the Japanese struck the tiny atoll. There was no radar warning system on Wake and the Marine gunners and fighter planes had no chance to get into action before the bombing and strafing shocked them into the realization that they were at war. In that first Japanese attack, twelve marines died, some of them Ed's classmates. One survivor said he could see the Japanese pilots' faces. They were smiling, dipping their wings in mock salute. It enraged the defenders and they swore they would take a heavy toll if the enemy returned.

Well, they did return. And the handful of men in the Marine garrison —no more than five hundred against several thousand—sank a transport and damaged several destroyers. This with hardly any air support. The Japanese warships were so badly shot up that they pulled back and postponed their invasion. It was our first victory, and a damn near incredible one.

The next battle, on December 22, was a different story for the Wake garrison. The Japanese admiral, humiliated by the way the Marines had beaten him off, came back with cruisers, aircraft carriers and a large invasion force. The Marines hadn't a single plane left but they fought on. There was hand-to-hand fighting—Ed was part of it . . . his unit, running out of ammunition for the antiaircraft guns, fixed bayonets, charged out of their positions and fought with the Japanese on the beach and wiped out a unit of a hundred Japanese marines.

But the enemy had established a beachhead with over a thousand troops. The marine commander, out of ammunition and water, was forced to surrender, and the Americans, including Ed and his sergeants Guzzo and Goodwin, were taken prisoner. The Japanese renamed Wake "Bird Island." They had lost 800 dead, our side 120, but the sandy sliver of land deep in the Eastern Pacific was lost to them.

At the time it must have seemed as if nothing worse could happen, but it was only the beginning for Ed and his buddies.

Just as that awful day when the so-polite FBI man came calling was only the beginning for the ominous merger of the Tamba and Varnum families . . .

KENJI TAMBA · JANUARY, 1942

It was the New Year, but there was nothing to celebrate. It was decided that it would be foolish for Julie and me to move to a new apartment—not to mention the difficulty of finding anyone who would rent to a Japanese. So we lived in a state of silent disapproval with her parents. I stayed in our room much of the time, forced myself to go to class, sensing of course the rising hostility all around me. I hated it, felt it was unfair, but understood their feelings. The news was a series of disaster reports for the United States and its allies. Our navy, air force and army seemed irresistible, like some force of nature, our men showing the world that we were indeed children of a god, invincible in our victories.

I rationalized. We were forced into the war, I told myself. If there were intransigents around the emperor, outlaws, what about the American State Department and the British Foreign Office . . . they too had their hardliners who would not give Japan breathing space or a fair hearing.

What business was it of theirs . . . you get ridiculous when you start trying to have it both ways . . . if we had made a pact with Hitler's Germany and Mussolini's Italy? Alliances were part of a nation's life. One cannot always choose one's allies in world politics . . . As for China, that was an old story. The West never had any guilt feelings about *its* invasions of China, its domination of her economic life, its ignoring and breaking her centuries-old laws and traditions, insulting the people, not even looking on them as human beings . . .

I argued with Julie that in a real way the oil embargo and the freezing of Japanese assets amounted to acts of war. How could an island nation of seventy-five million just stand by and let itself be deprived of its life blood? How could our industries function without oil?

But even as I tried to make these points, arguing with myself as much as Julie, I couldn't ignore what I knew . . . that there were forces in Japan —the outlaws—who would never compromise, never seek peace, never keep the tiger on a leash.

So I was of two minds. Split. Deep in my heart, though, I felt a tie to my homeland. Such feelings have nothing to do with logic. I could only hope for a speedy victory, an armistice, a coming together of diplomats. Farfetched as it seemed, I tried very hard to believe in it, even though what I now saw of Americans, what I knew of them, told me that *they* would accept nothing less than victory. They would not stop until my people were beaten and punished. I hated the thought, I sensed it was inevitable . . . and wondered where, how Julie and I were going to survive in this horror . . .

YURIKO TAMBA · DECEMBER, 1941

In Shibuya Ward my family accepted the war. The newspapers and radio assured us the war was all but over. Concealed from us was the fact that the attacks on Pearl Harbor and other Pacific areas were made without warning. That would have been a violation of the *samurai* code of honor, the *bushido.* One doesn't spring from hiding and stab an opponent in the back. Except that, I was to learn a year later, that is just what our military did, and no one was told.

There wasn't much cheering. People, including my family, just accepted what the propaganda agencies put out—America was beaten and would soon come begging for peace. There was a reassuring "everything back to normal" attitude on the part of the average person. People were confident about the armed forces, the generals and admirals *and* the emperor. There were public apologies from doubters—"peace faction" spokesmen renouncing their position.

We gathered around the radio one December night and listened as a government announcer read His Majesty's imperial proclamation. What a ringing sound those words had coming from his mouth:

"To assure stability in Eastern Asia, to contribute to world peace, this is the clairvoyant policy formulated by our High Illustrious Imperial Great Ancestor and our High Imperial Grand-Ancestor his successor, a policy that we ourselves have constantly at heart."

The speaker was invoking the ancestors of the Son of Heaven. This was no mere war. It was a crusade, sanctioned by the gods.

My father nodded his bald head. My mother was attentive, silent. Saburo was breathing heavily as the rolling phrases went on:

"To cultivate friendship among nations and enjoy a common prosperity with all peoples, such have always been the guiding principles of our empire in its foreign policy . . ."

Some weeks later my mother took Saburo to Dr. Varnum's clinic. My brother was thin and given to frequent attacks of asthma.

As Dr. Varnum placed the stethoscope to Saburo's bony chest and told him to take a deep breath, he saw my brother glaring at him.

"What's that all about, young man? You look like a *Kabuki* villain."

"I don't want to come here any more."

"What is that?"

"You're the enemy."

My mother clucked her disapproval but said nothing. As I've said, Japanese male children, of any age, learn they can do anything, say anything and will be understood and forgiven.

"Breathe in."

"No."

"All right. Hold your breath. You'll strangle and won't that be too bad?"

Finally my mother was moved to speak. Ever so gently, she chided her son. "Saburo, Dr. Varnum is an old friend."

"No more."

"Tough guy, huh? You're underweight and your lungs aren't strong. You need vitamins."

Saburo, staring at the floor. "I don't have to listen to you."

"Okay. Then how about a swift kick in the rear end?"

Saburo leaped from the table and began buttoning his shirt. "You insulted me."

"And you deserved it. Hisako, I don't like bad manners, even in the family. And you know we've always felt close to your family."

My mother nodded. "Please behave, son. Dr. Varnum is trying to help you. You fall asleep in class. You always have a cold or a sore throat."

"I don't need any medicine. I want to be a soldier like Masao. We're winning, we'll teach the United States to laugh at us—"

"Who's laughing?" the doctor said. "Listen, young fellow. I can't waste my time on a two-bit *samurai.* Grow up and then threaten me. If I didn't like your parents so much I'd toss you out."

When he was gone, my mother bowed deeply and apologized for Saburo's rudeness.

Dr. Varnum brushed it aside, wrote a prescription for her, and muttered under his breath that he would have been happy to prescribe arsenic for my kid brother. Who could blame him?

What made Saburo's outburst peculiar was that in those early days of the war there was actually no organized animosity toward Americans. It was a strange time. Ordinary people just didn't know what to make of what was happening. Our armies, we were told, were winning all over the Pacific; the enemy was beaten and helpless; so what possible threat could a handful of Westerners be?

Some weeks later, the military police, the scary *Kempetei,* called on the Varnum clinic. Some have compared the *Kempetei* to Hitler's Gestapo. One of its former bosses was now our Prime Minister Hideki Tojo.

For a while the police were surprisingly easy on foreigners. Maybe it was because everyone was so optimistic. As the invasions went on and cities fell and the enemy surrendered, Japanese on the homefront lost themselves in bouts of drinking, eating and having a good time. Yes, it's true. The newspapers and the radio encouraged it . . . Japan was unbeatable, why not celebrate?

But when the police called on our friends, the Varnums, and they were not polite about it . . .

As my mother and Saburo were leaving loud voices came from the waiting room. Men were shouting, ordering people around.

Dr. Varnum and his wife walked out of the office while two policemen were yelling at patients to leave. One man wore a blue uniform. The other was in civilian clothing.

"Do you have appointments?" Dr. Varnum asked.

"I am Lieutenant Koga of the military police," the man in street clothes said.

"I can't talk to you during office hours. Please come back in an hour."

The uniformed man approached Adam and Cora. "We will conduct business now. Your residence permits, work papers and identification cards."

"This is ridiculous," Adam said. "My wife and I have lived in Shibuya Ward for more than twenty years. You know that . . ."

He was right . . . the uniformed policeman, a local cop named Tani, as a young boy had been a patient of the Varnums. He knew them both and his own kids had frequently been in the clinic. He turned to Koga, the plainclothes *Kempetei,* and said, "That is true, lieutenant."

Koga ignored him. "*Papers,* both of you."

My mother, the most peaceable of women, lingered on the veranda, watching with Saburo what was going on.

"I am not at war with anyone," Cora said quietly. "I am a citizen of the Swiss republic and we are neutral—"

"It doesn't matter," Koga said. "All foreigners must be registered again."

Dr. Varnum began to rummage through his rolltop desk, but of course couldn't find his papers.

"Adam, I believe they're in the house," Cora said.

"Dammit, I thought they were here." He glared at Koga. "You have a damn nerve coming in here without any advance notice. I suggest you be a good fellow and come back this evening. We'll have the documents, office hours will be over and—"

The plainclothesman grabbed Dr. Varnum and began to tug at him. "You will come with us. You are an agent of the United States. You are a spy."

"What am I spying on? Measles?"

This joke was lost on the policeman. He tugged again. "You will come."

"Get your damn hands off me."

Shaken but ever the peacemaker, Cora suggested that it might be easier if they searched for a few minutes in the house, found the papers and then went wherever it was the lieutenant wanted them to go.

But the police were now too angry. Even Tani looked stupidly irate, and the two officers began to drag Dr. Varnum to the door.

At this point my so-timid mother walked in, shuffling in her sandals and socks, a plain woman in a brown kimono. She bowed until her head almost touched the floor, then spoke to Koga.

"Please, sir?"

"What is it, woman?"

"Dr. Varnum is our friend."

"What about it?"

Saburo lingered on the veranda as a crowd of passersby, peddlers and neighbors, gathered to watch.

"So you are his neighbor," Koga snapped. "What of it?"

My mother said, "But he is not anyone's enemy. Nor is his wife. They are friends."

Koga and Tani, each with a firm arm on Adam's white coat, shoved him toward a waiting car. Apparently Cora's Swiss citizenship spared her. For the moment, at least.

She called out to Adam, "I'll get in touch with the Swiss consulate, they'll send someone, I was afraid of this . . ."

Most courageously, my mother trailed Dr. Varnum, muttering that the *Kempetei* should leave him alone. She stopped at the car, where Koga ordered her away.

My mother told me that as they shoved Dr. Varnum into the vehicle Koga asked Tani, the man in uniform, who she was.

"Mrs. Tamba. Her son is the major, the one they wrote about in the *Asahi Shimbun* the other day, the one who killed two hundred of the enemy in Malaya."

"And *I* cured him of chicken pox, goddammit," Dr. Varnum said. He waved to his wife and his patients and the car drove off.

My mother said his only hope was his association with our brother, a war hero. I hoped she was right. Otherwise . . .

Meanwhile another far more influential man than Dr. Varnum was cultivating *his* associations—and my father was the target.

Kingoro Hata, the member of Parliament, had begun to pay considerable attention to my humble father. Hata was influential and cunning and my father was in some ways a childlike man. Hata of course knew he worked at the palace, often served the emperor's visitors, and so might pick up useful information. Hata was not a man to let any source go untapped. He also was aware that my brother Masao was a rising force in the army.

Not surprising, then, that he invited my father to a *sumo* wrestling match in the downtown stadium in Tokyo, my dad in gray kimono and a loose black coat, Hata in a dark blue business suit, white shirt, dark blue tie. My father proudly described the evening match to my mother and I eavesdropped.

They watched a few bouts. The clash of big-bellied, ham-thighed opponents who fought with grace and delicacy and a remarkable sense of timing didn't interest me at all. Hata's and my father's conversation over pickled cuttlefish and beer was another story.

While Hata was telling my father that size alone didn't win matches, he went on to brag about the way our nation of seventy-five million was beating up on giants like America and Britain by superior courage and intelligence. Victory after victory, he said—Manila, Hong Kong, Singapore, Wake, Guam, the East Indies—proved it. Some members of the General Staff even regretted that an invasion of Hawaii hadn't been tried, he said. After all, the United States fleet was at the bottom of the Pacific, their people were terrified, they would sue for peace when they saw their homeland occupied . . .

My father obviously took it all in. Mr. Hata was a wise man—about war, about *sumo* and life generally . . . My father said he had been troubled by some talk he'd heard from a couple of the generals and wanted Mr. Hata's opinion. He said he'd overheard them saying that His Majesty had been reluctant to go to war, had even pleaded for negotiations and requested that America be told in advance before the attack on Pearl Harbor. Was that right? my father wanted to know. And Mr. Hata had quickly said that His Majesty was right, but that his divine spirit also told him the only way to defeat a cruel enemy was to strike first. One did not give a crocodile advance warning, Mr. Hata said, and then told my father he was glad he could confide in him. I remember much of what followed almost verbatim, because it both shocked and saddened me . . "Are you aware of the work I am engaged in?"

"You are a member of Parliament. And a rich man," my poor father said.

"I am more than that, I arrange things. I also stand at Tojo's service. And you can help. The way you helped me today. Gossip you hear at the palace. What this general said, what this admiral said. Who visits the emperor, news of victories."

"I hear very little, I am a servant," my father told him.

"You are an *intelligent* man, Mr. Tamba." My father's chest puffed out as he repeated this to my mother. "Not only that, your son Masao will be home from time to time. Any information he would like to furnish would also be appreciated."

Apparently it was then my father screwed up his courage and asked the great arranger if he could arrange a mistress for him, and Mr. Hata said *that* was "as easy as stubbing one's toe in a dark room, and much more pleasant." Mr. Hata was full of homey wisdom. My father's interest, it seemed . . . I blush to tell this . . . was one Fumiko, a servant girl in the palace. Mr. Hata said he would talk to her, and put the Plum Blossom House at my father's disposal.

War or no war, life went on as it always had.

JULIE TAMBA · FEBRUARY, 1942

My brother Chris, now a San Francisco-based United Broadcasting correspondent, complete with safari jacket, shoulder patch, combat boots, recorder and typewriter, had little to say to me, by phone or in person after my marriage to Kenji. And after Kenji had to register with the FBI, Chris saw less of us. He just wasn't comfortable around Kenji, and once he told me in private that Kenji's days were "numbered." Naturally I was furious. Before long, Chris had said, Kenji would be sent to a security camp in the desert along with all Japanese, citizens and aliens. The American public hated the "Nips" and there'd be no distinction made between the innocent or guilty.

Guilty of *what?* I'd asked.

"*Anything* will do," Chris had replied. "Maybe just being slant-eyed and having yellow skin . . . Now don't get mad, I don't think that way, I even sort of like Kenji, but I'm trying to give you a shot of reality."

"Don't do me any favors," I said, feeling miserable and angry all at once . . .

Chris got reassigned to Hawaii to report on the attempts of our armed forces to rally themselves after the shock of Pearl Harbor. We would hear his clear crisp voice on UBS, and I have to admit it made me as well as my parents proud. The guy was only twenty-three and already a full-fledged war correspondent. Not bad.

In one letter to my folks he told us about catching up with an old friend on a visit to an army hospital. Chris was interviewing some enlisted men, whom he said he liked better than officers, when a female voice asked him if he had permission to be in the hospital.

He didn't turn around but made some offhand comment about the working press and the Bill of Rights. Typical cocky Chris. But when he turned around he saw it was Carol, in a nurse's uniform, carrying a stack of bed charts. She'd been kidding him, and after some sort of strained if friendly greeting, she told him she was working hard and glad to be in the military, that it was also what her father wanted . . . he was trying to get back on active duty even though he was overage. Carol, he wrote, asked about me. He told her I'd married Kenji, that I was going to be hurt.

Chris said that Carol "looked magnificent. Her dark eyes were bright, her hair cut short, army-style." Carol's mother was Portuguese and she had her mother's dark Latin looks. He was less enthusiastic about Major Herb Kahn, the surgeon Carol was in love with and who was getting a divorce to marry her. Chris had a bad time accepting the fact that Carol had a mind of her own and somehow was managing to live without him.

Poor Chris . . . or rather poor world, I guess I should say, because Chris Varnum was going to take it by storm. I could only hope that along the way he would find some kind of personal happiness. I know he pitied me, but he was wrong. Oh God, how wrong he was . . .

KENJI TAMBA · DECEMBER, 1941

Closeted with Julie in a room on the second floor of Mr. and Mrs. Varnum's home in Glendale, I sometimes felt our marriage was in name only. They were decent to me—but distant, not able to hide their inevitable hostility, or perhaps resentment was the better word. It was as if I had stolen their daughter as sneakily as Japan had bombed Hawaii. There were long silences at the dinner table. Most of the time Julie and I would stay in the upper room, studying, listening to radio reports, wondering what would come next.

Mr. Varnum had all but given up speaking to me. A nod, a word. I said to Julie one night after we had made love that perhaps we should leave, hide away somewhere . . . or perhaps I should do as her parents asked and divorce her.

"No," she said. "Your trouble is you're too *nice* to everyone. Get *mad* now and then, okay? This will work out, I insist on it. I never saw a war big enough to stop two people who are in love. And you do still love me, don't you?"

Her solemn face masked her irrepressible good humor and optimism. Did I still love her? "More than ever," I told her.

"Even if I don't walk two paces behind you? And slide across the floor like a snake? And bow till my head touches the floor?"

"Yes, may the gods forgive me, but yes, even if." I had to smile in spite of myself. Julie could do that to you.

"You know," she said, "I have the feeling I get the princess treatment because I'm white, blonde and all-American. Trade in my saddle shoes for *geta*s and I wonder . . ." Then she mussed my hair and drowned my face in kisses. Oh, yes, how we loved each other. It was what kept me sane . . .

* * *

Then one day I received a letter from my revered teacher Professor Adachi. He had managed to mail it shortly after the outbreak of the war, when censorship mechanisms were not yet fully established. I had not heard from him all these months.

My dear Kenji:
Your old *sensei* has been informed that he is to be removed from Tokyo and taken to a village in Hokkaido, there to spend the war. I am considered "unreliable," a threat to the government.
Although I have not been beaten or tortured and will not be placed in true detention, I will be restricted to some obscure village. The area is currently under three feet of snow, and since I am too old to ski or ice skate I shall have ample time for reflection. Like the Buddha, I will try to lose my identity with the cosmos through enlightenment. Today I felt the need to set down some notions about the war and how our people are accepting it, so please bear with an old man. You were my first student and I will be rewarded if you share these meandering thoughts with me.
First, the newspapers and radio are glorying in our victories. Self-praise and self-congratulation are the order of the day. We are invincible, the press tells us. Generals and admirals are interviewed daily. They talk interminably of the victories at Pearl Harbor, Malaya, Guam, Wake Island, the Dutch Indies, and so on. Nothing can halt the inexorable advance of our armies. The Rising Sun is ruling Asia, and the "Greater New East Asia Co-Prosperity Sphere" is about to be realized. No one talks of the sneak attack on Hawaii, the war without warning, rumors of atrocities that have come to our ears, the apparent barbarism of our armed forces.
A ritual dance is taking place: Tenno Heika's name is invoked for all acts. *Our orders,* reads His Imperial Rescript, *are the orders of your officers and must be obeyed.* Leaders at the top really do not know who is in charge. They fumble, improvise. It is a paradox. Having no true plan, no balanced view, they have staggered blindly into war as the inevitable solution for the nation's problems.
So many of our political and military figures are robots. And those at the top, the effete Konoye, the sycophant Sugiyama, the bumbler Nagano, the half-mad Mastuoka, floundered abut until presented with a *fait accompli,* with the most barbaric of all solutions—war. And this political act arises from that miasmic swamp in which dwell the outlaws, the bandits and the killers. (Note the difference between Nazi Germany and Fascist Japan. In the former, the outlaws, armed bohemians like Hitler, Goering and Goebbels, *became* the government. In Japan, the outlaws were content to infiltrate the bottom, infect the middle ranks and allow

notable men of education, intelligence and charm to make war and condone savagery. It is a peculiarly Japanese phenomenon and it fills me with shame.) It is the rule of the higher by the lower—the lower orders of assassins and blackmailers, like your brother's father-in-law Colonel Sato, calling the tune. But that, I fear, does not absolve the Konoyes and the Sugiyamas who have danced to it.

And what of Tenno Heika? Our emperor is a symbol, a portable shrine, no more. It is impossible for me to think of a single decision that has emanated from his divine self. None. And his senior retainers? Spavined schemers who prefer a doomed war in preference to confronting the class struggle at home. Yes, these *genro* have decreed, better to bomb Pearl Harbor and unite the masses than face a mob of hungry peasants.

As you see, I am in one of my gloomy moods, for I find nothing to console me or lighten my dark and pessimistic view of the future. We will be a long time living down this shame, and casting off the rule of gangsters and weak-kneed functionaries . . . Forgive me if I have imposed on you, but I feel this is the last opportunity I will have to communicate with a rational fellow-countryman. I wish you all the good fortune you deserve, and forgive me.

I did not show the letter to Julie but told her some of what it said. She found it difficult to understand how we so-called good people could have let happen what Professor Adachi described. I wondered too.

That night we heard on the radio that the Philippines had been invaded by a huge Japanese force. Within hours the invaders were racing toward Manila, crushing Filipino resistance, threatening to drive the Americans under MacArthur into the sea.

We went to bed without speaking. It was safer that way.

YURIKO KITANO · JANUARY, 1943

My fiancé Hideo Kitano came back from Pearl Harbor a national hero. He was a deck officer aboard the aircraft carrier *Akagi*, one of the ships whose planes devastated the Americans and gave Japan its first victory.

In his sparkling white uniform, his chest bearing the Pearl Harbor medals, he came home to a hero's welcome, and to his reluctant bride-to-be, Yuriko Tamba. I remember us all listening to the radio as our announcers talked of our "soaring eagles" and "godlike heroes." Hideo said that he was proud to have been part of what War Minister Tojo now called *Dao Toa Senso*—the Great East Asian War.

Our wedding was smaller than Masao's, which was fine with me. The war made it inappropriate anyway to hold large costly weddings, so we were married at a Shinto temple with only the immediate families and a few friends attending, including Kingoro Hata, the great arranger, and his lady friend, a woman named Satomi who owned a geisha house. Mr. Hata did a lot of bragging . . . I hated him . . . about a new textile mill he had bought, and about investing in a munitions plant, opening a chain of teahouses since, as *he* put it, people would need places to relax and enjoy the fruits of victory.

My young brother Saburo was downcast when Mr. Hata told him the war would not last more than six months. The American navy, Hata said, was crippled, Japan would attack Hawaii again, occupy the islands and the United States would beg for peace.

"We will be generous conquerors," Hata told Saburo, my father and Mr. Kitano. "As befits a samurai nation. Our culture and our standards will open their eyes and they will never mock us again."

Saburo still hoped he would get a chance to learn to be a pilot and told Hideo he intended to fly a fighter from the deck of *Akagi* some day.

I wore a white kimono with a chrysanthemum-and-cherry-leaf design in watered silk, and the same wide white hat—the "horn hider"—that Michiko had worn when she married my hero brother Masao, who, of course, wasn't there. He was in Malaya leading his men to victory. My parents made us pray for him in front of the Buddhist altar every night.

It was decided—*not* by me—that Hideo and I could stay at the same inn at Lake Hakone where Masao and Michiko had spent their honeymoon. We would have a room with a view of the waterfall. My mind tends to reject . . . I cannot help it . . . the details of the ceremony—the nine sips of sake, the chanting priest, signing the register, cameras going off, the pop of flashbulbs. It was like a dream . . . a bad dream.

I changed in a hotel room from my bridal gown to a crimson kimono that was one of my favorites. I had wanted to wear a comfortable Western-style suit but my father said it was unpatriotic. We should be as Japanese as possible, Hideo was a war hero and should have a truly Japanese bride. I was to dress the part. And, yes, that was the right word—I felt like an actor playing a part, not revealing feelings behind the mask . . .

My sister-in-law Michiko helping me change, gave me a present—two pair of lacy satiny, pale blue panties. She said they made men very passionate, that Masao had bought them when he had gone to Malaya as a so-called salesman before the war. I must say that they did look nice on my smooth round hips, and came halfway down my thigh. I liked the feel of the satin and lace. I would have preferred a different object for my own passions, but perhaps I thought, I could imagine that Hideo was one of the handsome men in those romantic novels I'd been escaping into . . .

At the rail station my father asked Kingoro Hata to pronounce a few words to the newlyweds and guests, but instead of saying anything about us he announced that Singapore had just fallen and that surely Major Tamba had been crucial in that victory.

"The emperor's heart beats with joy," he went on, "and we must be grateful for that. Are not our lives and our deaths of value only insofar as they serve Tenno Heika? Now the Lion City of the Far East has been brought under the one roof—Japan! *Banzai!*"

Everyone echoed the *banzai,* and Hata promised to send us a gift of money. (He never did.) Kenji had always said he was a blowhard, which sounded exactly right.

As the train sat huffing in the station the guests bowed to us and we bowed back. No one, of course, kissed or hugged, that would have been indecent.

Like a good Japanese wife, I dutifully picked up the three valises we had brought and followed Hideo onto the train. Actually, in his stiff uniform, sword at his side, he probably would have had trouble with the luggage. Once in our compartment, Hideo took the window seat, loosened his collar and told me to put the bags on a metal rack above us. I stepped on the red plush seat and tried to get Hideo's heavy wicker bag settled there, but it kept slipping back on me, Hideo all the while gazing out the window. Finally an old man came into the compartment and helped me get the luggage secured above. When I bowed to thank him, Hideo stopped me, saying the old man was a farmer. The old man, apparently not insulted, sank into a corner seat and fell asleep.

As the train now moved slowly out of Tokyo Central Station, Hideo took off his tunic and gave it to me to put on a hanger, then took off his trousers and gave them to me to hang up.

"Neatly, neatly," he grumbled. "That's my dress uniform."

"Yes, honored husband." I felt like someone watching someone perform. He would never know . . .

The old man stirred . . . "A good wife, a good wife," then promptly fell asleep again, having given his review of my performance. I would have bowed my thanks if I had been allowed.

Hideo, now in his underwear, turned on his side, taking up two seats. Without looking at me he muttered that I should get him a blanket. Since there wasn't one in the compartment I had to get down one of our valises and find him a wool coverlet, which I placed over him. Then once again the old man helped me get the valise up to the rack above us.

Now, at last, my hero husband was in a state of near bliss. Like most Japanese men he yearned for a return to childhood, to being mothered, spoiled, allowed anything he wanted. This was his *amae,* that feeling of total dependence and acceptance and approval that Japanese mothers bestow on their sons, and it lasts all their lives. If Hideo had had a bottle in his mouth he would truly have been in heaven.

As though reading my mind, still with his eyes closed, he broke wind and said, "Get me a beer."

"Do they sell them on the train?"

"Sure. Find the vendor."

The old man smiled. "Two cars back, madam."

I made my way through the hazed cars . . . everyone seemed to be smoking, eating or drinking and the floor was littered with orange peels, papers, empty bottles. Finally I managed to locate a man selling snacks and got a beer for Hideo and a tangerine for myself.

When I returned I discovered that the old farmer had a wife with him. He'd kept her watching their luggage in the baggage car until the conductor convinced him they were safe. Now the two of them grinned at me as they admired Hideo's uniform, the ribbons, the braid. How lucky I was to have a hero of the Great Asian War as a husband!

The hero now opened one eye and held his hand out for the beer, then sat up in his underwear, scratched himself and gulped down the beer. I had seen funny movies of chimpanzees acting like people, and that is what Hideo now reminded me of. No, even in my best fantasies, I could not make him into one of the dashing heroes of my novels—

He was staring at the tangerine. "You buy that?"

"Yes. Is that all right?" I did not add, "My hero."

"Cover me," he ordered. "I want to sleep some more."

He then placed his stockinged feet in my lap, yanked the coverlet around his shoulders and began to snore. At least he controlled his lower digestive system, although he did belch loudly a few times.

Outside the window the gray wintry countryside flew by . . . rice farms, vegetable patches, factories, huddled wooden houses—the outskirts of Tokyo. I was cold, and felt alone, and I did not want this man to be my husband.

I gave the tangerine to the old man. "Please," I said, "I am not hungry . . ."

He bowed his head and took the fruit, then gave it to his wife to peel.

He allowed her to eat two segments, ate the rest himself. Perhaps only a lowly old farmer, but still a very Japanese husband. And would be so unto death.

KENJI TAMBA · FEBRUARY, 1942

I was still free to attend class at UCLA, the campaign to collect Japanese and sequester them in camps having not yet gotten underway, although rumors were constant. I did, though, carry two I.D. cards and tried to be unobtrusive as possible.

My friend Frank Yasuda took to wearing his ROTC uniform around campus, acting very American, assuring me that he would never be interned. How could they? He was a one hundred percent Yankee Doodle soldier. "But you, Tamba, you may be in trouble. Tough break." I tried not to listen to him.

Julie, over my opposition, had quit school. Nothing could dissuade her . . . she was determined to help support us working in the poli sci department and insisted on giving part of her small earnings to her parents as rent money for us. At first they refused but she would not budge. And so *she* was helping to support me. It was terribly hard for me to accept this, and of course her parents resented me even more.

"Don't take it personally, Kenji," Professor Aaron Shapiro said to me in his seminar classroom one March morning.

He meant the way students and others were now shunning not only me but Julie too. We drew hostile stares, whispered comments. But of course it was, to be honest, impossible to separate myself from where I came, from my country, from feelings of attachment that every person has from an early age about his people and nation, no matter how one may disagree with what their government does. I tried to tell Professor Shapiro this, but stopped myself, realizing that it made me sound as though I somehow approved of the high command, which I did not. But what about our ordinary sailors and soldiers and airmen . . . were they not decent young men who obeyed orders blindly and fought with fantastic courage? Moreover, I was not certain that Japan did not have at least something of an historic rationale. If the European powers, and, yes, to a certain extent the United States too, could build empires, consume whole backward undeveloped areas, impose their law with their flag, enjoy extraterratorial privileges, why not an energetic, growing, imaginative industrial power in Asia such as Japan? Why were we forbidden to do what the British and French and Dutch had been doing for a hundred and fifty years? Because we had yellow skin? What followed was as though my thoughts had been spoken rather than kept to myself.

There was a knock at the door, and Julie came in with the FBI agent I had already spoken to, Mr. Watterson. After Watterson identified himself, Professor Shapiro protested that this was a classroom, but I said I had no objection to talking to the agent.

When Professor Shapiro had left, Watterson sat at the table and asked Julie and me to sit down with him. I felt like a condemned man about to be read his sentence. I was right.

"Have you been notified of Executive Order 9066 issued by President Roosevelt?"

I nodded. Julie looked pale. She took my hand.

"I'll review its key points. All Japanese, whether aliens or citizens, are covered by it. It provides for removal, roundup and internment under supervision of the United States Army's Western Defense Command—"

"That's outrageous, it's . . . unconstitutional," Julie broke in, her face now red with anger.

Watterson took documents from his briefcase. "You are mistaken, I have here—"

"Senator Robert Taft thinks so," Julie interrupted again, "and he's a solid conservative Republican from Ohio."

"Senator Taft's only objection is that the law may affect persons other than those for whom it is intended. He has stated he had no argument with the law's intent. Congress has indicated overwhelming approval of Order 9066."

"It's rotten, not fair—"

"I am here to carry out the laws of the country." The FBI man was so polite I could almost believe he was sympathetic. "The law provides for the exclusion of Japanese from our cities, ports, and so forth. They . . . the Japanese . . . are to be placed in relocation areas which will be under military control."

"It sounds like something the fascists do," Julie said.

"Please, Julie, this isn't helping. Mr. Watterson, what will I be required to do? And when?"

"At the moment, you do nothing. But I must ask you some questions."

"Go ahead."

"Have you ever engaged in any acts of espionage against the United States?"

"No."

"Committed any acts that would give aid and comfort to the enemies of the United States?"

"No . . ."

I answered no to everything, affirming as I had already done that I was indeed a Japanese citizen, a government scholar and connected to the Ministry of Education.

"You've been cooperative, Mr. Tamba, I appreciate that. In a week or so you will receive notice to report for relocation. We don't know where it will be. There will be information on it—radio, newspapers, posters. Make sure you comply with all regulations." He got up. "Good day. And thank you."

Julie would not look at him. I got up and bowed. I felt it a crucial moment to show something of what I was. Julie all but yanked me down to my chair.

JULIE TAMBA · MARCH, 1942

My mind was made up. Wherever Kenji went, I'd go too. We hadn't yet been notified, but it didn't matter where they sent him. I'd follow. We were husband and wife, period. *No* argument. Except we had some angry arguments in my home—when Kenji wasn't around. My parents, ordinarily peaceable, were now aroused with the rest of the country. The newspapers were united in demanding the "exclusion" of Japanese. Stories kept appearing about acts of sabotage and espionage. There were stonings of Japanese-American stores, homes and school kids. It was awful. Ninety percent or more of the Japanese in California were citizens. *Citizens of the United States.* They paid taxes, served in the armed forces, farmed the land, worked as gardeners and shopkeepers. No one suggested rounding up Americans of Italian or German descent.

Frank Yasuda, his assignment to military duty held up because of his race, told us a pitiful terrible story. He'd been friendly with a priest in Los Angeles who ran an orphanage where most of the children were of Japa-

nese ancestry. Some were half-Japanese, others one-fourth. When the time
came to relocate these youngsters the priest asked an army colonel which
children should be sent. The colonel's answer was: "I am determined that
if they have one drop of Japanese blood in them, they must go to camp."

Camp. It had a weird sound, being something usually associated with
people packing swimsuits and tennis racquets for a month in the mountains. It was hardly that.

The most noisy adversary I faced at home was brother Chris. He'd come
back from Hawaii for a few days and was waiting for a new assignment.
He had connections with the military, and one evening, while Kenji was
in the library, Chris got on the phone and tried to find out where my
husband would be sent. Particulars weren't to be had, but Chris reported
that the camp would probably be in the desert, "Where they can't do any
harm . . ."

My father was reading the Los Angeles *Times.* My mother was darning
Chris's socks. We looked to be the ideal middle-class California family,
all geared up for the war effort, Quakers or no.

"What kind of *harm?*" I said, biting off the word.

"Whatever Japs do. I have a hunch they're being put into those camps
for their own good. The public has had it with them. Nobody trusts
Nips—"

"Oh, sure, Mr. War Hero Correspondent, how many spies and sabo-
teurs have we caught to date?"

"Go ahead, laugh, Julie, but there's evidence that before Pearl some of
those innocent-looking slants, guys posing as hotel clerks and jewelers,
were taking pictures and sending signals out to Yamamoto's boys."

"Well, then let them find those bad guys. Why jail several hundred
thousand innocent people? Women, children—"

"*Because* we're at war, sis. You seem to forget that."

"If they send Kenji to one of those prisons," I said quietly, "I am going
with him."

At which point my parents froze. Mother dropped the darning egg. My
father set down his newspaper and his pipe and stared at me as if I'd sworn
at him. "Did I hear you right?"

"That's right, you heard me right. I'm going with Kenji. I do know
there's a war on, but he's my *husband.* He needs me, I need him. And God
knows he's no spy or war criminal—"

"What do you think those places are, Julie? YMCA camp? The Girl
Scouts? Let's go, kids, first hour canoeing and rowing, second hour crafts?
Face it. You'll be behind *barbed wire,* looking down machine-gun barrels.
I mean it."

"I don't care."

My mother's voice had an actual tremble in it. "Julie, listen to your brother, please—"

"And to me," my father said. *"You will not leave."*

"Daddy, don't, please . . ."

"Can't believe it," Chris said. "I'm back for a happy three days with the family and I spend it trying to convince my sister not to go to jail. *Listen* to me, kid. Those places are going to be like death. Hot. Windy. Barracks, communal toilets, gun towers."

"Oh, Lord," my mother said, "you can't go . . . Walter, *talk* to her."

My father tamped his pipe. His silence always was worse than a spoken reprimand.

Chris stepped into the breach. "Why did you have to *marry* him?"

"I *love* him. That a crime?"

"No, but it was stupid, almost perverse . . . you had the whole male student body panting after you. Football heroes, Phi Betas, future Nobel prize winners, even Harry Onderman, the guy who ran the student laundry agency. And you, *you* pick the man whose brother probably dropped a few bombs on Pearl Harbor—"

"I told you, I loved him, I still do."

Christ was shouting now. "Then *stop* loving him. He's no good for you, he'll wreck your life—"

I got up from my chair, walked over to my brother and slapped him. "Be quiet. Don't you *ever* dare say that to me again."

My mother started to get out of her rocker, fell back. "Walter . . ."

My father's tone was low, and all the more frightening. "Julie, listen to me. Chris, you stay out of this."

"A pleasure."

"Julie, I forbid you to follow your husband into a prison."

"Daddy, you can't stop me."

He inhaled, rubbed his hand around his pipe and got up. "Then you and he must leave this house. Now. When he gets back from the university the two of you can pack and go. We've tried to explain the burden you were putting on yourself. Now you insist on ruining your life by going over to an enemy people—"

"Walter, that's enough . . . Julie will listen to you. She's just overwrought. I'm sure Kenji will understand if she stays here . . ."

And that, of course, was my Achilles' heel. Kenji would indeed *understand*, he'd even say it would be fine with him if he went off to camp alone. He'd rather have me safe at home and so on. I spoke for him . . . "No, Kenji and I agree, we're man and wife, we stay together."

"Then you will leave together. I don't want him in this house. He knew what kind of dreadful situation you were headed for. He went along. I can't ignore that . . ."

At this point Chris, who realized things were getting out of hand, even though he'd helped stir them up, stepped in. "Everybody settle down. Maybe I can arrange something. I don't know . . . a delay, a special deal for Kenji. And who knows, maybe relocation will be revoked."

"I doubt it," my father said, "and I am not certain it isn't the proper thing for the army to do."

"Okay," I said, "I guess that's it. Daddy, mother, I love you, I always will. But I'm going with Kenji. And if you want us out of the house right now, we'll go."

My father left the room then. He was never too good at handling his emotions. He always had this reserve. I made it hard for him to express his feelings. And once I cooled off some, I realized I wasn't angry with him. It was more like I felt sorry for him . . .

"Think it over, sis," Chris finally said.

My mother was crying.

"I'll be *fine*. They can't keep so many people locked up forever. Kenji and I are young, we'll manage . . ."

MASAO TAMBA · FEBRUARY, 1942

Although General Percival, the British commander at Singapore, boasted that his troops would now become part of "an epic in imperial history," he did not understand Japan's mission and the epic that *we* intended to write.

As I led my men south to Singapore I reread the words of one of my instructors, General Araki:

> The Imperial Army's spirit lies in exalting the Imperial Way and
> spreading the National Virtue. Every single bullet must be charged
> with the Imperial Way, and the end of every bayonet must have
> the National Virtue burnt into it. If there are any who oppose the
> Imperial Way or the National Virtue, we shall give them an
> injection with this bullet and this bayonet!

And so we did. Our enemies called us slaughterers, accused us of atrocities. But they would not understand that their opposition to the Imperial Way took away their right to protest . . .

I looked at my soaked, mud-splashed men as they pedaled their bicycles down the road, courageous, cheerful, and was proud of them but saw again the wisdom of our mission, the Imperial Way, as an inspiring force for each soldier.

One morning, before continuing the advance, our bellies full of rice and warm *miso*, I told my officers what I had long believed.

"We must view this war as a struggle between Asian brothers. Yes, it is so, the soldiers of Asia are really our brothers. They have been misled by the white man, our true and natural enemy. We must make the Malayans and Chinese and Indians regard us as true brothers, which we are. And so we fight them as unruly misled members of a family. In our family the good older brother, Japan, is obliged to chastise errant but not evil younger brothers. In time they will see the light, understand that what we do is for their own good, in *their* best interests. It is the age-old problem of any family, the father teaching the children . . ." The men seemed pleased by this simple but effective way of seeing our role, and accepting what we were faced to do. . . .

It pleased me that the British-led forces outnumbered us three to one. They had 85,000 men to defend Singapore, but no air support. General Yamashita's heavy artillery, guns from my own battalion included, pounded the approaches to the city from across the straits. I loved the loud sound of the crump of shells falling on Singapore. My blood pumped faster. It was better than in China. In China we had mostly fought corrupt bandits. Here it was the haughty and superior British who were feeling our fire.

I stood at the edge of the wrecked causeway and saw spires of choking black smoke rising from fuel tanks. Moments later I was in a lead boat as we traversed the straits for our last battle. Along the road behind us we had left windrows of the dead—British, Australians, Indians, Gurkhas.

Once ashore I was ordered to seize a British hospital on the outskirts of the city, to expel its personnel and use it as a battalion headquarters. Our planes had already strafed it. As my staff car raced down the road to the hospital I saw huddled groups of enemy dead . . . Australians, red-faced, long-jawed men. They had surrendered, my adjutant said, to a unit under my colleague Colonel Tsuji, the man who had spoken openly of his hearty contempt for the enemy.

"Resisters?" I asked my adjutant.

"No, sir. Colonel Tsuji ordered them bound in groups of three and shot in the back of the head. Ignoble deaths for ignoble men," he said. "They forfeited their rights to be treated under the rules of war."

More corpses littered the roadside. They, too, had been bound and shot. The smell was intense. "A defeated soldier should welcome death," I said. Our planes zoomed overhead, eventually to bomb Singapore. "Yes, if a soldier dies in battle, all glory to him. If he is shot after surrender it removes his guilt, and the shame of his defeat . . ."

Our engineers had cut Singapore's water supply, the bombing was incessant, soon the inhabitants would give up on account of thirst, starvation and disease . . . We saw Indian troops hanging from trees like long vegetables—small men, Gurkhas. My adjutant said he had heard that they fought fiercely and had been made an example of so as to remove notions of resistance from other Indian units. A nasty but necessary lesson.

"We must take the city," I said, feeling a bit weary. I heard small-arms fire crackling ahead, bursts from light machine guns.

"We will, sir."

"Well, we've run short of ammunition," I told him. "Our advance has been so swift that supply can't keep up with us. That damned city will surrender today, I swear it."

We pulled our car into the hospital grounds, up to a wide two-story building of pale plaster covered with a rusting tin roof. The Union Jack hung limply from a flagpole. Around the front yard—a rose garden, typically English—lay the bodies of Sikh soldiers, their turbans blood-spattered, their beards pointed inanely at the sky. Misguided Asians! To die for what? An English king?

My men dismounted from their bicycles and formed a perimeter around the hospital. Machine-gun teams set up tripods and belts and took cover. But there was no one to fight . . . A British captain, a doctor, in a dirty uniform, a thin man with ginger hair and a clipped mustache, emerged from the shattered front doors of the hospital carrying a broomstick with a pillow slip fixed to the end of it. A surrender flag.

He saluted me. I returned his salute and stood up in my car so I towered over him.

"There are only medical personnel and patients inside," he said. "I presume you understand English?"

His arrogant tone, even in defeat, irritated me but I controlled myself, said nothing. I could see the sweat coating his pasty face. His greenish eyes surveyed the rifles aimed at him, the machine-gun teams. Behind us more units were coming down the road.

"Your name?"

"Anderton, James, Royal Medical Corps."

"You will mount your bicycle, captain, and ride into Singapore with an escort of my men. Advise your commander that unless he surrenders at once to General Yamashita, all personnel and all patients will be executed." (These were orders from Colonel Tsuji, who had received them from General Yamashita.)

"I must protest, major. That is a violation of the rules of war. You appear to me to be an educated man. You cannot hold defenseless people, including women and wounded men, as hostages."

"You will do as I say or the executions will begin at once."

The officer got on his bike. Three of my noncoms mounted bicycles and rode with him. They would see him through our lines, then send him off to his commander, General Percival.

As soon as the party was out of sight I turned to my adjutant. "The city will of course surrender but we must make a strong impression on the British. We must educate them. You will take Company B into the hospital. All patients and medical personnel will be executed. They have surrendered. We spare them living with the shame of their actions."

"The women, sir?"

"Do whatever you wish with them." My men were entitled to a warrior's reward.

I saw faces at the cracked windows—a gray-haired nurse, a bearded man with a bandaged head, a blond man with an eyepatch. They meant nothing to me. *We* were engaged in a moral crusade. Punishment of the enemy was the most moral of acts. And so the screams of the dying patients and the doctors and orderlies, the shots that echoed from inside would never haunt me. Our mortal enemies, white men and women, were learning that their time was over. Asia for Asians was no longer a mere slogan. It was the rallying cry of the noblest war in history . . .

KENJI TAMBA · FEBRUARY, 1942

There was a story going around, some said from a BBC broadcast, that the Portable Shrine, as Professor Adachi had termed His Majesty, had heard about certain terrible acts committed by our soldiers in Singapore,

Hong Kong and elsewhere. Some unidentified peace-faction person at court may have told him. It was further believed that he broached these matters to Prime Minister Hideki Tojo, the former police chief.

"His Majesty must set his heart and mind at ease," Tojo was reported to have said. "These reports of so-called atrocities are lies. They are concocted by the enemy to distract the world from the crushing defeats suffered by the Americans and the British."

The prime minister was said to have gone on to say that at Singapore the British had surrendered nearly 200,000 men of many nationalities— a disgrace that could never be lived down. And so the wicked lies about Japanese atrocities.

It eventually was revealed that the Son of Heaven had indeed gotten wind of a BBC broadcast in which British Foreign Minister Eden had detailed atrocities. Tojo said that Eden had lied. No one had been used for bayonet practice. No one had been raped. The only deaths were those of men brought down in battle in a fair fight. What did these Caucasian liars know about *samurai* tradition? How dare they insinuate that Japanese soldiers would kill unarmed men and women? It was vile slander.

"Consider the carp, Your Highness," Tojo was reported to have said. "The noblest of fish. He fights with admirable courage when hooked, battles the angler to the very end. Yet when he is placed on the housewife's cutting board he awaits the stroke of the knife without protest or motion. Our enemies should take a lesson from the carp. When they are beaten, they whine like old women. They are not even worthy of a good stroke from a Japanese sword. Our men would dishonor themselves to waste steel on those who surrender and then weep."

Listening to all this, I couldn't help but bring the big issues and talk down to a personal level. After all, my brother Masao was one of those soldiers . . . could it be that he was implicated in killing innocent people? I tried to force the thought from my mind. Didn't I have enough trouble with the prospect of an internment camp facing my wife and myself . . . ?

YURIKO KITANO · MARCH, 1942

Although it was considered correct for a bride to move into her husband's home and allow his mother to enslave her, I refused.

Our house had plenty of room. Besides, Hideo's parents' home w much better than a large shack on the edge of Toshima Ward. The main room was only a six-*tatami* one. The extra room they wanted to give to us was the size of a chicken coop. I made polite excuses, and we apologized to Mr. and Mrs. Kitano in a roundabout way. I watched my father and Mr. Kitano, a postman, discuss over endless cups of tea the matter of where we would live. My father kept insisting that "Yuriko wants very much to live with you." Mr. Kitano kept saying he "wouldn't think of disturbing Yuriko's relationship with her parents." Hideo, true to form, didn't care one way or the other.

Both fathers, of course, were lying. Both knew that the other was lying. The discussion, though, was carried on in such a polite way that it seemed they were telling the truth. Actually Mrs. Kitano was drooling to get her claws on me, give me orders, make me scrub the floor and rake the garden. Her husband didn't dare say so. And my father knew I didn't want to leave our comfortable house in Shibuya Ward and be my mother-in-law's serf, but he had to appear to think otherwise.

It was eventually agreed that I would wait for Hideo's return from sea duty on the *Akagi,* and then he and I would find a small place, maybe an apartment near the Kitano house. . . .

This spring everyone seemed to be having a wonderful time in Tokyo. In spite of so many men being overseas, the theaters and movies and dance halls and restaurants were never more packed. People seemed to be smiling and laughing all the time. Why not? The newsreels, newspapers and magazines were full of stories of our invincible army and navy. Every day came word of new victories.

At the same time, though, we on the home front were warned that there were spies in our midst, that *any* foreigner was suspect. Lies were being spread about our soldiers, about the way they treated conquered people, and it was the spies who circulated these lies, among other things. To counteract this we were shown newsreels of Japanese troops feeding smiling Filipino children, Japanese sailors handing out medical supplies to savages in grass skirts. We were a nation of generous, compassionate people. We were a great nation. It got to us all, including me . . . this sense or pride in ourselves and our nation. But so far as I was concerned, there were limits to patriotism—in my case going to work in a factory, which my parents thought I should do as a patriotic gesture.

"I am not a factory worker," I said. "I'll only hold back the war effort—"

"It doesn't matter," my father said. "The word has gone out to the palace servants. Either their children must serve in the armed forces or work in a factory."

"I'll have to wear those awful *mompei* bloomers. I'll look like a chicken." Yes, I confess it, along with all my wonderful qualities, I am also, along with my sharp tongue, a vain woman.

"Mr. Hata is arranging for you to take a job at the New Dawn munitions factory. It isn't dangerous. They make shell casings. Mr. Hata is a part-owner, he says it's easy work."

In revenge I overcooked the rice, and of course Saburo teased me wickedly, but I could see there was no choice. I wasn't much good for anything except being a wife and a mother, and my husband, thankfully, was at sea most of the time. I had no useful skills, could not type or take shorthand, and had been only a fair student in school, being bored too much of the time to concentrate. My father always said girls didn't need any education. Too much learning spoiled them for kitchen work and dusting.

As part of the preparation for my new job I had to take a physical examination to see if I was sufficiently fit to sort out metal shells or something equally demanding.

So I went to the Doctors Varnum office, noting that across the street from their stucco building stood Saburo and some of his school pals shouting out, "*Supai, supai, supai . . .*"

"Are you crazy?" I asked my brother. "The Varnums aren't spies."

"All foreigners are spies," Saburo said, and rejoined the ridiculous chanting, "*Supai, supai, supai.*"

I was in the waiting room, feeling glum, pitying myself. No romance, no sex, no home of my own, no husband—at least not one I could like —and now I was to be a factory worker and carry a *bento* lunchbox.

There were two gossipy old women in the waiting room and a crippled man who ran a cigarette-and-news kiosk down the street. He asked me through broken yellow teeth about my family, but I just was in no mood to talk.

Suddenly the door banged open and in charged a man in a trenchcoat and a black felt hat with two uniformed policemen. The man in the trenchcoat began calling for the doctor.

Dr. Varnum, in white coat, a stethoscope around his neck, came out. "Ah, Lieutenant Koga, you're early."

"Please get out of our way," Koga said.

The two old women got to their feet, bowed to the police, and hurried out of the waiting room. On the other hand, the old man from the kiosk grinned, apparently enjoying the invasion.

"I have office hours now," Dr. Varnum said. "Please sit down and wait until I'm finished."

Cora Varnum appeared then, a yowling infant in her arms. "Adam, don't . . . Can we help you?"

Koga leveled a finger at them. "You are spies—"

Dr. Varnum's protests were interrupted by a rock sailing through the window that nearly hit him in the face. I silently died of shame, knowing that Saburo or one of his pals had thrown it.

Koga ignored the assault, waggled a finger at the Varnums. "You will report to my office every morning at eight and furnish a full account of your activities of the previous day. Every appointment, every person to whom you speak, all telephone calls. Understood?"

"I am no enemy of Japan. I've lived here more than twenty years—"

"You are *not* exempted. All foreigners are under suspicion. Officer Tani is now assigned to this hospital, which we have reason to believe is a center for espionage. He will check on your visitors and listen in on phone conversations."

On the way out Lieutenant Koga stared at me, then said, "I am surprised that a daughter of Japan would come to this place of spies."

I bowed deeply to him. At least I knew how to handle pompous asses. You simply out-pomp them, Kenji used to say. "Dr. Varnum and his wife are friends of my family."

"And your family?"

"My father is Mr. Goro Tamba, a member of the Imperial Palace household staff."

Koga looked like he would choke as he sucked in air through his fat mouth.

"And, sir, my brother is Major Masao Tamba, a war hero. We are all long-time patients at this clinic."

Koga, sucking more air, backed away and bowed to me. Having run out of threats, he departed the premises.

Adam Varnum bowed to me, smiling. "Nicely done, Yuriko. And thank you. Now if you'll get your bratty brother and drag him in by the ears, I'll give the little galoot a lecture I think he badly needs."

I had no idea what *galoot* meant, but I agreed Saburo could use some discipline. Unfortunately, he absorbed little of what he was told and refused to apologize to the *gaijin*. We Tambas were a headstrong clan, no question about *that*.

JULIE TAMBA · MARCH, 1942

Frank Yasuda was pointing to a chubby G.I. with a Western Defense Command shoulder patch, a wrinkled blouse and a pie-plate helmet at the front of the bus. A rifle was slung over his shoulder.

"What about him?" Kenji asked.

"He's carrying a 1917 Enfield rifle. Useless. I bet he doesn't even have ammo. It shows how little they think of us. Big threats, all right," he said bitterly.

Frank Yasuda, a lieutenant in the United States Army, Kenji and I were on a packed dust-filled bus barreling along an asphalt highway to a detention camp in Manzanar, California. We were, as predicted, being "relocated."

The G.I. guard with his old weapon, the driver and I were the only Caucasians on the bus. Seats were packed with couples, kids and lots of older people. They were mostly farmers and shopkeepers. Yasuda, in his smart brown tunic and pink trousers, Sam Browne belt and peaked cap, was the smartest-looking person on board. Kenji wore a rumpled tan suit and a topcoat. It would be chilly in the desert, my grieving mother had said, and had knitted in record time a floppy woollen gray sweater. You can imagine the scene when I left, but my parents realized I was adamant, would never let Kenji go into a camp without me.

It especially bothered me that at the rear of the bus there was a Japanese man ill with some wasting disease, a man with a waxen face who was being carried aboard on a stretcher, for God's sake. *No exceptions,* the army had said, and there would be none. His wife sat by his side, patting his forehead with a wet cloth and talking to him in Japanese.

Frank Yasuda, bitter, would not be shut up. "So I say to this FBI guy," Frank was saying loud enough for the whole bus to hear, "*look* at me, Jack. I'm an American. An *officer.* And he says, sorry, you go, you're a Jap. I tell him ninety-five percent of these people are red-blooded American citizens, right? What'd they ever do against the U.S.A.? I don't see any German-Americans or Italian-Americans going into camps. He says, it's government policy, from the president down, plus the Congress, the army, the courts. Everybody goes." There were a lot of heads nodding.

Across the aisle from us a baby started to bawl. The mother, a reed-thin woman in a black coat, gave it a bottle. Other kids started to cry . . . It was really nerve-wracking for someone not used to being around little children.

"What do you hear about the camps?" I asked Frank.

"Sort of a cross between Alcatraz and Burbank. Mess halls, com-

mon toilets, wash houses. They say we'll have to fix the place up ourselves." . . .

The roundup of Japanese-Americans had gone pretty much without a
hitch, with some awful exceptions . . . like a man in Pismo Beach named
Murata, a hero of World War I, who had put a bullet through his head
rather than give in to "exclusion."

"Try to think of it as a sort of forced vacation," a young woman said
to us. She was pretty and had been a beautician in Pasadena, she told us.
"My brother says it isn't that bad . . ."

The bus rolled on. Dust began to choke us. The children continued to
howl, had to be changed on bus seats. Pretty soon the smell of urine
permeated the whole bus.

Kenji stayed calm, holding my hand, smiling at me. I'd forbidden him
to say one damn word about my decision to go with him into internment.
He kissed my neck. A good trade-off, I thought.

"Ah, old neck lover," I said. I thought of the passionate love we'd made
in Coronado and how now we'd be in a barracks with other couples all
around us. For how long, I wondered, hoping my feelings didn't show.

Kenji was saying, trying to be light, "I think I should have addressed
myself more rigorously to the teachings of Buddha."

"Can't see you with a shaved head, saffron robe and a begging bowl."

"Buddhists teach self-cultivation and inner discipline. We will need
it . . ."

"Nuts to that, my love. I'm for concentrating on getting us a warm and
private place to sleep."

I leaned against his shoulder and closed my eyes. I didn't want to think
or see. Not until I had to . . .

Later I would learn that at just about the time Kenji and I were being
delivered to Manzanar camp in the desert, Ed Hodges and his marine
buddies from Wake Island were being transported in the belly of a Japanese freighter to the mainland of Japan.

Ironically, for all their talk about respecting courage in the enemy, it
seemed that it was because the Wake garrison had resisted so strongly,
taking a heavy toll of Japanese, sinking ships and the resisting attacking
forces, that the survivors were singled out for especially brutal treatment.
Starvation, beatings, summary execution. The Death March of Bataan
was at least partly because Japanese officers were so enraged by the way
American G.I.'s stood up to them.

I don't know the name of the ship that brought Ed, Guzzo, Goodwin and other prisoners from Wake to Yokohama harbor, but it was a hell ship, all right—full of stench, filth, disease and death, was the way the survivors described it.

Almost *thirty percent* of British, Australian, American, Canadian and New Zealand troops captured by Japan died in Japanese camps. The death rate in Nazi camps was four percent.

Ed's buddies would tell about a day when three men died, clutching at their throats in the foul air of the hold. They were Ralph Guzzo and Verne Goodwin, Ed's sergeants, and they told how they kept needling each other to keep their sanity . . .

"We been fed today, Ralph?" Goodwin asked.

"You dumb ridge-runner. How come you don't remember? We had your favorite meal. Hog belly and grits."

"You jokin', Ralph."

"No, I ain't. I had a lasagna with lots of ricotta, the way my old lady makes it. I wiped up the sauce with Italian bread."

A young Marine from second platoon said he had just drunk his own urine.

"How was it?" Guzzo asked.

"You ain't missed a lot, sarge."

Ed and the other officers started what they called the daily "hootenanny"—banging mess tins and cups against the sides of the ship, chanting for water.

A hatch opened. The face of a guard they would come to know too well, Sergeant Ozawa, nicknamed "Froggy," appeared.

"Son-of-a-bitch assholes." Froggy was a real linguist. He'd spent three years in Hawaii, gone to high school there and worked on the pineapple plantations.

"We have men dead from thirst, sergeant," Ed called.

"You like water? All right, you *get* water." And Froggy sloshed them from a bucket, water falling in a long silvery arc. Men tried to lick it from their bodies, from each other, from the excrement-fouled floor.

That night three more men died, raving, feverish, to be reduced to rotting corpses.

As Ed was making his horrible passage to Japan, Kenji and I were trying to settle in at the Manzanar camp in the California desert.

It was, I tell you, a dismal place. The sun beat down on a flat scrub desert. The March wind kicked up dust. Our shoes soon filled with gritty stuff. Rectangular tar-paper barracks raised several feet above ground on cinder blocks, a sort of town square, a long communal bath house, a large mess hall. Around all of it was a barbed-wire fence, and at regular intervals there were watchtowers with G.I.'s manning machine guns.

It was *crazy*. At the moment Kenji, Yasuda and I got off the bus, towers were still being nailed together. I wondered if anyone would think about escaping. Where would one go in that expanse of dead land?

It was a barren expanse of nothing, mountains in the distance, a great blue sky, and a clutch of huts with loose black paper flapping in the wind, broken steps, no semblance of streets or sidewalks. The guards, we noted, were kept outside the fence, and most of them seemed young and, understandably, ill at ease. They were what the army called "limited service," men with physical shortcomings that kept them out of active duty. They really weren't a bad bunch. They talked to us, joked and tried to be friendly. Some of the men said the guards were kept outside the fence to keep them from trying to seduce Japanese women. I didn't want to believe that . . .

Frank Yasuda was assigned to a barracks for single men, and we watched him coming toward us carrying his duffel bag on one shoulder, a cardboard suitcase in the other. Two young Japanese men, sawing wood in front of the building, greeted him. We stopped and listened.

"Army, huh?" one asked.

"U.S.A., buddy. They won't keep me in here long." Frank grinned and sat on his duffel bag.

One of the young men, a Nisei like Frank, told Frank he ought to join the Japanese-American Citizens' League, a pro-American organization determined to prove its patriotism, and to work on U.S. government agencies to wipe out detention camps.

The other young man was a Kibei, an American-born Japanese who had had most of his education in Japan. Talk about split personalities. The Kibei had come back to the United States filled with pro-Japanese feeling, and tended to look down on other Nisei. Many of them seemed to feel that they had seen the light during their schooling in Japan. In the camp they formed tough cadres and they became a thorn in the side of the JACL.

Actually, I sort of felt sorry for them, and I think I understood their anger. They'd soaked up Japanese traditions and culture and now they were back in America. Many Nisei, Americanized like Frank Yasuda, looked down on them. So they in turn considered the Nisei as stooges of the Americans with no sense of pride. Naturally the internment policies seemed to the Kibei to justify their hostile feelings. It was a real mess.

The Kibei guy, who was sawing wood, was saying to Frank, "Burn that uniform, Yasuda. It won't do you any good."

"Okay, what will?"

"Break the hell out."

"Where? It's all desert out there."

Suddenly the Nisei was staring at Kenji and me, and put down his saw.

"What team are *you* on?"

"I'm Japanese," Kenji said. He bowed. "Kenji Tamba, Ministry of Education. This is my wife, Julie Tamba."

Jaws visibly dropped. "We're newlyweds," I said. "We thought this was a nice place to spend our honeymoon." Forced humor, not exactly brilliant.

"Good luck," the Nisei said. His name was Anamai. The Kibei boy— he was rugged and stocky—was named Ito.

"Don't get too upset with guys like Ito," Anami said. "You know how Kibei are. Talk tough, do nothing. We'd ask Tamba to join the JACL but he isn't even a citizen."

Ito said, "Stick with us, Tamba, we'll be running this camp in a week."

We left Frank Yasuda at the bachelors' barracks and walked to a long dark barracks building where some children were playing hopscotch. They stared at me and giggled.

The barracks chief, a middle-aged Issei—Japanese-born but an American citizen—named Dr. Makioka told us to take one of the corner rooms. We would learn that Makioka, a stubby man with a shaved head and a perpetual smile, wasn't an M.D. but a physiotherapist, a massage and manipulation man. He may have been a chiropractor, I'm not sure. Once he gave me a soiled card that said "Naturopath"—whatever *that* was.

"There's another American lady in this barracks," Dr. Makioka said. "From San Joaquin Valley. Mrs. Harada. Good luck, Mrs. Tamba. Your room is at the end, north side."

It was about fourteen feet square with no door, but an opening cut into the unfinished plasterboard, from which hung a gray sheet. It led to the central corridor that ran the length of the barracks. There were no sinks or toilets or showers in the buildings. These were a hundred feet away in the "ablution center." Fancy talk for *un*fancy facilities.

Kenji and I dropped our valises and stared at the cell. There is something especially depressing about raw plasterboard, complete with nailheads and streaks. There was a tiny window at the rear. The panels did not reach the ceiling so we looked up at splintery wooden crossbeams. There was a single naked bulb hanging from the beam. On the floor were two folded canvas cots and two straw-filled sacks passing for mattresses. There were also four olive-drab G.I. blankets, two stained pillows, no sheets or shelves or closets.

"My fault—"

"Silence. If you love me, you'll stop that stuff. Got it, husband?"

"Got it."

I was playing Jean Arthur. Maybe Kenji bought it, maybe he didn't. Never mind . . . stop thinking and start unpacking, I told myself. Luckily my mother had insisted on giving us sheets and pillowcases—snowy white and spotless. They would really help. Kenji was already scrounging crates for temporary shelves, and we rigged a cardboard shade for a bulb and even managed to plug in our faithful old Philco radio. Kenji also went out to see about getting tools and lumber to put in permanent shelves and build a divider more effective than the gray sheet.

I was stacking our clothing and setting up photos of my folks when an American woman knocked at the partition. "I'm Mrs. Harada," she said. "We seem to be in the same boat."

I introduced myself, and she asked what my husband did.

"He's a student at UCLA. I was too."

"Mr. Harada is—was—a farmer." She was in her forties, suntanned with uncombed gray hair. She was once a pretty woman, I could see that. "They took our farm."

"Who did?"

"Okies. Local farmers. Mr. Harada bought this rocky land, nobody wanted it sixteen years ago. He worked twenty hours a day clearing stones and scrub, he put in irrigation lines, he planted orange trees. All by himself. We never had children. The farm was our child. I think the others were jealous."

"Oh?"

"Yes . . . how could that *Jap* succeed and make money and drive a Buick when *they* barely made a living? It never dawned on them they didn't work as hard, or maybe weren't as smart. After Pearl Harbor I knew it was all over."

"What happened?"

"They burned down our barn. Now this. We'd just packed our bags and started to leave when some of the neighbors came over, demanded the keys to Mr. Harada's car, his farm machinery, everything. What could he do? We were leaving in a few hours. Now they've moved into our house. We'll probably never get it back . . . all my furniture, my nice things . . ."

What could I say to her . . . ? "My husband thinks this is temporary—"

"What's the difference if you lose everything? What can we go back to?"

"There are laws—"

"Doesn't matter. You whites . . . I mean, most whites . . . don't want

us and the Japanese can't stand us. We're intruders. Whites hate any
Japanese who marries an American woman even more. I wish I had better
things to tell you. Maybe neither of us should have come here. I see from
these pictures you have a family. I have nobody I could have stayed with
. . ." Mrs. Harada shuffled out then, and I had the feeling she'd probably
been drinking. Speech slurred, movements slow. I was glad to see her go.

I said nothing about her to Kenji when he came back with a hammer,
some nails, old boards and two paper cups of coffee he'd gotten from the
mess hall that he said was run by a guy who'd owned a luncheonette on
Westwood Boulevard and remembered Kenji.

Kenji then rummaged in his duffel bag and came out with a buff-and-
blue UCLA banner that he tacked on the wall. I laughed and clapped in
appreciation.

"Couple of old Bruins," I said, "they just can't get us down. Not for
long anyway . . ." He kissed me, and I kissed him back. To hell with
privacy.

Later we switched on the radio to grim reports from the Philippines—
more surrenders, more defeats. All along the Pacific front the Japanese
were now in control. They seemed unstoppable, a whirlwind. A double
disaster was being reported . . . the Dutch navy had been destroyed in the
Java Sea and the British had evacuated Rangoon.

"I can't listen any more," I said, and switched stations until I got the
scratchy sound of a record playing somewhere in Los Angeles. It was
Glenn Miller's "Moonlight Serenade," just about my favorite.

Suddenly Kenji had me in his arms, dancing me around the littered
floor in the midst of our suitcases and packing crates and the cots, and
we kissed each other again, a public spectacle and who cared . . .

Kenji was whispering in my ear, "How can I ever make this up to you?"

"You'll do your best, starting tonight. Now please shut up and let's try
to make this place a little more livable." Dr. Makioka had found us a
rickety stool and promised us better mattresses in a few days. Mr. Harada,
the farmer whose land had been stolen, came by, introduced himself,
bowed, and was amazed to hear that Kenji was a *real* Japanese. *And* a
government official. He welcomed us with a rare present—some homemade orange marmalade from his farm.

At dinner I realized how valuable his gift would be as long as it lasted.
We lined up like prisoners outside the mess hall and were served on metal
trays. Rubbery half-cooked frankfurters, canned beans, cottony white
bread, a stewed peach floating in syrup, and cocoa with powdered milk.

Japanese especially love fruit and vegetables and rice, and there were few if any of those. There was a shortage of fresh foods for a good reason, Mr. Harada said. So many expert Japanese farmers had been driven from their land, who would grow it? His wife, he said, had decided to skip dinner and rest (with a bottle, I guessed).

That night there was a camp council meeting and Frank Yasuda, wanting to play a leadership role, asked us to be there. We told him we were just too bushed. To tell the truth, never mind the good front we had put up, we were pretty depressed. It was *wrong,* wrong, wrong of our government to do this. I didn't care how many excuses they gave. It was especially hard to believe that a man like FDR would have gone along with it . . .

YURIKO KITANO · APRIL, 1942

I was pregnant with Hideo's child, and, no surprise, I was not happy about it. Maybe if I'd loved Hideo, even liked him or respected him. The best I could manage was to feel sorry for him—which was not what you wanted to feel about the father of your child.

When Dr. Cora Varnum got back laboratory tests to confirm that I was bearing a child I felt sick. I had to talk to someone, and went looking for my mother, a wise woman even if she was careful to conceal this fact from her husband.

She'd be on a food queue, I knew. In spite of military victories and the boasting in the newspapers, food was in short supply. There were even some hints that rationing would be imposed. We were told to grow vegetables in our gardens, and the neighborhood associations, the *tonarigumi,* were already overseeing food distribution. So much food was going to our soldiers and sailors that even rice, our *gohan,* was sometimes in short supply. People could panic over this . . . life without rice would be no life at all . . .

My mom, sure enough, was standing on line outside the local fishmonger's. There wasn't much for sale in the wooden bins—squid, razor clams, eel, although my father told us that there was always plenty of carp and bluefin tuna at the palace, not just for the imperial family, but for all the employees, and sometimes he'd bring home a chunk of fresh tuna.

My mother was not happy with the selections, saying to another woman, "The fish look old and smell bad."

"Yes, the best goes to the officers."

"*That* is as it should be," my mother said haughtily. "My son is an officer, and so is my son-in-law. They deserve the finest."

Other women nearby clucked, smiled. Some knew that Mrs. Tamba was the mother of the hero Major Tamba, and her words were to be treated with respect.

I waited with my mother, and told her about the laboratory tests. She, not surprisingly, called it a blessing. I said she was wise, but she was also a very traditional Japanese wife, which I had momentarily lost sight of. When I told her I thought carrying Hideo's child was not exactly my idea of a blessing she was shocked.

"What are you talking about? How dare you even *think* such thoughts . . . ?"

"Hideo beats me when he's drunk. Is that a reason?"

My mother shook her head vigorously. "That only proves he respects you, my child. If he beat you when he was sober, then you could worry. He doesn't really hurt you, does he?"

"I have bruises all over my thighs. That is hurt—"

"He'll change once you give him a son. Nothing makes a man happier than a son."

"He also treats me like a servant, worse. My brothers, even Saburo, were kinder to me."

I was sorry I'd upset my mother, who looked pale as the fish dealer, Mr. Kurita, recognized her and out of deference to the mother of Major Tamba reached under the counter and found a fresh mackerel for our dinner.

I carried the newspaper-wrapped parcel and walked along with my mother, who stopped off to buy vegetables and *soba* noodles.

Suddenly as we turned into our street I felt dizzy and had to stop.

"Rest a moment," my mother said. "It's from carrying the baby."

I am not the sort to cry, but now I couldn't help it.

My mother tried to comfort me, even though it was exactly what I didn't want to hear. "When he comes back, you will find a place for yourself. You can be his wife, bear his son, begin to live your life. Everyone says the war will be over by the end of the year."

"I can never be happy living with him."

"Yuriko, happiness is not necessary for a good marriage."

In that case, I thought, mine should be pure ecstasy . . .

I had to sit on the bench at the bus stop, and my mother looked worried. She saw my pale puffy face, the unusual tears.

When I got up and we continued toward our home I came out with the words I'd been holding back, not wanting to shock her but having to let it out and who else to talk to except my loving mother. I prayed she would understand . . .

"I don't want Hideo's child. I want to have it taken from my body. Women do it all the time these days. He doesn't have to know—"

My mother looked as if I'd blasphemed against the emperor. "I will hear none of that, Yuriko. I forbid you to think of such a thing. You will have Hideo's baby and keep bearing children until there is at least one male child. That is the end of this conversation."

I could only stare at the wartime posters on the walls and kiosks exhorting people to work harder for Tenno Heika and to support our soldiers. There were pictures of the Rising Sun shooting its rays all over the world. In my misery I indulged myself in such irreverent thoughts as could a nation of 75 million people rule the world . . . What if the Eskimos or the Zulus decided they didn't want us? . . . I was about to bring up the matter again when my mother's hand went up.

"Silence. One more word and I will tell your father. As soon as we get home you will write a letter to Hideo and tell him the news and how you cannot wait for him to come home."

She was interrupted by a noisy crowd that had gathered in the square where some little children were playing on swings and teeter-totters.

"What's happening?" my mother asked a man selling coconut slices.

"*Look,*" he said, and pointed east.

A single airplane was flying low over the rooftops of Tokyo. It was very strange. Around the plane were a series of gray puffs in the air. Not clouds. Explosions. Antiaircraft guns? To the rear of the low-flying plane was a smaller one that I recognized as one of our fighters.

It was half-past noon, a sunny spring day. Suddenly a series of loud blasts rocked the air. The dark plane flew on.

"What can it be?" asked my mother.

"The Russians," the coconut man advised the crowd. "Oh, yes, they are breaking the peace treaty. It was bound to happen, those communists. Russians, yes, no doubt."

No one seemed to want to leave the square, apparently hoping to see another Russian plane. There was none. But there were more explosions, then silence . . . followed by the wail of sirens. When they stopped no one had moved to the shelters—actually, the one nearest our street was a good mile away and useless.

Yes, all agreed, it was the Russians, and my mother and I, unconcerned, walked on home.

It took the newspapers three days to admit that the raid was conducted by *American* bombers flying from *American* aircraft carriers. First the *Domei* news agency assured everyone that the emperor, the imperial family and the palace were all safe. It was three days later that they got around to admitting the raid. Four days after that anti-American posters appeared, emphasizing that the treacherous Americans had mercilessly machine-gunned civilians, bombed hospitals, killed innocent children. Any American flier captured would be put to death. It was the *Americans* who were barbarians, and swift death was the only just penalty for them.

My parents and I sat somberly in our house, listening to the radio. My father, reading from the newspaper, said that the raid convinced him more firmly than ever that Kenji had betrayed his family and his emperor by marrying a woman who came from a nation that stooped to killing innocent women and children.

We later learned that eight of the Doolittle fliers were captured and sentenced to death. Three were executed, although I heard from my father that palace rumors had it that the emperor personally commuted the death sentences of the others. My father, shaking his head, said sometimes it was difficult for an ordinary man to comprehend the mind of a god . . .

I confess that I cared less than I should have about the American raid, about the atrocities their fliers were said to have committed, or what was going to happen to the men who were captured. I was too intent on myself.

I dreaded Hideo's return, thought I would die before I could bring his child into the world, and more than anything I wished Kenji were at home. I had always felt better when I talked to him, but he was thousands of miles away in a prison of some kind, the Varnums told us, and who knew when I would ever see him again . . . ?

JULIE TAMBA · ARRIL, 1942

We learned about the Doolittle raid at the camp, and reactions were mixed. The JACL members hoped it would bring Japan to its senses. What few of us knew was that the actual damage was marginal.

Kenji was sober, quiet and reflective. "I'm afraid the time will come when not a handful of bombers but fleets of them will bomb Japan," he told me as we sat in our cell. I was sewing one of his shirts, repairing the sleeve. We'd volunteered for the school, Kenji as an athletics instructor, me as a kindergarten teacher.

"Maybe it will bring Tojo and the rest of that mob to realize they can't win," I said.

He was tuning the old Philco, always hunting for newscasts. "That is unlikely. Once on a chosen road they don't change."

"Forty-seven *ronin* again . . . but for God's sake, this isn't medieval vengeance, this involves the lives of hundreds of thousands of people—"

"I tell you one bombing raid won't sway them. It will only harden their determination."

"Well, what about the people, *they* may not exactly take to getting bombed."

"They have no say, you know that . . ."

I couldn't think of anything to say to that except that maybe when the war was over Kenji and people like him could change things. He didn't exactly looked thrilled at the prospect, and I thought I at least partly understood. He felt he was out of step with most of his country, including its educated class.

"But you know," I said as I dropped his shirt on the bed, "I don't understand . . ."

"Don't understand what?"

"You've told me Japan is the most literate country in the world. Smart people. Don't they realize they're being lied to?"

"We are raised to obey."

"There are limits to obedience."

"Not in Japan . . . father to older son, older son to the rest of the kids. Above the father his boss, the big bosses, and the emperor. And those in charge use the emperor's name to excuse and explain everything. I believe this rule by generals, and always in his name, embarrasses him. But what can he do?"

"He's the emperor, isn't he? He *could* speak up."

"It is impossible."

And Kenji then went on to say that certain of the young militarists in the past had actually talked about *arresting* the emperor, taking him prisoner, or replacing him if he didn't give in to what they wanted . . . One lunatic group even decided he should be killed if he stood in the way of their notion of Imperial Japan. Kenji's old teacher, Adachi, called them outlaws, and they sure were. But it still didn't answer my question—why didn't anyone dare oppose them? Why didn't some good people speak up and denounce them? And if the emperor was so widely loved by the ordinary people and his name was needed to bring reform, why didn't he get tough and tell off the bad guys?

It didn't work that way, Kenji said, getting tired of my badgering, or lack of understanding, or both. The emperor signed papers, issued Imperial Rescripts, attended high-level conferences. But decisions, it seemed, were made for him. Others acted, he okayed their acts. It didn't sound like too great a job, I said, especially for a god, then shut up, realizing Kenji had enough of such brilliant talk . . .

My brother Chris was in Hawaii when he learned about the Doolittle raid. He and some other correspondents were at a press center when word came in about the sixteen B–25's that had flown from the deck of the carrier *Hornet*, firebombed Tokyo and then made their way to Chinese airbases.

Chris wrote that the usually blasé newsmen stood up and cheered, delighted that at long last America had struck back. He said it was hard to describe the fury of Americans there against the Japanese—fury still combined with an edge of fear. Not only had this little Asian nation all but destroyed the Pacific fleet, they had seemed unstoppable, with one triumph after another and trumpeting their victories to the world, daring the United States to take them on. Well, finally, they'd tasted some of their own medicine.

Chris wrote that he and the other correspondents were drinking to the Doolittle raid, toasting the air force and the navy when a telegram arrived for him:

DEAR CHRIS. HERB AND I WERE MARRIED TODAY
SAN FRANCISCO. DID NOT WANT YOU TO LEARN
FROM ANYONE ELSE. HOPE YOU ARE WELL. BEST TO
JULIE AND KENJI. WARM WISHES FROM MRS. HERBERT
KAHN

Chris said he tried to be offhand about it, bought a round of drinks and called to arrange an interview with someone at fleet headquarters. On the inside, he felt like he'd been bombed.

MASAO TAMBA · APRIL, 1942

Malaria sent me to a hospital in Singapore and I returned to Tokyo to recover, and more importantly—I seem to have an unusual capacity for shaking off illness—to report to the War Ministry on the conquest of Malaya.

Curiously the meetings that followed lacked purpose and direction. My superiors seemed smug with our victory. What else was there for us to prove? Where to attack next? Well, an attack on India, for one thing, and I strongly urged such a campaign. From what I had seen of Indian troops they were brave but not while fighting under the Union Jack. Others in the High Command favored an invasion of Australia. A third faction wanted us to declare war on the Soviet Union. Why not? they argued. Russia was reeling, her armies decimated by Hitler.

Colonel Sato said we suffered from the "victory disease," too many triumphs, too much land to digest. The emperor had told Lord Privy Seal Kido that "the fruits of victory are tumbling into our mouths too quickly." He said this on his forty-second birthday, April 29, 1942, as we celebrated the capture of Rangoon. Forty-eight hours earlier all allied forces in Java had surrendered. We were unbeatable. We ruled the Pacific and much of Asia.

"We face two goals now that the first operational phase of the war is over," Sato said to me. We were in his office, smoking American cigarettes and studying the wall maps. The phone rang continually . . . Sato was in constant touch with journalists, parliamentarians, junior officers. Among them were the hotheads who wanted us to "teach the communists a lesson" and attack Russia. Sato would humor them . . . Yes, yes, the Soviets would be conquered in due time, he would say. Meanwhile it was prudent to adhere to our nonaggression pact. "First phase ended, the second must now begin," my father-in-law said. "Consolidation and exploitation of conquered lands. We need resources, the loyalty of the people, cheap labor. Asians marching together. At the same time a speedy peace with the United States now that we have bloodied the giant's nose. The trouble is, our troops are the world's best fighters but as administrators our officers lack something. Damn it, Rangoon falls, Manila falls, and our soldiers mostly rape women and loot. Not the way to gain the support of native populations."

I told Sato that Singapore had been a special case. Our anger was directed at the British. I agreed that we would go easier on leaders who cooperated. Like a man named Sukarno who had been freed from prison in Java, Sato said. He had agreed to head a new freedom government allied to Japan. There would be others like him.

"And this settlement with the Americans?" I asked.

"One knows so little about the Americans. We could use your brother Kenji to tell us how they think. I can't believe that after Pearl Harbor, Wake, Guam and the Philippines, all terrible defeats for them, they have any fight left."

"Well, colonel, I have no interest in colonial administration or peace offers to the Americans or anyone else. I want to know where we move next."

"The navy has its eyes on New Guinea, a jumping-off place for an invasion of Australia."

"The navy is generous with army lives, colonel. Don't they know we're still fighting in China?"

Colonel Sato said the navy had an alternate plan, authored by Admiral Yamamoto—the "mid-Pacific strategy." It called for luring the American navy—what was left of it—out of its haven in Hawaii, and destroying it in one huge battle. Admiral Yamamoto felt that our naval gunnery, torpedo capability, carrier-based fighters and bombers and battle tactics were superior to those of the United States. The time to strike was *now,* Yamamoto argued. The longer we waited, the shorter the gap between our navy and theirs would become as their industrial capacity spewed out ships and planes.

"Mid-Pacific?" I asked. "Where?"

"A dot of coral called Midway," Sato said. "Yamamoto wants to land an occupying force there and use it as a staging area to seize Hawaii. This would suck the Americans into a sea battle they couldn't win."

"And the Australia and New Guinea strategy?"

"There's the trouble . . . others want us to proceed in that direction and cut American supply lines in the Coral Sea." Colonel Sato turned and squinted at the wall map. He used a pointer. "They want us to garrison these. The Solomon Islands. They are under the British flag. I saw a report on them a few days ago. A place called Guadalcanal is the most likely.

A Japanese copra trader sent us a signal. He says the most interesting feature of Guadalcanal is a cricket pitch! Can you imagine that, Masao?"

"That is typical."

I didn't like the confusion Colonel Sato described. I was a warrior and proud of it.

I found Michiko well into a pregnancy, cheerful, obedient and now with a housemaid, a countrywoman named Reiko, a gap-toothed, slightly retarded girl of sixteen. I was glad my wife had help. It gave her time to refine her painting. I must say, she was quite good. A dealer on the Ginza wanted to show her floral *sumi* work but of course I wouldn't hear of it. Michiko asked if she could use an assumed name so that no one would associate her art with the Tamba family, and then I agreed. She would be Kiko Suzuki.

My wife never asked me about the battle for Malaya, the fall of Singapore, the shame we inflicted on the British. Why should she? Such matters were of no concern to women.

She touched her head to the floor in my presence, bowed low to open the door, cuddled me close to her breasts at night, which I liked very much.

One evening, full of rice and sake, I lay back on a *tatami* mat and read a secret report from the War Ministry. It warned us not to discuss certain matters with civilians or any members of the press, especially neutral journalists—Russians, Swiss, Spaniards and so on. Michiko served me plums in syrup. Outside pink blossoms, our beloved *sakura,* bloomed on the lone cherry tree in our tiny garden. Michiko massaged my feet, fretted that I would be ordered back to duty before she could fatten me up. My skin had been yellowed by atabrine and sometimes my teeth chattered at night.

The secret report concerned a summary of charges that were being disseminated about our occupation forces. The British and Americans were flooding the airwaves and their newspapers with them. The report characterized them as despicable lies unworthy of a response. It was said that in Borneo our soldiers massacred the entire white population for sabotaging the oil refineries. In Hong Kong we were alleged to have killed hospital patients and raped nuns. In Singapore 70,000 citizens of Chinese descent were said to have been rounded up. Five thousand were imprisoned, most of them for the crime of wearing a tattoo that suggested membership in secret societies. Many of these Chinese were used for living bayonet practice—just as we had punished similar criminals in Nanking.

Well, war was war, and the *bushido* said that a man who does not fight
to the death has no rights and so can be treated with any degree of cruelty.
I was certain most of what the report said was true, and I wondered why
we kept denying it. Why not tell the whole world the truth? What better
way to create fear in our enemies, and at the same time justify our acts
as the honest fulfillment of the warriors' code? If we weren't afraid of
death, which to us was "light as a feather," why should others be? And
if the Chinese and Britons and Americans were afraid, didn't that prove
our superiority?

I was sitting in the elegant officers' bathhouse with my father-in-law some
days after what people now call the Doolittle raid. As we sat on wooden
stools and scrubbed ourselves with sandalwood soap, a radio blared a news
report:

"Any foreign airman who dares to harm Japanese civilians again will
be put to the sword. After the cowardly strafing and bombing of women
and children by the Americans, the Imperial government will punish to
the fullest any acts of barbarism . . ."

"Sixteen planes?" I asked Sato. "Why are we so upset?"

"Oh, matters of morale."

"Were women and children killed?"

"A few, I suppose."

The bath felt marvelous. How I had craved a decent hot bath when I
was in the field, caked with mud and sweat, racked by malarial fevers and
chills.

"The people must be on guard," Sato said. "So must we. These peace-
faction traitors are shrewd."

"I had no idea there were any left."

We talked again about Yamamoto's plan to capture Midway and destroy the American navy. Apparently some naval officers were having
second thoughts. The two-edged operation might be a mistake, they
thought. Such strategies, with double, perhaps contradictory, goals were
dangerous.

The colonel then said that while he wanted me to stay in Tokyo, the
general staff preferred that I take command of a battalion in the Solomon
Islands, or at least organize defensive positions there.

I laughed as we lowered ourselves into the scalding tub. "You want me
to guard a cricket field?"

"I have a feeling Guadalcanal will be important," he said. "The Americans will guess we're after New Guinea and Australia. They may evade

Yamamoto's trap and steam toward the Solomons. If they do, you'll be part of the force that ends the war. Once they are beaten there they will have to sue for peace."

"I would like to fight Americans," I said. "The British and the Indians and the Chinese—they had no stomach for cold steel and massed fire. But the Americans on Wake Island fought like demons."

"But also surrendered." Sato stretched his pudgy arms.

"So it appears this war can be won soon, colonel?"

"Yes . . . do you recall how the liberals and the soft-hearts and pro-Americans derided us? The Cherry Blossom Society. The Dark Ocean Society. We were right! All that we wanted will come to pass. This war can be won, and it *will* be won. It will be good to see the new world that emerges from our victory, a world free of corruption and weakness. No slavish imitation of the West. Honor, duty, courage, everyone in his proper place. What we sought in 1936."

"And Tenno Heika?"

"He will be the heart of the new Japan. Our divine presence. Of course he will rule only in accord with our desires."

"A new shogunate?"

"An emperor who symbolizes gods, the state, the people. As only the descendant of Amaterasu can."

"And you . . . and I . . . and our friends—"

"We will guide him. Make decisions for him. Traitors—liberals, socialists and internationalists—will be purged in the same way one takes a strong laxative and shits out impurities . . ."

It was a peculiar way to put it, I thought, but said nothing. I wanted most of all to get back to war—talk of the peace seemed to me premature.

JULIE TAMBA · APRIL, 1942

Kenji and I were on our way to the barracks when we saw a crowd gathered outside. The camp ambulance, a rickety van with a red cross on its side, was parked in the street. It was cold, it was *always* cold at night in the desert. Wind whipped the dust into angry spirals.

"What's going on?" I asked a young man.

"Someone's sick, the American lady."

We hurried up the creaking steps toward the rear of the long building where the Haradas had their cell.

A Nisei doctor with a stethoscope around his neck was standing alongside a cot in the Harada room. A half-dozen people, including the naturopath, Dr. Makioka, were looking on. Mrs. Harada was sprawled on a cot, her arms dangling over the sides. Her eyes were open but she didn't move.

The doctor listened to her chest, turned to Mr. Harada. "I'm sorry, I can't help her." He held up a dark bottle. "She took all of these. We're too late."

Harada dropped to his knees and buried his face in his wife's chest.

Good Lord, that woman had been guilty of nothing—*nothing.*

Kenji put his arm around me and walked me out to the sounds of Mr. Harada's quiet sobbing.

"They didn't hurt anyone, it's so awful . . ." I could hear Dr. Makioka saying something about notifying the camp commandant, getting certificates signed, the possibility of an FBI report . . . the camp was federal property. So irrelevant, so goddamn *unfair* . . .

Two nights later Kenji, Frank Yasuda and I went to a meeting of the camp council called in response to Mrs. Harada's death. An outcast in life, in death she was now accepted as one of them. (I almost said *us.* I was definitely beginning to feel that way).

We gathered in the mess hall under dim lights, the smell of cheap frankfurters and cabbage permeating everything. The mess hall detail, mostly women, was mopping up.

Ito, the American-born, Japanese-educated young Kibei, along with some of his friends had taken over the meeting that had begun as a protest against lousy medical facilities but had now degenerated into a shouting match between the Japanese-educated Kibei and the more Americanized men like Anamai who were affiliated with the JACL—the Japanese-American Citizens' League.

The three of us took seats on the benches in the back of the mess hall. I guessed that over seventy-five percent of the people were men. Even among the Nisei women weren't exactly liberated. Most of them stayed in the gloomy barracks, sewing, washing, working to make life more comfortable for their men.

"*Inu,*" one of the Kibei leaders, was saying, "That's what you are, Anamai, a damned *inu.*"

"It means *dog,*" Yasuda told me, "but it really means stool pigeon. If I were Anamai I'd belt him."

Ito went on shouting at Anamai and other JACL members who sat together. "What a bunch you are . . . spineless stooges. You say you're the camp leaders? We'd be better off with no leaders. Dammit, we have rights. By God, we'll get the goods on you. Informers. FBI spies. You give in to anything the Americans want—"

Yasuda was on his feet. He was wearing his uniform—suntans, gold collar-bar, the crossed rifles of the infantry. I felt awful for him . . . playing soldier for an army that wouldn't have him.

"Hey, buddy, slack off," Yasuda was saying. "What do you want the leaders to do? Start a riot? Go on hunger strikes? We know we've got a rough hand. *Nobody* likes it here. But if I read Anamai right—and look, I'm JACL myself—they're figuring things'll ease up. Give the Okies a chance to get it out of their systems. We'll be sprung, they'll need us to work the farms, to do factory work, and I'll be back with my old division in three months—I'll bet you."

"You, Yasuda? You're the biggest pet dog of all. How can you wear that uniform?"

"I'm an American, I don't like the way I'm being treated, but I'm not turning yellow dog either."

Another Kibei youth said, "*They* don't think you're an American, Yasuda. And you came here the easy way, on a bus. How about some of us from Terminal Island? They kept us in hot boxes. Our wives, our kids. No water, no sanitary facilities. Treated us like cattle. That's your America, Yasuda—oh, *excuse* me, *Lieutenant* Yasuda."

Yasuda was walking to the front of the hall where the camp council was —both the Kibei and the JACL men.

"Hey, stay back there," Ito said. "You're not on the council."

Kenji and I admired him for his guts, his sticking up for what he believed. It was plenty tough, tougher in a way than for us.

Yasuda stood in front of the leaders now. "I say we draw up a petition, tell 'em how much we can help on the outside. We *aren't* spies or criminals. There's all kinds of work we can do. What good are we cooped up in the desert?"

Anamai clapped his hands. "Right, Yasuda. That's just what we plan to do. We've got friends in Washington. FDR will wake up and realize the army conned him into this."

"That's right," Yasuda said. "How about it, Ito?"

"No."

"Why?"

"Because you . . . you and the others like you . . . you're *traitors.*"

You didn't call Frank Yasuda a traitor. He leaped at Ito, and a brawl broke out . . . Kibei against Nisei.

"I feel I should be in there," Kenji said, "except what side would I be on? Frank is right but so is Ito. These people should not be in a prison. They aren't enemies. I feel guilty—"

"Baloney, you're guilty of nothing, except maybe marrying me. Please just get in there and stop them."

And Kenji did just that. Strong and trained in unarmed combat—in spite of his peaceable noncombative attitude—my husband pulled bodies apart, ducked blows. He shoved Ito to the floor and pinned Yasuda's arms. Within seconds the battle was over.

Ito looked strangely at Kenji. "The Ministry of Education, huh? I didn't know they taught you guys karate at Tokyo Imperial University."

"They didn't. Anyway, I don't think there's any gain in brawling among ourselves."

Ito and the other Kibei eyed him with new respect. Ito said, "I wish I were you, Tamba. I'd get back to Japan and get some licks in—"

Anamai spoke up. "You're not one of us, Tamba. What does an outsider think?"

Kenji told them we should be firm about decent treatment, medical care, all those things, but that Frank was also right. The Americans would come to their senses. I only hoped he was right.

Frank Yasuda, wiping blood from his nose, nodded agreement. "Someday we'll be on their side, we'll show 'em a few things about courage."

Kenji's answer was to bow to Ito, to Anamai, to Frank, and they returned the gesture. He seemed to transform them into the best of what they were. I had myself, as if I needed more evidence, quite a husband

The truce didn't last. The next morning we learned that there had been attacks by Kibei gangs on some JACL leaders suspected of being informants. Several men were waylaid and beaten. A blacklist had been drawn up. In the dead of night the G.I. guards had had to enter the camp and take off JACL leaders and their families to protective custody in the military camp outside the fence.

Kenji and I felt awful about this as in the light of the desert morning, with the sun baking the dusty land, we walked to the schoolroom. In the square outside the school about thirty children had gathered for the morning flag-raising. It broke my heart when I saw the Nisei teacher raise the flag that was supposed to stand for freedom and fairness and then hear the children, prisoners inside the chain-link fence, recite the pledge of allegiance.

. . . and to the Republic for which it stands, one nation, under God, indivisible, with liberty and justice for all.

"What's going to happen?" I said to Kenji.

"I wish I knew . . . are you sorry you came here with me—?"

"Never. And don't dare ask me that again." But as I said it I felt a new rush of love, and respect, for him. It helped me get through the day, to offset the fear and anger that came with every morning.

Yuriko Kitano · MAY, 1942

My mother, my sister-in-law Michiko, my brother Saburo and I had come to the gardens of the Meiji shrine to see the cherry blossoms. It was April, a misty day with sunlight darting in and out of low feathery clouds. Sometimes a single tree with thousands of pink blossoms would look as if it were illuminated in one celestial beam. We took our blossom-viewing seriously.

Saburo ran off, shied stones at ducks in one of the Meiji garden ponds, and we three women paused to admire a particularly lavish trio of trees in full shimmering bloom.

"Masao says that the *samurai* chose the cherry tree as their favorite," Michiko said. "He told me that a blossom is like the death of a warrior. The tree sheds the blossoms in the breeze while they are still in their prime, not after they have faded on the bough."

A warrior's death is supposed to be beautiful, I thought, but of course didn't say anything. I didn't want to upset my mother. But no wonder Japanese men can celebrate early death if they're cherry blossoms . . .

"Father says that the war will end soon," my mother said as we stopped to look at one enormous tree that seemed bowed beneath its weight of flowers. "The Americans have surrendered in the Philippines. Your father heard the generals saying that the enemy can't fight much longer. That will be good. All our children can come home."

As she walked ahead with Saburo I asked Michiko if she missed Masao very much.

"With all my heart, I long for him."

"I'm jealous of you."

"Why, Yuriko?"

"Because I don't miss Hideo—"

"You mustn't say that. It isn't right—"

"But it's true. I hate it when he comes home."

"Yuriko! I shouldn't even listen to you!"

"He beats me."

"Because he loves you."

I stared at her, wondering if I really knew my sister-in-law, what went on in her head. She was a good mother, an accomplished artist, a woman with a decent education. But to approve of my getting beaten? To call it husbandly love?

"He doesn't know what it is to love, but maybe I don't either."

She looked stunned. "You mustn't let your mother hear what you're saying. I'm ashamed to hear it myself."

"I don't care, and one day I'll tell Hideo. At least then he'll have a good reason to beat me."

I looked at the green-and-pink park and thought of when I was a little girl. "I wish Kenji was with us," I said. "He always carried me on his back or bought me a present. A fan, or a paper puppet—"

My mother looked at me. "You mustn't talk about Kenji so much, especially around your father."

"Why not? He's my brother."

My mother turned away, pretending to be absorbed in a dwarf cherry tree with lush blossoms. The crowds were larger now, mostly women and children, but some men in uniform too. Even civilian men had taken to wearing a kind of silly brown uniform—knee britches, puttees, peaked caps—to show their support of the war. "I wonder what Kenji's wife is like," I said to Michiko.

"She looked pretty in the photograph, tall and blonde and with kind eyes."

"I hope to meet her, I want to be friends with her."

Michiko smiled as if she wanted to agree with me but was afraid to— even though my mother and Saburo were out of earshot. As anti-*gaijin* as my father was, I could imagine what it had been like to have been raised in the home of Colonel Sato, that enemy of anything not Japanese. And my brother Masao, although younger than Sato and better educated, was almost as violent in his feelings.

"Masao says it's a disgrace to your family," Michiko whispered.

"What is?"

"Kenji's *gaijin* wife."

"Why?"

"Masao says we're better than other people. When he was in China he
had two of his soldiers court-martialled for marrying Chinese women."

"But Americans—?"

"He says it's just as bad."

"But we send students to study in America, we imitate things they
have—"

"Masao says we're allowed to do that only to better ourselves, but *not*
to marry them."

"Well, if Kenji married Julie, I know she's a good person and I want
to meet her. I bet *they're* in love." I couldn't resist pressing her. "Are you
in love with Masao?"

"I . . . we . . . yes, yes, of course . . ."

It wasn't exactly a ringing declaration and I suddenly was sorry to have
been so pushy.

"Were you two talking about Kenji?" my mother asked as she came up
to us.

I bowed my head. "Yes, mother."

Michiko bowed her head. "Yes, Mother Tamba."

"You must not. Do you want me to tell your fathers? You know how
angry they will be."

Imagine, not able to talk about her own son. It was sad and wrong, I
felt.

"It is your father's hope," my mother said to me slowly, "that this
foolish marriage of Kenji's will end. Look at what it has done to him. He
is in prison now."

"Mother, his being married to an American is not why he was sent to
the prison," I said. "The Americans arrested all Japanese people. Whether
Kenji was single or married he would have been interned—"

"Oh, no, your father heard at the palace that they were especially angry
at Japanese with American wives."

There seemed no logic to my mother's talk or to the rumors my father
had picked up. "Well, I don't think the marriage will end," I said, "and
if Kenji is happy he has a right to stay married even in prison. Didn't Dr.
Varnum tell us that his niece volunteered to go to the American jail with
him? Doesn't that prove to you how much they are in love?"

Michiko sided with my mother. "My father says the Americans want
to humiliate Japanese people, to make them look like cowards. So we'll
have to punish them and win the war quickly."

I said nothing more. Kenji's letters spoke only about his affection for
his wife. I was a little jealous but I was also very glad for him.

Saburo had crawled behind the bench I was sitting on, stuck his hand through the slate, tugged at my *obi* and ran off, quite pleased with himself.

I was furious, but my mother thought it was *cute.* Thankfully Michiko's baby Maeko started to cry and we decided it was getting too cool and might rain and headed for the bus station.

As we did, we spotted an older man in uniform, a veteran of the China campaign, standing on a tree stump making a speech, assuring us that if we all worked harder and prayed more and did good things for Tenno Heika the war would end in a month.

I wondered if our soldiers and sailors felt so sure.

JULIE TAMBA · JUNE, 1942

At Manzanar Camp there had been a roundup of the militant Kibei leaders, including Ito. The army had shipped them out in a heavily guarded bus to an "isolation camp" in Utah. True, these men weren't popular with the majority of the internees but most also felt the punishment was too harsh, didn't fit the "crime." They were separated from their families, confined miles away and treated like criminals.

Kenji was against it, and I took the other side. "They threatened other Japanese, they beat up JACL men, they wanted a revolt in the camp."

"I know," he said one morning as we walked to the school where I taught a kindergarten class. "I can understand their anger. Most of the men would volunteer for military service, like Yasuda. Or work on the outside."

I suppose I felt less intensely, but I was glad to see Kenji be a little less *understanding* of the injustices we'd . . . well, we Americans . . . had put on him and other loyal Japanese. About a half-hour later Dr. Makioka, the naturopath, knocked at the schoolroom door. With him was an American man in a business suit that I recognized as Watterson, the FBI agent from Los Angeles. Had he come to Manzanar just to see Kenji?

Later, after we'd collected Kenji and were sitting in the mess hall, I almost fainted when I found out why Watterson had come.

"Mr. Tamba," he said, "our governments, through the International Red Cross, is arranging a swap of prisoners—"

"And I'm included?"

"Your name is on the list."

"I'm only a student—"

"Because of your status as an employee of the Ministry of Education you have been placed on the official list. In a few weeks there'll be a ship sailing for Japan. You will be escorted to New York and put aboard."

"I find it hard to believe."

Watterson smiled. "Even during a war certain rules are observed. Diplomats, business people, teachers, a variety of VIPs will be sent back to Japan. Your government, in turn, will send Americans to the States."

"What about me?" I asked, recovering from my astonishment.

Watterson looked at the letters in front of him. "I'm not sure what provision has been made for non-Japanese wives—"

"If my husband goes, I go."

"I'll have to ask if it's permitted—"

"Oh, it will be. Ever study Latin, Mr. Watterson?"

"I have, but I've forgotten it . . ."

"*Amor vincit omnia.* Love conquers all, in case you've forgotten that too."

"Well, I'll give whatever help I can, Mrs. Tamba," and he handed Kenji a letter of notification, instructions on where to report. It turned out there was no one else in the whole camp who qualified for this free trip to Japan. Whatever, I was determined to go along, I wouldn't let Kenji out of my sight.

"You don't have to do this," he said. "Maybe you ought to stay in California—"

"Are you kidding? You're stuck with me, husband. Here, Japan, I don't give a damn."

"It won't be easy in Tokyo, Julie. I might even have to join the services."

"It's better than being in prison here."

"And fight against your country? Would you like that?"

"I can't . . . I won't think that far ahead. Besides, you'll be a real American expert. Maybe you can beat some sense into them. All those outlaws you talk about. Make 'em see they can't win."

He just looked straight ahead. "I'm afraid you're innocent, Julie. About my people, I mean . . ."

"*And* optimistic." I kissed him on the lips. "See? I said we'd have an exciting life. Jail. An ocean trip. The Far East. How lucky can we get?"

His answer was to keep quiet about the deep misgivings he felt.

YURIKO KITANO · JUNE, 1942

Hideo had been at sea for a long time, a deck officer on the aircraft carrier *Akagi.* I didn't see much of his family. They treated me, of course, as a poor relation, the typical attitude toward a daughter-in-law.

Since I had already graduated from high school and never prepared for university, my parents decided I should go to work, except I hadn't been trained to do anything. One day a neighborhood association leader told me I'd been selected for a great honor—I was to work in a munitions factory. My father agreed, since as a palace servant he had to see that his family was beyond reproach. Saburo teased me about becoming a "slave." Masao thought it was a splendid idea.

I won't forget that first day at work. I had to dress in those hideous *mompei* bloomers, a kind of khaki pantaloon tied below the knees, supposed to make women less enticing and so keep everyone's mind on the war effort. I looked like a brown toad.

I took a bus to the factory, which was in the southern part of Tokyo, and noticed that people were looking drabber, sadder, puzzled. Ever since the air raid of April all new precautions were being taken . . . inflated barrage balloons flew over Tokyo, in parks and squares there were sandbagged bunkers and antiaircraft guns. The *tonarigumi* (neighborhood associations) sent people around to show us how to make our homes fortresses against air attack. A few days before I went off to the factory, a strutting old man, a retired bookkeeper, came to the houses on our street and told us to start digging holes in our garden, saying that each family member could crouch in a hole, pull a flat rock over the top and be safe. "You will even be safe in your home if you follow orders," he said. "All you need do is make a little house inside the closet—cushions, *futons*— and hide inside it. Like a bird in a nest." No one, least of all my mother Hisako, dared ask this idiot how a paper-and-wood house would protect us from fires and explosions.

Outside the New Dawn munitions factory, where I had been assigned by the Ministry of War Production, it seemed that half the employees were digging furiously in the hard earth. After registering and getting my I.D. card I was assigned to a long wooden table where seven other girls and I inspected shell casings that tumbled off a conveyor belt, looking for defects, dents, misshapen forms. The light was dim, the air foul, the noise deafening. It was a shock for me, a middle-class snobby little girl who had attended a good school, whose father worked at the palace, whose one brother was a war hero, whose other was a scholar . . .

That first week I barely talked to the women on either side of me. One was a silent woman of middle age whose name was Mrs. Kurusu, a war widow. The worker on my left was a pretty young woman, perhaps three years older than I. She had laughing eyes and a perfectly round face. Her name was Midori, and I could tell by her drawling accent that she was from Osaka.

Midori and I became friends out of a mutual hatred for our foreman, a bandy-legged old man named Umezu. He would waddle up and down the aisles shouting at us, insulting us, admonishing us to work faster. He was also not above cracking us across the back or the arms with a wooden cane.

One afternoon when Umezu had been whipping his cane against the legs of a young farm girl who dropped a box of casings on the floor, Midori and I decided to speak up. We told him he had no right to hit us, that we worked as hard as we could and that the girl he had made cry was doing her best. To our amazement he backed off. He stared at me and I stared back, while the other women bowed, even fell to the floor. Such behavior has always offended me. I hated doing it for my husband Hideo, I hated seeing my mother do it and I didn't much like it when Michiko played the role to Masao.

When Umezu scuttled off in his bandy-legged walk Midori whispered to me, "He respects you."

"No, he doesn't," I said. "He knows who my brother is."

"Your brother?"

I told her about the famous Major Tamba, a hero, one of the conquerors of Singapore, veteran of the China campaigns, a soldier who had been cited for bravery five times. Yes, it was no secret among the factory foremen. I was a Tamba of Shibuya Ward.

"Then why do you have to work this way?" Midori asked.

"My family says it's my patriotic duty."

"Rich people get anything they want even though there's a war."

I tried to explain to her that I wasn't rich, that my father was a servant, but she seemed slightly awed by me. I liked her. She was funny and vigorous and didn't let the vile factory with its noise and stench depress her.

On our lunch break that day as I dawdled over rice and fried squid, lukewarm tea from a thermos, I told her I was pregnant with Hideo's child, that he was at sea on the aircraft carrier *Akagi* and that I rarely heard from him. I also admitted I didn't like his parents.

"Ah, but you love him, your navy husband—"

"I hate him."

Midori almost choked on a pickled turnip. "You . . . what? How can you say that, Yuriko?"

"It's not hard. He hits me. He gets drunk. He goes to whores. He thinks he can do anything he wants. He once told me that in the navy his superior officers abuse him all day so when he comes home it's only *fair* that he abuses me."

After lunch as we approached the table for our next load of shell casings, Midori said, "You won't think me bad if I say something?"

"Such as—"

"If your husband is so mean to you . . . you could get a friend . . ."

"Oh, well, there are some things I just can't do, although it's an idea. By the way, I have a friend now. You."

Her round face glowed and her eyes looked faintly wicked. "A *man* friend, Yuriko. Not everyone is in uniform. There are men around. I have no family. Just an uncle in Osaka and I never see him. So I found myself a man—"

"But you aren't married, and I am." As I said this, I felt a little shiver in my belly, a funny weakness in my legs. As if I were anticipating something . . .

"Who'll know? You're at work all the time. Your husband is somewhere in the Pacific."

"But that would be dishonorable—"

"Yes, but it could be fun."

I was silent a moment as Umezu waddled past. Busily, I picked through the next load of metal casings, tossed two aside, shoved the others onto the moving belt.

"Maybe I could fool my parents," I said, "but my brother Masao has eyes in the back of his head. He's like the spirit of the wind. He's everywhere. If he found out I was seeing another man he'd cut my head off."

Midori made a comical face. She crossed her eyes, bared her teeth, and put a wooden spatula that we used for separating the shells between them. "Yaaah. *Samurai.* Come on, Yuriko, how would he know?"

Was this place what my life was going to be for the rest of the war? Midori's hints that I find a friend were already having their effect.

". . . Yes, you'd better start having some fun," Midori was saying, almost reading my mind, "or you'll end up like the old women here."

While I was at the munitions plant it turned out that my husband was at sea with one of the greatest armadas ever assembled—greater even than the fleet that had attacked Hawaii.

Hideo and his bunkmate Mori and the rest of the junior officers and of course the enlisted men had no idea where they were headed.

One of his shipmates later told me that he wasn't much of a sailor, that he got seasick, and inflicted cruelty on his inferiors as a coverup for his own failings. My husband, my hero . . .

Much later we would hear by letter and reports of those who survived about Admiral Yamamoto's strategy for bringing America to its knees. It consisted of two audacious parts. One was a sea and air strike at the American navy. The Americans would be drawn into battle in the open sea. They couldn't run and hide and would be overwhelmed by an attacking force that included eleven battleships, eight carriers, twenty-two cruisers and hundreds of support vessels, not to mention over three hundred of the world's best airplanes. How could the Americans, so badly wounded at Pearl Harbor, possibly handle this assault?

The second part of the plan would be an invasion force on Midway Island, which up to that point no one had even heard of. There would also be an invasion far to the north on the Aleutian Islands in Alaska. *Yamato Damashii.*

The great admiral himself was to command the battle far to the rear, fittingly aboard the largest warship in the world, the battleship *Yamato,* unsinkable, bristling with guns, the mere sight of which would terrify the American sailors . . .

A few days later the ships' companies would be officially informed by their commanders that they were sailing for a scrap of coral called Midway Island, that they would there destroy what remained of the American navy and then proceed to occupy Midway.

Hideo sent me a letter telling me to send future letters to a place called "Island of the Rising Sun." I looked at my atlas and could find no such place. Not surprising. So confident were our admirals that they would seize Midway that they had already chosen a new name for the island that would become the dagger pointed at America's heart.

And so *Akagi* steamed into the night, carrying Hideo and these men to carry out the destiny they believed in—without question. They would, they thought, rule the waves the way they ruled their wives, and the emperor would take care of them the way their mothers always had. Such thoughts, of course, were all but treasonous to the way we were raised and what we were taught to believe. Sometimes I couldn't believe myself the things that came into my mind.

JULIE TAMBA · JUNE, 1942

Some time in June, I would learn from the International Red Cross, Ed Hodges and his men, the prisoners of Wake Island, arrived in Yokohama, the big port city. I even got eyewitness accounts, and they were awful . . .

It was a hot June day when the prisoners came out of the hold of the ship, tottering ghosts. Behind a barbed-wire fence women and children stared at these wraiths in rags. Japanese guards hit the men with cudgels if they moved too slowly.

A sergeant named Ozawa, but known to all the men in Ed's section as Froggy because of his wide flat mouth and walleyes, emerged as the resident tyrant. He spoke good English, claimed to have worked on the pineapple plantations in Hawaii for three years, where he had developed a grudge against white people. He stood on the loading dock and gave it to the POWs: No work, no food. Be glad they had a chance to work for the emperor. They'd work in the open, where Japanese civilians would see them and realize how inferior the western *white* men were.

The men were pushed into columns of five and marched off to a warehouse two miles from the docks, and a Sergeant Verne Goodwin, barely able to walk, began to sing "Goodbye Mama, I'm off to Yokohama," which the others quickly took up.

The Japanese guards mistook guts for clowning. It was a gap of understanding that saved the men's lives.

YURIKO KITANO · JUNE, 1942

My brother Masao was spending more time in Tokyo than he liked. He'd left Malaya and Singapore where our troops were now the rulers. Through Colonel Sato's influence he not only had been promoted to major but was a member of a military planning council.

Like Kenji, Masao was intelligent, but his talents obviously were very different. Fearless and a born leader, he would have risen high in the army even without his father-in-law's backing. Sometimes he frightened me, and I didn't approve of many of his cronies, but he was my older brother and I was proud of him.

One night he and Michiko and I took a stroll through Shibuya Ward. Hideo was still at sea, although there were reports that the great battle for Midway Island was over and that Japan had won another huge victory. We even heard rumors that the American navy was finished once and for all, and of course everybody *wanted* to believe it.

Michiko's baby girl, Maeko, was just a few months old and was carried in a sling on Michiko's back, where she slept peacefully, in spite of a summer drizzle, street noises and the heat. I've always said that if there is one thing we Japanese excel at it's sleeping . . . we can snooze just about anywhere at any time of day. I don't know why, but it starts when we're infants. You hardly ever hear a Japanese baby cry. It's too busy sleeping.

So while Maeko slept on, Michiko and I walked together, two paces behind Masao. Soldiers—older men in soiled uniforms—manned an antiaircraft gun inside sandbags. The guns had been placed smack in the center of the playground in the square near our house. As we walked by Masao snapped a command to them and they promptly got to their feet and bowed low. Masao told them he'd have them beaten if they didn't look more alert.

As we approached the Shibuya Ward clinic we could see that there was some trouble on the veranda. A single light shone inside—normally the clinic was not open at night except for emergency cases. A group of kids was watching Dr. Adam Varnum and his wife as they talked heatedly with a man in civilian clothing and a uniformed policeman—it was the dolt Tani who lived down the street from us. Suddenly the kids started to yell rhythmically and thrust their fists at the Varnums . . . *"Supai, supai, supai."*

We stopped in front of the veranda, and in the dark—a partial blackout was in effect—we waited.

"I am no *spy,*" Dr. Adam Varnum was saying. "I run a hospital—"

"And I'm a Swiss," Cora added, "my country is neutral."

The civilian then grabbed Dr. Varnum by the arm. "You will come with us, you're an American and you're a spy—we can prove it."

"That's right," Tani said. "This is Anti-Espionage Week. All foreigners have to be questioned. Both of you will have to come with us."

It was crazy. Just a few weeks back my timid mother could get these police dogs to back off just by saying a few words on behalf of the doctors. Now this . . .

"You have acted in suspicious ways," the plainclothes man (a Lieutenant Koga) said. "You have been heard playing foreign music on a phonograph. You read subversive books. You are incorrect people. We have information that you attempt to get information from the people who come to this clinic."

Tani added, "We're going to cut down on your medical supplies, which should stop people from coming here—"

And the police now started to drag Dr. Varnum down the steps. "Dammit, take your hands off me," he told them.

"Adam, please, go with them. I'll call the consul."

"*No.* This is my clinic and these people aren't going to do this to me or you."

Lieutenant Koga yanked a short club from his jacket and raised it. Cora screamed.

Masao walked to the edge of the veranda and said quietly, "Take your hands off him."

Koga squinted in the dark and saw the figure of an army officer. Masao moved closer. The hospital light glinted on his major's leaves, the ribbons on his chest, the curved sword.

Koga bowed so low his forehead almost touched the wooden boards of the porch. Tani nearly prostrated himself.

"As the major will observe," Lieutenant Koga said, sucking in his breath, "we are merely putting into action the government's response to American atrocities. This is, as the major knows, Anti-Espionage Week. We must teach these *gaijin* a lesson. Just as Admiral Yamamoto taught their navy a lesson at Midway. I mean the Island of the Rising Sun . . ."

Masao let him blather on, then, "Do you know who I am, lieutenant?"

"No, sir."

Tani, bowing, doubled at the waist as if hinged, said, "Why, sir, that is Major Tamba."

"The hero of Singapore? Oh, *yes,* I should have known . . ."

"Good evening, Masao," Dr. Varnum said. "Will you please advise this loyal member of the *Kempetai* that I have no time, let alone the inclination, for spying."

"The doctor is right," Masao said, his voice steel. "You will leave him alone. He is an American, but he remains our friend. Leave."

"Sir, I have orders—"

"My orders will be to slice your backside with my sword if you don't get out and stay out."

Koga and Tani bowed, bowed again, backed away.

When they'd gone off Dr. Varnum invited us in for tea, returning our bows—an old Japan hand, he knew how much we Japanese disliked the feel of a moist hand or a public embrace. Michiko and I joined Cora in the living room, Masao went into Dr. Varnum's study and we could hear their voices . . . Dr. Varnum thanking Masao, Masao telling him that he and Cora were still our friends.

MASAO TAMBA · JUNE, 1942

It was simply impossible for me to think of Dr. Varnum and his wife as enemies. I'd known them all my life. Besides, I privately hated the civilian groups and secret police who had never been in battle.

After I'd gotten rid of them, we sat in Adam Varnum's office and smoked cigars . . . the last of one of Kenji's gifts, mailed to the doctor before the war.

"The fragrance of the noble leaf," Dr. Varnum said. "It's like a narcotic. I shouldn't admit my weakness, but there it is. I'm more human than medical about my cigars."

I agreed and we chatted about many things . . . Dr. Varnum knew much about tropical medicine. It was what had brought him to the Pacific and eventually to Japan many years ago. Sometimes he seemed to regret that he had not chosen a life of resarch, but then he would say, "I decided I preferred people to bacteria."

"We are learning about tropical parasites that can attack the body," I said.

"Yes, I imagine so. Your soldiers are spread across the Pacific. How's your own health, Masao?"

"Good, doctor. My malaria seems to be under control. We need little. Rice, fish, a sip of sake. That is one reason why we can't be beaten. We fight on one-third of what it takes to sustain meat-eaters. If we had to we could live off the land."

"You may have to, my friend."

"I beg your pardon, Dr. Varnum?"

He leaned forward and flicked ashes into a wastebasket. "Masao, we get radio reports from the Swiss consulate. Cora has friends there."

"What do these reports say?"

"There are signs that your navy took a beating at Midway."

I laughed. "Midway? You mean the Island of the Rising Sun? Doctor, we have conquered it. We sank half your aircraft carriers. Any day now the government will announce the details of this victory. I tell you, doctor, the war is nearly over."

From the inside room, my daughter Maeko let out a loud cry . . . evidently Dr. Cora Varnum was examining her.

"That sounds like a high C," Dr. Varnum said. "Why don't we join the laidies? I know your daughter gets the best of medical care at the military hospital, but you won't mind if an old friend looks her over?"

"I would be honored. How can I not accept the care of a man who taped my ankle so many years ago?"

Yes, I truly liked him . . . he was almost one of us. But he could never understand us. I also had some difficulty about these Quakers who did not believe in war. I remembered Colonel Sato asking if all Americans were Quakers and hated to fight. I knew this wasn't true, but I said that maybe it did color American thinking. So far they had shown very little appetite for fighting and less for dying.

But I did not question Dr. Varnum on the matter. One still must have respect, and I did respect Cora and Adam Varnum.

Yuriko Kitano · JUNE, 1942

My father told us how he served tea to His Majesty and Professor Hattori today. We were at dinner and as we ate our fourth portion of rice for the day we complimented my mother on the fine smooth quality of the long grains, the perfection with which each shiny grain had been boiled, the way the mounds of rice, steaming and fragrant, rested in their porcelain bowls. There wasn't much to go with the rice—a slice of smoked mackerel, a side dish of *miso* soup and a pickled white radish. But the meal was delicious. We even had rice soaked in green tea for dessert.

Professor Hattori was a famous biologist, and the emperor was a scholar of marine biology . . . it was more than his hobby, it was his passion. My father, always discreet, had left the tea tray on the laboratory table at which His Majesty and the professor took turns peering into a microscope. Just then, he told us, Prime Minister Tojo and a naval aide entered the laboratory, bowed and asked permission to speak. The emperor didn't get up from his high stool but just kept studying the specimens on the slide. The war, it seemed, could wait on his specimens. Tojo waited, bowed again, and spoke up, "I have the honor and pleasure to inform His Majesty that the victorious Imperial fleet is returning from Midway. It seems the Americans were trapped as they slept and that their destruction is now total. We anticipate detailed reports at any moment."

My father, from long practice, had developed a remarkable ability for reproducing in his stories to us the actual dialogue that went on at the palace. This confirmation from the prime minister about Midway was impressive . . . and while I had to be pleased along with the others, I'll also admit to a twinge at the thought that this might mean that Hideo would soon be home . . .

Later after dinner my mother sent me out to bring Saburo home. He still was a problem, wandering about the neighborhood, getting into fights. At dinner he had sulked and complained that the war would be over before he had a chance to fight. If the reports on Midway were true—and how could anyone doubt them?—the United States would surrender before the year 1942 was over. We'd had a lively discussion at dinner and when I helped my mother clean the table and wash the dishes she again said how wonderful it was that Hideo had been part of the victory at sea and she prayed he would be home in time for the birth of our child. I've already said how I felt about *that* . . .

I was quite round now, feeling the life beating inside me, loving the child but not its father-to-be. In the dim street, under the glow of tiny lights from shops, I watched people queue up for rice cakes, newly baked from spring rice and considered a delicacy by many people. I remembered, though, how Kenji used to joke that these cakes were indigestible and probably caused numerous deaths by strangulation and rupture of the bowel since no gastric juice could dissolve them. How I missed Kenji. So bright, and he could make me laugh, although with most people he hid his humor and acted like a scholarly sobersides.

Saburo, when I located him, was with his gang of blue-uniformed boys hanging on to a chain-link fence, watching air cadets drill and cheering them on. I felt sorry for the kids, especially Saburo. They were so young, and yet growing up too fast in a world of war and death. Thinking it was so romantic. I wondered what would happen to them when they had to face up to reality . . .

JULIE TAMBA · JUNE 10, 1942

After a week's internment . . . *internment,* I can't believe it . . . at a hotel in Virginia, Kenji and I went to Jersey City with forty Japanese citizens and went aboard a Swedish steamship, the *Gripsholm.*

We were told we were heading for the port city of Lourenco Marques in the Portuguese African colony of Mozambique. From there the Japanese government would provide a ship to take us to Yokohama. The Italians would have a ship to take Italian and German deportees to Genoa. In turn American nationals who had been trapped in Japan would be transferred from the Japanese ship to the *Gripsholm* and returned to the United States. . .

We waited for eight sweltering days in the steamy port. Apparently all sorts of diplomatic problems fouled up our departure. The *Gripsholm* seemed to be a fine ship, painted the colors of the Swedish flag, blue and gold, and it had a huge sign, DIPLOMATIC, on its hull so that it wouldn't be attacked at sea. The Swedes were polite and considerate, but there were thousands aboard, three times more, we heard, than the ship's normal complement. Kenji and I, as junior members of the passenger list, were given a tiny cabin with a narrow double-decker bed, no private toilet, and a bathtub that would have given a midget claustrophobia. Air didn't seem to penetrate the sealed walls of this hotbox so we kept the door open as much as possible.

It may sound nutty to say it, but Kenji and I were actually happy in that cabin that smelled of oil and sewage. The big thing was our privacy, which we had more of than in a long time. Kenji could joke that we'd been given a room that the sailors' union would probably reject as an insult to Swedish seafaring men, but I was grateful for the time we could be next to each other, make love and not have a whole barracks listening in.

The New York skyline at dusk, even when the dim-out was in effect and at night when all we could see were the black silhouettes of the soaring buildings, was really exciting. I'd never seen it, and Kenji was equally impressed.

Mostly we all kept to ourselves. The three Axis groups in particular wanted it that way. The Germans talked in their loud voices, jogged a lot, did calisthenics *endlessly,* gathered in blonde, red-faced groups. One of them, a military attaché, demanded that the swimming pool be filled at once so he could have his morning dip. The Swedes obliged him. The Italians stuck together too, mostly complaining about the food. What did Swedes know about pasta? The Japanese, the largest contingent, were clannish even among themselves. As soon as it became known that Kenji was a mere student, a civilian, and one married to an American, we were snubbed. It was, of course, much harder on Kenji than me.

The big news on board was the battle of Midway. Kenji and I read every word in the newspapers and listened to the radio every chance we got. According to the American reports the Japanese navy had suffered its first devastating defeat in four hundred years. The war was turning. The most powerful armada ever assembled had been beaten by the U.S. navy, with a big loss of ships, planes and lives.

The Germans and Italians sneered, made sarcastic comments, avoided the Japanese diplomats and businessmen and military people. It looked to me like the Axis, the three-way alliance that was supposed to rule the world, was a kind of fragile arrangement, if you went by the representatives aboard this ship. Clearly they didn't have much use for each other.

We read the accounts of Midway—the heroism of American marine pilots, the Japanese carriers sunk, the retreat of the Imperial navy, and again Kenji had mixed feelings. I wasn't surprised, but I didn't always handle it too well.

"I'm afraid that thousands of my people are dead," he said to me as we stood at the rail sharing a New York *Times.*

"Well, then maybe they ought to call it off."

"It isn't that easy, Julie. I've tried to tell you . . . the military runs Japan. They'll lie about Midway, to their own people, even the emperor. They'll fight to the end and people will think they're winning when they're losing."

An Italian journalist walked by just then, chattering about the fall of Tobruk in North Africa, the Nazi drive into the Soviet Union. I saw him buttonhole a German businessman and heard them both agree that the British and Russians were finished and the Americans had better get out of the war while they could.

Kenji and I looked at each other, saying everything without needing to say anything.

We waited in the muggy harbor, waiting for orders to sail. We were prisoners, we couldn't leave the ship. A barbed-wire fence went all around the dockside area. Armed soldiers patrolled. My God, they acted like they needed protection from *us* . . . It was a nightmare time. Julie Varnum, all-American Southern California girl, an enemy of the people? I grabbed hold of Kenji's arm, so tight he winced. But of course he understood. Probably better than I did.

Kenji . . . my husband. Lines were deepening in his golden brow, the skin I loved to kiss, to stroke. He was so beautiful. But now he seemed in pain. At least I could understand that. He was tormented by his deep national feeling for his people, at the same time full of hatred for the militarists who had shoved the country into a horrible bloody war. He didn't want millions to die, but he confessed that sometimes he wondered if that might be the only way Japan could ever be recognized as an equal ... "No," he would quickly say, "I don't really mean that. But the West" ... he would look at me, hoping not to upset me ... "the West, yes, even your wonderful country, Julie, bears some blame. Too many westerners still think Asiatics are *born* inferior, and you can tell by the color of the skin." And then he would shake his head violently and add that he was not making excuses for what Tojo and his men had done ...

"Lies." A Japanese man in a gray suit suddenly was on us. His name was Mr. Doihara. He was pointing to the *Times* in Kenji's hands. "Why do you read that, young man?"

"Because I can't buy the *Asahi Shimbun,* sir," Kenji said, trying to humor him.

"Then you should read nothing."

He told us he imported machine tools, that he actually liked Americans but was sorry for them. He hadn't, he said, been able to "convince them they were doomed." He had his own "sources" about the war, including Japanese shortwave broadcasts. No doubt about it, he told Kenji, at Midway the American navy had been wiped out. Japanese forces had occupied the island and also grabbed the Aleutians. So now they had created "a giant pincers that would crush the mainland of the United States."

"Your wife is German?" this all-knowing jerk asked.

"I'm an *American,*" I said, quickly.

He bowed. "I have many American friends. I bear them no ill will. But they must realize that the war is over—"

"I'm afraid not, Mr. Doihara," Kenji said. "It is just beginning."

Doihara left us alone after that, but I saw him huddling with Japanese officers, whispering to them when Kenji and I walked by. We were outsiders, pariahs.

We sailed from Jersey City on June 18. No sooner were we underway, passing the Statue of Liberty, steaming for the open sea and then south toward Africa, than a group of Japanese naval officers actually tried to take command of the ship.

It sounds hard to believe but it's true. In starched white uniforms, peaked hats, swords slapping at their sides, they climbed onto the bridge, forced their way into the captain's quarters, stopped some petty officers on deck and proceeded to give them orders. One Japanese commander brought out a set of international signal flags and began to send messages to a junior Japanese officer on the bridge.

On the second day at sea the Swedish exec officer ordered an end to this nonsense and put out an order that if the Japanese navy men didn't stay out of the way of the Swedish crew they would be thrown into the brig. A shrewd fellow, he did allow a ceremony . . . if it could be called that . . . on the captain's deck, with much bowing, nodding, grinning and heavy breathing, and that was the end of the Japanese officers' attempt to seize command of the *Gripsholm*.

Kenji and I had watched this comic affair with astonishment—not so much at the Swedes' successful effort to assert their will but at the gall of the Japanese military.

"But they gave in so easily," I said. "They caved right in."

"They knew it was hopeless. So long as protocol was observed they were willing to submit. It isn't always so easy to convince them, I'm afraid . . ."

Later that day while we were walking the deck, we passed a group of Japanese—men, women, civilians, military—doing calisthenics under the barked commands of a Captain Sumitomi, one of the brass hats who had tried to take command of the *Gripsholm*. The busybody Doihara saw us walk by, went into a huddled conversation with the naval officer and then the two of them came up to us. They did *not* bow.

"You are Mr. Tamba?" Sumitomi asked.

Kenji bowed. "I am, sir."

"You must join the exercise class."

Kenji turned to me. "Do you want to, Julie?"

"No."

"My wife is not interested."

The captain said, "You are *Japanese*. You are a government functionary. Tenno Heika expects you to show your unity."

Kenji looked flustered. The Japanese in the calisthenics class were staring at him. I could see the struggle going on inside him. As for me, the truth was I'd been feeling kind of lousy . . . the heat, the waiting, the sudden change in my life. Kenji knew and understood this, yet he also wanted to be part of the Japan he had left . . . Kenji once told me that Japanese really hate being alone, separate. They crave large groups of their countrymen they can sort of immerse themselves in. They love their crowded cities, they enjoy traveling in huge groups, individually lost in a sea of faces and bodies. They can't wait to be in a crowded classroom or a military unit, merging their personalities.

Kenji, thank God, was different, but he still had some of the same basic grounding. Anyway, enough to be part of this group of countrymen.

"What do you think, Julie?"

"I think," I said, smiling a bit too brightly to cover my annoyance, "I think we can get all the exercise we need walking. If you need more, you can always chase me up and down the rigging."

Captain Sumitomo and Mr. Doihara looked shocked. But then what could they expect from a *gaijin* wife?

Kenji kept a straight face as we continued our constitutional. The Germans stared at us, confused, disapproving. The Italians, though, were friendly and invited us to eat with them. But Kenji still seemed under a strain . . . tense, uneasy.

It turned out I didn't have much of a stomach for an ocean voyage. I got miserably seasick and had to spend more time than I wanted in a deck chair. The cabin, hot and cramped as it was, lost its romantic setting when my stomach was in my mouth. Kenji brought me endless cups of tea, tried to divert me with his quiet humor. We talked some about our friends and families, especially Ed Hodges, and Carol and my brother Chris. But nothing really turned the trick. Julie Varnum Tamba was one sick—and, frankly, scared—girl having to grow up in one very big hurry.

YURIKO KITANO · JUNE, 1942

How I could be attractive to *anyone* in ugly *mompei* I don't know. Well, at least the bloomers hid my bulging stomach.

This warm summer day I started out by lying to my mother, telling her I had to work an extra shift at the munitions factory. Midori and I went into a subway lavatory and powdered our faces, lined our eyes, straightened our hair. It surely was a relief to get out of the filthy factory, away from Umezu's snarled commands, the overworked people. We had spent part of the afternoon digging air-raid ditches in back of the factory, and my hands were blistered. I'd almost backed out of the secret meeting Midori had arranged but she had convinced me . . . didn't I want to be convinced? . . . that it would "do me good" to meet another man. Not just a man, she'd said, but a foreign man—a *gaijin*. Safer, that way, she'd added, which made the whole excursion seem even more forbidden. I've

always been sort of crazy, I guess, but this was really acting it out . . . I'd
lied to my mother, and if I were ever found out I would bring shame to
the family, which I did not want to do. Hideo would divorce me—was that
so bad?—except divorce would mean I'd be disgraced and probably
thrown out of our house. But I *needed* . . . needed a kind word, a smile,
someone just to *talk* to . . .

We rode a streetcar to Asakusa, walked through narrow streets and
came to a café called the Purple River. Small and plain, it had a threadbare
purple curtain in the doorway—the only explanation for its name. Or
maybe the only reflection of the name.

"I'm worried," I said to Midori.

"Who'll ever know?" was her simple reply.

I envied her. "I will, I'll know—"

"Good. Then it will make you feel better. That husband of yours doesn't
deserve any better treatment. You told me so."

Well, that wasn't exactly true, but I had been indiscreet with her
. . . I hadn't heard from Hideo for a month but I did know that *Akagi*
had been part of the great victory at Midway. The radio and newspapers
just two days ago had told us that the victory over the Americans was
total, the enemy had lost many ships.

I didn't know what to believe, and right now was too nervous to think
about it as Midori and I entered the dimly lit cafe. Two men were seated
in the back at a western-style table drinking tea. They got up and bowed.
One was a stocky young Japanese with a withered leg whose name turned
out to be Muto. He was Midori's boyfriend, and she'd told me he was
"political" and did secret work. What that meant I had no idea. The other
young man was named Hans Baumann. He was thin, kind of sickly
looking, but also rather handsome. We Japanese tend to think of westerners as fat, gross, clumsy, big-nosed, giving off the smell of meat-eaters. Did
you ever see those drawings by some of our printmakers of Dutch sailors,
or the Americans who came with Perry? Huge, disgusting men.

But this Hans Baumann was thin enough to satisfy any fish-eating
Japanese, and with a fine-boned face that was almost feminine. Certainly
not threatening. He was chalky white with a blond mustache that drooped
sort of comically and blond hair that came to just below his neck. He
looked like a religious person or a poet, was my first impression.

"Hans, this is my friend Yuriko Kitano," Midori said.

Baumann bowed again. "I am delighted to meet you, Yuriko."

I bowed too, feeling ridiculous in my work bloomers. Then to my
surprise Midori and Muto excused themselves, said they had to look for

an apartment and felt it would be better if we were left alone. I really thought I was going to die.

"Please sit down," Hans Baumann said.

Shivering on the inside, I did so. He ordered tea and smiled at me. "You are very pretty."

"These awful clothes," was my brilliant response.

"You make them beautiful."

He spoke excellent Japanese, almost without an accent. I asked him how he had learned it, trying desperately to divert the conversation from myself.

"I'm a journalist. I've been in Japan for two years and have made it my business to speak and read Japanese."

"I've never known a journalist. And to speak and read our language . . . my brother told me that when the Jesuits came to Japan they had such problems learning our language that they decided it was invented by the devil to keep the Japanese from becoming Christians . . ." I was talking too fast, rambling. Still, he seemed interested in what I had to say. The only other man who had ever paid any attention to me was Kenji.

"Well, I don't believe the Japanese language was invented by the devil," he was saying. "And I believe one's religion is a matter of choice."

"Are you a Christian?"

"No."

"I thought all Europeans were Christians."

"I was born one," he said. "But I have no religion in the usual sense. I'm an atheist, which doesn't make me exactly popular in the West or the East."

I wasn't sure what an atheist was, but didn't say so. He asked did I know any other Europeans or any Americans. I told him about Dr. Varnum and his Swiss wife, and he seemed to have heard of them. And I told him about my American sister-in-law, and how we'd heard that she and Kenji were on a ship at this moment bringing them to Japan and how I was looking forward to their arrival. "Of course, the rest of my family doesn't care for the marriage," I said. "We Japanese, as you probably know, look down on the *gaijin.*"

"Yes, I know . . . Do you look down on me, Yuriko . . . ?"

It seemed strange for him to be calling me by my first name. Many Japanese husbands spend a lifetime and never refer to their wife by name. It's *you,* or *do this.* He asked if Midori had told me anything about him, when I didn't answer his first question.

"Just that you were nice and intelligent—"

"And lonely."

I said nothing, although I wanted to say how I felt . . .

"I've heard your husband is at sea. Do you miss him?"

I hesitated. "I should not be sitting here drinking tea with you . . . a stranger. I shouldn't tell you anything about my husband or how I feel . . ."

"Would you like it better if I talked about myself?"

"Oh, yes, that would be easier."

So he told me he came from a city in Germany called Bremen, a port like Yokohama. He had no parents, his father had died in the first World War and his mother had abandoned him to relatives. He had studied hard, worked his passage to Japan and was a correspondent for magazines in Germany, Austria and Switzerland.

"How do you like it in Japan?" I asked.

"More now than before, Yuriko."

"You must not pay me compliments. It makes it more difficult . . ."

He nodded, seemed to understand. We sat there, sipping tea, saying nothing, and I felt my heart beating under the ugly khaki blouse. When he did speak his voice was soft. He did not raise his voice, and he did not touch me. He did look directly into my eyes, as if he were really interested in me. Hideo scarcely glanced at me when he was home, I was a piece of furniture or a rock in our garden.

I told Hans Baumann I had to leave, that my parents would wonder why I was so late and that I felt badly about lying to my mother that I was working late.

He didn't try to argue with me, but it was also clear, I thought, that he was disappointed as he walked me to a bus stop. It was dark now, no street lamps were lit, just a dim glow from tiny shops along the narrow street in Asakusa that showed people lining up for newly baked rice cakes.

"May I ride home with you?" he asked.

"Please, no . . . I don't want anyone to see me, I have done a bad thing—"

He laughed quietly. "Yuriko, I have not even held your hand."

He had not, it was true. And at that moment, the two of us waiting for my bus in the dim damp night, I wished fervently that he had.

"May I see you again?" he asked.

"I don't know, Midori must have told you that . . ."

"What?"

". . . That I am carrying my husband's child. You could have guessed from my shape."

"The *mompei* hides it. But that's no reason for us not to be friends."

I bowed to him. "You are kind, I have enjoyed your company." I wanted him to kiss me. I craved it.

Finally he did touch me, took my elbow to help me get on the bus, then waved to me. I could see him smiling as the bus pulled away, and wondered if I would ever see him again . . .

MASAO TAMBA · JUNE, 1942

It is getting increasingly difficult to keep the truth about Midway from the public. People keep asking questions—where are our heroes? Why are there no photographs of the American ships sinking? Why no victory parade?

The truth is that we have suffered a terrible defeat.

My father-in-law Sato and his friends are seeing to it that as little as possible leaks out. The newspapers and the radio are under orders to be silent about our losses. And they are considerable. I've seen secret reports: four aircraft carriers sunk, including the *Akagi,* on which my brother-in-law Hideo Kitano was serving, 3,500 seamen and pilots lost, three hundred planes shot down. Who could imagine that the Americans were that strong?

Yamamoto overplayed his hand. He made a serious strategic error, we in the army feel. He sent the fleet out with a double mission—defeat the American navy and invade Midway. It proved to be too much for his forces. And the American marine pilots had surprises waiting for him. I still can't imagine how they managed to sink *four* of our carriers.

But none of us are discouraged. The Americans tell the world that this is the turning point of the war, that we have had our last victories. They do not understand *Yamato Damashii,* the unbeatable spirit of Japan. They will still feel the cut of our sword.

Today I was at a planning meeting where we discussed the strengthening of island bases in the South Pacific, new landings that will allow us to cut off the Americans from Australia and the Philippines. I am itchy with all this planning business. I am a field soldier. I need to be back with my division, confronting the enemy, the way we did in Malaya, and Singapore, and the Philippines.

We returned to the planning rooms and reviewed the occupation of certain islands and the strengthening of existing bases. I was the junior officer present, but they were all eager to get information from me. My combat duties in China and Malaya have made me a valuable adviser.

But what excites me is that I am to command an assault force that will land at an island in the Solomons group. It is called Guadalcanal.

JULIE TAMBA · JUNE, 1942

The slow passage to Africa goes on and on and on . . .

We docked at Rio de Janeiro but couldn't leave the boat. Almost four hundred more Japanese who were living in Brazil came aboard now and the *Gripsholm,* already crowded, became suffocatingly packed. We ate in shifts, the water supply was reduced.

Kenji and I were not, as I'd worried, snubbed by all of the Japanese. Unlike Doihara and the military, the ordinary people were really kind and considerate. Every day Kenji would give me a lesson in Japanese. Sometimes some of our shipmates joined these deck classrooms and encouraged me to use the right accent. We laughed a lot and while hundreds of thousands of people were suffering and dying in different parts of the world we sailed along under our neutral flag, eating regularly, playing cards, taking the ocean breezes. . . .

Months later I would learn from Aunt Cora what Ed Hodges was going through while we were sailing along, and I felt guilty as hell—except I didn't need to . . . things had a way of evening themselves out.

Aunt Cora was the first non-Japanese to make contact with Ed after he was brought to Yokohama in that filthy prison ship. Being Swiss she had an official position with the International Red Cross. The Japanese were careful about what the neutrals thought about them. They wanted their side of the war to be reported in a way favorable to them and gave the Red Cross and other neutral agencies a lot of room to operate in. Dr. Joachim Reinhold, a Swiss physician working for the IRC, had kept asking for permission to visit a POW camp, and when it was finally granted he asked Cora to go with him on a supervised tour of a POW barracks in Tokyo.

Their Japanese driver took them to an abandoned rusting warehouse near the railyards. He was, Cora told us, a talkative old man, and said that Prime Minister Tojo had announced that all prisoners must work or starve. But, he added, he'd read in the *Asahi Shimbun* that these prisoners were well-treated, got good food and medical care. They didn't deserve it, though, because having surrendered they had no rights and could just as well have been left to die. Real nice.

Armed guards examined the papers presented by Aunt Cora and Dr. Reinhold and were told that the visit would be no more than fifteen minutes, plenty of time to see for themselves that the POWs were in tip-top health.

The warehouse was cold and gloomy, almost no lights coming through filthy windows. The men slept under rags on triple-tiered bunks. The POWs' heads had been clean-shaven and they had a sickly pallor even though most of them worked out doors. In the center of the room was a "smoke stand"—a big sand tray the men were to throw their butts and matches into, something permitted only after working hours.

A Japanese sergeant was joined by a Japanese lieutenant who took Cora and Reinhold into the sleeping quarters. The men ate there too. At night a wheeled cart of slops—usually cold chunks of rice and a stinking fish stew, mostly heads, tails and bones—was wheeled in. The prisoners called it "the Good Humor truck." God, you had to have a grim sense of humor to call it that . . .

The visitors would be allowed to talk to a small group of prisoners—there were four hundred men in the barracks—and then leave packages from the IRC. Cora said some of the men appeared to have been beaten and cut. They had bruises on their faces and arms, and one, an American marine sergeant named Guzzo (Ed's buddy) had a bloody bandage on his head.

When Aunt Cora asked Sergeant Guzzo what happened to his face, he hesitated, looked at his guard and said he'd fallen from a hoist he was operating in the railyard.

At that time Ed Hodges was in fairly good shape. He'd survived the awful passage and stayed in condition by exercising and jogging when they let him. But Cora noticed that his gums were bleeding and there were sores around his mouth. Dr. Reinhold complained to the Japanese lieutenant that many of the men seemed malnourished. The officer said anyone who worked was well-fed. Besides, these men had no rights. There was, the officer told them, a "select group" of American and British prisoners who were writing for Japanese newspapers and radio stations, providing English language articles so that "everyone will know the truth." They were, it turned out, Quislings who furnished copy for Tokyo Rose.

When backs were turned Guzzo whispered to Reinhold that there were thirty-five men in sick bay—dying, diseased, getting no medical attention. Cora didn't mention it to the Japanese officer out of fear he would suspect Guzzo, and she saw Ed warning the sergeant to can it.

When packages were handed out, Ed managed to pass a scrap of paper to Aunt Cora: "LT. E. HODGES, GLENDALE, CAL. TELL FAMILY I'M OKAY."

Cora was shaken by her visit to the barracks. The Japanese had gone out of their way to make the awful place presentable, but the misery of the prisoners couldn't be hidden. The Swiss consul would convey the information to the United States, she decided, and send a telegram via diplomatic pouch about Lt. Hodges.

She tried not to think about what would happen to the prisoners once she and Dr. Reinhold left.

YURIKO TAMBA · JUNE 25, 1942

My son Hiroki was born a week before the neighborhood association staged the "great victory parade" to mark the destruction of the American fleet at Midway.

I've come to believe the real strength of our country is its hardworking people, especially since my time in the factory—not the bloodthirsty ones at the top. I now have more respect for a wrinkled old woman who has spent her years in the rice paddies than for an army of pompous officers. I know this puts me at odds with my brother, whom I love as I must, but that is my peculiar situation. And it is why, as I stood on the veranda of my parents' home and watched the victory parade, I felt a sudden pain in my heart . . . I did not want Hiroki to grow up to be one of those who lived only for power and conquest. Strange ideas for a Japanese girl, you might think, but as you may have noticed, I am a bit strange anyway. I tend to think for myself, but try not to show it . . .

There were drummers and flute players, people in ancient Japanese costumes, kids dressed like *samurai* in cardboard armor, wielding twin swords like their hero Musashi.

In the playground across from our home, where an antiaircraft battery now stood, my father was asked to introduce the member of parliament, Kingoro Hata, who had come to Shibuya Ward to tell everyone they had to work harder for victory.

From the veranda, holding little Hiroki, I was able to see Hata get out of his black limousine. A beautiful woman, her hair done up geisha-style, was in the automobile. She had a serene face, almost like a statue. Not a young woman but stunning. She was, as we all knew, Hata's mistress— Satomi, the owner of a geisha house, the Plum Blossom. She stayed in the car.

I felt very lonely. I would have even welcomed Hideo at that moment. His baby son wanted the caresses of a father, although Japanese men aren't much at touching and kissing and stroking their children—it is considered unmanly. There was another reason I felt uneasy, even afraid of my feelings . . . I thought of Hans Baumann. I remembered how gentle he had seemed, and his interest in my life, my family. I felt guilt and excitement as I thought of him . . .

Hata was making a bombastic speech about the way the war was going: "The American fleet is rotting on the ocean bottom. Japan will *never* be invaded, I can assure you," he said. No nation on earth could overcome the Son of Heaven and no people could defeat the children of a god.

Applause. We had a terrible need to believe in His Majesty and our soldiers and sailors, no matter how extravagant the claims. Still, there were questioners:

An old woman asked in a loud voice, "If we won a great victory at sea, Mr. Hata, why can I not see my son who fought there?"

The crowd stirred. I wondered the same thing. The battle had been fought more than three weeks ago. Why no letters from the men who served on the ships? Why no letter from Hideo? The old woman was saying that her son was a stoker on a destroyer and—

"They will be home soon," Hata loudly interrupted. "And, madame, it is not your place to question the divine decisions of Tenno Heika."

The last thing I saw was my little brother Saburo leading a file of schoolboys soliciting money for the families of war dead. I wondered how many yen Mr. Hata and his geisha friend gave to that worthy cause. Damned little, I suspected.

My baby smelled sweet and clean. I wanted him to grow up in a peaceful world. I wondered if Hans Baumann, that pale man from a strange land, might be able to tell me things that would make me more hopeful. As soon as I was strong enough to go back to the factory (it was agreed by the family that I would return to work and that my mother would look after Hiroki) I would try to see Hans Baumann again . . .

MASAO TAMBA · JULY, 15, 1942

I paid a visit to the tomb of the forty-seven *ronin.*

In the mists around the Sengaku-ji Temple I contemplated the graves of those warriors who redeemed the honor of their *daimyo* by killing his murderer. Foreigners and other informed people forget that this remarkable event took place late in our history—it was in 1702 that Oishi Yoshio cut off the head of the evil lord Kira and placed it on his master's grave . . .

I mention the relative closeness in time of this heroic deed to emphasize that the forty-seven *ronin* woke up a sleeping Japan to the realization that *bushido* was *not* ancient history, that the spirit of courage and honor still was imbued in Japanese warriors.

As I prayed and lit incense, I reflected that I was part of a divine army that was again reminding the world that modern *samurai* were not to be mocked, ignored or pushed into some dusty corner of history. *Bushido* lived again. The enemy knew it by now.

That night I made love to my wife Michiko, who is surely more beautiful than the prostitutes her father takes me to, but she is still a wife. A good one, I agree . . . she keeps the house clean, cooks rice as finely as did my mother (not too damp, not too dry) and is attentive to our daughter Maeko. But a man who lives on the edge of death needs more comfort than a wife's body, her prescribed areas of entry. That is all good and fine and perhaps sufficient for a farmer or a metalworker . . .

And so Colonel Sato took me again to Satomi's Plum Blossom House, where I spent the rest of the night with the former *maiko.* She sang in my ear. Her tongue found every part of my face, every opening of my body. I came to climax, roaring, bucking like a he-goat.

I did not get home until dawn. Michiko was feeding the baby and was not angry. Seeing her serene and beautiful, a loyal wife, I felt a twinge informing her that I was leaving by plane for the Solomon Islands in two days to assume a new command. She did not cry, though. She understood.

* * *

On the flight I thought about the stage we had reached in the war. At the highest levels of command, generals and admirals brimmed with confidence. Midway was a temporary setback. The United States was struggling to get its navy in fighting shape. We had been advised by our agents and by neutral informants such as the Soviet Union, who observed their neutrality pact with us, that President Roosevelt had given first priority to the defeat of Germany, which meant that the bulk of American arms and troops would be sent to Europe. Good news for us! The dregs of the United States forces would be fighting us, and what could they do? We occupied a heavily fortified string of islands across the ocean, places bristling with guns. How could they invade and conquer them, and then attempt to subdue our impregnable island fortress of a homeland? Meanwhile we grew stronger every day—oil from the Dutch Indies, rubber from Malaya, rice from Indo-China, cheap labor from Korea. It would have made sense for the United States to sue for peace.

But they were difficult to predict. What would they do next? Reading an old illustrated manual on the martial arts of the *samurai,* I tried to find some lesson in it, some clue to how and where the Americans would strike . . . There is a form of combat called *bujitsu* in which two swordsmen face one another in a kneeling position, thereby limiting freedom of movement. Each man is armed with a sheathed sword. Arguments have raged for centuries over the best method of *bujitsu.* Does one attack first? Or should one wait for the opponent's first move and then counterattack? Volumes have been written and illustrated about the correct mode of fighting *bujitsu.*

It seemed to me that the Americans and ourselves were now in that position. The oceans were our "seated position," limiting freedom of motion. But how to attack? Perhaps that had been the mistake of Midway. By moving the offensive, we suffered the enemy's punishing counterblow. Puzzling. Perhaps the Solomons, especially the tiny islands of Guadalcanal and Tulagi, to which I was being dispatched to shore up defenses and create strategy, would provide an answer.

We had been on the islands since May 5. The British occupiers, who with typical English blindness had built a cricket "pitch" but had failed to emplace artillery, had been captured or had fled. When I arrived with my staff there were five thousand Japanese troops on the islets, mainly Imperial marines and construction workers building an air field.

I immediately held staff meetings, assuring the commanders that more forces would be landed, that the completed air strip would insure our defensive posture. It was unthinkable, I told them, that the Americans would dare attack us. Every book on military strategy I had read stated that amphibious assaults against heavily dug-in positions defended with automatic weapons and artillery could *not* succeed.

Again, it seemed, we and the enemy were like two knights, kneeling and facing one another, awaiting the first stroke in a *bujitsu* match . . .

I tried to sleep in my tent under mosquito netting. Tulagi and its sister Guadalcanal were cursed places. The stink of rotting vegetation permeated our clothes, our skin. Clouds hid the 8,000-foot peaks. Rainfall was intense, providing little relief from the heat. Tropical birds screeched throughout the night and every known variety of biting insect attacked us.

I realized, of course, that ordeals far worse than a wasp bite or a soaked cot might be waiting for us . . .

YURIKO KITANO · JULY, 1942

My husband Hideo finally came home, six weeks after his ship, *Akagi,* went to its grave.

He seemed almost bleached, thin, less apelike. He had lost much of his arrogance, he did not speak much, but he did seem to love Hiroki. He would hold him until the child wet or cheesed, then hand him to me. He also cried at night after drinking a half bottle or more of sake, mourning his dead comrades. He told me how he and his shipmates stood at attention in a lifeboat as *Akagi* descended into the ocean and sang "Kimigayo," our national anthem. It was impossible not to feel for him, and for perhaps the first time to see him as a person who could be hurt like the rest of us.

Sometimes he would grow silent, fall flat on his back and just stare at the ceiling. He was also drunk a great deal. Over and over he would mutter, "How? *How?* How did they do it? They had so few planes. We sank all their ships. They are cowards. How . . . ?"

He would turn on his side and cry like a child, and I felt I had to lie with him, enfold him in my arms and mother him. He expected it of me, I could not deny it to him. So I rocked Hideo in my arms, and dreamed of Hans Baumann . . .

Eventually Hideo was sent to a port on the inland sea for duty aboard a cruiser, and I was alone again, Hiroki spending his days with my devoted mother while I worked at the munitions factory. In that impersonal atmosphere, I dared to express some of the ache I felt when I thought about Hans . . . I had secretly now begun to think of him in that more personal way, calling him by his first name and daydreaming—nights too —about seeing him. Finally I told Midori, and she reacted quickly, as I knew she would.

It was not so easy to lie to my family about Hans. They believed me. Everyone was working long hours. The day before, Midori, who saw the boy Muto almost every day, had arranged to get a message to Hans, and now here I was, riding the bus that hot summer's day to his flat. Riding along, I found it difficult to think of our country as being at war. People were taking vacations, going to the beach and mountains, lingering over tea, seeing movies. There's a myth among the *gaijin* that we Japanese are in love with death, that our young men die so willingly, anxious to give up life for the emperor and not caring anything about life. That's an exaggeration. The generals, and their lackeys, spread this impression. But what was happening that summer said something else. People were swimming, traveling, walking in the parks, enjoying their children. Girls wore their brightest kimonos as soon as they could get out of the *mompei*. Our word for war is *senso*. It was hardly ever spoken. Midway? Another victory. Guadalcanal? No one knew where it was.

My heart was light, though beating very fast, as I got down from the bus near a western-style cafeteria in Minato Ward—and there was Hans, waiting for me on the corner. Crowds of people, gaily dressed, swarmed into the restaurant, and just as many seemed to be coming out. The women, now in oversupply, looked like brilliant butterflies.

Hans took my hand, saying it was too nice to be indoors. Why not walk to the Hie shrine, where a festival was to take place, honoring the god Onamuji and his "monkey messengers"? He bought us paper containers of fried squid that we ate as we walked along.

I apologized for my get-up and said that next time . . . I was getting awfully bold . . . I'd wear a kimono, a yellow and black one, my favorite. He said I was the most beautiful girl in Tokyo, and when he took my hand as we crossed the street I squeezed his palm.

We had never kissed or even touched one another so far . . . but he smelled so clean, and his eyes were soft and understanding. With Hideo I mostly felt he was looking past me or did not see me at all. With Hans it was quickly as if he and I were the same person. We merely touched and our flesh seemed to unite.

At the shrine we sat near the gates and rested. People were sitting on the grass enjoying picnics, and for a moment I felt guilty, leaving my son with my mother and being, as I saw it, unfaithful to Hideo. But I *craved* Hans's company. He made me feel . . . worthy, something more than a servant and a receptacle. I felt *alive* with him . . .

I told Hans that one would never think our country was at war. Everyone seemed gay, so full of life. People were joking, calling to their children . . .

"Yes," he said, "people are about living. Too many of their rulers specialize in death. The people don't want this war, they never did."

"Then it should end."

"Those who have the guns and power won't let it end. I'm for a world when power will belong to the farmers, the workers and students, and mothers like you, Yuriko."

I told him I thought that sounded fine, but wasn't too sure how it could happen. He only looked at me, smiled and said nothing. I asked him if he lived far from here. He didn't. If we got tired we could go to his flat, he said. And then, having asked about it, I felt ashamed of myself, but no use denying it . . . deep in my heart was a need to be alone with him.

Hans put his arm around me. People ignored us. There was so much gaiety, so much happiness around the shrine. War? Impossible. This was July—sunny, hot, full of life.

We walked to the outer gardens of the Meiji shrine, and there under a row of cypresses, as night fell on the city, Hans took me in his arms and kissed me—my forehead, my hair, my eyes, my lips, my neck. He put his tongue into my mouth, and I felt faint.

"I'm afraid. I must not do this—"

And protesting, weakly, I kissed him back, our tongues touching, all of us touching. I felt we had merged, and it brought an excitement that surpassed anything I had ever known—in pleasure, and fear.

JULIE TAMBA · JULY 21, 1942

Lourenco Marques . . .

I'd never heard of this port on the east coast of Africa, and here we were, wilting in the July heat, waiting for transfer to the Japanese ship that would take us on the rest of our trip.

When the *Asama Maru* came into the port, flying the Rising Sun flag, all the Japanese on the dock—we'd disembarked—stood at attention. The military attachés led cheers for the emperor, and everyone began singing "Kimigayo."

Kenji did not cheer. He sang in a subdued way. We were told that the United States ambassador to Tokyo, Mr. Grew, was aboard the ship and that the *Gripsholm* would bring him back to America. There was also an Italian merchant vessel in port to take the Italians and the Germans to Europe. The Italians talked a great deal about getting a decent meal, and the Germans predicted that the war would soon end and everyone could get together and fight Bolsheviks. They already had another war lined up before this one was finished. Terrific.

Kenji and I stared at the African laborers, handsome black men, carrying our luggage aboard. They seemed from another world.

It turned out that not all the Japanese on board were unfriendly to us. The civilians—business people, teachers and so forth—were warm and interested, and seemed impressed that Kenji was associated with the Ministry of Education.

But the officers, *never* without their swords, avoided us and herded their wives and children away when they saw us. Even as we climbed the gangplank of the *Asama Maru,* trailing a giant African who carried our trunks and bags as if they were trinkets, the uniformed muckamucks ignored us.

Kenji tried to ignore their attitude but I could see he was hurt. Captain Sumitomi looked the other way when we approached. Kenji was not included in the military conversations. His bows were not reciprocated. And, once again, I knew it was my fault.

Once he tried to say a few words at the bar with some young officers who were talking about the victory at Midway. Kenji had tried to give them the American version of Midway. The young officers stared at him, took their drinks and left the bar. He was a pariah and traitor to them. And I . . .

So it was lonely on board the *Asama Maru.* We managed to pass the time playing cards and word games, me struggling with my Japanese lessons, the two of us laughing at my problems with the strange language. We even got to like the awful cramped cabin, but you could take just so much of it.

One day Kenji and I were in deck chairs on this Japanese ship—God, I felt alone and *alien.* I'd put down my notebook and picked up the phonetic dictionary Kenji had gotten for me, puzzling over some difficult characters. As I concentrated on the figures, wondering if I would ever get even a slight understanding of this impossible language . . . sorry, Kenji, but it really is—love you, not your lingo, darling . . . a boy of about five ran up, grabbed the notebook and ran off with it.

Maybe a lot of frustrations spilled over in me, but I took off after the boy. He dodged me and began to rip pages out of the notebook. A brat is a brat, on that at least East and West do meet . . . I grabbed him, pulled the notebook from his hands and yelled at him. "Hands off, kid, learn some manners—"

At which point his mother sailed up, a fat woman in a green dress, grabbed him, hid him from the insults of the *gaijin* witch and proceeded to bawl me out, in Japanese, naturally.

Kenji was there now, trying to smooth things over, saying that the notebook was important to me, that I was trying to learn Japanese . . .

By now a small crowd had gathered. People clucked and looked pained, as if I had committed some crime against the youth of Japan. People at the rail who were watching the frolicking of porpoises turned away to witness the uncivilized behavior of the American woman. I was steaming.

"They forgive you," Kenji said.

"Forgive *me?*"

And now people were laughing as the boy whimpered and hid behind his mother's skirts, she patting his shaved head and assuring him (I presumed) that the next time he wanted to steal someone's notebook and make confetti out of it that would be just nifty with her. There was much bowing, apologies all around—none to me—and Kenji and I retreated back to our chairs.

"Can I ask a dumb American question, beloved husband?"

Kenji knew I was a storm about to break.

"Why didn't anyone discipline that little monster?"

"Julie . . . he didn't do anything so terrible. I'm afraid American and Japanese kids aren't so different in some ways—"

"Bull, my beloved. He stole my book. Ripped pages out of it. Wouldn't give it back. Thought it was a great thing to do and—"

"He's a child, Julie."

"So what? If he doesn't learn now, when? He's the kind who could grow up and shoot prisoners."

A dark shadow covered Kenji's golden face. "No . . . you don't understand—"

"What? What don't I understand?"

"The boy was feeling his *amae*—"

"*Amae?*"

"It's a Japanese concept, it's not so easy to explain—"

"Try me, scholar. I'm not stupid, you know."

Kenji sat on the lower part of the deck chair and leaned forward. It was a very hot day. We were sailing toward the Indian Ocean and our port of call, Singapore.

"*Amae* . . ." Kenji wrinkled his brow. "We all have it. I mean, mostly all Japanese males do . . ."

"Great—but what *is* it?"

"A sense of dependence . . . no, it's more subtle. *Amae* is the feeling that all infants have when they are at the breast of their mother. Dependent, completely passive, an overwhelming need to be loved without returning that love, an unwillingness to leave the warm place, the protective flesh of the mother."

"But *all* infants feel that way at some time, whether they're breast-fed or not."

"Yes, yes, but for many reasons, cultural and biological, in Japanese people this sense of *amae*, of indulgence, acceptance, safety, comfort, gets prolonged throughout adult life."

"And so spoiled brats."

"That's too simple, Julie. It is more than being spoiled, the way you mean it. It's actually a force that, well, that shapes our character. I'm not defending it, I'm trying to explain it. Look, the Japanese male grows up convinced that every person he meets bears him goodwill and will indulge him. And since he is the recipient of eternal love from his mother, he can be indifferent to the feelings of others."

"Is this *your* theory too?" I was not exactly delighted by this lecture.

"No. One of our psychologist evolved it. It's a theory, but one that has a great deal of truth, and it does make for problems, I realize. It blurs standards . . . the child may very well have stolen your book and tried to destroy it but—"

"By his lights, by this—what d'you call it?"

"*Amae.*"

"*Amae* . . . yes. He has the *right* to do what he wants and devil take the hindmost. If ripping pages makes him feel good, fine, terrific. Besides, he figures I'll approve of his male behavior. Right?"

"More or less—"

"Do *you* believe in this theory?"

"There's some truth in it, as I've said."

"But, Kenji, if everyone in Japan, the men anyway, are convinced they have everyone else's goodwill and approval and all that matters is the nice warm feelings they're after, what happens when people start competing? I mean, a woman has only two breasts and one warm body. Suppose six guys want it?"

"That is why we have a strongly disciplined society. To keep such needs satisfied in an orderly fashion. Beyond that, *amae* is remarkably flexible, and paradoxical. It makes us docile and violent at the same time. We can be unrealistic in what we seek but very clear-sighted about it. We can be spiritual yet materialistic. It's a useful tool, a way of life that has let us survive, prosper. Remember we are a poor nation, crowded, tiny in area. *Amae* has helped us survive—"

"At what cost? Those soldiers who murdered civilians in China and Malaya. I know you hate to hear this, but the death marches . . . the killing of hospital patients . . . is that the end product of *amae?*"

"In its worst form, yes . . ." His voice was almost faint. "They assumed that they would be indulged, I believe that. There's always the mothering breast . . . the emperor's will do . . . to assure them they are loved, and in the *right*. I told you that along with this image of a world there goes a sense that the rights of others can be ignored."

I couldn't believe this was the whole story. Kenji wasn't like that. If the Japanese craved everyone's goodwill, why the hell did they go around bombing and killing and starting wars? Was that a way to win friends and influence people? I decided to cool it for a while. We weren't going to settle the origins of the Japanese spirit in five minutes, and carrying it on could ruin our night . . .

In the cabin as we dressed for dinner—more rice, more dried fish, more salty vegetables—we laughed as we tried to move around each other. I tried to joke. I asked Kenji if he'd seen a Marx Brothers movie called *A Night at the Opera*—especially the scene where dozens of people are crammed into a tiny stateroom.

"A manicurist comes in," I told him as he struggled into his shoes, "and she asks Groucho if he wants his nails long or short, and he says 'You better make them short, there isn't much room in here.' "

He didn't laugh.

"Not funny, huh?"

"I'm not sure I got the point . . ."

"Ah, well, chalk it up to cultural differences. It was crowded, see? Short nails—more room? As if the length of his nails made any difference."

"Oh. Yes. I'm sorry . . ."

I smiled and kissed him. Who said we had to be the same. *Vive la différence*, isn't what what I'd always said? . . .

We kept bumping into each other. The room was smaller than the one we'd had on the *Gripsholm* but at least we had what passed for a bathtub. Actually, it was just about right for small birds but it was welcome.

I struggled out of my dress, put on a bathrobe (ah, Julie, enlightened rebel, still partly inhibited Quaker girl). "May I ask you something?" I knew I shouldn't but I pursued it anyway.

"Please, yes, anything."

"Why didn't you stick up for me out there?"

"When?"

"When? When I had to face down half of Japan because that kid stole my notebook."

"It wasn't an issue, Julie, I *tried* to explain—"

"But there's right and wrong. I don't care about his need for *amae* or whatever it is."

"I told you why it was not a matter of great importance—"

"Not good enough, pal." Careful, Julie.

"You'll have to learn to accept us *with* our failings or things you can't understand. Just as I accept Americans and their failings. Your people did jail thousands of their own citizens because they had yellow skin. I accepted that—"

"Maybe you shouldn't have."

"It was not my place to object."

My head was spinning. I sat beside him on the bed. "But . . . sometimes the truth hurts and has to come out. I don't mean just that boy. I mean people like Sumitomi and Doihara. They go around repeating lies to each other. They keep saying they've already won the war. You know that isn't true, they can't win—"

"Other things matter." He turned on one arm, stared at me, silently asking me to cut it out, to stop baiting him.

"Like what?" Have you ever rubbed an itchy eye because it felt good but you knew you'd be sorry later? That was me.

"Our honor. The face we show the world matters."

"What kind of face is it after Pearl Harbor? Or Nanking?" At least I didn't accuse his brother too.

"We have a different code, some day you'll understand—"

"Sure, sure. The Chinese loved being bayonetted. It made those Japanese boy-men feel warm and cozy. Is that it?"

"*No.* Please, Julie, it's more complicated . . ."

I hugged him then. "Kenji, *you're* no *samurai* blowhard. You told me you were wise to Mushy—is that his name?"

He laughed. "Musashi."

"Yes. The one who split open the head of a thirteen-year-old boy. Some hero."

"All armies can behave brutally. I don't condone things that have happened. But to be obvious, Japan *is* my country. And I wish . . . I wish . . ." Torment showed in his face. He shut his eyes, held me close.

"What?"

"I don't know, maybe an armistice, an end to this—"

"Kenji, my love, you don't know Americans as well as you think you do if you think they're going to roll over and *quit.* Chris writes to me from Hawaii. The navy can't wait to take on the Japanese navy. Midway was just an opener, he says. This is going to be a long and bloody war and the people who started it are going to have to pay the piper."

"Julie, at some point I must defend my people even when they've behaved very badly." He sat up. "Let's stop this, Julie. My head is splitting."

"Right. We have much more important things to decide. Such as who gets the bathtub first tonight."

"Agreed . . . I ask only that you be a little tolerant of me."

"Likewise, sport."

He kissed me. I kissed him back. We didn't bathe right away. On the narrow iron-hard cot we made love, and it was especially deep and satisfying.

YURIKI KITANO · JULY, 1942

My father, saddened by Masao's departure for distant islands, was at least cheered some by Hideo's return. My parents insisted that Hideo and the baby Hiroki and I spend a great deal of time with them. They didn't say as much, but they knew Kenji and his strange wife would soon be living with them and they didn't look forward to it. But they were uncomplaining, unemotional people. I'm sure they were upset by the prospect of an American woman living in their house. Having Hideo and me around would give them some assurance, a sense of a traditional family.

My father especially liked it when Hideo wore his starched white uniform and the colorful ribbons and medals he'd earned at Midway and

Pearl Harbor. But to my amazement my father, who spent his days around the palace, where he picked up gossip and rumors, was still not aware that Hideo's ship, the *Akagi,* had been sunk until one night, as they sat smoking and sipping sake in the rock garden at the rear of our house, Hideo told him. My father seemed stunned.

"Then your victory is even more to be admired," he said, trying to recover.

Hideo nodded. "I'll be reassigned."

My father dropped the conversation, his brow furrowed and he dragged on his cigarette. Seeing them quiet now, I brought Hiroki into the garden, where he promptly fell asleep on my back, snug in his carrying case.

My mother took him from me, then cradled him, kissed him, Hiroki sleeping through it all. "You must never punish him," she said to me. "He's too wonderful . . ."

My mother fussed over Hiroki, crooned to him, took delight in his good looks, his good behavior. I loved my child too . . . but I couldn't help wishing he had another father . . . Hans was in my mind, right or wrong, he was there. This man who was *interested* in what I said and did, who even made me laugh when we talked about the factory. I had once wanted to quit the factory, but the truth was that as terrible as the place was it gave me a convenient excuse to be away from home, to be able to see Hans. Hideo, I was sure, suspected nothing, and neither did my parents. It was my patriotic duty, all agreed, to examine shell casings, to stand all day at the wooden table, and to eat cold lunches. I nodded dutifully.

"I heard Colonel Sato say the other day," my father was telling Hideo, "that Midway is of no importance anyway. The strategy now calls for an invasion of Australia."

"Good, good," said Hideo, who puffed on his cigarette. At times I felt very sorry for him. He was not educated, he had barely passed his officer's training, he seemed . . . well, lost . . .

"Yes, yes," my father went on. "The first step will be to conquer New Guinea. Anyone who looks at a map can understand that. A wild country, filled with black savages. Once New Guinea is under our flag . . . one more corner of the world beneath our roof . . . then the road to Australia will be open to us."

"They say Australia is very big," Hideo said.

"No matter. Look at China. We are conquering it. Look at the Pacific, even bigger. Nothing can stop us, the colonel says so. He met with the General Staff last week. Once we've fortified New Guinea we'll dare the Americans to invade. And that will be the end of them, it will free up our forces to invade Australia . . ."

None of this interested me, it seemed a lot of fairytales. I had suspected earlier that we were being told lies about Midway . . . why had Hideo been kept in barracks in Yokohama for so long, why did he cry so much about his lost ship and his dead comrades . . . ?

Hideo and my father talked about Masao. Was he in New Guinea? No, my father told him, Colonel Sato said Masao had gone to some island called Tulagi to make sure it was properly defended.

"Don't worry about Masao," my father said. "He's a *samurai*. Wherever he is, we will win. He took Singapore by himself—well, with a little help."

They smiled and laughed and got drunk on sake. It's strange about our men. Sober, they are proper, they observe rules of behavior in public. They bow just the right way, keep their emotions in check. Drunk, they weep, laugh, act like children, roll on the floor. Hideo had a very small capacity for drink. He loosened his stiff collar now, belched loudly, excused himself.

"Where is Hideo going?" my mother asked.

"Man's business," my father informed her. "Yes, he's a real man."

I knew, of course, that he was off to a whore and later he would come back and expect to nestle in my arms.

Watching him go off, my father stared at the sand and rocks of our garden. "I envy him his youth and his daring," he said. "All I do all day is serve tea and count linens."

And suddenly I saw my father in a new light . . . as a man with sorrows and feelings. It was, sad to say, a startling revelation.

MASAO TAMBA · JULY 25, 1942

There is something about this island I do not like. Not at all.

From the air it looks like a tropical wonderland—bright green trees, soaring volcanoes, winding rivers. It is also feverish, dank, stench-ridden, as if Nature herself is dying here.

I have been told that my assignment is a brief one—survey the terrain, position the troops, move on. My hope is I will be sent to New Guinea. I suspect the allies will strike there. If we can subdue them, wipe out the

Australian and American forces, we can threaten Australia. But of what value are these insect-infested Solomon Islands?

The men stationed here are mostly engineers and construction workers. I prefer the Imperial marines. I have asked for reinforcements but no one seems to take my requests seriously. At night my officers and I, after a day of training with the troops, pore over maps. What, I ask myself, can these islands mean to anyone? Tulagi is a scrap of earth. Across the strait is the much bigger Guadalcanal, a useless place with few paths, scruffy plantations, and ugly black savages in grass skirts who ignore us and can't be made to work. Even when we executed a few by example it didn't help.

About all I've seen accomplished is the finishing of a primitive runway on Guadalcanal, the erection of a signal tower and a camp for pilots and air crews. True, Guadalcanal is our most southerly base. It is inconceivable to me that an American attack would succeed. Or for that matter even be launched. For one thing, with our air strip complete, we now have an effective land-based air arm. There is no way the Americans can match that if they try to land. They will be supported only by carrier-borne craft. I'm inclined to believe our intelligence reports that say despite our losses at Midway, American losses were also grievous. And their ships are spread thin across the Pacific.

So we wait, play cards, smoke, drink, try to summon up radio contact with Tokyo. The news is good. The Germans are marching through the Crimea and the Soviets may topple any day now. Yes, Russia is neutral, but we hope for a quick German victory to put pressure on the British and the Americans and force them to back off in the Pacific war.

I suppose I should feel confident, at ease. But this damn jungle bothers me. The men seem corroded, feverish, sapped by the heat, the damp, the bug bites. And still, no one in Tokyo has honored my request for reinforcements.

There have been a few cases of venereal disease, picked up by our men from the black women, whose ugliness would be a barrier to anyone of sensitivity. I have had these men punished. A better alternative is in one of the enlisted men's tents—a safe and clean substitute are life-sized inflated dolls representing beautiful Japanese women.

"Sanitary and satisfying," I told our medical officer. He didn't think it was funny, and was surprised that I would. Actually, I was a little surprised myself.

Kenji Tamba · AUGUST 1, 1942

We were told that in a few days we would be docking at Singapore, the Lion City of the East, which Japan now occupies, thanks no doubt to soldiers like my brother.

The weather turned hot and humid, sleeping was difficult and the noisy fan in our cabin did little to relieve the heat. Also, by now water was being rationed.

Julie was mostly good-natured about the voyage although we'd had our tense moments. She'd perfected an ingenious scheme for bathing and doing our laundry at the same time. I'd catch her crouched in the ridiculous tub (not much bigger than a pot) washing her lovely cream-colored body, the water making her long yellow hair gleam, and then scrubbing my socks. The best of famous American know-how, and I was the fortunate beneficiary.

Mostly we'd laugh, try to ignore the heat and the clatter above us—there always seemed to be platoons of Japanese kids running around in wooden sandals. I'd sew buttons on our clothing or try to fix the wind-up alarm clock that my brother-in-law Chris had given us . . . "This is not what the man of the house does in my country," I told my wife. Actually I'd gotten rather good at buttons.

"Suffer, buster."

"Why this *buster?*"

"It's an expression," Julie said. "Don't ask me to explain. It's as subtle as your tea ceremony. Please God, don't let them turn off the water until I've rinsed my panties . . ."

"I'll make this up to you, Julie. We'll share the biggest tub I can find. A quiet inn in the mountains, lots of pure hot water from a natural spring, fluffy towels—"

"And privacy. Just you and me."

Suddenly she was feeling sick to her stomach. I helped her out of the midget tub, wrapped her in a towel and she promptly vomited into the tiny sink, tears clouding her eyes.

"What a spoilsport," she said. "Here I am having fun in my bath and scrubbing our underwear and I ruin our fun."

She looked pale. Beads of sweat covered her forehead. I kissed her.

"You must go to the ship's doctor at once," I said.

Dr. Fujitani, a tiny man in a white coat two sizes too big for him, examined Julie. He was sympathetic and seemingly more interested in my American wife's background than her ailments. He had gone to Pomona College for two years, thought the war was idiotic and dared to say so.

"Yes, yes, UCLA," Dr. Fujitani said. "Lovely campus. I dated a Nisei girl from UCLA. I went to their track meets."

It was an effort to get him off college memories and onto the matter of my wife's illness. I pressed him. Did Julie have only an upset stomach or a parasite or—?

"Oh, no, nothing of the sort. Mrs. Tamba is pregnant."

We stared at each other, then hugged one another.

"That explains the nausea. It is natural. Try to eat boiled foods. No raw fruit or vegetables. Exercise daily. Do not smoke. Think restful thoughts. You are in excellent health, Mrs. Tamba."

We walked out on deck, arms around one another's waist, not caring what the other passengers thought. They never, as is our custom, showed affection in public. Men and women pulled back even from the touch of a hand. Some raucous boys laughed at us and started to shout *"gaijin"* at Julie. We didn't care.

The sea was like liquid steel—gray blue, almost oily in appearance, full of deep secrets. We circled the deck, and in a corner near the lifeboats embraced and kissed again. And again.

"War is hell, isn't it?" Julie asked me.

"What . . . oh . . . ?"

"I promise I won't confuse you. General Sherman said it. In our Civil War."

"You're making fun of my ignorance—"

"I am *not*. Let's see . . . the exact quote goes, 'There is many a boy who looks on war as all glory, but boys, it is all hell.' "

"Ah. Which side was he?"

"Union. The man who marched through Georgia."

"It is still all hell . . . except we are together."

She kissed my ear. "That's what I meant. People are dying and we're so lucky. You're the best man I've ever known, Mr. Tamba. You put up with me. You let me kid you, you're taking me home into God knows what. I know this isn't easy for you. Your family won't exactly jump for joy when they see the wild *gaijin* with her blonde hair and blue eyes. I'm putting a burden on you and I know it—"

"No, no. You're the brave one. And my parents will like you." (Did I believe that?) "When they hear you are having my child, they'll welcome you." (I did believe that.) "You'll see. You'll be a real Japanese wife. Kimono, *obi, tabi* socks, *geta* sandals, a fan. Not so bad, Julie. And I adore you. I love you so much . . . I wonder how our men can live the way they do, ignoring their wives, staying away from home. Not this man. If you are my Japanese wife, I'll be—"

"My American husband."

We held hands, circled the deck again. We talked about our honeymoon, remembered how we had made love in the hotel in Coronado . . . did it happen there? . . . how we craved the private bed, the secret room where we could devour each other with passion, cry and shout our joys, feed our love on each other's bodies . . . I did not have the heart to tell my beloved wife how cramped and public and uncomfortable a Japanese house can be, or that women keep a cloth nearby to stuff into their mouths so as to stifle their cries of passion when they make love?

We talked about our child to come and made plans for him and decided he would go to UCLA, or if he preferred, to Columbia or Harvard. Professor Adachi had attended both universities and I said I would consult him as soon as we were settled.

"He's a little young to be a freshman, isn't he?" Julie teased.

"He may be a *she.* I won't complain."

"Right. I have to stop thinking like a Japanese. Women count also, don't they?"

"As they always have in my mind."

I promised to consult with one of the ship's cooks and get him to bake a rice cake flavored with almonds, a delicacy guaranteed to strengthen the child within my wife. My child. Our child.

YURIKO KITANO · AUGUST, 1942

I couldn't help overhearing a conversation today between Dr. Adam and Dr. Cora.

I was the only one in the waiting room—I had brought Hiroki to the clinic because he had a summer rash on his bottom—and was waiting quietly when I heard their voices.

At first I could not believe my ears. Then I huddled in the corner, wanting to hear more. They were such good people, so kind to everyone, that their words filled me with sadness.

"I admit it. I forced you into this life," Adam Varnum was saying. "And what is it? A prison life. Maybe I should have opened a practice in

Los Angeles, turned down the Society of Friends, raised a family in California."

"We waited too long for a child of our own," Cora said.

"My fault, my fault—"

"No, Adam. We made the choice. Then . . . my operation, one of the penalties of advancing age, even for a doctor."

"I never let you have a child so you could be a mother. Too much on my mind. Keeping this place going, battling for funds, fighting the damn bureaucrats. And now, trying to survive. Forgive me—"

"There is *nothing* to forgive. I love these people as much as you do. I don't blind myself to their faults. We can never be one of them. We're outsiders. Still, I admire them and want to help them, it makes up for what we've missed."

"My levelheaded *Schweizerin* . . ."

I felt so guilty, but it was revealing to hear them talk, people in their forties (although Cora looked much younger), and hear them sigh as they kissed.

"They say that after two thousand years of neutrality and democracy all that the Swiss have to show for them is the cuckoo clock," Adam was saying. "I know differently."

A joke of some kind, but not too clear to me.

"Cora, did I ever tell you how yodeling was invented?"

"No . . . Adam, cut it out . . ."

"You have to do *something* in Switzerland."

She laughed briefly, then her tone became serious as she talked about her visit to the American prisoners and how a young man had given her a name and an address. It wasn't too clear to me, and my English is only fair although I studied it in school for many years.

Then Hiroki woke up and let out a howl, and Cora came out and asked me into the office. I wondered if they suspected how I had overheard them.

They fussed over the baby and Cora applied a yellow salve to his buttocks and he howled again. They both asked about Hideo, about Masao, and if I knew the exact date when Kenji and their niece would be arriving.

I said I didn't, just that they were coming, but I liked talking about our family. It pleased me that the Varnums would in a way be related to us now.

Cora was surprised that I was still working at the munitions plant. I think I almost stuttered with nervousness as I said I didn't mind the work, it got me out of the house and kept me from worrying too much about Hideo . . .

Adam showed me a photograph of Julie's brother. His name was Christopher, Dr. Varnum said, and he was a blond, handsome young man. He must have been very well-educated because he was a war correspondent for the American radio station and he was with their marines now on some island.

"Is he married?" I asked.

"No," Adam said. "He's had a lot of girl friends, I gather. He writes that he knew your brother at UCLA, and he especially hopes your family will be good to his sister."

"Oh, we will." (I would, anyway.)

Adam reminded me that the life of a Japanese wife in her mother-in-law's house was never easy, and for a *gaijin* daughter-in-law it could be even more difficult. Cora said that the International Red Cross had advised her that they expected the *Asama Maru* to arrive in Yokohama in about ten days. The ship bearing my brother and his wife had left Singapore and was steaming north, in waters that our Japanese navy controlled. So passage would be safe, they said.

I couldn't wait to see Kenji and his wife, and I wondered why our countries had to be at war. It all seemed a terrible mistake . . .

Cora gave me a present—a little pot of English raspberry jam—for the baby, and then they both kissed me. I didn't mind. Not at all. Bowing was fine but Hans was teaching me the loveliness of the touch of someone's lips.

MASAO TAMBA · AUGUST 7, 1942

Now it is we who have been caught sleeping. I had warned Colonel Sato that the Americans will not simply fade away and leave us to our island bastions.

Yesterday a huge American invasion force steamed around Cape Esperance and blasted Tulagi and Guadalcanal with their batteries.

I wanted to make a fight on the beaches but headquarters decided otherwise and they were probably right. My ill-trained construction workers were not fit to meet the invaders so we decamped and retreated into the marshes and mountains of the interior.

The truth was our intelligence had shamefully failed us. Had I been an intelligence officer attached to the South Pacific command I would have slit my belly and paid the price for my stupidity. The Americans, big guns blazing, planes zooming overhead, invaded the Solomons without a shot from us in return. We would have to fight doubly hard to extricate ourselves from this disgrace.

Yet even as I watched the terrifying display of firepower from the enemy, I had a sense of hope. All the guns and bombs in the world would not force us from these islands. Our supply lines were of course much shorter. More troops would soon come in. And what I saw of these marines—my first look at Americans in combat—told me they would not measure up to my men. They seemed overburdened with gear. They were hesitant and clumsy as they clambered down landing nets, stepping on each other's fingers. They fell into deep waters. A few drowned. Many cried out in pain when they suffered cuts from the sharp coral reef.

On the beach at Tulagi—*Beach Red,* they had named it—they seemed to mill about aimlessly. Supplies were disgorged from landing craft as if vomited up—crates, vehicles, weapons in a never-ending stream. Meanwhile, the sea and air bombardment, while driving us inland, took only a few lives and served to increase our determination to hold the high ground.

Through my binoculars from our bunker at the eastern end of the island I could see American officers puzzling over maps, trying to figure out why their landing had been all but unopposed. I had set a trap for them, a series of escalating dugouts on a red clay cliff overlooking the British cricket pitch. The flat surface of the field would be a temptation to any attacker. When he reached the cliffs we would have a bloody surprise for him.

And of course they came—a battalion of the best fighting men in the American forces. By now they had control of the town of Tulagi and it was clear that they meant to sweep the island and then mop up on Guadalcanal and seize the airstrip.

More men waded ashore. They seemed surprised, perhaps a bit disappointed that we had given up the beaches without a fight. I actually saw two men tossing a baseball and laughing. Well, they would have laughed less if they knew what we had waiting for them. The terrain, for example. Once dug in, entrenched, reinforced with artillery, we could annihilate them. My men traveled light, needed little in the way of food or medical care, had become jungle creatures. These heavily laden Americans in their hot green combat suits and heavy boots, their odd-looking weapons, would not last long. Fever would take its toll, malaria, parasites, the miasmas of the hellish island . . .

Of course I was bothered by my order to pull back without a single shot in answer to the invaders. On Guadalcanal our airfield workers fled so quickly that the marines found their breakfast rice warm in their mess tins, and indeed, stumbled on a massive refrigerator filled with good Japanese beer. The Americans seemed to have no respect, no sense of dignity. On the side of the refrigerator they had painted a sign: TOJO ICE FAC-TORY: UNDER NEW MANAGEMENT. Such clowning augured well for us. Fools, I believed, do not make good soldiers . . .

And so we burrowed into the cliffside above the cricket field. I was convinced that massed fire from our protected positions would teach these stumbling *gaijin* what it meant to fight Japanese marines. Without their bombarding planes and ships to help them they would taste fire, drink blood, feel their guts spurt from their bellies and either die or run . . .

My defensive position was, I believed, impregnable. No one could outdo Masao Tamba at preparing a defensive complex. In the tall trees around the field I had posted snipers. On the face of the cliff and on its crown I had positioned some two hundred men, two companies of the toughest Imperial marines. They had machine guns, grenades, rifles and ample water and rice and sake. Each dugout was reinforced with layers of felled trees interspersed with earth that were superior to concrete in absorbing shell fire. They bent but did not break. They took thousands of bullets and grenades and afforded us firing slits from different angles.

I sent only one order to the men by my subordinate, Captain Shiga. "Tell them," I said, "to defend these posts to their death."

Behind the fortifications were my reserves—two thousand men, a rag-ged collection of workers, supply corpsmen, cooks and civilians. They were commanded by my officers, men who had fought with me in China and Malaya. They were to hold the high jungle ground, while those of us in the dugouts would smash the marine attacks.

They came sooner than I had anticipated. They raced across the cricket pitch and we cut them to pieces. And still they came. Our fire was massed, accurate and devastating. Yet these Americans refused to turn tail. At night I could hear them digging in, posting guards, shouting taunts at us —the worst of these—which revealed their barbarousness, was "Hirohito eats shit." (I shudder even as I use these words.)

I consulted with my aides. It seemed to me we had little to fear from these crude big-noses, so I ordered a counterattack. Half our men would storm out of the dugouts and mount a bayonet charge against the sleeping marines.

We charged out of the cliffside, firing rockets and small arms, scream-ing, blowing whistles, our officers waving swords to lead the advance. It was not cowardice but practicality that made me remain in the common dugout. Should I die, there would be no field grade officer to command our small unit.

But the marines were not taken by surprise. Huge men, they rose from their foxholes and engaged us in mortal combat, first with small arms, then with bayonets, then with their fists. Under the glare of rockets they grappled with our men, and for every stroke of the sword they took, they responded with bayonet strokes, mighty blows with their rifle butts. They were bold and strong and they died shouting curses at us.

And they were not afraid to die. We had met a worthy foe. I had been wrong about the courage of these American fighting men.

By morning the field was covered with chunks of raw meat—the remains of bodies, Japanese and American. Flies formed clouds over them. Carrion birds tore at the dead flesh. The stench was nauseating. I noticed that the Americans were meticulous in removing their dead and wounded. Far behind their lines I could see a hospital tent, vehicles, much coming and going. There was a hospital ship offshore, a luxury we did not have.

"Advise the men we will attack again," I told my adjutant. "Tell them that the Americans have shown weakness by caring for the wounded. We give our lives without regard for these matters."

But it was not our turn to attack.

The next day, having cleared their dead and wounded, the Americans stormed the heights, and died under a hail of bullets, tumbling in bloody heaps, losing arms and legs and heads, disemboweled corpses, faces turning into squashed red masks . . .

And still they kept fighting. They could approach our position from only one direction. A flanking attack or an assault from the rear was impossible because of the impenetrable jungle, my snipers and the tangled terrain. So they scaled the red wall of the cliff. Men died, clutched their smashed heads, their bleeding bodies. And a few would battle their way to our dugouts and drop sticks of dynamite into them. Others hauled up a terrible new weapon, a flamethrower that roasted my men alive. By the end of that awful day almost all of my defenders had been blown to raw red bits. Others were turned into charred offerings. Still others went mad and raced into the open air to be cut to pieces by bullets.

Our men in the frontal positions were all killed. They had fought until they ran out of water, rice, ammunition, and I had to control myself to keep from weeping as I saw them overwhelmed. By nightfall all two hundred of the defenders were dead, either in their holes or on the cliffside.

My mind keeps returning to a vision of Corporal Amano, one of my best noncoms, whirling in circles, a human torch, flames swirling from his shaved head, his uniform crisping, turning to ash, blisters of blood and flesh popping on his charred figure. *He whirls, whirls, spins as the marines pump bullets into him . . .*

After that I ordered my commanders to pull back. It made no sense for all of us to die at the cliff. There were stronger positions inland. There were rivers to protect us, caves to hide in. We rallied our men and left during the night. In three days of fighting, we estimated, we had killed more than a hundred Americans.

After three more days of fighting—the marines trailing us, hounding us—we joined forces with the reserve units. Of my two thousand men, only *twenty-three* were taken alive. Apart from myself, my staff and a cadre of noncommissioned officers, every Japanese in that first battle had died for the emperor. Could I not be infinitely proud of them?

And yet at night, in a lean-to of palm fronds, eating canned fish and soggy rice, squatting on my helmet, I had nothing to tell those who had survived. This had not been China, where we cut through the Chinese bandits like a sword of flame, turning the earth crimson with their blood. This had not been Malaya, where the British and Indians heard our first shots and threw down their guns and ran.

These were a different breed of soldier we were facing. So it would be our divine duty to kill them all, to convince them of the immorality of their courageous fight. And if we lost . . . well, there are worse things than defeat. A death with dishonor is one. Surrender is another.

As we sat under the fronds, hammered by furious rain, trying without success to raise Tokyo on our shortwave set—everything rusted in this fungus-cursed place—I found some dog-eared maxims of battle in my tunic and read them aloud to my men. We drank the last of the sake by candlelight. We could hear the guns of the American fleet pounding away at Guadalcanal.

"I will read from *Hagakure*," I told the shivering men. "Save a cup of wine that we may drink to the wise words of its author."

The men nodded.

I read: " 'The way of the *samurai* is found in death. If the choice is between life and death the *samurai* must choose death. There is no more meaning beyond this. Make up your mind and follow the predetermined course. Day and night, if you make a conscious effort to think of death and resolve to pursue it, and if you are ready to discard life at a moment's notice, you and *bushido* will become one. In this way, throughout your life, you can perform your duties for your master."

The men sighed their agreement. We finished the sake, posted sentries, slept.

The next day, as if in answer to our courage and our prayers, we learned on the radio that our navy had smashed an American invasion fleet off Savo Island, not far from Guadalcanal. I could tell from the report that this was no new misrepresentation like the Midway disaster. We had truly whipped the Americans—four of their cruisers and a thousand seamen lay in the mud of the straits off Savo. For the time being their marines would be without naval support. The defeat was a double disaster for the Americans. Their fleet was crippled. Meanwhile more of our troops would be landed.

"Fellow officers," I said, "we shall have our day. Let these round eyes learn how it will be to fight us again, when we have more men, more arms, and a renewed spirit."

We gave thanks to Tenno Heika and drank his health and knew in our hearts that we would hold the island forever.

JULIE TAMBA · AUGUST 20, 1942

We docked in Yokohama today. What a relief to be on dry land again. Full of Kenji, our happiness, I had no fears, no worries about my new home. Kenji was cheery and encouraging. We had weathered the glares and snubs of the posturing military types (tin soldiers, Kenji called them) and had become friendly with several civilians including the chirpy little physician Dr. Fujitani, who gave me vitamin B pills and warned me that beriberi was widespread in Japan because of the rice diet. I had asked Kenji at dinner a few nights before we ended our voyage, why the army and navy officers acted so apart, so differently.

"Rank has its privileges," he said. "But more than that. The *samurai* were supposed to have been finished off in the Satsuma rebellion in 1877. A *samurai* army—rebels, students, hotheads, led by a reactionary soldier named Saigo—tried to defeat the national army of conscripts in the service of the Meiji emperor. Remember, Julie, that the emperor was modernizing Japan, rejecting a lot of the old feudal business. Anyway, these draftees, the emperor's army, defeated Saigo's Satsuma gang. Saigo committed *seppuku* and the other *samurai* fell to the government soldiers' bullets."

"But that should have done them in."

"It did and it didn't. As a fighting force they were through. But their traditions lingered on in the military. Fight to the death. Never be taken alive. Suicide rather than shame. Saigo, a traitor, is honored today. There's even a statue of him in Tokyo."

"Confusing, isn't it?"

"And depressing. I try not to think of it. I'd rather think about us."

Kenji stroked my hand as we lingered over soggy rice cooked with bits of anonymous fish that tasted vaguely of library paste. Two adorable little girls at the next table giggled and covered their mouths as they watched us holding hands. I wondered what our child would look like. Would he (or she) suffer for being a mixture of races? Me, the pale-skinned blonde Californian with my cowlike eyes (Kenji said they were full of life) and Kenji, lean and golden, with his narrow black eyes, the shadows that formed subtly on his cheekbones? All I wanted was a healthy and happy child, one who would be enriched by both cultures. I believed in it and looked forward to it.

"*Samurai* has been the curse of Japan," Kenji said in almost a whisper. "You would not believe the rules that were devised to perpetuate it. A warrior must always be perfectly groomed—toenails trimmed, hairknot oiled and perfumed. To die with neglected grooming is to be despised by the enemy. There were even rules against artistic accomplishment. Although, in fact, some *samurai* were poets."

"Why not? Look at David."

"Who?"

"King David. He was a poet, a musician and a nifty dancer. But he was also a warrior."

"But he wasn't Japanese."

"No, darling, not unless he kept it a secret." I said it with a mock-serious face, which he looked into, then began to smile. Ah, his American kidder . . .

We switched our attention to a mauve-colored dessert. Either old bread pudding or young tapioca. We moved it aside and sloshed our insides with green tea. Actually I was beginning to crave tea, it seemed to settle me down, quiet my nerves. Kenji said I'd fit right in . . . "I've heard that we have one hundred and thirty-two types of tea. Our tea ceremony, as you know, is a religious observance. We even honor tea with a title, *O-cha.*"

"Well, here's to *O-cha*," I said as we lingered over dinner, watched Japanese businessmen dance with their mistresses. Several of them had brought lady friends aboard and were now dutifully returning them to original owners, was my guess. A four-piece band played soupy renditions of "Stardust" and "Cheek to Cheek." Somehow I wanted to hear a *sa-misen* or a *koto*, to see some geisha girls. It was all so western. I said to

Kenji that maybe the *samurai,* in trying to hold onto old traditions, had something on the ball.

"The old *samurai,*" he said, responding to my opening, "in the seventeenth and eighteenth centuries weren't all bad. They were often philosophers and scholars and administrators. Cruel, yes, but at least with a role in society. The militarists corrupted the system. They hate intellect, art, the gifts of the mind. Oh, there are exceptions. Yamamoto, a few others. But most of them really distrust intelligence. They even warn their soldiers not to look too smart. They want their men to train, to fight, to die and no questions asked."

Poor Kenji . . . he was so torn—one moment miserable over the old tradition of combat and class, and then feeling he had to defend it. That became even more obvious at a "lecture" the next night delivered by the strutting Captain Sumitomi. We sat in the back row. I tried to melt into the wall, being, as usual, the only Caucasian in the room. Kenji provided a running translation for me and it was pretty much what I expected. Captain Sumitomi warned the returning Japanese that they would be expected to work hard for the emperor and win the war. As people who had the privilege of serving His Majesty overseas, of being exposed to the *gaijin,* they were now in a unique position to offer their knowledge of the outside world to other Japanese. But in that very knowledge, Sumitomi went on, "there lay traps and temptations." Perhaps some of them had contracted bad habits in America and England and other foreign places, the way people can catch rare diseases in tropical countries where they have little immunity. They would have to examine their consciences to see whether "un-Japanese" ideas had infected them.

"Like not wanting rice four times a day?" I whispered to Kenji.

"Nothing that serious," he said. My husband was becoming a jokester.

Sumitomo then was pointing at the women, a group of Japanese *hausfrau*s who grinned, tittered and covered their mouths. The tone shifted from stern to paternal, the captain chuckling, slapping his riding crop or whatever it was, against his boots, strutting on the raised platform. When he was *finally* finished, all rose, applauded and bowed deeply. Me included. When in Rome . . .

When Kenji and I left, Dr. Fujitani joined us for our last constitutional around the deck. The sea was calm. You could hardly believe we were in a war zone. But the calm was understandable. The American navy and air force, the forces of the other allies, had been neutralized, kept far from the shores and waters of the island empire.

"What were the women giggling about?" I asked Kenji and the doctor.

"Captain Sumitomi was reminding the women about their wifely duties according to the rules of Confucius," Kenji said.

"What was so funny?"

"They laughed as a sign of respect," Dr. Fujitani told me. "Very old rules."

"Such as?"

Fujitani raised his hand. " 'Approach your husband as you would Heaven itself, for it is certain that if you offend him, punishment will be yours.' "

"Were you getting that all down, Kenji?"

He took my hand. "Every man learns those rules, every woman has to obey them. Let's see . . . 'the lifelong duty of a woman is obedience. She must be courteous, humble and conciliatory, never peevish and intractable, never rude and arrogant.' Sumitomi wanted to make sure the women got over any seditious notions of equality."

"Boy oh boy, am I ever in trouble," I said and squeezed his hand.

Dr. Fujitani, eager to enlighten me further on the duties of the good Japanese wife according to Confucius, took up the lesson. " 'You must be ever attentive to the requirements of your husband. You must fold his clothes and dust his rug, rear his children, wash what is dirty, be constantly in the midst of his household, and never go abroad but of necessity.' "

"Wow," I said, "go directly to jail."

"I beg your pardon?"

"A sort of joke, Dr. Fujitani. But nothing about Sundays and Thursday afternoons off? Nothing about Mother's Day or time off for good behavior?"

"Mrs. Tamba has quite a sense of humor, doctor," Kenji said, careful to smile when he said it. "She knows that these are old rules and that Japanese men treat their wives decently."

"Well," Dr. Fujitani said, "women expect nothing else . . . it's their job to cook, sew, raise children, clean the house and obey. They like it that way and so do we." He was not smiling. I shut up for once, but was boiling on the inside.

"Confucius was a good man," Kenji said, playing peacemaker, "but he wrote things that especially related to *his* times, although some of it is practical and applicable today—"

"Such as?" I asked, reverting to my old self.

Kenji said, "He believed that there were five dreaded maladies that afflict women's minds," Kenji said innocently. "Indocility, discontent, slander, jealousy and silliness—"

"The sage went further than that," Dr. Fujitani jumped in. "He said that these ailments infected seven or eight out of every ten women and . . . well, indicated the relationship of women to men."

"And you *believe* this?"

Dr. Fujitani shrugged. "It is a way of thinking. It is a concept. One can examine it and analyze it and perhaps reach no conclusion . . ."

This was what passed for Japanese logic, at least in a debate, I was learning. I asked Kenji whether he agreed with the great Chinese teacher and the inspirer of so much behavior in Japan.

"No, of course I don't believe it," he said. "I mean, women are not inferior. We all have our roles. Without women how could the human race go on? Besides, they're prettier than we are."

I'm not sure his comment—almost as evasive and vague as Dr. Fujitani's—reassured me too much. But I was excited about our imminent arrival, the prospect of meeting my new family, Kenji's family. I was, literally, about to come face to face with a new life. Confucius or no Confucius. Julie Varnum Tamba had arrived.

KENJI TAMBA · AUGUST, 1942

No one from my family came to meet us in Yokohama.

Julie was surprised and I think hurt, but I tried to explain that my father could not take a day off from his job at the palace, Saburo was at a technical school and my mother and Yuriko were probably occupied with the new baby and household chores.

I was surprised by the lack of military security at the docks. Welcoming families and friends were allowed to flood in past the gates, seemingly without credentials. There were newspaper reporters and photographers all over the area and of course they tried especially to interview me and Julie.

"Ah? You are German? Swedish?"

For some reason Julie was always assumed to be an ally or a neutral. She was tall, blonde, and altogether American-looking, but many of our people found it hard to accept that one of the enemy would willingly come to Japan. There was, however, no overt hostility toward her from the journalists. Indeed, they all smiled a great deal, tried to use their English and asked good-natured questions. I wondered if my family would be as accepting . . .

We were both struck by the holes in the ground all around the port. "What in the world?" Julie asked. "A convention of moles?"

"Air-raid shelters . . ."

They looked pitiful and ridiculous. The "shelters" were about ten feet long and three feet deep. They were everywhere—in empty lots, in front of shops and public buildings, in gardens and parks. Orders, it seemed, had come down from the highest level of government to start digging, and I wondered at the defeatist attitude it indicated. Up to now our rulers had been so cocksure, forever telling the people that Japan would never be bombed again. The Doolittle raid was quickly dismissed as a mistake, something that could never happen again.

There had been a heavy rain and the "shelters" were half filled with muddy water. Mounds of wet clay bordered each pit. People dug, squatted alongside the holes examining them and a few teenage kids were actually lying down in the muck and staring at the sky.

"No roofs?" Julie asked.

"Those will come later, I guess. We are the world's greatest improvisers."

Julie seemed downcast, not only because of the failure of anyone to meet us but also at the sight of the rusting, dirty appearance of Yokohama. The war was draining all our resources, the impoverishment on the home front reflecting it. Trolleys creaked along on rusting wheels. Bicycles rode on flat tires. Taxis and trucks belched black smoke from charcoal burners. People seemed dressed in drab colors—grays, khakis, blacks. The flowery kimonos of a few years earlier were no longer in evidence. And everywhere —queues. People lined up at kiosks for a newspaper, at grocery stores for their rice ration, at beer halls where they could get a weekly ration of weak brew. The queues seemed interminable—blocking streets, spilling into the curb, rounding corners, vanishing down narrow alleys.

And the people . . . they looked thin and weary—and the war was not a year old. The reason for it was no mystery. The hungry maw of the military machine ate up food, medicine, clothing, creature comforts. The millions of people clopping along in wooden sandals, just as they did under the shogun and the *daimyo,* would bear the burdens and suffer.

I managed to engage the services of a creaking taxicab and after much arguing the driver agreed to take us to Tokyo. He said the trip would eat up his week's gasoline ration, so I promised to pay him extra. He helped me load and tie our bags to the roof of his aged taxi and strap boxes to the rear, and I wondered if the ancient automobile might fall apart under the strain, but by going under twenty miles an hour and creeping up hills he managed.

Julie asked me about the mobs of people everywhere. If so many of our men were overseas, "how come the country seems to crowded?"

"It's the waiting."

"Waiting?"

"We Japanese are the most patient people in the world. The common people, the ordinary men and women will wait forever. Look—lines outside a restaurant at ten in the morning an hour before it opens. Crowds around bus stations and trolley stops."

"But where are they all going?"

"Who knows? Jobs, perhaps. Shopping. Many of them travel just to keep in motion. To see a relative, a friend, to get their minds off the grayness of their lives."

I asked the driver about the people around the terminals.

"Most of them go to the countryside to buy food," he said. "A woman will spend all day traveling to farms, to the country to buy a radish or a pumpkin. Life is better outside the cities. The farmers keep their best things to sell directly."

His explanation had an ominous ring to me. Was there actually such a shortage of food? Was the country as poor and as depressed as it seemed? I'd been gone only a year and Japan looked different, smelled different, sounded different. An oppressive gray cloud seemed to have settled now over people. I saw no joy, no enthusiasm. We passed a broken-down trolley car, crowds waiting patiently around its door as the motorman and an engineer tried to get it to function again. They waited, waited, *waited.* Not a sound rose up from their ranks, not a protest, no laughter.

We did, though, at last get underway on the pitted highway to Tokyo. Jerry-built factories and warehouses lined much of the way, and I could see Julie staring, puzzled and a bit pained, at the pervasive drab of the roadside scenery. True, here and there was a patch of green—a lonely vegetable garden, a tiny rice field. But of the picture-book charm of Japan with which I had regaled her, the parasol pines, the craggy mountains, the lacy waterfalls, the clouds of blossoms, there was almost nothing. Telephone and electric lines formed spidery traceries against a leaden sky, from which there seemed to be a complete absence of birds. A sense of something harsh, metallic permeated the air.

"Why so silent?" I asked, although I knew.

"It's . . . new."

"I know. It isn't very pretty, is it? The war . . ."

"Yes. But why are the women wearing those outfits? Sort of like Turkish harem pants."

"Ah. The *mompei.* So they can work better and not distract the men. They're deliberately shapeless. Otherwise the men would let their minds wander."

The driver, who had heard the word *mompei,* spoke up. "It is unpatriotic to wear kimonos or brightly colored clothing. It makes His Majesty sad. All thoughts must be about the war."

I didn't translate that last for Julie.

Julie Tamba · august 21, 1942

First, the streets.

This narrow winding alley was to be my neighborhood for three years. I tried to locate the quaint, the exotic and the charming, and failed.

The houses somehow seemed thrown together without any plan. Unpainted wood siding, small verandas, blind walls, thatched or tin roofs. The predominating colors were the gray of weathered wood, the dun and dark brown of the roofs. The dirt street itself was without sidewalks, a barely asphalted pocked gutter. Here and there was a tiny shop. Vertical drapes over the doorways advertised what kind of store it was. The only relieving note was a tiny park and playground opposite the Tamba home. It was filled with kids, and they were endearing as they played on the slide, the seesaws, the jungle gym. They looked incredibly clean and well-dressed, full of spunk and laughter. Some older women looked after them —no child, I saw, was allowed to cry very long. The slightest fall or frustration was met with instant affectionate attention.

"The children," I said to Kenji. "They look much happier than the grown-ups."

"They don't know about the war."

"But you're supposed to be winning the war."

"The adults sense it will be a long one. They obey and they carry on."

While Kenji and the driver unloaded our baggage—they refused to let a pregnant woman help, although I suspect your average Japanese gent would have gladly let his wife do the manual labor, it went with the job classification—I waited for them to finish, feeling horribly out of place in my beige summer suit, my two-tone shoes, looking too tall, too pale, too *American*. Some kids gathered to stare at me, snickered and pointed at my hair.

While Kenji settled with the cabdriver I looked at the house, as simple as a log cabin—hand-hewn poles and frames, almost like a large South Sea hut. There was obviously no basement, the house standing on piles of natural stones. But the natural colors, the grain of the woods, were attractive. Under the outer veranda I could see a bench, a place to leave shoes before putting on the mandatory slippers, or if one liked, just remaining in one's socks. Kenji had briefed me on all this, but here it was . . .

"The Tamba home," Kenji said. "Where I was born and raised. Do you like it . . . ?"

I forced a smile, which I'm sure wasn't lost on him.

"Oh, it's much bigger than it looks. Inside there are three large rooms and a kitchen. *And* a bathroom with a big wooden tub and all the sanitary facilities. And wait till you see the garden."

A gangly schoolboy in a blue uniform and a peaked cap came running around the corner, saw us and put on his brakes like Pluto in a Mickey Mouse cartoon. He was painfully thin but as handsome as Kenji. Kenji smiled and nodded. I knew what he was waiting for—the first bow from a younger brother.

"Saburo," Kenji said.

"Hello, Kenji." The lad's face was as immobile as a papier-maché mask. He bowed slightly. Kenji bowed back.

"May I present my wife. Julie, Saburo."

Being of a somewhat daring nature I offered my hand. The younger brother recoiled as if I'd thrust a pit viper at him, staring at me as if I were some weird alien from another world. *Who was I? What was I doing here?* And go *away* . . .

"I'm not exactly in the mood to bow to teenagers, Kenji," I said, "even if he is a Japanese male and your brother."

"Then smile?"

"I *am* smiling."

The two brothers didn't touch, embrace, shake hands. No exchange of affection. But I could see the warmth and feeling in Kenji's eyes. Saburo, sullen and confused, seemed to be struggling to smile to welcome his brother. He was saved from further such effort when two women appeared on the veranda of the house. One, I realized, had to be Kenji's mother, wearing a gray kimono and white socks. Her prematurely gray hair was bound in a bun. She had a too calm, sort of resigned expression, but you could tell that she'd once been pretty. She was, Kenji had told me, in her

late forties, but she could have been sixty. The other woman was young
and vivacious and startlingly beautiful. Obviously sister Yuriko.

We approached uneasily. At the bottom step Kenji bowed twice, to his
mother and his sister, and then introduced me. I bowed, as deeply as I
could, considering the child inside me. I had a peculiar thought . . . would
all this bowing put a crimp in his tiny spine? Pregnancy puts strange things
in your head.

There was a further moment's hesitation to inspect this invader from
another planet. Hisako and Saburo acted as if I were so foreign, so *different,* that they had no prepared attitudes, no means of dealing with me—
even though, thanks to Kenji's drilling me, my Japanese was fairly good
by then.

Only Yuriko smiled. And how I welcomed *that.*

"We are happy to see you," Yuriko said, not at all shy or apologetic.

Her mother then managed a suggestion of a smile.

Saburo lolled against the gray board siding, his eyes not meeting mine,
his weedy figure sprawled.

"Come," Hisako said. "You are tired."

"And the best thing in the world for that is a hot bath," Yuriko said
quickly. "I'll get it ready."

I smiled at her, sensing an ally . . . or maybe I was being unfair to Hisako
and Saburo. After all, I *was* one of the enemy. I'd stolen number-two son,
made a part-*gaijin* of him. Why should the welcome mat have been
thrown out for me?

The interior of the house was charming at first glance. I've always liked
minimal designs, things that are functional and utilitarian. What could be
more barren and yet pleasing to the eye than a Quaker meeting house? My
parents never believed in ostentation, conspicuous consumption, flashy
possessions. The Japanese had the same idea.

My only problem was that there seemed to be no place to sit. Walls,
floor, roof . . . where doth the daughter of Glendale rest her weary butt?
As though reading my mind, Yuriko magically produced soft plum-col-
ored cushions and we squatted on the floor, staring at each other.

Yuriko then presented her baby son Hiroki to me, to handle, stroke,
kiss. He was a handsome clear-eyed child. I know it sounds like reverse
racism but there *is* something about Oriental kids. Their eyes. They look
so sharp, knowing, aware of the world. Kenji says it's because up to age
five the Japanese child is master of his universe—pampered, indulged,
petted, never disciplined, and so develops a deep sense of security. This
celestial state ends once a male enters school, wears a uniform and has to
act toward his teacher the way a boot obeys a marine drill instructor. Still,

that early conditioning has its effect, and I remembered Kenji's lecture on *amae,* the search of the Japanese male for the all-encompassing love that the mother gives . . .

"I hope you have a boy also," Yuriko said. "It would be so nice. Two cousins to play, to swim, to fly kites, to go to school."

I really took to this lady. She'd taken the day off from work, changed from the *mompei* to a gorgeous red kimono with a black *obi* in celebration of Kenji's homecoming, *gaijin* in tow.

Saburo had disappeared. Hisako had set water to boil in the kitchen (were we to be honored with rice so fast?) and Yuriko excused herself to help her mother and start the fire for our bath, slinging Hiroki into a kind of papooselike sack on her back.

The main room's light was dim, a shaft of milky morning sun coming through the partly opened sliding doors that led to the veranda, another beam of light from the doors that looked out on the garden. It was a big room, barren as an empty canvas. *Tatami* mats covered the floor, lovely woven things. There were no windows but the rice-paper *shoji* screens, off-white and translucent and divided into pleasing rectangles, slid on runners to let in light and air. There was a single low black lacquered table over a pit in the midst of the room. But what impressed me was the total absence of decoration. My head had been full of images of bright scrolls, prints, paintings, vases, pottery, flower arrangements. So I was surprised to see that the room had no decoration except for the sacred alcove, as Kenji had described it, the *tokonama,* at one end.

"You seem hypnotized," Kenji was saying.

"It's lovely. I can't . . . well, it's so different . . ."

"It's in the Zen tradition. Refined simplicity, the virtue of emptiness. The *samurai* believed this. Life was to be reduced to basics—"

"But no place to sit, or lie down or read a book."

"You're sitting."

Squatting, was more like it. I would also soon learn that girdles and garters and stockings were of little help in learning the Japanese indoor way of sitting.

"But . . . a desk? A table? A place to toss clothes the way any American kid does?"

"Japan's secret weapon," he said. "Closets." In a swift, deft and almost invisible move Yuriko had produced four cushions. Then like a magician making objects materialize Kenji went to the north wall of the room and indicated a complex of drawers of different sizes, all in finely grained wood, each with wooden knobs. He proceeded to pull them out, reciting the contents like a litany . . . "Floor cushions, *futons,* tableware, scrolls, lamp, clothing, books, extra *tatami* mats, all one's heart desires." He pointed to the steps leading to the upstairs room. "More closets built into the steps. Not an inch of space wasted."

It occurred to me that the arrangement was something like the Japanese character. I mean, on the surface simple, uncluttered, barren, but beneath the facade and hidden in locked closets all sorts of surprising stuff . . .

We sat now around the low table in the center of the room. Street noises filtered in—kids yelling, dogs barking, the cough and rattle of old cars, the *clang-clang* of the motorman's signal from a trolley a block away.

Yuriko in a stumbling English and I in a hesitant Japanese managed a dialogue of sorts over the hot green tea, which I found delicious, with bite and character and a wondrous capacity to ease fatigue. I told her my baby was due in February. She said she couldn't wait, that her sister-in-law Michiko had a little girl Maeko, older than Hiroki, and Yuriko wanted to have birthday parties with all three children. I sensed a sort of sadness in her. Every now and then she would lower her eyes and she barely talked about her husband Hideo, promoted to lieutenant and at sea. In her letters to Kenji she rarely mentioned him. I didn't ask questions.

Kenji, talking to his mother, seemed a different person, respectful but distant. To me he was almost always warm and affectionate. And we *laughed.* No laughs with Hisako.

The conversation had gotten around to Masao, the family pride and joy, now a major, a combat commander, a man the general staff relied on for opinions, strategy and so forth. His father-in-law Colonel Sato had said that Masao could be a general someday, maybe even a high-ranking member of the general staff. The Tambas didn't come from one of the old noble clans like the Satsuma or Chushus but Masao's brilliance and bravery were well-known, I was assured. Hisako got to her feet, opened one of the magic drawers and pulled out a scrapbook—the life and times of Masao Tamba, reflected in newspaper and magazine articles, photographs and artists' renditions of big brother's exploits as a modern *samurai.*

"Well, Julie, that is my brother," Kenji said, and with pride, as he turned pages: Masao in uniform, sword raised, outside a city gate in Nanking. Masao bare-chested, winning a *kendo* contest. Masao in Malaya, posing with grinning fellow officers, holding captured British flags. Masao on some Pacific island, planting the Rising Sun in a village of grass huts. There was even a child's comic book—cartoons in gaudy colors and with balloons for dialogue telling how Major Tamba conquered Singapore. I wondered what it had been like for my husband to live under the shadow of such a holy terror.

I politely scanned the clippings and photos and drawings, noting that the great Masao looked very much like Kenji—lean and sharp-featured, except there was a set to his jaw, a hard edge to his mouth. I had the feeling he didn't smile much.

Hisako lovingly took the scrapbook, rewrapped it in its silken red folder, tied it with a silk cord and returned it to the closet. *Those closets.* The Tambas' whole world seemed hidden in them.

Yuriko finally left to prepare the hot tub for us, and Saburo slouched into the house, brushed past us with only a few curt words between himself and his mother. I asked Kenji what went on.

He smiled. "She wants him to clean his room—"

"My God, it sounds like Glendale. My mother was always after Chris to get rid of his old smelly sneakers and make his bed."

We lingered, sitting cross-legged on the *zabuton* cushions, sipping a second cup of tea. It was cool, the air full of the aroma of natural fibers, aromatic wood, a scent of herbs.

I was staring at a section of the ceiling that was panelled with handsome wood—beautiful, age-darkened, grained, as if part of nature had grown right there into the house. I asked Kenji about it.

"Oh, yes, the grain in each panel is the same, a continuation of the previous panel. All the sections came from the same tree, a cryptomeria. We consider that the best kind of building—the use of the same tree, the same design. When you go to the lumberyard you find bundles of wood for home-building cut from the same tree trunk and tied together so that the natural conformation of the grain is maintained. Although it dies to serve our needs, the tree's essence is preserved."

I stared at the magnificent ceiling. It wasn't at all showy . . . in the half light you had to focus carefully to make out the marvelous designs in the grain.

"Kenji," I said, "it's lovely . . ."

"I'm glad you approve," he said as he held my hands and we kissed briefly. Out of the corner of my eye I thought I caught a glimpse of Saburo, the junior terror, peeking at us from the kitchen. Again, it seemed a brat was a brat, East and West.

And the bath.

Kenji had explained to me that even working-class people often had the luxury of a bath in their homes. As a middle-class family, the Tambas had a pretty good arrangement for their daily ritual. Neither war nor shortages could keep the Japanese from their blessed tubs. And who could blame them?

First we went to our room, once Yuriko's room, on the ground floor rear. It was even more spartan than the main room, a four-*tatami* room, with the usual *shoji* screens, sliding doors, paper walls, and the drawers containing our *futons,* blankets, floor cushions. It was dark and kind of dank-smelling. In fact, an unpleasant odor permeated the moist air, and I soon learned it came from the lavatory just outside our rear door, an arrangement my delicate American nose wasn't too happy with. Plumbing was a communal sink in the lavatory and of course in the kitchen. But the outdoor "convenience" was primitive and unnerving to an American girl spoiled by American Standard. A slit trench in a ceramic pit, in short, a squatter, was going to prove hard to take.

I paused in our room, subdued. The main room, where Kenji's parents lived, slept, ate, entertained, carried on their daily lives, was wide and long and filled with that mysterious light. Our room was dark and airless. And the odors from the adjacent john—the *benjo*—didn't help. I didn't want to be a pill right off the bat so I didn't say a word to Kenji about what seemed to be an overworked septic tank. Anyway, the hot bath soon took my mind off it.

In a shed attached to the rear of the house, on a raised circular wooden platform nested this wondrous round affair fashioned of dark cypress wood not nailed together but tightly bound by thick woven reeds. Attached to the lower part of the tub was the simplest sort of heater—a rectangular copper box that Yuriko was stuffing and stoking with charcoal sticks. As she worked she told me that she had developed a touch or a feel for the temperature of the water. (Don't ask me how the Japanese do it but they can bring a huge amount of water to a boil with the tiniest amount of fuel in no time at all.)

It looked delicious and, thank God, smelled even better. The charcoal was smokeless and glowed inside the copper chamber. Kenji told me that a ceramic tube conveyed the heat to the water and that inside the tub a few transverse wooden bars would keep us from burning our bottoms against the entryway for the heat.

We had now changed into light kimonos and sandals. On racks nearby were bars of sandalwood soap and washcloths. There were also two huge earthenware jugs filled with warm water. Kenji explained that we would *not* soap ourselves inside the tub, a filthy Western habit. No, this would be done by using the warm water as we squatted on stools, scrubbed ourselves clean, washed the soapy water from our bodies and then climbed a little ladder into the tub for the comforting embrace of Yuriko's magical fire-making.

"Enjoy it," Yuriko said, then whispered, "I am so glad you are here.

I have looked forward to it . . . and I always wanted an older sister." And then she quickly left us.

Soaped, washed down, wet and a bit chilly, I ascended the stepladder. Kenji watched me. He also cheekily kissed my butt, which I loved. He moaned some too.

The sexiness that flamed in me for a minute was boiled out of existence the second I felt that scalding water. I howled, tried to pull back, but Kenji nudged me forward and I made the plunge, convinced I was the main course for dinner. Boiled California *gaijin* served in its own juices.

"*Yoww, ooo.*" I could feel my arms and legs, my breasts, my belly blistering away.

"It's only just over a hundred degrees," said my unhelpful husband. "It relaxes you."

"Sure, like being cooked to death . . ." But he turned out to be right as we faced each other in the fetal position and laughed and kissed. Once I'd adjusted to the watery inferno, gave in to its hot embrace, and Kenji's, I felt like I was in heaven.

"This isn't hard to take," I said.

"I'm glad," Kenji said. "It's a ritual. Purification. And no work, no sitting in dirty water. We are clean, pure, passive—"

"You weren't so pure and passive when you kissed my rear end."

"My beloved Julie, I couldn't bear to look at your beauty without some act of respect." He even smiled when he said it.

We reached for one another then, utterly at peace, touched hands, touched all over, and I began to laugh out loud. "I'm a convert, I *love* it."

"You see," he said, "you are becoming Japanese already."

KENJI TAMBA · AUGUST, 1942

So far, so good, as the Americans say.

My mother was distant—*confused* is a better word—but Yuriko was wonderful in her reception of my American wife.

I was most of all concerned about my father. He had never sent us a congratulatory letter after our wedding. Even when we were interned he had not responded to my letters.

This evening he came back late from his duties at the palace, looking tired and preoccupied in his dark suit, changed to a kimono, settled onto a floor cushion, set his rimless spectacles on his nose, lit one of his many cigarettes and began to read the *Asahi Shimbun.*

"It's time to meet my father," I told Julie.

"Do I bow low? Forehead on the floor?"

"It's a good idea. You remember the words? 'I am honored to meet you, father of my husband.' "

"I'll manage."

"He is a gentle man."

We wore kimonos, Julie looking tall and slender in the dark green one I'd bought for her in the ship's store on the *Asama Maru.* We entered the main room. We bowed. I got to my knees and prostrated myself. After all, I had been away from home more than a year. I had married against my father's wishes and I was something of a slacker, a younger son who was not serving Tenno Heika.

Father, of course, did not rise. He barely set his newspaper aside. "Ah, Kenji. It is good you are here. I greet your wife. Was it a pleasant voyage?"

Julie understood it was not her place to speak. It was hard for her, but as I had explained to her, being a daughter-in-law in Japan is not one of the easiest jobs in the world. And being an *American* . . .

"Most pleasant, father."

"That is good."

"I am told . . . your wife . . . is expecting a child."

"Yes, father."

"That is good. She can visit her uncle, Dr. Varnum."

My father meant no discourtesy. Japan is a rank-conscious society, and he was incapable of finding the right level, the right step on the ladder, for my strange blonde American wife.

Dinner made things a bit easier as we sat around the low table, food brought from the kitchen in relays by my mother and Yuriko. With Hideo at sea, Yuriko and the baby spent several evenings a week at our house, where she was only too glad to help. There was a huge bowl of rice and side dishes of pickled eggplant and cucumbers, slices of fried sea bream, and to finish off, a clear soup with bean cake floating in it. We ate quickly with little conversation.

Eventually talk did get around to Masao. My father had learned from Colonel Sato that my brother was in the Solomon Islands, a "tropical paradise" in the southern Pacific, commanding a battalion. He had already fought American marines and had driven them off the island with heavy losses to the invaders. Saburo nodded his enthusiasm and said it was

stupid for our enemies to pursue the war. They were already beaten. Julie
was silent.

Yuriko asked if Colonel Sato had any news about her husband.

My father absentmindedly said he thought Sato mentioned that Hideo
had been assigned to an aircraft carrier. Perhaps the *Soryu,* maybe the
Akagi.

Yuriko, serving tea and rice, said that Hideo had told her that the *Akagi*
had been sunk.

"Then it's the *Soryu,*" my father said irritably.

Julie was restraining herself but looking agitated, and I knew why
. . . she was silently saying to me, *How can you let them carry on with these
lies when you know the truth?*

I spoke up. "Father, the *Soryu* was also lost at Midway."

"Was it?"

"It was *not,*" Saburo said.

Julie could no longer restrain herself. "But it was. Four of them.
Akagi, Soryu, Kaga, Hiryu. They all were sunk. The whole world knows
that . . ."

Silence. Eyes downcast, heads shaking, industrious eating . . .

"That's only what the Americans say," Saburo said.

I translated for Julie. She said nothing.

"Saburo is right." My father belched and picked his teeth. "Colonel
Sato says we won at Midway and we are winning the battle of Guadalca-
nal. More American ships have gone to the bottom. The sailors call it
Ironbottom Sound—a graveyard for Americans."

My mother began to clear plates from the table, and Yuriko got up to
help her. Julie volunteered but my mother would not hear of it. I'm not
sure if this was meant as politeness to a tired guest and new family member
or that she was at a loss about how to treat this unnatural creature.

Later Yuriko would tell me about the whispered conversation that she
and my mother had in the kitchen, as my father, Julie and I sat tensely
at the low table . . .

"I don't know what to say to her."

"Just be friendly."

"She is very strange."

"She seems nice."

"A daughter-in-law is supposed to be only a step above a servant. She
obeys her husband's mother. She waits on her. Kenji's wife should do what
I want her to do. But I can see she never will."

"She volunteered to clean the table and wash the dishes—"

"She didn't mean it. I don't like having her in this house."

"But mother, Kenji has no job, where will they go?"

"Kenji brought this on himself. He will have to do something about it. I could see that your father was getting indigestion during dinner."

"It was the pickled eggplant. Too spicy."

"You take care how you talk to me. And don't be so friendly with the *gaijin.*"

"But I like her . . ."

Later things relaxed some. My father was not a man to turn away from a pretty face, a womanly figure. Masao and I had suspected that he had been hungering for another woman for a long time. It was natural that he should smile at Julie after dinner and escort her to the *tokonama,* the honored niche in the corner of the main room. He spoke to me in court Japanese and I translated while Hisako detached herself, grumbling, and began sewing a shoulder patch on Saburo's school tunic. He was no longer a mere member of the eleventh form, he was a private in the "badger battalion."

"My father says the *tokonama* is the alcove where we display our treasures," I said to Julie. "The wooden pillar at the side is made of rare mahogany. It's called a *tokobashira.* Actually it's just the bare part of a tree trunk stripped, polished and with the grain untouched. Some artists carve the sides into an octagonal design, we prefer the natural form of the wood."

"It's lovely."

"My father also points out the scroll. It's an heirloom of the Tamba family and was given to a merchant retainer of a *daimyo* who was my father's ancestor, Tadao Tamba. He was at the siege of Osaka Castle in 1615. Father says it has been authenticated."

We sat for a while on the veranda and watched lights flickering in houses, street vendors making their last rounds, selling brooms, pots, sweet potatoes, noodles, soft drinks. Birds chattered their night song. Swallows darted across the summer sky.

Saburo came out for a last game of catch with one of his friends. He'd done his homework . . . he was a lazy student . . . and Julie tried to talk to him, telling him how she and I met during a baseball game and how I'd gotten the winning hit, that latter a bit of fiction.

He pouted, looked away and pounded the shapeless ball in his frayed mitt. "I don't have to talk to her," he said to me.

"You could be polite," I said. "Your English is good. And her Japanese isn't bad."

"I'm not studying English anymore. I'm going to cadet training for the rest of the year."

Julie tried to ignore him, and I could have killed him. Before I could say more, though, he'd run out for his game of catch.

We watched the glowing sky, and I thought how peaceful it seemed. People had apparently forgotten the Doolittle raid of April or passed it off as a meaningless show by a desperate enemy. Peacefulness could also be translated as weariness . . . people were undoubtedly tired from long hours of work, shortages. They missed their sons.

My father came out now, puffing a cigarette and stretching, then launched into a speech on how excellent His Majesty looked and felt these days, how he gave everyone courage and joy . . . "His Majesty is setting an example for the nation," father said. "He has given up his English breakfast of bacon and eggs to show his patriotism and his rejection of foreign things. He will not even play golf and may never again wear his English trousers."

Julie tried to stifle a smile when I told her this.

Exhausted from the trip, the tensions of introducing Julie to the family and in a real sense reintroducing myself, I suggested we go to bed early.

Bed was adjacent *tatami* mats and thick *futons.* It was hot in the small room. Mosquitoes bit us mercilessly until I rigged some netting over our mats. We could hear Saburo in his upstairs room, thumping the floor as he did exercises to build his muscles. He'd told my father he would enlist as a pilot trainee as soon as he became seventeen.

Julie now realized in the most acute and poignant way that there is no privacy in a Japanese house. The wall that separated us from our parents was a divider, a mere screen of translucent white rice paper with the *shoji* design.

We could hear my parents talking, grunting, my father's belches, as if they were in the room.

"Kenji," Julie said, wincing, "how can we ever make love again?"

"We'll be quiet."

"But I like to make noise. You know me."

"We'll have to stuff cloth in your mouth the way they did in the old days."

"Just try it."

"Then we shall have to let my family know that I married a lustful woman. They won't care. We are open about sex."

"Sure, we could sell tickets."

To shut her up, as she would put it, I did my best to make her forget her weariness and unhappiness with our quarters. At first she resisted, and then, sighing, abandoned herself to the love that no cultural difference, geography or even war could diminish.

JULIE TAMBA · AUGUST, 1942

I went alone to visit my aunt and uncle, with Kenji's blessing. He felt he might intrude on the reunion with my relatives. Besides, he was going to start looking for a job. He had an appointment with Kingoro Hata, apparently a man of some influence, a member of Parliament and distantly related to Hisako. I think Kenji also felt embarrassed at being unemployed, at not being in the military, at not finishing his studies, and although he would never say so, of bringing a kind of shame down on his family by marrying a barbarian.

Anyway, here I was in my rumpled beige suit and low-heeled shoes, strolling the dusty street in a five-minute walk to the Shibuya Ward clinic where Aunt Cora and Uncle Adam had worked for so many years.

People, no surprise, stared at me as I walked along, but they were at least polite. Several of the women even smiled, although some children in a playground called out, *supai, supai, supai* . . .

Sure. *Spy.* I guessed anyone looking Western was just assumed to be one, but here, unlike my country, even nationals of enemy countries were allowed to walk about free as air. Maybe they just didn't have the room to cast people off to camps like we did.

I noted an ominous thing . . . a large excavation was being cleared in a park not too far from the Tamba house. On a truck there was a menacing antiaircraft gun waiting to be placed in the pit. Older men in khaki uniforms were working like ants, filling sandbags with earth. It didn't seem right to have this scary gun in the midst of a playground . . .

The clinic turned out to be a squat dirty white stucco building, very different from the weathered wood houses that surrounded it. The outer walls were cracked and patched. The roof was of some rusted corrugated metal. Instead of *shoji* screens there were Western-style windows, a few of them broken. A blind man with a crippled boy as his guide and a pregnant young woman were sitting on a veranda, waiting.

Aunt Cora and Uncle Adam greeted me with noisy affection. I'd seen them only twice before during their rare visits to the United States, but they were legends in my family. Cora—her maiden name was Martens—was born in Geneva, Switzerland, but was no stern Calvinist, as you might expect from someone coming from that city. She was a birdlike pretty woman with coquettish brown bangs, cheeks like round pink balls, and she talked with a French accent. Uncle Adam was a gruff cigar-chomping bear who looked sort of like my father but was bigger and heavier and darker complected. His thick hair had turned white over the years.

While I waited for the morning office hours to end the Varnums gave me some letters that had been sent to them through the International Red Cross, and I sat in a rose garden under a trellis and sipped some green tea and made contact again with my parents and my brother.

It was warm and peaceful in the garden, and in spite of the noise and crowding of the whole city I was impressed how the Japanese managed a corner of tranquility with a tiny garden, some rocks, a bench, a lantern. Uncle Adam was certainly no Japanese but he had apparently learned how to make for himself something very Japanese. Outside there was a patchwork of helter-skelter wooden walls, the faded weather-beaten flanks of dwellings and shops, an odor of sewage, the howls of dogs and the yowling of a cat. But the garden was homey, restful and a fine place to catch up on one's mail.

My parents' letter was affectionate, short and unforgiving. They had tried to stop me from marrying Kenji, from going into the Manzanar camp with him, and especially from going to Japan. I'd gone against them on all three counts . . . They told me that Ed Hodges was a prisoner of war, he'd been captured at Wake Island. The Red Cross had no other information so far as they knew but they'd lost touch with Ed's mother after my marriage to Kenji. Chris was in the Solomons covering the fighting there, in the thick of it. They actually heard him on the radio several times a week and they said he was considered one of the bright young war correspondents. Good for Chris.

My father wrote:

> We miss you terribly, and we still can't accept what you've done.
> Kenji is a fine man, no doubt, and so don't misunderstand our
> feelings about that. But look what you have brought on yourself.

God knows when we will see you again. God knows whether you
will be safe in Japan, our enemy. Eventually Japan will be
subjected to bombings and perhaps even invasion. What will
happen to you? What kind of life will you be able to make for
yourself, and Kenji for that matter? Your mother and I love you
very much, Julie. We love you not only because you are our own,
but because you are a fine person. We respect you, but . . .

It was hard for me to go on. I had not yet told them that I was pregnant.
Of course I would have to. Would it only make them more unhappy?
Probably. But it was *my* life, not theirs. I could understand their feelings,
but did they really understand mine? I *loved* Kenji, he loved me. There
was *no* argument about that. If they could accept that fact everything else
should follow. Or would it? Maybe I was being impossibly naive . . .

My mother had added a note suggesting that perhaps I could find a
monthly Friends meeting in Tokyo and go to it for guidance and support.
She said that the fellowship of the Society might offer "sustenance and
guidance in the trials that face you." God. Or perhaps I should consider
coming home for the duration of the war? Kenji could follow me when
the war ended . . .

I turned to Chris's peppery letter, which as usual was mostly about
himself. My modest brother. Kenji and I both had brothers who could do
no wrong and were making a very good thing out of the war . . . Chris
had managed to avoid military censorship and gotten the letter out via an
air force pilot who in turn got it to a Red Cross courier. He wrote about
things I'd only heard in the radio reports on the ships coming to Japan
and rumors we'd picked up since our arrival.

Dear Sis,
First I hope and trust you and Kenji are okay after what I have to
assume is a safe arrival in Japan. No news of your ship anywhere.
I guess after you transferred to the Japanese ship you were under
tight censorship. Please note my APO number and write to it.
Aunt Cora can get it sent out. Strange how the mails keep
functioning even with all hell breaking loose all over the
world.
    When the L.A. office assigned me to the South Pacific I griped,
having no idea that I'd be thrown into the middle of the bloodiest,
meanest action of the war to date. I landed with a marine division
on Tulagi, moved to a hellhole called Guadalcanal and have been
up to my eyeballs in the most awful butchering you can imagine. I
don't sleep too hot. My stomach is a wreck. At first the Nips just

disappeared into the hills and let us land and pile up supplies. There was no room on the beaches for an extra rifle. Then all of a sudden the Jap commanders changed their minds and decided we had to go. They hit us with everything. Every damn night they try to sneak more slant-eyed types in under cover of darkness. And then they attack. Most of the fighting takes place around an airfield that the Japs started and we captured. Every night they throw more men against our machine-gun positions and every night we mow them down. The perimeter of the field is like a butcher shop. The bodies pile up, and still they come, crazy nuts, screaming little bastards, officers waving swords, dying like ants getting sprayed with Black Flag. Which isn't to say our own marines aren't taking a beating too. Every time I see the dead body of one of our kids I want to tear apart this whole lunatic fanatical Jap enemy. Last night, for God's sake, the Japs tried to cross a jungle stream and take one of our positions. I swear we killed eight hundred of the crazed bastards. I never saw so much blood, so many corpses. Thirty-five of our marines died. I wish we'd killed eight thousand Japs. I mean it. They're not human. We found the body of a Jap colonel. He'd slit his own belly with his sword after the attack failed. Good. One less of them.

Why do I tell you all this? Well, I think you have some serious tough rethinking to do. Kenji is a good guy, I always felt that way. He's decent. He may even have been against the war. But look at what he comes from. Look at what *his* country is doing, the crimes his holy god of an emperor is condoning. What kind of place will Japan be after this mess is over? I've seen their ships and their guns shooting down planes, machine-gunning survivors in the water. They don't deserve anything but destruction, and by God I'll help in any way I can by reporting the truth to see that they get it. *Julie, get out. Get out while you can.* Pack up, go home, and maybe Kenji can come stateside, take out his citizenship papers someday. Do you really want your kids raised to be half-killers who run like they *love* it into machine-gun fire for no damned reason other than some god tells them to? I tell you, Julie, I've gotten to hate these bastards and I mean really *hate.* The only good Nip is a dead one. Not Kenji and a *very* few like him, but . . .

There was no reason for me not to believe Chris's account of the fighting in the Solomons. Kenji had told me about the Japanese soldiers, the dedication of their officers, their willingness, eagerness, to die rather than surrender, the indifference to the suffering of prisoners and the wounded.

But Kenji wasn't part of that. He and his old teacher Professor Adachi saw another kind of Japan that had been terrorized by the outlaws. Kenji had told me that the emperor himself was a peaceful man but was manipulated by militants.

I was getting a headache. My stomach was queasy. It was a relief when Uncle Adam and Aunt Cora joined me in the garden and their maid, an old farm woman named Sachiko they'd adopted, served us more tea and rice cakes.

"Newsy letters?" Uncle Adam asked. He lit a cigar, waved to Officer Tani, assigned to making sure the clinic wasn't a *supai* base, who had returned to grin at us and accept a rice cake. Kenji had brought a box of White Owls for my uncle but he wanted to give it himself, all nicely wrapped.

I told them that my family wanted me to come home—my parents and Chris. And then I told them I was three months pregnant and that in *no way* would I ever leave Kenji.

"We'll do all we can to make you comfortable," Aunt Cora said. "The clinic is well-equipped. I will deliver your child."

"I'm so glad you're both here," I said. "I have to admit I'm a little scared."

Uncle Adam puffed on his cigar. "Any change is hard, Julie. Japan is a different world."

I read them some of Chris's letter about the fighting he'd seen.

"If I can understand it," Adam said, "they're two people. A nation with a split personality. On one side you have flower arrangements, *haiku* poems, moon-watching and the cherry blossoms. On the other a bloody rage, a lack of basic humanity that still stuns me. It takes some getting used to."

Aunt Cora asked how my in-laws had treated me.

"Except for Yuriko they obviously wished I wasn't there."

"You'll have to be patient," said Cora.

"The understatement of the year," Uncle Adam said. "No matter what you do you'll still be a *gaijin.*"

"I hate that word already."

"Better to try to understand what's behind it, Julie. They have an almost pathological fear of foreigners. White faces, big noses, strange smells, peculiar ideas about eating and sex. When we first came here it took months before anyone would let us treat them."

Aunt Cora laughed. "Adam and I used to say that they brought their children here not for us to cure them but to scare them. 'Look, baby, see the disgusting *gaijin?* If you don't behave, we'll let him eat you.' "

"That's right," Uncle Adam said. "We're freaks, intruders. If not *gaijin* we're at least *ijin,* strange people."

"Or *ketojin,*" said Cora. "Which means hairy barbarian. *Seiyojin*—west sea people. As if we came from the ocean floor."

"Whatever they call us," my uncle said, "whatever they feel, they also treat foreigners courteously. Even in the thirties, at the height of militant nationalism, foreigners were treated pretty well, apart from an occasional visit from the police. Look at me. I'm not in jail. They assign that idiot cop to grin at me from across the fence, but what of it?"

"I hope my in-laws get the idea," I said.

"They will," Aunt Cora said. "You're a rare bird for them to take into the nest. It's not so much that they dislike you. You're simply not one of them—"

"Who said I *was?* But I *am* Kenji's wife."

"Does Kenji know how you feel?" Uncle Adam asked.

"Sure . . . he's great . . . but, well, I wish he'd sort of speak up more, especially to that snotty kid brother."

"It isn't really his place to do so," Uncle Adam said. "Not in his father's house. It will take time, Julie."

I hugged him. "Thank God I have you two. I may need a shoulder or two for a good cry now and then."

Cora said, "Don't expect too much from Kenji in front of his family, Julie. He's a second son. That doesn't count for much. Masao is the king of that house. You'll just have to get used to it."

"Masao! I know all about him. He's a bloodthirsty killer, he murdered civilians . . ."

Uncle Adam got up and shredded the butt of his cigar into the roots of a rose bush. "More contradictions," he said. "I'm willing to believe some shocking things about Major Tamba's war record. Cora gets reports from the IRC and we have access to Western news broadcasts through the Swiss consul. But Masao is not a bred-in-the-bone villain."

"Isn't he? What *is* he, then?"

"He's a *product.* In the old days if a commoner offended a *samurai* in the slightest way, the *samurai* could lop his head off and not be punished. What Masao and his troops do comes right out of that code."

"Well, that proves to me Kenji is more of a man. He had the good sense to say no to that garbage. Masao still lives by it . . ."

And I told them more about my letter from Chris, the suicide attacks, the piles of dead Japanese soldiers, the acceptance of death, the suicidal refusal to quit.

Adam nodded. "All true, I'm sure. But how will you feel when I tell you that Masao came here when he was on leave and intervened to keep me out of prison? Many Americans have been jailed. But one good word from Major Tamba to his superiors and Cora and I remained free to practice."

"That's because he knows you. You treated him when he was a kid. You're useful to the people around here, including his family."

Adam lit a fresh cigar. "Yes, maybe so, but if he had let me be carted off to a lockup he'd be burdened with shame. One doesn't let that happen to friends. Again, Masao is two people. Just like Kenji is. Maybe someday they'll work it out . . ."

Aunt Cora brushed her bangs back. "It may sound strange, Julie, but there are quite a few Americans, British and other enemy aliens walking around, never jailed. There's a whole community of American nuns teaching school north of here. American and British women married to Japanese men—like you—have been left free."

"But my in-laws act as if I'm Typhoid Mary."

"As I told you," Adam said, "you're an intrusion. They haven't been able to mesh you into their lives."

"I wish Kenji and I didn't have to live with them, but he has no money and no job. He says it's impossible to find a place. And what if he's drafted?"

"Unlikely," my uncle said. "They won't want him."

"Why?" I asked, privately relieved.

"There'll be suspicion he's tainted. Too much exposure to the enemy U.S. And with you as his wife—"

"That's just fine with me. I'd have thought they'd want every able-bodied man they could get their hands on."

Uncle Adam laughed. "Oh, no question, this country is a mass of contradictions. Dear Julie, Japan has its share of draft-dodgers. For all the patriotic talk there are thousands of rich men's sons who don't fight and rich men's daughters who don't work in factories."

Cora then suggested that I come in for a physical examination. She said I looked peaked and that some vitamins might be in order. The rice-and-pickled-vegetable routine was not the best in the world for an expectant mother.

My health was excellent, she said, after looking at my rising tummy, listening to my lungs. Everything pointed to a normal delivery. I had, after all, lots of California sunshine in my system.

And so we are dug in at Guadalcanal. More of our men arrive. We attack again. The marines kill more of us.

Who could believe these overfed Americans could fight like this? Where have they found the courage? They are not a people of the gods. What is their line of descent? A mixture of every known race and religion, a stew of "others." They are big and clumsy and they stink of butter and yet they fight like tigers.

If I survive to see Kenji again I must ask him about these marines. Maybe they train them in some special way, or give them whiskey to make them fight. It is incredible that they can accept the punishment we inflict and keep fighting back. Our dead pile up under the muzzles of their guns. They come out of their holes and bunkers and fight us hand to hand. And, to be truthful, all our training in martial arts is rarely a match for their brute strength, the way they wield their bayonets and rifle butts. I am no longer certain it's sufficient to tell our soldiers that Japan has never lost a war, that the gods are on our side, that we must gladden the emperor's heart. Not when these Americans are as courageous as we are, stand to their guns, cut us into scraps. They have named the airstrip we started Henderson Field, after a pilot who died at Midway. Oh, yes, we know the truth about *that* encounter by now. We were beaten and retreated. What lies will be told about Guadalcanal? Still, I am a loyal officer.

Which is why it was so surprising to me that I had this terrible argument with Colonel Ota yesterday. He's a pompous sort who talks big and makes sure he stays in the rear. He was also responsible for sending a thousand of our best men to their death three weeks ago at the Tenaru River. Ota's strategy will divide our forces—a mistake, as any military student knows. The main unit under my command will strike at the rear of the marines' lines after a circling movement. A smaller unit will hit Henderson Field from the west, while a new group of Imperial Marines will attack the airfield from the opposite side. It *sounds* good and looks fine on a map, but I pointed out that the Americans had scouts out spying on us. They learned their lesson, it seems, about intelligence after Pearl Harbor. We have seen their observation planes hovering over our formations . . . even in the jungle we cannot hide thousands of men or keep our landings secret.

"I have a feeling, colonel," I told Ota, neglecting to bow, "that the marines will not be fooled."

"Do you, Major Tamba? Please explain yourself?"

"There is high ground clear of the jungle at the rear of the marines' defense line. If they know anything about our movements they will place machine guns on that ridge. There is no way we can penetrate it," I said.

"Then we will die attacking it. Major, it is not like you to talk of defeat. What has happened to the Dragon of Malaya?"

"Dragons do not just spout fire, sir. They also think, they plan. They seek victory, not a shameful defeat."

"No defeat is shameful if one fights with courage and then dies."

Despite my training, I confess I was getting sick to my stomach at hearing this old record. I looked at my officers and noncoms squatting on the packed earth, cleaning weapons. Exhausted, poorly provisioned, many fought with bandaged wounds, shaking with malaria and dengue fever. Their armpits and crotches were infested with parasites, worms, bugs and bacteria they had no resistance to. They lived on three scoops of rice and a slice of dried fish. Their teeth were rotting in bleeding gums. They died of dysentery, shitting their lives away. We had become an army of defecators, an army eaten by insects. I loved my men, I did not want them annihilated in doomed attacks. It would be better, I argued, to wait for the next landing of men and medicine and food, then plan a wide encircling movement, cutting off the American supply lines. We knew that their navy had been cut to ribbons in the straits. The sea lanes were filled with their dead sailors and wrecked ships. Why not gather strength and later devise a better strategy?

Colonel Ota would not hear of it. Each day was a waste of time, he said. Had we lost a thousand men at the Tenaru River? Surely the marines had lost just as many. "I don't give a damn if you are the son-in-law of Colonel Sato," said Ota angrily. "I don't care about your past exploits, Major Tamba. You will get off your ass, rouse those slackers in your battalion, and lead the assault on the rear of the American lines. Tenno Heika demands no less, as you should know."

I wondered how he knew His Majesty's mind so well. But I should have been used to it. My father-in-law always seemed to be talking in the emperor's name as well. "I will obey you, of course," I said, and still did not bow, "but I cannot believe this attack can succeed . . ."

On the night of September 12 I sent my best men forward against the Americans' defense line, "Bloody Ridge." Offshore our naval guns pounded the marine foxholes. We gained not an inch and lost forty men. There was no surprise in the attack. The marines had simply turned their guns around, dug in, faced us and poured fire into our ranks.

The next night we attacked in greater force, softening the enemy with mortar shells, taking a heavy toll. Some of the Americans were in units that had not slept for two days and were running short of water and

ammunition. But they fought back savagely. We came out shouting our
*banzai*s, setting off firecrackers and flares.

> U.S. Marines be dead tomorrow.
> U.S. Marines be dead tomorrow.

My men slapped their rifle butts and kept chanting this taunt as they
tried to pierce the defenses. We sent bright green flares into the sky and
the entire length of Bloody Ridge was illuminated in a sickly light. We
could see the marines in their dugouts, behind their machine-gun emplacements. They would not retreat.

Once my assault company isolated the men at the top of the ridge, only
to be cut down by a machine-gun unit that came to their comrades' rescue
at the last minute. I saw my men fall like stalks of dead chrysanthemums
in an autumn field. Bodies piled on top of bodies, masses of torn flesh,
rivulets of blood, faces turned into red gouges.

Meanwhile I learned on our field radio that the attacks on the airfield
had been no more successful. Both attacking columns ran headlong into
massed fire. American planes took off and strafed us, destroying our
retreating men with machine-gun fire. Never, not in China, not in Malaya,
had I seen so many of our dead in so small a space. The flanks of Bloody
Ridge had become a mass grave for hundreds of our soldiers.

I confronted Colonel Ota. "We will retreat, and you can report me if
you want and you can go to hell." I called him many names, cursed him
for staying in his tent as his soldiers were slaughtered. He did not say a
word.

We left six hundred dead on the slope. The Americans suffered many
less dead, I knew. Ota and other high-ranking braggarts had said they
would be breakfasting on American rations that morning. All we tasted
was blood and dirt.

Our superiors had been so cocky that they had even refused to bring
enough food, actually convinced they would be eating the Americans'
rations.

Starving, exhausted, sick with fever, we began a long retreat through
some of the wettest, vilest jungle terrain on earth. Three days later my
executive officer confronted me. Sheets of rain were making it impossible
to move. Trails were flooded. We shivered from malaria, starvation, the
night's cold . . . I heard some men say they should have died in Bloody
Ridge rather than suffer the shame of this retreat.

"Sir," said my exec, "there are twenty men who can go no further.
Wounded . . ."

"Where are they?"

"In the clearing near those huts."

"Can we carry them?"

"No, sir. The men who can walk are half-dead. None of these men can be helped. We do not have enough medical supplies, we have no corpsmen left."

"We will do what must be done."

I could not ask my executive officer to perform the act. I loaded three automatics and waded through yellow mud to the native village where I saw my wounded men stretched out in the battering rain, some bleeding to death, some with bandaged stumps of arms and legs, some shaking convulsively.

I drew my gun and walked toward them.

A few began to pray. Most shut their eyes, waited. Some were so near death they did not understand that Major Tamba walked among them, easing their entry into heaven with a single shot.

We continued our retreat. To attempt to storm the marine positions again with our soldiers would have been suicidal. I often wondered as we sloshed our way through the green hell why we did not do exactly that. Ota never once mentioned the possibility of all of us dying on the barbed wire and on the slippery slopes, and in the ditches surrounding Henderson Field. What had become of the boast we would die in combat?

I saw my men digging for roots, munching grasshoppers and white grubs, chewing on clumps of bitter grass. Every day more died of malaria and diseases unknown to us. And whenever we were visible, emerging from the jungle, the American fighter planes would ravage us with machine-gun fire. We made it a standard practice to shoot the severely wounded.

On September 24, after reaching a coastal haven, I accompanied a party of high-ranking officers on a flying trip to the island of Truk, where the largest battleship in the world, our *Yamato,* stood at anchor. Aboard was the architect of Pearl Harbor, *and* of Midway, Admiral Yamamoto.

I lingered in the background, a junior officer, as my superiors pleaded their case with Yamamoto. He was aging, squint-eyed, his manner curt. We noted that while we of Guadalcanal had seen our men starve, die of thirst, bleed to death, twist in the agonies of disease, these lofty naval officers looked sleek and healthy. The best sake was served to enhance elaborate meals. Stewards could not do enough for them. There was even a masseur aboard, motion pictures, evenings of entertainment and heavy drinking. So much for the asceticism of our commanders. It was just this kind of self-indulgence, conspicuous luxury that had led me as a young officer in 1936 to support the mutiny.

Yamamoto told us that he would provide aerial and sea cover for us. Thousands of fresh infantrymen would be landed. If necessary he would bring the *Yamato,* an unsinkable ship the size of a city, alongside the island and pound the Americans with its great guns. He also promised that the hateful Henderson Field would be bombed into a pile of rubble.

In our last meeting with him someone let slip that one of our army staff officers in New Guinea had stated that Japan now had no chance of winning a war of attrition, which was what the Guadalcanal and New Guinea campaigns had become. Strangely, Yamamoto made no comment. But other gold braids uttered brave words about the unbeatable spirit of Japan—*Yamato Damashii*—and the absolute necessity of retaking Guadalcanal. I bowed my head in agreement. What else was there to do? Besides, I believed we could win. And if by chance we lost but died bravely in combat, would we truly have lost?

On the flight back, we got roaringly drunk and sang an improvised song in which we renamed the great battleship "Yamamoto's Yamato Hotel, where whores serve bigger whores."

KENJI TAMBA · SEPTEMBER, 1942

Only after my father's urgings did I finally agree to see Kingoro Hata, the member of Parliament. Long ago Professor Adachi told me Hata was not much better than an outlaw, a corrupt conniver who was making money on the war through lucrative contracts for uniforms, food and medical supplies. At one time Hata was a member of the Japan National Socialist Party, which sounds ridiculous . . . he was certainly no socialist, no more than the Nazis who called themselves National Socialists. I'm sorry to say that scoundrels like Hata had succeeded for too long in gulling too many of our people.

So I went to see him only out of respect for my father, who obviously felt ill at ease with my wife in the house and hoped I'd get a job and move

out. Where we could move to I had no idea. Tokyo had no available
dwellings, and as gloomy as the atmosphere was in my father's house, at
least it was a home for my pregnant wife. Julie and I would be fortunate
to find a rabbit hutch.

Hata, it turned out, was attending a rice harvest festival, a *matsuri,* in
a nearby district, and his secretary told me that if I hurried I could catch
him there since he would not be back at his desk that day. So I took a
clanking trolley out to Shinjuku and found the Shinto shrine where the
matsuri was taking place. Prominent was a chauffeured black car with
lace curtains at the windows parked at the edge of a rice field—the only
car within view and obviously Hata's.

I was startled by a woman's voice calling to me from the car.

"Mr. Tamba?"

I walked to the gleaming automobile with its official license plate and
the Rising Sun flag. The curtains parted and I saw a beautiful hard-edged
white face. It was the geisha proprietress Satomi whom my brother had
told me about. Her features looked like carved ivory. Her voice was
musical, almost like the sound of a *samisen.* She wore a high black wig
and a bottle green kimono.

"You are back from America?" she asked.

I bowed. She was a geisha mistress and I was a scholar, *and* a male,
and yet I felt inferior to her.

"Yes . . . I hope to talk to Mr. Hata about finding employment."

"I wish you luck. What word do you have from your brother?"

"Only that he is in the Solomon Islands."

"Ah . . . and I hear *you* have a *gaijin* wife."

"I do," I said somewhat belligerently. "And she is with me in
Tokyo . . ."

She finally smiled. "I was always told you are a most unusual and
intelligent man. Your wife is beautiful, I am sure."

"And intelligent."

"One would expect nothing less from the wife of a Tamba."

I bowed again and walked toward an outdoor shrine at the edge of the
rice fields. Several dozen farmers in conical hats, sandals, worn gray work
clothes had gathered around. They had lined faces and muscular arms and
legs. The older people were bent at the waist, permanently disfigured in
the service of eternal *gohan,* the rice that gave us life . . . An elderly Shinto
priest stood in front of the shrine to Inari, the rice god, and was offering
a prayer for "long ears with five grains," wagonloads of the precious
short-grained rice. He prayed that evil spirits and demons would stay
away from the harvest and that rats and mice would be chased away when

the rice was stored in great baskets. People prayed, bowed, and applauded the words of the priest, who then stepped aside to let Hata speak.

Kingoro Hata, in frock coat, striped trousers and a stiff collar, walked to the center of the shrine, proceeded to say how appropriate it was that he be there to represent His Majesty, since Inari was not only the god of rice but the patron of merchants, and he, Kingoro Hata, in his humble way was doing all he could as a merchant to help Japan win the war. Rank hypocrisy was rewarded with applause. He then went on about the sacred duty of the peasants to produce more rice and bigger harvests "to feed our soldiers," and he assured them that the war was being won.

My stomach turned and my head started to throb. How long could these greedy bastards get away with this . . . ?

Studying the weatherworn faces of the farmers, I understood better than ever what Professor Adachi meant. Our suffering people had been fed (along with their rice) a stew of lies and of fantasies, of allegiances to a false history that had now sent their sons to die dreadful deaths in hellish places. Worse would come. Much worse. And for this they could thank men like Hata and Sato and perhaps my brother. . . .

There was a group of drummers at the shrine and when the thumping and chanting began Hata took his leave. The farmers got to their knees and bowed to the crafty schemer and my stomach tightened.

I waited for Hata at his car, and in spite of the loathing I felt I also forced myself to bow. I owed it to my father, even if I choked.

Our conversation was brief.

"Kenji, my boy, you are in a difficult position but I will ask around and see what I can do. After all, you have a talent for languages. But . . . all those years in America, and of course, the problem of your wife . . ."

"There are men in high places with American or British wives."

"But they have little influence. You are young, Kenji. The best for you would be to join the army."

"I have inquired. It seems I am regarded as unreliable."

"A pity."

He then suggested I become a member—a nonpaying job, of course—of the Imperial Rule Assistance Young Men's Corps. Huffing into his car to sit alongside the geisha, Hata explained that his party, the National Socialists, and all "right thinking" political groups had recently been merged into the Imperial Rule Political Association, which was the *only* legal party. "It has made it possible for those of us who follow the Imperial Way to neutralize liberals, socialists, traitors and the villainous peace faction. The Young Men's Corps, the *Yokusan Sonen Dan,* mobilizes the energies and enthusiasms of the people, like these good farmers. We're like the patriotic parties in Germany and Italy, but of course they have no god to show them the way."

I told him I doubted I was equipped for work in his party, he shrugged, sent his regards to my parents and my brother and ordered his chauffeur to drive off.

I could hear him and Satomi laughing as the car moved off.

YURIKO KITANO · SEPTEMBER, 1942

In the two months that my American sister-in-law had been living with us we'd become dear friends. I especially loved it when she taught me the newest American dance steps! The best was the Lindy . . . She laughed when I called it the "Rindy." Julie had bought jazz records with her and we had an old windup player, scratchy and undependable and run down, but I adored the happy music it reproduced.

Of course we were disobeying the new patriotic code, which said we were to reject foreign music, art, literature, food and clothing. Well, we did it anyway. We cranked up the machine and danced, always when my father was away, to Benny Goodman, Artie Shaw, Tommy Dorsey, Glenn Miller. I was crazy about them. I think my favorite was Benny Goodman's "String of Pearls." I wish I knew the words to it. It sounded so Japanese . . . maybe because we love pearls and produce the best in the world . . . But I also liked "One O'Clock Jump," the way it got faster and faster and the room seemed to rock with the beat. And I loved "Sing, Sing, Sing," which went on forever.

Julie said she had once heard Mr. Goodman play at a college concert in Los Angeles. She said he looked kind and intelligent and obviously loved to entertain people.

I was teaching her Japanese and she was improving my English. I guess you could say we'd become loving friends. We shared secrets and feelings and because we were so honest with each other she even admitted to me what she hated the most about our house—the toilet, the *benjo*.

One day Julie was almost in tears, saying she would never get used to the squatter in the alcove set apart from the rear veranda. She'd dropped

261

a small purse into it by mistake, and she was furious. Like most Japanese privies in anything but the richest homes, it's nothing more than a ceramic slab with a slit in the middle. I told Julie that Japanese were clean people and that the thought of letting our precious rear ends touch a seat someone else had sat on horrified us. Which explained the squatting position, less comfortable but more sanitary.

She shook her head and said she'd try to get used to our strange habits. We laughed then as I promised to help her overcome her fear of the dread squatter. And we put on records and danced to Glenn Miller and Artie Shaw and Tommy Dorsey. I took off my kimono, she took off hers, and in our underkimonos we held hands, changed hands, did all the steps until the house shook. It was fun, but I wished I had a man to dance with. Hideo was still somewhere off the Solomon Islands, who knew where, and I hadn't seen Hans Baumann for some time. He'd just disappeared.

JULIE TAMBA · SEPTEMBER, 1942

I'd volunteered to shop with Hisako, who was silent as we walked down the pitted street. I'm afraid she didn't approve of me or my introducing Western music into the house. Well, in a way I could understand, but I also felt this business of getting on with each other was a two-way street. As we walked along I saw the antiaircraft gun across in the playground was now assembled and manned behind layers of sandbags. It didn't look like it could stop a model airplane, the kind Chris used to make with balsa wood and glue, and the soldiers in the battery looked unkempt.

I also noticed that refuse was collected less frequently, that the Japanese, such models of cleanliness in their homes, didn't seem to mind the piles of loose garbage in the street.

A troop of school children, girls in light blue smocks and boys in dark blue blouses, marched by shouting slogans and waving bamboo sticks. They couldn't have been more than eight or nine. What did the future hold for them, little kids promising death and destruction to the enemy?

But I wasn't afraid, not anymore. By now I'd come to see the truth of Uncle Adam's talk about the Japanese schizy attitude toward foreigners, their thinking on so many other subjects too. There was the meat-eating, big-nosed *gaijin*. Look out, baby, mama will feed you to the white bogeyman! On the other hand there was the courtesy, if restrained, I was generally treated with. Yes, I never really found anyone in the neighborhood, apart from an occasional nosey cop, who didn't smile, greet me when introduced and act as if I had a right to be there. Oh, the government promoted campaigns against foreigners. Kids, including my snotty brother-in-law Saburo, sometimes threw rocks at Uncle Adam's clinic and ran after some poor old French nun or Dutch missionary shouting *supai, supai, supai.* But you got the feeling it was more a game. The propaganda bosses passed the word on to neighborhood associations, and the children went into their act. It didn't appear that anyone took it too seriously.

It wasn't often that I shopped. Hisako wouldn't *hear* of me buying anything for the house. She was convinced, among other things, that I'd be cheated. So now I was something of an attraction as I lined up with a group of women outside Mr. Kurita's fish store. The women laughed, smiled, pointed at my braided yellow hair, tried to get me in a conversation and I struggled to respond. No, I was not a German, not English. *An American?* This wowed them. Their day was complete. And not a sign of animosity or word of reproach. No one wanted to lynch me, jail me or accuse me of stopping the oil shipments or freezing Japanese assets. They did, though, keep their distance, touching of course being out of the question, but the smiles grew broader and even if they had no idea what I was saying they seemed delighted.

I was asked in English by a pretty young woman, "Where are you from?"

"California."

Which set off titters. They had, most of them anyway, apparently heard of California. One older woman said she had cousins in Los Angeles. And not a word about the internment camps, no anger.

Mr. Kurita had to ask the ladies to keep moving and talk less, since the supply of fish was limited and he was closing early. Many of the shops did that, there was less and less to sell.

Hisako, I noticed, was smiling at me for the first time in weeks. She was human, after all, a decent hardworking woman, and she liked the attention. God knows she never got much from Goro, my father-in-law. I never once saw them touch, let alone kiss or otherwise indicate any feeling for one another. Still, I guess it was there—in their own fashion. They respected one another, but it would have been vulgar to indicate affection. What went on for them behind the *shoji* screens that separated us at night, who knows? I'm sure, though, they slept soundly on their little wooden pillows, those neck-breaking *makuras,* cylindrical hard cushions mounted on wood boxes. One thing, I discovered, that the Japanese do better than anybody is sleep, which was a break for Kenji and me . . . we could make love without too much worry about rousing his parents. Or at least so I thought.

Squid, abalone, bream, eel and yellowtail were all the fishmonger had to offer, and the catch was rationed. Hisako bought a tiny bream she would fry, a slice for each of us on top of the eternal rice. I felt sorry for her and guilty too. Kenji and I were freeloaders. We contributed nothing. I had no money. I couldn't work. Kenji had been pounding the pavements, wheeling his bicycle around Tokyo for weeks trying to get work.

The least I could do was volunteer to carry Hisako's shopping reticule, and she accepted. Leaving the fish store, she said to another woman—I picked up most of it—that rich people had no trouble getting the best fish. She was talking about a woman in a maid's uniform who had gone to the rear of the shop and was sold a thick tuna steak—expensive, rare, a delicacy. But neither Hisako nor the other woman seemed too upset. Like most Japanese, they sort of just accepted privileges of rank—that was the way life was—with overlords and underlings. I remembered that when Kenji dared say to his father one night that Tojo was rumored to live like a Roman emperor and his wife was notorious for her love of luxuries he was given a stony stare and no comment. Rank had its privileges in civilian as well as military life . . .

Hisako made out better in a store that specialized in pickled vegetables. The Japanese, I had learned, pickled anything that grew. No sooner does the tree bear fruit or the vegetable mature than someone drowns them in brine. My mother-in-law bought a white *daikon* radish pickled in bran and salt, guaranteed to raise your blood pressure. The storekeeper bowed to both of us, and as a bonus offered a tiny *umeboshi,* a pickled unripe plum. I found it godawful but Hisako told me it was good medicine and that if the baby gave me a headache I should press an *umeboshi* against my forehead. I smiled winningly but decided I'd stick to unpickled aspirin.

As we were coming out of the pickle shop I saw Aunt Cora coming toward us. She, too, had been on her shopping rounds and she was looking sort of peeved as she left the cubbyhole of a pharmacy that served Shibuya Ward.

Cora grumbled that medical supplies were getting harder to come by. Even staples like iodine, laxatives and peroxide were in short supply. As she spoke we saw on a street corner an old farmer selling rice from his own paddies from a burlap bag. Cora spoke to him and laughed as the transaction was completed and the rice was wrapped in a cone made of old newspaper. "He says it's the finest rice, the best *kome.*"

"I thought rich was *gohan.*"

"Only after it's cooked. Don't get me started on the names for rice. We'll never finish our shopping."

Aunt Cora was going to try the dispensary at a nearby private hospital, where she had some friends, to get supplies the clinic was short of. She bowed to say her good-byes, then remembered something.

"Julie, I had a call from the Red Cross this morning."

"Yes?"

"Did I tell you about my visit to the prisoner-of-war camp?"

"You mentioned it."

"Did I tell you about the young officer who gave me a slip of paper?"

"I don't think so."

"My friend Dr. Reinhold called from the IRC. They contacted his mother. She had no idea he was alive. I mentioned it now because she lives in Glendale. A Mrs. Hodges—"

I thought I would faint. "Ed Hodges . . . ?"

"Yes. He gave me a scrap of paper—Lieutenant Hodges, L.A. Sure enough, he's one of the marines from Wake Island. Do you know him?"

"Oh . . . yes. Yes, I know him very well. Kenji knows him too. He was . . . a friend of mine. Where is he?"

"A huge warehouse near the docks. It's an awful place. Dr. Reinhold and I have asked over and over to visit the men again but we keep getting turned down."

"What did he look like?"

"A tall man, blond hair, light brown eyes. He's not in very good health, none of them are."

"Can I see him?"

"I'll try. If they give us permission for another visit, we can try to arrange something. Sneak you in." Cora paused. "How well did you know him?"

"He was my boyfriend. *Before* I met Kenji."

"I see . . . Oh dear, I've upset you."

"I'm just glad he's alive." My mind spun. Kenji . . . Ed . . . me. Kenji and I were free to shop, talk . . . and Ed, a good man I'd rejected . . .

Officer Tani, the policeman stationed at the Varnums' clinic, walked by, saluted, bowed and asked to see my alien card. He'd seen it a dozen times but that didn't satisfy him. I went through with the ritual, showed it to him and he squinted at it as if he'd never seen it before.

My mother-in-law, who'd been negotiating with a peddler selling hand-made brooms, came up to us then and began to scold him, and I tuned out, thinking in a sort of daze that I would have to tell Kenji that Ed was in Tokyo, and that he needed our help . . .

KENJI TAMBA · SEPTEMBER, 1942

Yesterday a boy came to our house, asked for me and gave me a note that bore an address in Minato Ward and the name of my old *sensei,* Professor Adachi. *Please come to see me.*

I had heard that he had been jailed at the outbreak of the war with other so-called liberals and peace-faction people. I'd learned of it in a letter from Yuriko and was afraid he'd be in jail for the duration of the war. Now here he was apparently free to send me a note.

I did not tell any of the family, not even Julie, that I was going off to see Professor Adachi . . . after all, maybe it was a trap? Someone playing a joke on me? Better not to involve them until I knew more.

It was a gray humid day when I found my way to the house in Minato Ward—actually a concrete office building of some three stories with a shabby printing shop on the ground floor. I parked my bike in the rack outside and chained it. (In the old days you could leave a bike unchained. Customs had changed with the war, theft was becoming more common.) I checked the names on the slots next to the buzzers and found no Adachi, only a dentist, a lawyer, a machine tool shop, and something called Edo Sugar Export. It seemed the most likely. I buzzed, was buzzed back, the door opened.

The building was old and dingy, the corridors smelling of mold and mildew. Paint and plaster peeled from the stained walls, a single dusty lightbulb lit my way to the top floor. Edo Sugar Export was at the end of a cracked tile hallway. I knocked at a wooden door with a wire-enforced upper section made of opaque glass. A stout young man wearing a radio headset answered the door . . . an odd piece of headgear for someone in the business of exporting sugar, I thought. I presented my card and bowed.

"Tamba," I said.

He bowed a bit lower than I had. "Yoshiro. Please come in."

As I entered I heard a familiar clatter. It was the sound of a teleprinter. Yoshiro escorted me through a dim gray high-ceilinged room to another room, opened the door for me, bowed again and left.

Professor Adachi rose from an old wooden desk cluttered with leaflets, documents, books, notepads and long sheets of teletype copy. He smiled at me, the same pleasant expression I had seen so often in my classes at Tokyo Imperial University. His face was as round as an apple, with pink splotches on his cheeks. His head was bald, except for two white cottony puffs above his ears. He wore rimless spectacles with steel temple pieces. Often when lecturing, I remembered, he removed them and chewed on the metal. Now he wore a threadbare white shirt—I could see stains on the pocket—a frayed black tie and gray trousers that could not possibly accommodate a single new crease.

We bowed.

"Kenji, my boy. How good to see you."

"*Sensei.* I am honored that you sought me out."

Next to parents and ancestors, no one traditionally is revered in Japan as much as a teacher, especially a teacher who opens one's eyes and gives one guidance. Adachi had been that to me. I loved him and respected him. *Sensei*—teacher—is a title of high honor and respect that especially applied to him. He asked me to sit and offered me a cigarette and I recalled he was a chain smoker and that during lectures ashes would dribble onto his vest, stubs burn his fingers. He was periodically assailed with hacking coughs and often threatened to leave Japan for someplace warm, dry and sunny. He never did, of course.

I filled him in on the last year and how I was a man with a wife, a child on the way and unemployed. An Imperial scholar with an American wife wasn't exactly in great demand. He told me how he had been *jailed* after Pearl Harbor. Two jailbirds. He'd kept silent about the attack but some of his prewar writings had attracted the attention of the military police, the *Kempetei.* They'd dragged him from his *futon* in the middle of the night in front of his wife and locked him up in a prison near Kobe. They sounded worse than the FBI.

"They didn't know what to make of me," Adachi said. "After all, I'd helped revise national school curricula and the emperor's brother knew me from the university, so I was questioned, jailed for a while, then classified as a harmless crank, and freed."

"And the Edo Sugar Export Company? Mr. Yoshiro is your sole employee. A sugar exporter wearing a radio headset?"

The gentleman in question had retired to another room. The door was half-open. Now I heard the sounds of a radio crackling. Shortwave? Static? Did I hear scraps of *English?*

"The only sugar that passes through these walls is the single lump for my morning coffee, a habit I learned at Columbia."

I said nothing, waiting.

"You are probably ahead of me, Kenji. We have been financed by certain political figures. I cannot name them. You need not know who they are. No, *not* Americans. We deal with some of my old colleagues in government who hoped for a democratic Japan. Our job is to collect data on the progress of the war—not from Japanese sources but from the West. We have access to newspapers, magazines, radio broadcasts and other data. We read it, digest it, send it on and—"

"Hope that some day the truth will reach someone's ear at the palace."

"That is our hope."

"What if you're caught?"

"We will probably be hanged." He lit a fresh cigarette with the stub of the old one. "One can be ready to die for truth as readily as our military leaders do for their misguided cause."

He had put it well. The guilt I felt over not serving, the churning in my mind about the war, my early private hope that Japan could win quickly and then settle differences with America . . . all these might be resolved some by working with him.

"If you're inviting me to join you, I accept."

"Splendid. You can tell your family you're working for an import-export house. Of course you will not mention me. Say that Yoshiro is your superior. He's unknown, one of my former students. You handle accounts, keep records, whatever comes along.

"Our protection, in a peculiar way, is the mindless confusion of these military bureaucrats. I suspect this firm—as it were—is registered somewhere in a Tokyo office and some bureaucrat has us filed under food trading."

"Then we are the beneficiaries of their incompetence?"

"Yes, in a sense. It's odd how the West views us as an absolutist state on the order of Germany. Not so. Since the mid-twenties, when these virulent policies infected us, there have been eighteen cabinets, fourteen prime ministers, twenty foreign ministers, five army chiefs, six navy chiefs and numberless personnel changes in other high offices. A unified plan and purpose? What drove us into war was an *absence* of leadership, a lack of common design and common sense."

He dragged deeply on his cigarette, coughed, and went on. "The irrationality of our politics, the perversity of state decisions, the persistence of lies and myths, these are what propelled us to Pearl Harbor. Tojo himself admitted that we stumbled into war like so many sleepwalkers. I prefer the analogy of a drunken man falling down a flight of stairs. Did our leaders want war? Yes. Did they try to avoid it? Yes. Paradoxical but true."

"But that is surely a simplification, professor."

"Oh? What does the returned scholar think?"

"The men at the top, the military commanders and advisors to His Majesty, are not stupid people. They had excellent educations. Many studied in England, the United States, Germany. A man like Admiral Yamamoto cannot be regarded as a criminal or a psychopath—"

"More paradox, I agree. Compared to the Hitlers and Himmlers and

Goerings, a collection of thugs, drug addicts, emotional freaks and demented murderers, our leaders are a remarkably refined group. What then?"

"Your old theory? The outlaws?"

"Exactly. Wandering, scurrying in and out of the offices of the men in power, rarely at the top or even formally associated with government. Sometimes they are in uniform, but at a lower level—like the esteemed Colonel Sato and his colleague Commander Endo—"

"And my brother?"

"No. Not Major Tamba. I think too well of him. But he has allowed himself to be used by the outlaws. God help us, and him. We are still paying the price for those legends about heroic wandering *ronin* when the truth is they were by and large a mob of depraved bandits who preyed on the poor. Jesse James and Robin Hood, in legend at least, gave to the poor. Our peripatetic robbers existed to suppress the peasants in the name of greedy noblemen. And today they have put us into a war no one wanted."

I was grateful, but uneasy, about what he had said about Masao. I believed he was basically a good and brave man, my brother, and yet . . .

"The outlaws influence all ranks, run away with policy, and the men at the top—including our benign emperor—find no way to thwart them," the professor went on, perhaps inspired to launch into his old professional rhetoric by seeing me, a former student. "It's the *samurai* business at work —the sword-wielding, avenging, honor-bound wanderers. What a bad historical joke. These devotees of brothels, these self-inflated petty criminals prating about our glorious destiny, our *obligation* to rule the world. Was ever a nation of honest, industrious people sold out in such fashion by such scum?"

For a man who would walk the plank if discovered, Professor Adachi seemed to be having a fine old time. I wondered if I would be as lighthearted when I went to work for him. I wondered how Adachi had been able to get away with such talk at all . . . I suppose the outlaws regarded him as an eccentric fool, with a single gear to his motor.

"Kenji, did you ever try out my theories on your teachers in Los Angeles?"

"I'm afraid not, sir."

"Perhaps it was just as well. The Americans have reason enough to be wary of us, indeed, to hate us."

He abandoned the lecture and wanted to know more about Julie, her family, her brother who was a war correspondent. He even seemed to recall hearing Chris's voice on a broadcast from the Solomon Islands. I filled him in and then we agreed that I would start work the next day. The pay was minimal, but it would help my parents buy food and it would contribute to the upkeep of the house.

As I got up to leave, Yoshiro came in with a sheet of scrawled notes. He had just monitored a newscast from an American shortwave radio station in San Francisco—listening to such a report was punishable by imprisonment and perhaps worse. Professor Adachi scanned the notes and read aloud: "Our crack *Sendai* division has been cut to ribbons on Guadalcanal. Half its officers are dead. Over thirty percent fatalities. General Maruyama has conceded defeat in the face of the American marines' counterattacks. The American flag is still flying over Henderson Field."

"A bad day—"

"But out of it perhaps a better one will come," the professor said.

I got back to my parents' home eager to report on my job with the Edo Sugar Export Company, only to find my mother in a state of distress.

Julie was at the central police station. She had been taken in for questioning. I was, of course, horrified, and demanded to know what had happened. As near as I could tell, it went something like this . . . Officer Tani, the idiot, had asked to see her residence card and other identification papers. She had obliged. But somehow he had decided that she had insulted him, hadn't been properly respectful or some such. After my mother and Julie had returned from shopping Tani had come back in a car with Lieutenant Koga, the plainclothesman from the *Kempetei*. Julie was rudely hustled into the automobile and taken to the military police building in central Tokyo.

I asked my mother why she hadn't told Dr. Varnum and his wife or at least called my father. What? And endanger ourselves? The best thing we could do was to distance ourselves from my wife, she said, to act as if she weren't part of the family. And of course if she were a spy we would have to accept the inevitable. And how would it reflect on my father? Wouldn't his palace superiors think badly of him, even consider dismissing him . . . ?

Angered and flustered I had no time to respond to her incoherent wailings. I was glad no one else was at home to witness her hysteria. Except what could I have expected? She was afraid.

"You see, Kenji, the trouble is coming already," she cried after me as I got on my bike and rode off.

* * *

I was allowed into the police building and kept waiting for about fifteen minutes. Then Koga appeared and led me into an inner room. And there was Julie, on a couch, sipping from a glass of water. Koga and a captain of the *Kempetei* were also on hand.

The captain spoke excellent English. Julie got up quickly and we kissed, which clearly revolted both of the policemen, no doubt reinforcing their prejudice.

The officer lifted a looseleaf notebook from his desk. "I must read to you, Mr. Tamba, an editorial from the *Mainichi* which reflects our views and will explain why your wife was called in for questioning."

"I've heard it already," Julie said, "it isn't much—"

"Madame, you must behave with more respect," he said. "You are an enemy alien. You walk the streets due to our liberal laws and above all because you are married to Major Tamba's brother. That is the *only* reason you are not in prison. Please sit and be silent."

I motioned to Julie to do as he said. I knew she was furious, but I also wanted her to go along with the situation. It could get very serious if she didn't. The officer was looking for an excuse . . . He cleared his throat and read on:

"News has come to us that a British resident of Tokyo, allowed by the grace of His Majesty to be at liberty, used a piano to hide a secret radio transmitter. Any foreigner not playing music on a traditional Japanese instrument is suspect. Let us purge foreign influences. Spies are in the street, in the shops, in the theaters and cafes. Be on the alert for any foreign face and any foreign speech. Keep alert for anyone acting in an unusual way. In that manner the war will end in the expected victory even sooner than we expect . . . ."

Julie stared at the ceiling and shook her head in disbelief. I tried to signal her not to.

"Your wife is behaving incorrectly," the officer said to me. "And let me remind you, Mr. Tamba, that under the shogun Ieyasu, the *samurai* were authorized to cut off the heads of anyone who behaved incorrectly."

Luckily this morsel of shogunate wisdom was in Japanese. I did not translate for Julie.

"What can we do, sir?"

Julie threw her hands up. "Good God, Kenji. They picked me up because Officer Tani heard me playing Benny Goodman and Artie Shaw records. I was teaching Yuriko, *your* sister, to do the Lindy. They seem to think there's a shortwave transmitter in the RCA victrola. It's crazy."

"I can assure you that my wife is no spy—"

"She will be under surveillance, Mr. Tamba. Officer Tani will now

divide his time between the Shibuya Ward clinic and your home. He is
to have access to all those in your home—the possessions, the building
itself."

"Major Tamba will not approve—"

"He will understand. As will your father. It will be a thoughtful surveillance."

And with that he dismissed us. So Julie was suspected of spying because
of "One O'Clock Jump" and "String of Pearls" . . .

As we walked down the steps of the police station she made it clear she
did not think it funny. She balanced on the crossbar of my bike and we
made our way through late afternoon crowds.

"Those pompous jerks," Julie said.

"It's their job, they could have arrested you," I told her. "You got off
easy with a lecture on the dangers of American music."

"It isn't funny, damn it. By the way, you don't sound too sympathetic."

"Forgive me, Julie, I know it's been unpleasant, but may I remind you
that in California I was put in a concentration camp. As were hundreds
of thousands of American citizens who happened to be of Japanese descent. I'm sorry about the hour and a half you spent in a police station
but I don't think they're comparable," I said as I weaved my way past a
bus, got caught between two honking cabs, found myself trailing a horse-
drawn flatbed loaded with sacks of cabbages.

Julie said nothing, obviously fuming. But I felt that old need to defend
my country. I sighed, found a side street on whose cobblestones I could
coast downhill. "Maybe I'd be better off in uniform like Masao. This
business of balancing my life between two loyalties is a lot harder than
balancing this bicycle—"

"But you don't *believe* in the war."

"But I *do* believe in Japan." I had to . . .

We kept silent the rest of the way, until we arrived at my parents' home,
and I told Julie about my job at an exporting company involved in food
trading. She said that was nice but didn't think it fitted my training. I
couldn't tell her the truth . . . better for her not to know . . .

That night after dinner while we sat by ourselves in the garden Julie told
me that she'd learned that Ed Hodges was in a prisoner-of-war camp in
Yokohama, that her Aunt Cora had seen him and he looked in bad shape.

I felt miserable, but also resentful that somehow I was being blamed.
"Julie, I did not capture Ed. I did not attack Wake Island. I am against
this war—"

"Yes, I know . . . well, can we at least try to see him, maybe help him
there? You do know him—"

"Julie, if I show interest in a prisoner I'll be arrested, so will my family and it will make things even worse for Ed. You're being watched right now. You heard the police. Let your aunt visit him, she's in a better position to help than any of us. At least right now . . ."

"Okay, *okay* . . ."

She sounded hurt, angry, and I could understand that. But I also confess to a certain irritation with my lovely American wife. Yes, she was being very American, showing a trait that I had learned to admire and at the same time find somewhat presumptuous in my American friends—and, yes, even in my American wife. Americans are not only sure the world can be made better but that it can be made that way overnight. And the only problem is that somebody refuses to get on with the job. Americans are such optimists, or maybe in some ways such children. Julie saw a bad situation for her friend and mine, Ed Hodges. Her so very American reaction was that something should be done right away, that we somehow could manage it. A nice romantic notion, but the facts, for now at least, were all against it. How to make her understand this . . . ?

Dinner was more silent than ever. Yuriko was working late again, putting in an extra shift at the factory. Saburo began to go on about how he was going to enlist next week—idle talk, since he was still underage.

My father did relay some palace gossip about the fighting on Guadalcanal. Apparently the American navy was taking a beating trying to protect their marines on the island and attempting to hold off the landing of our reinforcements. Our troops, father said, were now on the island in overwhelming numbers and would soon proceed to destroy the Americans.

"Oh, yes," father said, "His Majesty was briefed, and all the news was good. The Americans have only one aircraft carrier still afloat. Ten thousand more of our best men have landed on the island. Marquis Komatsu, our great admiral, is sending his submarines into action. He has already sunk an American carrier. The *Wasp,* I believe."

My mother said, "I only pray Masao is safe."

"He is," Saburo said. "No one can kill Masao."

I said nothing, but I could see the pain on Julie's face, and the anger. When my father mentioned that he had heard that a final death sentence had been handed down on three of the Doolittle flyers who had bombed Tokyo, Julie got up and left the table, not to return that evening.

When I went to her late, she turned aside my embraces and would not talk to me.

I thought of telling her the true nature of my work with Professor Adachi but decided it would only be a self-indulgence. The more she knew, the more she was in danger. Sleep did not come easily that night.

I felt we were moving apart, that our effort to cross the bridge, to be one in spite of the war, might be failing.

YURIKO KITANO · OCTOBER, 1942

My husband was home on leave, more moody and brutish than ever. But he did get some real pleasure out of our son Hiroki.

The factory gave me a week off because of Hideo's leave, a special bonus for the wife of a hero, so I was able to spend much time with the baby, and with my husband, getting pleasure from the former.

Only Hiroki's babbling or laughing could get Hideo out of his shell. He would recline on a *futon* in the main room of our tiny house and reflect on his good luck in having a male son. "A man is not a man until he has a son. Your brother Masao may be a famous warrior and a major, but *he* has only a daughter. So I am the better man."

I said nothing and offered my breast to Hiroki, who always seemed hungry, greedy, sometimes hurting me, but I enjoyed the feel of his strong sucking lips. We shared a pleasure nobody could take from us. When Hideo and I made love, if that is the correct word, he ignored my breasts, never kissed them, and went directly to his pleasure.

"When I die, Hiroki will pray every day at the Buddhist altar where there will be a picture of me to my memory," Hideo was saying.

"You must not talk of death."

"I am not afraid. The son will continue the Kitano name. He will own this house and everything I have, but most of all my good name."

Usually Hideo spoke little of the war. He had been aboard a carrier called the *Shokaku* with his friend Mori and told my father about victories over the Americans at places called Savo Island, Cape Esperance, and other places in the Pacific. I tried not to listen.

Hiroki was already crawling, and Hideo was critical of this, saying that a baby ought not be allowed such freedom before it was a year old. I picked Hiroki up, took off his heavy diaper—he actually smiled when it came off and I didn't blame him—and held his little bottom out the door so he could learn that after eating came the elimination of body wastes. I whistled the same tune in his tiny ear and already he had learned that the response to this was to urinate and defecate. My son was so smart.

Fed, cleaned, purged, the baby could now be presented to his lounging father, who played with him briefly, then suggested we all three go into the bath. I bowed, slid across the floor, and began to fire the charcoal burner attached to the wooden tub.

We took turns holding Hiroki on our knees, jiggling him, splashing him, and he seemed to delight in the play. I think babies know more than we imagine. Hiroki seemed to understand everything, even, apparently, that the strange man in the house was his father.

Watching father and son, all three of us naked in the caress of the hot water, I felt a certain guilt about my renewed visits to Hans, who had reappeared without explanation of where he had been. Well, this was wartime and people were secretive . . . We had never done more than kiss or hold hands, but just seeing Hans had made me unfaithful, a bad woman —I could be divorced or even killed for my crimes. Yet I craved Hans.

That night Hideo forced his sex on me and I felt nothing as he entered me as if I were a rubber doll, gasped, spent himself, toppled aside. A kiss from Hans, a stroking of my hair by my "lover" awoke far more in me than these mechanical couplings with Hideo. It was, literally, criminal of me to think this way, but it was true.

Sometimes Hideo's friend Mori came by—they had both been promoted to lieutenant—and they would get drunk on sake, start to cry, or laugh, or fight, and talk about all the Americans they had killed and the ships they had sunk. Then they would stagger out of the house, giggling, and go to whores. I would bow my head, hold the baby close and like a good Japanese wife not complain. Besides, I was relieved to be left alone.

A traveling troupe was staging a Noh play at a local theater and when I told Julie about it she got excited and we decided, the four of us, to attend a performance of *Dojoji,* a Noh classic.

In the lobby Hideo and Kenji talked some about the war. Apparently, our navy had sunk or damaged many ships around the Solomon Islands. Hideo also told Kenji about Admiral Tanaka's race through a trap set by the Americans . . . "He had only eight destroyers, six of them stripped for transport work, and some cruisers. He ran the gauntlet through a dozen American warships, and he tricked them into firing at each other. Three of their heavy cruisers went down and a fourth was damaged." Kenji asked why, if that was so, it was so hard for us to shove the Americans off Guadalcanal. "Those damned marines," Hideo said. And would say no more as we walked into the theater.

Kenji did not translate any of this for Julie. Kenji and I sat on either side of her, and she was immediately intrigued with the stylized set, the bridgeway with its three pines, the main stage with audience on two sides, musicians on one side, chorus on another, the *shite* pillar, the gazing pillar, the *waki* pillar, the flute pillar.

"It's so *simple,*" she said, "and so perfect."

I told her about the Noh tradition . . . showing off, I guess . . . how in the fourteenth century a kind of purified drama was developed, something like opera, with masks, music, dance, mime. And although on the surface bare and austere, Noh is full of hidden meanings. Hideo wasn't interested in the play and to be honest I preferred a good American film, although there *is* something mysterious about any Noh performance—the grotesque masks, the elaborate costumes, the chanting, the sounds of flutes and drums. Julie loved it also.

The play, *Dojoji,* is an eerie thing. Kenji and I tried to interpret most of it for Julie, and she was puzzled by some of it, as I was, but still seemed to be enjoying herself, and she was a close observer, remarking on the way the actors moved, barely lifting their feet from the floor like Zen priests.

It was hard to explain what the play was about, but Kenji and I tried during the performance . . . At the *Dojoji* temple the abbot and the other priests are waiting for the hanging of a new great bell. A woman dancer enters. Although women are forbidden to witness the ceremony of the bell she lulls the servants, then leaps into the bell. The actor playing the dancer has to be an acrobat and perform the leap while in mask, flowing wig, heavy kimono and a crested outer garment. What the servants and priests don't know is that the female dancer is really a serpent-demon who has come to work revenge on a priest who wronged her. Years ago the spurned woman, in a jealous rage, turned herself into the demon, then with the magic of evil she roasted the priest alive while he was in the bell. The abbot, a wise old man, suspects that the "dancer" is the same demon returning to place a curse on the new bell. When the bell is raised the dancer-woman-demon-serpent inside begins to shake it. Everyone cowers in terror except the abbot. With chants and spells and prayers he forces the demon out of the bell. Then there's a struggle between good and evil, first the demon prevailing, then the abbot. Finally, using his rosary and prayers to overcome her evil, he drives her away. The last scene is really horrible. The woman is cooked in her own roaring fires, then drowns. The final words are a rhythmic chant:

> The breath she vomits at the bell
> Has turned to raging flames

Her body burns in her own fire
She leaps into the river pool
Into the waves of the river Hitaka
And there she vanishes
The priests, their prayers granted
Return to the temple . . .

The actor playing the old abbot stamps his foot from his position at the *shite* pillar and once more the temple is safe from vengeful demons and the bell can ring in all its haunting splendor.

When the lights went on I had to wake Hideo, who had snored through the last half of *Dojoji*. Afterward we walked down a darkened street on our way home, and my husband stopped to urinate in the street. Kenji tried to stop him but he paid no attention. When Kenji and Julie left my husband did not bow, merely grumbled that he needed a shot of whiskey after the play. I trailed him three paces behind like a loyal wife, wishing I had spent the night with Hans.

JULIE TAMBA · OCTOBER, 1942

It was past eleven but the streets were full, people shuffling and clopping, coming or going to factories, coming out of theaters and bars.

"One thing got to me," I said to Kenji. "Why was the demon a woman?"

"That's the way the play was written by Nobumitsu—"

"She was the only villain in the play."

"It's only a *legend*, Julie."

"Right. Men, masters. Women, slaves. And male priests wrote your history—"

"Julie, I thought you enjoyed the play."

"I did, I'm sorry." I took his arm. It was kind of stupid of me to sound off about Japanese life and customs. Our own tradition hardly exalted women either. Better remember what a lovely man I had for a husband . . . and father-to-be . . .

* * *

A few days later I got another letter from my brother Chris. He was still
on Guadalcanal. He said that after death and horrors that he'd never
imagined the Japanese must be wearing down. They had, he wrote, taken
a heavy toll of American shipping, outsmarting and outgunning the best
warships in our navy, but we had managed to land reinforcements. And
the suicide attacks of the Japanese soldiers, led by fanatics who believed
that their divine emperor would protect them, were reducing the Japanese
forces to bands of half-mad marauders.

"We'll hang on here, sis," Chris wrote, "and every Jap we finish off
makes me happier. Admiral Halsey is right when he says we have only
one mission—*Kill Japs, kill Japs, kill Japs.*"

He told me that stories were coming back about the treatment our
POWs were receiving at Japanese hands. On Bataan there had been the
terrible death march. In camps all over the Far East our men—and
Britons, Dutch, Australians and others—were being starved and beaten.
Chris had seen a secret intelligence report that said prisoners at Wake
Island—he was thinking of Ed—had been brutalized just because they had
fought back so hard and embarrassed the Japanese. There had even been
summary executions of POWs in violation of every international treaty on
the treatment of prisoners.

Chris reported he'd also had a bittersweet reunion with our friend from
UCLA, Carol, now Carol Kahn, having married an army surgeon, Major
Herbert Kahn. Carol is a *captain,* highly regarded by her colleagues and
the patients in the field hospitals.

Chris wrote:

> The guy she married seems a good enough Joe but he's *thirteen*
> years older than Carol, fat, bald, with a mustache. Jewish guy from
> New Jersey with two teenage boys. He must have been dippy about
> Carol because he divorced his wife and lost contact with his
> children. Anyway, he's a hell of a surgeon, saved more lives out
> here than a trunkful of holy medals and I'm glad Carol found a
> husband. Well, I tried to be glad. The major is a little standoffish
> with me, maybe he knows or guesses I was there before him. Hey,
> I like the guy, and we have a drink every now and then. But when
> the shelling lets up and there aren't too many wounded marines
> coming in, I sort of resent him, I admit it. I liked Carol a lot more
> than I let on, but I try not to wallow in self-pity over a busted
> romance. There's too much else around here to feel bad about. Any
> chance of you coming stateside and getting out of that deal? I can't

believe you choose to live with them. I wonder if I'll ever be able
to look a Nip in the face again and feel anything other than a
desire to smash it. Sorry, sis, but them's my sentiments . . .

Chris's letter upset me, made me think of the worst things that might
happen to Ed. Made me thing about my own situation, and wonder if I'd
ever be able to explain Kenji and me to my brother. . .
Then I got what was almost good news . . . Dr. Reinhold, the International Red Cross official, was unexpectedly called for a camp inspection,
in answer to his repeated requests. It happened so fast that Aunt Cora
wasn't invited, but Reinhold gave her a report on what he'd seen and she
now filled me in as we sat in the clinic garden. She'd just examined me,
and the verdict was that the baby seemed to be thriving on my rice diet,
supplemented by Uncle Adam's vitamins.
"Did Dr. Reinhold see Ed?" I asked.
"No, but that may be good news."
And she told me that two of Ed's sergeants . . . I remembered the names
from when Ed was in OCS at Camp Pendleton, Sergeant Guzzo and
Sergeant Goodwin . . . had told Dr. Reinhold that Ed had been sick for
a time with a bad fever, but the men had looked after him and when he
got better the Japanese had put him on what they called detached service
in the dispatcher's office of a railyard. He and three other men with
university educations had been sent there to help run trains, keep
schedules, supervise other POWs in loading and unloading freight cars.
They all lived in a shack near the dispatcher's office and had a pretty good
deal. Only one guard was assigned to the special unit. From the description, I sensed that it was possible that I could visit Ed. The Japanese
apparently allowed several such special units a good deal of freedom.
There were even, Guzzo angrily told Dr. Reinhold, some POWs who were
working as writers and broadcasters for Japanese propaganda radio.
Guzzo obviously considered them collaborators. What the men in the
warehouse wanted more than anything, Sergeant Goodwin told Dr. Reinhold, when the guards were out of earshot, was a radio. Dr. Reinhold said
it would violate his neutral status if he tried to smuggle one in. Before
leaving Dr. Reinhold tried to get the name of the railyard where Ed was
stationed but no one seemed to know . . . one morning Ed and some other
men were simply ordered to pack their kits and move out . . .
As I listened to Aunt Cora's story I wondered if it was true or had it
all been cooked up to get rid of Dr. Reinhold. Maybe . . . I had to face
it . . . Ed was dead and this was a cover story. Dr. Reinhold had said he
had evidence of beatings and torture of officers and noncoms, of isolation

in hotboxes, of starvation rations. Guzzo, Goodwin and some of the others, he'd said, looked underweight and infected with parasites and sores. He couldn't explain the invitation to visit the warehouse, except that maybe if the Japanese had been defeated at Guadalcanal and felt the war was going against them they were now trying to behave a bit more humanely.

I wanted to believe the best, and asked Kenji what he thought. I shouldn't have been too surprised that Kenji was getting a little tired of my worrying over Ed, although he tried not to show it . . .

Masao Tamba · NOVEMBER, 1942

I had to shoot five more severely wounded men today. They died so bravely. A sixth, Corporal Itagi, a young man from Osaka, begged to be killed also. He has malaria and shakes from head to foot. His teeth chatter and make awful echoes in the cave. He'll probably die tonight. Outside, the rain never stops. We do not bury the dead any more. We roll them into a flooded ravine. The jungle, the torrent and the ants finish off their remains. But it is not a bad death to go back to nature. We all are fashioned from earth, and to earth we return, a purification of flesh and spirit . . .

My own wound is troublesome. It started on my left forearm, a glancing bullet from a marine rifle during our last charge at Henderson Field. The Americans have a new semiautomatic rifle, and it has made a difference. Sometimes I wish it had killed me, but I live so that we can fight again. The wound just will not heal, we have no drugs, no bandages and our last medical corpsman was killed weeks ago. We keep being told about new supplies landing with new men, but they don't come. For a while kegs of rice and medical supplies and ammunition were floated ashore but the Americans learned about them and blasted them out of the water . . .

The wound. Now it has turned a bright orange. Blisters and running gouges. It is an infection I have never seen. It is also very painful but I have learned to ignore pain, fatigue and fear. There isn't much feeling in my left hand and I cannot flex the fingers. The orange growth on the arm festers and smells badly. I pick maggots from it every morning. One of my lieutenants, a former biology student, says it's a bacterial infection but he has no idea what kind. I have tried to cut away the orange stuff with my trench knife, but in a day the infection is back, the pain is worse. I am well aware that the infection may spread internally and kill me.

My mind rejects that we are being beaten. Our navy does keep punishing the American ships, hitting, running, landing men. I am told we have over fifteen thousand soldiers on Guadalcanal, but of course many are too ill or wounded to fight. The Americans will not bend, will not retreat. One of our colonels put it well when he reported to General Hyakutake, our commander, that we failed because we underestimated the enemy's fighting power . . . Hyatukake, in turn, reporting the disaster of Guadalcanal to the emperor, said he deserved "the sentence of a thousand deaths" for our failure. General Kawaguchi says he feels "as if his intestines have been cut out." Hypocrites, all of them. They have not been up to their knees in blood and shit and brains and bones the way my men and I have . . .

On our rusted radio set my signalman had some good news today. The War Ministry is determined to win back Guadalcanal. Twelve thousand men of the crack 38th Division will be landed to reinforce us, to resupply us and to break the Americans' backs. Henderson Field will be ours and the Rising Sun will replace their flag. Yes, I believe that will happen. I must believe it.

Late today, during a downpour that made it impossible to see a meter through the jungle, my aide caught one of the starving men eating the liver of one of the wounded I had shot. I killed the cannibal with one shot from my automatic, blowing his forehead apart.

As I pulled the trigger, drenched with rain, watching him topple into the ravine with the blood of a human liver on his lips, I thought of my wife Michiko, my daughter Maeko, and my peaceful home. Odd.

YURIKO KITANO · NOVEMBER, 1942

Hideo's leave was over, and on the night before he left he beat me with his fists, making sure he struck my body so that no one could see the bruises and warning me to be silent about it. He was drunk, yes, and in the morning said he did not remember doing these things. I let it go. At least he was leaving.

When he'd gone Michiko brought her little girl Maeko to our house, and my mother, Michiko and myself had a wonderful time dressing the children up, watching Hiroki crawl after his little cousin, watching them share toys, laugh and eat. They took my mind off the sorrows of my marriage . . . I had resolved to look for Hans Baumann again. This time he had been away a month or more . . .

The talk eventually got around to my brother Masao. Not a word had been heard from him for many months. Our newspapers said we were smashing the American army on Guadalcanal and that soon the men fighting there would be on their way home. Why then had we heard nothing from Masao?

"I pray he isn't dead. My oldest. It would destroy your father," my mother said.

"My father asked at the War Ministry," said Michiko. "They have no word. Communication is hard and not many letters get out."

"Perhaps they're forbidden to write if we're losing," I said.

My mother and Michiko chided me for even thinking such thoughts. "It would be very sad if Masao were to die without a son to carry on his name," my mother said, making me feel even more rotten. But Michiko bowed her head in apology. "I am sorry, Mother Tamba."

"When he returns you must do anything he wishes, please him in every way and create a son for him."

"I will try."

"There are old women in the countryside who know about plants and herbs and seeds that will make a woman produce male children. We'll go to see one of them someday," my mother added. Of course I didn't believe this folklore but said nothing . . .

Julie was not at home. She had gone with Dr. Cora Varnum to see a man at the Red Cross. She was so secretive about the visit . . . I think it had to do with her American friend whom she believes is a prisoner in Tokyo or Yokohama.

My mother, taking advantage of Julie's absence, looked about as if to make sure she was not there, then said, "It is hard for me, the *gaijin* woman in my house. She will bear a child soon, and it may very well be a boy. But our Masao, the jewel of this house . . ."

Michiko promptly began to cry, and I wished again she would not accept so passively such insinuations from my mother. My mother was very old-fashioned and did deserve respect, but Michiko was like a servant in front of her . . . She had wanted so much to please Masao she had even stopped her painting, and she was a woman of genuine talent. Michiko seemed born to be made miserable, and it made me mad.

"Don't cry," my mother said, "it will only make me cry. I have a bad feeling we may never see Masao again—"

"I will pray for him," Michiko said. "Yuriko, you and I will go to the temple in Ueno Park and pray for Masao and ask the Bodhisattva to place a son in my belly. We can offer Kannon a boy's doll, a little soldier in uniform." She actually began to smile, making herself, and my mother, feel better. Yes, I would go with her, but I would be thinking of Hans Baumann.

KENJI TAMBA · DECEMBER, 1942–JANUARY, 1943

By way of press reports and Professor Adachi's secret radio receptions we now know the truth of Japan's defeat on Guadalcanal. The vicious fighting has all but ended in the Solomons. Japan had a total of 40,000 men on Guadalcanal and Tulagi. Twenty-three thousand died there. We . . . yes, *we,* regardless of my feelings about the wrongness of the war I still deep down identify with my country, my brother . . . we were fortunate to evacuate most of the survivors but it's estimated that thousands of starving diseased Japanese soldiers are hiding in the jungle and caves. Naturally I wonder if Masao is among them. As a field officer, one would think some word would be forthcoming about him, but neither my father nor Colonel Sato can learn anything about Masao.

Among our generals Guadalcanal is now known as the "Island of Death." This of course is not heard on any of our official radio reports or printed in any newspapers. It is part of the secret information that finds its way to Professor Adachi's ears.

Admiral Yamamoto, in spite of losses inflicted on the Americans, has conceded the loss of two battleships, three cruisers, twelve destroyers, sixteen transports and hundreds of planes. Always a reluctant dragon, Yamamoto and Admiral Tanaka have told their superiors—but *not* His Majesty—that Japan's fate is sealed. Tanaka has written to friends that Guadalcanal proved to us the strength and character of the enemy—I could have told them that.

I tried phoning Colonel Sato today and could not get through. Then

Yoshiro came in with notes he'd made on the latest Allied radio report. The Americans and Australians say that the battle for Papua in New Guinea has ended. Buna Mission and Gona have fallen after last-ditch stands by our men. The last survivors put on gasmasks to protect themselves from the smell of putrefying bodies. And when the Australians had killed the last defenders at Buna and overrun our positions there was evidence that we had resorted to cannibalism to stay alive.

Yet at the Imperial Palace, in the grand rooms and halls, on the picturesque wintry grounds where snow covers the stone bridges and massive walls and peaked roofs, life goes on as if all were going well for our armed forces.

If any word of defeat has reached Tenno Heika's ears it is couched in language that conceals the extent of the disasters. Courtiers and officials come and go. Ladies of the court in traditional dress shuffle and mince about in sandals. The royal family conducts levees, fetes, dinners. My father counts napery, polished silver, sets chairs, serves tea. It's heartening, he has told me, how calm Tenno Heika is, how even-tempered even in the face of discouraging news. The servants agree among themselves that while we have suffered losses the war will be won. We wait for a final great battle and peace will follow.

On a snowy day, I waited for my father outside the Ishi Bashi gate of the palace, having received word at my office that he wanted to see me.

Snow covered the stone walls and the bridges and moats, and I was reminded of the photographs of the army mutiny of February, 1936 that showed soldiers setting up machine guns and taking positions in the great plaza amid a storm of snowflakes. It chilled me to recall that Masao, as a cadet, that Colonel Sato, then a captain, secretly backed the mutineers.

As such notions swirled in my head, like the snow that so delicately fell on the stony plaza, I saw my father emerge, and with him was a tall woman wearing a quilted blue coat. I could not see her face. They bowed —she bending much lower than he did—and she went off, slipping slightly in her *geta*s.

I crossed the street and bowed to my father. He was gazing at the woman, who, I was to learn, was his mistress Fumiko, a buxom maid at the palace, arranged for him by the fixer, Mr. Hata. My father told me all this quickly, with no apologies. Apparently my mother even knew about it. I hoped Julie wouldn't find out. And I shuddered to think what she'd do to me if I ever strayed. Well, she needn't worry, I never would. We might have our problems, but *that* was not one of them . . .

My father and I stopped at a stand selling *soba,* and each of us slurped the piping hot buckwheat noodles. The *soba* was served with a soya sauce and a dab of tongue-curling *wasabi,* grated green horseradish. My father treated me. He knew I earned little in my job at the "sugar exporting company," and that meals at home had become routine successions of rice, barely livened by poorhouse scraps of fish.

Casually, he then told me he had overheard General Sugiyama and others—his job was to serve them tea—talking about the enormous casualties inflicted on the Americans at Guadalcanal and that in spite of the withdrawal of Japanese forces the campaign could be accounted a *victory.* His Majesty, advised of the end of the Guadalcanal battle, had called the matter "regrettable" but was in a good frame of mind. The crushing of Japanese forces at Gona and Buna in New Guinea apparently was not discussed or at least my father's attentive ear had heard nothing of those places. Illusion, delusion, misinformation seemed the order of the day in the palace.

We finished the last of the *soba* and proceeded to walk the snowy streets, me wheeling my bicycle, which could not get much traction in the snow since I was riding on the rims. Besides, my father seemed eager to walk slowly, and to get something off his mind.

"Your mother wanted me to tell you something."

"Yes?"

"Now that you're working . . . she thinks you and your wife should move . . ."

I had been anticipating this, but not until after Julie had given birth. It shocked me, but I also remembered my place in the family and the rules of behavior regarding second sons. "It would be difficult, father. There are no places available in Tokyo. I receive little salary and the baby—"

"Your wife makes your mother unhappy. I know this is not easy for you to hear, but it is so. She is not like a Japanese daughter-in-law, it is hard for your mother to give her orders—"

"When has Julie ever refused to help?"

"Your mother feels she does so with resentment. Kenji, this marriage is against everything we believe. You *know* that. It is an honored tradition that parents select a son's wife through a go-between. That is how Masao married Michiko. That is how Hideo's family and ours agreed on Yuriko's marriage. You chose to disobey these rules and marry a *gaijin*—you have made life difficult—"

"I understand, but Masao carries on the name, his children will—"

"Masao has no son. And Masao may be dead. We must face that. Kenji, it was your *oya on* to your family to have married a Japanese woman selected by me. It is now your duty to act honorably, to leave us and let us live our separate lives."

We stopped at a busy crossing. A few Christmas decorations—pine branches and willow branches—dangled from store signs. The city was covered with a pale mist—snow, dust, dirt. Yet it was haunting, beautiful. People were packed five and six deep at the traffic crossing, patiently waiting for a signal from the policeman. I sensed again that feeling of security and protection, of safe haven, that Japanese cherish in crowds—why we go on vacations in groups, avidly join our factory associations, cling to one another. When the cold wind whistles and the snow falls, when fire and earthquake strike, when we struggle against the floodtide we seem to find reassurance in the knowledge that there are hundreds of thousands like us, all in the same fix. I sensed it, as I say, but I no longer felt part of it . . .

My father had surely placed me in a desperate position by referring to my filial obligations, my *oya on.* Much of Japanese life is based on such obligations and their reciprocals. And now as my father and I trudged the snowy streets at the end of the work day I realized that I was in the trap of an ancient tradition. I had received an *on* from my parents and had failed to fulfill it, my obligation. For this I would forever be held in low esteem by my family, except Yuriko, who understood me and liked Julie.

I told my father again the hardship it would be for us to leave now, and by the time we approached the street leading to our home, he seemed to have relented . . . he was not, after all, a cruel man but he did live by a rigid code.

"Then perhaps after the child is born," he said, "after the *gaijin* woman—"

"Father, can't you learn to call my wife by her name?"

"Someday, perhaps." He sounded unhappy, struggling to hide his affection for me.

"Is it only mother who wants us to leave?"

"No, I agree."

"Then I will try to honor your wishes, but please do allow us to stay through the birth of my child—"

"I will talk to your mother." Then suddenly, as we came up to our house, he said, "Do you recall, Kenji, the day you and Masao won the kite-flying contest in Ueno Park?"

"I do, father, yes . . ."

"I was very proud of both of you. Didn't you design the kite? A carp chasing a minnow?"

"I did. It was red and gold. Masao laughed at me. But when he saw how beautiful it was he insisted on helping me fly it."

"I remember it so well. A sunny day. We ate cold *soba* after the contest. After you and Masao won prizes. What were they?"

"Toy soldiers."

"Yes. Little *samurai.*" He paused outside the veranda. We could see the dim light inside, anticipate the warmth of the *kotatsu,* the hot bowls of rice, cups of hot green tea. As the snow beat at our faces my father smiled and for a moment I almost thought he would touch my arm or my face, but of course he did not. He could not.

"I'm glad you were happy that day, father."

"I have had many happy days with our family. But this war . . . come, let's go in."

I took off his sandals as he sat on the small bench in the foyer, put on his slippers—a good second son. I hoped I could continue the performance until the birth of my child.

JULIE TAMBA · FEBRUARY, 1943

The baby was due any moment. I went to see Aunt Cora and Uncle Adam every other day, not so much because I needed medical treatment —I seemed to be thriving on a rice diet, but wondered if my stomach would droop permanently the way Japanese women's are supposed to do on account of so much clotted rice—I just enjoyed their company and they often had word from the States, news of the war that Cora would get through the Swiss consulate.

This morning there was a letter from my parents and one, surprise of surprises, from Captain Carol Kahn.

My parents' letter was warm, brief. They'd stopped asking me directly to come home, but still tried in a roundabout way . . . no reason that Kenji and I couldn't be together when the war ended, why prolong my misery in Tokyo . . . ? I'd told them—not exactly the truth—that I was very comfortable in the Tamba house in Shibuya Ward and that everyone was swell to me. Of course I didn't give them the details about the frigid rooms in the winter, the flicker of heat from the *kotatsu,* the weight of the *futons* we had to wrap ourselves in to keep our teeth from chattering, the diet of rice forever, the smells from the john with its honeybuckets (ha!), the lack of privacy, with Hisako and Goro sleeping on the other side of the paper divider, or charming little Saburo

clomping around in wooden sandals above our heads. Picture-
postcard notions of gracious Japanese homes, the *shoji* screens, *tatami*
mats, elegant woodwork, floral decorations—not my life at the Tamba
house.

My parents sent me some newspaper clippings about Chris Varnum, the
hot young war correspondent. He was due home for leave, my folks said,
and they really couldn't wait for his homecoming.

Carol's letter:

> I can't tell you enough about Herb. We work together in the
> operating room and it's an inspiration to me how he dedicates
> every ounce of strength and skill to saving lives. We get guys with
> limbs missing, bodies torn apart, head wounds. They've fought
> hard to hold this miserable island, and now that we've just about
> secured it the goddamn Japs keep hitting back, picking off patrols,
> sending suicide squads into our lines. What can they gain? No one
> can figure them out.
>
> Herb and I go to our work every day together. It's funny how
> this makes you feel about the Japs—maybe I shouldn't tell you
> this, but it makes you *hate* them. Chris—I see him every now and
> then although lately he's been covering the navy and been at sea—
> has probably told you the same thing. I know you feel differently
> but damn it, I won't lie about my feelings. Of course I don't hate
> Kenji. Herb says there was at least one encouraging sign toward
> the end of the fight for Guadalcanal. The Japanese evacuated more
> than 20,000 men from this hellhole and Herb says this proves they
> aren't all ready to die in suicide attacks and may be losing some of
> their stomach for war. Well, enough of that . . . I'm enclosing a
> photograph of Herb and yours truly and would love to hear from
> you. How's Kenji? Chris said you were pregnant. Wish you all the
> best, honey. I mean that. Hey, you ever think about UCLA and
> movies in Westwood Village and jitterbugging? Seems a few
> thousand years ago . . .

The photo she included showed a sort of paunchy guy, bald-headed,
with a black toothbrush mustache. He looked good-natured, and he had
his arm around Carol, who looked pretty much as she did when she was
a student, except that her dark brown hair was clipped short. They both
wore wrinkled suntans. They looked happy and I envied them, even
though they were living in the "green hell" where so many thousands of
our men had died. They knew where they stood. No complications, no
mixed feelings.

KENJI TAMBA · FEBRUARY, 1943

Yoshiro picked up an American radio broadcast today that told about an American naval victory in the Bismarck Sea, off the island of New Britain. A disaster for us.

With Guadalcanal gone, the Imperial High Command was apparently making an effort to reinforce our troops on New Guinea. The emperor had himself, we learned, expressed the desire that the army and navy not "make the same mistakes" in New Guinea that they had on Guadalcanal.

According to the broadcast American bombers had sighted our transports under a clear sky and proceeded to pound them with a new bombing technique, dropping the bombs from low altitude the way a boy scales a stone across a lake. These "skip bombs" played hell on the tightly packed ships. More than twenty ships, most of them destroyers and heavily loaded transports, packed to the gunwales with troops, were blown apart, sent to the bottom. Japanese planes, launched from support carriers, were now no match for newly designed American fighters, and over sixty of ours were shot down. The communiqué said that *less than two hundred* of the fifteen thousand men destined for New Guinea got there. The Americans cut them to pieces.

The handwriting, it seems to me, was on the wall, but no one at the highest levels of government seemed able or willing to read it. Adachi shook his head.

"When?" I asked, knowing there was no good answer.

YURIKO KITANO · FEBRUARY, 1943

Hideo came home from a navy hospital. The whole upper part of his body was covered with burns and he had a row of bullet wounds on his upper back. It was a miracle that he was alive. His parents cried and I felt for him too, but not as a wife for a husband. Why lie? He was thin and yellowish green and he drank even more than before. At night he and his friend Mori, who had lost his right arm and was being discharged, would sit in our house around the charcoal fire and get drunk on sake.

I would cradle Hiroki in my arms, feed him and wish that I had married someone else. Was that terrible of me? Hideo Kitano was a war hero who had been through hell. But I could not like him, feel for him. I never did, I never could.

"Those bastards," Mori said, "the way they shot at us . . ."

They would spit into the *kotatsu,* roll around the *futons.* Sometimes I wondered if Mori did not like men better than women.

Hideo ripped off his kimono and showed the vivid red-and-white scars that covered his shoulders and chest. He'd been lucky—plunged into a burning oil slick, finding a hatch cover and floating away to where one of the destroyers cold pick him up. Mori had been found unconscious in a lifeboat.

One night when Mori wasn't there . . . he'd gone back to the hospital to have his arm treated . . . we were huddled around the *kotatsu* trying to keep warm, and suddenly Hideo simply broke down and began to cry. He'd only had a little to drink this time, but less and less had begun to affect him more and more. It would have been impossible not to have felt a sympathy for him, not to try to comfort him. He was mourning over his dead shipmates, the dead soldiers they were taking to New Guinea. "The water was all red with our blood," he said. He cursed the Americans for being so bloodthirsty, and when I dared to say that we had started the war—I don't know that I'd ever said that before—he insisted that we had been forced into it by the humiliation the Americans had forced on us. How, he didn't say, but I knew he was sincere, that he meant it, that he had been taught and, as Kenji had told me, brainwashed by the top government officials in the military. He and so many others . . .

He came to me now for comfort, not sex, and I could not deny it, even though as I held him, sobbing and sniffling in my arms, I also could remember the beatings and insults. But I was to forgive that, as the world was to excuse whatever atrocities our forces may have committed against our foes. Just as we were to believe that the war was being won, no matter if it was not. Our men simply could do no wrong . . . But just now Hiroki began to fuss and cry and demand my breast. And here he was in competition with his father, who had pulled apart my nightdress and was sucking at my nipples, burying his nose and mouth in my small breasts, whimpering like an infant. When I told him that Hiroki was hungry, had to be fed, he said the baby could wait, that he needed me, and when I tried to get up, to remove him from me, he swung his arm and hit me on the side of the head, then collapsed to the floor, dead to the world, and began to snore.

I couldn't stand it any longer. It was impossible even to feed my baby, the milk wouldn't come. I had to get away, get out of there. Our next-door neighbor, a nice elderly woman named Mrs. Motoda, knew all about my situation, about Hideo's drunken rages and fists, and I ran now to her door, found her awake . . . who could sleep with our battles going on? . . . left my son with her and told her I was afraid to stay at my own house. And then I ran off to find a trolley . . . to go to Hans Baumann . . .

It was bitter cold. The wind whipped across the darkened streets—the war had forced a cutback on the use of electricity, coal was rationed, the streets were dirty, in contrast to our tradition of immaculate cleanliness. On the trolley car the conductor looked hard at me, and I felt he was seeing right through my coat to my nightclothes, and I pulled my coat tighter around me. But there was no way to hide the teary streaks on my face.

I didn't care, though, I had to try to see Hans. It had been months since I'd heard from him, and I was taking a chance that he wouldn't be at his home, but I had to go anyway. When I got to his building it looked deserted—it was a three-story ramshackle wooden affair at the end of a street that was not much more than a muddy alley. All right, if he wasn't there I'd have to go back, but at least I'd tried . . .

I opened the door of the building and ran up the creaky stairs to the top floor where Hans lived. I rapped at the door. A light went on. The door opened a crack. And then wider, as he saw it was me.

"Yuriko . . . come in." He was wearing a blanket thrown around his robe. He looked pale and cold, but to me more handsome than ever. "Come *in,* I'm delighted to see you. I'll try to start the fire again."

It was truly freezing, and all he had was a small copper brazier with a few sticks of smouldering charcoal. He pulled it close to the low couch and told me to sit down, then heated some water for tea.

Suddenly I let loose, the tears came. He sat down beside me and took my hands in his, said nothing, waiting. I couldn't hold back any longer, and told him about Hideo, the beatings, the drunkenness, and even as I told him I felt guilty for doing it, a part of me thinking I ought to have been more tolerant of my husband, he was suffering in his own way, had seen awful things like shipmates drowning, machine-gunned, roasted alive in burning lakes of oil . . .

"Yuriko, stop trying to be a saint. You have your needs and feelings too. We all do . . ."

We sat close together on the couch and sipped tea. I asked him where he had been, and he told me more of what he was doing . . . gathering information about Japan for German colleagues, but not the Hitler regime, which he said he hated, even though it was supposed to be an ally of Japan. I told him how badly Kenji and Julie had said the Germans aboard the *Gripsholm* had behaved, how they had snubbed everybody, especially the Japanese.

Hans laughed and poured some sake for us, which warmed even better than the tea, and he told me that he was one of many Germans who hated the Nazis and were working for a kind of democratic socialism to take power after the war, which he expected the Germans to lose. Before I could ask him anything more he had embraced me and kissed me, kissed my mouth, pressed me back onto the sofa. I was looking right into his eyes and I wanted him very much, but I also was terribly afraid . . .

Hans got up to add some sticks to the fire, and I sat up and looked at the map of Asia that he had on the wall. I tried to find the place where Hideo had been, and where Masao might be, although the family, as I told Hans, thought he was dead—even if they didn't want me to know it . . .

And suddenly I felt faint, and Hans was there, holding me and then lowering me to the couch and lying down beside me. He pulled the *futon* over us.

"Try not to think such things," he told me. "You need some relief from your grim thoughts, we all need our escape."

His hands were caressing my breasts, he began to remove my clothing —my coat, my robe, the nightdress . . . he found my thighs, and I received him and I was full of nothing but the joy of him.

"I will be punished," I began to say, but he sealed my lips with his, mingling our tongues, and I felt warm and truly in union with him. Did I also love him at this moment? I surely thought so . . .

MASAO TAMBA · FEBRUARY, 1943

Colonel Ota took his life today.

I confess I never liked the man but his death did him more honor than his misguided life as a soldier.

We did not try to stop him. The fifteen of us who live in this cave deep in the mountains stood there—what a collection of ragged, half-dead remnants of human wreckage we are—and bowed our heads while Ota committed his expiation, disgraced forever by our defeat and his poor leadership.

His orderly had fashioned a robe out of the remains of an American parachute and draped it over Ota's spindly body. The colonel then sat cross-legged at the mouth of the cave, recited the Shinto prayers and asked for his ceremonial dagger.

The man was a terrible field commander but he could have given lessons in the proper mode of committing *hara-kiri*. The code states that in taking one's life one must not topple to the side or subject oneself to spasmodic, jerking, blood-spattering movements. In this regard the suicide was masterful. Ota fell forward, his head in line with his knees.

He had done this well, using the dagger to cut only his stomach muscle without touching the bowels or any inner organs. That way little blood was visible. The wound was shallow and needed only an inch or two of the gleaming blade. He fell forward with grace, unflinching. I then had the honor of performing the final stroke. I unsheathed my saber and took off his head with a single downward blow that would have earned praise from Musashi.

"Farewell, colonel," I said. "Go to the gods."

That night we ate white grubs and the roots of a wild yam. I knew that cannibalism was common among men hiding in the cave a thousand meters from us. I'd seen the corpses with their livers and hearts cut out, and tried my best to keep my men from eating the dead. Sometimes I had to beat them and wondered how long I would be able to hold them off.

A few days later the survivors of the unit in the other cave launched an attack with two rusty rifles and bamboo spears against a marine outpost, and they all died, screaming their *banzai*s, cut down by machine guns.

I am wondering now if some of my men regard me as a coward for trying to keep us alive. There is little hope that we can be evacuated from the island. We did succeed in getting twenty thousand men off, and when I volunteered to lead the rear guard units that would protect their evacuation I knew I would be stranded.

My lower left arm was amputated a week ago. I bit on a green branch while my sergeant cut the gangrened lower half of my arm from my body, hacked at the bone, cauterized the stump with a burning brand. I am proud I did not cry. No sooner did I begin to recover from the fevers and agonies that the infection had sent through my body than I developed a painful infection in my left eye. It is apparently a tropical organism of some kind, and it seems to be eating at the eye itself, and I have trouble seeing. We caught a Melanesian native the other day and tried to ask him how to treat the infected eye. Is it a worm? The egg of an insect? Is there some native remedy for it? The man could tell us nothing. We shot him. . . .

Now I am all but blinded, but I still try to rally the men, send parties out searching for food. We will try to stage a night raid and steal food from marine patrols, perhaps kill a few of them—although that would probably guarantee our destruction. I am personally determined to live, to fight again. Ota's suicide charges proved futile and destructive only to us. The marines kept killing us. That idiot—I honor his death, not his life—kept sending my men into frontal charges against protected positions. And we died by the thousands, blood-spattered, ravaged bodies piled high . . .

The last radio report we heard before the batteries died and we lost contact with the outside world said that Guadalcanal was not a defeat, not a retreat but a "clever redeployment" of troops. The commentator said that it was merely one of many islands and the loss of an island did not matter to a great empire like Japan.

I wonder where he was when he made the broadcast, or if he has ever seen these Americans fight.

KENJI TAMBA · FEBRUARY, 1943

My father told me that some months ago His Majesty went to pray at the holiest of holy places in Japan, the shrine at Ise dedicated to the sun goddess, the founder of our race.

Colonel Sato was a member of the official party that accompanied Tenno Heika and told my father that the emperor was pensive, his aides reassuring him that the war was being won and that the defeat at Guadalcanal was at worst a minor setback.

The emperor entered the wooden hut surrounded by giant cryptomeria trees and prayed for the continued "fertility and well-being" of his beloved people. In the sanctuary he was met by the high priestess of Ise, who was related to him. In the holy place he gazed into the mirror of the sun goddess, his ancestor, and saw Amaterasu's face. At least so said my father. I knew the legend, and I did not believe a word of it.

Sato, in a gossipy mood, also told my father that he had heard from certain palace officials a disturbing report . . . that the Son of Heaven had suggested to his advisors that he really never thought of himself as a god and suspected that this notion had been deliberately fostered by various superpatriots and military leaders. He was, Sato had heard, uneasy with the concept that he was "above the clouds" and had no obligations to speak out, to take issue with others. The emperor's advisors keep reassuring him that he is indeed a god, and that it is crucial to the conduct of the war that he maintain his position of divinity. After all, the generals and admirals argue, his brave soldiers find it easier to die for a god than a mere "organ of the state." It was suspected, Sato told my father, that Hirohito was looking ahead to a time when he would have to deal with foreign powers, after the war ended. Being a mere mortal who was a functionary of the state would make things easier for him . . .

This suspicion worried the extremists. It sounded as if His Majesty was becoming defeatist, was depressed at the downward trend of the war. So, argued Sato, it was all the more important for true patriots, those who deeply loved and admired and worshipped the emperor, to keep reminding him that he was in truth a god. Comments like those of Admiral Yamamoto, reeling from the beating his navy had taken in the Solomons and New Guinea, must be kept from the Imperial ears . . . "We must keep Yamamoto and other faint hearts from spreading their treasonous words. Yamamoto says we are now hostages to fortune . . ."

Tensions between Julie and me had been building, and erupted during the "celebrations" for New Year's, 1943. Actually it began the day after New Year's when we came to my father's house and saw Yuriko tying three branches to one of the wooden pillars on the porch. Yuriko said it would not be a proper New Year's without them, but she'd had trouble finding them.

"Bamboo, pine, plum tree," she said. "Aren't they pretty?"

"Oh, yes, great," Julie said a bit tentatively. She was very pregnant and uncomfortable.

I tried a little pedagogy. "The pine tree symbolizes strength and long life, the bamboo is vitality and resilience. And we honor the plum tree because it blossoms in the snow and teaches us courage and endurance."

"I wish I had more of both," Julie said, patting her stomach but meaning more than that, I knew.

"You're doing great," I said.

"Am I?"

I felt nervous for her. She was bloated by the child, ungainly in her padded coat, shuffling in wooden clogs. We'd spent an hour trying to buy vegetables on the outskirts where some farmers peddled their wares, and all we'd come back with was a shriveled cabbage and one *daikon*. We were both very tired.

In the doorway Yuriko, before leaving for a night shift, stretched a straw rope with neatly folded paper bows tied to it.

"And this?" Julie asked.

"The *shimenawa*. To welcome the gods of the New Year."

"I'm glad someone's welcome around here," she muttered to me.

We had brought belated gifts for my family, things Julie had been hoarding since our arrival. Actually we exchange gifts at Christmas, a ceremony we learned from the West. Even though most Japanese are not Christians they enjoy buying presents, wrapping them in fancy paper, decorating a tree with ornaments and displaying Oriental-looking Santa Clauses. This year, of course, these celebrations were being downplayed, both for economic and patriotic reasons. So Julie and I compromised with gifts to mark our first New Year in Japan.

It was smoky and cold in the house, and my father sat at the *kotatsu* as close as he could get to the glowing charcoal in the hibachi below it, his nose buried in his newspaper. My mother was at a low writing table composing a letter to Masao. She wrote every other day, although she had no idea if the letters ever reached him, or even if he were alive.

It was one of the coldest days we had yet had. All of us seemed to be living in long woolen underwear and layers of outer clothing. Despite the hot baths we did not, I fear, smell too prettily. Our clothing was imbued with smoke, and the closeness of the house and lack of ventilation did not help. In the poorly lit room I could see my father squinting at the newspaper, holding it a few inches from his weak eyes, my mother laboriously thinking about what she wanted to say to her son.

Julie and I bowed deeply and waited. My father nodded at us and managed a stiff smile. My mother did not look up from her writing.

"Happy New Year, father. Happy New Year, mother," I said.

Julie echoed my words. Her Japanese was quite good now, good enough for going to shops, getting around the city, making small talk with my family.

My father coughed, and nestled closer to the fire. He and my mother wore their quilted robes. I set my knapsack down. "Julie and I have brought you presents," I said. "To celebrate our first New Year in Tokyo."

My parents looked up. At least they were no longer openly hostile to my wife—mostly they seemed to regard her as some kind of unfathomable eternal stranger. She would never be fully accepted, I realized, so I welcomed this relatively passive attitude on their part, but I was under no illusions about how deeply their inability to accept her hurt Julie.

We looked at each other . . . who would make the presentation?

"Go ahead, honey," Julie said.

"But you selected them—"

Just then Saburo came down from his upstairs room wearing a woollen scarf around his head and a heavy coat. If the downstairs was cold, the flimsy upstairs room was like the Arctic, and he had so little fat on his bones to protect him from these winter chills.

Julie wrapped our presents—shiny red paper, gold ribbons—but was up against the expertise of my family . . . package-wrapping is an art, a compulsion among us Japanese to make the *exterior* of a gift as beautiful as the gift itself. Perhaps more beautiful, another example of our emphasis of appearance over reality . . . My father undid the wrapping with little pleasure on his face, and found inside a handsome leather wallet.

"Thank you, my son."

Julie fidgeted. He had made a point of not including her.

My mother's gift was a portable sewing kit in a leather box. She sucked in her breath and smiled.

"I hope you like it . . . mother," Julie said. "I got it in a department store in Los Angeles. I brought an extra one along and was saving it for you . . ." She seemed to be struggling for conversation, and who could blame her—the atmosphere was tense, not celebratory.

My mother nodded at her, probably already worried about a reciprocal gift.

Saburo was holding his present as if it were a bomb about to go off in his hands. He looked at it, looked at us, then left the room. "I'll open mine later, I'm studying."

"We . . . we . . . have not provided presents," my father said, embarrassed. "Because of the war, and Masao . . . we decided not to celebrate. Not that we do not appreciate these gifts . . ."

"We thought we would not spend the money on presents but on a donation to the goddess Kannon and ask her to be merciful to Masao," my mother said quickly. "We leave prayers with her and burn incense and ask the priests to make an offering."

"Yes," my father said. "Tomorrow."

I bowed. "We understand, father. We are concerned about Masao as well."

"I pray this letter reaches him," my mother said. "It is not fair the way the war takes our best children."

Julie spoke to me in English. "But not the bad ones like guess who."

"Julie, please." She looked angry, she *was* angry.

"I need a bath, a real scalder."

We filled the metal furnace with charcoal, also in short supply, and I poured buckets of frigid water into the wooden tub for her. In our room, I helped her out of her clothes and into a quilted bathrobe, and she shook as if afflicted with the ague.

"Join me?" she asked.

"In a few minutes, you should at least have the luxury of all the hot water by yourself for a few minutes."

I helped her into the tub then, kissing her full belly, and making her laugh. "Our little child," I said, "keep him warm."

"I wish he'd hurry up. He might give us a few laughs around here."

"Enjoy your tub." My poor Julie . . . with her smooth white flesh stretched and misshapen by the child inside, yet still moving with grace and strength. She smiled at me, looked over the edge of the steaming water and made a comical face. "Just call me lobster-back. Oh, oh, oh, this is so *good*. Almost as good as sex. Now, now, I said *almost* . . ."

I kissed her, then went to our room to index some material Professor Adachi had given me, documents that could get me in serious trouble—when I heard a scream and commotion coming from the bath.

I ran out of the room, pulled aside the *fusuma* panel and ran into the bath. Julie was standing in the tub, the wooden dipper in her hand. I could hear Saburo's howling, and the clatter of wooden clogs as he raced upstairs.

"The little *rat*," Julie shouted. "A goddamn Peeping Tom!"

"Who?"

"Saburo, that's who . . . I caught him, the little darling, sneaking a look through the crack in the *fusuma* and let him have it, a dipperful of hot water. That miserable little . . ."

She started to climb out of the tub. "Hand me my robe, Kenji. I'm going to have it out with that spoiled brat right now. And I don't care what Mama-*san* and Papa-*san* think—"

"Julie, please, it was wrong but—"

"But *nothing*." Julie got into her robe and stomped into the main room, my parents acting as if nothing had happened. My mother was sealing her letter to Masao. My father was shaking his head over some item in the newspaper about, he said, nearly five thousand geishas being out of work.

Saburo was at the veranda door. He'd opened his gift, thrown the paper on the floor and was twirling the metal propeller of the toy plane we had given him, a model of a PBY flying boat.

Julie, beside herself, took in the scene and proceed to lay down a barrage against the outlaw Peeping Tom. My parents said nothing, further infuriating Julie, and Saburo, not looking any of us in the eye, said, "She's lying."

Ah, the power of *amae*. In my young brother's mind was the firm conviction that all his acts would be understood and excused, that he had the *right* to presume that others loved him, *indulged* him, would give him the benefit of every doubt. I had tried to tell Julie about this phe-. nomenon the Japanese male exhibits all his life, but she'd had little sympathy with it at the time and now, as a victim of it, would have even less.

"Ask precious why his shirt is wet," Julie said. "I hit him with a dipper of water. Go ahead, *ask* him."

"She is of no interest to me," said Saburo, about to protest more until I stepped forward.

"Tell the truth," I told him.

"I am. I'm not afraid of you. You're a coward, and I'm not afraid of her—" Saburao smashed the airplane to the floor and stomped on the frail metal. "And I don't want your toy, it comes from *America.*"

My parents were smiling.

"Well, someone's got to do it," Julie said, rolled up the sleeve of her robe and advanced on Saburo, who suddenly was looking uneasy. I knew, as Julie didn't really, how deeply disgraced Saburo would be, and never live it down, if he were struck by a woman, especially a *gaijin.* He spaced his legs, went into a karate stance, arms at the ready, palms flat. He had had training in the martial arts and frail as he was, Julie would never be a match for him. I was forced to put myself between them. "Please, darling . . ."

Saburo took the opportunity to run past us, and my parents appeared pained.

"*Damn* him," Julie said, fighting back tears. I went to her, but she moved away, furious with me as well as with them.

As I followed Julie to our room, my father said, "Thank you for the gifts. You realize it may be some months before we can repay the *gimu.*"

We lay in each other's arms, shivering in the cold under the *futons.* I kissed her a hundred times and she kissed me back, but she was more unhappy and confused than she had ever been in this unhappy confusing situation.

"My God, Kenji, I can't believe it. The big deal to your father wasn't Saburo's rotten behavior but when he could give us some presents to even the score. And you didn't exactly stick up for me—"

"Darling, you know about Japanese males, how they're raised to believe they can do no wrong, especially to—"

"Outsiders? Then why are the people so polite to me in the street?"

"They feel no threat. You haven't moved into their world. Julie, I tried to warn you how it would be."

She raised herself on one elbow. Behind the paper wall I heard my mother opening the wall closet and taking out the *futons* for their night's sleep. Saburo was upstairs, presumably studying, but I often heard the floor shake with his masturbatory exercises, which had no shame connected with them.

"Well, damn it, Kenji," Julie said, "*you* don't behave the way Saburo does."

"I've been away from home for many years, have lived in America. And remember, I'm Master Cold Rice, second son. I try to overcome my old need for *amae,* for dependence, indulgence. Have I succeeded?"

"You bet you have," and she promptly kissed me again. "You're better than any of them . . . all of them."

"Don't praise me too much, it's been easier for me. Besides, if you praise me so much you may reactivate my *amae* and then—"

"Oh, shut up, Cold Rice, and warm up this poor pregnant *gaijin* lady . . ."

Which I did. Afterward, lying close, her roundness against me, I whispered that she was going to give birth to a *sumo* wrestler, and we both laughed.

"I also promise you," I said, "I won't, as you would put it, spoil our son. He'll be treated properly—"

"And if she's a girl?"

"I'll love her just as much."

Just then the baby kicked and Julie smiled. "He . . . she . . . sure is healthy and kickin'."

"It's the *gohan,*" I said, and kissed her belly.

JULIE TAMBA · FEBRUARY, 1943

Our son was born on Valentine's Day, February 14. He was big . . . eight pounds, one ounce, and roaringly healthy, confirming Kenji's faith in rice diets.

Little Taro—as we named him—couldn't wait to get out, but the labor was painful and I went to the clinic in the middle of the night gritting my teeth.

Aunt Cora and Uncle Adam had no sedatives for me. It was cold in the delivery room. A little before daybreak, when I thought I would die either of cold or pain or both, Taro, screaming, slimy and dark, emerged from me. He looked much like any baby, neither Oriental nor Caucasian, just stained, wrinkled and with a sort of flattened head and wisps of dark hair. I loved him at once and so did Kenji. We named him Taro after Kenji's dead grandfather who had been, I was told, a nice gentle man who'd worked as a cook at the palace.

Washed and cleaned up, Taro was placed on my chest so I could stroke and kiss and admire him. Kenji came into the room, knelt at the bedside and said that this was the happiest day of his life.

"How about our wedding day?" I asked.

"My two happiest days," he said, smiling as I had never seen him smile before.

He said that his mother would come to visit later with Yuriko, who was going through one of her moody periods. His father, no surprise, had smiled on hearing that I'd given birth to a healthy *boy*.

"He smells like a rose," Kenji said. "May I kiss him again?"

"Of course."

The baby thrust out his arms in that spastic shivering motion characteristic of infants, and reacted to Kenji's kiss. Or at least we both believed he did.

Kenji laughed. "We're a strange people, I sometimes think."

"Now *whatever* makes you think that, darling?" and I reached for his ears, pulled his face down and kissed him.

When I let him go he said, "We hate to be touched, kissed. But with children we make an exception. *They* can be hugged and touched all the time. I can't resist him . . ."

We seemed so happy, the three of us. Uncle Adam came in and presented Kenji with a cigar. "It's usually the father who is supposed to hand them out but I know they're all but unattainable so I make this sacrifice for the big event. But you better pay me back someday—"

"It will be my *gimu.*"

"Like everything else."

Aunt Cora had managed to locate a tiny electric heater that she put on a wooden stool and pushed up close to the bed. She stayed with me, said she'd try to send Red Cross telegrams to my parents and maybe to Chris, who was covering the navy now and she wasn't quite sure how to reach him.

"You look so happy, Julie."

"I am."

"I'm sorry the facilities are sort of primitive—"

"So long as himself came out okay . . . Isn't he gorgeous? Does he have the spot on his back?"

"He does. The trademark. It vanishes after a few years. Did it worry you?"

"Heck, no. I love the idea that he's a mixed grill. And his hair—what color do you think it will be?"

"Impossible to know. It's dark brown now but it can change. The main thing is, he's healthy and strong. We'll have you home in a few days and you'll be able to nurse him."

Home. Could we move? Could we find anything livable? For all the lack of privacy in the Tamba house, the john, the drafts, it was a decent house. I'd had a glimpse of how the *real* poor lived in Tokyo. Chicken coops didn't appeal to me, especially not now. And it had been so good to be around Yuriko, who now spent more time with us whenever Hideo was on duty.

Aunt Cora, fussing over me, even spoonfed me *miso,* a broth with chunks of bean curd in it, then had to return to the clinic. They seemed to be getting an epidemic of industrial accidents—fractures, abrasions, burns. People, after all, were exhausted, working harder, making them vulnerable to injuries.

"Oh, things are difficult everywhere," she said. "There was an item in the paper today . . . they run a daily report on the status of the geishas. There are thousands of them out of work. Poor hothouse flowers! All a geisha is trained for—dance, song, serving food and drinks, chitchat—is not much use during wartime. So the factories and offices are getting these butterflies who can't type or spell, much less think for themselves. It's really sad. Suicides have been reported. The government is trying to retrain them but how do you train some girl who has been taught to spend half a day putting on makeup and fixing her hair?"

"I know a little about it," I said. "Goro . . . Kenji's father . . . was reading about them the other day. Maybe there won't be any more geishas.

Women aren't dolls . . . ask one who's just had a baby. By the way, Aunt
Cora, what about Ed Hodges? Has the Red Cross arranged any new
visits?" She said they hadn't. "Well," I said, "I'd still like to see Ed. I'd
be grateful for anything you or Dr. Reinhold can do." She said she'd keep
trying. Also, she thought it was a hopeful sign that people had seen more
groups of POWs working in the streets than ever before. Apparently the
men had been brought to Japan from prisons in Malaya and the Philippines and other places, the idea being to provide cheap labor at home and
at the same time make the Japanese people aware of the "inferiority" of
the enemy. Dr. Reinhold told her that these men sometimes worked
virtually without armed guards. Being Caucasians and in prison dress,
there was no point in their escaping. Where could they hide? It was
conceivable, she said, that Ed might be on such a detail. The Japanese
assigned security to prisoner officers, and if a man tried to escape or broke
rules he was killed on the spot and the officer in charge severely punished.
Still, the relative freedom given these labor details might at least help us
find Ed . . .

I slept a lot, and felt confident and cheerful, proud of my motherhood,
ecstatic over my healthy son. His mixed heritage especially delighted me.
He'd be different, good, and we'd raise him to be *proud* of his two cultures.
Unlike my brother Chris I knew better than to hate the Japanese, to lump
them all together. It made no sense, no more than lumping all Americans
together. There were good guys and bad guys and in-betweens on both
sides. I saw so much to *admire* in Kenji, and in the people in the street.
Right now I even appreciated my in-laws' occasional efforts to reach out
to me. Sure, they didn't make it most of the time, but that, I felt, was on
account of how they were raised and taught. They were *not* cruel people.
Yuriko was special proof of that. I had come to love her, and felt for her
in her loveless marriage, especially when by comparison I had so much.

In the outside room Kenji was talking to Uncle Adam, who I was told
had gotten a stunning report from the Swiss—an entire German army had
surrendered at Stalingrad. And the Japanese newspapers were running full
reports of the battle, and, it seemed to Adam, they were enjoying the
Germans' embarrassment and misery. He said that Japan, in spite of its
loud anticommunist stand, needed the Russians for trading and prayed
that they would stay neutral. And this was oddest of all—they seemed to
think of the Russians as a sort of ace in the hole that would come in on
their side if the worst came to pass and they were on the verge of
defeat. Maybe it was because so many in the Soviet Union were Asiatics
too . . . ?

I kissed Taro's fuzzy head, watched his eyes open, try to focus, and decided they were definitely Oriental—black, slanted and delicate, and I loved him even more for it. He was *mine,* and Kenji's . . . *ours.* I said a little prayer that he'd be able to grow up in a world without war and prejudice. He dribbled then onto my breasts. A down-to-earth young man, bringing me back to the realities of here and now.

KENJI TAMBA · FEBRUARY, 1943

Dr. Adam Varnum and I were sitting in his consulting room after my first glimpse of my son—*my son.* It sent tremors of joy and excitement through me. And if I were to be honest, I would admit a certain pleasure in accomplishing something important that my hero brother had *not* managed. Master Cold Rice had a *son* . . . He was so perfect, so strong and handsome. At least now, I thought, my parents would accept Julie as one of them . . .

I always enjoyed talking to Dr. Varnum. He was, like many Americans I'd met, open, hiding little. And life was getting to be hard for him and his wife at the clinic—shortages of medical supplies, even bandages, harassment from the police, stupid Officer Tani peeking into windows at women or "borrowing" cigarettes from Cora.

"I can't complain," Adam said. "I'm not in jail and I could be at any moment. I honestly believe that Masao's interceding a few months ago saved my old neck."

"He was honored to do it. It was a *giri* for him, as you know—an obligation he owed to someone who had done him favors. Just as I have a *giri* to you and your wife—"

"Nonsense, Kenji. I treated you as a patient because your mother brought you here."

"That, yes. But I owe you a much greater *giri.* Remember it was *you* who told me about Julie."

"Well, Kenji, as I understand it, such a *giri* must be repaid with exact equivalence, and there's a time limit on the repayment. How do you propose to handle it?"—he was smiling—"by introducing me to the chief lady-in-waiting? Or Kyoto's number-one geisha?"

I laughed. "No, that would not be an equivalent. None of them could match my Julie. But I will try . . ." I turned serious and embarrassed.

"You have done so much for me I'm ashamed to come again, as a patient this time."

"What's the trouble, Kenji?"

"Headaches . . . I haven't told Julie, I don't want to trouble her. She has more than enough problems with my family. But I have been troubled with a pain over my left eye and the left temple."

Dr. Varnum examined my eyes, took my pulse, probed at my head. I told him I felt nothing, that the blinding nauseating attacks usually came after I had undergone stress—a family argument, long hours where I worked, worries about Masao and Yuriko.

"Do you see flashing lights? An aura?"

"Yes. Before the pain starts. First just a throbbing, then an awful ache. And then as if a knife were being driven into my left eye. My eye turns red and tears. Sometimes it gets so bad I have to lie down in the dark."

"Migraine, probably . . ."

"I never had them before this year."

"Brought on, as you said, by tension and anxiety. In your case, Kenji, there's plenty of reason for it. You're two people, sometimes at war with each other. Japan—America. Julie—your parents. You—her parents."

I nodded. "Yes. And after Julie and I argue I sense the pain coming. As if someone turned a switch in my head. You're right, the headaches seem to be triggered by these conflicts I can't resolve . . . I have never told you, doctor, but after Pearl Harbor I prayed that Japan would win. Then I changed my mind. I hoped for a quick armistice. But I knew the Americans would accept nothing short of victory. I know that much about them . . . and I did not blame them. And in knowing that, and guiltily, privately wanting them to offset our forces . . . well, I began to hate myself. I was violating my ingrained obligation to the emperor and my tradition. Can you understand this?"

"Of course. Look, this will sound farfetched, but maybe your obligation to the emperor *and* your country can be repaid by working for peace. I've heard he isn't a warlike man, that in fact Tojo and his people dragged him into the war."

"I have heard that too. But is he so powerless? Is he really just a puppet?" I held my head in my hands. The headache was intense, searing. A stabbing pain, boring into my left eye.

Dr. Varnum put a hand on my shoulder. "Kenji, you are, after all, Japanese. Don't apologize—"

"I have never denied it, I am *proud* of it." Was I, though?

"You must be, you have a right to be. A remarkable tradition. Admirable people. Cora and I certainly wouldn't have spent twenty years here if we didn't love this country. Your problem is you see the warts . . . see them too well, and you're torn."

"You think I'm like one of those demon-infested wretches in the Noh plays?"

"Maybe . . . your writers understood. Kenji, you have got to learn to live with your affection for your country and the ability to see what is evil in it. You must *not* feel a traitor or less of a man for your insight. Good lord, Yamamoto himself, I'm told, opposed the war."

"It is an irony, doctor. But I've still got a damn headache."

He hugged me when I got up, then found some pills in his cabinet. "Last of the wine. An ergotamine derivative. Be careful with these. Two at the onset of pain, one two hours later, and a fourth four hours after that. No more than four in a twenty-four-hour period, and never more than eight in a week. They won't kill you, but they constrict the blood vessels, and they'll tend to make you nauseous and sluggish. Okay?"

"You are very kind to me—"

"*Stop* it. You and your family were the first Japanese to welcome us into your home. You, your brothers and Yuriko were like our own kids. Don't try to take on yourself *all* the burdens of the nation. Be happy . . . and patient . . . with Julie. And your family. And for God's sake, be happy with your son."

I smiled. "That is the easy part."

"She truly loves you, Kenji." He looked very serious.

I nodded. "That sometimes makes it all the more difficult for both of us."

MASAO TAMBA · MARCH, 1943

We are the last.

The detachment in the other cave, twenty-one men, are all dead. They made a final suicide attack and were wiped out. We hid like cowards, unarmed, starved, sick with malaria and parasites while the marines wiped out our comrades.

We could hear the Americans' voices . . .

Burn their asses . . .

Cut his damn cock off . . .

This one's for me, look at the damn monkey . . .

My men keep telling me that I must not die. So they have hidden me deep in the cave. They bring me the heart of the sago palm, giant grubs, wild yams . . .

But I have decided to die.

My left eye is blind. Whatever it was that was eating at the pupil—a parasite or an infection from an old wound—has finally blotted out my vision. I tried to clean it with a saline solution but it did not restore my vision. I see shapes and lights but can't make out faces or any details. It is only a matter of time, I believe, before I am fully blind in that eye. I joke with my men that I am like Lord Nelson, missing one arm and one eye.

"But he lived to fight again and win battles," my sergeant said. "As you will."

"No. Ota, idiot that he was, was right about something . . . it is a myth, a lie that we will ever be found. We should have died in a last charge, killed the enemy, redeemed our honor."

The sergeant reminded me that the Imperial General Staff did not want everyone to die this way . . . otherwise, why had they gone to such efforts to redeploy twenty thousand men from Guadalcanal instead of ordering them into doomed assaults?

"It is a matter of honor," I whispered. I was on my back on a pallet of palm leaves, naked except for a breechclout. "Lift me up, sergeant. Find my sword. I will do with one hand what Ota did with two. No blood, no mess. I will fall forward and die like a soldier."

The men—there are twelve of us left—began to stir uneasily. They got to their knees. Some butted their heads against the earthen floor of the cave. One man began to throw up. He was nineteen, and I knew he had eaten a dead man's flesh that morning. We did not bury the dead. The men devoured them. I had to be forced to eat a broth made of someone's heart. At least all that would end for me now.

They carried me to the mouth of the cave. I requested that I be seated facing the Imperial Palace to the northwest. No tears came to my eyes. I was too full of pain, of fevers that never left.

"We cannot let you die . . ." the sergeant said.

"Where is my sword?"

I had to be propped up, my back against a sago palm, a violation of the procedure of *hara-kiri*. I turned to the sergeant. "I will be unable to cut my jugular vein. The moment I fall, cut off my head. And be strong. One single stroke. Then bury me outside the cave, with my head facing Japan."

At that moment, as the sergeant tried to position me for my death, we heard voices . . . very well, it would be done for us. I was relieved, let the marines come. We would fight with bamboo sticks and swords, die the way I preferred a Japanese soldier should—

But what we heard were Japanese voices.

The jungle brush parted. From behind a wall of green vegetation appeared a black face—a native. He gestured, then stood aside.

A Japanese marine, a young lieutenant, appeared, followed by four heavily burdened enlisted men. The officer walked up to me and bowed.

"Major Tamba?"

"Yes."

"I am Lieutenant Inoue of the Imperial marines. We have landed a boat at the eastern end of the island. A submarine is waiting for us. We will leave when it turns dark. I regret what you have suffered. I was sent here on orders of the War Ministry to find you and bring you back home."

I was helped to my feet, I returned his bow, very nearly fell on my face . . . "I was about to take my life," I said, not realizing that my voice had become no more than a hoarse croak. The young man looked puzzled, straining to understand me.

"Major Tamba was about to commit *hara-kiri*," my sergeant said quickly.

"He must not. He is needed for a new invasion. More battles are to come." The officer signaled to his men to break out supplies of food and medicine, and I asked him what was happening in the war.

"Victories," he said. "We are preparing to drive the enemy out of New Guinea and Malaya. Only a matter of time."

"Good . . . I offer my humble thanks to His Majesty for this *ko-on*. It shall be repaid."

Fine sentiments . . . except the effort it took to stand up and speak them bent me double with spasms of retching. What I really craved was a soft warm ball of cooked rice and a cup of sake. Not such a heroic thought for His Majesty's warrior.

KENJI TAMBA · MARCH, 1943

Some time after the birth of my son Kingoro Hata invited me, along with my father, to his private club to congratulate *us*. The club was called the Patriotic Businessmen's and Industrialists' League for a Greater Japan, and Satomi, the geisha mistress, was on hand to wait on us, seeming sullen and even resentful. She apparently was feeling out of her element, which was the Plum Blossom House, and wore a severe black kimono to show it. Her hard-edged face was coated with powder, bright red daubs on her lips. She wore the wig of a high-ranking geisha, and shuffled about serving us sake and rice cakes and later whiskey for toasts to my son.

I had never quite figured out how Hata was related to my mother, an obscure connection that, as I understood, went back to my mother's village near Sendai. Hata himself was of humble origins. He had risen to his high estate through a sort of creative cunning. At various times he had belonged to ultranationalist secret groups, some with a veneer of respectability, others clearly collections of gangsters dedicated to murder and blackmail in pursuit of power for its own sake. This was his time, ready-made for his kind of operator, or fixer, as the Americans would say.

"Oh yes, oh yes," Hata said, as we reclined on the *tatami*s. "The Black Dragon Society, fine fellows. And the Hundred Million Hearts Society— all beating as one." He smiled, clearly pleased with what he considered a clever turn of phrase.

He drank toasts to my son Taro and said he would send us a valuable present—a crude and un-Japanese thing to do—bragging about it, and said there might yet be a job for me in some patriotic home-front group. I told him that my work with the Edo Sugar Company was satisfactory. My father looked embarrassed at my rejection of what he felt was Hata's generosity, and it occurred to me that Hata might have some idea or at least suspicion of my work with Professor Adachi. Did he smell a rat? Was he toying with me?

"Oh, the Black Dragons, a fine group," Hata pressed on. "It had its origin, you know, as the Amur River Club . . . we demanded our rightful expansion into Manchuria, leadership in Asia, anti-Westernism, cultivation of the virtues of the *Yamato* race—"

"And . . . have these goals been fulfilled?" I asked, and as I did so I caught a smile from Satomi. She was in her late thirties, a handsome woman. I had been told she and Hata were partners in geisha houses, teahouses, cafes, real estate ventures. The war was certainly not hurting their business in spite of unemployment among geishas. They were nicely diversified.

"I had my connections with other groups," Hata said, draining his sake cup and waggling it at Satomi to be refilled. "The Blood Pledge Corps, for example."

The sake was making me bolder. "Didn't they murder Baron Takuma Dan and Junnosuke Inoue?"

"They were pardoned, Kenji. I knew fellows in the Cherry Blossom Association, the Dark Ocean Society, and as your father knows, I helped *found* the Imperial Rule Assistance Political Association. You'll recall, Kenji, I once asked you if you'd be interested in joining their young men's corps."

"I apologize for my lack of enthusiasm," I answered solemnly, hoping he did not detect my sarcasm.

"No matter . . . I am sure sugar trading is essential to our war effort."

He did not mask his sarcasm, making me uneasy again, but, as I said, the rice wine was loosening my tongue too. "As essential as geishas?"

Satomi tittered.

"To what do you refer?" Hata asked.

"I have heard that the government is closing the geisha houses. That must be a heavy blow for Madame Satomi."

Satomi smiled—a hard red line across her lower jaw. "Only for ordinary houses. There is a steady call for my girls among government officials. You needn't worry about me, young man."

Hata cackled at that. "A black market in geishas! Kenji, my lad, do you think Tojo and the cabinet and the generals are suffering from shortages . . . of food or women? Never. The evenings are full, I assure you. I've been to a few. Satomi's ladies are in abundant supply. The Plum Blossom House is still in business, invited guests only, of course."

Well, if Hata was being indiscreet, I would take some risks too . . . "I am told Tojo's wife is an avid collector of gifts—jewels, furs, antiques." Adachi, of course, had told me this.

"Why not?" Hata boomed. "Why should we be penny-pinching and miserable because of the war?"

"A lot of Japanese men are dying—"

My father suddenly found his voice. "My son Masao may be one of them." His eyes began to mist.

"Ah, my heart goes out to them," Hata said quickly. "But the sufferings of these men who die so nobly for Tenno Heika should not deter us from living. I am sure His Majesty would not disapprove, especially for his closest aides."

"I am told he is a Spartan and unostentatious man," I said. "That he rejects indulgence and is a faithful husband and father and lives simply. It is even rumored, Mr. Hata, that he doesn't really think he's a god any longer . . ."

We were all surely drunk by now . . . what they say about Japanese men getting that way is true . . . and we had had shots of whiskey on top of the sake.

"He is a god, all right," Hata was saying, his voice clotted, almost as if he were gargling. He ran his hand down Satomi's back, let it linger on her buttocks. "If *we* say he's a god he's a *god* and what better way for a god to behave then by being nice and moderate in his tastes . . . ? I'm also sure he's pleased that in spite of the war some of us can have a good time . . ."

I suppose you could say Hata was an engaging scoundrel . . . corrupt politicians like Tojo and his cronies took bribes and accepted favors from industrialists and tried to appear models of honesty and self-denial. Kingoro Hata had no such compunctions, he boasted openly about getting rich on the war and didn't seem to care who knew it . . . Engaging for a moment, if you had had enough drink to anesthetize your sensibilities . . . Hata now asked Satomi to sing for us and she seemed put off—after all, she was no mere geisha but an entrepreneur. But she dutifully got her *samisen,* sat in front of us and sang a little song about creation, a Shinto version.

I saw her only dimly . . . a white-faced, black-robed form, and heard her tinkly nasal voice and wondered if she were as cold and calculating in bed. Did such women ever experience real love, reach true orgasm, join freely in the sexual union with generosity?

> Izanagi, old god, asked his wife
> Of her body, how it was.
> Izanami, old goddess says,
> It has one place that is not
> Fully formed.
> Izanaga replied his body had one
> Place, formed far too big . . .
> So they decided that he take his too big thing
> And put it in her place that was unformed
> And give birth to the land!

We all laughed and applauded, yes, me too, proper Imperial scholar Kenji. Julie was always saying I was *too* good . . . she should have seen me now. No, she shouldn't . . . Hata drank more toasts to my son, to my family and I was thankful he made no reference to my *gaijin* wife. Ultrapatriot that he said he was, he did not seem upset by Julie, and it occurred to me that Hata was looking ahead, far ahead, to a time when someone like me with access by marriage to America might be useful . . .

We dined on excellent fried eel spiced with ginger, and mounds of the best rice I'd had in months. My father thanked Hata for the honor. How could we ever repay it?

"By keeping me informed," Hata said easily. He looked at me, and not so drunkenly. "Do you know an old man named Adachi? A teacher at the university? I believe he was jailed for subversion . . ."

I tried to control my fear, summon up a plausible answer. "He was my teacher at Tokyo Imperial University, yes."

"Ah, so. And where is he now?"

"I don't know."

"They say he's a big peace-faction man. If he is he had better hide, or much better, kill himself."

I said nothing to that. My father then put in cautiously, "Is there really such a thing as a peace faction? I can't understand anyone being opposed to our patriotic war. We are all one with His Majesty."

"There seem to be a few such fools around," Hata yawned. "They will be dealt with at the proper time. Yes, even those in high places—" Hata broke off to direct Satomi to play the *samisen* again. She bowed, plucked at the strings, and a soft eerie noise filled the semidark room of the private club. A waitress in a red kimono slid across the floor, doubled over and served bits of *sushi*.

"High places?" I asked, genuinely curious now.

Hata must have been very drunk or he would not have gone on as he did, lowering his voice . . . Tojo was having a difficult time with some generals . . . gossip in Parliament had it that the conqueror of Malaya, General Yamashita himself, had tried to convince Tojo of the advisability of suing for peace, despite the early victories Yamashita believed the war couldn't be won . . . Tojo was said to have stripped Yamashita of his command and exiled him to Manchuria . . . Surely no news like this had ever leaked to the public. I was astounded.

"And there are others," Hata went on, "generals who dare question the wisdom of the war. Itagaki has been sent to Seoul to keep him out of trouble and shut him up. Homma, conqueror of the Philippines, has been exiled in China and our prime minister is in control . . ."

"That is good," my father said. "If a disloyal general can't escape Tojo's reach, there's no hope for the minor traitors."

I swallowed my sake, took a fresh cup, drank again with Hata and my father to the health of my newborn son, realizing as I did that I was one of those "minor traitors" my father referred to.

I wondered how much Hata did know about me, and Professor Adachi

... I knew that men had been beheaded for less than we were doing. I did not want Julie widowed, my son without a father, my life ended when I was just beginning a career I might be proud of.

But Hata at least *seemed* dissolved in alcohol, and now he was telling Satomi to send for women, he wanted to spend the night at his club with a young virgin. He also offered to "make arrangements" for my father and me. I looked at my father, and it was obvious he would have liked to accept but was embarrassed in front of me, a second son and, perhaps worse, an intellectual. I would have liked to tell him to go ahead, but of course said nothing.

JULIE TAMBA · MAY, 1943

Taro is a lusty three months old, a vigorous child and like all Japanese babies, I'm told, a grade-A sleeper, which makes things easier for us. I nurse him, happy that although my diet is lacking in protein my milk flows. It better, because he's greedy and hungry all the time.

The fifth day of the fifth month of May is Boys' Festival Day and I think it marks a sort of turn for the better in my relations with my in-laws. Male children, as you've heard, are gods. The Honorable Brats, I might privately call these spoiled little men. I am determined Taro won't grow up a selfish, self-loving little tyrant like Saburo. He'll be like Kenji. At least that's what I hope for.

Still, I guess there's nothing wrong with celebrating Boys' Festival, and it did help melt some of the Tamba elders' reserve where I was concerned. At least a boy was a boy, even if he was a mixed breed. Besides, some diplomats and professors married *gaijin* women, and their children were honored—provided they were raised as children of the sun goddess. I would make no such concessions, by god. Taro would share the best both his parents had to offer—and nuts to *samurai* craziness. Of course I keep such thoughts to myself, even from Kenji, at least for now. I'm learning a little bit about shutting the mouth when discretion is the better part of valor, as they say.

Kenji bought a beautiful six-foot red-and-gold paper carp that we flew from the center pole of the Tamba house to tell the world . . . well, the world of Shibuya Ward . . . that here lived a new male child. There were smaller flying carps for Goro's and Hisako's three grown sons. I've learned that the carp symbolizes maleness because of its courage, because it has strength and tenacity and a true fighting spirit. When it's caught and put on the chopping block—so the popular legend goes—it lies there and bravely accepts the knife. I didn't like this part and said so . . . I didn't want *my* son offering his tender throat to anyone's bloody blade. He was, after all, half American, and Americans weren't death lovers. No "in death is life" stuff, the way some suicidal officers yelled around the bar, for me and mine.

Taro sleeps in the same room with us, burbling on his own *futon* and his own *tatami* mat. He seems to crave them, happy when he smells the fresh straw of the mat. Personally I wasn't too thrilled with straw pallets, especially with the consequences of having sex on these scratchy pads and picking up the peculiarly Japanese affliction known as *"tatami* burns," sort of like the strawberry guys get on their hips and legs from a hard slide into second base.

But Taro seems to thrive on his *tatami,* enjoys his swaddling clothes, the huge padded diapers and, when I give him the chance, urinating or moving his bowels into a tiny potty.

Hisako has been a real help to me, changing Taro, taking him for walks strapped to her back. She's overcome her early reserve about this not-quite-Japanese son of her son and I'm glad for it, believe me. Watching her cradle Taro in her arms, sing-songing to him, wiping his eyes, dabbing his lips with a sugared rag, I can't help remember her bleak reception only three months earlier v hen I'd come home from the clinic with Taro.

Today Yuriko was really happy . . . she brought her son Hiroki to meet his new cousin Taro . . . to tell the truth, they didn't seem too interested in one another, but Yuriko pretended they were. Also, Hideo was at sea again, and she was much happier. While I watched Hiroki warily inspect his cousin, I couldn't help thinking maybe he saw him as a future competitor for the kingship of the Tamba house? . . . Hisako and Goro, standing off at a distance, might be thinking the same thing. Hisako had shown she could take real pleasure in her new grandson, but sometimes Goro acted as though I'd brought a live alligator into the house. Okay, maybe I'm exaggerating, but it's there. No such reservations by Uncle Adam and Aunt Cora about Taro. Treating him as if he were their own grandchild. Sure, it's true my parents had given a cool reception to Kenji, especially when I said I wanted to marry him, but they came through right away with a loving letter and a lot of baby stuff and even Chris said he was delighted to be an uncle, and congratulated Kenji as well as me on the great event. All in all, we came off pretty well . . .

MASAO TAMBA · MAY, 1943

Three weeks after my rescue by the Imperial marines my left eye was removed in a crude operating room aboard a navy transport. During the surgery that was done without anesthesia we were strafed by American fighter planes. A dozen of our sailors were killed and buried at sea. They died in part because of rescuing me and some survivors of Guadalcanal. It humbled me. How could I scream when an infected eye was removed?

I had also developed gangrene. There were no laboratory facilities aboard the ship, and the doctor said he had no idea what organism had infected me but that if I let it continue the infection would spread and kill me. A fat man who drank too much, he could only mutter, "These unknown infections have a way of getting more evil as they progress. As the Christians, or the Jews, I forget which, say in their holy book, 'If thy left eye offend thee, pluck it out.' " He had been educated at the University of Hawaii, he told me.

So I subjected myself to the scalpel again. Afterward he trimmed the stump of my left arm, sawed the bone to a flat termination, cauterized it, sewed up the skin and doused me with whatever disinfectant he had on hand.

Dr. Orishi then pronounced me, minus a left eye and arm, "a superb specimen of a man. You are without an ounce of fat, your ribs poke through your chest and you have survived two painful operations and much loss of blood, but essentially you are still healthy."

I was interested to hear it. "One eye, one arm, and I was once the best *kendo* fighter in my division."

"Life has other diversions. You have given more than your share to the emperor, you deserve a rest."

I told him I had no intention of retiring, that one reason for my rescue was that the generals wanted to make use of my knowledge of jungle warfare and the defense of islands.

"Hmmm," he mumbled, and reached for his bottle, "one would think the Americans are sick of losing so many of their soldiers. If they try to drive us from all our island bases they'll all die . . ."

I tried to tell myself I believed that too . . .

The voyage home seemed endless . . . stops at our island bases in the Marianas—Saipan, Tinian, Guam, all of them stoutly defended—and then a circuitous route to remove us from the probing eyes of American planes and submarines.

We docked in Yokohama and I walked off the ship at night to a tomblike city. No one smiled, no one greeted us. No brass bands, no school children shouting *banzai.* Welcome home.

For six weeks I was kept in isolation in a hospital that was more like a prison. I was interviewed, briefed, given secret reports to read. I learned that the Chinese were getting more arms from America and were fighting back; that the British in Burma had launched a counteroffensive and that the American navy and air force, for all the blows we had dealt them, were growing stronger each day—more ships, more planes, more men. New Guinea was virtually theirs; so were the Solomons. They were a giant industrial power, I knew. And privately I also knew we could probably not defeat them. It would, of course, have been a violation of *bushido* to say this to anyone. Even to myself . . .

My father-in-law Colonel Sato was allowed to visit and brought news of my family. The birth of Kenji's son did not make me celebrate. Perhaps because I had no son of my own, and he, a younger brother, had a male child, even if a mongrel one. But what future for such a child? He could not properly carry on the Tamba name. Sato agreed and said my father took small pleasure in Kenji's infant, though he did add that the child was healthy and handsome. As for the *gaijin* wife, she was too independent and outspoken. Sato was also puzzled by her. He said one of the problems in dealing with her as a woman in the same way one would deal with a Japanese woman was that she was just too blonde and too tall. He was not being funny. It was as if the obligations that applied to our women —like obedience, modesty, silence—could not be imposed on someone so unlike what a woman was supposed to be . . . "Her legs are too long," Sato said glumly. A woman's leg should bulge at the calf, the ankles should be pleasingly thick. Nothing, he said, excited him more than a heavy, slightly bowed leg in a woman, such as his mother's or his late wife's. "Satomi is tall but her legs are heavy and solid," he said. "Your *gaijin* sister-in-law's legs are much too long and thin. It is a wonder to me how Kenji was ever attracted to her. He is, after all, a Japanese man, though sometimes I wonder about him . . ."

We sat in a glassed-in veranda warmed by early spring sunshine. Sato had brought me a quart of Scotch whiskey—members of the general staff never lacked for excellent beverages and fine foods. I had heard from other wounded officers at the hospital that the top-ranking military men and cabinet members participated in lavish parties, feasts, evenings of entertainment. Many were even getting rich on the war. These were, of course, some of the reasons that drove us as young officers to support rebellion in 1936. I reminded Sato about this.

"But matters are different now," he said. "We are at war. I know about these rumors, but we should keep things in perspective. As long as the enemy seeks to destroy us we must fight on, support our leaders, prepare for final victory."

It was what I wanted to hear, to believe . . . I was half a man, one eye, one arm, but I was beginning to revive, to crave another combat command. I wouldn't sit around an office the rest of my life, go to meetings, listen to the squabbling and scheming of armchair generals. I belonged in the field. I grieved for every dead soldier who had served under me and I honored their memory in the Buddhist temple at the military hospital by praying each morning for the repose of their souls. But it wasn't enough. I was a soldier, I needed to fight and lead. . .

Sato's account of Admiral Yamamoto's death intensified my feelings. American planes had tracked him down in the Solomon Islands. "They knew his flight plan," the colonel said. "Those new planes, the P–38s, chased his Mitsubishi bomber over the upper Solomons and forced it to crash. The escort of Zero fighters was, I'm sorry to say, overmatched by the Americans."

"He will be badly missed," I said.

Sato looked at me. "A brilliant strategist but also a defeatist at heart. He did not have the true spirit of *Yamato.*"

"What about the war elsewhere?" I asked Sato, and he told me that Kiska and Attu, two small islands in the north near Alaska, had been retaken by the Americans. The battle at Attu, a bleak fogbound outpost, was especially bloody. Of our 2500 defending troops, only *twenty-eight* were taken prisoners, the others dying in *banzai* charges that cost the Americans a thousand dead.

"We must keep making them pay. It's the only way to force a surrender," Sato said. "Remember, there is a peace faction in America too. They cannot accept such losses . . ."

I wondered about our own losses but said nothing. I had decided I must try to believe in victory.

"At least the Solomons and New Guinea campaigns have taught us," said Sato, "that heavily entrenched positions, deep dugouts and multilevel fortifications with massed enfilading fire from automatic weapons cannot be overrun. We are strengthening all the island outposts. The Americans will make other amphibious landings—where, we aren't certain—and they will be mowed down like grass. Sea landings against fortified positions must fail. Our mistake was allowing the American marines to get footholds on Guadalcanal. We should have ringed the beaches with dugouts, tunnels, firing positions. Then we made things worse by attempting frontal assaults on their positions. It will not happen again."

An orderly came by, bowed and served us green tea. They knew me well at the hospital. Major Tamba, hero of Nanking, Malaya and Guadalcanal. I was uneasy with this attention, remembering my dead comrades.

"What disturbs me about these island dugouts," I said, "is that we are letting the enemy call the tune, make the aggressive move. At Pearl Harbor, in Malaya, in Hong Kong, it was *we* who released four hands and crushed him—"

"But if I remember my Musashi correctly he wrote that if the enemy attacks we must make a show of strongly suppressing his technique. He will change his mind if made to bleed sufficiently. We then alter our spirit and defeat him by forestalling him with the spirit of the Void."

"And you think that the next time that he invades, a defensive posture will suppress his technique and bring him to his knees?"

"I am certain of it."

I yawned. My empty eye socket did not hurt but it itched maddeningly. A healing process, the doctor said. Actually it was my stomach that had been most damaged by my ordeal on Guadalcanal. It was in a constant state of upheaval. I retched, experienced cramps and diarrhea, and the doctors could not stop it. They told me that a prolonged lack of rice had upset my digestive system, and so I was unable to gain weight. Well, I hoped my new diet would speed up recovery. I hated being sedentary in a hospital.

"You and I have roles to play in creating an unquenchable spirit in our army," Sato was saying. "Japan *cannot* be beaten. No amount of arms, no industrial empire, no horde of big-nosed barbarians can defeat *Yamato Damashii.*"

He insisted I join him in drinking to this speech. My stomach growled in protest.

As far as Tenno Heika was concerned, Sato went on, he was determined to keep fighting in spite of rumors that his divine presence was losing confidence in the military. Lord Privy Seal Kido, one of the men closest to the throne, had advanced a unique theory . . . if Japan were to be defeated too quickly there would be anger against the emperor, even from leaders who had sworn that they would bring victory to Japan. So . . . even if defeat awaited Japan, and that of course was unthinkable, Sato said, the people would have to be made to suffer and die in great numbers. This, according to Kido's peculiar logic, would assure the perpetuation of the god-descended royal line.

"In any event," Sato said, "*our* goals remain the same. We must conquer, unify and enlighten Asia. Even if Germany fails to unify Europe, our road toward the domination and rule of Asia will not be impeded."

I yawned again, fussed with my eye patch.

I mentioned casually that I had heard that MacArthur was promising he would return to the Philippines and drive us out.

"Mad ravings," declared Colonel Sato.

A week later I was transferred to a small medical facility north of Tokyo for field-grade officers that was like a country inn. I was fitted with a prosthetic metal arm, painful and unwieldy, but I forced myself to try to learn to use it. And gradually my strength did increase . . . I even learned to engage the metal claw as a weapon in combat with another one-armed officer, a Major Fuchida who had lost his right arm at Rabaul. Both of us often wondered whether we should have died with our men. I'm sure it was a strange sight . . . the two of us in white judo garb and black belts circling, thrusting with our metal forearms.

I did, though, refuse to wear a glass eye, sticking with the black eye-patch.

"Now you are a one-eyed dragon," Major Fuchida joked.

"One eye here and one overactive asshole," I said. "And *that* is driving me crazy."

My bowels were still not in order, I seemed to be squatting seven, eight times a day. The physicians said I had some damned tropical parasite, and so they tried to purge me with castor oil, cascara seeds and other natural remedies, and still the damned worm or fluke thrived in my guts and sent me into spasms when I crouched over the pit.

Fuchida and others also had been to one degree or another afflicted by digestive disorders, all of us agreeing it was a lack of rice, at least properly washed and cooked rice, that had outraged our innards.

"When I got off the boat," Fuchida grumbled, "I had no desire to see my wife and children. I ordered the ambulance driver to take me at once to my favorite restaurant in Minato Ward, the Golden Hall, a place that cooks the best rice in Tokyo. I sat there by myself eating bowl after bowl of rice—nothing on it, no fish, no pickle, no sauce—until I felt at peace with the world. Only then did I think of my wife . . ."

Wife . . . Michiko, I knew, would be concerned about me and want to see me . . . it had, after all, been months. She apparently had cried and begged and finally after I had spent a week convalescing at the inn she arrived one warm May day with my mother and my daughter.

To have not one but *three* women confronting me, with my wounded comrades looking on, felt unmanly and degrading. I would have preferred to have seen them at home, but Michiko carried on so, according to her father, that I finally gave in. A private room, a beautiful eight-*tatami* room looking out on a formal garden, was reserved for this meeting. I sat on a red cushion as the three entered, and through a waterfall of tears Michiko said to our daughter Maeko: "Bow to your father, child. On your knees and elbows, as low as you can get. That's right, little one. Let your head touch the floor."

All three fell to the floor, their heads touching the *tatamis.* Their hands were extended and flat. Their knees were locked together.

"You may get up," I said, honored by their respect. I was pleased to see that my American sister-in-law, whom I had not met, had not infected them with American notions of greeting—sweaty handshakes, womanish embraces, wet kisses, pattings and kissing. My inner organs would not have been able to tolerate these.

"We are so happy to see you, Masao," my mother then said, speaking first.

"We are glad you are so well," Michiko said, as my daughter began to howl. She was obviously frightened by the patch over my eye and the metal hook of my left arm that rested in my lap. I couldn't blame her, but all the same, her yowling was unnerving. "Here," I said, and offered my baby daughter a morsel of sugared plum. She promptly shrank behind her mother.

"I have brought you something," Michiko said, and unwrapped a flat package, then slid across the floor, lowered her head and handed me a framed watercolor painting that she had done herself. It showed a shrike, the bird that impales its victims on thorns, sitting on a willow branch with a dead fledgling in its beak.

"Very good," I said, though in truth I am hardly an expert and wasn't sure whether it was good or not. "And your calligraphy has improved."

"Mr. Isamu says I am talented."

"I'm sure you are, you must keep at your work . . ."

Michiko smiled and retreated, pleased with my approval. In the past I had rather cruelly scoffed at her painting, calling it schoolgirl's work, preferring that she run the house and concern herself with my needs. But what were my needs now? I was hardly ever at home. I had a shivery, almost pleasurable premonition of my death in battle . . . I squinted at the watercolor. It was of pale hues of brown and gray and just a touch of black, everything orderly and understated.

"Your father will come tomorrow night when he is off from work," my mother said. "He tells everyone of your heroism—"

"I do only what the emperor expects of me." Did that sound humble or like boasting?

Suddenly my mother began to weep, then sob in wet spasms, pounding her head against the floor. It embarrassed me, and I only hoped that Major Fuchida in the adjacent room would not hear her going on about my missing eye and arm, and tried to stare into the garden at a rock formation that suggested a flight of wild geese, at a row of *bonsai* trees. They didn't calm me or divert me from her crying.

Michiko then got caught up in the weeping, hitting her head against the floor, and now I knew what Fuchida meant by preferring a bowl of decent rice to having to face a wailing wife.

"You *must* stop," I said, embarrassed and upset, even though I appreciated her concern.

Finally they did subside, and my mother was able to talk about Saburo and his eagerness to attend cadet school and become a pilot even though he was underage and not strong. She went on about Yuriko and her factory work and even some about Kenji. My brother apparently had found a routine job with a food trading company. The military had rejected him, as had the government, in spite of the efforts of Kingoro Hata, who I thought could fix anything. No one in an official position, it seemed, wanted a young man with an *American* education and an *American* wife. Kenji, my mother hinted, had become somewhat estranged from them, even though his wife had learned to speak our language and their son Taro was a good child.

"And Yuriko's husband?" I asked.

"Hideo is at sea again," my mother said. "She spends her free time at our house with Hiroki, your nephew. Also a fine boy."

Boys. I looked at my daughter, a perfectly formed, beautiful child, laughing now, playing with the red paper Michiko's painting had come wrapped in. She was, truth to tell, an irresistible and endearing girl. If only she were a boy . . .

My mother asked, "Will they make you go to war again?"

"No, I will insist on it."

Her mouth trembled. "But you have already given so much. Michiko's father says you can stay in an office here in Tokyo—"

"I am a soldier, mother. It's all I know."

My daughter, only thirteen months old, walked remarkably well . . . an energetic, well-coordinated child. She could also say several words and I complimented Michiko on the progress Maeko had made.

"She is intelligent, dear husband. Like you."

Hisako quickly added: "Yes. She has your brains and your strength. Even Colonel Sato is impressed."

My wife told me that Maeko wasn't allowed to crawl, that as soon as she could stand she was taught to walk by means of a silk sash looped under her arms. Now she scuttled about the room, sturdy on her feet, babbling in a tiny voice . . . "Daddy. Daddy, boots? Daddy, chair?"

"I taught her the words," Michiko said.

"And she has already been weaned," my mother said. "I told Michiko that a child must be weaned at eight months, and eight months to the day we took her away from Michiko's breast."

"Did she cry?" I heard myself asking with some astonishment.

Hisako said, "At first she howled terribly, but I told Michiko to put pepper on her nipples and that cured the baby of wanting to suck."

Michiko blushed. "Your mother also helped me to understand that it was selfish for me to want to keep nursing Maeko, that the pleasure I got was greater than the baby's and that to nurse a child too long is to ruin it."

"What does she eat now?" I asked, again surprised at my own interest. I had been through combat, seen my men cut into chunks of bleeding meat, seen them die of thirst, starvation, disease, seen them eat their comrades' dead flesh, and here I was, touched by the sight of my tiny daughter, wanting to hear about such mundane and womanish things as her diet . . . The child was staring at me with knowing black eyes, yet so innocent and pure and loving that I was somehow uneasy.

"After weaning she was fed the water in which we boiled the rice," Michiko was saying. "But now she eats what we eat, lots of rice and whatever else we have—fish, vegetables, a sweet now and then."

"And your next child will be a boy." My mother gulped back tears, trying not to look at the metal claw in my lap. And then the tears began to flow again.

"Be silent, mother," I said firmly. "There is nothing that your tears can do to bring back my arm or eye. I accept these losses as part of my *gimu.* Tenno Heika will understand. You and father and Michiko must understand."

Maeko came to me then, smiling like a morning flower, and rested her chin on my knee. The glinting metal of the prosthetic hand obviously now fascinated her. She touched it, then pulled back.

"Maeko, *no,*" Michiko said.

Maeko didn't cry. Instead she touched the claw again, at once attracted and repelled, as children will be by a frightful picture in a book.

"That's all right," I said. With my right arm I lifted Maeko into my lap and held her against my chest. Ah, she was so soft and warm. I pressed my lips to her silken cheek. She was like something precious from a garden, a cherry blossom in the fullness of its bloom.

"She is very happy with you," Michiko said and began to cry softly, without the hysterics of my mother.

And, to my astonishment, my eyes filled as well. It was unmanly of me and I knew I should be ashamed for showing so much affection for a girl, but I could not resist my child.

YURIKO KITANO · JUNE, 1943

I went often now to Hans's apartment straight from the factory, just hoping he would be there. He had no telephone and I was never quite sure when he would be traveling or at the dingy flat. I had a key and he told me to feel free to visit whenever I wanted to.

This night the room was empty. There were unwashed dishes in the sink, the remnants of a meal on the kitchen table. The room was always a mess—Hans didn't seem bothered by this, but I decided that even if he did not come home I'd clean it for him. I would enjoy doing it for him.

I washed the dishes and the cutlery, swept the floor, smoothed the narrow couch on which we had shared our love and began to put his papers in order. He had a black German-made typewriter, and I dusted it, sharpened his pencils and filled the inkwell. I thought it exciting and fun to be the friend of a journalist.

It had turned dark and I was about to leave when I heard him at the door. My heart pounded and I ran to let him in.

He seemed startled at first, then smiled, and we kissed and held one another. He was unshaven and smelled of sweat and his clothes looked as if he hadn't changed them in several days. In a small satchel that he unpacked after we had kissed again was a camera and lenses.

"You acted frightened when you saw me," I said.

"Did I?"

"Yes. You looked pale, as if you did not want to see me here?"

"I am *always* happy to see you, please believe that."

He told me he had been on a trip to some of our ports, collecting information on the Japanese shipping industry for an article for a Berlin magazine. Although he was an accredited journalist with identification papers from our officials and the German embassy he had been stopped on several occasions.

"It was pretty bad in Kobe," Hans said. "They didn't believe me, took my films, kept me in prison overnight, roughed me up a little. Finally the German consul got on the phone and they let me go. He assured the police that I was a Nazi party member—"

"But you're *not,* you told me you hate them."

"That is our secret."

"Secret?"

"Yes."

"But if the police come here and see some of your writings against Japan's ally, Germany—"

"No one comes here. I'm a penniless writer. They know me at the press club. They've seen my Nazi party card, my little lapel pin."

We squeezed in together in his wooden tub after I'd brought the water to steaming, and we were wrapped together, turning pink, then red, playing with each other's bodies, until Hans began to moan . . . telling me that no woman ever had made him feel so good . . .

And now Hideo did not exist, nor did my marriage oath. All was replaced by our two bodies coming together, then Hans inside me, and me all round him, and we discovered we were one body, thrusting and receiving, flesh to flesh, and it was time out of time, nothing for either of us except ourselves . . .

Julie Tamba · June, 1943

The war seemed to settle into a sort of slow violent dance of some kind. Kenji had access to some source, more stuff about battles and strategy than Aunt Cora could get from the Swiss consul, and he said that the latest American invasion was in a place called New Georgia in the Solomons. Now the Japanese military was getting edgy, wondering where they'd be hit next.

None of this appeared in the newspapers. The war was as good as won, the papers said. The people were assured that by the end of 1943, the "great final battle" would come and Japan would rule Asia, just as she was destined to do.

The really exciting event came at the end of the month—Masao's homecoming. I was nervous about it . . . Major Masao Tamba, hero of . . . you name it. Kenji's older brother. Family darling.

"Masao is not a bad sort," Kenji said. "He is the very bravest man I know. He is a soldier, it's part of his upbringing. He was off to military school when he was a boy, it's his life."

Okay, let it go at that, I didn't want to rock any boats at the homecoming party. The Tambas hired street musicians, two men and two women in purple kimonos, beating drums and piping on flutes, eerie music. The red-and-blue drums were decorated with golden *mitsutomoe* symbols— three shapes like commas in a circle chasing each other's tail. Kenji told me the *mitsutomoe* could signify the three treasures of Buddha—the Buddha, law and the laity. I could never figure out what happened to Buddhism after the Japanese militarists got hold of it. I'd thought Buddhists were supposed to be against violence. Maybe I don't know enough about it, or maybe it proves that religions can be twisted by rulers who have the power to say it's what they want it to be.

Out on the exterior veranda of the Tamba house were the parents, Goro and Hisako, Saburo, Yuriko, Michiko and the kids—Michiko's Maeko, an adorable child, and Yuriko's Hiroki, a pudgy little thing. Kenji and I stood to one side, as usual a bit out of things. I'd slung Taro on my back and good Japanese kid that he was, he snoozed. Even the cymbals and bass drums of the street band didn't wake him up.

Lots of local kids, Saburo's schoolmates, had come to see the hero. They waved rising-sun flags, and one of them wandered around with a drum with a slit in the top collecting money for war widows and orphans.

Suddenly, with much honking, an army staff car drove up—chauffeur, flags, the works. The driver hopped out, opened the rear door, and out came Colonel Sato trailed by Major Tamba, my esteemed brother-in-law and the guest-of-honor.

The two of them wore rows of medals and ribbons, carried long swords and sported decorative braids—*fourragères*, I think they're called—looped through their epaulets. I can't say I took to either of them, preening, it seemed to me, like something out of Gilbert and Sullivan, oriental version. Okay, naughty thoughts, but damn it, I needed some outlet . . .

There was applause from the crowd, drum beating, banging of cymbals and flute trills. Everyone on the veranda bowed. I knew of course that sons by custom deferred to fathers—I'd seen it with Saburo and Kenji . . . *father, may I speak, father, may I leave? . . .* Not Masao. It was Goro who bowed to his son and then to Colonel Sato. Hisako, Yuriko and Michiko hit the deck, heads touching the ground, palms apart. I'd be damned if I would.

"Bow," Kenji whispered. He was bent at the waist himself.

"How about a curtsey?"

"Please, Julie. Not now."

I bowed.

Goro smiled. "Welcome home, eldest son. Welcome to our home, colonel."

The warriors nodded and trotted up the steps. Both men sat on the wooden bench. Michiko and Yuriko got to their knees again, removed their black boots and placed slippers on the honorable feet.

I could not help staring at Masao. Mutilated, he was nonetheless a commanding figure. Alongside him, Sato looked like a fat doll. Masao . . . lean, pale, handsome in an icy way . . . I could just see him leading men in battle, not giving a damn about his own life, a man whose courage and brutality combined into some kind of cutting weapon. I might not approve of him, but I was sure he was brave. Still, in spite of Kenji's excuses for him—his training, dedication, loyalty—none of it made me accept murdering civilians in Nanking, shooting Indian soldiers in Malaya and God knows what else in the Pacific Islands, and I thought of my brother Chris's angry letters . . .

The two uniformed men didn't look at me, for that matter they didn't give the time of day to any of the women. No kisses, not even smiles for Hisako and Yuriko and Michiko. The colonel and the major walked . . . strutted? . . . across the main room, hardly glancing at the feast that Hisako had labored over, the extra tables, the mounds of rice, the fish and vegetables and the casks of sake, and went on into the garden at the rear.

I lingered, slinging Taro to a more comfortable position, and watched as Masao and Sato took seats of honor on the low stone bench in the garden. Goro followed them and sat on the steps. Kenji stayed in the doorway. Some of Saburo's little friends poked their heads over the wooden fence. Saburo shinnied up the cherry tree and settled himself in the lower branches, not taking his eyes off Masao, obviously worshipping him.

Yuriko came by, carrying a tray of sake cups, playing a role, although I knew she didn't much like it. It was interesting, the way she and I had more in common than she and, say, Michiko.

Masao and the colonel were drinking toasts, fast, saying their *kampais*, banging down empty cups that Michiko would immediately fill. Sato would finger his bright ribbons and medals, and I wondered when he'd last heard a shot fired in anger. From what Kenji told me he hadn't held a field command since China. Nowadays he manned a desk at the War Ministry, spied on his superiors and kept up his contacts with such customers as the Dark Ocean Society and the Purple Cloud Pavilion— the names for these gangs were really something. Talk about euphemisms . . .

"We drink to the coming victory," said Sato, and Masao raised his cup. Goro mumbled something and tossed down his sake. "I drink to our heroes of Guadalcanal and New Guinea," said Sato.

Again cups were emptied. Saburo watched, his eyes wide. He called down from the tree, "Masao, tell us about the Americans you killed. A thousand? Five thousand?"

Masao seemed ill at ease with the metal hook in his lap. The upper arm maneuvered it, dropped it to his side, tried to find a comfortable position for it. Often his right hand would rest on top of the metal contraption as if trying to quiet it, to hide it. I began to feel something for him . . .

"Never mind, radish-head."

Sato took over. "We killed them by the thousands. They learned what it was like to fight the emperor's troops."

Sato's tongue was well-oiled by now and he was rambling on, laughing, smacking the hilt of his sword, spitting on the raked sand. "After Guadalcanal I can assure you there will be no more invasions of our islands— *none.* They cannot take such losses. They know how Japanese soldiers fight. Like all Americans they worry about their lives too much."

"That is so," Goro said thickly.

Masao, the only one of them who had been there, was silent. His one eye stared into space, seemed hazed and unfocused.

"They will all die," Saburo hooted from the tree. "Isn't that right, Masao? They're all cowards—"

"No, radish, they are brave men."

There was a noticeable shifting of butts and thighs, some coughing from Goro. A scowl appeared on Sato's face. Kenji half-smiled at me, as if to say, *See?*

"Brave, yes," Sato said. "*Some* of them. But they don't know how to die *and* they have nothing to die for."

I just couldn't take any more of this. I knew I was violating every code of behavior for a woman, but I couldn't stop. I stepped forward, rested against a pillar and slung Taro around. "Colonel, why do you think Americans have nothing they'll die for?"

Sato looked at me as if I'd crawled out from under a rock. "What did you say?"

"You think Americans are afraid to die and that they aren't brave, and—"

"Kenji, discipline your wife."

Kenji touched my arm. "Julie—"

I tugged away. "Colonel, since I'm a *gaijin,* I don't have the good sense or manners of a Japanese woman. So you can talk about this with me."

He turned his round bald head away.

Masao managed a thin smile. "Say what you wish," he said. "Go on."

"Your own troops didn't all stay to die on Guadalcanal," I said. I was soaked with sweat and scared.

"Our men died gloriously," Sato said. "You must not step on their sacred memory—"

"They died by the thousands there and on New Guinea," I said, my voice shaking. "I'm not glad about that, but it's true. And your navy evacuated thousands rather than let them be massacred, which was sensible. But the Americans beat the tar out of you on Guadalcanal—"

"*Not so.*" Sato's voice rose. "Not so, it was our victory."

Kenji bowed to the colonel. "My wife is upset, she must defend her country and the soldiers who serve it as much as you speak up for the Japanese soldiers—"

"But she distorts the truth."

"With all respect, colonel, who holds Guadalcanal now? Who controls New Guinea? Whose navy has mastery of the seas?"

Sato roared now. "If you weren't the brother of Major Tamba I would have you jailed for such remarks—"

Masao put his claw on Sato's braided sleeve. "My brother means no offense, he is not a soldier. He does not understand strategy." He winked at Kenji. "What we engaged in was strategic redeployment. Look at me. I lived so that we could fight again on other islands."

Kenji pressed on. "New Georgia has been invaded. The Americans plan to retake the Philippines. Their navy gets stronger every day and they have new fighter planes."

Goro got to his feet and literally prostrated himself in front of Sato. "Accept my apologies for my son's behavior. He is ignorant and rude—"

"He's telling the truth," I said.

"I will not listen to any more of this. Masao, your father is not to blame." At that, poor Goro got to his feet and bowed again. "I hope the feast we serve will make up for my son's thoughtless remarks."

This time I held my tongue. I felt I'd gotten Kenji into enough hot water.

Yuriko and Michiko came to the rescue, each took one of Sato's arms —he was quite tipsy by now—lifted him to his feet and escorted him into the house. He would have the seat of honor with his back to the *tokonama* that had a new scroll with a poem in praise of summer. Hisako had also arranged peach blossoms in a celadon vase.

"Ah, an escort for the old battleship," Sato said, "two lovely little sloops."

His daughter and Yuriko smiled and practically lifted him up the steps.

Masao now came over to Kenji and me.

"How do you know these things?" he asked Kenji.

"There's information about, my wife hears things from her aunt."

"Ah, yes. The Swiss hear the *American* broadcasts. But what if they tell lies?"

I put in, "What if your side does?"

Masao smiled like I was an idiot child. "You don't understand—"

"I understand very well, major."

"You may call me Masao."

"You see, Julie, my brother is welcoming you into the family."

"Yes, you are my brother's wife, you have given him a male child, but you don't understand . . . Look at me."

"I'm sorry for what you've suffered—"

"Again you misunderstand. I don't want you to be sorry. Suffering is nothing, suffering teaches us to deny the material world. You see me, missing an eye and an arm. It would appear I am ruined, not much of a man any more. I assure you, I will fight again. And it is the same with our army and navy. Yes, we have lost minor islands like Guadalcanal, Attu, Kiska. We have lost ships, planes, courageous men. But are we defeated? Do we surrender? No, and we never will. We have millions ready to die for the emperor. This is a god-ruled nation. We trace our lineage to the sun goddess Amaterasu. How can America . . . a nation of people who do not even worship the same god, defeat us?"

Well, he'd asked . . . "With more planes, more ships, more bombs, and men who are *just as brave as yours.*"

"But *we* will not surrender. We will find more men, and more—"

"Like *me,*" Saburo shouted down from his perch.

Masao smiled. "Yes, a million like Saburo. Have you seen the children marching in the street, drilling with bamboo spears? How can any country prevail against such spirit?"

Kenji shook his head. "I'm sorry, elder brother. You do not know the Americans."

"I fought them."

Masao fixed his one eye on Kenji. It was an odd look. It wasn't a hostile gaze or contemptuous, I could see that he respected Kenji. As for me, I think he just dismissed me as a crazy *gaijin.* And if Masao respected Kenji, it obviously was mutual, even if they disagreed.

Hisako called from the porch, breaking the tension, telling us dinner was ready, that the colonel and Masao must be hungry.

I hoped that the colonel would choke on a fishbone. He had taken over the Tamba house. Michiko especially was fussing over him, flitting about, making him comfortable on floor cushions and sort of propping him with his back to the *tokonama.* He was drunk by now, toppled over once and had to be righted. Terrific . . .

"Pay no attention to my father-in-law's words," Masao was saying to Kenji. "He has the peace faction on his mind. I want you to sit next to me."

Kenji smiled. "I won't be fed last? No Master Cold Rice?"

"I will guarantee it."

They ignored me. I followed after them, dutiful Asian wife. But I'd be damned if I'd shuffle as I went to the kitchen to help Hisako, my honorable mother-in-law who glared at me. "I know you do not think the way we do but it is wrong of you to insult our honored guest."

I kept the lip buttoned, then and through dinner, grateful when Yuriko, who kept on playing a part, entertained us with sad songs on the *samisen.*

By the end of the evening I had changed much of my feelings about Masao. I didn't agree with him and I couldn't forget the stories about Nanking, but there was no denying the power and integrity that he had. Once he even smiled at me and looked at me as if he were trying to figure me out. I felt like telling him the feeling was mutual, but again was a good girl and kept my mouth shut.

* * *

When Kenji and I left we were exhausted and Taro was howling to be changed, to suck at my breast. At the Tamba house Kenji and I lay on the *tatamis* and *futons* in the dark, not saying anything for a while. Then I tried to snuggle up to him. "Was I too awful, honey?"

Kenji groaned, then stroked me. "No . . . I was the one who offended. I shouldn't have debated with them, not tonight. I know better . . ."

"Kenji, why should it be so one-sided? I mean—"

"Please, Julie. My head hurts."

"I'm not surprised. My God, that Colonel Sato . . . I hate him, I really do, and I hate it the way they treat you."

Kenji turned to me. "Julie, I'm not really worried about all that . . ." And then, patiently and slowly, he told me about his dangerous work, and I understood what he meant. I think I had sensed that he was doing something special and had never quite bought that stuff about an Edo Sugar Export Company, it sounded too made up. I just couldn't see Kenji as a clerk or nonentity.

"I'm working with my old teacher, Professor Adachi," Kenji said quietly. "He's gathering information on the war and on foreign government policies for people who can and want to change things. Which is why I should be careful about what I say and do. I've no right to bring suspicion on myself because if I do I also risk bringing it on Professor Adachi and others like him."

I shivered, even though it was a hot sticky night. Here I was wanting my own feelings fulfilled by Kenji, and he could be jailed, or worse, for it. We had the sliding doors open, and mosquitoes flew into our room, hummed and buzzed and I thought of an old Robert Benchley story . . . I love Benchley . . . about "Lillian Mosquito" who can sound as if she's in your ear when she's fifteen feet away, so you keep smacking your ear till it turns red, but when Lillian Mosquito *stings* you, you never hear her coming. I tried telling it to Kenji but it didn't go over too hot.

KENJI TAMBA · JULY, 1943

New Georgia, Lae . . .

More American landings, more failures of our troops to hold onto these island positions. And still the High Command talked about victory.

On the home front, Adachi briefed me, millionaire manufacturers and warlords, the corrupt group around the palace, did not suffer. They feasted, drank, had their evenings with whores and geishas.

From Kingoro Hata I learned that my father had acquired a mistress, which didn't surprise me. Fumiko, the maid at the palace, had agreed to a weekly stipend and gifts to supply my father with what he craved. Hata had arranged for a room at the rear of his friend Satomi's geisha house to be used for these liaisons.

"I assure you," he said to me one morning as we met in downtown Tokyo, "your father has never been happier."

"And what does he do for you in return?"

Hata was candid. "He supplies me with information he overhears at the palace, bits of conversation, opinions. He serves tea and rice cakes to the generals and admirals when they come calling. They are loose-lipped in front of your father, whom they, forgive me, consider part of the furniture."

"I would think that as a member of Parliament you would know things on your own," I said, bristling.

"My dear Kenji, they tell us civilians as little as possible. We were not even aware of the Amano scandal."

I shook my head.

"Yes. My fellow parliamentarian. The one who cut his belly last week. The official announcement was that he had died a natural death. Your father overheard the story at a luncheon when the Lord Privy Seal entertained military aides. It seems that Amano, who was in the forefront of those urging the war against America, had a change of heart and he wanted us to sue for peace with the United States and attack Russia."

I shook my head again.

"Amano attacked Tojo in private, called for an immediate withdrawal from Pacific bases and a declaration of war against the Soviet Union. This was nonsense, because we have a nonaggression pact with the Russians. Tojo had him arrested, interrogated and he had the good grace to commit suicide. I am told he fell forward in true *samurai* fashion, then had his servant cut off his head. The man was not altogether bad."

"And my father heard all this and told you?"

"Yes. He feels that my help in arranging his meetings with Fumiko are surely worth bits of such information."

"Does your friend Satomi also charge him for the use of the room?"

"Why not? We must keep everything on a businesslike basis. You must notice how relaxed your father looks."

What I noticed at the moment were pinched faces, old women and wounded men, and I wondered how we had let ourselves to be misled, betrayed and used by people like Hata. Adachi's thesis, I decided, was too academic . . . On the other hand I had to admit that my father did have more spring to his step, seemed more animated at dinner. He even laughed some, and managed to smile at Julie now and then. He was less distant with Taro and seemed to enjoy it when all three of his grandchildren, Taro, Maeko and Hiroki, were at the house together and would get on his knees and play with them as if he were in his second childhood.

Once when his kimono flapped open I saw some large red "*tatami* burns" on his thigh. No doubt about it, Fumiko was giving him his money's worth at the Plum Blossom House.

I did not joke about this or even mention the mistress to Julie. She would not have thought it at all funny. Besides, I owed my father some filial loyalty. By his code he was doing what every Japanese male dreams of doing, and in a way I was glad for him.

MASAO TAMBA · NOVEMBER, 1943

Tarawa . . .
I did not even know the name at first. Why there? What did the Americans have in mind?

Miserable at my desk job, sick of meetings and strategies that are not strategies but fantasies, I learned today of the American invasion of one of our strongholds in the Gilbert Islands far to the east. This is their long-awaited general Pacific offensive. I look at the map and I think I understand their objectives—to break through our outer defenses, move from the Gilbert Islands to the Marshalls, affording them air bases and fueling stations for their ships, then press westward to the Marianas. We will make them pay. As we have made them pay on Tarawa.

I had asked for reassignment to a combat command. But Colonel Sato ·etoed it. He wants me here. I think he wants to make sure his daughter Michiko bears him a grandson before I die.

Today I saw a report on the fortifications on Tarawa. The island is actually an atoll, the main part called Betio. The whole scrap of coral is only three miles square and worthless. We fortified it with British-made eight-inch coastal guns that I helped capture at Singapore, protected by over a hundred pillboxes, machine-gun posts and bunkers built of coconut palm trunks six deep, sand, coral and steel. We had five thousand men on Tarawa. Nearly all of them are dead.

But before they died they took a fearful toll of the invaders. The massive bombardment by American naval guns and the aerial bombing barely dented our fortifications. Set in sand and logs, the pillboxes shook, bounced and recovered. All guns were operative when the marines stormed ashore, and they died by the hundreds in foolish frontal attacks. I would have thought they would have learned from our mistakes on Guadalcanal.

The coral reef barrier and the tides were our allies. The Americans were cut down en masse by our gunners, taught a lesson in tactics. Many of the marines had to walk seven hundred yards across the treacherous reef into the teeth of machine gun and artillery fire. They had no cover. The low tide that exposed the reef also left them naked. At no time during that first day was a single landing craft able to get to the beach. We killed or wounded more than a thousand of the five thousand who landed. Corpses choked the beach, burning vehicles, the amphibious craft and tanks they prized so highly, piled up.

But still, damn them, they would not give up. They landed more men, burned our defenders with flamethrowers, destroyed our snipers with grenades. No, Colonal Sato was wrong, marines did not lack for courage, as I had learned on Guadalcanal. I tried to warn my superiors, they told me the American people would tire of the huge losses. Wrong. Wrong.

I have in front of me now the last report on Tarawa. The scrap of land is lost to us and from it the Americans can move on to Makin, to the Marshalls, the Carolines, the Marianas. Each island will cost them dearly, but . . .

Admiral Shibasaki's last signal from Tarawa reads: *Our weapons have been destroyed and from now on everyone is attempting a final charge. May Japan exist for ten thousand years!*

Brave words. Brave fellow. He was burned to a pile of cinders along with three hundred of his best men. The marines sealed the entrances to his blockhouse with sand, then pumped gasoline down a venting shaft and threw in grenades.

Of 5,000 of our men, only one officer—may his name live in shame—was taken alive, along with 16 enlisted men and 129 Korean laborers. The Americans lost 1,300 dead out of an attacking force of 18,000. All this death for three square miles of sand. We can only hope there will be more hesitation before they try to invade an island again. We can hope . . .

"It is only an insignificant scrap," Colonel Sato said to me.

"But they defeated us, colonel."

"Imagine what is going through their minds. If a small island like Tarawa can create such casualties, if they need *eighteen thousand men* and a fleet and air support to defeat us, what will they require to retake the Philippines? Or Malaya? Or the East Indies? Let alone any crazy dream of invading our homeland. They would need an army of twenty million men, more planes and more ships than even the United States can build. So I tell you we must view Tarawa as a victory for us. It has taught the Americans a lesson. They cannot go on forever shedding their blood and losing their materiel and best troops in such so-called victories. They kill five thousand of us? Fifty thousand more will take their place, ready to kill, to die."

To die, yes . . . *I* should have died on Guadalcanal. I should have died on Tarawa. Colonel Sato, and people like him, are beginning to turn my stomach.

JULIE TAMBA · DECEMBER, 1943

Chris was able to get uncensored letters to me via the Swiss consul in San Francisco. They would include his letters in the Swiss diplomatic pouch delivered to the Swiss Embassy in Tokyo, where Aunt Cora would pick them up.

Chris had missed the "big show," as he called it, on Tarawa, but had landed with the marines in a later invasion of an island called Makin to the north. He had also interviewed marines who had been at Tarawa . . .

> . . . visited Tarawa a week after the battle. Hard to believe anyone survived. And the faces of those guys who fought there. Full of pain, exhaustion, shock. They had seen their buddies die by the hundreds, mowed down by murderous gunfire. We seem to have made every mistake in the book and the Nips knew it. The tides were never right. The bombardment of the Jap dugouts was a flop. Our radio equipment was wrecked by salt water. The amtracks aren't armored. Air support was lousy. I get sick to my stomach when I think of those mass graves filled with kids. As for

> the Japs, bunkers full of 'em, burned into hunks of charred meat.
> And I don't give a *damn*. I'm told that back home people have
> been shocked by Tarawa. What does this mean for the rest of the
> war? These damned Japs will not quit, will not accept that they're
> beaten. Kill 'em all, I say. I really mean that . . .

He went on about the horror of watching an American carrier, the
Lipscomb Bay, go down off Makin in a huge cone of flame after being
torpedoed by a Japanese submarine. More than six hundred Americans
died with the ship. He watched it all from another ship, he and the other
witnesses raging and not able to help the doomed men.

> . . . this is a war to the bloody end, sis. This is a war where
> we'll have to kill and keep killing until these little bastards
> understand that they're beaten. I just hope that the people stateside
> don't get down on our action after Tarawa. If anything it makes it
> more important than ever that we stay at it until the Japs are on
> their knees begging for mercy . . .

It was a terrible, scary letter, and it made me realize what Chris never
intended . . . that both sides were brave, and that this war was being
fought, just like Kenji and his professor said, for the big shots in the
military and industry. But I was still an *American* girl, and I couldn't just
say both sides were equally wrong. I couldn't. Damn it, the Japanese
started the war . . .

I lingered at the clinic, waiting for Aunt Cora and Uncle Adam to finish
up with their patients. Nowadays they mostly treated old women and
children. Adam was increasingly upset by the shortage of medical supplies. He was also still pestered by the police, but at least was never taken
in for questioning.

There was also a brief letter from my parents, who mostly wanted
photographs of Taro. When I wrote to them I lied a little. No, a lot. Yes,
things were fine at the Tamba house, there was plenty of food, the war
hadn't really reached us, and so forth. No problems between me and the
Tambas, between me and Kenji. Why saddle them with stuff they couldn't
do anything about? Besides, I'd made my own bed, how could I gripe
about it? Especially to my parents, who'd argued so hard against the
marriage and then my decision to stick with Kenji when war broke out
and he got interned. I should tell them the details of the *benjo* and meals
of rice on rice? I had Taro to share with them.

Aunt Cora, bustling about in her white coat, her hair tied up in a kerchief, now was motioning to me, Taro on my back, to come into the garden for tea. Uncle Adam, puffing one of the last of his precious cigars, joined us.

We talked about the Tarawa and Makin invasions, and Adam said that if those defeats couldn't convince Japan's rulers of the folly of the war probably nothing could. "It should be obvious to everyone from the emperor down that they can't win," he said. "The man is no fool, the men running the army and navy aren't fools. They *must* see the handwriting on the wall."

Officer Tani grinned at us across the wooden fence, saluted, mumbled something incomprehensible. Aunt Cora offered him a rice cake, which he accepted with a formal bow . . . Seeing Tani, I thought again about Ed. I doubted he had a fool like Tani guarding him but really cruel and vindictive men.

"The story going around the neutral embassies," Uncle Adam said, "is that Hirohito is considering options for peace. He and Kido, you know, the Lord Privy Seal, know that they can't surrender right now. Too much opposition. Besides, to surrender while Japan is relatively untouched, cities intact, people not starving, will, they figure, bring no sympathy from the United States. But if they wait until they've been bombed, are in much worse state, maybe they'll get a better deal."

"God," I said. "Wait until thousands more suffer, including civilians, before doing the right thing and saving their own necks?"

"That's about it, Julie."

"Tell her what the Swiss consul said about Kido's plan."

"Yes, well, it goes like this . . . They want Germany to keep fighting and winning. That will put off the pacifists and traitors in Japan. Any move for peace mustn't come from these peace-loving types, Kido says. But of course there has to be a *secret* Imperial plan ready to be put to the Allies at the right time."

I thought of Kenji's work for Professor Adachi . . . he and the professor would probably be considered part of the hated peace faction. I realized much more how dangerous Kenji's work was . . .

Some advisors to the emperor, Kido included, Uncle Adam said, believed that the war had already been *won* by Japan. No matter what happened, Japan had broken down the "encirclement" by the United States, Britain, China and the Netherlands. The Asian countries "liberated" by Tokyo would never be the same. So a surrender, with face-saving at some later date, would be a pill they could swallow. Provided, of course, the military went along.

"In fact," Adam said, "they're feeling so cocky about things that they'll insist on self-determination for all Asian nations, except Manchuria, which of course will remain theirs."

"Very generous of them," I said.

"*And* they think they have a trump card," Aunt Cora said. "Right, Adam?"

"What? A secret weapon?" I asked.

"Yes . . . and it's called the Soviet Union," Uncle Adam said.

I must have looked as dumb as I felt, and was glad for the momentary diversion of Taro playing with my hair, pulling at it.

"I hear and read that there's a feeling among Kido and others near the top that Russia is the secret weapon to keep Japan from being isolated because of race. Russia is an *Asian* nation, Stalin is *oriental* in his thinking. And since they have a nonaggression pact with Moscow, why not a formal alliance at a later date?"

"Hey," I said, "that sort of fits with Kenji's story about a politician who had to kill himself because he wanted an invasion of Russia."

"Well, who knows? . . . Kido has circulated a memo that any surrender would not be a surrender of spirit, just a bow to American technology. And while they bow they will secretly shake hands with the Kremlin and wait for the day when they can fight again. The Asiatic races against the white race."

"That sounds pretty wild," I said. "If you're talking about Asiatics, what about the Chinese?"

"As I said, who knows?" Adam proceeded to puff up a storm from his stogie. "How are things at the Tamba estate?" he asked.

"About the same," I said. I didn't feel like going on about the old stuff, and was sure they didn't particularly want to hear it.

"And you and Kenji . . . ?" Aunt Cora put in.

"He's got those headaches. He's caught in the middle, I understand that, and I think it's easier for me than him."

"You could stay with us," Aunt Cora said. "All three of you—"

"I wouldn't think of it, Aunt Cora. The clinic is overcrowded, you have your own problems. And besides, Kenji would be humiliated. He feels bad enough he can't find a house for us. Even Yuriko's dumb husband Hideo got her one, and Michiko was given a place by her father. It hurts him."

"Naturally, he is a proud man, Julie—"

"And I love him." I hoped I didn't sound like I was protesting too much.

"Do you want to go home?" Adam asked abruptly—his usual fashion.

"No." Was I absolutely sure?

"It could be arranged," Cora said. "You could wait out the war, then you and Kenji could be reunited—"

"I . . . I couldn't take the baby from him, and he needs us so much. He's a pariah to his family. He'd be miserable if I left—*and I would be too.*"

"Then that's that," Uncle Adam said.

There was a sort of awkward silence, and then I asked Cora if she'd gotten any word about Ed Hodges. I still felt I should try to see him. To help him if I could.

"Well, Dr. Reinhold has gotten me a list of places where the POWs work. Most of them are on the Yokohama docks and they're not too closely guarded. It's sort of like an honor system—the American officers have to see to it that no one tries to escape. If anyone does, the officers are punished. Besides, where could they go?"

"Well, let me know," I said. Adam walked me out of the clinic then. On the street an air raid drill was going on. Women and children, directed by the shouts and whistle-blowing of an old man in a World War I uniform, raced about in no particular pattern, dragging hoselines, filling buckets, pumping away. They cheered one another, didn't seem discouraged when the ancient hose leaked streams of water and cut down the flow from the nozzle.

I noticed that my mother-in-law Hisako . . . aging, contending now with a gloomy husband and a *gaijin* relative . . . was among the hose pullers but looked grim-faced. Who could blame her? For all her chilliness to me, I really felt for her . . .

Uncle Adam and I stood watching for a while. Finally he said, "The government feeds these people lies on lies. You'd never know there was a Tarawa. But one thing they do tell them the truth about."

"What's that?"

"That there will be more bombings, that they will have to suffer. They are smart to do it, because it almost certainly will happen, and when and if it does they won't be caught by surprise. It's better for them this way."

He looked about us. "Paper. Wood. Straw. If ever a city was built to be turned into a bonfire this is it. Are you sure you want to stay?" He was looking at Taro's rosy face. My son's chubby little hand was tugging at my hair, he seemed intrigued by the blonde strands.

"Yes, uncle. *I'm staying.*"

"Then, as the Friends say, 'My peace I give unto you.'"

I smiled and finished it. "'Let not your heart be troubled neither let it be afraid.'"

He kissed my cheek and I left then, waving to Hisako, who had now seen us. She waved back, and once again I felt a rush of pity for her.

MASAO TAMBA · FEBRUARY, 1944

Kingoro Hata, a man who knew how to make a war work for him, kept a seaside villa in the fishing village of Hayama, where His Majesty also maintained a house. I was invited for a weekend, along with Hata's mistress Satomi and some of her prize geishas, including a young woman named Kiku, with whom I had enjoyed several evenings. I was pleased that my father-in-law Colonel Sato was not able to join us.

We strolled along the pebbly beach. It was chilly and we wore heavy coats. I was in civilian garb.

"Certain faint hearts," Hata was saying, "have been telling Tenno Heika to surrender now. Their point seems to be that Japan is intact, so do it before it is too late. Cooler heads have prevailed."

"I am a soldier, not a politician," I told him.

Hata wore a tight black greatcoat and black army boots, although he had never heard a shot fired in anger and was a soft overweight man. Now he gave forth with another extreme notion . . . that a prolonged war might be a good idea since it would thin out the population, get rid of a lot of the weak, the defectives, the burdens of the state. And if Japan were to truly suffer, to be bombed, have millions killed and many others left homeless and impoverished, then we wouldn't need to apologize to anyone. Such so-called punishment would atone for any of Japan's imagined wrongs. The books would be balanced, and such deaths would permit us to rise from the ashes and start again with no need to say we are sorry.

"I wonder if our dead soldiers and civilians would appreciate such grand theories."

"But major, wouldn't their deaths be more glorious than most lives? Eternal happiness in the Yasukuni shrine, prayers, honors." Hata used his cane to flip over a pulsating starfish.

We approached his villa, surrounded by tall pines with a magnificent view of the bay. Once inside we sat down to tea and were waited on by Satomi and Kiku. Satomi then joined us and began to reminisce about her younger days in Akasaka, the delicate "floating world" of the old geisha houses . . . "It's all going," Satomi said. "The girls could sing beautifully, play the *samisen,* dance and wear the Shimada hairstyle. We allowed no coarse unmannerly girls. And our kimonos! Each was a work of art."

Hata, bored by her recital, tried prodding me for details about the American invasions, and although I normally was close-mouthed I'd had a great deal to drink and told him some of the latest battle news, none of it good . . . "The Americans have driven us off the Marshall Islands," I said.

"Is that strategically important?"

"Yes and no," and I launched into a long explanation about why the loss of Kwajalein, Majuro and Jaluit wasn't crucial to our defense. I didn't like myself for such rationalizing, walking around a subject. It was out of character for me. It came from too damn many hours at the War Ministry, surrounded by blowhards like my father-in-law. I had better get back with my dirty, unshaven, hard-bitten foot soldiers or I'd end up like him. I stopped the double-talk. "The island of Truk was bombed into rubble by carrier planes. We are saying nothing about it. Admiral Koga ran. The Americans wrecked the harbor, shot down three hundred planes, sank much of our shipping. Truk is finished, they have neutralized the Caroline Islands."

Satomi's *samisen* notes pinged and echoed in the hardwood room. I could hear the gentle lap of the seawater on the pebble beach outside Hata's villa.

"What does all this mean?" Hata asked. He meant what did it mean for him. He was also interested in drawing me out in such a way to make me vulnerable, to make me compromise myself and so be beholden to him. To hell with him.

"It means that our outer defenses have been wrecked. The Americans will probably bide their time and when they are ready they will invade the Marianas on our back doorstep. Guam, Saipan, Tinian. All in bombing range of Japan. There have already been carrier strikes against these places."

"Major, I must say that sounds to me like defeatist talk. Surely our generals have a plan for stopping the Americans—"

"Several. Except that the army and navy can't seem to agree. The navy wants to draw the Americans west and then crush them from our island bases. One decisive battle. They argue that our outer islands are, in effect, unsinkable carriers while as we have shown, their carriers can be sunk."

"And the army?"

"They say that the Marianas and Palau, like the Marshalls and the Gilberts and the Solomons, cannot be defended. They want a decisive land battle on Formosa or the Philippines. Evacuate the small islands, consolidate and make a stand further back."

"And whose side are you on, Major Tamba?"

I looked at him. "I don't care, I only want to be in the field again. If we are given the choice of death or death we must choose the one that is most honorable. For me that is with my men."

Hata gave up pressing me at that point. Later I retired to a darkened room with Kiku and her sister. Their bodies were smooth as flower petals. Their breasts were sweet and firm and their inner thighs were like silk. At first I had little interest. I needed assistance of a most subtle kind before I could respond like a man.

Early the next day, when I telephoned the duty officer at the War Ministry, I learned that Prime Minister Tojo, feeling the weight of his prediction that the United States navy would be "wiped out," had fired the chief of the army, General Sugiyama. He, Tojo, would now head the army.

I decided to let Hata find out this news for himself. He was going over what looked like account books with Satomi. A clerk and a fixer.

My stump pained me, and the damp air did not help. Satomi, seeing my discomfort, brought me a decanter of Scotch whiskey and a glass. In her hard-edged businesslike way, she was someone to be admired. She never prattled on about holy missions, glorious wars, divine rulers. It was all double-entry bookkeeping to her. Very refreshing.

I crossed my legs, sipped the Scotch. It was warm and relaxing. My stump often jerked involuntarily when I was tense, but now it lay against my side. I would ask the two young women to spend the night with me, and hope to forget for a while the sickening schemes of men like Hata, and, yes, our generals and politicians too. They disgraced the men who fought and died. They disgraced their emperor and their sacred nation. I deeply believed that.

JULIE TAMBA · FEBRUARY, 1944

The bus dropped me off at the Shinko docks in Yokohama after an hour's bumpy ride from Tokyo. A swirling powdery snow veiled the port.

Underfoot it was slippery, ice patches forming on the cobbled streets. The air froze muddy holes and the wet snow seeped through my sandals and soaked my *tabi* socks.

I had tried to hide my face—a quilted hood over my head, a thick woolen scarf covering everything but my eyes. I bent over to hide my "unnatural" height. I'd come here on a gamble, not wanting to wait any longer in my effort to see Ed Hodges. It had been a year since Aunt Cora had learned that Ed was in Tokyo. Then the Imperial War Prisoner bureau had without warning or reason stopped Red Cross visits and even halted the delivery of Red Cross packages. But what Cora had heard from Dr. Reinhold about prisoner treatment was pretty scary. I couldn't let any more time pass. Damn it, Ed was my *friend.* I owed him at least a try at finding him and helping him. All right, and maybe I was still feeling a little guilty over that Dear John treatment I'd given him.

All I had to go on was that he might be at any one of a half dozen locations along the Yokohama docks. So now on this snowy, bitingly cold day I trudged the Yokohama docks looking for some POWs. My eyes— too pale—were all that showed behind the layers of thick clothing. Dr. Reinhold had told Cora he believed that some men were being worked at the New Dawn Warehouse in Shinko, unloading cargo.

A railroad siding cut diagonally across the area from the pier to the warehouses. A chain-link gate was open. To my surprise, people moved back and forth freely, with only a solitary policeman on duty. People streamed out of ferryboats, crossed the tracks, waited patiently, covered with mantles of snow, for trains that were late, buses that broke down. In a way I felt I was one of them in my quilted hood, floppy coat, sandals. I had a half-Japanese son at home, a Japanese husband, and I had even gotten used to all the rice. But of course I really *wasn't* one of them . . . probably never would be . . . they were kindly and sadistic, gave oranges to POWs, or so I'd heard, and conducted death marches. They bowed and they brutalized . . .

Suddenly I saw some tall men in dark quilted coats working the cargo nets from a rusting freighter. There were white *P*'s on their backs and I heard English being spoken.

"Move it, Guzzo, move it." . . . "Stand back, pogey bait, I got me a full load." . . . "Lady wit' a baby, comin' through." . . . "What's in them, Guzzo? Anythin' worth eatin'?" . . . "Lasagna and pepperoni. Two hunnert crates of 'em. The Nips are gonna give it all to us."

Men were working the nets, unloading them, stacking wooden crates on pallets. A Japanese woman, bundled in layers of rags, drove a forklift truck with a double blade. She maneuvered the truck so that the fork entered the open spaces at the base of the pallet, lifted the load, turned, and chugged off to the warehouse. Only two elderly guards were at the far end of the dock, smoking and laughing.

When they got up once to nudge one of the POWs with a wooden club I heard . . .

"You shit today, Guzzo? . . . "You bet, Corporal Araki." . . . "You got cigarettes for me?" . . . "No, sir, maybe next week. You guys let us get packages from home, we'd get butts, you'd get butts, we'd be buddies. Right, Goodwin?"

Guzzo and Goodwin. Ed's platoon . . . But no Ed, that I could make out.

I turned away, still hearing their voices.

"Figured out what's in them, sarge?" . . . "I give up. Talcum powder? Silk stockings?" . . . "Nah, it's some kinda white chemical. Can't eat it. Ain't worth stealing."

I decided to follow the forklift to the New Dawn Warehouse. The crowds were larger now, people shuffling through the snow to the ferryboat. The forklift belched its way, bumping on the cobblestones to the far side of the rusting metal shed. I went after it, and was soon lost in the crowd of dockworkers, passengers, vendors and school children.

The truck stopped at an entrance to the shed. A conveyor belt had been set up there and POWs in black coats with a large *P* on the back were manhandling crates, tossing them to the belt and shoving them into the warehouse. Their breath formed clouds of steam. The snow was heavier now. The men working the rollers wore no gloves and blew on their hands. There was no guard in sight.

I saw Ed.

He came from the opposite side of the warehouse and was carrying a clipboard. I pressed myself against the metal flank of the shed and stared at him to make sure.

Ed. Ed Hodges.

His face was chalk-white and thin. There were dark circles under his eyes, hollows in his cheeks. His chin was covered with a ragged blond stubble. There was a halt to the unloading. The forklift truck was emptied, and chugged back to the pier. A second small truck was being loaded at the dockside. The three men at the conveyer went into the warehouse.

Ed flapped his arms and stomped his feet. The snow drew sort of a feathery curtain between us. I still didn't see any guard but I heard voices inside the shed. A guard was shouting at the men, using American profanity he'd no doubt picked up from the prisoners. Great imitators . . . *Move ass, Johnson . . . Marine, shithead, work better . . . You want chow, Johnson, you work . . .*

An old Japanese couple, the man in the lead, the woman trailing, shuffled by. They were ankle-deep in snow. They *smiled* at Ed and even bowed slightly.

In Japanese Ed told them good morning. *Ohao.* They grinned. I walked from where I'd been hiding against the building and approached Ed. We stood on opposite sides of the conveyer. I pulled the scarf from my face and yanked the hood back.

"Ed," I said.

He blinked, wiped snow from his eyes. "My God . . . *Julie?*"

"The same."

"I . . . don't believe it. How . . . ? How'd you find me?"

"Luck. Oh, Ed . . ."

He ducked under the rollers of the belt and stumbled toward me.

"I live in Tokyo," I said inanely.

"I know. My folks wrote me. But how'd you find me?"

"Aunt Cora's Swiss. She knows the Red Cross people. They helped. But are you . . . okay?"

"A damn sight better off than a lot of my men . . . How about you?"

"I guess you know. I came here with Kenji."

". . . You look great, Julie . . . any kids?"

"A son. Taro."

He looked faint.

"Christmas comes a little late this year," I said, and handed him cigarettes, plum jam, a pen, a pad, woollen socks and two copies of *Newsweek.* "Don't ask me how but Kenji always seems to have American reading material."

Quickly he hid the gifts in his clothing. "You learn this pretty fast. I mean, how to hide stuff. Thanks. And thank Kenji . . ."

The jar of jam disappeared in a sleeve of his coat. The magazines were inserted one in each sock. The cigarettes went in a wool undershirt that peeked out from beneath his blue POW shirt. The pen and the pad were stowed in the lining of his cap.

"Don't you get searched?"

"Used to. Things have eased up some. They don't kill us anymore, just beat the hell out of us. Sometimes the guards are pretty good. You never know."

"Ed, I feel awful—"

"Why? Jesus, I feel great, seeing you." He put his hands on my arms. His hands were bony, red and calloused. "Hey, this war won't last forever. I've made it this far. I damn well intend to be around when we clean up at the end."

"I've heard some bad stories. About beatings, torture . . . ?"

"It happens, but the guys protect each other."

"If they find the things I gave you will they punish you?"

"No, just steal them."

"Ed, I'm feeling peculiar. I'm so glad to see you, and I wonder what you think of me, you know what I mean . . ."

"Hey, I think you're great. Now cut it out . . . besides, here comes a load."

The forklift was rumbling across the cobblestones. Two of Ed's fellow POWs came out of the warehouse, blowing on their hands. I yanked up the hood and pulled the scarf over my face.

"I got only one question," Ed said quickly. "Do you love Kenji?"

"Yes. He's a good man, Ed. He's—"

"Enough, kid. I think you better take off."

The POWs were staring at me and I heard one say, "Jesus, a *broad,* and she sounds like an American . . . ?"

"Julie," Ed said. "Please go. And it might not be a good idea to come back here. Anyway, we're moved around all the time. There's scuttlebutt we're supposed to go north and work in the mines."

"Oh, God, I hope not."

The small truck with its load of wooden boxes came up to the conveyor.

Ed's men stared at me, still trying to dope out who, or what, I was.

A guard in a quilted khaki coat and a peaked cap came out of the warehouse and stared at me. He couldn't see my face but I was one suspiciously tall Japanese lady.

"What going on?" he said. He was carrying a long wooden club as he shuffled through the snow. "What you do, Hodges?"

"Nothing, Froggy."

The man stopped. "No *Froggy* crap. Sergeant Ozawa. Who is the woman?"

"I don't know. She said she's lost. Wants to find the train to Kobe."

"You, beat it," the guard shouted at me. "Do not talk with prisoners. *Go.*"

Froggy ran at Ed and hit him in the back with the club. "I say no talk. Everyone work, dammit. No work, no rice."

I felt the pain in my own back.

The detail began unloading crates. Ed picked up his clipboard. I looked back once to see Ed rubbing the small of his back. I saw the guard had raised the club again and I wanted to scream. If I'd had a gun I would have shot the guard between the eyes. I knew now what my brother Chris meant about learning to hate.

The train back to Tokyo broke down twice. Once I almost got a seat but a mob of schoolboys in blue uniforms jostled and shoved me and nearly dragged me from the momentarily empty space.

"*Supai, supai,*" a kid of about twelve said.

They all laughed and I thought I would faint.

That night I told Kenji about my trip to Yokohama, about Ed, how he looked, how the guard beat him.

"I'm sorry, Julie—"

"Why are they so damned *cruel?*"

"I can't justify it, just explain it. It's in the code of *bushido* that Masao taught me . . . 'Bear in mind the fact that to be captured means not only that you disgrace yourself but that your parents and family will never be able to hold their heads up again. Always save the last bullet for yourself.' To them a military prisoner is subhuman, worthy only of contempt, treatment as a slave. I hate it as much as you do, but don't make me feel guilty for the madness of *bushido.*"

"I don't blame you, darling. Believe me . . ."

"I believe you've been looking for Ed for a year. Maybe you're sorry you picked me over him, maybe you—"

"Kenji—*no.* You're my husband. This is my child. Ed is an old friend I cared about. I still do. It's got *nothing* to do with us, and you better believe it."

He looked at me, then suddenly pressed his palms to his temples and I knew that the migraine was at him again.

"Kenji," I said, "come here and hold me. I need some *amae* too. And I warn you, believe me when I say I love you."

His hands came down from his temples, he even smiled a little as he came to my side of the *kotatsu* and we held each other under threadbare *futons.* Hisako had been hinting that it might be a nice idea if I repaired them, but I'd resisted. Well, tomorrow I'd be a good girl and get out my sewing kit. It wouldn't kill me, after all, and it would help to make some peace in the Tamba house.

"I love you, Julie."

"Master Cold Rice. *And* cold feet."

"Nag, nag." He was real pleased with the American humor. So was I, and proceeded to reward him as best I could, shifting Taro to the side to get at his father.

Yuriko Kitano · April, 1944

This time there was no question, and I knew I would have to tell Hans. As usual, I had left Hiroki with my mother . . . sometimes it would be with my mother-in-law . . . and invented a story about an extra shift at the machines to explain being away for hours. Fortunately my parents believed me, and besides, they were too tired at night to investigate.

Hideo, thankfully, was away again. It was a cool spring night, and I'd come to Hans ashamed, as always, of my *mompei* bloomers and the grease on my face. By now there were callouses on my hands too—not very romantic. It was past eight when I arrived at Hans's place, and quickly went behind the screen, took off my clothes, bathed in a wooden bucket of hot water that Hans had prepared for me, and changed into a fresh kimono. When I came out I put on a lacquered wig, added a touch of lipstick and some white powder. Hans put a Japanese record of *samisen* music on the windup player and I danced to it for him, using a fan in the traditional fashion. I wanted to please Hans, especially when he came to me, knelt in front of me, parted my kimono and began to kiss my thighs. I wanted to respond, to make love with him on the funny sagging couch as we had so many times before, but now I could not, I felt sick to my stomach . . . and I knew I could no longer put off telling Hans my secret . . .

"Darling," he said, "don't you want to make love?"

I was trembling, perspiring badly. "Hans, I believe I am pregnant with your child . . ."

". . . Are you certain?"

"There is a woman doctor, a foreigner, a friend of my American sister-in-law. She has examined me and has sworn to tell nobody. My family must never know. If they did I would have to kill myself—"

He kissed me, then put his arm around me. "Yuriko, if you want this child I want you to have it. I want it too . . . Perhaps I could take it and—"

"Hans, with your blond hair and blue eyes and long nose, I'm sure our baby would be handsome, but I am also sure people would suspect." I tried to smile, then abandoned myself to him as we lay together, and he was gentle, as always . . .

Later Hans got up and poured some of the German brandy for us and I sipped mine from a tumbler. "Yuriko, people get divorces, even in Japan."

"Oh, Hans, you know so little about us. Yes, a man can divorce a woman whenever he wants. He goes to a city clerk, signs a paper and the wife is ordered out of the house. But a woman . . . she is bound to a husband forever, so long as he wants her. And if I should go ahead and have the child my parents would disown me . . . it would be a child of mixed blood, be looked down on as worse than a foreign child. It would be unfair to the child—"

"But Kenji's child . . ."

"Even his baby my parents don't truly accept, especially my father. But at least Kenji is married. And he is a man. That makes it easier for them to stand the shame . . . Hans, I cannot keep this baby."

He looked at me, put his arms around me, said nothing. He did not have to. The way he held me told me that he understood, and that he was grieving for the loss as much as I.

JULIE TAMBA · MAY, 1944

Kenji has told me that he has learned about a major American assault to drive the Japanese out of New Guinea. General MacArthur has launched surprise landings all along the island's northern coast. The major port, Hollandia, has been captured, and Kenji says that the defenders, more than ten thousand men, didn't stand and fight the way they have before. They mostly ran off into the hills. "Maybe," Kenji said, "they're losing their appetite for dying for Tenno Heika in suicide charges."

That sounded like good news to me. It was offset a few weeks later, though, with some very bad news I got in a letter from Chris . . . Carol's husband, Major Kahn, was killed in the Hollandia invasion. Chris wrote that he ran into Carol outside a field hospital in Hollandia:

> She looked awful, which isn't surprising. Living on nerves. She told
> me that the major was killed during the landing. The Japs had
> abandoned the place but they'd mined the harbor. The major
> insisted on going ashore with the second wave, guys from the 41st
> Division. A lot of them got it in the shallows that day. The
> amtrack Major Kahn was in hit one of the Jap mines and Kahn
> and five other medics got blown up. They buried Major Kahn in
> the G.I. cemetery, and an army chaplain, a rabbi named Goldstein
> who went to Stanford, said prayers and gave the eulogy. Major

Kahn was really well-liked. Three generals came to the funeral, but
what counted most was that the enlisted men from his outfit made
their own plaque with the Star of David. I made Carol have a
drink with me at the officers' bar and she said she never loved
anyone the way she did Herb Kahn. They were planning to live on
the Monterey Peninsula after the war, where Herb would set up a
practice, and they wanted kids. God, when I think how I treated
her in San Francisco, but that's old cold potatoes now . . .

Chris went on to say that almost all the Japanese-Americans were out of
the camps by now, trying to get their homes back:

Hell, the army even has formed a special combat unit of those guys
to fight in Europe. I bet the guy who was at UCLA with us, the
gung-ho ROTC officer, Yasuda, is part of it. Didn't we all play in
a softball game a couple of hundred years ago? Ed, Kenji, Yasuda,
me? And you and Carol sitting under a tree cheering for us?

At the end Chris asked if I'd heard about Ed, if I'd seen him, and I knew
I'd have to tell him about the only meeting we'd had. Afterward I'd tried
again to see him, but I never could find the work detail along the
Yokohama docks, and one day Dr. Reinhold told Aunt Cora that he'd had
some word that Ed's group had been moved north to work in the coal
mines in Hokkaido.

Today Yuriko confided in me that she was pregnant, and *not* with her
husband's child.
I was diapering Taro, patting his pink-gold behind with powder, kissing
his fat neck and his sturdy arms.
"Look," I said, pointing to his lower back, and the blue-black marking
above his little rear end. "The Mongolian spot. Proof of citizenship."
Yuriko smiled weakly. She'd taken a day off from work, saying she felt
sick. Hiroki was slung over her back, as usual fast asleep. She patted his
rump. "Hiroki's is almost gone, it disappears after a year or so."
She watched me quietly as I put a fresh diaper on Taro, put him down
on the floor and let him play with Hiroki. The cousins got along fine,
crawling, grabbing at each other, squealing with joy.
We sat on the veranda and Yuriko suddenly said it . . . that she was
pregnant and the man was a foreigner.
Wow. My head swivelled. She told me then all about Hans Baumann.

"You're sure it's his child?" I tried to keep my voice down. Neighbors loved nothing better than eavesdropping. Nothing was secret. Houses were cheek-by-jowl, backyards faced one another.

"It is not Hideo's. He was away. It is Hans's child."

"Do you love him?" Why did I ask that? Did it make it easier if she did?

"Oh *yes,* Julie. I do. I've never understood what it can be like with a man you really care for. I know better now what you and Kenji have . . ."

And I understood now those "extra shifts" at the factory, the long nights when Yuriko was supposed to be inspecting shell cases. She'd carried it off so well, and I was rooting for her. Damn it, she deserved some happiness. And now this.

"What are you going to do, honey?" having a pretty good idea even while I asked.

She lowered her head. "I cannot have the child."

She said it like a death sentence. But couldn't she go away and have the child, turn the baby over to this Hans?

"No, no, there is no way." Yuriko was crying now. "I want Hans so much. And I want his child, but I can't have it . . . Julie, you must help me . . ."

I put my arms around her and kissed her. I'd come to think of her as a kid sister. She's been the only one who'd welcomed me to the Tamba house, she was sweet and funny and smart.

"I'll help you, Yuriko, no one will ever know."

She nestled against me. Our infant sons toddled down the steps, crawled into the garden and began to fling fistfuls of pebbles and dirt at each other. Yuriko jumped from the step. Japanese kids are kept squeaky-clean. Sandals, socks, spotless clothing. The Japanese say they love nature but they sure don't like dirt. I let Taro wallow around and watched as Yuriko, with someone named Hans's child in her womb, dusted Hiroki's fat legs, kissed the top of his round head and hugged him.

"Will it hurt?" she asked.

"I don't know, Yuriko. But we'll do it the best way, and I'll look after you."

On her knees still, she pressed Hiroki to her breast, rested her face against his. "You and my son, and Hans too . . . I love you all so much . . ."

Masao Tamba · May, 1944

A week ago I said good-bye to Michiko and our daughter Maeko and prayed at the Shinto temple at the Yasakuni shrine with my father-in-law, then left for Saipan.

Michiko was hysterical our last evening together, she bowed in front of her father, hugging his feet, begging him not to allow me to return to battle.

"Masao has asked for this honor and I will not dissuade him," Colonel Sato told her, for once talking plain and straightforward.

Colonel Sato had assigned me to the 43rd Division on Saipan as an aide to General Saito. I was very pleased. Saipan was where we believed an American strike was imminent. I closed my ears to Michiko's wailings, bought an expensive geisha doll for Maeko, packed my kit and left Tokyo the last week of May.

Once on Saipan I toured the defensive positions in a small truck and decided that this place could be the butcher's block on which we smashed the bones and carved the flesh of the Americans. The war might be lost, but here they would pay a fearful price. This was no flat, low-lying atoll like the Gilberts or Tarawa. Saipan was a mountainous swampy place, dotted with sugar-cane fields and ravines. There was a treacherous coral reef and a shallow lagoon. And many limestone caves in which we could hide artillery and machine guns. And we had 32,000 men on Saipan.

This would be no easy target like Makin or Biak. I at once put men to work stringing barbed wire and chopping down palm trees to bolster the gun emplacements, packing sandbags, burying mines on beaches. All we had learned at Tarawa would be utilized here, the strategies multiplied. I did not fear the Americans' aerial attacks and offshore bombardments. Secure in our caves, protected by palm trunks and thick cushions of sand, we could withstand such blows and destroy the landing forces.

Thirty-two thousand men! I looked forward to battle and wondered if this might even prove to be the turning point of the war! My doubts began to fade. Yes, we might *still* win.

We had abundant supplies of ammunition and food. There was also a native population, fine-looking Malayo-Polynesian people of mixed blood, whose women made good sexual partners for our men. We also had thousands of Korean laborers building fortifications. They were a surly bunch and we had to shoot several to keep them in line.

There were also some magnificent vistas on Saipan. I admired the spectacular view from the Morubi bluffs at the northern promontory of the island. From those heights I could watch the white surf pound against the black rocks below, sending up foaming explosions, the rhythmic roar of the ocean sounding like a divine music.

Once I drove there by myself, one-armed, one-eyed Major Tamba, a legend of sorts among my new soldiers, also a martinet and, I hoped, an inspiration. My superiors left me alone. They knew I had faced more bloodshed than they had, had known death a dozen times and continued to draw my sword. China, Malaya, Guadalcanal . . .

The cliffs helped soothe my mind, the view helped clear it. Looking at the Morubi cliffs, I also thought, what a good place to die.

On my dispatch book I wrote a *haiku* that I hoped would be read at my funeral.

> High cliffs face
> The roaring sea,
> Fearless, eternal . . .

JULIE TAMBA · MAY, 1944

In Tokyo there always seemed a street that looked poorer than the one you'd just left . . . Anyway, this was certainly the case of the alley I'd brought Yuriko to an hour ago. Her friend Midori, who originally introduced her to Hans, she told me, had found a midwife for us. There was no sign on the doorway. There wasn't even a door, just a flapping black cloth. Downstairs was a tiny coffeehouse with no customers. A drunk slept in the doorway. Two aged women pushed a wooden cart full of flammable refuse.

Yuriko didn't want me in the room when the abortion was done. She said it was something she had to endure by herself, she didn't want me to be any more involved than I was. There was no arguing with her. Hans had offered to be with her too but she'd even turned him down. I got the awful notion that she saw the abortion as some form of private *hara-kiri* . . . Anyway, the most she'd let Hans do was wait at the address in Nihombashi, a few blocks from the railway station.

So I left Yuriko—she seemed unbelievably calm—with a blowsy woman of about fifty with a pock-marked face and bowed legs, and her teenage assistant, and after paying them cash in advance, waited in the rain . . . it had just started . . . outside the coffeehouse.

The rain had now become one of those pervasive warm spring drizzles, half-rain, half-mist, that sort of surrounded you and everything else. I looked at my watch—Yuriko had been in that place for an hour, and I was getting very worried . . . When I looked up I saw a thin white man approaching me from the main street that led to the station. He was wearing a finger-length navy blue jacket and a black peaked cap, the kind of outfit that I somehow always associated with European workingmen, unionists. Once he got closer I could see that he was a pretty good-looking guy, in an undernourished sort of way, with a long nose, blue eyes and straw-colored hair. Obviously Hans Baumann, about whom I had some definitely mixed feelings, regardless of Yuriko's enthusiasm for him.

"Mrs. Tamba?"

I nodded and he offered me his hand, which I took without too much cordiality. It was a smooth hand, obviously not a dockworker's or something like I'd thought at first.

He was nervous, fidgeting, and I let him stew for a minute before answering his question about how Yuriko was. I told him that I had to assume that she was okay, but didn't know yet. We moved under the canopy of the coffeehouse and he offered to buy me a cuppa, as one of my UCLA friends from back east used to call it, and I declined. I couldn't help looking on this man as the problem, as the cause of the awful ordeal that Yuriko was going through. I know, I know, it takes two to tango and all that stuff, but Yuriko, I felt, was the innocent in this deal.

He lit a cigarette, looked at me. "I know what you must be thinking, Mrs. Tamba, and I don't say you are wrong. I take the blame . . . but I did want her to have the child, I offered to take care of it—"

"Oh, come on, Mr. Baumann, you know very well that's impossible in Japan. They'd roast her alive if they ever found out, and besides, how would you manage it? Yuriko tells me you're some sort of journalist, but not exactly set up to keep and raise a half-oriental, half-white child." I felt myself getting hot under the collar, maybe working off some frustrations on Hans Baumann that had nothing to do with him . . . "Don't you Germans believe in contraceptives?"

His pale cheeks took on a visible flush. "I know what you are saying, Mrs. Tamba, and I agree. I should have been more careful. There are no good excuses here, except one . . . that passion sometimes makes its own rules, and that I truly do love Yuriko, and she loves me. I don't know, maybe I wanted a child and didn't want to admit it to myself. But after the war, who is to say we can't be married? After all, Mrs. Tamba, you married a Japanese, and had his child—"

"Yes, but *after* we were married. And while I'm no sophisticated lady, I think I had a little more experience with the opposite sex than Yuriko has had."

It was hard to stay too mad at him, or at least not to see something of what Yuriko must have seen. He was so damned polite, so agreeable. What a change, especially from hideous Hideo.

"I wish you would also accept," Hans was going on, "that it has not only been sex between us. We respect each other. She has told me that she has never been happier, and I can assure you it's been the same for me. Please at least try to believe that."

"Suppose I accept everything you say. Let me tell you, a mixed marriage is no bed of roses anywhere, and that goes double in Japan. If you really feel about Yuriko as much as you say you do, you'll stay away from her. Otherwise you're going to destroy her and maybe yourself too."

"I can't promise you that. We love each other—"

"You're a grown man, Mr. Baumann. You know very well that love isn't enough . . ." My God, listening to myself I heard an echo of the words my parents had said to me when I told them I was going to marry Kenji . . .

He tossed his cigarette away and turned to indicate that Yuriko had appeared just outside the door, huddling inside her gray coat, obviously trying to fight back tears. When she saw Hans she put on a smile and came to him and they hugged, a rare sight to see in public in Tokyo. After a while, and some words that I didn't hear, standing as I was off at a distance, Hans tried to unwrap her arms from around his neck. She didn't want to let go of him, digging her hands into his sleeves.

"I've got to go, darling. And you must, you should be at home." He looked at me, asking for help if not understanding. "Mrs. Tamba is a good friend, she will take care of you—"

"But I don't want to go, I'm afraid I won't see you again. I want to go with you."

"Come on, honey," I said to her, taking hold of her arm and pulling her away. We had made up a story for her parents about the upset stomach, throwing up, Yuriko sending word to me that she was feeling sick. "They're going to be wondering where you are, we have to get back."

I continued to pull her away, her tears no longer held back, and the last we saw of Hans was as a solitary figure standing there in the spring drizzle, not moving, and finally I could feel for him too.

In one way I half-blamed myself for Yuriko's misery. She'd been led to expect too much, looking on Kenji and me as some kind of storybook lovers, East and West in glorious union, the kind of marriage she had wanted, the touching and kissing, and open show of affection. Instead she'd gotten the standard Japanese issue. And whatever Hans was, or wasn't, he obviously supplied the tenderness and passion she craved . . .

I located a smoke-belching cab, and put my arm around Yuriko. We rehearsed our story for her parents again. She had a bad stomach, had to miss work, was okay now.

"You must believe me, Julie," she said, and this time her eyes were clear and her voice was strong. "I love him. He is a good man."

KENJI TAMBA · JULY, 1944

It was a hot summer. At Professor Adachi's office I pored over new accounts of the fighting on Saipan. I knew that Masao was there, determined to play his role, literally to the hilt . . . Colonel Sato had presented him with a new sword before he flew off to Saipan. My mother wept, Michiko wailed, but Masao had been adamant—he was sick of the wrangling and backbiting between the army and navy, and he wanted the surety of action. He also told me the day before he left that Prime Minister Tojo was in trouble. Tojo, an army man, was hated by the navy. And one afternoon Adachi said that the move to get rid of Tojo did not come from "peace faction" people but extreme nationalists . . . As my *sensei* put it, "no matter how extreme someone is, there is always someone more so." Right now they were calling for Tojo's head but he seemed to believe he could survive, that Tenno Heika still had confidence in him.

Yoshiro brought in a transcript of a BBC broadcast saying Burma was falling, our starved troops were collapsing and the British and Australians were driving the remnants of our army north, having their revenge.

Adachi went on to say there were moderates but they had to walk carefully. He named the rather effete Prince Konoye as one of them. Also, an Admiral Okada, a former member of the *genro*, the council of elders, hated Tojo and had opposed the war and had years ago nearly been assassinated by the mutineers of 1936. Okada, Konoye and even the chameleon, Lord Privy Seal Kido, once considered an ally of Tojo, had apparently swung over to the moderates who believe the war is finished for Japan and that continued resistance will only mean continued misery and ruin for the people.

"Everyone hates Tojo's guts," Adachi said. "And rarely has a public figure so merited that sentiment."

He stroked his pate, toyed with the cotton puffs over his ears. "Kenji, when the Americans build airbases on the islands they have targeted, our suffering will just begin. And for what? Greed, archaic notions of conquest and glory."

Bicycling home from the secret office, I met my father and his mistress, Fumiko, coming out of an eel restaurant. It was early evening. I'd stopped to buy a glass of lemonade from a street vendor when I spotted my father alongside a tall, rather stout broad-faced woman. She wore an elaborate kimono for a servant, dark blue with yellow lapels and a yellow *obi* and a red chrysanthemum design at the waist.

The heavenly Fumiko, donor of *tatami* burns.

I bowed to my father. He bowed to me. He looked uneasy. Fumiko, who seemed taller and certainly broader than I was, bowed very low to me. She had a flattened nose and thick lips, her bust was very large by Japanese standards, and her hips were thick and rather shapeless. Maybe I imagined it, but I thought there was a cunning . . . calculating? . . . look about her. She knew what she was doing.

"My son, Kenji Tamba."

She bowed again. "I am honored."

"This is Miss Fumiko Yamaguchi. She works in my section at the palace."

I must have allowed a smile to linger on my face. I'm certain she was aware I knew her role in my father's life.

"You are handsome, like your father," she said. She had a squeaky voice, at odds with her bulk. "I met your brother Masao once and he is very handsome also."

The truth was neither Masao nor I looked like my father. He is round-headed and short. We favor our mother, who has a long narrow face.

"I am pleased to meet someone who works at the palace with my father," I said stuffily. I was sounding like a Western censor and realized that was foolish.

Goro, however, beamed. "Yes, yes. And excellent news today at the palace. A bulletin posted in the servants' quarters announced the Americans have been driven from the island of Saipan, the British are retreating in Malaya."

I had long ago stopped trying to contest the lies of the propaganda agencies so I said nothing. Meanwhile, Fumiko Yamaguchi was fingering a pearl necklace that had a genuine luster, Mikimotos pearls perhaps. She was taunting me. Obviously, her look said, she could not afford such pearls, they had been purchased for her by Mr. Goro Tamba, father of four, husband of Hisako Tamba of Shibuya Ward.

And Goro Tamba was now telling his son to "advise your mother that I will be late. Fumiko and I have errands to perform for the assistant chamberlain. We must replace some crockery."

I bowed, at the same time thinking of the American expression I had heard more than once in the States concerning "a crock."

Later, after a dinner of rice balls and vinegared cabbage, I told Julie about my interesting encounter. She punched me, not so playfully. And not so amused. I should have kept it to myself.

We made love that night, quietly as possible, so as not to disturb my mother, who slept alone until after midnight, when my father came home after his "crockery" mission.

MASAO TAMBA · JULY, 1944

"Annihilate the enemy with one blow."

Such were the orders from General Saito, our supreme commander on Saipan. In mid-June we had watched the marines come ashore—a seemingly endless flotilla of amphibious vehicles, landing some 20,000 of these tireless Americans. Why did our propaganda people persist in calling them cowards and blunderers, men afraid to die? I never knew braver adversaries in my life.

My battalion was part of the first *banzai* charge down the slopes of Mount Tapotchau, to drive the marines into the sea. My soldiers fell in heaps of dead. Men with faces blown away. Legless, armless corpses. Bodies cut in half. And the terrible stench of burning flesh. After three-fourths of my attacking force was cut down by the marines, Saito reconsidered these assaults and pulled us back into our dugouts and pillboxes, assuring us that the Imperial Fleet was coming to our rescue. It sounded like another Guadacanal.

"West of the Marianas in the Philippine Sea," the general told a meeting of officers, "the most powerful fleet the world has ever seen is steaming to relieve us. They will engage the Americans there and the decisive battle will be won."

Among the warships in the fleet was the *Taiho,* Japan's newest aircraft carrier, and serving aboard it was my brother-in-law, Lieutenant Hideo Kitano, my sister Yuriko's husband.

Admiral Ozawa commanded this fleet. He was one of our best seamen, and he predicted that the battle of the Philippine Sea for the relief of Saipan and the protection of the Marianas would equal in significance the 1905 defeat of the czar's navy in the Straits of Tsushima.

A disturbing piece of news cast a shadow over our commanders, and myself. A navy pilot I spoke to said that a new American fighter plane, something called a Hellcat, could outfly and outshoot our Zeroes. "But no matter," he said blandly, *"Yamato Damashii* will prevail, a divine wind will save us, the spirit of Japan will conquer . . ." Drunk with sake, he told me all this as we squatted in a lean-to, and I thought again how little we really knew, and how much we had already deceived ourselves. I would tell that to no one, not my fellow officers, not to my men, not in letters to my family, but the worm of doubt was again nibbling at my brain. How long could we go on waiting for this decisive battle?

On July 6, General Saito, as a result of his failures to repel the marines, committed ritual *seppuku.* Before taking his life with the short sword he sent his apologies to the emperor and instructed his staff officers to undertake one last *banzai* charge against the persistent Americans who had been killing us in such great numbers, blasting us with machine guns and artillery, flushing us out with flamethrowers.

"Take seven lives for every one you give," Saito told them, then punctured his stomach and fell forward.

On the morning of July 7 we assembled all our men at the crest of the hill line on the northernmost point of the island. We had already shot the wounded. I studied the skirmish lines as they formed around my men. Crippled, blind men—myself a fit leader, mutilated as I was, for this charge of starvelings and ghosts—and I saw that many men held only bamboo spears. Half were sick with malaria and dysentery. We did not number more than three thousand out of an original force of some 32,000 well-armed men.

And we died by the hundreds. The marines poured fire into us from a range of twenty yards, but we still came on. I cut an American officer's head off with my sword, disemboweled another, a helmetless blond-haired man who stared at me with fixed blue eyes as his intestines, bluish ropes, burst from his belly.

We fought until we cut a hole in their lines and drove them to the beach, fired our last rounds and waded over piles of our own dead. We overwhelmed artillery positions, destroying field guns so that astonished crews picked up carbines and used them as clubs to fight us off.

We redeemed our honor. We showed how to die . . . And I realized how much we were hated . . .

I don't know how I escaped. I battled to the beach with two men from my headquarters company. At night, with no ammunition or water, we floated out to sea on a crate. I cannot forget the sounds from our dying. It was as if the Americans were killing them not once but twice and three times.

We drifted out to sea at night and paddled our way to a rocky ledge at the Morubi bluffs and found shelter in a cave where the surf rushed in. We ate limpets and barnacles and found puddles of rainwater. There were just three of us—myself, my batman Sergeant Noguchi, and a sergeant from headquarters company. He had only half a face, the left side was a red scar. We lay in the rocks, on beds of seaweed. We let the waves break over us and we clawed at the jagged cave wall, yanking off barnacles and limpets and anemones and chewing on them until some made us vomit and I found myself fingering my dagger and Noguchi, staring at me, asking the question with his dimming eyes. The other man soon died.

And then from where we hid in the cave we could see the bluffs, the rocky ledges that faced the sea, where I had written my *haiku*. There was movement above, masses of bodies . . . I realized then that the Japanese civilians on Saipan, thousands of them, mainly women and children, were walking, as though in a trance, to the edge of the black rocks. I could hear a loudspeaker with someone—an American interpreter or maybe a captured soldier—telling them:

"Give up, give up, you will not be harmed. You will be given food and a safe place to stay. Don't jump. We repeat, *don't jump.*"

With that a woman holding a child by each hand went off the cliff onto the wave-lashed rocks below. A wailing noise arose from the surging mob, a wave of lament.

We should not have been surprised. We had told them that the Americans were savages, rapists who would murder them, eat their flesh, ravage their daughters . . .

I was revolted, yet could not take my eyes from the cliff from which bodies kept falling—some stumbling, some in running leaps, some holding hands and descending in arcs to the deadly black rocks, the pounding surf . . .

I spotted an American patrol boat trying to get close to the shoreline. A sailor—he appeared to be Japanese, perhaps one of the Nisei Kenji had told me about—was shouting through a loudspeaker but his words were lost in the roar of the waves, the lament of those intent on death. Soon the boat could not navigate, the waters around the rocks had become so clotted with corpses.

"I cannot bear to look," Sergeant Noguchi said. "Even those who hesitate and resist are pushed by people behind them—"

"We *must* look," I said. "We owe them witness . . ." But I was thinking, Is this the ultimate consequence of our code of *bushido?*

A party of American marines had taken cover behind a wrecked half-track . . . some of our soldiers *were still firing.* It was as if they were a rear guard charged not with saving withdrawing troops but insuring the ceremony of destruction at the cliffs. Rapid-fire blasts from a machine gun cut them to pieces . . .

Sergeant Noguchi killed himself that night, gulping salt water until he began to choke, vomit, and finally die in a paroxysm. I was barely alive, surrounded by the bodies of thousands of my countrymen. But I was alive, I would not kill myself or even try. Was this my disgrace . . . or was something subtle, something unknown happening inside me that resisted the code I devoutly believed in . . . ?

YURIKO KITANO · AUGUST, 1944

We were warned that someday American bombers would come. In indirect ways the radio and newspapers told us that certain islands close to Japan had "been given" to the Americans at a fearful price.

We were required several times a day, and on lunch and cigarette breaks, to work at digging air-raid shelters. For weeks after my abortion I felt weak and dizzy, ate little and slept less. But of course I wouldn't claim an exemption. We were directed with bamboo poles, from the factory benches, to the street, given shovels and told to dig holes and ditches. The foreman assured us that these holes would save us from the bombers.

While we worked a radio played martial music at us, and Umezu, the old foreman Midori and I were convinced was a little crazy, paraded up and down thwacking backs if the work didn't go fast enough. The radio announcer—I got to hate his voice—was describing the last days of the heroic civilian population on an island called Saipan.

. . . rather than surrender to the American savages, women chose to destroy their children . . . young girls put on their funeral clothes, arranged their hair with oil and combs and went to their death. It was a lesson in courage and honor and devotion that stunned the Americans . . .

"Have you ever heard such craziness?" Midori asked me. We dug the shovels into the resisting clay, created mounds of wet earth, cursed the foreman, the factory and, yes, the war.

"More coming," I said.

The announcer was reading a statement of "imminent victory" from the new prime minister. I knew Tojo was out of office and a man named Koiso was prime minister. My father said he was a wise old general and that he would find the road to victory that Tojo couldn't find.

The words droned on: "The indomitable spirit of the Hundred Million marches on. United, the people will rekindle their determination and launch themselves, crushing the enemy. By seizing Saipan and other islands close to Japan, the United States is digging its grave. As its navy approaches the Rising Sun, the final blow will be dealt them and Japan's invincible fleet will turn the tide."

Midori said, "Don't they ever run out of it?"

Umezu shouted at us to talk less and work more. We made faces at him and pretended we were hard at work.

Suddenly I saw my mother shuffling down the pocked street, disheveled, her face smudged. She stopped to talk to Umezu, favoring the tyrant with a bow he didn't deserve.

The foreman turned and called to me. "Yuriko, out."

"Thank god," I said to Midori, "maybe I'll get the day off. I don't care what the reason is. I've had enough of this—"

Whistles blew. Women laid down their shovels, lined up—we had to march in military style—and lockstepped into the factory. I walked toward my mother and I could see she was crying. My first thought was—Masao.

I bowed to her but she did not bow. In one hand was a yellow sheet of paper.

"Hideo, Hideo . . . your husband Hideo . . ."

"He—?"

"Yes, he is dead."

Now, whatever our cold relationship, I felt a terror overcome me. He was gone. He had been part of my life, creating my child . . . and a stab of guilt went through me, like the abortionist's knife . . .

Is it also sinful to admit I felt a secret relief that Hideo was gone? I don't know. Hiroki will never know his father, but would he have if Hideo had lived? How often would he have been at home, or away from his drunken companions . . . ? I tried without total success to put away such guilty thoughts . . . as well as my love for Hans . . .

We sat in two rows on floor cushions and faced the altar in my parents' home. It was decided that the small house Hideo, Hiroki and I had shared was too little for the funeral. In the *tokonama* was a scroll heralding the coming of summer. There was a white porcelain vase with a willow branch in it. On the Buddhist altar was a photograph of Hideo in uniform with a black cloth band draped over the frame.

We ate and drank for four days. People called on us and the Kitanos, his grieving parents. I am certain that they felt I did not cry enough over their son's death.

Julie helped my mother Michiko and me wait on the guests, pour sake and beer and whiskey while they took turns praying. A priest from the naval academy said prayers and made a speech about Hideo's "glorious death for Tenno Heika." He would "be rewarded forever," the priest said. A further reward would be the victory over the Americans that Hideo had helped bring about even in his watery death.

Until then we did not know how or where he had died. As he did so much else, Kingoro Hata was the source of this information, bustling in on the last day of mourning, bowing in front of Hideo's photograph, bowing to my parents and the Kitanos, then squatting on a cushion. He drank to Hideo's memory and said he had glorious news, that he had secured from the navy department an account of Hideo's death and he would be honored if he were permitted to read it.

People sucked in their breath, nodded, smiled appreciatively, and Mr. Hata read from an official document:

Lieutenant Hideo Kitano of the Imperial Navy gave his life for
His Majesty on June 18, 1944, while serving on the aircraft carrier
Taiho.

Before being destroyed by an overwhelming assault by American
ships and planes, *Taiho* exacted an enormous toll on the aggressor
fleet. The battle took place in the Philippine Sea and was a major
defeat for the Americans. *Taiho* contributed to this defeat, its
planes downing hundreds of American aircraft and sinking
numerous warships.

Admiral Ozawa tried valiantly to go down with his ship, but was
rescued by his subofficers. May Hideo Kitano's soul find everlasting
glory. The Imperial Navy extends its condolences to his family and
adds his name to the long list of heroes.

My in-laws were sobbing, as was my mother. Hiroki, crawling about,
looked frightened.

My father spoke up. "We will miss your son," he said to the Kitanos.

My mother added, "Yes, he was good to our daughter."

My father: "And fathered her splendid boy."

More tears, more shaking of heads.

Hata dabbed at his forehead. "The noblest way to die."

"There is no better death," my father said.

Kenji and Julie were sitting to my right, saying nothing. They, of
course, knew another side to the story.

"Ah," my mother sighed, "if only we could hear some news of Masao,
Mr. Hata. Do you know anything of my son?"

Hata had nothing to report about Masao's fate. Nor did Colonel Sato,
who arrived late and confided that once the Americans got close to the
mainland our navy would wipe them out.

Kenji looked drained. I could see him rubbing his temples. The headaches again.

KENJI TAMBA · AUGUST, 1944

The days of mourning for Hideo have gotten on my nerves. Too much
hypocrisy? I do feel sorry for the young man and his parents, and for
Yuriko, for the conflicting feelings I know she must have.

But Colonel Sato and Kingoro Hata turn my stomach. Adachi, as Julie would say, "has the goods" on Hata. Making a fortune in war industries, selling uniforms that shred and contaminated canned goods to the armed forces. He and his mistress Satomi have been buying real estate, for the time when they can cash in. Hata has one abiding interest in the war—to get rich.

Sato is a different breed. Long a mover and shaker behind the scenes, he has kept up his contacts with outlaw groups, all of whom keep pressure on vacillating officials, and thereby on the Emperor.

"Yes, yes," Sato was telling my parents and the Kitanos, as we squatted on cushions under the dead gaze of Hideo, "we have pure hearts and a shining sword. There will be no surrender. Tenno Heika will be restored to his rightful place at the center of political life and Imperial rule will prevail . . ."

The last thing the outlaws and their military cronies want is an emperor who thinks and acts on his own. They want a puppet who signs papers and sanctions their bloody plans. I wondered about that man in the palace so happy with his biology books . . . did he have no idea he had been led astray by scoundrels?

"As a youth at the Golden Pheasant Academy," Sato was going on, "I learned that Japan must be first in Asia, first in the world. Our history proves it. Never defeated in a war. Our soldiers more courageous than any others. And here the proof of their valor, the young Lieutenant Kitano." He wiped his mouth. He was full of sake.

My father said softly, "We are the people of Jimmu—"

"I drink to Jimmu," Sato said. "The first emperor of Japan . . . founder of the Imperial dynasty . . . Do you remember the grand ceremonies in 1940 when we marked the 2600-year anniversary of the founding? How glad we made His Majesty's heart . . ."

"Yes, Jimmu descended from the sun goddess Amaterasu," my father said like a schoolboy. "So His Majesty is also divine—"

"Can there be any doubt about it?" Sato said.

Julie, who had been fidgeting during these perorations, muttered "Yes," and it was overheard. Sato looked as if an icicle had been jabbed up his nostril. He glared at Julie. "You doubt it? Well, you are not one of us. I will not listen."

My mother left the room. My father bowed to Sato. "I apologize for Kenji's wife."

Sato waggled a finger at me. "Your wife may voice such notions, Kenji, but be careful. Do not agree with her."

Julie looked furious. My temple throbbed. A needle was poking into my left eye. Dr. Varnum had warned me—tension, being torn in my loyalties, could trigger the pain of migraine.

An embarrassed silence. Michiko said she would take the children into the garden for some air and gathered up Hiroki and Maeko. Taro slept like a hibernating possum on Julie's back, content, oblivious to the anger and tension in the room. Saburo had been slouching in the doorway, resting his splinter of a body against the door frame, his arms folded. He had not done any crying. He hardly knew Hideo. Suddenly he loped across the room and stood, legs apart, in front of me.

"You're a coward," he said. "You don't fight. You favor the enemy. You could be shot . . ."

People seemed stunned by the outburst, except Sato, who clearly enjoyed it.

Julie nudged me to respond.

"I'm going to be a pilot," Saburo shouted. "I'll avenge Hideo and the others. I'm going to enlist. To make up for the shame you give the family—"

Julie was on her feet. With one swift sharp move she cracked her palm against Saburo's cheek—the worst insult for a male, to be hit by a woman. If Saburo had been older and carrying a sword I suspect he actually might have drawn it and struck Julie.

"*Beat it,*" Julie said between clenched teeth. "Don't you dare say things like that about my husband and your brother."

Saburo was so shocked he didn't know how to respond. He gasped and touched his cheek. Eyes wide, he looked at Julie as if she were a bear or a dragon. Then, realizing what was expected of him, he raised his hand to strike her—

I leapt from my cushion and grabbed his ankles, sending him to the floor. Tackling him, as in American football games. While I wrestled with Saburo—he was like a live eel—and my mother howled, and Sato shook his head and the Kitanos averted their eyes to avoid the shame of seeing two brothers fight during the period of mourning, Julie ran from the house with our son, followed by Yuriko.

My mother entered the room then and knelt in front of my father and began whispering to him.

I let Saburo up, he swung at me, missed, and I grabbed hold of his right arm, put his wrist behind his back and held him. In fact I am stronger than Masao, more agile, a better athlete. I just always hated to fight.

My head started to feel better once I had Saburo under control. "Behave yourself," I told him. "Don't accuse people of bringing shame. And show some respect for my wife."

"I hate you, *I hate your wife.*"

In a now weary voice my father said, "Kenji, let your brother go."

"Only if he promises to behave with Julie."

"I promise nothing."

My father was more insistent. "Let Saburo go."

I did and he ran to his room.

"We will talk about this later," my father said. "We should not insult Hideo's memory by unmannerly behavior."

No one appeared concerned about Saburo's behavior. He had started the fight. As usual he would get away with it.

When the guests had left, my father took me into the garden. He was furious, but controlled his anger, which only showed in the furrows on his forehead, a slight twitching of his left cheek.

"Your mother and I feel there are too many people in this house . . ." he began without prologue.

"You want my wife and me to leave?"

"It saddens your mother's heart to see the strife that has come here because of your wife—"

"My wife has a right to her opinions."

Goro sucked on his cigarette. "She is not one of us. She never can be."

JULIE TAMBA · AUGUST, 1944

I sat on a bench in the park across from the house. It was terribly hot. The park was now occupied by two antiaircraft guns. There were sandbags piled around two huge pits. Several artillerymen in faded uniforms lolled about, smoking, drinking from canteens. They looked like older men, out of shape. Not very warlike. They didn't seem much worried about aerial attacks.

Yuriko came hurrying up to me. "Julie . . . I heard my parents talking, they are going to ask you and Kenji to leave the house."

I wasn't exactly surprised. "Maybe we should—"

"*Please* stay. I can't afford the little house any more. Hiroki and I are moving back to the main house."

"That will give them more reason to invite us to leave."

"No, you must stay." Yuriko put an arm around me, and one of the soldiers stared at us . . . he couldn't make sense out of it, *gaijin* woman with long legs? Japanese baby? Japanese girl? And why in the name of eight million gods were these people *touching* one another?

"Julie, you're my best friend. You know about Hans, you know about the baby I gave up—"

"Yuriko, you know I love you. My first friend here. Sometimes I think you're my only one."

"And you are my best friend. When I come back to the house with Hiroki I want him to grow up with Taro."

I saw Kenji coming out of the house, looking for us. He was smiling at us, appreciating our friendship. "The Shinto priest is here, we should be in the house for the evening prayer."

The three of us crossed the street, and I swung Taro around in his sling, stowed him on my back.

Back at the Tamba house the priest lit incense and the pungent smoky fumes filled the room. Yuriko and her parents and Hideo's parents went to the altar. Kenji and I kneeled at the back and listened to the tinkling of the bells—to summon the gods—and the priest began to intone the prayer for a dead hero.

For some reason his praying upset Hiroki, who let out a yowl, and that spread to Taro, who woke up and let loose a few yowls, and even Maeko, the oldest of the three kids, began to sound off. All in all, a pretty noisy lament for a hero . . .

KENJI TAMBA · SEPTEMBER, 1944

Professor Adachi invited me to his bathhouse for a scrub, shave and dunk in the scalding waters. We squatted on wooden stools, scrubbed ourselves with hard bristles, shaved in front of the room-length mirror and talked quietly about the way the war was going.

Adachi knew about my situation with my family, that Masao was missing on Saipan, but didn't probe into personal matters. Instead he talked about the information he had on the war.

"The Marianas are finished," he said as he maneuvered his straight razor, removed hairs from his nostrils. He was no less a patriot than the Satos and Hatas of our nation, but what a difference. I had also learned he had been an expert *kendo* fighter in his university days and had even served briefly with the army. But he hated the conniving secret societies, the cold-blooded secret killers, the chauvinist aggressors.

"New reports?" I asked.

"Yoshiro contacted me last night. Guam has fallen. The Americans are building new airfields to service their bombers, the B–29s."

"Do our military leaders know this?"

"They know it, but they say that bombing raids on the mainland will only mean the end of the Americans, they will be beaten to death on the anvil of *Yamato Damashii.*"

"They have been saying that for two years. Does the emperor know—?"

"It comes to him in droplets. Kido, Konoye, a few others hint at the truth, but the military still make the final decisions."

Later, as we sat in a teahouse, I was startled to see Colonel Sato come in. He of course noticed me, came to our table. I rose and bowed and was obliged to introduce Professor Adachi.

It was a charged moment. I wondered if Sato knew anything about our work . . . he was always making threats against "peace-faction traitors." Now he was face-to-face with a leader of one.

"Adachi, Adachi . . ." Sato frowned. "Why do I know the name?"

I explained that my *sensei* had been on the faculty at Tokyo Imperial University but now ran a small business.

"You cannot teach any longer?"

No answer . . . I invited him to join us for tea, hoping he would refuse.

"My views were regarded as incorrect," Adachi finally said.

Sato grunted, crossed his legs. "Incorrect?"

"I questioned the wisdom of the war."

Adachi's nerve stunned me, but he was a wise old bird . . . he must have strongly suspected that Sato suspected him. After all, if the colonel wanted he could easily investigate him and learn that he had not only been dismissed but *jailed.*

"I am a harmless old man," Adachi said. "I hurt no one. Kenji will tell you that I even enjoy buying and selling sugar."

Sato drained his green tea. They stared at one another. I tried to change the subject. "Is there news from Saipan? Can we still hope that Masao is alive?"

"He is my dear son-in-law, but if he is dead we will accept his fate. What more glorious way to die? Don't you agree, professor?"

"Death is an enigma," Adachi said. "I cannot presume to judge any man's death."

Sato squinted through his sunglasses at Adachi as if to say, *I know about you,* then got to his feet. He did not bow as he left us.

"I am worried," I said to Adachi. "He suspects us."

Adachi ordered a pot of tea. "Perhaps . . . but he has more on his mind than the likes of us. Their war is destroying them, and since it is all they believe in, all that they live for, they have larger worries on their mind."

I was still worried.

JULIE TAMBA · OCTOBER, 1944

Two new words were heard more frequently. *Yami,* the blackmarket, and *yase-gaman,* strength through thinness. Great for a model maybe, not a person.

The *yami,* which means darkness, meant we had to scrounge for food every chance we had. There was no meat, butter, milk or eggs. Fruits and vegetables were priced sky-high and available mostly on the *yami* from illegal dealers and street peddlers who got them from farmers who made their way to Tokyo to sell produce.

Strength through thinness. A bad joke. Actually there wasn't even a real rationing program with cards, allocations and so on. The neighborhood associations, the *tonarigumi,* were made up of political hacks who decided who got what. Sure, we were luckier than some families . . . my father-in-law's prestige helped us to larger rice rations—they were down to a third of normal—and Masao's name could produce a bit more fish, an extra turnip. Still, the *yami* was for us like most everyone else the basic source of food supply.

It was a day like many others, Yuriko and I prowling a back alley where we knew farmers came with vegetables to sell on the *yami,* that I was arrested.

Yuriko and I had been negotiating . . . haggling was more like it . . . with a farm wife over a head of cabbage. A policeman zeroed in on me. For two years I'd been more or less left alone. Stopped and let go. Not this time. And I was not being arrested for black-market purchases—no one else in the alley was bothered—but for *espionage.* I just managed to tell a terrified and angry Yuriko to hurry home and get word to Kenji before I was shoved into a police car by two uniformed men.

My Japanese by now was nearly fluent and I protested, loud and clear. I showed them my alien card, I told them that my father-in-law was an employee of the palace and that my brother-in-law was the war hero Major Tamba. Their answer was to grin at my *gaijin*'s Japanese, and I remembered Kenji's warning that a foreigner speaking Japanese, even speaking well, sounds like a foreigner first, last and always. These guys found my efforts, it seemed, real funny. I wasn't laughing along with them.

At a *Kempetei* office, a red brick building in Minato Ward, I was hustled into an interrogation room and told to sit down. I stared at wall posters. Tojo was down, Koiso was up, a shaggy-haired mustachioed old bird. Of course the obligatory photograph of the emperor also gazed down at me, a not unkind face, with spectacles, sort of academic-looking.

A character named Koga, a lieutenant in civilian clothes, came in. He didn't bow—a bad sign. He was the same officer who had nearly wrecked Uncle Adam's clinic. He kept wiping his glasses but never putting them on. Strange.

He sat at his desk and studied my identification papers as if looking for the plans to the Kobe naval base. He bit his lower lip, then pointed a finger at me: "Mrs. Tamba?"

"That's me."

"You are a spy. Do you understand?"

"I'm *not* a spy, and I understand Japanese."

"You are a spy."

"What have I been spying on?"

"We have reports that you talked to prisoners-of-war illegally. In Yokohama. Do you deny it?"

Ah, so . . . someone had seen me with Ed at the street outside the warehouse. Kenji had told me that Japan was now full of informers, brown-nosing the authorities by snitching. The report on me had apparently collected dust in some pigeonhole. I guessed that Aunt Cora kept making repeated inquiries to the International Red Cross and the connection had been made with me, once I was seen with Ed on the Yokohama dock.

"I did see some POWs in Yokohama," I said.

"What were you doing there?"

"I went to try to buy a crib for my baby boy, I'd heard there was used furniture for sale there—"

"But you spoke to prisoners."

"It was an accidental meeting. I don't even remember what we said or

who they were. There were these Americans unloading supplies. That's
all."

"You have a child?"

"A son. My husband is Mr. Kenji Tamba of Shibuya Ward. And my
father-in-law works at the palace."

"We know that. We have a report on you. What has saved you so far
is your family connection. It is difficult to believe that so illustrious
a person as Major Masao Tamba would harbor a spy in his parents'
home—"

"You can ask him, he'll vouch for me."

I felt pretty smarmy, trading on Masao's name and fame, but I guessed
I was in a box and I owed it to myself and my son and husband to survive
this the best I could. Still, Masao might, for all I knew, be blown to pieces
on Saipan, and I was pretty sure he had no love for me, and I was invoking
him like a family god. Maybe I was getting more Japanese than I thought.

Koga, wiping away at his specs, got up, told me I could go but that I'd
be under strict surveillance and I'd better be ready to show my identity
papers at all times and I'd also better not talk to other foreigners, especially POWs. Violate any of these rules and I'd be subject to arrest. He
didn't bow at the end of his speech. Neither did I.

Kenji, barreling at full speed on his bike, met me at a Shinto shrine at the
edge of the district, and didn't exactly thrill me with his first words, which
were where was Taro. I mean, I'd just been put through the third degree
and I wouldn't have minded a little tender loving care directed my way.
Anyway, I assured him that our son was with his mother. I then filled him
in on what had happened as we sat on a stone bench in the peaceful
surroundings of a little park complete with a bright red *torii* gate, a couple
of stone lanterns and, of course, immaculately trimmed shrubs. Kenji was
now holding my hand—a definite show of tender loving care—and told
me that the authorities these days considered all foreigners spies, including
their so-called allies. "Yuriko," he said, "told me that even her friend, a
German, had been picked up for questioning." I was sort of surprised that
Yuriko hadn't told me, except that she probably was uneasy talking to me
about Hans ever since the trip to the abortionist and my hotheaded words
about him.

Kenji asked me if there were any questions asked about his work, and
added that I should be careful never to say anything about what he did.
He also said he wished he had never told me anything, that it just put me
in danger. "I'm your wife, Kenji, we share, you and I. Good stuff and bad.

Please, that's why we have so much more than these others . . . All right, maybe it's not better, by some standards, but it's ours and it's what makes us special . . . at least, I hope we're special." I think he wanted to kiss me then—I know he did—but of course he held back.

He looked very seriously at me, and said he had been worrying about me lately, that I'd seemed preoccupied. "Well, most of all," I said, "I worry about our baby. I mean, they say it's just a matter of time before Tokyo will be bombed. And the family, your parents, have made no bones that they want me out of the Tamba house, which I won't pretend makes me exactly happy, even if when I get myself calmed down I can sort of understand it . . . you've helped me a lot there . . ."

He looked even more seriously at me. "Julie, do you want to leave?"

I'm willing to bet that no Japanese man living would have asked his wife that question, ever. God, I adored him. "No, Kenji, I couldn't stand being away from you and Taro. So that's that."

We got up from the bench and I perched myself on the crossbar of his bike as he pedaled between wagons, carts, creaking taxis and a few private cars. As we rode along he said, "I was thinking, maybe we could move. That little house Yuriko has . . . we could ask the Kitanos . . ."

"Good," I said. "Sure. Let's face it, it would take a lot of pressure off everybody concerned. And at least we could make love without an audience."

KENJI TAMBA · OCTOBER, 1944

Saburo, all of seventeen, marched—I'm sure that was his gait, a march —into an air-force recruiting office and got himself into a cadet training program. He was still a thin, not very strong boy, and I had doubts about his eyesight, having more than once caught him faking an ability to see objects at a distance when I pointed them out. But he was clever and persistent, and the recruiting officers agreed to take him. My mother was near-hysterical. My father was accepting, perhaps even proud.

That evening Saburo and I sat in the garden together—a rare moment for us—smoking and talking. Julie and Yuriko had taken the children to see a traveling theater group that had set up down the street. Saburo puffed importantly on his cigarette, and seemed especially excited, and welcomed my companionship, happy to be telling someone about how he managed to get himself accepted by the air-force officers.

"A captain asks me if I know what *shichisho hokoku* means, and I tell him, to be reborn seven times to serve the country, that any *samurai* knows that. Then he makes me do exercises, measures my chest and tells me to read the eye chart. I didn't do it so well. Without my glasses I have real trouble, and you can't wear glasses if you're going to be a pilot . . ."

I had to admire him—he might be underweight and impossible at times but he was a fighter. "Then what?" I asked.

"Then I told him I was Major Tamba's brother, and he woke up. He said they'd make an exception in my case."

Not to mention, I thought to myself, that they were desperately short of able-bodied men.

"The captain told me that something called a special-attack force was being organized . . . a new way to use planes in battle. I think I'll be trained for it. I had to read something by Prince Shotoku about the Lord being heaven and the vassals earth. What does that mean, Kenji?"

"It means Imperial commands are supposed to be obeyed because they come from God. That's what the military says, anyway."

Saburo looked at me, not sure he liked what I had added. "Well, the captain also told me that at Saipan a pilot crash-dived his plane right onto a torpedo that was headed for the *Taiho.*"

"And?"

"He died, but he exploded the torpedo."

"Saburo, the *Taiho* was sunk. Your sister's husband died on it."

His eyes glowed. "Yes, but if there had been fifty like that pilot maybe *Taiho* would have been saved and the American ship sunk instead." He tossed a stone at an alley cat prowling along our rear fence. "He asked me if I knew what body-hitting was, and I said it was like in *kendo* or *karate.*"

"Were you right?"

"Well, not exactly. He said in the air force it's when you can't fly anymore, or you can't get back to your base and you smash into the target. Like the pilot that killed that torpedo."

"Did he tell you, Saburo, who makes the decision to crash-dive or not? I mean, did he say those orders are given when he goes out or it's left up to the pilot?"

"No . . . he didn't say. What's the difference? A brave man would know what to do."

Listening to him, looking at him, frail and belligerent, I loved him, was even proud of him—and I wanted to cry for him.

JULIE TAMBA · OCTOBER, 1944

Kenji just got word that the Americans landed in the Philippines. He told me that it was supersecret news and to tell nobody. He and Professor Adachi had to be doubly careful. The Japanese radio didn't report a word about General MacArthur's making good on his pledge to return to the Philippines. Instead they went on about a naval victory over the Americans at Leyte Gulf, claiming that lots of U.S. warships had gone to the bottom—no details—and that the two biggest warships in the world, Japan's battleships *Yamato* and *Musashi,* had caused all kinds of damage to the American ships in the battle of Leyte Gulf.

"A lie," Kenji said. "*Musashi* was sunk."

Privately I thought it was sort of fitting. I'd learned that Musashi means sword-fighter, avenger, was the name of the Jesse James of Japanese literature, a hero to most Japanese kids. Now the battleship named for him lay at the bottom of Leyte Gulf . . .

"Are you really so pleased . . . ?"

"What?"

"The look on your face . . . you look like you are glad that—"

"Maybe I am."

Rarely had I seen Kenji look really angry. His voice was tight as he said, "All those dead young men. Is it their fault? Where is your compassion for them—?"

Now my hackles were rising. Or maybe a lot of pent-up frustration and anger was taking over. "What about your compassion for the dead Americans? They didn't ask for this war. It sure isn't *their* fault . . ."

Before Kenji could answer, Taro, whom I had cradled in my arms, let out a yelp, thrusting his arms out as well as pursing his lips. He was hungry . . . about the only food that seemed to be plentiful was pumpkin, sort of odd-shaped green gourds, and I think the steady diet of them was giving Taro the runs. In the main room we could overhear Goro and Hisako . . . and I hoped they couldn't do the same with us . . . talking to the old man Isamu from the neighborhood association who was telling them that on orders of the emperor he was authorized to distribute two sunflowers to each family on the street. Perfect. The rice ration was down to three hundred grams a day, new clothes were so shoddy in quality that they disintegrated when you washed them . . . Kenji had once said that Hata was probably selling the stuff to the army . . . but never mind, folks, the emperor has proclaimed that all will be set right with two sunflowers per family . . . Martial music was coming in from the street—our stirring summons to the evening "air-defense oath of certain victory." Which oath really meant an hour of digging, manning pumps that were lucky to manage a half-inch stream.

As Kenji got up to go a siren wailed . . . they wailed almost constantly, not signaling an actual raid but a practice. The constant noise got on people's nerves, mine and Kenji's included. I didn't get up to go with him, I told him I'd sit this one out, that he could tell Isamu that Taro had a fever.

"Does he?"

"No, Kenji. He has diarrhea. Besides, I'm a little tired of pumping water out of a dry bucket—"

"Julie"—his face was literally getting dark—"it may not be much but these precautions may just save our lives, and the life of our son—"

I couldn't stop myself, and out came, "Well, I figure we've got nothing to worry about. After all, any country that can invent the paper house and live in it hasn't anything to fear from a few bombs—"

Thankfully, before Kenji could react to that dumb crack, Taro took over with a piercing howl that I tried to quiet with some dry rice, which he promptly spat out. "Kid has no taste, no likes rice. Obviously a born traitor—"

"Julie, do you think it fair to insult my people? Yes, my people. Maybe you would have been happier with Ed Hodges, with his *American* child . . ."

And I woke up with that jolt to realize that I'd gone too far, way too far. I'd hurt Kenji, I'd hurt a man that I loved and whose child I'd given birth to. Again, Taro let out a world-beater and I gave him a smack on the rear.

"Julie, *no.*" I'd violated the essential Japanese in Kenji, I knew it and I couldn't stop. Hisako had been listening in—she'd have had to've been deaf not to—and now she came shuffling in, carrying her sunflower. Taro yowled, I smacked his precious bottom again, in full view of grandma this time, and she nearly died. Never, never, never do that to a male child . . . "Don't you hit my grandson," she said, and I informed her "I'll do what I want, he's my son—"... "Not in my house," said Hisako, "I forbid it ..." Kenji now tried to mediate but it was no use. "Give me my son's child, I must comfort him—" ... "I'll use him for a beanbag if I want to." ... Finger leveled now at Kenji, she said, "She will ruin our son, she is not one of us." ... To which I responded smartly, "You bet I'm not," and promptly, finally, broke into tears that made Taro's look like child's play, which, of course, they were. I slumped to the floor, gave up Taro to Kenji, who came to me and offered to hold him. God, I felt like a complete bitch. I was coming apart, I was ashamed but I couldn't seem to control myself. Without another word I tried to make a quick exit and ran all the way to the clinic, where I proceeded to pour out my troubles to poor Aunt Cora, who quickly dismissed a patient to help me out.

"Julie," she said, "I've said it before, if you're really miserable and want to leave I can find a Red Cross ship or maybe a neutral one ..."

I looked at her, tried to get hold of myself. Leave? The answer to that was the same one as before. I loved Kenji. I couldn't leave him. The question was, how long could he stand me ... ?

KENJI TAMBA · DECEMBER, 1944

I never, of course, bothered Professor Adachi with my family problems. Such matters are the obligations of blood relatives to resolve. Adachi was my teacher, not to be burdened with talk of my wife's and my conflicts, my mother's unhappiness ...

I concentrated on the work, and one day late in December a man in a black business suit came to the office. I wasn't introduced to him by name, and he was identified only as "the assistant secretary." Professor Adachi asked me to read him our latest reports from the battle areas. So I read him a summary as of that morning, including the encirclement of Japanese forces in the Philippines that was underway, the attempt to land reinforcements for Field Marshal Teruachi's troops that had failed, and the conclusion that American control of air and sea was complete. Professor Adachi told me to tell the losses, which I did. "The Americans claim we have lost 56,000 in the Philippine campaigns, including losses at Mindoro and Visayan as well as Leyte."

The man cleared his throat, told us in formal Japanese that "this visit must remain secret." He sounded titled, I thought, someone close to a palace official, perhaps a member of, or a person who had contracts with, the Eleven Club, the closed group of hereditary peers. Ordinarily Professor Adachi would have had little patience with such people, but if they could be allies, he had no choice.

The man asked about American bombing plans, if we had any information about that, and I told him, once Professor Adachi had nodded his authorization to me, that the Americans were now flying B-29s from airstrips in China, that they had bombed the oilfields in Malaya and Sumatra, but that they were also having maintenance problems on account of the long distances from homebase. As a result they had decided to move their main B-29 base to the island of Tinian in the Marianas. And, I added, "As you know, they have already bombed Tokyo twice."

"Ah, but with little effect."

"The attack, it's true, on the Masashima aircraft factory was ineffective, few bombs hit the target, but only one of their planes was shot down. The cloud-cover this time of year makes it difficult for them to select targets—"

"Then we have little to fear."

"Sir," Professor Adachi said, "the Americans appear to be building up a force of bombers in the Marianas that can bring wide-ranging damage to Tokyo and its citizens. Perhaps a single high-level precision raid on a factory may not be effective or too damaging, but widespread bombing of a city and its people . . ."

"And the Soviet Union?"

Neither the professor nor I could follow the question.

"I refer to the last conference among Roosevelt and Churchill and Stalin. Do you have any knowledge about what was discussed?"

"Rumors, mostly," Adachi said.

"Did Stalin stand by his neutrality pact with us? We must assume he will honor it, we have behaved most generously to the Soviet Union."

Professor Adachi let cigarette smoke drift upward, let the tension build before he answered. He wanted his information, rumor though it might be, to hit this titled functionary full force. "We believe," the professor finally said, "that Stalin has promised the United States that once Germany is defeated he will declare war on Japan . . ."

The caller looked shaken. "But that is impossible, professor. Moscow has assured us that relations remain friendly. There are even hints that . . . that they would be willing to perform as go-between in the event that . . . I believe you know . . ."

He could not quite say it.

"In the event that we should sue for peace?" Adachi finished for him.

"You should not use that phrase. Let us only say that if circumstances were, theoretically, to become such that an approach to the United States was indicated, an approach to reevaluate our relationships and so forth . . ."

Apparently he was a diplomat. Only a court-trained type could so skirt around what he truly meant to say. And, of course, our language reinforces such evasions and circumlocutions.

The professor saw him to the door. "Can this information be gotten to His Majesty?"

"An effort will be made . . . it must first be passed through lower levels, of course, and in utmost secrecy. You and your aide are sworn to silence under penalty of death if you should reveal any of what has passed between us today. As far as you are concerned, both of you, this visit never took place."

"Depend on us, sir. But please make certain that those in power, no matter what their rank, understand that to save our people this war must be brought to a conclusion. The alternative is national suicide."

Once again the caller looked shaken, even more than before, as he thanked us and left.

When he had gone I asked Professor Adachi if he felt we had gotten our message across, and whether it would really be passed on to where it could have some meaning and effect.

The professor shrugged. "I can't say. These aristocrats make me uneasy. They have never cared about the common people. They may just say let them burn and die, we will survive, as we always have."

It was a chilling appraisal, but I reminded the professor that the man did seem genuinely upset.

"And he should be. But mark my words, Kenji, we will never see him again, and no matter what happens we will never know if this meeting did effect events. All we can do is work, gather information, and hope."

MASAO TAMBA · JANUARY, 1945

People look at me like a ghost come back to life. Especially my family, who thought I was surely dead. I felt like a ghost, one of a handful to survive Saipan.

I drifted out to sea, was picked up by native fishermen, who dumped me on an uninhabited atoll where I lived on sea creatures, killed birds with a slingshot, drank rainwater that collected in palm leaves. The fishermen were glad to be rid of me, obviously afraid of my metal arm and one eye. I think they considered me some kind of demon, and perhaps I was.

By now I was losing my sense of shame for not dying on Saipan with the others. Besides, *someone* had to live to fight again. So now I had staggered through the carnage of Guadalcanal and Saipan and I had seen the Americans at their worst—or best . . .

Alone on this sun-baked and rainy atoll I hid from probing American ships, watched endless flights of their planes pass overhead, and prayed for rescue. I was a wraith, thin as a young bamboo. My metal arm rusted and infected the stump and I had to discard it. Barefoot, wearing only a breechclout, I moved about the island, catching crabs and lizards, devouring them raw, often while alive, and cut down young palm trees with my knife to get at their soft hearts.

Sometime in December a Japanese freighter, the *Sakura Maru*, responded to my signals with a mirror and picked me up. I nearly died aboard on three occasions, suffering from a recurrence of malaria that rattled my teeth so hard my mouth bled and shook me out of the narrow cot. Dehydrated and infested with parasites, I lay in shock for days. I was brought ashore a month later after the freighter ran a gauntlet of bombs and torpedoes and delivered its cargoes to Okinawa, where it was forced to stay in port for repairs.

It was in an Okinawa hospital that I learned about our new "special attack" planes that were now active around the Philippines. Apparently the air force had devised a new strategy with a plane that itself was a bomb, loaded with explosive, designed to detonate on contact. Of course this meant the death of the pilot, but, I was informed, recruiting officers were flooded with young men eager to die this way. And the tactic had given the Americans pause, confused and frightened them.

"They call them *kamikaze,*" an air-force major told me as we lay side by side on cots.

"Divine wind," I said. "The typhoons that destroyed the armadas of the Great Khan."

"Well-named," the major said. He said he knew about me and was amazed to see me alive . . . the word in military circles was that I had died on Saipan. He himself had been shot down in the Philippines, suffered severe burns and had been evacuated to Okinawa.

"And the general staff feels it can turn the war around with these planes?" I asked.

"We say there is no question about it." He went on to say that since the late summer the air force and the navy had been developing these "special attack" units. The pilots were using Class 99 light bombers and Class 4 heavy bombers, the "flying dragons."

"I'm an infantryman," I said. "How do those things work?"

"They convert the bombers to single seaters, room only for the pilot. Then they're packed with heavy bombs. The 99 carries an eight-hundred-kilogram navy bomb, the Class 4 gets two of them. Then the nose of the plane is fitted with a long detonator fuse that explodes on contact."

"No chance for the pilot?"

"He fulfills his *chu*. He is with the gods."

"Used against warships only?"

The major peered through the bandages covering his burned face. "No, they are being used to bring down B–29s too. It's called body-ramming. The arithmetic is with us. We lose one obsolete plane and one pilot. A B–29 has a crew of eleven, and it is much bigger and more expensive than our old bombers. A good exchange for us. In the case of a naval vessel it's even better for us. One plane, one pilot. And a cruiser with hundreds of Americans is sunk."

He sounded so sure of things, I almost began to have some hopes again about winning the war.

Back home in Tokyo I found it difficult to be with others. I was wasted to one hundred and five pounds, and was ravaged by diarrhea.

I had also lost all sexual urgings. At night I wanted Michiko only to hold me. I was more a baby than a man. It was as if I had reverted to infancy, when all needs are met, when no pain is inflicted and one is loved unconditionally. I was grateful to Michiko for playing this role of my mother.

Nor did I do any better in trying to arouse my body to sexual pleasure with courtesans. Satomi and Kingoro Hata now employed both geishas and prostitutes, although the supply of the latter was far greater. Geishas, by government edict, had been ordered out of their robes and wigs and forced to go to work. Whores, many of them widows, orphaned country-women, were in great supply. None tempted me. In fact, their pungent womanly odors, hidden hairs, oily apertures made me feel sick. Perhaps it was their fish smell, reminding me of those fishermen, the raw fish and animals I ate on the atoll.

Saburo, I learned, was now in training at Chofu Air Base, and remembering what the major had told us in the hospital, I was, to be truthful, afraid for him. When he heard that I was back in Tokyo he wrote me a letter full of innocent enthusiasm.

> Honored older brother,
> At the start of each day's training we recite the Imperial Rescript and the Imperial Mandate. I tell you this so you will know how truly we follow *Kodo*, the Imperial Way.
> How glad I am you are home and well and will live to see Japan's victory!
> We sing "Kimigayo" twice before going to our planes, and then we sing "Going Out to Sea."
> On every holiday we bow to the Imperial palace. In addition to our flight training, which I love, we are taught aggressiveness, the proper attitudes in life and death, the benevolence of the Imperial house and belief in final victory. We have been given more and more training in *kamikaze*.
> I cannot wait to meet the enemy. I am one of the youngest men in the unit. Many are university students and they laugh at me but I don't care. Wait till we're in combat. They'll learn about the courage of the Tambas!
>
> Your devoted younger brother,
> Saburo

Yes, I felt pride, but even more fear. So young . . .

I saw little of Yuriko. Since Hideo's death aboard *Taiho*, she had, it seemed to me, become arrogant, short-tempered and aloof. Did she also have a boyfriend? I suspected but did not probe. She had taken to wearing Western clothing in the evening, after work, things Kenji's wife had given her. Once the Women's Patriotic Society stopped her in the street and lectured her on her bad taste. She laughed at them. There was little I could or wanted to say to her.

My father, having an affair with one of the maids from the palace, was rarely home at night and had also taken to drinking more than was good for him. But all of us, including my mother, accepted his drunkenness and his liaison as his due. My mother even told me that he was better-humored now that he had his friend Fumiko to endow him with *tatami* burns. It was one of the few times I was able to laugh or smile about anything.

One evening I asked Kenji to accompany me to the Yasukuni shrine. He was reluctant but, good-natured fellow that he is, he agreed.

When we got there I noticed that the bronze gates of the shrine to our war dead were gone.

"Taken to a munitions plant and melted down to make spare parts for our aircraft," Kenji said in response to my questioning expression.

"The shrine is our symbol of military power—"

"Then what has happened to the gates should be a warning to us."

I managed a wry smile. "Master Cold Rice, that is fancy talk, but I tell you the Americans are in for some surprises."

I knelt in front of the shrine to the war dead, left some prayers written on rice paper in the gates and joined the Shinto priests in a new prayer, denouncing the "haughty enemy," asking the gods to ensure the overthrow of the Allied forces and to reinforce in us the "august powers of the deities."

Kenji only watched me, said nothing, although I knew what he was thinking. It was bitter cold and we huddled in our coats as we walked through a snowy landscape amid swirling flakes, and said nothing.

JULIE TAMBA · JANUARY, 1945

The Varnums' clinic was still open, still functioning, but only just. They were doing the best they could, with their terrible shortage of supplies, still trying to treat the poor people of the neighborhood, widows especially now, along with the *Eta*, the wandering souls from the slums and countryside whom everybody shunned. Everybody, that is, except a couple of *gaijin* named Dr. Cora Varnum and Dr. Adam Varnum.

I had gone there this chilly day after a boy had come to tell me Aunt Cora wanted to see me. We sat shivering in the Western-style living room in back of the clinic, where Aunt Cora brewed some English tea she could still get at times from the Swiss consul. She then proceeded to tell me a story about how the day before a young man named Kwon had appeared and delivered a letter. He said he was from Seoul—Korea was a Japanese colony—and that he and his classmates had been promised all sorts of chances for advanced study if they would come to Japan. What they got was forced labor in the coal mines on Kyushu Island. They had it relatively easy, though, as pit bosses, ordering around American prisoners. He said the work was long and hard and the Japanese beat the prisoners and there was danger from mine collapses and gas explosions. After a while, Kwon told Cora, the Koreans formed a sort of bond with the American POWs, both sharing a hatred of the Japanese. As Cora went on, I knew what was coming . . . how could I miss it . . . the coal mines and American POWs . . . anyway, being a skilled electrician Kwon had been ordered to Tokyo to work in an airplane factory, and before he left an American prisoner had given him a letter addressed to "Mrs. Varnum, c/o Swiss Consul." He had delivered it and left, asking Aunt Cora not to tell anyone that he was an illegal messenger.

The letter, written on rice paper with a pencil, was from Sergeant Ralph Guzzo, and he'd certainly taken a chance getting word out of the camp at the coal mines, and the Korean had taken just as big a chance delivering it. It read:

> Dear Mrs. Varnum,
> I remember you from when the Red Cross came to the warehouse
> maybe a year and a half back. My name is Ralph Guzzo, and I'm
> a POW marine sergeant. A few months ago your niece, she's
> married to a Japanese, came looking for our C.O., Lt. Hodges.
> They had a talk at the Yokohama docks and then she had to take
> off. This letter is to let her know he's not in such good shape.
> I'll keep it short, Kwon's a good guy and if either of us gets
> caught . . .
>
> Well, this Kyushu deal is bad. Lots of snow and rain. Guys get
> killed in roof collapses cause the Nips don't know how to shore up
> the face and their drilling equipment is lousy. The Koreans
> smuggled in parts—wire, condensers and batteries—so I could rig a
> radio. We hid it during the day and pulled it out from under the
> honey buckets at night. We could get the BBC and the Mosquito
> Network and Tokyo Rose.
>
> Somebody—who knows who?—blabbed. I built the radio, so I
> fessed up, but I wouldn't tell them where it was hid. They beat me
> and shoved water and pepper down my nose and put me in the hot
> box. While I was in it a kid from Texas got caught using the radio
> one night and they took him and cut off his head. They said they'd
> kill every tenth man if we didn't own up where other radios were.
> Of course there weren't any others.
>
> Anyway, Lt. Hodges took over then and told them he'd have
> them brought up on war criminal charges and the first one to hang
> would be the Jap C.O. They beat the lieutenant and cut him and
> hung him from a beam in the barracks. When they cut him down

they beat him again. That was about a month ago. We haven't seen him since, but the Japs claim he's still alive. We try to believe that.

If you can get the Red Cross out here maybe the Japs will ease up some on us, and if the lieutenant is still alive maybe they can get him out of wherever he's being held. He's the best we've got.

> Sincerely,
> M/Sgt. Ralph Guzzo
> USMC

It was too horrible to absorb all at once, or at least to react to. Cora said she and Adam would go to see Dr. Reinhold the next day. I asked her what if the Japanese refuse to look into it, or let the Red Cross. Uncle Adam looked into the wintry yard with its trees without leaves, a tangle of old rose vines, hard-packed earth. "I don't know," he said. "As the threat of bombings gets closer to reality, they may get even tougher on the prisoners . . ."

My first impulse was to try to go to Kyushu myself, I was an American married to a Japanese, maybe I could help in a way others couldn't. When I said as much to Cora and Adam they shook their heads and told me it was really a crazy notion, that I'd never make it and what made me think they'd care what a *gaijin* girl married to a Japanese who came to see an American POW had to say . . . They made sense, but I didn't give up the idea.

Instead, I tried to concentrate on a letter I'd gotten from Chris, which was like an antidote to the awful news the Korean had brought out of Kyushu. The heart of it was that since her husband Major Herb Kahn had died, he and Carol had been spending a lot of time together on Tinian Island, where he'd gone to cover the B–29s, and it seemed he had stopped being so self-centered and really cared about Carol and was helping her over this rough time. He also told me I ought to get out of Japan if I could, that the air force was "gearing up" for raids on Tokyo. Well, we already knew about that, and I had decided I wouldn't go.

KENJI TAMBA · JANUARY, 1945

The evening started all right, even pleasantly. Except for my mother, Julie and I had the house to ourselves . . . we hadn't moved, the Kitanos had put some relatives into the little house with Yuriko and her child, but at least I was now paying a little rent that I earned from my work with Professor Adachi.

My father was no doubt with Fumiko in her flat in Shitamachi or with Kingoro Hata at the Plum Blossom House. Masao, still suffering from his stomach problems, was out, probably with Colonel Sato. I had managed to trade some writing paper and pencils from the office for charcoal, which was a welcome change for my mother to burn instead of the twigs and old boxes in the hibachi. Julie was singing the UCLA fight song to Taro, and when I came in she looked up and told me, "I'll make a Bruin out of him yet." She gave him to me then so she could prepare our dinner, and I held him close, enjoying the feel of his sturdy arms and legs.

Julie said the day had gone better than most with my mother, who "actually let me help her out some, dusting and mopping. *Gaijin* women are good for something." She quickly smiled when she said it, and turned to stir the rice and taste a few grains. She also had a dish of fried whitebait, a treat from the fishmonger, and some pickled carrots. But she had had another ugly incident outside the fish store, a woman collecting her children and shouting the usual epithets at her. As she told me about it she seemed to be unusually tense, and her voice showed her anger.

As a diversion I tuned in Radio Tokyo, which was broadcasting Tokyo Rose's report that General Yamashita had matters under control in the Philippines, that his troops were confident, MacArthur's landings on Luzon had been repelled with staggering losses to the Americans in men and ships and planes. Once again, we were to believe the war was being won for losing.

After dinner, during which Julie had become ominously quiet . . . my wife was not typically close-mouthed . . . she announced out of the blue that she had heard terrible news about Ed Hodges in a POW camp in Kyushu and that she intended to do something about it, maybe even try to go there herself. I pointed out that this was impossible, that as she knew, she was under surveillance and wouldn't get as far as the railway station.

"Then you'll help me. You're smart and can figure out some excuse to get to Kyushu—"

"Julie, please . . . you know this is foolish talk. I'm sorry for Ed too, you know that. But there are some things that we can't do. We could never get near him."

"But we *owe* him more than just feeling sorry. You're an expert on owing, you've explained it to me often enough. You owe your parents, you owe anybody who does you a favor. My God, don't I owe an old friend something too?"

I got up and went to her, but she drew away from me, told me not to touch her. She was getting more Japanese than I wanted, at least about not touching.

"Julie, I am trying to talk some sense to you. You would be put in jail the moment you tried to go, your child—"

My mother came in just then, having, of course, heard some of our words. "You must keep your voice down," she said sharply to Julie. "The neighbors . . ."

By now Julie had slumped to the floor, had turned her back to me, her body shuddering with her weeping. And I realized that more than Ed Hodges was once again working on her, working inside her. It was a terrible burden for her, being here. I knew that, and while I sympathized and even felt guilty about having let her come, I also had private feelings of resentment that I could not control. She *had* come. Life was not easy for any of us. I was not accepted by my own family, was suspected by my brothers and Colonel Sato—I tried to stop such negative feelings, surprised that I had allowed them at all, asked my mother to leave us and went to my wife.

But Julie would not turn to me, would not move, would not even allow me to put my arm around her. And finally she said, in a voice whose tone, or lack of it, said more than her request, to leave her alone.

Without another word I left her and went out of the house into the very cold night. I wandered the streets, took a bus to Akasaka and moved as if in a trance to the first whore I could find. She was standing slouched in a doorway under a green paper lantern and I walked through the beaded curtain with her, not saying a word.

YURIKO KITANO · JANUARY, 1945

I have been seeing Hans almost twice a week. We make love often, though he now uses a protection.

When I am with Hans my edginess is gone . . . Julie would call it a kind of bitchiness, an American term, which she says I am entitled to. I do know that it is not important what we do together as long as we are together. Without much money, we always find something pleasing to occupy us—a walk in a park, a movie, a puppet play. Hans does receive occasional payments for his magazine work and for writing reports for the Germany embassy in Tokyo. It is never much, but he almost always manages to bring me little gifts like a bar of soap, a handkerchief, a scarf.

Each time I see Hans, so thin and pale, with his increasingly unruly shock of blond hair, I *crave* him . . . a very un-Japanese, unladylike acknowledgment. And he is tender with me, at the same time that he does things for me Hideo would never have considered, and about which, until meeting Hans, I was totally ignorant of. He *pleases* me, and I hope I do as much for him. He assures me I do, which makes me even happier . . .

I have told Hans about the letters from Julie's brother, the warnings of mass bombings of our cities. He says we shouldn't worry, that the Americans are more likely to go after Kobe and Nagoya and Yokohama, where there are airplane factories and steel mills. Tokyo, he says, is a city of restaurants and teashops, with nothing of military interest. I only hope he is right . .

As we walked back from a movie this evening, we were stopped by a policeman, and Hans was ordered to show his alien card and journalist's pass. When the police saw he was a German citizen they bowed and wished us goodnight, as they usually did under such circumstances. As we walked on—it was bitter cold—a siren went off. Searchlights streaked the skies. But people did not seem afraid. No one ran for the holes and ditches that were supposed to save us. Just the opposite—people came outside, staring at the moonlit sky, pointing to the south, where we could see flights of American planes.

"To Yokohama," Hans said. "The port. Don't be afraid, they've come a long way, they can't waste bombs on Tokyo." He kissed my cheek then and told me he had to meet some people. I didn't press him about who they were, but he often had to go off to such meetings, and I did not know that although he was posing as a loyal German, and therefore an ally of Japan, he was working against the German government, against Herr Hitler, and I suspected against our own military as well . . . "Hans, I respect what you are doing, I respect and love you, but I don't want to be on Kikaigashima, an exile on Devil's Island."

He smiled at me, trying to reassure me. "Actually, it's not possible," he said. "It isn't Kikaigashima anymore. They call it Iwo Jima, and nobody goes there except soldiers."

The American planes droned on, yet none of our planes went up to meet them. Nor did we hear any antiaircraft fire.

Before Hans left me I told him I was much more afraid for him than of the American planes. I would kill myself, I told him, if anything happened to him. I meant it.

MASAO TAMBA · FEBRUARY, 1945

Colonel Sato had arranged a reprise of a previous feast at the Plum Blossom to celebrate, he said, our victories on the island of Iwo Jima. I could not eat, not with my ravaged stomach, but I went along for the diversion. It was better than doing nothing at home, and my good wife deserved a night off from the ghost I had become.

The naval officer Commander Endo was there and some others whose names did not register. Endo, my father-in-law and the other officers quickly began drinking toasts to our war dead, and to General Kuribayashi's valiant defenders of Iwo Jima.

"The marines will never climb Mount Suribachi," Colonel Sato was saying. "They advance, they are thrown back, they have lost two entire divisions. Eventually they must rethink their strategy. As for an invasion of our homeland, that wild notion will be banished from their calculations forever. If one speck of volcanic rock like Iwo Jima cannot be taken, how can they possibly think of an invasion of Japan?"

Endo and the rest agreed. I said nothing, but I thought there was sense in some of my father-in-law's analysis. I had seen the bravery and persistence of the American marines as he had not, but the Americans were not superhumans. They could sustain only so many losses. We were showing them how to die, and we knew more about that than they did. On the other hand, if Iwo Jima should fall . . .

Suddenly we heard the sirens, and were assured by Endo that they meant nothing, but by now he and Colonel Sato were well into their cups and the conversation skidded into the weighty question of why geishas do not wear underpants. Endo apparently had the answer. "There was this fire," he said with slurred speech, "at a geisha house in the Pontocho district of Kyoto . . . the girls got to the roof but they didn't jump off because they were too ashamed to let the crowds see that they had no panties on and so they all burned to death—"

"Excuse me, gentlemen," Satomi said, "but no such fire ever took place in Pontocho. It was a department store in Asakusa. The salesgirls were worried that people could look up their kimonos if they jumped and so they died. It resulted in the Wear Panties Movement."

This intelligence convulsed Endo, Sato and the others, but I confess I did not laugh. Nobody cared or noticed.

"Why *don't* geishas wear panties?" Endo suddenly asked. "Some of us like the pleasure of taking them off, it's very nice the way they slide down the thighs . . ."

Satomi had the answer to that too. "It is because going to the bathroom in a kimono and *obi* is difficult enough without having to struggle with underpants. So my girls wear a *koshimaki,* you know, the plain silk wrapper around the waist."

The sirens wailed again, louder and louder. Colonel Sato somehow managed to right himself and go to a telephone. When he came back he informed us that it was "merely an incendiary bombing of the outskirts."

Endo, dismissing the matter, turned to me and asked about the meaning of the attack on Iwo Jima, from the Americans' point of view, as I saw it. Being the only one there sober, I suppose I was the right one to ask, since at least I could put two sentences together and not be diverted by the question of geisha panties, yes or no. I told him that Iwo Jima was seen as a midway airfield for their B–29 bombers, the flight from the Marianas was too long, and, I said, "we are told that the Americans may soon have over four hundred of the big planes on the islands. So to overcome the problem of the huge distances between the islands and our homeland, Iwo Jima will be a way-station—"

"Ah, but they will never take Iwo Jima. I predict that Kuribayashi's network of pillboxes on the slopes of the mountains and the death toll among American marines will take care of that," Colonel Sato said, then raised his glass and muttered, "The marines will be driven into the sea, the invasion will fail, they will never even try to invade our homeland, they will sue for peace and give us what we need and are entitled to . . . the rule of Asia . . ."

All drank. Satomi, seeing me looking glum and not drinking, came to me and bowed. "Does Major Tamba desire anything?"

"Nothing, Satomi."

"The virgin?"

"No."

"Whiskey?"

"Satomi, I will rest here. Perhaps one of your women could play a song for me . . . 'Going Out to Sea' . . ."

"At once, major."

The women took their seats at the *samisens* and began to pluck the taut strings and sing in lovely mellow voices.

> If I go away to sea
> I shall return a corpse awash,
> If duty calls me to the mountain,
> A verdant sword will be my pall;
> For the sake of the emperor I will not die
> Peacefully at home . . .

I had been forced to accept that there would be no more battles for me, but there would also be no dying "peacefully at home." There would have to be one last occasion to wield a sword, to atone for not having died in battle with my men. I had tried, but had never been able to accept this . . .

KENJI TAMBA · MARCH, 1945

The Swedish consul's office secured a blurred copy of the photograph, and one of Professor Adachi's couriers brought it to us—five American marines in battle dress raising the American flag on Mount Suribachi.

Professor Adachi said, "Iwo Jima has fallen to the Americans, at a great price on both sides. Twenty thousand of the Japanese garrison wiped out, twenty-five thousand Americans wounded and at least six thousand dead. All for a few square miles of volcanic ash."

"I can't believe the Americans will pay the additional price for an invasion," I said.

"Perhaps not, but someone must stiffen Tenno Heika's spine, and put some sense into the heads of his advisors."

"Is there any hope, *sensei?*"

He tugged, as he so often did in moments of stress, at the white puffs of hair over his ears. "I am told that Konoye has actually told the emperor that the war is lost. Lord Privy Seal Kido agrees, as does Prime Minister Koiso. But the three Ks are afraid of the military . . . they do not want to appear to be in front of His Majesty, or risk arousing suspicion about themselves, thereby inviting reprisals. Konoye talks about communism being a threat if the war goes on and Russia comes in on the side of the Americans. It is smart of him to use this cover. Of course, short of an invasion, Tenno Heika is secure in the love and loyalty of his subjects. The reason to end this terrible war is to save our people from destruction."

"But who," I asked, "is going to call for peace and not be arrested or worse? My brother Masao tells me that the army has a new slogan—One Hundred Million Will Die Together."

"Your brother is an interesting man, or at least so I have gathered from what you have said. On the one hand he is everyman's military hero, a descendant of the fiercest of our *samurai* traditions. Still, he is an intelligent man, as you have said, and he has suffered terribly in battle. He has many good qualities. I believe you should talk to him. His father-in-law is the influential Colonel Sato . . . Yes, Kenji, you must talk to him . . ."

I took the photograph of the flag-raising on Iwo Jima and bicycled out to Masao's house at the edge of the Shibuya Ward that very evening.

He was sleeping, as he so often was these days. Michiko was feeding Maeko. Their maid Reiko was washing the supper dishes. Michiko was always glad to see me—she had never been rude to Julie. She was gentle and decent, although she had none of Yuriko's spirit. She did, though, have talent, and I asked her if she were painting again, and she said she had no time but wanted to, and that Masao approved of her work and had no objection to her selling her *sumi* work. I squatted on the floor near the *kotatsu* and asked about Masao's health. She said he was weary all the time, slept a great deal, which I knew, and took pills to relieve the pain in his stomach, although nothing seemed to help, and he would not eat.

Masao stirred and groaned, and Michiko went to him and cradled his head. It was upsetting to see this hero brother of mine, a man I may not have agreed with often but always could respect and look up to, now reduced to this state . . . As Michiko stroked his face, I could scarcely look on the former Dragon of Shansi, now a wreck of a man . . .

Maeko followed the maid into the kitchen, and I turned back, drawn and repulsed, to watch my brother . . . and memories flooded into my mind . . . memories of the day four years ago when I had gone to the barracks to tell my brother about my scholarship which would mean my return to the United States. I remembered watching him in a *kendo* fight, beating the best men in the batallion—merciless, strong, lithe as a panther . . .

Masao, having heard my voice, was now awake and lifted his head from Michiko's lap to face me. "Master Cold Rice, is it you?"

"Yes, elder brother."

"Forgive my appearance. I am glad to see you . . ."

Michiko asked if we would like some tea, and if we would like to be alone.

"Yes," Masao said, "make some tea for us, green tea, strong, the way Master Cold Rice drinks it."

Michiko left for the kitchen, and Masao eased himself to a sitting position. I made a move to help him but he held up his hand to stop me, proud and independent even in his condition.

"I'm happy to see you," he said again, his voice no longer strong, more like the croak of a water-bird. "Do you still collect enemy reports—don't worry, I would never inform on my brother."

I told him I knew that, and then, taking a deep breath, I took out the photograph from my pocket and showed it to him . . . the American marines raising their flag on Mount Suribachi. He stared at it, as though not quite comprehending, or not wanting to. "Our garrison on Iwo Jima is destroyed," I told him. "The way is now clear for the Americans to launch bombing raids from the Marianas. How much longer can we allow our people to be destroyed? And to risk the destruction of our cities?" I did not mention Saburo, but he was on my mind, as I knew he must be on Masao's. But we still thought so differently . . .

"I understand the price paid for Iwo Jima," he said. "But they will pay a thousand times over if they invade our homeland."

"But thousands and thousands of our people will die—"

"We must accept that."

"Masao, you can't speak for everyone. Please, talk to your fellow officers. Talk to Colonel Sato, he has influence, tell them that it isn't too late to seek an honorable peace. I believe there are people in the palace itself who know this but they fear the military—"

"And with reason."

His face now seemed set, almost animated. He seemed a man yearning for a heroic ending—his own. Cheated of death twice, he apparently hungered for a kind of martyrdom, or at least what he considered an honorable death . . . And yet I also reminded myself that he had twice chosen to live . . . perhaps there was still reason to hope he would choose to do so again . . .

Michiko came in now with a lacquered red tray, china cups and a teapot. My brother and I said not a word as I put the photograph back in my pocket, drank my tea, bowed and left.

JULIE TAMBA · MARCH, 1945

Chris married Carol Kahn in mid-February but I didn't learn about it until the first week of March when one of his letters arrived via the Swiss diplomatic pouch.

Today I was sitting, as I often did, in the park across from the Tamba house, keeping an eye on Taro, fat and happy and still padded in his winter clothing, playing with two baby girls, daughters of the fishmonger Mr. Kurita.

My happiness watching my son was tempered when I thought about what was happening between me and Kenji. Ever since the night of our big fight when he'd gone off into the night—I never asked him where and he never volunteered—our relationship had changed, we hardly ever made love and I was scared to death that we were growing so far apart that we'd never get back together again.

Kenji and I were still in love . . . I believed that, but was being in love enough with everything else that we had to sustain? I put it out of my mind for a moment as I read Chris's description of the wedding at an old hotel on Hawaii. My parents were there—I couldn't help feel a little jealous of their no doubt glowing approval of Chris and Carol compared to their frosty reaction to Kenji and me. Not that my parents had stopped caring about me . . . Chris reported that my mother wanted to know if he'd heard anything more about me, that they were real worried about the bombings of Tokyo. Chris said he tried to reassure them some by telling them bombings were and would be restricted to industrial places, and that the Tamba home was well away from such target areas. He also enclosed a photograph of himself and Carol. Somehow they looked sort of subdued for a just-married couple, and I could understand it . . . Chris wondering if he could live up to Major Kahn in Carol's eyes, and Carol maybe still feeling a little guilty for remarrying. I figured, though, that they'd get over that. At least those kinds of problems didn't seem on a par with what Kenji and I were going through, and then once again I reminded myself to cut out the self-pity, that we both had gone into our marriage with our eyes wide open, as they say . . .

Sitting there in the park, I showed Taro the wedding photos, pointed out my father, looking more stooped and gray now, in his dark blue best suit, and my mother. I said the words "Grandpa, grandma," and he studied the pictures and looked at me for some help. He knew, of course, that Hisako and Goro were his grandparents, and that's the way he referred to them, but who were these pale *gaijin* people? Not surprising that he was confused.

I got up from the bench and let him lead me around the corner to a favorite little alley of craftsmen. Above us a wonderful red kite in the form of a whale floated serenely on the March breeze—I'd seen some boys flying it behind the park.

"Kite, kite," Taro was saying, "want kite."

And like a true Japanese mother, at least to this extent, I right away wanted to give my male child his heart's desire. Well, why not? If my marriage was going to be saved, if it was going to survive the war, the homesickness, the sense of being an outsider, this fat happy lovely child was going to have a lot to do with it. I also thought of one of the teachings of the Friends—that members of the Meeting have a responsibility to bring under the loving care of the group all the children of the Meeting. It made sense. Kids really give us so much, and never had I felt this more than now.

We passed an alcove where Mr. Ikita carved his wooden combs, an atelier where the Asami brothers dyed silk for kimonos, creating colors unbelievable in their beauty, and then on to the kite shop, where Mr. and Mrs. Shigemasa were painting kites for the cherry blossom festival. They let Taro take a brush and splash paint on scrap paper any which way he wanted, unusual for the Japanese, who like everything just so. The Shigemasas, in their cubbyhole of a shop, were real artists— he with a snowy beard, looking sort of like an underfed oriental version of Santa Claus, she with her gray hair in a tight bun and a twinkle in her eye.

Taro picked out a kite showing a fire-snorting *samurai* in a helmet and wielding a baton. Frankly I'd have wished for a little more peaceful motif, I'd had a bellyful of fire-breathers, but Taro was all boy, and how different, really, was this from all-American kids playing Cowboys and Indians? Mr. Shigemasa got up and bowed and, I'd bet, charged me less than his usual price, being an old friend of Kenji's father.

"You know, Mrs. Tamba," he said to me as we were leaving, "for us a kite is more than a toy. It is also an offering to the gods, and in the old days the characters on the kite said words of thanks to the gods. So when your son flies this kite he is also reaching to the gods . . ."

The way it worked out, Taro never saw the kite fly.

KENJI TAMBA · MARCH, 1945

It was some time after midnight, around twelve-thirty on the morning of March 9, that I awoke to thudding noises, along with the heavy hum of big planes.

Yuriko was sleeping upstairs with Hiroki, she'd gone to bed early after an argument with my mother, who had apparently learned about her visits to Hans Baumann and wanted my father to discipline her. But Goro, ironically, was in Shitamachi, a working-class suburb, with his mistress Fumiko. What was acceptable for her husband was not acceptable for her daughter.

Julie was already awake, lying in Japanese style with her child fast asleep tucked close to her breasts. "What is it?" she asked me, and I told her it was another air raid, probably only the factories . . .

So far the B–29 attacks had concentrated on the industrial belt from Tokyo to Yokohama, and although terrifying they hadn't managed to knock out their main target, the Masashima aircraft works. Even the raids of the "black snow" hadn't managed—although they had a special and depressing effect . . . It was the last week in February and there had been a huge snowstorm that covered all of Tokyo with a pure white coat. And then once again came the B–29s raining incendiaries and explosives all over the white snow. Fires and detonations caused great clouds of snow to rise and fall again, blackened. For two days snow and bomb damage had nearly paralyzed the city, but the people stoically went back to work, got the trains running again, opened the shops. Schoolkids walked by in formation, as always, mothers wheeled tots, peddlers appeared selling their noodles, sweet potatoes and pancakes. There had been serious damage to some districts, though, especially Kanda, near my old university, but according to my father, "The people at the palace say these raids are a sign of American desperation." What ridiculous rationalization, but I believe he believed it, and maybe they did too, or at least some of them.

That had all been five days ago.

Now on this morning of March 9 I heard once again the deadly drone of the big planes, saw flickering lights in the distance, heard bombs exploding.

But there was something else, something new.

There was the wind. It was an unnaturally warm night, coming so soon after a February snowfall. And with the abruptly milder weather a wind was rising. The sky was clouded and starless. There was something like a sniff of typhoon in the air, but what frightened me was the wind—gusty, violent, knocking over trashcans and crates, sending refuse skipping down the street, slamming shutters and unlocked doors.

Standing outside my house, I saw Mr. Kurita coming up to me. He smelled of fish, as usual. A paunchy man with drooping eyes, he had lost two sons, one at sea, another on Saipan.

"Shitamachi," he said, pointing. "They are bombing it . . ."

Shitamachi? This was a downtown suburb of Tokyo on the banks of the Sumida River. At the turn of the century it had been a rich center of culture and entertainment but now it was mostly a working-class area where three quarters of a million people lived and worked in lath and clapboard wooden frame buildings. It was a densely populated part of the city, the flimsy buildings side-by-side, or at best separated by narrow alleys.

"Ah, perhaps the river will help," said Mr. Shigemasa, the kite-maker, who had just met us. "They can pump out the water . . ."

Now my mother, Julie and Yuriko walked onto the veranda. Yuriko was holding Hiroki in her arms. Julie had slung Taro—sleeping, as ever —onto her back. The women stared at the flickering lights in the distance.

To the east the sky was a sickly yellow-green, giving off pulsating waves of light, like an aurora borealis but much brighter.

Searchlights streaked the eastern sky, long fingers of light picking out the shapes of American planes. It surprised me, and others, that the bombers were flying so low, surely in the range of antiaircraft guns. But there seemed to be little firing. The battery in our park was silent. The crew was manning it, shouting orders, wheeling the muzzles of the guns around but not firing. The B–29s were out of its range.

Suddenly great cones of fire shot up from the east and the sky over Shitamachi and the Sumida River became a panorama of orange, yellow, red and gold. Flames burst upward, subsided, then appeared in another part of the horizon and I realized what was happening . . . the fierce wind was whipping the fires from place to place, leaping over rooftops, consuming whole areas, then roaring in whirling forms to another section of the city

"Oh, my God . . . all those people, " Julie said, her face white.

My mother looked, was unnaturally calm. Or frozen.

Yuriko asked about the shelters she had helped build, and a woman laughed bitterly. "Shelters? Those holes in the ground? Look, the children are filling the ditch across the street."

A dozen young boys and girls, many in night clothes, had crammed themselves into an open trench in the park. They did not seem frightened, almost as though it were a game.

I thought of my father in Shitamachi with his mistress, prayed he would be safe, but saw that the sky above the eastern part of the city was on fire. Could anyone survive that inferno?

The skies were so bright that now we could see the silvery planes clearly as they moved eerily in and out of the searchlights, passing through columns of smoke. These were no factories burning, these were thousands and thousands of paper-and-wood homes. Sirens wailed. The wind roared. Chunks of metal and wood debris clattered down the street. The kids in the trench were singing, but now I thought I could hear—it must have been an hallucination, a trick of my mind—an accumulation of pained shrieks and moans, as if every soul in the conflagration were crying out to be spared this fiery death. Of course it was my imagination . . . we were miles from the heart of the blaze. I prayed that the river would save Shitamachi. Perhaps the wind would subside. Perhaps our undermanned, ill-equipped fire fighters would somehow bring the fires under control . . .

But the Americans had planned the raid too well. The planes had come in low, and at high speed. The emphasis had been on incineration, deliberately setting raging fires in a congested area. And the wind now took up where the B–29s were leaving off. At the moment I felt anger, Japanese anger. Never mind that we were getting back what we had given, this seemed cruel and I was *there* with *my* family . . .

A fire brigade ran across the street. Pumps were set up, hoses run to the canal. There did not appear to be enough water in the canal (where the dyers washed their cloths) to put out the fire in a hibachi. Still, people shouted orders, tripped over each other, tried to extend the hoses. As yet we seemed untouched by the blaze. Perhaps we would be spared? In previous fire attacks our district hadn't suffered . . .

Old Isaku, the air raid warden, climbed upon a trash bin and called to us through a megaphone: "You know what the orders are. Each family is to defend its own home. Fill buckets. Get hoses out."

We seemed to symbolize our condition. Women, children, the elderly would now pay the price for the lunacies of the outlaws, and the revenge of the Americans . . .

I squinted east. It was getting worse. The light was much brighter, the giant bursts of flame, swirling in rising cones, much nearer to us. Evidently the fire had leaped across the Sumida River and was now engulfing parts of Bunkyo Ward. And it was traveling at a demonic pace, gorging itself on whole neighborhoods, on the wood-and-paper homes—

I snapped myself out of my trance . . . "We must pack things," I said to my mother, Julie and Yuriko.

"I cannot leave this house," my mother said quietly.

Yuriko turned on her. "Mother, *listen* to Kenji."

"Our family scrolls and the altar," I said, "clothing, cooking things. Get all our valises and *furoshikis* and fill them. I'll rig Saburo's cart to the bicycle."

As I spoke there was a violent orange burst in the northeast, a display of monstrous fireworks, long strands of bright flame shooting upward. A fuel dump or a chemical plant had probably been ignited . . .

People started to drift into the street from other areas. They were scorched, covered with soot, their clothing in shredding patches. A man in a uniform, hobbling on a crutch, went down the street carrying a child on his back, muttering to himself, not realizing that the child was a blackened corpse.

Julie gagged and ran into the house.

Yuriko started to cry, then took my mother's arm and they started carting things out.

And still people stood, and stared, and cried in a kind of paralyzed fascination as more flames shot up, more planes roared above us, more burned and dying people crowded into the street.

A blinded policeman, his clothing burned from his body, his legs a mass of black blisters, was being led by a teenage girl naked except for a blanket knotted around one shoulder.

"The plain side," the policeman said, the colloquial term for Shitamachi . . . the lowlands near the harbor were the plains—flat, packed neighborhoods of workers . . . "the plain side," he muttered, "is destroyed, thousands dead, people can't escape—"

Suddenly he crumpled, his burned legs gave out from under him, the girl began to wail.

Dr. Varnum and his wife came around the corner now, and Cora knelt promptly down and took the girl by the hand. The policeman . . . he was her father . . . was dead.

"The clinic may be safer," Dr. Varnum said, "we're putting up children and the injured. Kenji, tell those kids to get out of that damned trench and come with me."

He began to select elderly people, those who lived alone, people who had trouble walking, and began leading them to the clinic. I got most of the children to vacate the trenches . . . if the fire spread they would be roasted alive.

On the veranda Yuriko, Julie and my mother were stacking valises, cardboard boxes and *furoshikis*. Isaku saw them and wagged a finger at me. "You know the rule, Mr. Tamba. Protect your own house and *stay.* If each family puts out the fire in his house then the fire will be defeated."

The old fool probably believed what he was saying. He had had this dinned into his ears for months. His fire fighters raced back and forth with meager hoses, buckets and barrels filled with water, sandbags and wet *tatami* mats, and waited . . . they would die in place, like the soldiers on the islands.

I helped run a hose to the canal and told my mother to go to the Varnum's clinic. Julie had strapped Taro to her back (amazingly, he *still* slept). Yuriko had done likewise with a howling Hiroki.

"I will not go to the clinic," my mother said. "I will wait for your father here."

Yuriko touched her hand. "Father will be all right, mother."

We were all lying, walking around the truth. We did not even know the address of his trysting place. For him to survive would have been a miracle. We could only hope.

Julie went back into the house. Yuriko pulled Saburo's wooden cart to the front and she and my mother started stacking boxes on it and tying them down.

Suddenly as I came back from the canal I sensed that the air had grown hotter. Not a few degrees higher but truly hot—as if a blast furnace had been opened, as if I had walked past a giant oven. It was terrifying, this abrupt change from the mild March air. An unnatural heat seemed to fall from the sky. People began looking at one another, waiting, frightened by the rise in temperature, the heat that came from nowhere, unrelated to climate, some kind of demon's manipulation.

The flames and the brilliant colors in the sky were now nearer, seeming to explode in patches, sudden bursts of orange and yellow, floral displays that splotched the black night, took weird shapes, bloomed again.

At the end of our street, beyond the park with its silent antiaircraft battery, on the opposite side of the canal's wooden bridge, was a house somewhat larger than the others of our district. It was owned by a widowed merchant, Mr. Onishi, a retired tea dealer, an aloof man who never participated in local affairs and lived with two concubines, neither of them attractive. I was watching the scorched and stunned people crossing the bridge, many of them sobbing or incoherent, when the roof of the Onishi house exploded into a long sheet of flame.

Those of us in the street could only watch and draw back, our faces lighted by the wall of fire that rose up from the roof. It took only seconds for the house to collapse on itself in a wall of flames. Driven by the winds of near-typhoon strength, the wooden walls, the carved wooden doors, the thatching, the paper walls became one instant giant bonfire. The fire fighters, paralyzed for a moment, waited, then spurred on by Isaku's shouts, turned their hoses on Onishi's house. It was like trying to put out a forest fire by urinating on it.

In seconds the blaze had leaped across the bridge and consumed Mr. Kurita's fish store, the grocery shop and three small houses, one of which was the home of our mailman. On the front veranda of the Onishi house the retired merchant came stumbling out on his knees. It was impossible to help him. He was naked. He held his arms out, as though in some mute appeal, and then he too burst into flame. The air in him, his very blood, seemed to have been ignited, turned into a fiery ball and vanished in an orange sun . . . Two women, barely identifiable in the inferno, staggered as far as the veranda and then they too were consumed. The fire, spreading from the roof downward to earth and then driven by the wind, seemed to burn their feet and legs first, soar upward and devour them in ravenous gulps. They did not have time to scream.

I ran to my house. Julie was hugging Taro to her breast. Yuriko came running out with a small vanity case—her beloved cosmetics. My mother was the calmest of all. She had carefully stacked the Buddhist altar, the scrolls that were changed each season in the *tokonama,* boxes of jewelry, her bridal kimono, my father's clothing, cooking utensils on top of the cart. Above them all she placed the framed photograph of the emperor.

"Masao . . ." she said. "We should find him—"

It was no time for speeches, but to look for my brother now would mean we would all surely die. Masao lived a mile away, where our ward adjoined Minato. He was no safer than we were. It would be suicidal to look for him now. I looked at my mother—her scored face, the strands of gray hair falling to one side—being tested to the limit, and I was ashamed that I had so little to offer her . . .

"I think we must leave," was all I said.

"To where?" asked Julie.

"Away from the fires, they're burning to the east and the northeast. It could be the bomb that set off the Onishi house was a stray. If we're lucky and we move toward Shinjuku, to one of the parks, we may be safe for the night. Then we can return if—"

The alley along the canal, the street of craftsmen where Julie had bought a kite for our son, suddenly went up in flames. Again there was that incredible vault from one burning patch to a new site. I turned away, got on the bike.

"Hold the cart steady," I said. "I'll pedal as long as I can. Julie and Yuriko, push behind me."

My wife's face was streaked with soot. She came to me and kissed me. "I'm sorry . . ." she said.

"Julie, you once told me I didn't bomb Hawaii. So I'll tell you now— this is not your doing."

I pedaled off then, legs straining, lungs aching from smoke and the deathly hot air that hovered all over the city. Taro was strapped to my back. I cradled Hiroki in my arms.

Julie and Yuriko pushed the cart as we moved uphill and away from the wind-lashed inferno. The fire fed on itself, forming great swirling columns, relentless, pitiless.

We passed people roasted alive in the "shelters" the government had guaranteed would save their lives. The serpentine canal that wound through our quarters was choked with bodies, people boiled alive or asphyxiated by smoke and burning air.

We finally came to a Shinto shrine where people had sought the protection of the gods under a long wooden roof. It had been a vain appeal to the deities—the flaming boards had collapsed on their heads and left scores of them dead under the wreckage.

Many had given up. Who could blame them? They could walk no more, they could breathe no more. They squatted in doorways, lay on street corners, mothers huddling to protect children, and waited for the fire.

The horror was too great for tears. We found ourselves numbed, concentrated only on survival. My legs were semiparalyzed as I kept pedaling to get to higher ground to save my wife, my sister, my mother and the children. I didn't have time to think of my father or Masao. Saburo was in Kyushu at his training camp, he would learn about the firestorm. No doubt it would harden his determination to die for his country. Death bred death. The Americans were teaching us that they could be more than our equals. We were being paid in kind for Pearl Harbor, Bataan, Singapore, Hong Kong, Nanking—and the interest had been compounded.

At about five in the morning the all-clear wailed. To my astonishment some people were leaving their homes, going to early jobs, carrying briefcases and *bento* lunch boxes. At the edge of Shinjuku we came to a community of squatters and refugees, a junkyard that seemed to be under the rule of some kind of criminal group—rough-looking hoodlums wearing red headbands, some consortium of the underworld, draft evaders, pimps, thieves . . . the scum always seem to survive.

From a high point, where we had paused to catch our breath, I could see the eastern sections of the city burning. The flames were over everything now, an immense flickering orange-yellow blanket, burning low on the horizon, sending up bursts of black smoke, obscuring the dawn, turning the sky rose-red. The wind was somewhat less frenzied, perhaps the fire would finally be contained . . .

The *yakuza* who ran this squatter city demanded money from me as rental, and I gave it, but I also let them know I was connected to the palace and the army—it was the only way to keep my family from being molested. The sight of Julie's fair, if sooty, face excited and confused them. I especially worried for her.

"Well," Julie said, "it seems the hideous *gaijin* has done it again." Even at a time like this she could joke. Faced with disaster, we become stoic and calm. Americans tend to joke, to minimize tragedies. I don't know which approach is better, but right now I thought Julie's was. She was every bit the woman I'd thought she was . . . and whatever trouble there had been between us had, I felt, literally gone up in smoke this night.

What we had "rented" was a rusting wreck of a boxcar on a weed-choked railroad siding at one end of the filthy muddy village of refugees, drifters, honey-bucket collectors and beggars.

We unpacked our possessions, my mother spread *tatami* mats inside the boxcar and she and Yuriko rigged a primitive fireplace outside the boxcar, suspended a pot on a metal hook. Yuriko then went off to find water. No matter what disasters befell us, we would have our tea and rice, it seemed.

Refugees kept wandering in, falling on the spot and refusing to move another step. No police official appeared, no ambulance, no city official, no one but the victims now homeless.

Inside, Julie was kneeling on a mat, changing the children's diapers. I went to her and kissed her neck. She took hold of my hand and squeezed. In the midst of all this we understood how much we needed one another. It's true . . . more than lust validates a marriage. Tonight we especially understood that. And I thought with shame of my angry transgression. And tried to shut it out of my mind . . .

"I'll go back to the street, maybe our house was saved," I said with more hope than I felt.

Julie only looked up briefly, nodded. I knew, though, that she felt my own doubts, and wouldn't show it.

"I must find Masao. We'll look for my father . . . that's my first duty . . . You'll be safe here, I'll bribe those *yakuza* . . . and I think they're duly impressed by my connections. They may be thieves but they're still afraid of the emperor and the army—"

"Kenji, please, stay awhile. You can't get into the eastern part of the city for another day anyway."

I looked to the east and knew she was right, then began to unpack our belongings. *Futons,* cushions, pots, a tea kettle. We had a little money and the women's jewelry. I worried about Yuriko, she was so pretty and young, and widowed, and the thugs who ran the camp had eyed her lewdly. Julie they were a little in awe of, uneasy with. But Yuriko . . .

When she came back with a pail of water, struggling through the mud, her face covered with ashes, I talked to her.

"I am not afraid, brother," she said firmly. "I have lived some myself, you know. Don't worry about me."

"You are Masao's sister, I see."

She smiled. "No, more like you, Kenji. I won't look for trouble, but I won't run if it comes. I'm ready . . ."

She opened her tattered coat and showed me a five-inch dagger in her belt. "Those *yakuza* do not frighten me."

We would go on. It seemed the Tambas of Shibuya Ward were still a family.

JULIE TAMBA · MARCH, 1945

Taro held my hand and walked beside me. With a child's resilience, he seemed unaffected by the new and primitive surroundings. He was chunky, athletic, curious, as handsome as his father, and eternally cheerful. I squeezed Taro's hand, lifted him and kissed his cheek.

"Daddy come home?" he asked.

"Yes, pumpkin, soon." Kenji had finally insisted on going back and looking for our house, trying to get food for us.

Outside the boxcar Hisako was patching together a *futon* cover, stuffing it with rags, sacks, cotton batting, anything she could salvage. It was a cold March, and if the old house had been chilly, the freight car promised to be a refrigerator.

I squatted next to my mother-in-law in true Japanese style, picked up a section of the ripped cloth, found a needle and thread in her sewing basket and began to work on the other end of the coverlet.

"A woman is selling old curtains near the gate," Hisako said. "Perhaps we can trade for them. We can use them to stuff the *futons.*"

I told her I would trade anything I had. Jewelry I certainly didn't need.

"No, save that, it's valuable, we may need food," Hisako said quickly.

"I have other things I took from the house, I'll get rid of them . . . underclothing, extra sandals."

She sighed. She had seemed to have aged ten years in the last two days. She bit at a thread, knotted the ends, rethreaded the needle, sewed swiftly and expertly. My stitches were a crazy quilt compared to hers.

Taro and Hiroki found a rusty tin can and began to beat on it with sticks, chanting a nonsense rhyme about "Monkeys in a tree, can't see me."

Hisako looked at them, and was able to smile.

Yuriko lowered herself from the car. She had put on lipstick and washed away the soot. "I'm going to the city—"

"Too dangerous," Hisako said. "Wait . . ."

"I can't wait." She did not add she wanted to look for Hans. She didn't need to.

As she walked away, Hisako frowned and said, "I don't like what I hear about this man I know she is going to see. He is a *gaijin*—" She looked at me with a quick smile. "Well, you are a good *gaijin,* and a brave person, Julie. There is much sorrow in my life, but I am glad that Kenji has a good wife, and that you have given him a good son. You are courageous to accept our suffering."

We had both come a long way in first tolerating, then understanding and even having respect and affection for each other. I was grateful for her kindness. Maybe we'd cross the bridge all the way someday. One thing was for sure, at long last, united in homelessness and maybe starvation, Hisako and I were finding a true common ground. East and West were coming closer in the Tamba family.

MASAO TAMBA · MARCH, 1945

My home, and Colonel Sato's which adjoins it, was not much affected by the firebombing of March 9.

We were in an enclave of parks and open spaces that act as firebreaks. People streamed by our street, some falling as they walked, others seeking water, grass, anything to ease the pain of their burns. Michiko offered them water, running to them with pails and a tin cup.

Colonel Sato came by to tell me he was, finally, disturbed by reports he had gotten from the military offices. It was now estimated that 100,000 people were dead and numberless thousands wounded and homeless. Sixteen square miles of Tokyo had been incinerated. Almost forty percent of the populated areas of the city had been ablaze. Of the great buildings of Tokyo only a handful were left intact—the Imperial palace, Radio Tokyo, Dai Ichi and San Shin—there was some method in the Americans' madness . . . did they really believe they could invade and conquer us? Did they believe these great structures would wait for them . . . ?

"Many are leaving the city," Sato interrupted my thoughts. "And not only because they are homeless. They are afraid of new fire bombings, but they also fear something else . . . an American invasion."

I looked hard at him. Had he read my thoughts?

"It seems not everyone is willing to die for Tenno Heika." His voice was low and serious. So was mine when I said that it seemed we hadn't done our job as well as we should have. And once again I felt the tremors in my gut. Yes, I should have died on Guadalcanal, on Saipan . . .

"The Americans receive credit for this," Sato said quietly, shaking his head. "They have set out to break our spirit. Low-flying planes, firebombs, choosing a night when the wind was fierce. A well-planned exercise. And they will do it again. Not only Tokyo but our other cities too . . ."

"Then perhaps those who speak of peace . . . ?"

"I did not mean that, major. Death will, in the end, make us stronger. The bombings will fail, the invasion will fail if we all make clear that we are prepared. Only then will they be convinced they can't win."

Privately I had trouble believing this . . . did the colonel, or was he now speaking the new official line . . . ?

He ordered his car brought around, and we made our way through debris-littered streets, past burned bodies, lost children, people wandering about as if in a daze, to Shibuya Ward.

As we crossed the bridge over the canal I could see that the street of craftsmen was now a row of charred timbers. Not a shop was standing. One of the few buildings in the neighborhood to survive was Dr. Varnum's clinic, and in front of it some thirty people waited quietly for medical attention.

I saw Cora Varnum, carrying two infants in her arms, come out of the stucco building and talk to some women crying, and I wondered if the children were dead.

Colonel Sato said, "Those people are a problem."

"She is a neutral," I said. "And she and her husband do much good for the people. They have for years."

"He may be a spy."

It seemed idiotic for us to be pondering such matters. Our city was being committed to the torch and we were discussing whether Adam Varnum might be a spy. I suppose it kept our minds away from certain unpleasant facts.

My parents' home, where I was born and raised, no longer stood. A huge black-gray square now existed where once there had been a street of pleasant wooden dwellings. Across the way the big Onishi house, the tea merchant's, was a ghostly shell. But at least several stout wooden pillars were standing.

As Sato and I got out of the the car Kenji came up to us wheeling his bike. Pale and sweaty, he halted and bowed to us, then turned and stared at the charred ruins. He said nothing but his eyes were blazing with anger —directed at Colonel Sato.

I asked about the family, especially our mother, and he filled me in on the grim circumstances.

"Does His Majesty know the extent of suffering of his people, colonel?" Kenji asked, looking directly at the colonel.

"He prays for them, he feels their pain. But we do him an injustice if we linger over these setbacks—"

"A city burned, tens of thousands dead . . . setbacks?"

Kenji's face was as tight and angry as I had ever seen it and I had a terrible fear he was going to attack the colonel. My brother might be a peaceful man, but also a man of strong feelings, and he was extremely strong. I'd never told anyone, but more than once he could get the best of me in a fair fight. He just tended to lack concentration, would grow bored and walk away just as he was getting the best of me. But if sufficiently aroused, as now . . . ? His only words were to me now, saying we must find our father.

"In Shitamachi? But it's still smoldering—"

"If you won't go with me I'll go myself," he said.

He was a brave man, my peace-loving brother. Had our ages been reversed perhaps he would have been the warrior and I the scholar? I wondered . . . ?

"I will go with you," I said quickly.

Sato offered us his car. There were staff meetings all day, he said. We would drop him at headquarters and then go on to Shitamachi. Moreover, he knew the address where our father had his assignations with Fumiko. Kingoro Hata owned the building and had set the maid up there. Sato scrawled the address for us and we drove off.

"The Kitanos are dead," Kenji said flatly.

"Hideo's parents? How do you know?"

"I went past their home this morning. An ash heap. They were burned to cinders. Mr. Kitano had stored kerosene in the house. It destroyed the whole block . . ."

I insisted on driving. Even with my metal hook I handled a car well and had been practicing *kendo* for a year, using the prosthetic arm as I once did my left arm.

We drove through streets still smoldering, great heaps of cinders, charred building posts, burnt cooking pots, the remnants of vehicles, toys, street signs. People wandered about in a daze, poking in piles of ashes. I had seen my share of death. I had lived through Guadalcanal and Saipan. But now as we approached the Sumida River I saw sights that broke my heart. The dead choked the canals, jammed the watery passages under the bridges. Several steel spans had collapsed. People must have crowded on them for safety, caught between hell and the high water. Leaping from the spans, they fell into the boiling river and were drowned.

Ambulances and army trucks were parked along the banks. Rescue teams were pulling corpses from the Sumida River and the canals, stacking them, trying to make identifications. With the help of a police officer, who bowed when he saw my rank . . . did I still deserve such respect? . . . we found our way to a residential district at the western edge of Shitamachi. Nothing. A cindery, smoking refuse heap.

We could go no further with the car. Kenji and I got out and followed the policeman. Tokyo, of course, had no street numbering system, no sequence, no proper street names. Homes are referred to randomly and a description of some kind is needed to locate them. Even cab drivers have problems, and usually a half-dozen questions must be asked before a dwelling is located.

Fortunately we found an old man hobbling on a cane who recognized the description of the house. Yes, it was one of six houses owned by a rich man in Parliament . . . Mr. Hata?

I nodded. "Show us this house."

He also said yes, he did know of a woman named Fumiko Yamaguchi, a lady who worked at the palace. She was a friend of one of his neighbors . . .

Kenji and I only looked at each other.

The old man limped down a side street, picking his way past charred bodies, dead animals, the wreckage of wood-and-paper houses—and halted at a square of blackened earth. There was nothing but hot ashes.

"The house of Miss Fumiko."

I gave him some coins and thanked him. I told the policeman we did not need his services.

My brother and I stared at the pile of ashes. This had been my father's trysting place. Here he had come to fulfill his needs, to enhance his self-respect.

Kenji turned to me. "There is nothing . . ."

"The swirling fire must have struck right here and spread." Not a spoon, not a cup, not a woman's comb or a bit of jewelry . . . Had my father and his mistress been ignited in the midst of their passion? Perhaps a shocking, to some obscene, thought . . . but it seemed to me a better way to die than most others. I would keep such thoughts to myself . . . I am sure Kenji would not have appreciated them.

"Can we be sure this is the house?" Kenji was asking.

The old fellow on the cane, eavesdropping a few meters away, nodded vigorously.

In the ruins of the street Kenji found a metal tea tin. It had no lid, was charred to blackness. "For mother," he said quietly. "We will fill it with ashes from this place. Some of them are father's. She will appreciate it. We will buy a porcelain urn and place the ashes in it and keep it in the *tokonama.*"

Then he did what I could not . . . knelt, dug his hands into the warm ashes and came up with something—a bronze ring.

"The household minister gave them to all members of the staff on Tenno Heika's fortieth birthday," Kenji said. "It proves that this was the house. We will put the ring in the ashes . . . And we will always have his memory. Do you remember, Masao, when he took us to the baseball game one day? He didn't understand a thing that was happening but he was glad to see us having a good time."

"I remember." And I suddenly remembered a great deal about my father, and fought back unmanly tears. He had always favored me, indulged me, given me anything I wanted. I was the king of the Tamba house, the eldest son . . .

"I want to pray," Kenji said.

We knelt in the ashes, clasped our hands, bowed our heads and prayed for the eternal rest of our father's soul.

Kenji carried the tea tin with our father's ashes as we walked back to the car, and I drove us past more scenes of desolation. We were still silent as we reached the edge of the great circle of fire in Minato Ward, where the palace grounds, with their sloping Cyclopean walls, bridges and turrets looked unharmed, secure and eternal.

All of us will have to die, I thought.

YURIKO KITANO · MARCH, 1945

We held our father's funeral in Masao's house.

It would have disgraced his memory, we all felt, to mourn for him in the confines of that rusting freight car we had been living in.

Dr. Adam Varnum invited us to stay at the clinic but my mother and Kenji would not hear of it. It would be too great an insult to our honor as a family. So about a week after the fire we gathered at Masao's house to pay honor to our father. It was a week during which the American planes came again and again, dropping firebombs on Nagoya, Osaka and Kobe. Our air force seemed to have disappeared, our antiaircraft was helpless. And yet except for Kenji and Julie I don't think I heard anybody say they wished the war would end. They *wanted* it to end, but didn't dare to say so. Me included.

Only one good thing . . . well, partly good . . . came out of the great firebombing of March 9. My factory was destroyed. It burned for an entire night, but three of my girlfriends working the nightshift died in it. Worse, one was Midori, the girl who had introduced me to Hans. I was told they never found her body. Apparently Umezu, the old foreman who used to pull down our *mompei* bloomers in the *benjo* while he claimed he was looking for stolen items, had bolted the door of the factory when the sirens went off. He didn't take the warning seriously and was afraid the girls would use the sirens as an excuse not to work. He and so many others paid for his stupidity. It was terribly sad, but with so many disasters it was hard to cry anymore.

At Masao's house we sat in two rows facing one another on either side of the altar. Next to the family stela was a photograph of my father in his palace uniform. The frame was draped with black. He was younger when the picture was taken, had more hair, an unlined face and the same gentle eyes. There was also a pale blue porcelain urn containing his ashes.

Masao, heir to the Tamba name, prayed first, kneeling in front of the altar and bowing his head to the floor. Then he looked at my father's photograph and said, "Great Buddha, protect the soul of our father, Goro Tamba, on his journey to everlasting life, to his reunion with his ancestors and with the gods."

Kenji whispered to me: "Eldest brother mixes up his Shinto and his Buddhism." Kenji knew everything.

"Why?"

"Shinto says that death leads to the world of the *kami,* where mortals and gods live together. Buddhists say death is just part of a path and we encounter it many times. The final goal is Buddhahood and deliverance."

Kenji, the irrepressible scholar, even at our father's last rites.

Julie got sick during the ceremony and went out to the *benjo*. Who could blame her?

All the men, including Kenji and some of my father's colleagues from the imperial household staff, got drunk and told stories about my father. The deputy imperial household minister sent a wreath of white chrysanthemums. Farewell, Goro Tamba, and I wished I could have felt more about his death than I did . . .

JULIE TAMBA · APRIL, 1945

Kenji, Taro and I were still in that damned boxcar. Yuriko and Hiroki went to stay with Masao and Michiko, where they had a tiny room. Masao, now the head of the family, had to look after his sister and his brothers.

Of course he had never had much to say to me and his relationship with Kenji was still sort of strained, I thought. Sometimes it seemed that even though he was a war hero he envied Kenji . . . his mind, his frankness, his willingness to challenge the conventional wisdom.

Masao and Kingoro Hata scouted about to find a new home for us but it was just about impossible, people were doubling up, living ten and twelve in houses built for four and five.

It was April now, the cherry blossoms were beginning to bloom in the park . . . it was a relief to look at them, made me feel as though there was still *some* beauty that just couldn't be burned or bombed . . .

Luckily Kenji was still able to bike to his office, working long hours, bargaining for food, trying to help us make our boxcar livable until someone found a home for us, and one day he told me that the Americans had invaded a large island very close to Japan, a place called Okinawa.

"I think it means that they plan to invade Japan," he said too quietly as we sat with Taro at a low table eating some rice and *tofu*—fish had all but vanished from the markets. Hisako was dozing in a corner of the car.

"Won't Japan surrender now . . . ?"

He shook his head, then told me about the *kamikaze* attacks on the American navy, and how these suicide bombing missions by Japanese pilots were taking a terrible toll on the U.S. fleet. Tokyo's radio's claims were exaggerated, Kenji said, but there was no doubt that these human bombs were in the process of destroying the American navy around Okinawa.

"I think Saburo is with the force attacking the American navy off Okinawa," Kenji said, barely getting out the words. "He telephoned Masao a few nights ago and said he was at an airbase in Kyushu. I'm afraid to tell my mother, I don't think she can stand much more. Last night she said she saw my father's ghost . . . it had no feet, it came at two in the morning, she said, when the grasses were asleep—that's an old peasant tradition. She said the spirits of the dead appear at streams, and she was at the water spigot when she saw him and that when the festival of Bon comes in July she wants us to take Goro's ghost to a better house than this." He looked at me and tried to smile.

"She's right," I said, "it isn't fit for a ghost. I'm sorry, darling, a lousy joke, but I'm afraid your mother isn't the only one who's getting sort of looney." And now I tried to smile brightly, fooling nobody . . .

I began staining a few days later and went to see Aunt Cora, and right there while I was on the table I miscarried.

I cried in Aunt Cora's arms for a long time, and was only grateful that I hadn't told Kenji I was pregnant. He had his limits of endurance too, and I'd not been really sure at first—with all the bombing it didn't seem unnatural that nature would shut down normal body functions too. Then when I knew, it just seemed a little crazy in the midst of all Kenji had to put up with. Still, I *wanted* this baby, and I hated losing it.

"You'll have other children," Cora said, hugging me. "The fire, the way you have to live now, it takes its toll . . ."

Yes, on everybody, it seemed, but Cora and Adam. God knew where they got their strength, I thought, as I got dressed. Dressed? I was down to underpants full of holes, bras that were tied with a string, a faded kimono patched and repatched. I'd sure gone native—another dumb bit of forced humor, I told myself. And yet I needed it if I was going to survive.

Uncle Adam, puffing on a cigar—he was still getting his supply—came in and suggested I spend the night at the clinic, but I told him I really couldn't. He asked about our "new home" and I told him the Toonerville Trolley had nothing on it. He smiled at the memory of the comic strip, and Cora then said I could move in with them, that "our offer stands."

"I've thought of it," I admitted, "but it wouldn't be fair to Kenji. Or you, for that matter."

Sitting in the garden, looking in the yard across from the Varnums' at a cherry tree in bloom, Uncle Adam spoke without looking at me. "Julie, we're worried about you, and Taro and . . . well, Cora and I have made our lives here. Really, it's our home. But you . . ."

"Are you saying I should leave? You've mentioned it before, and I admit I've thought of it—"

"There's nothing to be ashamed of. You could get home, wait for the war to end, then be reunited with Kenji—"

"It would be wrong," I said. "Besides, I happen to want to save our marriage. What would be left if I ran off now?"

"You love him?" my uncle asked.

I bit my lip. There had been times when I wasn't so sure, and we'd had that awful stretch when we weren't even sleeping with each other. But yes, I did love him, and my child. I admired his mother . . . and I wasn't a quitter . . .

Adam was pacing in the garden, snapping dry twigs from bushes, nodding to the women in the adjoining yard. "Julie, forget it—I think it's me who's the problem. I'm feeling old these days. Lately I've even been forgetting the names of some of my patients, or what disease they have."

Cora was having none of this. "Did it ever occur to you, *old* man, that with all the different people we see you'd need six secretaries to keep names and symptoms straight? Stop depressing Julie, for God's sake. She's got enough real trouble without your imagined ones . . . but, Julie, just keep this in mind. We get rations from the consul, you must let us share them. And if you do change your mind, let us know. There's a Swedish ship sailing for the Soviet Union in two weeks. Neutrals are routinely taken to Vladivostok. Maybe we could make some arrangement for you. But I'm not urging or even encouraging. What you and Kenji have is pretty special . . ."

I got up to leave, thanked them, and said nothing more. What could I say? Of course I wanted to go home. Of course I couldn't.

MASAO TAMBA · MAY, 1945

This morning the postman brought me a letter from my brother Saburo that had a lock of his hair and an account of his training and his mission.

I was now the head of the family and Saburo was obliged to account to me. I was proud of him. Weak, spindly, always subject to diseases as a child, bullied by his schoolmates, he had turned into a brave young man, perhaps about to become a true hero.

I stroked the fine black hairs, pressed them to my cheek then returned them to the envelope. They would be part of our family heritage. But did I feel nothing else with this pride? I knew I did, and it was fear for my little brother—an inglorious thought not to be made public.

When Colonel Sato and Kingoro Hata visited me that night I read parts of the letter to them as Michiko and our maid Reiko scurried in and out, waiting on them, and my wife looked on and listened.

> Training has ended for me, honored brother. Now I am ready to play my role in winning the war. I have accepted the kicks, slaps and beatings from my instructors. How else prepare for death? I have been taught disregard for my own life. The mission is simple. Enemy vessels at anchor or underway will be destroyed by collision. Thus they cannot sustain their attacks, their numbers will decrease, the war will be won. We have been told we are the spirit of Japan, land of the gods. My squadron commander says that a man's life is lighter than a feather, and our mission is heavier than Mount Fuji. I have received the white silk cloth to wrap around my head, and on it is a poem I want to send you now so that it will be printed on a scroll for the *tokonama.*

The colonel and Hata raised their sake cups to Saburo. I read the poem:

> Isles of blest Japan!
> Should your *Yamato* spirit
> Strangers seek to scan,
> Say, scenting morn's unlit air,
> Blows the cherry, wild and fair!

Hata emptied his nose into a silk handkerchief, Michiko was sniffling in a corner of the room, holding our daughter Maeko close to her.

"That is what makes us invincible," my father-in-law said. He switched to whiskey, drained a cup. I saw his face redden, his eyes bulge. Lately he had become more of a drunkard and somewhat irrational. He kept forgetting names, places, went on about the odd eating habits the people had developed. Butter, he said, was being made from silkworms. People were learning to boil grass, fry locusts and there was even a man in Osaka who was finding a way to make flour out of earth.

Hata declared, "Yes, even though many die, Japan will live on."

My father-in-law and I understood that Hata and his mistress Satomi had every intention of living on. They were buying up land as fast as they could, speculating in foreign currencies, hoarding valuables, cheating the government with adulterated cloth and boots made of cardboard.

"Live on?" boomed Sato. "Live on? You shit-eating toad, you're the one who will live on after kids like Saburo die for you—"

"I am ready to die also, colonel," Hata said with a disgusting show of sincerity.

"*You* are a fat bastard," Sato snapped at him, "and a damned traitor."

The colonel waddled across the floor and threw himself at Hata, trying to strangle him. Michiko screamed but I reassured her—the men were too fat, too old and too drunk to do any harm.

"Traitor, liar, schemer . . ." Sato was spewing. He had his hands on Hata's neck, but it was a fat thick neck and it resisted Sato's best attempts at strangulation.

"Dear husband, perhaps the honorable deputy should leave."

It was the first outright suggestion about guests (or almost anything else) that she had ever made to me, and I was surprised and glad to hear it. I'd had enough myself. I also felt a new affection for Michiko. Now that I hadn't the ability to enter other women, *or* my wife, I felt more kindly to her, perhaps because the old master-slave relationship no longer made sense with a master whose sexual capacity was only a memory.

"Yes, Mr. Hata," I said, "this was an unfortunate affair—"

"I meant no insult to your brother, we honor those who die."

He got up and Reiko helped him straighten his clothing. He belched, then rambled on about the glorious death of Japanese civilians on Okinawa, whole farm families dispatched with hatchets and hoes and clubs by their fathers to keep them from the Americans. After all, Hata said, it was well-known that the Americans would rape women, burn babies, and so the acts of suicide and murder were noble and elevating. I was finding myself getting sick in my guts . . .

Michiko helped her father to his feet. He and Hata bowed at each other, the battle of the *tatami* mats already forgotten. I was ashamed of both of them. The letter from Saburo in my hand was a reproach to such behavior, and I felt oddly detached from them, from everything, like Saburo aiming his bomb-laden plane at an aircraft carrier . . . ?

A few days later the colonel brought some encouraging news about Okinawa and asked me to go to the Sengakuji shrine with him, where our forty-seven *ronin,* the masterless *samurai* warriors who avenged their *daimyo's* murder and then committed suicide, are buried.

It was a clear May morning. We had just gotten news of Germany's surrender—May 7. We also had a new prime minister, an old admiral named Suzuki, who was deaf and feeble. He was a slender reed acceptable to both the military and the peace faction, all believing he could be manipulated.

Michiko and Maeko came with us. My daughter, something of a tomboy, had a kite with her, a red-and-gold butterfly, and she kept asking me to fly it for her.

"Do not bother daddy," Michiko said.

"Fly kite now."

"In a while, Maeko," I told her.

Colonel Sato and I walked ahead of them toward the stone shrine. A few people prayed in front of the urns. It was easy to understand their need for renewed confidence from old heroes. Tokyo had been bombed again and again, those damnable fire raids, low-flying planes unloosing tons of jellied gasoline and igniting the city.

We spoke of many things—or rather Sato did—the success of the *kamikaze* pilots, the crippling of the American fleet, the defeat of Germany, the new government.

"We can expect a lot of belly talk from old Suzuki," said the colonel. "Publicly he'll blather that the war must go on, pressing ahead for victory, but I don't trust him. He will also work secretly for peace. He's told the foreign minister that he has a free hand. I don't like that."

I said nothing. People made way for us. Sato and I were bedecked with medals, braid, ribbons. Many bowed—but some turned away.

"Whenever I'm at Sengakuji, my faith is restored," Sato said ponderously. "How can a people like ours be beaten?"

I didn't tell him. Behind me I could hear Maeko complaining to her mother for not being able to put the kite together, and Michiko was telling the child to wait for her father to do it. Heroes, after all, do have their place.

"Yes, we can break their backs on Okinawa," Sato was saying. "Every day the news is better."

I said that although their navy was suffering losses, they did seem to be winning on land.

"Ah, but they will be isolated, without ships to protect them. That is when we counterattack and wipe them out."

"Perhaps."

Sato stared at me. His eyes were red-rimmed and thick-lidded. He'd become a very heavy drinker, much more than a nighttime tippler. He looked bloated and dissipated.

"Masao, my son, even if our soldiers die, what better way to show our love for the emperor?"

Except, of course, mostly what he was showing these days was his huge belly . . . We talked about the sinking of the battleship *Yamato* off Kyushu. The world's heaviest warship, with the hugest guns ever put aboard a vessel, was supposed to be unsinkable and in a final grand gesture, it had been dispatched to rescue our men on Okinawa. She didn't get far. Struck by aerial bombs and torpedoes, *Yamato* exploded in a geyser of flame and sank in half an hour.

"A glorious way to die," Sato said.

"And the battleship *Musashi* is also gone," I said. "And *Mutsu.*"

"The navy is betraying us. I never trusted those stiff-necked admirals. We have done our job. Why have they failed in theirs?"

I thought of the way I had once listened to him, followed him in supporting the mutiny of 1936, listened to him and those like him plot murders and make threats. I had watched him operate behind the scenes, twisting the minds of his superiors, always assuming that he and he alone knew His Majesty's thoughts. Now I not only wondered if he was ever right—I questioned whether he was ever sane.

Around us worshipers gathered in front of the tomb of the forty-seven, paying reverence to that act of loyalty that so moved our Japanese hearts. Women in gray kimonos and men in khaki wartime garb burned incense and prayed.

"Yes, the *ronin,*" Sato said. "What better model for us? Loyalty. Dedication. The path is chosen and one proceeds, no matter what the dangers, no matter what hardships. Is that not the story of this war? And do we not fulfill our duty to the world by following that path to its end?"

"What is the end, colonel?"

"If it be death, we accept it."

I turned away from him. Colonel Sato had me in his debt for much of my career, but I could no longer swallow his blatherings. If he had been a field officer and fought and bled alongside his men . . . but as it was I could not stand with him at the Sengakuji and contemplate the destruction of Japan.

I saw Michiko trying to get the butterfly kite aloft for Maeko. She was clumsy and constricted in her kimono and *geta* sandals, tripping, letting the kite bounce erratically along the ground, not able to run fast enough to let it catch the wind and rise.

"Excuse me," I said to Sato, "I promised Maeko . . ."

"Of course." But he trudged after me, not yet finished with schemes, plots and counterplots. As I would learn . . .

I went to Michiko and took the wooden spool, unraveled a few meters of cord and jerked the line. I was always good at flying kites. How long ago that seemed . . . I had this happy vision of Kenji and myself as teenagers with Saburo, a squirt in short pants running after us, racing to see who would get his kite aloft first, and my mother and Yuriko spreading a picnic lunch in Ueno Park under a willow tree, and my father resting against the tree reading the *Asahi Shimbun.* I remembered that Kenji and his wife had bought a new kite for their son Taro but that it had been burned in the fire—

"Daddy, daddy, it's *up,*" cried Maeko.

An odd sight I was, in uniform and glistening boots, patched eye, metal arm as I ran across the meadow and maneuvered the red butterfly into the sky. Michiko clapped her hands and laughed, and Maeko toddled after me, her eyes alight with joy.

I did not want her to die.

YURIKO KITANO · MAY, 1945

Hans had gone off again on one of his trips. Since he had no telephone, I had to take my chances visiting him. And since I no longer had a job . . . the factory destroyed by fire . . . I had much free time to wander about looking for food, trying to find a new place for us to live.

I found him at home one warm day at the end of May, a few days after we heard that firebombs had actually fallen on the emperor's palace. Kenji had found out about the damage even though it was never mentioned on the radio or in the papers. The Imperial family, Kenji said, were living underground in rooms like fortresses. It seemed hard to believe that Tenno Heika could be as vulnerable as the rest of us.

Hans's apartment had been damaged by the air raids, but was still livable . . . and two people who felt like we did about each other could make love just about anywhere. Look at Julie and Kenji . . .

We had come together, clutching at one another, nearly tearing each other's clothes off—very un-Japanese, you might say, but you would be wrong. In bed a Japanese woman is still a woman, regardless of our storied romances and artificial prints. We were in bed immediately, snuggling under the threadbare *futons* on the familiar sagging bed, merging our flesh as if desperate to rediscover each other, and afraid we might never have another opportunity.

After that first explosive coming together, we repeated the loving act, Hans moving me, changing my position, kissing me, kissing every part of me . . . And then I was doing the same for him. And all without shame or restraint, which came out of our feelings for each other, not from any upbringing or differences in cultures. As I suspected Kenji and Julie had also discovered, a man and a woman who deeply cared for each other could come from different planets and it would make no difference.

Afterward we lay together, breathing heavily at first, then our breath slowing, feeling sated, unbelievably at peace, and then Hans told me something of how his work was going, and how when the war ended we would be together. I didn't press him too much about details . . . but in the evening he did allow me to see him develop photographs, and told me that he had been to Yokohama and had taken pictures of the devastation on the docks. He said that no more than about fifteen percent of our biggest port was usable now, that the rest was a smoking ash heap, and he wondered how Japan could keep on fighting . . . or if it would . . .

"What will you do with the pictures?" I asked him, finding it hard to speak at all as he was kissing my neck, my ears, exciting me again. And I would not let him off so easily, beginning to stroke his legs, which I loved, so smooth and covered with a golden fuzz . . .

"I'm taking them to some friends tonight," was all he would say, and I knew there was no point in pressing him, that his position was as it had been before, that to let me know too many of the details of what he was doing would only jeopardize me. And so we proceeded to communicate again in the way we did best—we made love, and got into the wooden tub, and then later I made some *miso* and we sipped the strong brandy that Hans had gotten from friends at the consulate. They were very upset, Hans said, that Germany had surrendered and had no idea what their status would be—which didn't bother either of us. I had no love for any German but Hans, and he hated the Nazi regime. He felt defeat was the beginning of a better Germany, and thought the United States might be playing an important role in that. I didn't quite follow how or why, and he didn't go into details, but I did begin to wonder if perhaps Hans was not only working for the Germans opposed to Hitler but also for the Americans . . . ?

I decided that was a peculiar notion that I wasn't able to handle, and pushed it out of my mind. I wanted all my senses, all my feelings to be concentrated on the happiness that we were able to share, even if only for brief periods of time.

"You look too serious," he told me, laughed and kissed me and we nearly ended up in the floppy saggy bed again, but he said he really had to go now, and in an opposite direction from where I was staying, so we went outside and parted, reluctantly, and I stood there a while, watching his back as he moved away down the littered street, a khaki bag holding the films he had taken slung over his shoulders.

There were no lights in the street because of the raids, but there was a bright moon, what Saburo in one of his letters had called a bomber's moon. I shuddered at the thought.

What happened next is a horrid nightmare, worse than the firebombs, worse than the loss of my child—and, yes, than the death of my father. I heard raised voices. I turned. Hans, I could see, was waiting for a trolley to pass, and two men in civilian clothes had come up to him. One grabbed the bag from his shoulder, then wrapped his arm around his neck, the other man bent his arm behind his back, unslung the bag, took out the envelopes with the photographs, threw the bag to the street . . . it all happened like a movie I didn't believe, didn't want to believe . . . I started to run to Hans, but he had wrenched himself free and was himself running up the street toward an alley—shots, like toy pop-pops . . . there was a kiosk at the head of the alley, and my Hans fell there, crumpling in a heap. Still . . . dead still . . .

I heard screaming, it came again and again. And it was moments before I realized it was coming from my own throat. Windows opened, people came out of houses, went quickly back in. I ran toward Hans, saw a black car pull up and the two men were dragging Hans's body into the car. There was a third man in a policeman's cap at the wheel of the car. I called out to them to stop, and one of the men pointed his gun at me . . . "Get away, go home. You saw nothing . . ." And then the car was speeding away, taking Hans, and I felt my knees grow weak and the world begin to spin . . .

I am not clear how I managed to get back. When my thoughts finally began to come together, I thought of killing myself, adding my body to those in the Sumida River, but I must have kept running until I was back and then I was undressing and lying down beside my mother, seeking something from her that she could not give. I did not talk to anyone, not even Kenji, who came from his and Julie's side of the blanket that divided our primitive quarters to ask if I was all right. Thankfully I had Hiroki to care for, and I took him from my mother and pressed him to my breasts. He was all I had left now . . .

Somehow I forced myself to go out the next morning with Julie on one of our usual foraging expeditions to find food. My mother was getting a small pension from the Imperial household ministry that helped us buy things that had escalated in price. We walked through the black market where a farm woman was selling camotes, those big purple roots that we could boil or roast and that Julie said tasted like glue. I guess she was right, but I didn't care. I didn't care about anything, and I told Julie, after she asked me over and over what was wrong, about what had happened during the night. She was terribly upset for me, even though I didn't think she ever really approved of Hans, and asked if Masao couldn't perhaps find out something, but I told her I saw Hans shot, that I knew he was dead.

She led me to a Shinto shrine and held my hand, saying nothing, just being with me and giving me her support. I loved Julie . . .

"I want to kill myself," I told her.

"You listen to me, little sister. Don't you dare talk that way. I know how you feel . . . at least I can try to imagine . . . but you have a son, like I do, and I tell you, let those damn admirals and generals who started this thing cut their bellies open. They *deserve* it. You and I have to live, to raise our kids . . . don't you dare let me catch you even thinking about . . . well, just don't even think it."

I looked at her, wanted to hug her. This *gaijin* woman who had married my brother and chosen to share our miseries was the closest person in the world to me now . . . closer even than my son. Yes, she was right, I tried to tell myself. But more than once in the days and nights that followed . . . especially the nights . . . I looked at the dagger I had gotten to protect myself and my child, and fought back the terrible urge to use it on myself.

KENJI TAMBA · JUNE, 1945

On June 15 we moved to a tenement in Shinjuku Ward, a mile from the junkyard. Masao had managed to find it for us, once the home of a lieutenant he knew who had been killed on Iwo Jima and whose family had gone to the country to escape, they hoped, the air raids.

Saburo's latest letter came to us only a few days after we had moved into the new home. The lock of hair he had sent to Masao was meant as an omen of death, which I understood but did not tell Julie. Fortunately

—Saburo no doubt did not think so—his mission had failed. His plane went dead on the runway, and he was sent for more training.

This new letter had another lock of hair.

It seemed that Saburo could not wait to die.

We also got a letter from Julie's brother Chris that hinted that perhaps not all Japanese were so eager to die for the sun god or to take their own lives according to some ancient and outmoded precept. Chris, who had been on Okinawa, got his letter to us by way of the usual roundabout route —back to San Francisco and then via the Swiss diplomatic pouch to Cora Varnum. I had my own information about Okinawa from my work with Professor Adachi that our troops were holed up in caves and pillboxes, and told by official propaganda that the *kamikazes* would soon wipe out the American fleet—one plane, one ship was the slogan. But the 32nd Army was being killed, regardless of what the top brass said. Chris's letter, which I read in one hand on a rattling trolley car while I held Taro— protesting that he was, as usual, hungry—with the other, gave a more personal and significant perspective, I thought.

> . . . We have an official interpreter in our group, a Japanese-speaking navy officer named Dave Lewis, and he listened to some intercepts of the chatter between *kamikaze* pilots before they crashed—and I have to tell you that these guys are hurting us bad, no denying that—but what the Nips were yelling just before they bought it wasn't any of the long-live-the-emperor stuff . . . no, and you may find this hard to believe, but a lot of them were saying just what a lot of our guys say . . . *"Mother* . . ." Can you beat that? It seems that when you're about to check out it doesn't matter what your culture or background or national origin, you're a man who wants his mother . . . Who knows, maybe there's hope for us all yet . . .

After that rather sardonic but, I thought, perceptive last comment, Chris went on to say that a Japanese nurse and two of her aides had surrendered to the Americans. They'd been told by their officers that American leaflets urging surrender and promising decent treatment were lies and that they'd be tortured, but they didn't believe it and were amazed to find that not only were the leaflets right but that they were even treated like guests and that they'd been badly lied to. They were also, Chris discovered when he talked to the nurses, very bitter about the lies . . . "Some of the bastards," Chris went on—and I have to admit I still wince at the names he calls us, yes *us*—"seem to have decided it's not all that hot an idea to die for Hirohito."

> Oh, they're still killing themselves, but at a place called Oroku the Jap commander actually asked for a cease-fire, in return for which he and his men would commit suicide. We gave them the cease-fire, and he got himself an "honorable" death. God, it makes you kind of sick.

Julie and I just looked at each other, not, of course, wanting to talk about this in public, but we read each other's mind without too much trouble. She obviously agreed with her brother, and in a way I suppose I did too, but I understood what was at work with the commander, an understanding I could never expect Julie to share. It was tragic, but the whole war was tragic too . . . I felt sadness and anger all at once.

Chris finished with talk about his wife Carol back on Tinian at the base hospital there, what a great job she was doing and how proud he was of her, and also once more urged Julie to come home.

That last, of course, as always, made me feel guilty and upset. I think Chris knew it would have that effect, and to be honest, I resented him for it, even though I also realized he was sincere in his worry about Julie. But so was I . . .

At home, in the hot, noisy place we now lived, I heard the neighbor's radio . . . everyone played their radios all day at top volume, as though trying to drown out the reality of our surroundings . . . giving out the latest government line:

> . . . even should Okinawa fall, we have no fear of the future. The Americans may attack the mainland, but when they do they seal their fate. We are prepared. Our plans are in place. Our Special Attack Corps' secret weapons have been tested successfully on Okinawa. When the Americans land, if they are so foolish as to do so, they will be wiped out by our killer weapons . . .

Julie slammed the sliding door shut, trying to stop the invasion of the noise that too many were still believing. I told her that at this very moment we believed the emperor was asking his aides to sue for peace through the Soviet Union.

Julie looked at me, her hair in disarray, furious. "I wish him good luck," she said. "But is anybody really listening to him?"

My wife had asked a question I could not answer.

MASAO TAMBA · JUNE, 1945

My brother Saburo died the second week of June. The word from the war office was surprisingly detailed, I suppose as an indulgence of a retired "hero." He had been flying a Shiragiku White Chrysanthemum plane, an old-fashioned midwing monoplane that carried a single 250–kilogram bomb—I knew that much myself, that all the *kamikaze* pilots flew such dated machines that were no better than slow training planes. Saburo died, said the war office letter, in a massed attack on a picket line of destroyers off the west coast of Okinawa. He, and two of his comrades, had sent a destroyer to the bottom with the cry of "Long live the emperor" on his lips.

> Your brother wore his black-hooded robe and his white
> headband, and carried a spray of cherry blossoms. He died in
> glory, defending his homeland. We regret we are unable to return
> his body or articles of his clothing, but we know he sent you a lock
> of his hair, which you will keep forever as a family heirloom that
> honors us all.

Reading the letter in my office at planning headquarters, I was unable to show my true feelings. I wondered whether the fine sentiments attributed to my brother, the descriptions of what he wore, all of it, were not just a bit too perfect . . . I had been told by Kenji some of what his wife's brother had said about the last words of *kamikaze* pilots, and while at first it had angered me and I did not believe all of it, I had to wonder about it. After all, I knew the capacity of my leaders, and even colleagues, to indulge in deception, including self-deception . . .

Well, to hell with them now. My thoughts were on my little brother, the loyal puppy who had overcome every obstacle to become a warrior— ill health, bad eyesight, the ragging of schoolmates. Lesser men would never have achieved what he had, and my pride in him could not possibly be dimmed by the other questions in my mind . . .

Questions . . . Kenji's about whether the cause justified the death of our brother, not to mention all those others, including my own men . . . and my own about whether those people that Colonel Sato said were looking for a face-saving way to end the war, including the weathervane Lord Privy Seal Kido and the aging Suzuki, whether these were so wrong, and if not and if they were to prevail, what then justified my brother's death . . . ?

Saburo's photograph went on the altar in my mother's house, alongside those of my father and Hideo Kitano. Only the immediate family participated in the brief funeral services. All Saburo's schoolmates were dead or in uniform or had disappeared for one reason or another from Tokyo.

As we sat on cushions on either side of the altar, my mother weeping quietly, I looked at Kenji, and between us were words of sorrow and anger, words of recrimination and frustration that we could not utter. Perhaps should never utter. Silently I think I resented his questions that he had pushed into my mind, and his *gaijin* wife. Yes, resented, because deep down in recesses I hated to explore . . . I wondered more than I could admit if he was not right . . .

KENJI TAMBA · JUNE, 1945

Adachi had a daring idea. From what I told him, he sensed with me that regardless of what he said, or rather didn't say, my brother might have been weakening in his support of the war, or at least was having doubts. I would not soon forget the look he gave me at our brother's funeral . . . and while he said nothing, I felt certain that there were some regrets, doubts, about the sacrifice. And about those who continued to try to justify it. I knew my brother, and I respected him, as I always had, even though we had disagreed.

Yes, if Adachi and I were right, perhaps logic dictated that he be approached. He was, after all, a genuine hero, a valiant soldier, well-respected, and even though only a major he was a man his superiors listened to. He had almost daily access to men like Colonel Sato and Commander Edo, those diehard warriors willing to fight to the death of the last Japanese youth, like our brother Saburo, to vindicate their loudly voiced notions of honor and patriotism.

We were in our office. Yoshiro had listened to a late report from Okinawa, supplied by the American shortwave broadcast. Over a hundred thousand Japanese had died in the futile resistance, not to mention the American death toll, which was huge.

"You actually expect me to win Masao to the peace faction?" I asked, knowing that was exactly what he wanted me to try.

"Tell him how General Ushijima cut his belly open and died without proving anything," he said. "Ask him if this is a good legacy for Japan.

Then tell him that further deaths are a betrayal of the emperor's wishes, not a fulfillment."

I found Masao at a military gymnasium near Ueno Park, training young men, doing what he could do. Not surprising. He had long been frustrated because his injuries kept him out of further active service. He felt most comfortable, I understood, with young men, just as he always had, who would fight, who wanted to fight, rather than with tired old men. Looking at him now in shorts and undershirt and canvas shoes, trying to teach bayonet technique to a dozen young men with shaved heads, my mind went back to a July day in . . . when was it? . . . in 1941, only four years ago that seemed more like forty, and I saw once again Masao training and shaping young men for battle. But then he had no questions, he had all his wonderful physical abilities and air of command. Of course these young men, teenagers, were in awe of the famed and decorated Major Masao Tamba, little knowing what the tiger really was feeling; that what they were seeing was not the same man who had shaped young men a whole war ago.

I waited patiently while he addressed his charges, told them they were honored to enter the battle, speaking now in a low, almost gentle voice, his face betraying nothing of his feelings. As usual, I was the alien civilian, the outsider, and I knew what I was about to do would be the most difficult time for me and my brother. When Masao's orderly saw me he draped a tunic over his shoulders, adjusted his sword and bowed. Masao then noticed me at the entrance and came up to me.

"Ah, Kenji, did the sugar company give you the day off?"

"There is little to export and less to import."

Both of us kept a straight face, but the edge of sarcasm in his words, and the resentment in my reply, were evident to both of us. I obviously was not starting off well in my mission.

"May I invite you to the officer's bath? I realize your aversion to the officers' quarters, but it remains one of the few places in all Tokyo where one can get enough hot water."

"Thank you, elder brother, I would like that very much. I need a bath—"

"Ah, Firefly, you are a bad dissembler. You always were. You are here for a reason, and it is not to bathe. Nonetheless . . ."

His words trailed off as he led me down damp corridors to a locker room. His batman, an old infantryman named Ogata, followed us and in the locker room carefully took off Masao's clothing, gentle as a nurse with the metal arm. I was left to take care of myself, for which I was grateful. Afterward, Masao dismissed the orderly, who bowed and left the room.

It was now late afternoon. Long shafts of dust-laden sunlight slanted from high translucent windows. I took a deep breath. Perhaps he had suspected something of what I'd been up to for some time, but now it didn't matter. I had to tell him everything . . .

And I did . . . about the professor's office, our access to foreign newspapers and other data, our monitoring of American and British radio, the way we assembled information on the war and the diplomatic front for people in high places, none of whom I knew by name. I told him about the highly placed peace faction of moderates and old conservatives working to end the war . . . though I suspected he already had heard of them. After all, he wasn't without his own contacts.

When I had finished he looked at me as I had never before seen him look. There was not even condescension, or a shade of affection or a more-in-sorrow-than-in-anger air . . . no, none of that as he said the terrible words: "You have been a traitor, Master Cold Rice."

His voice was like ice, and my reaction was automatic. "Do not say that, elder brother. I am as loyal a Japanese as you. Those who betrayed our Japan are the traitors, those who attacked like cowards without warning."

He looked at me as though I had failed his lowest recruit exercise, but I would not be put off. "Masao, it's not too late—"

"For what?"

Here it was, there was no turning back now. "To work with us . . . ?"

"Poor Master Cold Rice, do you really think I would destroy my name, betray His Majesty . . . Don't you understand that the Americans want only our destruction." It was not a question. "I am afraid you are still an American at heart—"

"I am as Japanese as you, brother. And I am just as proud of it. I happen to believe that it is right to grieve for the dead—"

His face hardened even more. No doubt he thought I was censuring him about our brother's death. Awakening feelings of guilt in him.

"We all must die. If the cause is good—"

"And you and the likes of Colonel Sato and his friends decide that? Don't you know that Tenno Heika himself is considering peace terms? Oh, you are shocked? There are even men in the *jushin,* admirals, old retainers, who have been looking for ways to end this war—"

"There may be traitors at the palace, but nobody would dare suggest a surrender—"

"Don't be so certain. Masao, leave Sato, he is an outlaw, he and all the other plotters. You have dedicated your life to serving Tenno Heika. They are conspiring against him. And the country is sick of this war, people are turning against it—"

"I do not believe it."

"Believe this then. When the radio reported General Ushijima's suicide I saw people in the street smiling."

A shadow crossed his face, his jaw set even more. Masao had known Ushijima, the commandant of troops on Okinawa, who had committed *seppuku* at the mouth of a cave. The Americans, we heard, were less than fifty feet away when he disemboweled himself and an aide cut his head off.

"And did you smile too? Do you make light of those who commit *seppuku?*"

"No, I do not. But I am interested that so few are doing it. By the *samurai* code all the outlaws should be ending their lives too."

He moved toward me, a shaft of sunlight cast a bar of yellow across his thin face. "And am I an outlaw?"

"No, you only allowed yourself to follow them."

"I acted of my own will—"

"All right, but what matters now is that you help stop these people, the Colonel Satos, from plunging our people into a sea of blood. The Americans will send a million men to invade us, thousands of planes, warships. Their factories are intact, they will keep producing bombs until there is nothing left of *Yamato* . . ."

He turned away from me, locked his good arm with his metal limb, then came back. We were naked except for towels knotted around our waists. "Master Cold Rice, if I understand you, you have said I am with outlaws, that it is not you but I who am a traitor . . ."

I said nothing, because at that moment the look on his face told me nothing could move him. And then, without warning, he had spun around and cracked his metal arm against my jaw. I fell backward, my head banging against a locker. I was just aware enough to know I was stunned and losing consciousness. I slid to the floor, bleeding from the mouth.

Masao looked at me, sorrow mixed with anger. "Get up."

He was giving my head a chance to clear, and slowly I got to my feet.

"I don't want to hit you again," he said. "I think you should leave—"

But now I forgot about my mission, I wanted to prove myself. Master Cold Rice was tired of the insults, the snubs, the comments about his wife, the role he had been assigned as a secondary person all his life by his hero brother, who at this moment he wanted only to show once and for all that he was his equal, perhaps more . . . And without thinking further I advanced on him, and he swung at me again, only this time I was ready and parried the blow with my right forearm, caught the claw with my hand and twisted. Masao grunted, moved away, regained his balance.

He was smiling at me. "Well done."

We faced each other now in the traditional fashion. He was bent forward, legs braced, right arm at eye level, left hook swinging loose, ready to come around if he had the advantage of position.

Once more he struck at me, hit my forehead, then my neck. He mixed these blows with stinging slaps with his right hand, using the side of it like a cutting tool, smashing it against my nose.

"Enough," he said, "I do not want to kill you or humiliate you. You are not a trained fighter."

I caught my breath, wiped blood from my mouth. "Musashi said one must move in the shade when one cannot see the enemy's spirit. Brother, you must now move in the shade, because you cannot see my spirit. What is it? Fight? Die? Slink out of here like a whipped dog?"

"Musashi also says that when you and your foe contend with the same spirit, release all four hands. In this fashion . . ."

And he let out a shout and came at me, legs dancing, metal hand and right hand darting and striking, and hit my chest, tore the flesh of my right forearm, retreated, took position again, then charged.

As he raised his right arm I too used every advantage and hit him on his blind side with my right fist. I did it American-style, what American boxers call a right cross, swinging from the side of my body, turning my fist and snapping it as it struck his cheekbone.

Masao gasped as he fell back against a wall locker. He was more shamed than shocked by my blow.

I bowed. "My apologies, elder brother—"

Again there was his cry of attack and he came at me, swinging the lethal arm. But I learned to time its swing and anticipate the moment of impact, ducked under it and once more drove my right fist into the part of his chest just above the knotted towel. It struck the base of his rib cage—part flesh, part bone—and hit him with such force I thought I had broken my knuckles.

The wind went out of his lungs and he jackknifed. With his eyes turning to black stones he fell over a wooden stool, motionless, trying to suck air back into his lungs.

I kneeled next to him. Bubbles formed at the edges of his lips. He made wheezing noises. Gently I turned him over. His body was hard and leathery, but he was thin as a begging monk. It was odd . . . as boys I had been stronger but he had always won the fights. Now his collapse shocked

me as much as it did him. I even felt guilty, along with an undeniable elation. He was my older brother, and old habits of respect were deeply ingrained.

"Brother, can you hear me?"

His right eye opened. I had torn the flesh, left a bleeding red mark on
his cheek. "Master Cold Rice, if the Americans couldn't kill me, you
can't."

I believe he actually smiled, or tried to. "I'm sorry—"

"Why? You fought well. Musashi would have approved." He got to one
knee and rested there. "A pity you never wanted to be a soldier, Kenji.
You would have made a good one."

I patted his bleeding face with the towel, convinced I had broken his
cheekbone. Of course he was in pain but did not wince.

A murmur of low voices now filtered across the locker room. I looked
up to see Ogata and some noncoms standing in the doorway, stunned.
Ogata, the old batman, was the most upset.

"Get out," I said, "the major will call you when he needs you."

They did. They respected me.

I helped my brother to a stool and sat beside him. He rested his head
against the locker door. I realized then that it was not so much my fists
that had weakened him but the months of terrible deprivation on the
islands. He had been too generous in his praise, I had not deserved it. "I
regret our fight—"

"Nonsense."

"If you wish you can report me. Not only for striking you but for being
part of what you regard as a movement of traitors—"

Masao laughed. "Report you?" He touched his cheek. "That was a
decent blow. Like the Negro, Louis. I once saw the film of how he beat
the German Schmeling."

"I saw it too, but his best punch was a short left hand. They said that
it traveled no more than six inches but could destroy a man. I'm afraid
my clumsy right hand is not in his class."

We both laughed and he refused my help as he got to his feet and again
invited me to the bath.

"Do you want anything? Whiskey? Food? A woman?" He smiled.

"No, my brother, only to spend time with you and try to remember
happier times . . ."

Ever since the firebombings of February and March, I had been working three or four days a week at Uncle Adam's clinic. It was therapy for me to do something positive, for life, in the atmosphere of death that surrounded us. Uncle Adam would quote Freud about the two essentials of a good life being "work and love."

The love in my life was having a rocky time, but I don't think I ever got close to the break I felt coming that night Kenji and I had our big fight. And both of us could look at Taro and realize we had plenty to be thankful for.

One day Dr. Reinhold, the Swiss from the International Red Cross and a friend of Aunt Cora's, appeared in the waiting room with a Japanese man in a rumpled gray suit. They looked solemn, but most people did these days.

Dr. Reinhold introduced the Japanese as Dr. Kida, a member of the Religious Society of Friends of Japan who worked with the IRC. I bowed properly and took them inside, where we sat around Uncle Adam's scarred rolltop desk.

Dr. Reinhold cleared his throat. "Periodically," he began, "the War Prisoner Bureau supplies us with information on the status of POWs, including the names of men who have died while incarcerated. They've been doing this with more frequency since the B–29 raids. Perhaps some bureaucrats are anticipating an end to the war."

My heart shivered. I knew what was coming . . . "with much sorrow that I report to you that the name of Lieutenant Edward Hodges, Jr. was on the most recent list . . . the official report said that Lieutenant Hodges suffered a progressive paralysis of the nervous system and died of natural causes . . . Dr. Kida managed to get some conflicting information from a contact in Kyushu . . ."

Now Kida was talking . . . "My informants report that Hodges was beaten prior to being hospitalized, there was some dispute over a hidden radio. Due to the beating, he developed an infection that apparently reached his brain and caused the paralysis from which he died. Please accept my profound regrets, Mrs. Tamba. I understand from Dr. Reinhold that Lieutenant Hodges was a friend of both yourself and your husband . . ."

I didn't hear his voice or Reinhold's parting words to Uncle Adam or the clatter of sandals as some women came into the waiting room . . .

Aunt Cora took me to her bedroom, and I lay there a while, thinking about Ed, about the brutality that killed him, letting it all mix and take me over.

"They murdered him," I said to Cora.

She looked at me. "You must not condemn them all, but you have a right to your anger. We all do—"

"Cora, I'm leaving. I'm going to take Taro and go, I can't look at another Japanese face—"

"What about Kenji?"

"I'll tell him tonight. He said it was okay for me to go but I changed my mind. But the way I feel now . . ."

Uncle Adam loomed in the doorway.

"Julie, child," he said. "Whatever you do, don't close any doors."

I arranged to meet Kenji outside a shrine that was near his office. He was cheerful and seemed almost optimistic. I thought it was his fight with Masao, which he had told me about, and a good talk he'd had with his brother that had drawn them closer together. There was still a pretty nasty bruise over his left eye where the Dragon of Shansi had smashed him, and I think Kenji was rather proud of it. I was happy for him, though he called his success "lucky punches." Kenji, as so often, too modest.

"Good news," he said.

I tried to look interested, but I wasn't much of an actress.

"More peace talk. We have reports that there was a conference and His Majesty for once took the initiative. He has requested that the cabinet and the army seek a negotiated peace. They're approaching the Soviets again—"

"The Soviets? Uncle Adam says the Russians will move into Manchuria any day. They're waiting to hit the Japanese from behind, and your government thinks they can arrange a peace through Stalin?"

"Julie, it's movement, the *desire* to look for peace." He told me that the bitter-enders still dominated the army, but they were beginning to go along with the emperor's wishes, however reluctantly and with lots of protests. But if the Americans demanded unconditional surrender and removal of the emperor, well, that would upset everything. They would all die fighting—or at least so the army leaders insisted. The emperor was the key.

I shut my eyes. "Ed Hodges is dead." I said it abruptly, to shock, and I guess I did.

"How did you find out?"

I told him about the people from the International Red Cross and their account of how Ed died in Kyushu.

"Julie, what can I say? I know he was a good friend, I liked him too . . ."

"Neither of us even tried to help him." As I said the words I saw I was bringing back memories of that awful night when we'd had our terrible argument that started over Ed. Kenji's face went all tight, and once more I realized precious Julie was on the edge of going too far in her upset, of losing what she cared the most about. *Shut up,* I ordered myself. For God's sake, stop acting as if the war were just your special misery . . .

Don't shut any doors, Uncle Adam had said. I was just about to . . . I took a deep breath and nodded. Of course he was right, what could we have done? Really? But it hurt and I hurt, and there was no denying that.

"Kenji," I did allow myself to say, "the people who run this country are in love with death. It's all that seems to mean anything to them. We can all be destroyed if—"

"Not everybody, Julie. It's what I've been trying to tell you."

Enough words, we both felt. We walked toward his bike resting against a stone lantern, and I stopped and looked at him. "Just hold me a second, please."

And he did, and kissed me.

A siren wailed. Another damned raid.

I couldn't get the words out of my mouth, my fear, my hatred of the people who had started all this, murdered Ed . . . but I found the words for Kenji, the best man I'd ever known or ever would.

"I love you, Kenji Tamba. That's a fact, and no matter what *anybody* says, including me, don't you ever dare forget it."

KENJI TAMBA · JULY, 1945

I was having a game of Western-style chess with Professor Adachi, waiting for any news, but my head, and heart, were still filled with what Julie had said to me as we left the shrine. I wasn't sure if I would ever be able to appreciate what it meant for her to go through what she had

—and what I suspected was yet to come—but I had strong doubts if the roles were reversed whether I would have been able to be her equal. We would never be the same, with all that had happened, but if we survived it together we would both be better and stronger and closer for it. In spite of our troubles, arguments—we were not, after all, paragons—we were still living through, not being defeated, no matter how close we might have come. Compared to where we were now forced to live, that camp in California was like the Imperial Hotel . . .

The professor nudged me, it was my move. Japanese chess is similar to Western but the pieces have different names—no king or queen but a piece called the "jewel" that has moves much like the king. We also have some "gold generals" and "silver generals." Not surprisingly.

Yoshiro came in to interrupt us, to my relief, with a sheet of typewritten copy. We had been waiting for the text of the Potsdam declaration, the terms of the Allied powers for the surrender of Japan. Now they had been broadcast on the Armed Forces Network, and Yoshiro had made notes as fast as he could take them down in shorthand. Adachi put on his wire-rimmed spectacles and read:

> We call upon the government of Japan to proclaim the
> unconditional surrender of all Japanese armed forces. The
> alternative for Japan is prompt and utter destruction. The Japanese
> people will not be enslaved as a race or a nation. Occupying forces
> will be withdrawn as soon as a new order is established and
> war-making capacities are destroyed . . .

"What do you think, *sensei?*"

"They will reject it. The outlaws will exploit that it makes no mention of His Majesty. That will give the fanatics a chance to keep up their belly-talk of fighting to the last man. I'd have been much happier if it were explicit—the emperor remains."

"Perhaps they can get word to the emperor. Assure him he can stay on."

Later that day Adachi's pessimism was proved justified. The Suzuki cabinet had chosen to ignore the Potsdam proclamation, to act as if it did not exist. The press was instructed to publish extracts of the allied proposals without comment. But our newspapers did the extremists' work anyway, calling the proclamation "a laughable matter," claiming it would only strengthen the government's intention to "carry the war forward to victory."

Adachi and I speculated on what seemed to be threats in the proclamation. With our major cities already in ruins, why did the Allied statement talk about "utter destruction"? How much more could be destroyed?

In the early evening I met Julie at a puppet show in a square near our new home. Julie was sitting in a rear row with Taro on her lap. I stared at her. I don't think she ever looked more beautiful to me—fair, thin, no makeup, wearing a patched gray kimono and black obi, with Taro, fat and bouncy, on her knees. He was clapping his hands, bursting with joy at the mock battle of knights on the tiny stage.

The performance ended with applause and laughter . . . so innocent, a reminder for me of the pleasures of childhood—and I had a sudden image of Taro as a future recruit, being slapped and kicked for failing to perform *kendo* properly.

I quickly took him from Julie as the crowd dispersed and carried him on my shoulders as he laughed and banged happily on my head.

I told her about the Potsdam statement. I tried to imply there might be some hope, in spite of initial rejection, in Suzuki's desire for peace—secretly held—and loyalty to His Majesty. I said that Suzuki's silence was a move to buy time, to hold off the diehards, keep them guessing. He had to control them, make sure they didn't do something crazy. There were mad elements among the outlaws who hinted that an emperor could be *killed* if he acted against the divine dictates of Amaterasu . . .

We walked slowly, in no hurry to get back to the tenement. The warmth of my son's legs wrapped around my head, his little feet tapping at my chest as we walked on, put me in memory of bouncing on my own father's shoulders as we once, so long ago, walked through the zoo in Ueno Park. So very very long ago . . .

MASAO TAMBA · AUGUST, 1945

The Plum Blossom House was now closed, so Satomi entertained special guests at a house in Minamoto that she shared with Kingoro Hata.

Colonel Sato and I were welcome, Hata being a man who kept all his options open. He was even receiving guests of the peace faction. My father-in-law's old friend from the Black Dragon Society, Commander

Endo, the naval aide, was even being courted by Hata. It seemed Endo
had had a change of heart—the navy, after all, was weakening. They had
no ships left. The Americans had created an ocean bottom of rusting steel
and moldering Japanese corpses.

There was talk about the cowardice of the navy, about Admiral Yonai,
one of our greatest heroes, and now navy minister and assistant prime
minister, who was rumored in favor of accepting the Allies' terms.

"Hatanaka and the rest of us," Colonel Sato said. "We'll handle those
shit-asses when the time comes."

And before his ritual passing out from too much sake, he said that he
would like me to be present at the next meeting of the "Hatanaka Group"
—a cadre of officers who were rallying around the mysterious young
major.

"You are a true war hero, my boy," Sato said sleepily . . . "you will give
luster to the group . . ."

And he fell back and began to snore.

KENJI TAMBA · AUGUST, 1945

"They call it 'the shattering of the jade,' " Professor Adachi said.
"*Gyokusai.* Die but never surrender."

We were in a teahouse near our office, a place once frequented by
students.

"I've seen an abstract of the final battle plans," Adachi was saying very
quietly. "The gentleman who called on us that day . . . you remember him
. . . he got it for me."

"The important personage in the black suit."

"He had access to General Miyazaki's strategy for the last battle. All
approved by War Minister Anami. Every man, woman and child will be
mobilized. The *kamikaze* planes will cripple the American fleet. On land,
probably Kyushu, the army will throw twenty divisions into the battle. In
two weeks' time the invaders will be annihilated—so Miyazaki says. This
will insure Japan's victory. There is, of course, an alternate plan. A quarter
of the Americans will die while at sea, thanks to our pilots. Another fourth

will be killed on the beaches. The rest will be lured inland and destroyed in human-wave attacks."

"My brother has told me about these human-wave attacks. The Americans stand by their guns and cut our troops to pieces. During the last battles our men stayed in caves and pillboxes and died in them, burned alive with flamethrowers."

"The military mind won't admit defeat," Adachi said. "All along the shore fishermen and farmers and homeowners are building handmade forts, barricades, caves, underground storerooms. There are villages where each human being has a sharpened spear. A *spear.* Men are being trained to strap dynamite on their backs and throw their bodies under tanks. A sort of national suicide."

Adachi looked to the day of a democratic Japan, a free people, rights respected, a center of commerce, industry, education . . . But for this to happen the military would have to be beaten. Except so far they would not quit.

As we threaded our way through the streets to the office, Yoshiro, who had on his headset, was scribbling as fast as he could . . . he had picked up a shortwave broadcast from San Francisco.

Adachi looked at the notes and read aloud so as not to interrupt our radio operator:

> President Truman announced today that a weapon known as an atomic bomb has been exploded over the city of Hiroshima in Japan. He described the weapon as "harnessing of the basic power of the universe." He said, "The force from which the sun draws its power has been loosed against those who brought war to the Far East." Further, his statement said that the United States is prepared to destroy all Japanese factories, docks and communications.

We stared at one another. What in the world was an atomic bomb? And why Hiroshima, which had never been much of a military target?

Yoshiro, covered with sweat, kept scrawling notes, handing a page at a time to Adachi, who continued to read aloud:

> It was to spare the Japanese people from utter destruction that the ultimatum of July 26 was issued at Potsdam. Their leaders

promptly rejected that ultimatum. If they do not now accept our
terms, they may expect a rain of ruin from the air the likes of
which has never been seen on this earth.

"What do we know of this bomb? Perhaps Truman is deceiving us—"
"I think not."
Yoshiro had additional information from San Francisco. American
observation planes reported widespread devastation—fires, ash storms,
total ruination—in Hiroshima. There was, the radio report said, nothing
left of the city. The number of dead was unimaginable.
Atom bomb? What in the world was it?

JULIE TAMBA · AUGUST, 1945

Kenji told me about the Truman announcement, about the new weapon
that apparently destroyed a whole city and everybody in it. It happened
at 8:15 A.M. on August 6, he said. I found it hard to believe. Most people
in Tokyo hardly knew about it. They just tried to go about their lives. The
firebombs were as bad as we could imagine. An atomic bomb? A city
destroyed? Who could take it in? And the offical press didn't say a word
about the bombing of Hiroshima.

Kicking a red rubber ball back and forth with Taro, Kenji told me more
about the report from San Francisco, about the bomb that would obliter-
ate all Japan unless surrender terms were accepted.

Hisako now sat down on the rear step, holding her arms out to Taro,
who ran to his grandmother, asked her to kick the ball for him. I did not
want my son incinerated on account of the pride and conceit of some
medal-wearing general.

Kenji brought our radio to the window ledge. Neighbors peered over
the fence. It was a working-class ward, people whose sons had died. A few
faces peered over the back fence. We were objects of scrutiny, a once-
famous family (so the local lore went) fallen on bad times. The dead
husband had worked at the palace, a son was a hero in the army, and so
on.

"An enemy plane has dropped a new bomb on the city of Hiroshima,"
the radio voice said. "The city has suffered damage. Authorities are looking into the matter."

And that was all. Apparently they felt they had to admit that *something* happened. People had not yet had their tongues cut out.

Hisako led Taro by the hand into the house to get him a rice cake. Hisako always had a goody hidden away for Taro, Hiroki and Maeko. The kids were her life. Never mind our problems adjusting to each other, I saw in her a strength that just might get this country back on its feet again some day—if the madmen ever got it into their heads that they were beaten and surrendered before the whole place was turned to ashes.

We kept the radio on that night, waiting for news of Hiroshima. We speculated, tried to guess, wondered if perhaps it *had* been just one more B–29 firebombing. But the reports kept saying—*one plane, one bomb.*

That night Kenji and I took some comfort in each other, merging our bodies with a passion that we hadn't known for a long time . . . as though for a few moments we could destroy death and bombs with our own fierce love.

YURIKO KITANO · AUGUST, 1945

My mother and I had taken one of the family scrolls, a beautiful rice-paper hanging with a poem about winter to the black market to try to trade it for soap—there was none left in the shops.

A policeman flirted with me and my mother made a sour face and quickly pulled me away. "What is to become of you?" she asked.

"Very little." I was still irreverent, but mostly I was assuming an air to cover up my grieving over Hans. Inside I felt only emptiness. Much easier to be light and smart than let out my true feelings . . . I could do that only with Julie . . .

"Don't joke with me, you were spoiled by everyone in the family, especially Kenji. But I don't like your impertinent remarks."

"I'm sorry, mother." And I was, for us both.

We walked through an outdoor market of people in rags, shoeless, squatting in the dirt trying to sell or trade everything imaginable. One woman displayed three shriveled *daikon* radishes on a sheet of newspaper. An old man, half-asleep, was peddling chunks of crockery—half cups, broken plates, chipped bowls. A young girl, no more than eleven, offered sandals made of old canvas.

"You make my heart heavy," my mother went on. "You were not good to Hideo."

I said nothing. What could I say? She was right.

"Then you took up with a *gaijin,* a man I never saw. Just as well. One in the family is enough—I have almost gotten to like Kenji's wife, yes, I do like her, but it's just that she is so different, her legs are too long—"

"I'll tell her to walk on her knees."

"You are being insolent again."

"Mother, Julie likes you, she's been as good as a sister to me."

"I suppose so . . . But she is not happy . . . Kenji worries she will leave us, with our child—"

"Taro is her child too. And I don't believe she will ever leave Kenji."

My mother shrugged, paused at a stall run by an old woman. In a straw basket were chunks of what looked like homemade soap, grayish white, made from animal fat and ashes. My mother bargained with the woman but she wasn't interested in our fancy scroll, she was a peasant woman who saw no use for our wistful *haiku* about winter. Who could blame her?

We ended up spending more money than we could afford for some bars of the greasy soap, then walked back through the black market.

"You are still pretty," my mother said abruptly, "and young, and a member of a good family. As soon as the war ends I will ask Mr. Hata to be our *nakoodo* again and arrange a *miai* with a suitable husband. He may have to be an older man, maybe a widower, but rich and someone who will appreciate a young wife and take good care of Hiroki. But if he prefers I'll keep Hiroki in my house. We must do something about you. Since the factory burned down all you do is read magazines, listen to American music and smoke cigarettes—"

"Please stop this talk."

She frowned. "Having no father in the house is a burden. Your father would have disciplined you. Now I have no husband, you have no husband, and I cannot depend on Masao or Kenji anymore. Yuriko, you must find a good man. I am going to be very nice to Mr. Hata and make sure he locates a rich old man for you—"

"I will *never* marry."

"You will change your mind."

"I will not. I hated the *miai,* I didn't like a *nakoodo* and the idea of my parents selecting my husband. Even if Hideo had treated me well I would have resented the way he was chosen for me."

"Your sister-in-law has poisoned your mind with her customs. I do not blame her, but she is an unfortunate mistake that Kenji made—"

"He made *no* mistake. They love each other. We should be grateful to Julie for the happiness she has brought my brother."

"You talk only of happiness, love . . . there are more important things—"

"I agree. I have a better idea than a *miai* and a new husband."

"Oh?"

"Yes . . . Mr. Hata could send me to his mistress Satomi. She could train me to be a geisha and I could make the money you think is so important entertaining rich men, including the Americans once they come here." It was a mean joke, of course . . . the last thing I wanted to be was one of those living mannequins, a powdered and bewigged and painted wind-up toy created for the cold pleasure of strangers. But when I looked for a reaction I had the feeling that my mother thought it wasn't such a bad idea, that it would get me out of her house and provide a steady source of income to the Tamba household.

The pain of that realization turned my insides colder than ever.

KENJI TAMBA · AUGUST, 1945

Two days after Hiroshima *a second* terrible bomb was dropped on Nagasaki. And, as though to reinforce this disaster, the Soviet Union declared war on us. All along the vast Manchurian front the Red Army opened up ferocious artillery bombardments. Hundreds of Russian tanks and planes flew across the border, sending tired Japanese forces staggering backward. As always, the Japanese soldiers fought courageously, but the army, short on fuel and munitions, was no match for the Soviet divisions that came at them like a gray machine.

"So much for the Soviets as our honest brokers," Professor Adachi said. "Stalin lay in wait like a spider, letting the Allies burn and bleed us and themselves and now he enters the war so that he can suffer the least casualties, make the biggest claims and establish Russia as a Far Eastern power once more."

"Revenge for 1904?" I asked.

He tapped his desk. "And more. I don't give a damn if he grabs some worthless land—Sakhalin or parts of Manchuria—but I am afraid that this will see an upsurge of the influence of communism here at home." He let cigarette smoke envelope his tired eyes. "Damn it, Kenji, we did not fight so long, suffer so many deaths and battle the right-wing fanatics just to have the lunatics of the left take this country over. They are as adept at cutting heads off and starving their own people as the madmen of the right—"

The phone rang. It was Dr. Adam Varnum saying he needed volunteers to drive a medical convoy to Kyoto. The victims of Hiroshima were pouring into cities that were relatively untouched by the war. Kyoto had opened its hospital facilities, schools and public buildings to tens of thousands of victims. The International Red Cross was cooperating. Trucks were being loaded, the doctor said, with blankets, medicine, bandages for the burned, stunned people, moving into the cities between Hiroshima and Tokyo. Would I go?

I agreed at once.

Adachi took my hand. "Learn as much as you can. But be careful. Kenji, we are going to need people like you to build a new Japan."

I bowed to the old man. "I'll do what I can, *sensei.* And thank you."

As I left I heard Yoshiro telling him that the cabinet had again—*again?* —rejected surrender terms and that no new word was expected that day.

I met Dr. Varnum and his wife outside the Shibuya clinic. Under the supervision of the old friend of the Varnums, Dr. Kida, ancient, bearded, of the old school, a dozen trucks were being loaded.

Julie was working along with local volunteers packing the vehicles with crates of medicine, clothing, hospital bedding and whatever supplies of medicine they could get. I noticed a group of American nuns, teaching sisters who had been free to conduct their classes during the war and had never been interned, were also helping out.

"How well do you know the road to Kyoto?" Adam Varnum asked me.

"Well enough."

"It's full of craters and roadblocks," he said. "Dr. Kida says he knows shortcuts and backroads in case we're stopped anywhere. He's the head of the column and we'll take our orders from him. You will be his driver."

"Conditions are worse than anyone can imagine," Dr. Kida said to me. "There may be more than a hundred thousand dead and another hundred thousand injured. But the injuries are of a kind one does not associate with ordinary bombing. We have reports of people with their skin peeled away, eyes melted, peculiar dark burns, swellings, physical effects that are unknown to any of our doctors. People are still dying, convulsing. The city has been forced to send less serious cases east, which is why Kyoto is being used as a hospital area."

It was a scary and confusing recital. Julie volunteered to go too but

Adam vetoed it, for which I was grateful. Who knew when the next bomb would fall? Or where?

"He's right," I said. "I want you with Taro and my family."

"*My* family too," she said, and I wanted to kiss her for it.

A wagon drawn by two old men came up, loaded with blankets, bound with straw ropes. We were scratching everywhere for the wherewithal of life. I joined some older women who were unloading the blankets and stacking them inside a creaky rusted truck. Red crosses had been painted on the side and on the roof.

Adam Varnum came alongside me. "We have new reports from Hiroshima coming in. The government can't keep it a secret. It's worse than anyone suspected. There seems to be some awful after-effect of the blast —severe burns, internal hemorrhaging, nausea, vomiting, blindness, God knows what. There's no city left. There are fires still burning and bodies, bodies . . ."

"Can we do anything else? Would it make sense to drive all the way to Hiroshima?"

"Four hundred miles? We're lucky we were given the gasoline to go as far as Kyoto."

The trucks were loaded. Canvas tarpaulins were tied down. Dr. Kida stood at the cab door, a frail, dignified figure. What a contrast to the strutting Sato and the disgusting Hata. Another Japan . . .

"Let me help you in, doctor."

"Yes, the old bones creak a bit."

He was light as a willow branch. He thanked me and settled into the seat.

The Varnums were in the truck behind us. Engines coughed, groaned, turned over. I waved to Julie as we headed into a grim and unforgiving world.

MASAO TAMBA · AUGUST, 1945

It was 9:30 in the morning, August 10. I was sitting in a rear row with Colonel Sato in an underground air raid shelter at army headquarters on Ichigaya Heights.

I felt drained. Sato was restless, fondling his sword, sighing and groaning under the weight of his huge belly. It was breathlessly hot and damp.

We were there as two men from the planning staff, a desk colonel and a half-blind, one-armed veteran. Sato had kept his lines open to those who ruled from the bottom—the men Kenji called "outlaws." Sato had entree everywhere.

War Minister Anami came in. His words shocked the room—there were about fifty men present—into abrupt silence.

There had been an all-night cabinet meeting with Tenno Heika. *The emperor had accepted the surrender terms of the Potsdam proclamation.*

At first many did not believe the war minister. There were demands that others who had attended the conference be summoned. There were shouts that the army still had the "sacred right" to defend the nation. Sato nudged me with his riding crop. He said he had known about the imperial conference. He had anticipated that the peace faction would twist the emperor's will, bend him to their wishes. So I was not altogether surprised by the announcement. As we mingled in the corridors of the stuffy bunker more details of the meeting came out. Apparently Prime Minister Suzuki, caught between the military and the civilians, the military wanting to continue the war, the civilians leaning to surrender, had with Lord Privy Seal Kido's approval turned to the emperor and asked him to express his wishes.

This was unheard of, a violation of every rule of government, of protocol, of our way of life. Tenno Heika was not supposed to be asked his opinion on anything. He sat in front of the golden screen to symbolize the nation and the people. He was there to sign his name to imperial rescripts drawn up by his cabinet and advisers. Anami, we were told by an aide, was furious when Prime Minister Suzuki put the question of surrender to His Majesty. But the emperor had already made the decision for peace. The exact phrase he used, the aide said, was that "the time has come when we must bear the unbearable." He did not want his people to suffer any longer. Ending the conflict was the only way to rebuild the nation. He paid tribute to those who had died, was saddened by the prospect of his generals and admirals and statesmen being branded war criminals . . . or something to that effect.

Some at the meeting argued that the peace offer was unacceptable since it did not guarantee His Majesty's continued role. But Tenno Heika refused to back down on his decision. His life, his fate, he indicated, was of no importance. The people came first.

What it all amounted to was unconditional surrender, which was what the enemy had demanded in the first place. Suzuki's formal reply to the Allies, drawn up that night, said that Japan accepted the Potsdam terms, provided the declaration did not compromise "the prerogatives of His Majesty as a sovereign ruler." It was a face-saving effort.

I should have been full of pain over this shocking information. I was not. The war was ending, the nation had been terribly hurt by the enemy. What more could I do? I was a soldier, out of combat. My doubts, my frustrations seemed taken out of my hands.

I noticed then the mysterious Major Hatanaka walking out with some other junior officers. He nodded at me and raised his crop in salute. A slight young man, what I had looked like before the islands. There was something ascetic about Hatanaka, an air of serenity and certainty not granted to the ordinary man. Or did he cultivate that manner?

"An aloof fellow," I said.

"He knows you," the colonel said. "He has asked for us to attend the meeting."

"What branch?"

"None. His own group. Loyalists."

"Loyal to whom?"

"My dear Masao, you who have lost blood, a limb and an eye in the service of Tenno Heika should know. Loyalty to the Son of Heaven."

"But the emperor has surrendered."

Colonel Sato took my arm as we left the corridor and started up the stairs. Plaster flaked from the ceiling. Cracks ran jagged lines on the walls, like a chaotic road map. The bombings had left nothing untouched.

"Do not be so sure," my father-in-law said quietly. "His mind was poisoned . . ."

We passed a large photograph of the emperor. A kind, calm face. My father had always told me what a considerate and modest person he was.

"Poisoned?"

"Misled by traitors. We all know that all the success we have had comes from His Majesty's *heart*. Failures are the work of bad advisers. That's why I feel that Anami's account may be . . . garbled."

"But War Minister Anami thinks the way you do. He wants to fight on. One hundred million soldiers . . ." I was careful to say as *you* do, not as *we* do. At that moment I wasn't sure what I wanted.

"There is something fishy about all this," the colonel said as we entered his office. "An imperial conference should not be called until the cabinet is in full agreement on strategy. Prime Minister Suzuki broke the rules. The cabinet was not of one mind about surrender. Therefore the conference had no validity. For reasons unknown to me Tenno Heika opted for a dishonorable peace when Suzuki illegally asked for his opinion."

I closed the door. "Colonel, do you call a decision of His Majesty dishonorable?"

"Ah . . . no . . . I misspoke myself. Of course not. But you and I know that His Majesty was cunningly maneuvered into his position by liars. We shall get to the truth soon enough." . . .

There was a message for me, saying that Kenji had left with a medical convoy for Kyoto, where victims of Hiroshima were being assembled. And there were new statistics on the dead and injured in both Hiroshima and Nagasaki—"Forty thousand dead in Nagasaki," I read from the memorandum. "Again one plane and one bomb. Center of the city gone, the Mitsubishi ordnance works destroyed."

Sato eased his bulk into his chair and lit a cigarette. "Any word on the Manchurian front?"

I looked at some telegrams. "We are falling back everywhere."

He said nothing, but curiously looked almost jaunty.

That evening I played some games of *go* with Michiko and my little daughter. Maeko really didn't know how to play but she was very bright at age three and understood the moves of the white and black markers.

The three of us sat on the floor. It was a suffocatingly hot evening, the air heavy with insect hum and the muffled chatter of local radios. I had stopped listening. The news only seemed to get worse.

"Daddy, when I go to bed, will you tell me stories about the islands and the funny black men who wore grass?"

"I will, little one."

"And sing one of their funny songs?"

"I'll try, child."

Michiko said that nothing made our daughter happier than the moments I spent with her, telling her tales of the strange places I'd seen. Of course I never told her about battles or talked about death. It was as if I were narrating a travel film. She was a child. She was innocent. I wanted her to stay that way. And then I thought of the children who had been killed, burned to ashes in Hiroshima and Nagasaki. The horror stories came in hourly. They would not play any games of *go*.

That night I did not really feel guilt . . . I did not bomb the cities, I did not want us to lose, I did not want to see the nation leveled. I was a soldier . . . But did I not feel shame? Had I fought bravely enough? Had I failed in not letting myself be killed? Had I led my men honorably? Was I always loyal in deed and thought to Tenno Heika? If some were to feel that I had failed to fulfill these obligations I would be under a cloud of shame. But whatever the judgment of others, I would answer to myself. I would be the ultimate judge of whether Masao Tamba had brought shame upon himself and the Tamba name. And I would act according to that judgment.

JULIE TAMBA · AUGUST, 1945

Kenji had been gone for three days, and in his absence I had a crisis of my own on my hands about Yuriko. She had been getting more and more depressed lately, it seemed to me, and you didn't have to be Freud to see it . . . swinging in her moods from a kind of fake gaiety and I-don't-give-a-damn attitude to almost total silence, even with me, refusing to go out or sometimes even take care of her child, looking at him as though she hardly recognized him. She never spoke about Hans or the baby she had aborted, but I knew they both were there, their deaths dragging her down more than she could admit or know.

With her on my mind this way I thought maybe I was worrying too much about her, that after all we all had our problems, to put it mildly. But Yuriko was right there, and I couldn't push away my worries . . . especially one afternoon when I had been taking care of Taro and Hiroki and realized that I hadn't seen Yuriko all day, and had heard nothing from her room. Hiroki was asking for his mother, and I called up to her room, not wanting to disturb her but figuring I had to. No answer.

I called again, at the same time telling Hiroki that his mother must be asleep.

No answer.

I told Hiroki to stay put and climbed the rear steps. My tread—a heavy one, I always felt oversized and clumsy in Japanese houses—didn't bring any answering movement or noise from Yuriko's room. Mosquitoes buzzed in my ear, outside wagons clattered and peddlers hawked sweet potatoes and bottled water.

I found her sprawled on the *tatami,* arms apart, legs spread, her mouth moving slightly, her eyes closed. At her side was an empty brown bottle of insecticide we'd been using on the ants and roaches in the house. The bottle was empty. She was breathing faintly. There was saliva and mucus and rice on her lips and one cheek. At least she had begun to reject the poison. A good sign, I hoped.

I ran to the window and called Hisako to come up, then raised Yuriko's head, wiped her face, and asked if she could hear me. She seemed to smile, then went limp.

There was no milk in the house, no milk of magnesia . . . I remembered from a first aid course in the Girl Scouts that alkalines were an antidote for most insecticides. I tried to calm Hisako out of her hysterics and I told her to make a mixture of flour and water, and we forced it down Yuriko's throat. Again she began to throw up, her chest convulsing, her neck in spasms.

"Don't save me," she whispered, "I want to die, please . . ."

"Like hell," I snapped at her. "You're going to live, you threw up most of the stuff." I told Hisako to pulverize some charcoal and we shoved a spoonful of that into Yuriko's mouth. Same Girl Scouts taught me that charcoal absorbs poison, deactivates it somehow . . . I prayed that I was remembering right, doing the right thing.

She seemed to recover slightly then, but her pulse was weak and she was sweating even though her skin was cold.

"We've got to get her to the clinic," I said. And when Hisako said there were no cars or taxis I rushed out and managed to find an old man pulling a flatbed wagon. He helped me get Yuriko downstairs and to the boards and took us to the clinic, Hisako's wailing fading in the distance.

Aunt Cora quickly took charge, found a bottle of milk that had been provided by a nursing mother who, miraculously, had an abundant supply, and we forced it down Yuriko's mouth.

"I don't think an emetic is necessary," Aunt Cora said. "She seems to be coming around. The charcoal is doing its work, and I suspect she vomited most of the toxic matter. You saved her life, Julie . . ."

Two hours later Yuriko had recovered enough for me to talk to her in her hospital cot in the clinic, which she shared with women victims of the firebombings. At first she was frozen-faced, didn't want to say anything, but she held onto my hand and squeezed like she was afraid something awful would happen if she let go, like I was her lifeline. Then she did begin to talk, and said she was ashamed to have done what she did when she looked around the room at all the women who were suffering and surviving, but then she said in a voice so low I had to bend down to hear her, "I don't deserve to live, I don't want to—"

And that got me mad all over again, like the first time she'd talked about ending it all after Hans was shot down. At least then you could understand and forgive it, she'd just seen her lover murdered in the streets . . . but now, well . . .

"Look, Yuriko, I'm not letting you off so easy. I almost did something as dumb myself a while ago, more than once, when I was threatening to pick up my marbles and run home and leave Kenji. That would have been a kind of suicide for me . . . I didn't do it, I'm not going to do it, and neither, damn it, girl, are you. Besides, I've gotten to like you, even if your mother can take me or leave me, mostly leave me, I guess, and I'm too selfish to let a real friend check out on me. So you'll just have to stick around and shape up. Have you got all that?"

She managed the beginning of a smile. "You don't fool me, Julie, and I love you for caring. I think you are the best friend I have . . ."

"Okay," I said severely, but with a smile, "then let's not have any more of this stuff, or you'll have an ex-best friend. Is it a deal?"

Her answer was to squeeze my hand even harder.

Kenji looked and was exhausted when he came back from Kyoto.

"I never want to see things like that again. I can't really understand why the Americans did this. The war will end without those bombs—"

"That isn't what Masao was saying the other day." Kenji was carrying Taro on his back and Michiko was walking with us, pushing Maeko in a stroller toward a Buddhist temple. "Masao said that the army would never surrender, that they'd fight to the end. The Americans must have known that, all the dead on Okinawa. One island. Imagine the casualties if they had to invade the mainland. Maybe they had to bomb Hiroshima . . . ?"

He shook his head. "If you saw the people, listened to their stories . . ."

Suddenly we heard air raid sirens and froze in place.

"Don't they know there is nothing left to burn here?" Kenji said angrily.

People around us looked resigned, not frightened, which to me was most frightening of all.

We looked to the sky as the sirens wailed, saw only one high-flying plane. It appeared out of clouds, then disappeared in them.

Michiko picked up her daughter. "Is there an air raid shelter near here?"

"It won't help," Kenji muttered. He looked at me. "Maybe we've been lucky to survive this long, and maybe I didn't deserve it. I'm sorry for—"

"You don't have to be sorry about anything, damn it. I told you that a long time ago. You just remember who I am, the *gaijin* who loves you."

We hurried away from the temple and waited. Kenji told me that the

Hiroshima refugees in Kyoto had said that a small white parachute appeared first, then the explosion. We looked to the sky, saw nothing. And then on a street of burned-out stores we spotted scraps of white paper floating to earth. Kenji picked one up.

"From the plane . . ." And he began to read slowly . . . "Your emperor has accepted the surrender terms offered by the Allied powers. The war is over. Please cooperate with His Majesty and observe his wishes. The war is over. You will be treated fairly . . ."

"I don't believe it," Michiko said.

I looked at the clouds. "There's nothing there. They flew over to drop leaflets."

"It could be a trick," Michiko said. "I'm taking Maeko home."

Kenji read the rest of the message. "It's no trick, Michiko. And if they do intend to drop the bomb on us no one will be safe anywhere."

As we walked along the street, silent, I felt a weight lifting, I was breathing easier. At long last our nightmare seemed to be ending . . .

I kept my feelings to myself as I took Taro from Kenji, held him tight and took Kenji's hand, and held it tight. Not a word passed between us. Our thoughts were speaking without words.

MASAO TAMBA · AUGUST, 1945

It was eight-thirty P.M., August 14. The colonel and I were invited to attend a secret meeting in the war ministry. We sat at the rear of the room, part of the proceedings but detached from it. We knew most of the senior officers present, had been their sympathizers in February of 1936 and Colonel Sato had belonged to secret societies with them.

Major Hatanaka, the rather mystical young man, seemed to be in charge, although he was junior to many of the men present. I was younger than Hatanaka and had probably gotten my rank later, but I believed I had a better combat record . . . few in the room could match my service in China, Malaya, Guadalcanal and Saipan. At least I had that . . . Hatanaka was talking in a soft, persuasive voice. Yes, he had spoken with War Minister Anami and Anami had said we would all be tried as war criminals and that we must stand together, face the enemy judges and explain that the war was a defensive war, that a Greater East Asia was a necessity . . .

Sato shifted angrily. "Dung from a sick dog."

Hatanaka went on in his near-hypnotic fashion. Anami had decided to commit suicide. Voices rose, there were gasps. The war minister had always been a true friend of the young officers' group, a supporter of *gekokujo*, the rule of the top by the bottom. I really didn't give a damn whether he did or didn't. Mostly I found him a windbag and a faker.

Hatanaka was holding up his slender hands. "What a grand concept . . . the mass suicide of the whole Japanese officer corps . . . what an example to show the world—"

A lieutenant colonel I didn't know scoffed at this and said we'd be more like the laughing stock of the world, and nothing was worse to a Japanese officer than such humiliation. The laughter of our enemies would haunt us to the grave and the ridicule would echo long after we were dead, he said. I thought he was a windbag too.

We all knew by now that the emperor and the cabinet had decided on surrender, an unconditional acceptance of the Allied proposals. Tenno Heika was said to be recording the surrender announcement in a few hours. We were swallowing hard and spewing it up, the way my sister Yuriko—foolish child—had tried to swallow insecticide.

"Mass suicide," Hatanaka now called out, his voice ringing. "*Yes.* It will show the world what we are made of, and will exonerate Tenno Heika."

There were grumbles that Tenno Heika had been deceived, perhaps even drugged by advisors. Sato, the desk warrior, leaned his hands on the pommel of his sword and growled. No doubt the Americans were shaking with fear from the shock waves.

The angry lieutenant colonel stood up now. "Major Hatanaka, I personally asked around the war ministry. I tell you only some twenty percent of the officers want to kill themselves. The rest gave no opinion, which means to me they were not in favor of *seppuku*. You are too generous with other people's lives."

We sweated, waited. Men smoked, opened collars. No, we would not give up, was the consensus. We did not know the word surrender. We would change the emperor's mind, or so we told each other.

Hatanaka circled the room, then revealed a different strategy. What would we think if he told us that he had the compliance of the imperial guards at the palace, that they would let a party of us inside? We would secure the palace grounds. We would find any broadcast or statement

issued by Tenno Heika and destroy it. Then, for his own good, we would
protect His Majesty's sancrosanct person and win him over. The true
wishes of the emperor would then surface. He would broadcast not a
surrender but his firm resolve to go on with the war *and* sacrifice all his
loyal subjects for the honor of *Yamato Damashii.*

Murmurs, some protests, but mostly the group seemed to be in accord
with Hatanaka.

I stood up. "Major, it is a neat plan, but will the Tokyo Area Army
commander permit it to happen?"

Hatanaka looked me over. His eyes lingered on my metal arm, my
patch. It seemed I had suffered too much to think clearly, he said. I had
been a fine combat soldier but these were matters of politics and honor
and perhaps I did not understand . . . He said he did not fear any general
in any army. Once he was able to appeal to Tenno Heika, he was confident
he could prevail on His Majesty to abandon thoughts of surrender.

Well, the bastard was a better talker than I was. He was an actor,
and he gradually won everyone over to the support of his plot. Yes . . .
even his hero Major Tamba. Less from conviction than wishful thinking . . .

We slept briefly in Sato's office on *tatami* mats, waiting for Hatanaka's
signal. He and one other officer were to make the initial attempt to breach
palace security and get inside the walls.

It was sometime after two in the morning when the phone rang and a
voice I could not identify told us to come to the north gate of the imperial
palace, that the guards would pass us through.

We drove through a moonlit deserted city, wondering how Hatanaka
had managed to get into the palace and make it possible for us to follow
him.

My father-in-law looked at me. For once there was no bombast in his
voice. "You have done more than your share. You need not do this."

"I see the road ending."

He nodded, patted his stomach. "Frankly I'm too old and fat for this
sort of thing."

If he weren't careful I might even get to like him.

At the north gate our convoy of staff cars halted. A dozen or so of
us got out to wait for our next move or a signal. We heard a single shot
echo from inside the sloping stone walls of the enclosure. No one said a
word.

We waited. Finally the gate opened and Major Hatanaka came out with another officer, a colonel. Hatanaka's uniform was splattered with blood, and he was holding a sheaf of documents.

"For the salvation of the nation," he said, "I have killed General Mori. He died for a noble purpose."

I nudged my father-in-law with my metal arm, said nothing.

Hatanaka now showed us forged documents that ordered the imperial guards to take control of the palace and protect the emperor. Guardsmen brandishing forged orders were manning checkpoints, in this way gaining us safe entry to the palace. We were to find the recording of Tenno Heika's surrender statement and destroy it, then abase ourselves in the emperor's presence and plead with him to change his mind.

We followed Hatanaka through the gate as he flashed his faked documents to the unsuspecting guards. One portion of our group was despatched to the Obunko, the fortified underground library the imperial family had been using as living quarters since the firebombing of March. Colonel Sato and I were sent to the imperial household building, where we were told the surrender recording was probably hidden. Hatanaka was becoming shrill now, furious with a palace chamberlain and his aides who kept diverting his search by alternately mumbling excuses and mouthing threats. The chamberlain was a noble Tokugawa, not easily frightened by officers making a foray into places where they normally had no business.

"Damn you, the recording," Hatanaka was demanding of the chamberlain.

"It is not here, major, and you are in violation of your sacred oath—"

A young officer slapped the old man's face and threatened him with his sword, but the chamberlain didn't budge. The Tokugawa name spelled courage. He turned aside questions, demanded that the Tokyo commander General Tanaka be notified.

Sato was now saying to me, "This is a fool's errand, Masao. Tenno Heika's advisors have hidden the thing, and if I know them they have made duplicates and cached them in various places—"

Hatanaka shouted at him. "Then the offenders will be found and tortured until we learn where the recording is hidden." He turned on me. "And *you*, Tamba, I think you have been against us from the start. I've seen the look on your face. I killed General Mori and I will kill anyone who keeps me from saving the emperor's honor."

"Major, your mouth begins to look more like your asshole every time you speak."

He sputtered, found no words, turned and went off to another room to save the emperor's honor . . . I could hear wood cracking, swords razoring the air, draperies and curtain rods being yanked from their moorings. So this is what our noble young officers' corps had been reduced to—a gang of hoodlums wrecking furnishings, insulting old servitors and murdering superiors. At some point Hatanaka finally left, saying he was off to the broadcasting station to find the disc.

Outlaws. I thought of the way old Adachi had described our class. I could no longer altogether deny the validity of the term.

I walked to a window, pulled aside the drapes and looked to the interior roadway below. A black staff car with the insignia of a general officer had halted, and General Tanaka was stepping out of it. I recognized him easily by his guards' mustache. He had been a rival of War Minister Anami, but had fully supported the Great Asian War. The difference, it seemed, was that he knew the realities of the war, of winners and losers . . . He was moving back and forth, slapping his crop against his riding boots, ready to move into action. Two platoons of armed soldiers came trotting into the enclosure at double time.

We were near the end of the road, the dark cave from which there was no return, the whirlpool in the cold ocean depths.

I turned from the window and bowed in the direction of the Obunko . . . it was the least I could do to honor His Majesty. I was not proud of being even a passive participant in this last foolish act. I understood, however, what I now must do . . .

KENJI TAMBA · AUGUST, 1945

The radio was silent.

I tossed and turned on my *tatami.* Julie was awake. Only Taro slept.

I moved the selector, raised the volume, tried a different electrical outlet. Nothing.

"Something is wrong," I whispered, "not even music."

I tried calling Michiko but phone lines seemed to be down. I called Masao's office at the war ministry. A sleepy sergeant got on, telling me that neither Major Tamba nor Colonel Sato was at his desk. In fact many of the top officers had not appeared at the ministry.

At 7:20 the radio went back on, and an announcer said that the emperor would "graciously broadcast in person later that day."

"*In person,*" I said to Julie and my mother. "That must mean he is going to announce the surrender."

"Then those leaflets were right," Julie said. "Thank God . . ."

I paced, nervous, agitated, wondering about my older brother. At about eleven in the morning Professor Adachi telephoned me.

"Kenji, it's *over.* His Majesty will announce formal acceptance of the surrender terms at noon."

"Yes . . . it's good . . ."

"It was a close thing. A gang of outlaws got into the palace last night. Our source phoned me about it."

My heart began to pound. "What happened?"

"They shot a general and some others. They actually invaded the palace grounds and the broadcasting station and tried to sabotage the discs with the emperor's surrender recording. Fortunately General Tanaka, an old bandit himself, was able to stop them. I guess it takes a scoundrel to catch a scoundrel."

I forced myself to ask . . . "Was my brother among them?"

"I've no idea, Kenji."

A brief reprieve. I thanked him, told Julie I had to find Masao and left the house, pedaling as fast as I could through swarming streets. Not surprisingly work had come to a halt. People were gathered around radios in shops and cafes, on porches, at windowsills. The air was somber, charged with tension. I was drenched in sweat. My breath was short, my arms and legs dead.

Army vehicles were backed up on the streets leading to the palace as I approached it. I recognized the shoulder patches of the Tokyo Command. Most of the men seemed tense, fretful. At the plaza facing the palace a large crowd had gathered. People bowed toward the Cyclopean walls, the stone bridges, the turrets and towers, and I remembered how as a child I had begged my father to take me inside and he had on special days when the children of palace servants were admitted. Twice I even saw Tenno Heika, a calm dignified figure, always seeming a bit sad, as if burdened by his divinity.

Then a car drew up at the edge of the crowd being held back by a cordon of military policemen and palace guards, and two young officers, a major in a blood-soaked uniform and a lieutenant colonel, stepped out. I had no idea who they were. They bowed to an officer of the military police, they bowed to the crowd, they bowed to the palace, prostrating themselves on the hot pavement and touching their shaved heads to the ground.

Then they got up and calmly walked to the audience and began handing out papers on which were printed an appeal to "prevent the illegal and disloyal surrender of Japan."

The major had handed me mine, and as he did so his hands shook but his lean handsome face was set in a smile.

I read:

> The loyal officer corps calls on all subjects of Tenno Heika to do all in their power to prevent the illegal surrender perpetrated by dishonest traitors who have deceived Tenno Heika. Do not obey any announcement . . .

Staring at the young man, I said, "May I ask your name?"

"Hatanaka."

He and his confederate had used up their supply of leaflets, then stepped back several paces.

"Major," I called, ". . . do you know a Major Tamba? I am—"

I never finished my question.

Hatanaka, as calmly as if he were adjusting his belt, drew his revolver and fired a bullet into his forehead. He fell slowly. The lieutenant colonel bowed to the fallen major, drew his sword, plunged it into his middle and fell in a pond of blood.

A man I knew as General Tanaka, the Tokyo area chief, appeared and glared at the dead officers and shook his head. I went up to him and he stared at me, not knowing or giving a damn who I was.

"General," I said, "I'm the brother of Major Masao Tamba. Is he . . . was he with the people who went into the palace?"

"Your name?"

"Kenji Tamba. My late father had the honor of being a palace servant. Masao is his oldest son—"

"Come with me." He gestured with his riding crop to an enclosure around a bend in the wall and I began to run, turned the corner—

Masao had fallen forward in *samurai* style, with the short sword deep in his lower abdomen, thrust upward and producing only a trickle of blood. His head touched the earth. There was a faint sign of life, a slight movement of his poor emaciated back. He had taken off his shirt. Each bone of his spine protruded like dragon's teeth. He looked like a child. A group of young officers stood about, silent, respectful. They had taken off their hats. To my disgust that fat hypocrite Sato was nearby. He had been disarmed and was leaning his bulk against the flank of a truck. Apparently he had decided against the *samurai*'s way. He had let Masao make the ultimate sacrifice to the emperor while he had chosen to go on living and take his chances with a trial, perhaps a pardon or an escape. I wanted to kill him myself, but ran to Masao. A lieutenant tried to stop me but the general ordered him to let me pass.

Kneeling beside my brother, I lifted his head. He even smiled at me. The eyepatch had fallen away and I saw the red gouge where his eye had been.

"Master Cold Rice . . . I am pleased to see you . . . Don't look so sad. Death is light as a feather. But I didn't cut deep enough. Will you take my sword and sever the artery in my neck?"

I shook my head violently. "No, *no*. I want you to live—"

"I can't live, Kenji, I have dishonored myself. I am covered with shame—"

"No, you're better and braver than all of them. Masao, listen to me. There are thousands of officers, men of high rank, who will never commit *seppuku*. They'll go on living, they'll accept defeat and make new lives. You must do the same. I'll take you to an ambulance, we'll go to a hospital." I looked up. "Is there an ambulance here? An army doctor?"

Stony black eyes, grim mouths, a frigid silence was all the response I got. A voice called out, "He's a *samurai*, let him die the way he chooses."

I was desperate. I shouted at Sato. "What about you, you fat bastard? You led him on, you got him into your secret brotherhoods. He was a better man than you or any of them."

Sato turned his back to me.

"Masao . . . please, think of Michiko and Maeko, of our mother—"

"Tell them I died as I wanted to die. With a sword, and by my own hand."

He began to bleed more from the cut in his abdomen. A crimson stain spread on his clothing, on his belly. His blood drenched my hands as I held him. And then he lost consciousness. His eyes didn't close but his face became immobile, as pale and smooth as ivory, and his lips moved slightly. I undid the leather thongs that bound the metal to the stump of his left arm and held him close to me for a long time. As I did I was dimly aware of Colonel Sato being led by two officers into a staff car and being driven away, of the crowd moving away, of loyal soldiers forming a protective phalanx around the palace walls. I heard General Tanaka and some of his staff officers talking about the emperor's surrender announcement being broadcast then. Many of the officers were crying. Some were pounding their heads against the pavement, tearing at their collars, howling like animals.

And then I managed to shut them out, see only my brother as death closed in.

Once, just before he died, I thought I heard him utter a single word. *Firefly*. His boyhood nickname for me. The one I had always preferred to Master Cold Rice. The last time he had used it was when we had fought, and he had been proud of me.

Julie Tamba · AUGUST, 1945

Kenji was still gone, looking for his brother. Yuriko and I were helping out at the clinic, when the emperor's surrender broadcast came over the radio at the stroke of noon:

"This will be a broadcast of the gravest importance. Will all listeners please rise. His Majesty the emperor will now read his imperial rescript to the people of Japan. We respectfully transmit his voice."

Then the national anthem "Kimigayo" was played.

Everyone in the room got to their feet and bowed in the direction of the palace. Even people lying in bed struggled and had to be helped from the cots. An old woman in an advanced state of debilitation, nothing more than bones, lifted her hands to me. I raised her from the *tatami* and she smiled, and as I held her up she bowed toward her Tenno Heika. I did not bow, nor did my aunt and uncle. I wasn't ready for any love-feast.

Then came a thin high-pitched voice. People strained their ears, bent their backs. Uncle Adam, looking weary, his white coat flapping, turned up the volume. It didn't help much. It seemed the patients and the local people had trouble understanding Tenno Heika. We wondered why until Mr. Kurita explained to Uncle Adam that "His Majesty is speaking the old court Japanese. It's not easy to understand."

Still, the gist of it was clear, and Adam and Cora caught enough of it and even I managed to interpret sentences here and there:

> To Our good and loyal subjects: After pondering deeply the
> general trends of the world and the actual conditions obtaining in
> Our empire today We have decided to effect a settlement of the
> present situation by resorting to an extraordinary measure. Despite
> the best that has been done by everyone, the war situation has not
> necessarily developed to Japan's advantage, while the general trends
> of the world have all turned against her interest. Moreover, the

enemy has begun to employ a new and most cruel bomb, the power
of which to damage is indeed incalculable. Such being the case,
how are We to save the millions of Our subjects? Or to atone
Ourselves before the hallowed spirits of Our imperial ancestors?
This is the reason why We have ordered the acceptance of the
provisions of the joint declaration of the powers . . ."

The Voice of the Crane, as some called it, droned on, but that was it.
It was over. And he'd managed it, as Uncle Adam pointed out, without
once using the words "surrender" or "defeat."

The emperor also had fatherly words of advice for his subjects. They
were to cultivate "the ways of rectitude, nobility of spirit," and "work
resolutely to enhance the glory of the imperial state" and "keep pace with
the progress of the world."

Over the crying that now spread through the ward, Uncle Adam said
to me, "Don't anyone bet that they won't take his advice. There's nothing
they aren't capable of once they put their minds to it . . ."

Yuriko and I, stunned by the event, walked into the street where
hundreds had gathered, having poured out of the shacks and shops, some
with tears in their eyes, all talking in low voices and stunned as we
were.

Mr. Kurita now bowed to *me*. I guess I was the nearest conqueror
around, and it really embarrassed me. It didn't take his subjects long to
follow the emperor's instructions on how to behave. "I hope your soldiers
will treat us fairly," he said, "we bear them no ill will, there are stories
that they are fierce men and—"

"I don't think you need to worry, Mr. Kurita. You've always been good
to us, giving my mother-in-law and me a little extra mackerel or tuna. It
helped and we're grateful."

"For my friend Goro Tamba it was a pleasure," he said, bowing again.
God, I hoped this wasn't going to be a trend.

Kenji came pedaling his bike, riding on the rims, weaving his way
through the street crowds. He jumped off the bike and came to us, hugged
Yuriko and me.

"It's all over," I said.

"I know . . ."

For a moment I assumed his flat voice and slumped shoulders were just
part of the reaction so many were having to the latest news, but then I
saw the moisture in his eyes, and I knew without asking that it wasn't on
account of the surrender. I knew that he had found his brother, and that
the news was bad. I waited.

"Masao is dead," Kenji said so quietly I could barely hear him. "He took his life, he was with those soldiers who went into the palace."

And then Yuriko was in his arms, and I stood aside, realizing that this was a private family matter that this *gaijin,* even if a wife and sister-in-law, could not share and should not try to share. I hated to think of the moment when poor Michiko would learn about her husband's death, and even more Hisako. That woman had suffered and endured too much. Her youngest son, her husband and now her oldest and dearest first-born, all dead . . . and at that moment I hated myself for ever resenting her feelings about me.

Kenji looked from Yuriko to me, nodded and said he had to tell his mother. He also filled in Uncle Adam, who had just come out, and Yuriko and me about Sato's role in the unsuccessful rebellion and how he was arrested and taken away, which was the only good news of the moment.

And then he told Uncle Adam about Masao . . . Uncle Adam put his gnarled hands on Kenji's shoulders, his eyes seemed to cloud over, and without a word he turned and walked away. His silence spoke louder than any words about what he felt for Kenji and his family. When Aunt Cora had been told the news, she asked Kenji and Yuriko if they wanted her to come along to help out in breaking the news to Hisako. Both shook their heads, Kenji saying that it was his duty, he was now the eldest son, and Yuriko, through tears, said, "Our mother is a strong woman . . . stronger than I am . . ."

Hisako was just what Yuriko said, stronger than any of us. She behaved with reserve, dignity, although behind that face it was impossible not to imagine the terrible anguish she must be hiding.

The next day a fourth photograph, framed and draped with black, went into the Tamba family shrine. It showed a young officer, stern and much decorated. In a way, I thought, the House of Tamba was a miniature of what had happened to all of Japan.

YURIKO KITANO · AUGUST, 1945

They were the first American soldiers I had ever seen, except for the prisoners-of-war we sometimes saw cleaning the streets and working in railyards and the docks. But those men were thin and dirty and in rags, they moved slowly and weren't allowed to talk to us. The men I now saw were mostly big, in spotless uniforms, talking and singing and making jokes and giving candy and gum to the little kids they saw.

"Hey, baby," a huge redheaded man shouted at me from a jeep, "whatcha doin' tonight?"

I bowed my head and pretended I didn't understand him.

My mother, of course, had told me the Americans would rape me and if I struggled they would bite off my nose. "You must dirty your face, make your hair unkempt, and wear the *mompei*. Do not talk to the *gaijin* soldiers or they will think you are a prostitute and try to pay you, and if you refuse they will hold you down and attack you," she said.

None of these soldiers matched her descriptions, and I couldn't honestly say I was afraid. If anything, they reminded me of Hans, which made me even more open to them. I was sorry when they passed by our poor street, honking their horns, shouting a few words of Japanese to us. They couldn't have been friendlier.

"It's a trick," Officer Tani said, "they will make believe they like us and when we offer our friendship they'll kill us all."

When that first group of soldiers appeared the local police and a few veterans were still in uniform, and some of the *Kempetei*, including that awful Lieutenant Koga, also came and stood with their backs to the Americans, keeping us at a distance.

"What gives?" the redheaded man said to him. "Why the backs?"

I had to laugh when Koga, the most militaristic of policemen, bowed low and said in broken English, "We protect you, sir. We are making certain that no harm comes to you."

For this he got a pack of cigarettes, for which he bowed low.

I felt ashamed for him.

JULIE TAMBA · SEPTEMBER, 1945

This warm September morning I was helping Aunt Cora change the dressing on Mrs. Kurita's back—she had been burned in a firebombing—when I heard American voices in the street. We had seen a few GIs, and I always asked them if they knew a war correspondent named Chris

Varnum and the answer was always the same. "No, sorry, honey." Our neighborhood didn't draw much GI attention, not being exactly a showplace or a pleasure strip, and I was surprised that the Americans even came there at all. In downtown Tokyo, around the Ginza, the main drag, they seemed to be all over the place, MPs and sailors and marines, jeeps and trucks, lots of good-natured guys amazing the Japanese with their jokes and loud voices and gift-giving to the children. Were these indeed the barbarian conquerors who had come to ravage their daughters?

Whenever a GI would stop to talk to me I of course had a lot of tough explaining to do. They'd see me lugging Taro on my back, figure I was a German or a Swede or some other strange creature, then look sort of confused when I told them I was an American, a *Southern Californian,* and free to walk around and could speak Japanese and dressed like a "Nip." I let them imagine whatever they wanted about Taro. In fact, I sort of got a kick out of watching them guessing but not directly asking. And so far none of these knew about a Christopher Varnum but said they'd be glad to ask, and I always gave them the address of the clinic and our flat, hoping word would get to my brother when and if he showed up.

It was getting toward noon. Yuriko had been sweeping the veranda. I heard her voice rising and went to the window and, my heart jumped, I saw my brother climbing out of a jeep and Yuriko bowing to him. A crowd of kids had already gathered with their hands out. I didn't have any tears, I'd shed and seen enough of these. No crying for joy . . . what I did was burst out laughing.

My brother. Right here.

I hadn't seen him for over three years, when I'd gone to the marshalling area with Kenji. Looking at him through the window, I saw that he was broader, heavier, very tanned, his face lined. No more innocent hotshot correspondent.

I took a deep breath and went out to the street to my brother standing at the side of a jeep with a paunchy red-bearded man in uniform. It had to be his friend Jack, whom I'd heard about. There was also a sergeant, their driver.

For a moment we just stood and stared at each other. Three years. In different worlds.

I ran to him and we hugged and now he started to laugh, shaking his head, like me not quite believing what he was seeing. After we'd calmed down I introduced him to Yuriko, and he told her he knew a lot about her from my letters, which obviously pleased her.

"The little sister," Chris smoothly said, taking in Yuriko's lovely golden face, her alert eyes, her fine features. Even with a kerchief around her hair, raw hands holding a broom, she was clearly a beautiful young woman. No question that if my brother weren't married and, I had to assume, reformed, he'd have lost no time in going after Yuriko.

Jack Sutherton was now introduced to us. He was a beer-bellied hearty man with sun-squinty eyes. He said he'd take a look around the ward and leave the family reunion to the Varnums.

Aunt Cora and Uncle Adam came out, and for a moment didn't seem to recognize my brother. After all, their last view of him was on a visit to Los Angeles a long long time ago when he was a pesty runt in short pants and ragged sneakers.

"Walter's boy," Uncle Adam said, "my God, you're a tall one," and he hugged Chris. "Famous war correspondent, Julie tells us, and a genius at smuggling letters through Cora's friends, as we well know and can't thank you enough for."

"Thank God it's ended," Aunt Cora said, "and now *please* tell us all about your parents and your wife and everything else we've missed . . ."

We sat in the tiny hot garden, peaceful, no more of the terrible air raids, and sipped green tea and Chris talked and talked and talked. While he did, trying to field our barrage of questions, I noticed Yuriko silent and hanging back, the only Japanese in a reunion of these loud happy Americans (and one somewhat less boisterous Swiss) and I told her to come sit next to me.

"We're like sisters," I said to Chris.

"Then I want her for a sister too," he said, and smiled at me. I gave him a warning look in return.

Yuriko now added, "Our sons are best friends too."

Chris nodded, said that was nice, but he kept staring at me. "I don't see how you survived, kid. There are miles of this city with nothing left. I mean *nothing.* Somebody up there must like you, and I'm damn glad of it."

I laughed, then got serious and told him how decent the Tambas had been to me, glossing over our less wonderful moments, how they'd taken me into the house, the horrors of the junkyard and how no matter the humble and crowded quarters and scarcity of food they'd always looked after me and Taro and Kenji.

"Well, it seems the Varnums owe the Tambas plenty. Post Exchange, here I come—"

"Oh, that wouldn't be right," Yuriko said quickly, getting over her shyness. "Our family did for Julie what they would do for any member. Besides, Julie put up with a lot . . . ask her about the outdoor toilet and the cold and our everlasting rice."

We all laughed at her more accurate version of life with the Tambas. Smiling, she then left, saying she wanted to go home early to tell her mother that my brother had arrived and so that Hisako could prepare a celebratory meal, using all her charm on Mr. Kurita to get a decent fish from him.

Once she'd gone Chris let loose with his thoughts on the war. "Well, as Julie knows, I don't like Japs. Now before you jump all over me, let me just remind you I've seen things you haven't. Charging like crazies into our guns, killing their own wounded, strafing survivors in the water . . . You all *know* about the Bataan death march, and how they forced their own civilians to kill themselves on Saipan and Okinawa. *Listen* to me, damn it. I *saw* whole families, Japanese farmers, who'd beaten their kids and wives to death with axe handles and then cut their own guts out with scythes to please some son of a bitch of an officer who decided they all had to die. What about all *that?*"

I shut my eyes. "I knew about those things, Kenji was monitoring broadcasts and getting outside newspapers. But you can't lump everybody together. You know better than that . . ."

Uncle Adam looked at him. "Their army leaders were trained this way, Chris. Bloody militarists drummed it into them that they possessed the only truth. The leaders used the emperor's name, never allowing him to decide anything, manipulated the symbolism of the throne to dominate the people—"

"I'm not sure I believe all that," Chris interrupted. "And look at those *kamikazes.* I saw it off Okinawa. Our navy will never admit it, but I can tell you they raised holy hell with our ships. They sank and disabled more American shipping, from carriers to LCIs, than the admirals will ever own up to. And they damned near stopped us at Okinawa."

"Chris, for God's sake, Kenji's brother Saburo was one of those pilots. He crashed his plane off Okinawa and died." I couldn't quite get myself to say *my brother-in-law* and I was ashamed of myself, for Kenji's sake, not Saburo's, who, let's face it, had hardly been one of my favorites.

Chris sobered up at that and said he guessed he'd better keep his mouth shut, though it wouldn't be easy. I hoped he meant it.

Uncle Adam then told Chris he should keep something else in mind. "The Japanese lack neither brains nor courage. They have them in ample supply, I assure you. But peculiar traditions persist here. An island nation, a homogenous people, never defeated in a war, a familial society under a divine king ruled by a noble class who taught them that death is not to be feared. To admit defeat was all but impossible."

"Sure, until we dropped the big bomb and they realized they'd all be wiped out."

"Kenji says the government was looking for a way out long before the atom bombs were dropped."

"Yeah . . ."

"You're quite a cynic," Aunt Cora said. "And so young."

"No, Aunt Cora, I'm a realist. You saw the way they hemmed and hawed even after Hiroshima. I hear they couldn't even keep some crazies from invading the palace and threatening to blow the whole surrender. I may sound cold to you, but I'm glad it went the way it did. It just may teach them not to try it again."

I nervously switched the conversation then and asked about Carol, did Chris have some pictures. Luckily he did . . . she looked dark, pretty, sleeves rolled up standing outside a military hospital on Tinian where she was now the chief surgical nurse. That got things into a safer nostalgic plane and we were able to keep it that way until it was time to go home for dinner, and for Chris's reunion with Kenji.

Kenji and Hisako and Yuriko were waiting for us in the main room, and I was quick to tell Chris to take off his GI boots and put on the paper scuffs sitting in the doorway.

When we entered the paper-walled room we'd lived in ever since we'd left the boxcar Hisako immediately dropped to the floor, bowing low, nearly letting her head touch the boards. Yuriko bowed slightly, holding Hiroki, who was tugging at her hair. Taro ran to me and started grabbing at my skirts. Hisako, of course, had kept her two grandsons immaculate, their patched shirts and shorts laundry-clean, their shoes neat. How she did it I had no idea.

Kenji tapped his mother lightly on the shoulder and told her that Chris didn't need to be bowed to this way, that he was one of the family and could be welcomed as a friend. I studied her face as she got up and came forward, still somewhat bent, her face stoic, and no matter what her son said, to her Chris was the enemy in her house, the big-nosed round-eyed yellow-headed *gaijin* brother of the *gaijin* woman who had upset so much in her house by taking away her son. But at the same time she had her pride, and her manners, and she would go through with the welcome, like it or not. Quite a woman.

Kenji now went up to Chris and shook his hand and they hugged each other, while Yuriko looked on in surprise at such a show of affection between men, and Hisako watched with no expression but I had a pretty good idea what she was thinking. I lifted Taro up and showed him to his uncle, who kissed his cheek.

Hisako struggled to find her voice, then whispered something to Kenji, who translated for Chris. "My mother says she's honored to meet you and welcomes you to our house, which she is sorry is so small and not as good as the house that burned down."

Chris was getting a lesson in Japanese ways that he never bargained for, and looked sort of sheepish when he asked Kenji to tell Hisako he was glad to be here and sorry about all the bad things that had happened to her. Kenji translated for his mother, who bowed again, then went with Yuriko into the kitchen to finish preparing the dinner.

Chris had bought a musette bag filled with stuff like jam and crackers and candy and soap and toothpaste, all of which we badly needed. He handed them over to me, and we thanked him and then showed him the altar with the pictures, which he studied carefully and seriously. When we sat down around the low table, Chris began telling stories about "Dugout Doug" MacArthur, and said that although he'd never been too keen about the general he'd once had the chance to interview him and said without question he was a brilliant man who had a respect for democracy. "Quite a guy," Chris said, "and I'm betting he's going to fool a lot of the wiseguys who've been knocking him . . . me included. He's really so damn smart about how to figure the reaction of the people . . . when he arrived in Tokyo he told his officers not to wear any sidearms—a terrific psychological stroke. You should have seen the reaction of the Japanese . . . approving and awed about sums it up. And I hear that in the Grand Hotel, where he's set up his temporary quarters, when his aides tried to taste his food for him he'd have none of it, showing the Japanese that he had confidence in them. But the biggest thing he did was to keep the emperor in his palace. He knows the way the Japs—excuse me—the Japanese feel about their sun god and he doesn't intend to offend them. By leaving the emperor untouched he figures to really win them over."

As Chris talked we nibbled at the grainy GI chocolate, and Yuriko told how she'd been offered some Spam by a couple of GIs that had passed by earlier. She wanted to know if it was safe to eat, which got a big laugh from Chris, who told her that most of the guys in the army hated it but it really wasn't poison, no matter what she'd heard.

As we talked and laughed I could see that even in the short time he'd been here Chris was softening some. Definitely he was moved by Yuriko's warmth and Hisako's dignity. For sure these weren't the brutal crazy "Japs" he'd seen on the islands. Oh, I knew he had a ways to go . . . after all, I'd been here four years and I still did . . . but a change was beginning.

After dinner Chris and Kenji and I went into the dirt yard to talk, and Kenji told Chris about Professor Adachi and the peace group that had functioned at risk and had opposed the war and wanted to make Japan a democracy. He said he hoped the American authorities would at least consult with Adachi, that he had an awful lot to offer them.

Later, after Kenji went to meet with some of these people he had been talking about, Chris said, "A good guy, and bright as hell."

"You always knew that, didn't you?"

He looked at me and smiled. "Yeah, I guess I did, but I didn't always want to admit it. Looks to me like you didn't do so bad, after all." And then, getting serious, with Taro resting his head on his knee, Chris said to me, "Okay, Julie, tell me, how's it really been here?"

"Later, Chris, I assume we'll have time for that before you take off again. But you've already got an idea of the Tambas, and I'm here to tell that although it was rough, and I mean between Kenji and me sometimes too, we're not just together but more so than ever. I'm a very lucky *gaijin* girl, and I mean that." And then we talked about Ed, and what I knew about him and how he died. Chris got really sore at that and said he'd make a point of going to Kyushu and seeing the bastards swing who had done it to Ed.

And *then* he asked the big question, which I had been waiting for and wasn't sure how to answer.

". . . Are you going to stay on here, sis, or . . .?"

I told him the truth. "I just don't know exactly. Kenji is going to be part of rebuilding Japan, he deserves that chance. And one thing I'm positive of, I won't go anywhere . . . not even home, without him."

Chris nodded, watched Taro waddle across the yard and up to me and plump his ball in my hands. "Mama, play ball."

"Not bad, not bad," Chris said, and suddenly pulled Taro up to him and kissed him a good one. "The folks are going to love this one, Julie. Just don't keep them waiting too long, okay?"

"Okay," I said, and hugged him like he might disappear for another four years.

KENJI TAMBA · SEPTEMBER, 1945

Professor Adachi and I were standing outside General MacArthur's headquarters in the Dai Ichi building—it had once been an insurance building. A flag-waving crowd had gathered because a rumor had swept the city that Tenno Heika was leaving the imperial palace and calling on the general! It was hard to imagine . . . our emperor never called on *anyone*. People came to see *him*. He was untouchable, sacred, a being apart from the ordinary run of mortals. Yet the crowd did seem pleased to see that their god was also a man who could come into their world to see the famous man who now ruled Japan.

As we stood there we saw a troop of schoolboys walk by, bookbags on their white-shirted backs, and I wondered if one of them maybe was called Firefly for studying too hard . . . The kids were singing a nonsense tune that had caught on after the Americans took over Tokyo broadcasting. It had the same tune as "London Bridge is Falling Down":

> *Moshi, moshi, anonay?*
> *Anonay? Anonay?*
> *Moshi, moshi, anonay?*
> *Ah so, deska!*

"Hello, hello, are you there? Ah, is that so?" I'd no idea why, but everyone was singing it. American GIs and Japanese too. Adachi, watching the singing schoolboys, said, "Better a bit of American nonsense than those promises to kill barbarians. And I also note a gratifying lack of bamboo spears."

A procession of black limousines appeared, led by police on motorcycles, and people bowed to the lead car. Inside we saw a shadow, a bespectacled somber face—Tenno Heika.

As we walked on the professor said he had been to the meetings about a new constitution. "They have asked me to join a committee of Japanese citizens who will provide a draft. Of course the general wasn't there, but the Americans who were told us they spoke for him and that their opinions were his. They said he wants a democratic government . . . free elections, the vote for women, free labor unions, an end to the industrial *zaibatsu* that helped plunge us into the war. Also an end to military control of government, and free speech, a free press. Shinto will no longer be a state religion, there will be freedom of worship. And land distribution."

"Not the agenda of a reactionary tyrant," I said.

"I tell you, Kenji, these Americans continue to confound me. All I had heard about MacArthur was that he was an old-fashioned military autocrat. If so, he is a most unusual one."

We paused outside our office building. No longer were we clandestine and camouflaged. The "sugar export company" sign was gone. We were expanding our office, joining a new press bureau under the aegis of MacArthur's government. Adachi would soon be leaving us for full-time work with the committee drafting the constitution and he wanted me to stay on with Yoshiro to recruit English-speaking Japanese journalists for the staff.

"Will you do it?" he asked.

"I'm not sure, my wife . . ."

"Of course. She wants to go home, to see her family."

"We'll have to talk about it, I'll help you as much as I can. You know I want to. We will surely have to go to America for a while, that is, if her parents want to see me."

"Why shouldn't they?"

"They may still resent me for the suffering I put their daughter through."

"That will be for her to decide, if I may be so bold."

I nodded, hoping he was right.

We passed the *soba* seller, where my father and I used to stop on snowy evenings to enjoy the hot buckwheat noodles with soya sauce. And then it was time to say good-bye, my *sensei* telling me to keep Yoshiro on his toes and that he would come by now and then to make sure I was doing a good job.

We bowed to each other, then shook hands—the "odd habit" Adachi had learned at Columbia.

"My father is dead, and I honor his memory, but I feel I have found a new one," I told him.

He looked at me seriously, then turned and hurried off.

The next day I stopped at a kiosk to buy the *Asahi Shimbun* and read about the emperor's visit to General MacArthur. There was a photograph on the front page and it told a great deal . . . there was the general with no tie, in starched tan uniform, no medals, a tall eagle-faced man, and next to him Tenno Heika, short, in cutaway coat and striped trousers, the two of them facing the camera. The Son of Heaven appeared a bit ill at ease. MacArthur, an older man, looked almost benign.

It had a tremendous effect on our people, as did MacArthur's going out of his way to say complimentary things about Tenno Heika. It was also rumored that he had forced the British and Russians to give up their plan to try His Majesty as a war criminal. It seemed he believed that Tenno Heika had been used and dominated by the war-makers, and that only when he spoke at the very end and demanded that we accept peace terms had he acted on his own. I agreed with that. We were fortunate indeed to have this man in charge.

On my way home to get ready to meet Chris, who was still in Tokyo and was taking us to dinner that night, I passed a large building in Minato Ward that had somehow escaped the bombs, while all around it were the scorched frames of wooden structures, heaps of rubble and empty lots. The Blue Dream Hotel, as it had been renamed, was open for business, but a very different business than before. Now a line of American soldiers and sailors extended from the beaded curtain in the doorway all the way into the street.

It was a *joro* house, a whorehouse. And as I looked at the Americans on the waiting line I felt almost sorry for them. Conquerors, yes. But not too comfortable at it. Their jokes, whistling at women, tossing empty bottles into the street, weren't much like the way the students at Oregon or UCLA acted, and the swagger seemed skin-deep, a cover maybe for their embarrassment?

"Hemsley, y'all got a rubber?"

"I wouldn't be for knowin' but for you I'll look, buddy."

"Well, then be for lookin', damn it."

"Hey, Hopper, I wants me a fat-ass big-titted one I can lay me on like she was a feather bed."

"Clyde, onliest thing you ever laid on was an old sow."

Mostly there seemed to be southern accents, and two Negroes approached the queue, listened to the voices and accents and left after some glares and a few nasty words.

"Whatcha lookin' at, slant?" a soldier asked me.

"Shit, he looks young enough to maybe shot me, the fucker."

I realized it was no good staying here and quickly pedaled across the street, where I heard my name called. Parked at the curb was a shiny black sedan with the shades partially drawn. I approached it. The shades rose and I looked inside.

Kingoro Hata was sitting at the window, and next to him in a stylish Western dress and layers of pearls was his mistress Satomi.

This didn't surprise me, but then I saw at the wheel of the car in a rumpled black suit none other than Colonel Sato. I couldn't be sure whether he was actually working as a chauffeur or was merely now a business associate of Hata and the geisha mistress.

I did not bow. "Mr. Hata. Miss Satomi." I did not even address Colonel Sato. He was just as happy, I'd been a witness to his disgrace, and remembered too well how the son of a bitch had let Masao cut his belly open and die. Sato had chosen to live. In fact, it was fascinating that in this year of defeat so far the rate of suicide among military personnel was one of the *lowest* ever. So much for the traditions and legends they'd used to send so many young men to die.

"Kenji, dear boy," Hata said.

"How are you?" Satomi put in.

Sato knew enough to keep quiet.

"I'm fine, and you?"

Hata nodded at the line of customers. "Our newest . . . business. As you can see, Satomi and I are at the service of our American friends. We have opened six houses of joy and they are doing a fine business. Soon we will expand into real estate, and as soon as decent locations can be found Satomi will resume her labors as the favored hostess of the Floating World. Kenji, you must come and see me. Such a talented family, a pity so many Tambas died."

How I wanted to smash a fist into his fat face. Yank him out by the lapels and beat him to a pulp. A conniving lying bastard, he was hand-in-glove with the civilian and military outlaws, and now he was sucking the blood of our people and no doubt responsible for spreading venereal diseases among our young women and the Americans. He was a parasite and a liar. Man of broad face, indeed. And she wasn't much better. They made a perfect couple.

I glanced at the back of Sato's neck, still not acknowledging his presence.

"Ah, the colonel," Hata said. "He is helping us out. He has changed his name. He is no longer Colonel Sato but Mr. Nishida. Change of name, change of profession. Colonel, you know young Tamba, of course?"

Sato turned and actually smiled at me. Well, at least he had found his proper calling—manservant to two pimps.

At a small country inn, one of the very few spared by the bombing, Chris hosted dinner for Julie and me, Hisako and Yuriko. We'd left the boys at home under the care of Mrs. Kurita.

We sat on *tatamis* around a *kotatsu*, and the owner, a sprightly old

Korean gent with two spinster daughters, served us *bulkoki, kimchi,* and *mandu kuk,* all of it spicy and fresh. As he did, I told about my encounter with Hata and Satomi and Sato.

Chris laughed. "Sounds as if some of the rats are inheriting the earth."

"Not for long," I said.

The food was very good . . . a lot of Japanese look down on Koreans, but I like them and I like their cooking. They're survivors, hard workers, good people.

Chris had brought us presents almost every day . . . clothing, drugs, soap, food, blankets, and my mother and I wanted to give him at least something in return. So as we sat there letting our mouths burn with the spiced beef and peppery cabbage and dumpling soup I gave my brother-in-law Masao's own copy of Musashi's *Book of Five Rings,* beautifully printed on rice paper with many illustrations, some copies of Musashi's own sketches.

Julie told Chris how Musashi had been Masao's idol, the great swordsman and warrior. Now that peace had come, Julie said, we all felt that this book of the warrior should pass out of the Tamba family.

"I'm honored," Chris said, and I knew he meant it.

"It's a soldier's book," I said, "and I'm not a soldier. That's why I want this book to leave the family. Just as Tenno Heika, we hear, replaced a bust of Napoleon with one of Lincoln."

Julie took my hand then and we tried to kiss, but the garlicky hot sauce of the *kimchi* made us laugh too much.

Chris went on to tell us about Frank Yasuda, the Nisei we had known at UCLA who'd been interned with us. I remembered him very well, a friendly young man convinced that his government would never do what it did to him.

But several months after being interned Yasuda and other young Japanese were released so they could volunteer for an elite fighting unit in the U.S. Army known as the 442nd Regimental Combat Team. Made up entirely of Nisei, they fought in Italy and accumulated the most battle honors of any military unit in the whole army. Not bad at all for the "traitorous yellow bastards," as they were called when the war broke out.

"Yasuda's a major now," Chris told us. "Silver star, bronze star, the works."

We lifted our glasses to Major Yasuda, and as we did I couldn't help remembering that bus trip to the internment camp. Afterward I translated Chris's account of the Nisei hero Major Yasuda for my mother, who mostly seemed puzzled and had trouble following what I was saying. Her comment was that she was glad the war was over. Well, as usual she knew what was really important.

YURIKO KITANO · OCTOBER, 1945

My English, thanks to Julie, now made it possible for me to read well, write some and speak almost without an accent. Her nightly lessons helped take my mind off Hans, although I doubted anything could ever really do that. Kenji was always saying not to look back, that there was too much work to be done, and he would quote Professor Adachi about creating a new Japan. I listened but didn't really share his excitement. I was still too full of my own miseries.

Gradually, though, slowly, I did begin to come out of it. When the American soldiers flirted with me, I didn't resent it . . . I even, to be truthful, liked it, although I don't think I encouraged them. But I did begin to feel alive, which I hadn't felt in a long time. I was beginning to *want* to be alive. Chris, Julie's lively brother, who had been so good to us, had brought me some books by American authors and now I began to dip into them. I especially liked *A Farewell to Arms,* by Ernest Hemingway, and Mark Twain's *Tom Sawyer.* They showed me new worlds, but the people and their problems, especially in Hemingway, didn't seem so foreign to me. . . .

One sunny day I put on a gray suit that Julie and I had been sewing for weeks, a white blouse, stockings and low-heeled black shoes that Chris had gotten for me. It really felt good, if a little strange. My mother, though, who was at the pump down the street beating clothes against the flat rocks inside the trough, didn't approve when she saw me "all decked out," as Julie would say.

"Why are you dressed that way?" Mother would never approve Western-style dress, and I knew better than to argue with her about it. But I could at least give her a reason. "I'm going for an interview," I told her. "For a job with the Americans. I'm going to be a translator at Professor Adachi's office. Kenji helped arrange it."

"And you will not be home anymore?"

"Mother, I will be home as soon as I finish each day, and with the money I earn I can help you and the family. I know how you feel about women working outside the home but things are changing. They say that General MacArthur is even going to let women vote next year."

My mother looked at me, brushed back loose strands of hair. What she had gone through was in the deep lines of her face, and I hated to make her unhappy, even though we had argued over the years. But I could help her with the money I could earn, and I did want to be part of the changes that were happening, the new Japan that Kenji was helping to build . . . and then she surprised me . . . they say children always underestimate their elders, especially their parents . . . when she said, "Yes, I believe it may be all right. I will take care of Hiroki, as I always have. He gives me joy. And with you away I will be able to spoil him, as is his right. After all, he is your first son." And we both nodded and laughed and I felt closer to her than I could ever remember.

As I walked down our street to the nearest trolley stop, I turned and saw her bent double, sleeves rolled up, once again pounding away on the flat stones, and I knew that no matter what changes came to our country they would never replace the strength and loyalty of women like Hisako Tamba.

JULIE TAMBA · OCTOBER, 1945

My husband needed a break, so one glorious October weekend I made him take off a couple of days from saving the world and building a new Japan and take me and our son to the old shrine city of Nara, which I had always wanted to see anyway. It was no disappointment, the sun shining on the bright green cypresses and crytomeria trees and highlighting the wooden temple of Horyu-Ji with its incredible collection of Buddhas and Bodhisattvas.

Not surprisingly Kenji couldn't wait to give me one of his lectures, this time on the history of the place, but frankly I was too happy to concentrate, full of the pleasure of just being here with him and our son, *and* thinking about how he would look when I broke the big news that I had found out a day earlier—that I was pregnant, no question about it, said Aunt Cora.

I picked a moment in the lecture when he had given up on trying to keep me interested. We were holding hands, watching Taro chase an occasional squirrel and toss his ball against a stone marker.

"Kenji . . ."

"Mmmm?"

"I know this isn't something to compare with the ages, or the new Japan, but I have some news. It goes like this, oh husband. Julie Varnum Tamba, *gaijin* wife of brilliant Japanese man, mother of child Taro, is about to do it again."

Silence. My God, didn't he care, didn't he want another child?

I got my answer when he leaned over and looked at me like he wanted to devour me, or maybe like he never wanted to forget what had passed between us at this moment. But still, he looked so *serious*. "Listen, please, you better say something or I'll think you're sorry—"

"Sorry? I am crazy with pleasure and happiness. But I am also afraid. Don't you know why?"

I shook my head, although I thought I knew what was coming.

"I'm afraid because I think now you may decide you have to go back to America, and I don't want you to go, even though I suppose you'll have to for a while. I want to go with you, but I need to be here. Don't laugh, but I really feel like I'm part of something now. I can be proud as I always wanted to be of what I am . . . Does any of this make any sense?"

"Well, aside from it being the longest speech ever given by a husband to his wife who's just told him she was pregnant, yes, Kenji, it makes sense. But do we have to decide on timing and all that right now? I want to enjoy this day, this feeling inside me, our child. Sorry to sound like Scarlett O'Hara, but I'd really rather think about it tomorrow."

He kissed me, and said it was a deal . . . and we happily went back to the pleasures of the day, which included the delicious universal sound of crickets chirping, Taro discovering a spider under a stone and holding it up with fear and awe . . .

After a while, as the day began to slip away, Kenji took my hand, then put his arm around me. "Do you remember the Noble Eightfold Path that I taught you for our wedding?"

"Well, you start, okay? And I'll see if I can pick it up."

"Right knowledge."

". . . Right intention?"

He smiled. "Right speech."

"Right conduct."

"Right means of livelihood."

I was stumped, and he helped me out. "Right effort, mindfulness, right—"

"Right concentration," I said triumphantly. "Except that's something I doubt I'll ever get right—"

But I didn't have to, at least not then, because he had pulled me to him and stopped me with a bold kiss right there in the open, right on the mouth. We might still have been in that kiss if Taro hadn't broken it by tugging at my sleeve and saying he wanted us to come with him and watch some big boys flying kites.

Like a good and dutiful Japanese mother, I got up and went with him, and was glad I did, because the kites flying over the lush green fields were really magnificent, a dipping and swerving red carp, a wonderful green dragon, a blue fox. What a sight they were, swirling in the autumn sky over the temples of Nara.

Watching them, the unique *Japaneseness* of them, I thought that maybe I would never entirely belong in this place, no matter how much I had lived and learned here, and gone through here, and no matter even that I had a Japanese husband and soon two of his children. And Kenji, for all his scholarship and experience in America, would never be *American*.

But I hoped, had to hope and believe, that this would somehow work out. We were and always would be different, but like the French said, *vive la différence.* Together we make something new and better. And, if love didn't conquer all, as I'd once told Yuriko, the kind Kenji Tamba and Julie Varnum had sure could take you a long, long way.